The Folks

A Bur Oak Book

The Folks

BY RUTH SUCKOW

Drawings by

ROBERT WARD JOHNSON

Foreword by

CLARENCE A. ANDREWS

UNIVERSITY OF IOWA PRESS   IOWA CITY

University of Iowa Press, Iowa City 52242

This book is published with the kind assistance of the
late Ferner Nuhn, husband of Ruth Suckow, and the
Ruth Suckow Memorial Association.

Library of Congress Cataloging-in-Publication Data
Suckow, Ruth, 1892–1960.
    The folks/by Ruth Suckow; drawings by Robert
Ward Johnson; foreword by Clarence A. Andrews.—
1st pbk. ed.
        p.   cm.—(A Bur oak book)
    Originally published: New York: Farrar &
Rinehart, 1934.
    ISBN 0-87745-374-8 (pbk.)
    I. Title.   II. Series.
PS3537.U34F6   1992   91-40598
813'.52—dc20   CIP

CONTENTS

FOREWORD

BY CLARENCE A. ANDREWS

Ruth Suckow (1892–1960) is one of a small group of Iowa authors
of short stories and novels whose work attracted the attention of
major reviewers, literary historians, and critics. Her reputation is
based on eight novels, three short novels, five collections of short
stories, some stories published only in magazines, and several critical essays, all published between 1920 and 1960. A number of her
short stories and one short novel have been reprinted in two recent
volumes. In many of these her subjects are "the sparrows of Iowa"—
"ordinary" Iowans from farms and small towns, the people Ruth
Suckow would have seen or known as she grew up in Hawarden and
other Iowa towns where her father, a descendant of German immi-
grants, served as a minister, the people she made "extra-ordinary"
by writing about them.

In her first novel, *Country People* (1924), Suckow used "folk life"
as the basis for her tale of three generations of a closely related immigrant German farm family. But in later work her subjects became
"folks," working-class and middle-class people on farms and in
small towns and cities. In "The Folk Idea in American Life" (*Scrib-
ner's Magazine,* September 1930), Suckow noted the differences between these two groups and the reasons for the change in her literary
philosophy. "Folk art" or "folk life" was not the basis of American
civilization, she said. The true basis was the "folks." "Folk life" was
"the common existence, in its most basic terms, of a group of people
knit firmly together by common ties—usually the blood tie."
"Folks," on the other hand, had a common "likeness . . . in fortune
and aim rather than in blood. . . . In the term 'folks,' as in the

name the United States, the ideas of variety and plurality are inher-
ent, bound firmly into the whole." Martin Mohr said Suckow's
"'folk' were crude primitives bound together and steeped in the
mysticism of The Soil. ['Folks' are] middle class townspeople trying
to get ahead."

The Folks (1934) differs from *Country People* not only in the difference between "folks" and "folk" but also in length and complexity of
structure. "It seems that nowadays a novel must run over 500 pages
to get into print," a contemporary critic said. Its sections focus in
turn on individual members of the Ferguson family; the times of
these sections often coincide with the times of previous sections.

Suckow's five earlier novels had also been narratives of family life
but with less complex structures, beginning at one point in time
and ending at a later point, with the usual divisions into chapters.
Three of these novels focused on families; two focused on a single
character. All emphasized personal differences among family
members.

The Folks focuses on Fred and Annie Ferguson, their two daughters, and their two sons. Their relationships with each other and
with their relatives and other people cover approximately the first
three decades of the twentieth century. We meet the family about
1920, the beginning of America's dependence on automobile trans-
portation. They live in Belmond, one of Suckow's many small Iowa
towns not to be identified with actual towns. Fred Ferguson is a
bank employee of Scots ancestry; his wife, Annie, is of German
origin; their children are Carl, Margaret, Dorothy, and Bunny. Fred
and Annie are descendants of earlier settlers in the area, and both
have relatives in and near Belmond who appear in the novel.

Events in the lives of the Fergusons almost completely dominate
the story—although we learn that Belmond's second bank has closed
because of the depression and there are passing references to a greenhouse and a store, only the bank in which Fred Ferguson works is
seen at any length. The prosperity of the 1920s, such events as three
presidential elections or Lindbergh's flight from New York to Paris,
and the zany happenings which dominated the front pages of newspapers and the minds of many Americans in that decade—all are
missing from this novel.

Although the time span of *The Folks* is some three decades, the novel takes place in what might be termed a "long day" in the lives of its characters. The omniscient narrator's tale begins with Fred Ferguson inspecting his property on a bright, rosy summer morning, furnishes something of his family background, and then introduces in turn Annie, Carl, the older son, and the two daughters, Margaret and Dorothy. In this section the reader sees the beginning of the differences which will be developed in later sections—particularly those between Annie and Fred and between Margaret and her "folks." Annie is often unhappy with Fred, although she manages to keep her unhappiness largely to herself. An especially difficult encounter between the two is only partly resolved in a moment of passion which is unusual for Suckow:

> She let him unfasten her things, standing passive and acquiescent while he carefully and clumsily drew off the brown waist with its tight cuffs. Everything seemed to go very fast then, and breathlessly, quietly because of the children. This was the only way he had of telling her how he felt about her. . . . And then they were swept together in such an uprush of the old passionate appreciation of one for the other, as they had not felt since Dorothy was born . . .

But, the narrator tells us:

> . . . when they were laid apart from each other, quiet and appeased . . . all which the years had accumulated, the unanswered questions, the doubts, disappointments, small resentments, his failure to share her feelings, her lack of understanding of what was required of men, and the fact that she had never been quite one of the folks, filtered again darkly through their warmth of contentment like a minor strain of music under the major tune.

Bunny, the younger son—the apparent result of this encounter— appears briefly in the second section, "The Good Son," and in more detail in the fifth section, "The Youngest." "The Good Son" focuses on Carl through several years as he and the girls grow up. Carl earns a college degree, marries Lillian, his childhood sweetheart, and begins a teaching career away from Belmond. But all is not well here either. Carl's marriage is troubled to the point where Lillian contemplates suicide.

The third section—"The Loveliest Time of the Year," the wedding day of Dorothy and Jesse Woodward—is set on a June day. It is the most romantic piece of writing that the usually realistic Suckow ever completed. Only in this section of the novel is all well—there is no evidence of family dissension.

In "The Other Girl," the longest section of the novel, Margaret's romantic dreams, her problems with her parents and her college dean of women, and her subsequent rejection of Belmond lead her to Greenwich Village, a bohemian life-style, and a marred romance with a married man that, though continuing as the section ends, offers little promise for her future. The realism of this section contrasts strongly with the idyllic tone of the section immediately preceding.

The realistic tone is continued in "The Youngest" as Bunny brings the foreign-born, socialist-oriented Charlotte to meet his parents— a symbolic meeting forecasting the future of towns such as Belmond, which prior to World War I had been more or less isolated from changes taking place in the nation's cities. At the conclusion of this section, Margaret's and Bunny's decisions and actions have produced a serious strain on Annie and Fred's marriage.

To improve matters, Fred makes a major change: he leaves his job at the bank and takes Annie to southern California for the winter. There, Fred and Annie are shocked to discover that the fairy-tale promise of Dorothy's wedding has been destroyed by actuality; Jesse's gambling has cost the Woodwards their home. In the succeeding narrative of the trip, the normally serious Suckow turns lighthearted as she relates how the once socially aloof Mrs. Spencer, whose husband owned the Belmond bank, has forsaken the culture of her Belmond Shakespeare Club and is now addicted to matinees at the neighborhood motion picture theater. In the course of the winter, the Fergusons realize that even such events as the famed Tournament of Roses parade or the annual get-together of former Iowans offer no escape from life's problems.

Back home in Belmond, the cultural shock of the West Coast lingers as the "long day" of the novel comes to an end. Even though Fred feels that his and Annie's relationship has been improved by the trip, he realizes that the couple's era has ended and only "the darkening twilight" looms ahead. As for their children, he can only hope that they will do as well as he and Annie have done.

On the surface, then, for the Ferguson family and others, the quiet life in Belmond and the Iowa towns where Carl is employed, Carl's early promise, Dorothy's wedding day, Margaret's bohemian life in Greenwich Village, and the more flamboyant life-styles in southern California all seem at first to represent a kind of paradise— but beneath the façade all seems more like paradise lost. Although the novel doesn't mention the 1930s depression, this reader wonders if it didn't have some effect on Suckow as she wrote these last pages.

Despite the novel's pessimism, major critics praised it. Carl Van Doren in *The American Novel 1789–1939* said that Suckow had "studied contemporary life with honest realism" and in this novel "came nearer than any other writer has done to representing the whole of American life." University of Iowa Professor Joseph E. Baker wrote that Suckow's "scenes live . . . they catch the group spirit, the feeling, the atmosphere of the Middle-Western farms, churches, streets, homes, band concerts, schools . . . changing, as living organisms change with the growth of the [twentieth] century."

In these two respects *The Folks* continues to be well worth reading. Whereas some history books focus on the 1920s as a decade in which the United States left the horror and the triumph of World War I behind and entered into the boom years of Harding, Coolidge, Hoover, and Republican prosperity, and whereas other histories of the 1920s focus on such aspects as the rise of gangsters, violations of the Volstead Act, the disappearance of Ruth Judd, the "strange death" of President Harding, the Leopold-Loeb murder trial, the athletic abilities of Babe Ruth, Red Grange, Bobby Jones, and Gertrude Ederle, and the rise and fall of the New York stock market, *The Folks* shows us the world of average American "folks" trying to endure in a society in which the consequences of these events really don't matter. For the Fergusons the issue is whether this average American family can endure—whether the change in family status from "folk" to "folks" is for better or for worse. In the terms of *Country People* or *The Folks,* the answer seems to be that it doesn't make much difference.

This publication of *The Folks* by the University of Iowa Press with the help and encouragement of the Ruth Suckow Memorial Association is a fitting tribute to Iowa's finest writer in this centenary of her birth.

Part One
The Old Folks

THIS was going to be another of those fine September days. The good weather had lasted for over a week now. And yet things weren't too dry.

Mr. Ferguson wanted to get up. He was an early riser. That came from having been brought up on a farm, when it had meant getting up at daylight if he was going to do his part of the chores and reach school on time. He had been living in town ever since he was a young man, since before he was married; but he had never got rid of certain of his country ways.

He whispered, "Mama?"

There was a little sighing opening of her lips as she turned her head and then snuggled it down closer into the pillow. He always felt lonesome getting up without her. But it made his bones ache to lie here any longer. He got out of bed with elaborate caution, thinking he was being very quiet, picking up his shoes by the laces and creaking out of the room in his stockinged feet. His wife turned and sighed as he closed the door. All the children were asleep. They didn't have to get up the way he used to do. Mr. Ferguson went on through the empty hall and into the bathroom.

It seemed chilly on the shady side of the house in the morning, with some of the towels fallen from the rack into the bare porcelain tub, and the colored window with the fleur-de-lys on streaky greenish-white keeping out any sight of the trees and closing him in with the soap and tooth brushes and toilet paper. However, it was pretty nice to have a good bathroom in your house and not have to depend any more upon those outdoor contrivances. He hadn't actually known until last year when they had gone out to that little town in Ohio where Annie's folks had lived, how accustomed he and Annie had grown to their home comforts. Mr. Ferguson stood for several moments, slowly scraping the lather from his face, which he studied with great attention in the white-framed mirror, luxuriating in the sound of running water and the freshness of the air coming in through the raised window.

The stairs were shiny and hard to his stockinged feet. He sat down on the bottom step to put on his shoes.

The folding doors into the parlor were closed. He left them

for mama to open. She would want to attend to the rooms herself. But he opened the heavy front door. That changed the whole feeling of the house. The lawn spread out dewy and fresh and the early air came into the gloom of the hall. A wagon went jolting down the street, he could hear the sound of an engine on the railroad tracks beyond the leafy trees, and somewhere the clop-clop-clop of horses. Mr. Ferguson felt his proprietorship as he opened up his house to the bright day.

He stood on the porch looking things over, enjoying the sense of a good expanse of time before he had to go downtown. It seemed to him that the place looked pretty nice this morning.

He went out into the morning stillness of the lawn. His feet left frosty tracks in the thick dew. He went over to look at the apple tree. The heavy leaves had got somewhat faded and dry during this week of September. The apples had ripened. He felt of the fruit among the leaves. This had been a good apple year, an abundant year all round. The folks wanted them to come out some time this week and get some of the apples from the orchard, they said they were just going to rot out there; and then pretty soon Willie, Annie's youngest brother who lived on the old place in Ohio, would be sending them the usual box of fine eating apples from out there—he didn't know what they'd do with it all. Well, he'd go out to the farm maybe some time this week, take Carl along to help him, and get a nice barrel for Essie Bartlett and her mother, and a box of the best for Reverend Santley—that would take care of a little of the fruit. But this abundance all around gave a sense of ease and fullness. It meant good times for the farmers, and a good year for them at the bank. The cool bark of the apple tree, his own tree bearing his own apples, had a personal touch to his hand.

The barn stood empty. They didn't have a horse now. Although Mr. Ferguson wasn't yet ready to make the admission to his family, he knew he would be buying an automobile one of these days. Other folks were getting them. Mert Clute who had the agency kept after him—thought anyone connected with a bank had money. Now they had those fifteen hundred dollars coming from Grandpa Luers' little estate. Although he didn't like to make any plans about that, it belonged to Annie. He remembered her funny, scared look when he had said to her, "Well, mama, you'll have to think where you're going to put your money." He supposed it did make a difference to her, calling it hers, although he had never thought of such a thing before—just taken it for granted, and supposing she did, too, that whatever was his was Annie's. Of course she would take his word on any investment. He was pleased with the way he had handled her part in the estate. Annie hadn't liked it because she had seemed to be taking more than Louise; but that was all right; she had lived closer to the old folks and done a good deal more for them in their last days; Louie and Henry would have more than they knew what to do with some day, unless they got around pretty soon to having some children. The larger part of the estate, and the home property, had gone by rights to Willie and his wife.

Remembering Grandpa Luers' death last summer made him realize, though, that his own father and mother were failing. They were still out on the old place, were some of those who had never been willing to move into town. But Ben and Ella did most of the looking after things now. The old folks spent more and more of their time just by themselves in the rock house that stood across the driveway from the frame house that Ben and Ella had built. As far as practical matters went, he himself—Fred Ferguson—was now the head of the family.

Birds were chirping all around. There were still a few things left in the garden. Dew drenched the late summer flowers. He saw some things here and there that needed doing. Carl ought to mow the lawn again tonight. But on the whole, he had never seen the place looking better than it did this fall. There was still a little time before he would have to think about stocking up for winter. He might pick up some of the best of the apples for mama to use when she got time. He didn't like to see anything good going to waste, even if apples were almost a drug on the market. There would be somebody who would be able to make use of the overflow. Some of the apples had got spoiled, lying on the ground, but they would do for sauce. He supposed he ought to insist on Carl's doing all such odd jobs. He was afraid the children had almost too easy a time of it. But it gave him pleasure to get the neat, dry bushel basket from the nail in the barn and to hunt over the apples that lay almost rooted in the thick wet grass, and then to set the basket on the back porch where mama could find it.

Wandering over the lawn, he stopped to finger the plants in the white stone urn, the foliage and geraniums. That urn was another thing of pride to him—that, and the colored window in the bathroom. They were the two fancy touches that he had added to the place when it was made over after he and Annie had bought it from the old Bishops, just a little while after Carl was born. "Oh, make it big enough, there'll be others yet," his mother had told him, with her primitive shrewdness. She always said that German wives had lots of children; and she didn't quite like it that he and Annie seemed to be stopping with three. But even three kept him going in these days, and the house wasn't any too big. The rope swing, hard shiny ropes of tarnished tan knotted at the bottom, dangled from the big maple tree. He went over to find out what had become of the seat. The board with crotches at each end lay split in the grass. He picked up the parts that were dark and damp with dew. But he saw it was past mending. It was too bad the girls couldn't have their swing. He wondered if he couldn't get it fixed up for them so they could have it to play with after school. As he stood reflecting over the boards, the sense of protection grew deep and warm within him.

Beneath it was the memory of his various responsibilities that never let go of him nowadays. He had a different, wary, protective feeling about the bank since the old man Spencer, old J. T., had retired and left Richard at the head of things. Richard was pretty smart, but Fred Ferguson couldn't trust him the way he had the old man. He felt as if he could look away ahead into the future and see a little cloud of trouble that would have to be faced some day. But he said nothing about that to anyone, only determined to keep his eye on things. The church finances were in his keeping. He always had the feeling that he must look after the old folks, too, although of course Ben and Ella lived right out there beside them. Ben did pretty well with the farming—if anything, he was too slow, too careful; but he wasn't much good when it came to the money end of things. Grandpa Ferguson had a little deep-seated scorn of Ben—well, Grandma did too, she used that dry tone in speaking of him, in commenting on his and Ella's having no children. "I guess it ain't on our side," she said, with a small, triumphant malice. It seemed kind of mean toward Ben, he was good to the old folks; but when they wanted any real advice, even about farming, they went to Fred. And then there were all the other people, besides his own folks, for whom he took a certain responsibility. The church people. His father and Abner White were still the real elders. But they were getting old, and were both pretty tight-fisted. Fred Ferguson was the one to see to it that the minister got his little extra gifts of apples, chickens and wood, and that the parsonage was kept up to date and in order. He looked after the spinsters and widows—Essie Bartlett and her mother, Mrs. Dunn, Mrs. Rist. And a few others besides those in his own church. He knew how little Fannie Allison had in the bank, after all her years of teaching, and he had cautioned her against investing it in a fruit farm out in Idaho when Emmett Egerton, who used to be superintendent of schools, had got the notion of going out there and getting up some sort of real estate deal. The Spencers ought to be the ones to look after old Dick, but they didn't always do it.

But the growing of his responsibilities these last few years gave him really a deep, silent satisfaction.

He had an eye for his neighbors too. He could always look with pleasure at the white house across the street. The Gilberts, who lived there, were old people, but they were New Englanders, and they kept the place as neat as a pin. Right now, he could hear the faint, sharp sound of the axe from the back yard, where old Mr. Gilbert was chopping clean, trim sticks of wood for the cook stove. Those folks over next door weren't up yet. No wonder the man was always losing his job! They never had decent neighbors living on that side. And never would have, unless somebody bought the lot from C. E. Stark and put up a decent house there. This little jerry-made house, meant to be rented, fairly hurt Fred Ferguson with its look of flimsy seediness. Even if it was just built to be rented, Stark might have made a better job of it. He'd have thought with all the airs they put on, of being from the East and too good for Belmond—Missus, anyway—they'd be ashamed of owning such a place. But C. E. Stark was just about the meanest penny-squeezer in town. He even had old Abner White beat. "Yes, I'd like to tell her, when she can't see me on the street, after coming in the bank so big with her check book, that her twenty dollars had better be spent putting some screens on that place that don't let in all the flies in town—and give us some better neighbors." But he had nothing to say against his neighbors on the other side. The Morgans might have their peculiarities, but they were as good folks to have living beside you as could be found anywhere in town. Annie said he was too hard on this other family, they were both good-hearted; but Mr. Ferguson had an instinctive distrust of people who didn't own their own homes. It seemed as if they must be unsteady.

However, it wouldn't do to forget that they must get the children off in time for school. Mr. Ferguson went into the house to get the stove lighted. It was still fairly early, but he fidgeted around, and finally called up the back stairs:

"Mama!"

"All right! I'll be down."

Now everything was started going. She was calling the children. "Carl—come, Carl! Margaret—Dorothy—come, get up!" He heard the thud of little bare feet above him. Things went fast when mama was once up. He had made her a nice fire. He remembered that swing, and went out to the barn. And then at his work bench, looking out through the cobwebby window at the small, backyard familiarity of the alley, he sawed away happily while clean sawdust piled up and dribbled down on his trousers.

Mrs. Ferguson glanced out of the bedroom window to make sure that it was a really nice day, so that she would know whether to let the girls put on the pretty new dresses that she had made for them to wear when school began.

The weather was still the same. Nicer, if anything. She felt a sense of lovely, exalted contentment as she looked down upon

8

the lawn, saw the dewy richness, the lacing shadows of the trees. Everything was still green. They might have another whole week of summer.

But there was a touch of autumn dryness somewhere in the thickness of the leaves. It brought back a memory of last autumn, that lay deep within her, muted but still alive. She felt again the hushed chill of the little parlor in the old house in Woodbine; the service in the burying ground, sunny and quiet, where a few leaves fluttered, where the voice of the German preacher sounded devout and slow, where the September trees were thick and dark on the hills around . . . where new yellow clay was heaped on the mound that would soon be as grass-grown as the one beside it . . . and the family group turned away, leaving the old couple finally together, as they had been through most of their long lives.

That memory darkened the morning sunlight of the lawn. Right here in the pleasant comfort of her own house, with the busy day just about to begin, she had to feel again the wondering ache of that realization that time must pass, that households could be broken, old stabilities pass away.

And yet she didn't realize it. Not here in her own home. Everything was going on too busily. It was too much the brand-fresh present. The cleanly papered walls, the bright daylight shining of her hardwood floors, the rumpled white sheets of the bed, all denied it.

In the hall she met Carl.

"Hello, mama." He leaned fondly against her. He was always demonstrative with her when they chanced to be alone together.

She said to him, "Hurry down, dear. You mustn't be late for school."

She looked in at the girls. If they were awake, they weren't going to let on. But they were so pretty lying there, the dark head and the light, their little hands seemed so open and helpless, that she hated to tell them now they must get up. She never could get over her glad wonder that there should be two of them, just as there had been two at home, herself and Louie.

She knew from experience, though, that she had to speak as though she meant it.

"Come, girls. Aren't you going to get up? Come, Margaret. You'll look after Dorothy, won't you? Dorothy, you let sister help you get dressed. Mama wants to get breakfast. You know papa won't like it if you're late."

In her softness, she always had to put things like that on papa. But he didn't mind it. She couldn't be severe with the children just of her own accord—although sometimes she could be put out and cross.

Tasks seemed to be crowding upon her as she made the crooked turn of the narrow, steep back stairs. But with a pleasant, busy exhilaration. There was so much to be done this fall. The teakettle was rocking and steaming on the range. You could count on Fred to make a good fire.

Carl came down while she was setting the table, and hung around as he liked to do while she was at work.

"Mama, I was the only one yesterday to get the square root problem. Did you know that?"

"No, dear. Were you?"

"Miss Lingenfelder gave me a hundred. I bet I get one hundred on my first report card, mama. Don't you?"

"Oh, how can I tell, dear?"

"Why not?" he pleaded.

"Well, a hundred sounds pretty high. But I know you'll get a good mark."

"*How* do you know it?"

"Why, because you always do."

She was heating the frying pan—Fred always must have his two fried eggs—with an eye on the clock, but still more or less able to listen to Carl. He was mollified by that last reassurance.

"Mama."

"What?"

"Did you know that Uncle Ben had some collie pups out at the farm?"

"Yes, dear," she said hastily, "but you can't have one of them. You mustn't ask."

"But did you *know* it?"

"No, but I said—"

"Well, that's all I asked you, mama. I asked you, did you *know* it."

She saw Carl's look of proud, aggrieved virtue. It hurt her to refuse a single thing to her children. But they couldn't have that old dispute coming up again. If Carl had a dog, then Margaret would have to have a kitten. And they knew how that would go! Fred had said never again. Oh, dear, Mrs. Ferguson thought, why must those two children always be at opposite poles? When they had such a nice home, and everything was so lovely now? There was a little shame in her secret heart because she always wanted to side with Carl. She denied that indignantly whenever Margaret accused her of it. She only admitted it to herself, and as if she had her fingers crossed.

"Aren't the girls getting up?" she said.

Carl said quickly, "Do you want me to go and call them?"

"Oh, no, I guess they'll be down soon." Carl never could stand it to be out of anything, Fred said. But his failing of over-eagerness, his fearfully sensitive need of approval, always seemed to stir his mother's love for him to an aching tenderness. "You might go down cellar and get mama the butter," she told him.

"All right!"

She smiled to hear him go clattering down the stairs.

But while he was out of the way, she took the opportunity hastily to call the girls again. She wanted them to get down before Fred came in, because he expected them to get up just as soon as she called them, and to help her. And why *didn't* they get down and help her? Why didn't they *want* to, of their own accord—Margaret, anyway, her oldest daughter? The girls weren't nearly so willing as Carl. She defended him against Fred.

Finally they came trailing into the kitchen, when she had everything on the table. Margaret's whole idea seemed to be to get out of doing everything she possibly could. Dorothy was still too little.

"Are we going to eat in *here?*" Margaret said with disapproval.

"Well, you should get down and help if you want to eat breakfast in the dining room."

Margaret gave a little shrug to her shoulders, which her mother pretended not to see.

"Why, Dorothy—child!" Mrs. Ferguson couldn't help wanting to laugh. "Is that what sister did to your hair?"

All the little fair ducktails hung piteously dank, and one lock, tied up fiercely tight with a blue ribbon, curvetted out over that poor little forehead for all the world like the tail of the trotting horse Richard Spencer used to drive hitched to his red-wheeled trap.

"It looks nice!" Margaret cried with jealous quickness. "Mama, don't you dare to spoil it."

"It hurts," Dorothy begged. Her lip trembled. Under the drastic intensity of Margaret's ministrations, she hadn't been certain whether to come down proud or ashamed. But she knew now that she looked funny.

"Make it looser for her, Margaret!" Mrs. Ferguson begged.

She couldn't keep her fingers off that ridiculous ribbon, although she knew it never did to interfere with any of Margaret's notions.

"Mama Ferguson, you *have* spoiled it! I don't care, you told me to fix it. Oh, you *never* like what I do!"

Margaret grabbed the ribbon and threw it fiercely onto the floor. At that minute the grease began to burn.

"Take off the frying pan, Margaret. Quick!"

"I'm not going to. You'll say I did something wrong."

She ran into the dining room and the swinging door shook after her.

"Oh, dear!"

Mrs. Ferguson pushed the smoking frying pan over onto the reservoir of the stove. For a moment she stood distracted. Why did that child have to be so difficult? Her oldest daughter, who ought to have been her stand-by. Always so different, always at odds, and incalculable. She wanted to storm herself just as hard as Margaret did. But it was such a lovely day. She just couldn't have breakfast spoiled. It seemed as if they all ought to eat as a happy family in harmony with the beautiful sunshine. And then she wanted to get Margaret pacified before Fred came in and asked what was the matter. She pleaded, opening the swinging door:

"Margaret. Come. *Don't* be like this with mama."

Margaret was standing there all veiled, like a queer little nun or bride, by the fall of the soft marquisette curtain. Her eyes behind the shimmer of white had a wary, dark reserve.

"Margaret. Please! Now come out of there. Why, you know mama meant nothing against you. Do you want to spoil breakfast on this lovely day?"

Margaret's lips drooped sullenly. But she slowly consented to come out from behind the curtain, avoiding her mother's touch with a switch of her little body.

"Come back now. You don't want papa to see how you're acting."

"I don't care," Margaret said proudly.

"Well, just come back because mama asks you to, then. You can tie Dorothy's ribbon again."

"I don't want to."

Margaret waited a moment, after her mother had gone into the kitchen, and then opened the swinging door again with a little kick, and followed.

"Hasn't papa come in?" And he was the one who was always insisting that everyone must be on time! "No, Carl, I want you to begin eating." He made his appearance just as she was getting breakfast onto the table. She asked him, "What became of you?"

"Oh, I was fixing something out in the barn."

"What have you got on your pants?"

"Where? Oh, that. Just sawdust."

"What were you making, papa?" Dorothy begged.

"You go out in the yard after you get through breakfast and you'll see. . . . Can't you sit down, Annie?"

"In a minute. The rest of you go on and eat. I don't have to get anywhere," she added.

She liked to be up looking after them when she had them all seated at the table, and then afterwards to eat her meal in peace. Besides, Margaret still looked sullen. Her grievance had only been smoothed over. Fortunately, Fred didn't notice anything unless it was out so plain that he couldn't help seeing it. Now Mrs. Ferguson's exasperation had changed to wary defence of her child against her husband. She watched anxiously until she saw that Margaret had begun to eat. Then she sat down happily feeling that everything was all right after all, and that the sunshine wasn't going to be spoiled.

"What did you girls do when you were out at Aunt Ella's?" she asked.

Margaret wouldn't answer. Dorothy said with innocent vagueness, "I don't know." There were still marks of tears about her eyes, that Mrs. Ferguson at least could discern—papa would never see them; but already, little as she was, she seemed to be in secret feminine league with her mother to keep up the peace of the breakfast table.

"Oh, they got along all right," Mr. Ferguson said.

He laid down his napkin. He had never learned to fold it.

"Well, I guess I better go, Annie. Dick may be getting lonesome." Dorothy gave a soft little giggle. Dick, the janitor of the bank, was a family joke. "Have you thought what you wanted me to get?"

They made out their grocery list together. But Mrs. Ferguson always waited, with little evasions, for Mr. Ferguson to suggest the meat.

"How would it be if I brought home a good steak this noon?" He said that at least four days out of seven!

"We had that just day before yesterday. But it'll be all right," she said hastily. As he was leaving she added, "I'm going to need some eggs too, Fred."

"You better call up Ella right away then. Should have done it last night. Some of the folks'll be in, I guess, this morning."

"Well . . ."

When it came down to it, she just couldn't bear to tell Fred she wanted the eggs from the store today. That was the Scotch! It filled her with secret impatience whenever she ran against it. "We can get that from the farm. Don't need to buy it." How well she knew that canny saying! He didn't realize how it put her back in her housekeeping to have to wait for things to be brought in from the farm. She supposed someone would have to come in on purpose too, making her guilty. The Fergusons would go to any time and trouble rather than pay three cents! Now she couldn't get her cake baked this morning for the church social, she would have to put it off until this afternoon, and maybe the frosting wouldn't get hard. She pretended to side in with the Ferguson thrift, like a good wife, but in her heart that was not the way she wanted to do things. She wanted to be lavish, fine, abundant, like her sister Louie.

But Fred was quite innocent of her impatience and resentment. His masculine innocence always made her ashamed of the easy success of her feminine duplicity. Her heart melted in soft tenderness and shame when he gave her arm the little squeeze that was his regular way of saying good-bye when he went to the bank each morning. He didn't kiss her in front of the children, except when she was going away on the train, and then he was stiff and wooden with embarrassment.

But as soon as he was gone, she was much more busy and at ease with the children.

"You must go, girls!"

She held Margaret a moment, stroking her black hair, unable to part in anger.

"Dorothy's hair looks lovely. It was tied too tight, that was all—mama just wanted to loosen it."

"You didn't think I combed it nice."

"Yes, mama did too," she lied pleadingly.

She felt Dorothy's warm little kiss in response to hers. But Margaret seemed only to permit kisses without returning them. The child was so dark and different—the mother was baffled. At times, her own love seemed to stand off in hurt resentment for being refused. Then she got irritated. And the love itself fought with a coldness that would have horrified her if she had ever admitted it to herself in any but those off moments that she supposed didn't count. She had the knowledge that more was involved in Margaret's actions, like this morning, than had ever been unravelled—but she thrust it off, it made her afraid, upset her cherished belief in a simple, beautiful family happi-

ñess, with something that seemed alien. To deny all that, she
held Margaret longer than she did Dorothy.

"Carl! Where *is* Carl? Carl, you must hurry."

She went to the front door and watched as the two little girls
went off to school down the long cement walk under the full
September trees, so fresh in their summer dresses, Margaret's
green-and-white checked and Dorothy's blue. Other children
were passing. Carl went streaking past on his bicycle. She stood
listening while the last bell rang, far away but strong, beyond
the trees and the houses. The air seemed to shake with the last
reverberations. Then there was an emptied stillness in the morning streets.

Now she had the house to herself. Mrs. Ferguson paused in
the sitting room.

"Hm-hum," she said, half sighing, for no particular reason.

Then she went back into the kitchen. It was just a little bit
too warm from the fire in the range. But she didn't mind that.
It added to the feeling of sunny, solitary cosiness. There was
still some coffee left in the aluminum coffeepot. She poured herself a nice cupful and sat down at the table again, "in peace."
When any of the family were around, even Dorothy who seemed
like just part of herself, Mrs. Ferguson never sat down to this
luxurious little second breakfast in which she loved to indulge
herself all alone. It was one of her unacknowledged secrets, like
her opinion of Ella's cooking. On the wall hung this year's
calendar of the Farmers and Merchants Bank, with a scene of
cows in a meadow and a farmhouse in the distance, the kind the
bank always picked as appropriate to its title—only that this
was so obviously an English meadow and an English farmhouse.
Once Carl had asked innocently, "Papa, why don't the farms in
the pictures ever look like *our* farm?" Mr. Ferguson said, "Hm?
Oh, well, I guess they have to make a pretty picture."

How she hated to have to get right at those dishes! What she
really wanted to do was leave them just where they were until
she started to get dinner. But some of them might get in with
the eggs before noon and see her kitchen. She had never got
over the feeling that Grandma Ferguson's sharp eyes were upon
her housekeeping, even from out there in the country.

"Oh, hum, I suppose . . ."

She washed the dishes, with a noble air of busyness, and then went upstairs to make the beds, in the accepted order—but feeling a little ashamed of her weakness. The bedrooms were slightly chilly. That showed that it was really fall.

When she had finished upstairs, she went down to open up the front rooms. When she was first married, she used to keep her parlor closed on account of Grandma, although she detested all that meager, country way of doing things. She wasn't quite such a big fool as *that,* any more—at least!

She got her sewing and sat down in her favorite low rocking chair in the sitting room. Outside, there was the sense of the green grass and the trees, and the feathery thickets of late-blooming cosmos not yet quite dry from their early morning drenching of dew. But that only made it sweeter inside. Leisurely sounds came to her from the street. This was her precious hour of solitude. Almost no one was likely to come in in the morning. Her rooms were in order. She had set the plants outside near the back porch and had not yet brought them in. Her own things surrounded her, in the comfortable room, closed in by the soft white shimmer of the curtains that hung at the three long windows. Contentment breathed in the stillness. But she felt a stirring of that muted pain—a memory of the dark, bare chill of the little parlor at home, with the organ and rag carpet and plain wooden rockers. . . . Her parents had had so little all their lives. When Louie had come to choose something to remind her of father and mother, in place of the money she wouldn't take, there had really been nothing but the little old photograph album and the crazy quilt that mother had made from pieces of the best dresses of her daughters and daughters-in-law and granddaughters. Whenever Dorothy had had a new dress, she had always been so proud to keep out a piece of the goods for Grandma Luers! And yet, Mrs. Ferguson thought, she mustn't feel badly, for the old folks had been happy and contented in the three rooms—parlor and bedroom and kitchen—that Willie and Minnie had shut off for them as their part of the house. Minnie said they had always been contented—until Grandma died—then Grandpa was pretty lonesome. Grandma had accepted with such smiling, childlike joy the pieces of cloth they had all conscientiously sent her, because it seemed as if there was so little they did for her and Grandpa. Whenever Annie went to visit her, she brought out proudly from the big chest of drawers in the little stuffy bedroom, the pieces of lovely black silk dress goods that Louie was always giving her. "Ja, Louie she has everyt'ing all so fine!" "But, mother, why don't you get some of these made up and wear them? That's what Louie wants you to do." "Ach, what would I do that for? I keep them in my drawer where they stay good. Ja, maybe in one of them I get buried." But mother had loved pretty things. She had had more of an eye for them than Grandma Ferguson did! So simple, and yet with not a bit of that meager Scotch penuriousness—even with a childlike joy in extravagance! She kept the photograph of Louie in the long fur boa and hat with the ostrich plumes on the organ and loved to show it to everybody with a fond, delighted gloating. Now Minnie had all those beautiful pieces of dress goods. In the dark kitchen, with the one small window, and the faintly sour smell of food, Grandpa used to sit with his stockinged feet on the warm oven door, reading aloud from their German religious paper, while Grandma puttered happily at her cooking. They had seemed so far away—the old folks— and now they were both gone. But they were her folks just the same, even if she didn't talk about them much, and had lived here among Fred's folks. . . . Mrs. Ferguson leaned over to find a spool of blue thread in her wicker sewing basket.

All this time she had been guiltily aware that she was putting off calling up about the eggs. She hated to have to give that smiling, evasive, half-false account of what she was doing today. They thought she had it easy—Ella and Grandma did— with her washing done for her, help with the sewing, and this nice house. And right now she shrank from hearing Ella bring it in somehow—as she would!—that Margaret had put her foot in it while the girls were staying out there. "Did Margaret go to school today? Well, I thought maybe she was sick. I guess she don't like my cooking, that was the trouble!" What would she do if they had already come to town? She got warm all over in a panic. She thought of little devices—taking something from the secret hoard in her red plush glove box, of money Louie had given her, and sending Carl downtown in a hurry this noon—because she couldn't explain to Fred why she had neglected calling up so long this morning . . . only they were all gold pieces, and would look funny at the store. . . . She hadn't let the girls wear their new dresses while they were staying out at Ella's, deceitfully telling them that they had had the dresses for the first day and now it would be nicer to keep them clean for the end of the week. Now she knew she couldn't get her cake baked this morning—nor the graham gems she had meant to make for dinner, because she didn't want to get the oven going twice.

But when she called up Ella's and found the line busy, she put up the receiver with a feeling of lovely respite, a little while longer to sit here by herself and sew.

2

The two little girls went on down the street together. Margaret swished slightly, liking the sound of her crisp, fresh gingham skirt against the clean stiff embroidery of her petticoat. Dorothy, walking along demurely and wistfully beside her, looked up at her and then swished too. Margaret was hoping that someone coming along would notice how far below her waist her braids hung in the back. She was always hoping that some wonderful stranger would notice her dark eyes and her long braids and say, "Who is that child?"

The air was so sunny and nice and cool that it made her want to forget her grievance against her mother. But she couldn't, either, for it came too close on the secret humiliations of the last two days: her perception, uncertain and yet pitilessly keen, that Dorothy was the one everybody liked—Grandma and Grandpa, Aunt Ella, even Uncle Ben, although he was so nice to both of them, full of little jokes, setting them on the horses' big shiny backs and letting them ride to the trough in the evening, making excuses of errands (at which Aunt Ella scoffed) because he liked to drive them in to school. But Dorothy was the one he pulled onto his knee when he came in from his chores after supper, singing—

> "Over the hills and a great ways off
> The woodchuck ran and his tail dropped off—"

and then suddenly letting her down to the floor. Margaret sat severely looking through the Memoirs of General Grant. She had to pretend drearily to be above interest in Uncle Ben's songs. She didn't care to have him call out, "Come on, now, Mar'get, you next," as an after-thought. She could understand!

It was two days since they had gone down this walk to school. Now the tree branches arched above them, lofty and heavy with leaves; and just before they reached the corner, there was one branch that hung down all red among the green.

Dorothy gave a skip. "Isn't it nice to be both going to school? Sister. Don't you think it's nice?"

"Kind of," Margaret said briefly. "It would be if I liked my teacher."

"Aren't you sorry that old Prince got sick and died?"'

"No."

Margaret stared, trying to beat back the blackness of that word "died" that had terrified her ever since the folks had gone to Grandpa Luers' funeral.

"Why not, sister?" Dorothy breathed in soft wonderment. "*I* am."

"Because I'm not going to be sorry about anything."

She had made that vow after she had stopped crying in secret over her black kitten.

Now was coming the moment to which Margaret looked forward every morning. It was when they passed the old Spencer house. Richard Spencer's was the biggest house in town. But the old Spencer house, square and white, with the cupola and the arches above long shuttered windows, gave her the feeling of being almost in a story. It was not to spoil this feeling that she had consented to kiss her mother when she left the house.

Old Mr. Spencer was cutting the grass around the weeping birch tree with a big shears. Dorothy called out softly:

"Hello, Mr. Spencer!"

He straightened up somewhat, and pushed up his silver-rimmed spectacles on his big nose, looking at them judiciously.

"Hello! Let's see, I believe I know these little girls, don't I?"

"We're Fred Ferguson's children!" Dorothy said proudly.

"We-ell! So that's who they are! *Fred's* girls. That's right! They grow so fast I guess I can't keep track of them. What a nice little pair of them! So they're on their way to school, are they?" He reached over and put his hand on Dorothy's fair head, gently shaking it. "Where did you get those curls?"

"I don't know!"

Dorothy skipped along flushed and pleased with her boldness. "I think Mr. Spencer's nice, don't you, sister?"

He had called them a nice little pair, but it was Dorothy's curls that he had noticed. And they weren't even very curly. Margaret's pride in her long braids was suddenly gone. She loved Dorothy, her own little sister. But she wanted someone to notice *her*, to pick her out. And it should have been Mr. Spencer, because *she* was the one who liked passing his house and secretly put him among her own special people.

The instant they reached the school yard, Dorothy was surrounded. "Come on, Dor'thy! Come on and play." She let herself be trotted off between two of them, her soft face smiling and pleased, but not excited.

Margaret went up the walk between the boys' side and the girls' side, walking delicately, as if she were invisible. She didn't want Lucille or any of the girls to see her. The long stairway echoed hollowly. The cloakroom was empty. Standing for a moment in the doorway of the cloakroom, she could see the teacher at the desk reading, her hand shading her eyes, in that same old navy blue dress that everyone was so tired of having to look at. Margaret made a face. Dorothy had a pretty teacher, Miss Ludlow, who puffed out her hair and wore a shiny pink dress.

"Good morning, Margaret."

"Good morning."

"Good morning, Miss *Bar*-clay."

But the teacher did not insist upon it when Margaret made no answer.

She felt uneasy with Margaret Ferguson, always felt as if she weren't sure how to manage the child. She had looked forward to having Margaret in her room, because Carl had been one of her best pupils.

There were only two or three other children in the room, and they were all from the country. Miss Barclay didn't know that Margaret hadn't come in from the country this morning. The country children were allowed to enter early. It shamed Margaret to be counted among the "country kids," even for a day or two, but she liked the privilege of entering before the bell rang. She liked *any* privilege. Margaret slipped into her seat and opened her geography. She carefully laid her braids over her shoulders and let them hang down into the aisle. Irene said to do that, and the boys would have to notice them and brush against them going to the board. Irene, Irene, Irene! Margaret didn't want to play with Lucille and Edna Mae and the rest of the girls. Irene was the only one in the room who was different. She began to write a note to Irene, pretending that it was something she was copying out of her geography.

"Dear Irene, I came into school early, wish you were here there are only some country kids."

There were some flowers in her inkwell!—a sawed-off stalk of geraniums with the stems wet and dark from the shallow little well of blue-black ink. For a moment Margaret was all excited. Her dreams soared up and she was sure that it was Gardner Allen who had put them there. What Irene had said about the braids was really true—it had made him notice her. She put her face down to the warm scarlet of the geraniums. Eddie Whitby, one of the country kids, sitting just a few seats away, turned red under his freckles. Margaret saw his self-conscious look, and knew that *he* was the one who had brought her the flowers! He lived right down the road from Aunt Ella's, and whenever she was out at the farm, he would appear in the grove, and then pretend to be playing out there by himself when she took no notice of him. "What's he always around for?" Aunt Ella asked once. Uncle Ben said slyly, "Maybe he's took a shine to one of these girls." "That little snipper?" Aunt Ella demanded. Margaret's disappointment was so bitter that she couldn't stand it. It seemed to hurt her all inside. She sat for a moment, staring with blazing black eyes; and then picking up the geraniums, she marched straight to the wastebasket, with a regal gesture of disdain threw them inside, and came back to her seat without a glance at Eddie Whitby.

She put her head down on her desk. Nothing ever happened as she wanted it—nothing! The wrong people always liked her, and the ones who should have picked her out chose someone else. Gardner Allen liked Mildred Summers. *Mildred*. If there was anyone she hated in this whole room it was Mildred Summers. She hated those light curls that made everyone think Mildred was so sweet, when Margaret knew she could be meaner than any of the girls. She was always telling one what another one had said about her, and as if she sympathized with the one to whom she told it. Mildred was like the golden-haired heroines in the stories that Margaret resented as her natural-born enemies —she liked Rose Red better than Snow White, and Rebecca than Rowena; and it made her just furious that they always got second-best. "So Snow White married the prince and Rose Red his brother." Some day she was going to write stories that turned out the other way!

The bell rang. Margaret lifted her head. Eddie Whitby's freckled face was turned away, but she could see how red his ears were. Margaret felt fiercely that she didn't care. What right had he to like her when she didn't like him? She didn't care about a single person in this room except Irene. But of course Irene was the one—she *had* to be, just because she was interesting!—with whom the folks wouldn't let Margaret play. Her mother wouldn't let her ask Irene to the house.

The shouts in the school yard were louder for a few minutes, and then broke and scattered. The children were forming into lines outside. Then the whole school building seemed to shake under the marching through the halls and up the long stairways. Boys and girls poured into the room and noisily took their seats.

"Quiet, class—quiet!" Miss Barclay was saying nervously.

Margaret sat watching the inrush with bright dark eyes. Lucille and Edna Mae came in with their arms around each other. They were rosycheeked from running. They dropped panting into their seats. Mildred came in smiling as always. Margaret felt a painful tightening of her throat. She stared icily past Gardner Allen hoping that he was seeing her refuse to notice him. She wished he would stumble or something. She hated him because he was so good-looking. But she heard him plump down into his seat.

Miss Barclay stood at the desk waiting. There were three minutes after the last bell had rung. Irene hadn't come yet. Margaret suffered. Miss Barclay had her finger on the bell. At the very last moment, Irene came sauntering into the room and took her seat. Miss Barclay tapped the bell.

Margaret could breathe again. She used to cry at home for fear of the disgrace of being late. But Irene didn't care. She didn't care if she failed in arithmetic at the board. She seemed to rest in some deep, queer, smiling certainty of herself, that had nothing to do with things like school. Now that Irene was in her seat, Margaret was too shy to look at her. She crumpled up the note and hid it in her desk among the tablets and the schoolbooks. But when she passed Irene's seat coming from the blackboard, she whispered quickly:

"See you at recess!"

She stood with heart thumping as they waited for the gong to sound and Miss Barclay to tap her bell. Would Irene look for her? Margaret pretended that she knew all about the things Irene talked of, but she was afraid of revealing her innocence and letting Irene feel that she didn't really know any more than Edna Mae or Lucille. The big gong shook and resounded through the building. The long lines went marching out, past the teachers on the landings, into the bright September air. Margaret slipped out of line and stood near the big doorway. She was afraid the girls would want her to play, she pretended to be absorbed in picking some bits of rough mortar from between the warm bricks.

"Margaret! Come on," Lucille cried.

Margaret would not hear. Irene came past; and reaching out boldly from the cold torture of her shyness, Margaret took hold of Irene's arm and walked blindly past the girls.

"Let's go over again and get one of the windows."

24

The basement window was shaded and cool, with its wide cement sill, away from the September sunshine. Margaret didn't care if Dorothy did see her. Dorothy wouldn't tell the folks. And Carl couldn't see her from the boys' side. She and Irene were all by themselves.

"What shall we talk about?"

"Do you want me to go on with the story I was telling?"

"Oh, yes! Go on with that."

Margaret listened dreamily. Irene could tell stories just like a book, better than a book, because the story was heightened by the queer, husky fascination of her voice. There were two sisters, Helena and Phyllis, beautiful but poor, they were just little seamstresses in London. Margaret tried to see some resemblance between the two sisters and herself and Dorothy, as she always did with stories—glad because it was the older one this time who was really the heroine, while the younger one was "pretty but not beautiful." But more often she put Mildred Summers into the rôle of the character opposite to the one she had chosen for herself. It hurt so terribly to feel jealous of Dorothy, her little sister; but she could hate Mildred with a fierce gladness. From where they sat, Margaret could see the girls playing out in the wide yard from which the grass was worn off in patches.

Now Edna Mae and Lucille came up, hot and panting, their hair streaked across their foreheads.

"Aren't you going to play?"

They stared at Irene. They had forgotten all about not having made up too, since they had been so horrid about Margaret going to the Presbyterian Sunday School—didn't act as if they *had* to make up, because *their* Sunday Schools, the Methodist and the Congregational, were bigger.

"We're busy," Margaret said.

Edna Mae and Lucille stared and then ran off. Now they were mad! A thrill of perilous horror and delight ran down all through Margaret. She had set herself finally apart from them, and she didn't care. When recess ended, she went boldly back to the schoolhouse with her hand in Irene's cool, secret clasp that seemed always to be pressing a kind of meaning that she felt with fascinated uneasiness but could never quite make out.

At home that noon she was brief and distant with her family; and as soon as she could get away from the table, she ran outdoors to the swing that papa had fixed for them. She and Dorothy had broken the seat, working up. Higher, higher, a backward scrape of her foot through the dirt, a push, her toes almost brushing into the maple leaves. . . . Did she dare to jump from this high? If she thought of it she had to do it. She came down hard on the ground, shaken, her hands flat on the dust; but seeing Carl on the porch, she got up with proud trembling unconcern, slightly shook her skirt, and walked away.

"Margaret, aren't you going to wait for Dorothy?"

"Well, she can come."

"Margaret, please wait for her."

"Well, I *yam!*"

Margaret hurried along so fast that Dorothy had to trot to keep up with her. She was impatient now of everyone but Irene. She walked in a delicious haze, feeling a half-terrified superiority to all the houses on the street, because now she was friends with the worst girl in the room and mad at the other girls. Proudly, she did not even glance at the old Spencer house as they passed it.

After school, when the long line reached the end of the walk, Margaret turned off quickly with Irene, walking again as if she were invisible.

"Isn't that your brother?" Irene murmured, pressing her arm.

"I don't know." Margaret shrugged her shoulders. It made her impatient that Irene hung on her arm and kept looking back to see if that was Carl. "Come on, I don't want to let him see us."

"Why not?"

"Oh, because . . ."

She was ashamed to say that it was because the folks wouldn't like it if they knew she was going home with Irene. She felt deep down the joy and excitement of her wickedness. It served mama right for the way she had acted this morning. But all the time, when she was out at the farm, and Aunt Ella had acted as if everything that she did was unaccountable—never wondering how *she* felt about the *rest* of them—Margaret had been half homesick and craving the warm oblivion of her mother's acceptance. She could see the girls away off down the street. Now they were mad at her! The sense of defiant wickedness glittered above the humiliation of having just Eddie Whitby leave her the flowers.

They turned off on one of those little side streets that never seemed to lead anywhere and that had a shoddy, unnamed quality that Margaret perversely liked. She had always been wild to go home with Irene, and see how she lived, and yet afraid. The rutty road ended in nothing at all, and on one side of the road there were several little one-story houses under scraggy trees. Margaret had never been on this street before, and so she liked it.

"Which house do you live in?"

"That one."

It was painted a dingy pink. Margaret detested that nasty little rented house next door to her own, but this one had a fascination, because Irene lived in it, and she didn't know where Irene had come from or what her folks were like. The door was open, and Margaret could see inside, the wall paper pasted on the cracked walls, the sagging floor under scraps of dingy carpet. There was some story-book feeling about the place and the shaggy trees with their spread-apart branches. A trunk stood right in the front room. Margaret felt all the time as if she were just on the verge of some dark knowledge. It was like when she was down in the ravine near the railroad tracks, where there were old bottles and a twisted shoe belonging to no one, and a dark wet smell from the stream that soaked mysteriously through weeds and rubbish between steep bushy banks and ended she never knew where.

"Don't look over there," Irene commanded.

Margaret stared straight ahead. But she couldn't help giving just one quick glance next door. The grass was worn off the yard, the ground under a horrid old swing was scraped with dusty lines. Cans glinted rusty-bright from the litter of old boxes, broken chairs, a washing machine of a dark weathered color, in the back yard.

Irene said, "That's where that nasty little jackass of a Jennie Gowan lives. If she comes over here, this time I'm going to kill her."

Margaret shivered with delight.

"Come on, we'll go into the house and get some cookies."

Margaret walked with delicate, blind precision through the soggy disorder of the kitchen, learning with a gasp inside what places could be like, but wanting to know it. She ate the crumbly, brown under-part of the store cookie and pulled at the leathery marshmallow top stuck over with hard little shreds of cocoanut, fighting down the turning of her stomach with a kind of pleasure.

An old woman came out into the kitchen while they were there. Margaret gave a startled little jump. She looked with fearful awe at the bright dark eyes, small and stealthily acute, with a trickle of tears into the wrinkles of the brown leathery face from which rough white hair was pulled back and twisted. She remembered how Mildred had said about Irene the day school started, "We don't want to ask her to play with us, they're poor white folks, the kind that come from Missoury." She stood away.

"Who's this little girl, Reny?"

"Her name's Margaret. You don't know her," Irene said curtly.

"My, what a pretty dress!"

The old woman spoke with naïve, gloating admiration. While Margaret stood not liking to draw back, she drew a lean brown finger down the shining length of one of the black braids, handled the pearl buttons on the gingham dress, even drew up the skirt and touched the embroidered points of the white petticoat. Margaret began to tremble.

"Let her go. She don't like that," Irene said imperiously. "You go back into the bedroom. You don't need to come out here."

The old woman dropped Margaret's skirt. She shuffled off

with an anxious servility that the teary brightness of her eyes made furtively ominous. Margaret was glad to get outdoors. Her heart beat too fast.

"Who was that?" she breathed, touching Irene's arm.

"My gran'ma. I don't pay any attention to her," Irene answered impatiently. "She won't hurt you," she added grandly, to Margaret. "Come on. Let's play."

The awfulness of the house, barely glimpsed and fearfully imagined, seemed to give Irene a mystery of experience which made Margaret humble and uncertain. A splendor, shoddy and yet lustrous, hung about Irene, shone from her hands that were grubby and smooth and pale, with their secret touch, and glinted from under the heavy lids of her gray-black eyes. Margaret's legs were still trembling. She was imperious with the other girls, wanting to choose the games herself, often losing her fun when the others chose them; but with Irene, that was all in abeyance. She seemed to herself ignorant and colorless, and she had to feel her way along behind Irene.

"Shall we be those two sisters you were telling about?"

"No. I don't want to be poor. I want to be rich. I know another story about duchesses and countesses. We'll be them. I'll be Duchess Dorinda and you can be Countess Phyllista. Then we can be dressed in velvet and all kinds of rare jewels and go to balls in the royal palace. Listen. I'm Duchess Dorinda and the queen's jealous of me," Irene said disdainfully, "because I'm so much more beautiful than her. Everybody's in love with me."

"Like in *Snow White*," Margaret said.

"What's that?"

"Why, don't you know, *Snow White and the Seven Dwarfs*?"

"Oh, a *fairy* tale."

Irene went across the yard sweeping her train, and Margaret tried to imitate her. She felt chagrined and uncertain about fairy tales now.

"I want my di'mond ty-ara, Riggs!" Irene stamped her foot. "No! I said my di'mond one and you brought me em'rald! I dismiss you at once, menial!" she said grandly; and added in her ordinary tone, "I can't fool around with servants that disobey me."

"Aren't we going to wear long gloves?" Margaret asked eagerly. Mrs. Richard Spencer had worn long gloves at the dedication of the new Opera House.

"No. I'm not. Lord Ronald likes to see my arms bare."

Irene moved her arms voluptuously; and Margaret felt again, with burning humility, that there were things she didn't know.

"There's that nasty little jackass again!" Irene stopped and stamped her foot. "You get out o' here. Or I'll kill you."

It was that little Gowan kid, whom the children called "Squirrel-Eyes." She had come over to the edge of Irene's yard and was watching them greedily. She ran scooting back into her own yard shrieking, "You can't touch me, dassent touch me here!"—and then she sat in that old swing watching them with those funny eyes. She tried to yell at them, but pretty faintly, and she backed down and got ready to run when Irene looked toward her yard.

"Come, countess, let us get into our coach and drive away from this rabble."

"Oh yes, all right, let us."

All at once, Margaret saw Irene's face change, and she stopped playing. Her eyes got glinting and queer under the thick lids, and she began to smile. She pressed Margaret's hand quickly. Margaret looked and saw Carl standing out there beside the tree! He had that virtuous look on his face. He said:

"Mama wants you to come home."

Margaret stared stonily ahead of her. But anger ran through her in a fiery thrill.

"She does not!"

"She does too. She says you're to come home."

"You go away from this yard, Carl Ferguson. I *hate* you."

Anyway, he didn't dare wait for her! He said, "All right!" still virtuously, but he turned and made for home. He had seen where she was going after school and he had told! Margaret tried to keep on playing, but everything was spoiled for her. She couldn't be a countess any more. She was choking with the humiliation of being told to come home. The folks never wanted to let her do a single thing that she really liked. None of the other girls knew how to play the way Irene did, or could tell which was higher, a duke or an earl. They were just beginning the ball! Irene said, "Oh, don't pay any attention, kid, I wouldn't"; but she couldn't help it.

"*Don't* go, kid!"

"I've got to."

"Oh, pshaw! You don't have to do what your brother tells you."

"I *don't* do what he tells me. But I can't have any more fun playing. I'm going to go home and tell Carl Ferguson what I *think* of him."

"I won't like you if you go away now," Irene taunted.

The road and the shaggy trees were blurred with tears. But Margaret went away just the same. She would always be ashamed to come back here now. It seemed as if she was just walking in a vacant place where there was nothing but empty anger and torture. Because she had made the girls mad, and now Irene was mad at her too. Grandma and Aunt Ella didn't like her, and she didn't like them—or the folks, either. There was a kind of fearful exaltation in this loneliness.

When she went down her own street, her face was set and blind for fear she would meet Mrs. Viele or someone else she knew. She couldn't bear to go into the house, although she had started away from Irene's wild to have it out with Carl. Margaret crossed the lawn with stealthy haste. There was a hidden place near the corner of the house beside the drain pipe and the cistern. That was where she liked to sit when she was miserable. Water came out of the drain pipe clogged and soggy with leaves and half filled an old, dark, soaked wooden bucket. Between the cracks on the square cistern top she could see, far down, the somber black brightness of deep, deep water. On the other side she was hidden by the young pines that the folks had set out along the driveway between their house and the Morgan house. The tender green tops of the pine trees had a spicy scent in the sunshine.

Here she revelled in her loneliness. She thought of something that had happened a long time ago, and that mama would never know she even knew about, but that she never would forget just the same. It was when she was a little tiny girl, and Dorothy was a baby, and she had heard her mother say to some ladies who were calling, "Yes, I'm glad she's so fair, Margaret is so dark"; and she had gone and hidden under the porch, crept in through the broken lattice, and sat there among the leaves and smell of porch posts and damp black earth. She had felt her darkness like a disgrace—and yet she was proud of it, because it made her different. Perhaps after all she *was* adopted. She used to listen with childish acuteness, and it seemed to her that Grandma and Aunt Ella used to talk about "when Carl was born" and "when Dorothy was born," but never "when Margaret was born." It seemed as if her real home had never been this house, or anywhere in Belmond, but in some place that she had read of, or dreamed of. Maybe it was some castle. But when, a long time ago, Aunt Louie had sent her and Dorothy a fairy-tale book with beautiful colored pictures, and she had seen the little cottage of the Three Bears with its green door, at once she had had the queerest feeling—This is where *I* live. It seemed as if the memory of just such a place had always been in her mind. Once when she had worn colonial costume at the Washington's Birthday bazaar, of bright pink shiny cambric, Richard Spencer hadn't known who she was. And then he had said to mama, "Look out! I warn you, she's going to work havoc some day." Margaret didn't know just what "havoc" was, but she liked it because it sounded dangerous. When people always said how darling and pretty Dorothy was, giving her the principal part in the Children's Day exercises, Margaret suffered jealous agonies. But she had things to treasure up, like Mr. Richard Spencer saying she would work havoc, and Irene saying that she thought the boys were going to like Margaret better than Mildred when they grew up—special people, not just the ordinary ones like the people who belonged to the church, and the neighbors. She knew all the time, through her misery, that somewhere there would be a wonderful, shining, special fate for her.

There were voices on the back porch. Uncle Ben had brought the eggs. Margaret crouched down in her hidden place. "I don't know as there's as many as you want, Annie, but mebbe I can bring you some more Satidday or some such time." The slow sound of Uncle Ben's voice made Margaret think of going out into the barn with him, at milking, and seeing the dark soft eyes of the Jersey cow turning watchful from her stall. Mama's voice, too, gentle and bright: "Oh, these will be plenty, Ben. I hope you didn't have to come in just to bring them." "Oh, I don't mind a little trip to town now and then." It made Margaret long to run to her mother and bury her face on that soft breast. If she just cried, and didn't try to understand anything, but just cried. . . . But mama just couldn't believe that anything Carl did could be wrong. She might pretend, but Margaret could see through her. Margaret crouched down. The air was secret and close in here between the shiny evergreens and the house wall. Even through her nervous misery ran the sharp, dramatic feeling of that one red maple branch among the green.

3

Carl could still hear that awful crying from upstairs where mama had taken Margaret to have it out with her. He wandered around the house for a while feeling lonely and aggrieved. He stood in the pantry while he ate jelly from a glass. But it didn't taste good. Margaret was the one who had done all the disobeying. He had only done what mama wanted. Mama was the one who had sent him, but now that Margaret was making such a fuss, she seemed to be distracted and not to know where the blame lay. "I didn't tell. I just said I knew where you were. Didn't I, mama?" "Shut up, Carl Ferguson! You needn't ever speak to me again." A guilty feeling lay heavy in his chest.

He went out into the back yard.

He thought of going over to Harry's and staying there for supper. But supper was better here at home. He would always rather have Harry come over here. Mrs. Santley seemed to be afraid they were going to eat too much instead of not enough, like mama. Reverend Santley asked the blessing in a loud voice, straight along, with his hand over his eyes, but even before he got to the end he was holding out the other hand, and then he said in just that same loud voice, "Amen pass the bread." Papa's blessing was short, with his head ducked, as if he was kind of ashamed. Carl liked it when they had family worship out at the farm. When he ate with Grandma and Grandpa, they always asked *him* to say the blessing. Grandma thought he did it fine. He ought to be a preacher when he grew up.

"Uh-uh," he answered, remembering Reverend Santley.

"What are ye going to be?" Grandpa asked.

"Oh, I don't know. Maybe I'll be in Congress."

"Why not be a farmer? What's better'n that?"

Carl wished he could go out and see Grandma and Grandpa right now. Everything that he did was right there. He was Grandma's and Grandpa's favorite of all the children, and the rest of them knew it—some of the cousins tried to make fun of him. In a way, he felt more at home in Grandma's and Grandpa's old rock house than he did in his own house with his own folks. There was something about it that he knew better, down deeper, than anything else. Aunt Ella's and Uncle Ben's house was more just ordinary. He liked to go around with his grandfather to do the early chores, water the big horses when they came in hot and snorting from the field, go up into the great, dim, churchlike barnloft and pitch down dusty hay; and then he and his grandfather crossed the farm yard to the old rock house that lay golden and mellow in the evening light, washed their hands out in the kitchen in the cool soft water that came out amber-colored from the iron pump in the sink, and sat down to Grandma's supper of fried eggs, fried potatoes, bread and tea, and the little dish of brown, puckered apple pickles that she always put on the table.

Carl went back into the house. His mother had come downstairs and was getting supper. Her look made him feel anxious and dreadful. He hung around the kitchen longing for reassurance. After a while he said in a subdued voice:

"Mama? Is Uncle Ben in town?"

"I don't know whether he is any more."

"I'm going back with him to supper."

"No, Carl, you can't."

"Why can't I?"

"The girls were just out there."

"Not at Grandma's and Grandpa's, they weren't."

Carl waited. His mother went over hastily and felt of her cake. It was still warm. She would barely be able to get it frosted in time for tonight. She would have to take it to the church uncovered and let the frosting harden on the way. Carl had a terrible feeling of being to blame for everything. It was mean of mama not to say that he wasn't.

Supper was horrid. A cloud of disgrace seemed to hang over the table, and Carl felt that he was included in it, and that it wasn't fair. Margaret shot him one look of hatred from her swollen eyes. He tried to look virtuous, but he couldn't when mama didn't say anything to him. And she wouldn't because she didn't want papa to notice—she would cover anything up rather than have papa scold the children. Papa didn't see things most of the time unless he was told. Mama was being nice to Margaret to get her to eat. She had got Margaret to come downstairs and not spoil supper, but Margaret just took her fork and made patterns on her cream sauce.

As soon as he dared, Carl said "Scuse," and slid out from his chair. He wandered out across the lawn, not knowing just where he was bound for, and then sat down gloomily on the old chopping block near the alley. He wouldn't go into the house until the folks came and called him, even if he missed the church social!

Gee, if he could just see Captain come racing across the yard! He hated Margaret whenever he thought of having given Captain away. He wouldn't admit that Captain had done it. But he could never forget the stopped, awful feeling when he had been shown Margaret's kitten lying limp and dead on the grass near the apple tree. There was something about Captain's downcast, shivering tail that had given him away. Carl knew it, even when he had taken Captain off and was falsely pleading to be told that he wasn't the one. It was Carl himself who had taught Captain to chase the kitten. "Sickum, Cap!" he used to say just loud enough for Margaret to hear. It made her so frantic. It was just in fun . . . he thought it was in fun. He had never supposed Captain was going to hurt the old kitten. But he knew in his heart he had been furious and jealous when mama had found big dirty paw tracks all across the front room rug, and Margaret had cried in malicious triumph, holding up the kitten's little tiny paws, "They aren't Black One's!" But her wild sobs had convicted him of guilt, just like today. He despised Margaret for crying, but he was always frightened and made to feel unequal by the display of such passionate woe. He wanted to cry too, always, when he heard anybody else. Carl's ideal of himself was so high. It didn't include hurting anybody's feelings, and so it never seemed as if it could be himself who had done that. He just had to find excuses. There was nothing for him to say when the folks had told him it was their decision that Captain must be given away, and that neither he nor Margaret could keep a pet again—trying to make it fair that way. Carl didn't believe anyone *could* like a cat the way a person did a dog.

He wouldn't live in the same house any more with Margaret Ferguson! The folks would have to choose. Mama would have to choose this very night. Margaret was always somehow putting him in the wrong. His bright confidence, fostered everywhere else, at school and in church and out at Grandpa's, seemed to falter before her big, black, scornful eyes and drooping under-lip. He would go out and stay with Grandma and Grandpa, and come in and sit with them in their pew in church.

It was beginning to get dark outside. It was pretty cool out here on the chopping block. It was already dark in the narrow alley shut in with barns and trees.

Now, out on the farm, the darkness was spreading all around. Cattle stood in the big pasture. Tiny pools of water lay dark and still in the hollows their hooves had left among the black, moss-filmed hummocks in that swampy place. Uncle Ben was still doing chores, but Grandma and Grandpa were inside, and the deep-set windows of the rock house made lighted squares in the twilight. Carl thought that probably Grandma was out in the kitchen setting the pancake batter, with the door open to get the light from the dining room, and that Grandpa was in there, in his rocker, looking at the paper and shouting out to Grandma, "I see—" well, that somebody had put up a new barn, or that someone else had got his thrashing done, in the

Buck Township Items—"D'ye hear that, mother?" The big night was lonely around the place. Grandma and Grandpa looked at the paper a while and went to bed. And then, through the open window in his own little room, would come the chorus of frogs from that low place across the road in the meadow that was swathed in mist—"Hmmmmmmm . . . *hmmmmmmmm mmmm,*" always the same, just on two notes, up . . . down, a low vibrating, sorrowful music that seemed as if it was the night singing to itself, the dark blind roads, the dark wide pastures, the black fir trees out in the grove.

Carl shivered. A cold little breeze ruffled the berry bushes.

All at once the light went on in the kitchen. The windows flung down warm, slanted oblongs across the dark lawn. Carl felt as if he couldn't stand it any longer being out here all by himself. It seemed as if he really had gone out to Grandpa's to live and didn't belong to the folks any more. He just couldn't live if they all went off to the church social without him. Yes, he *had* wanted to tell on Margaret . . . no, he hadn't, either . . .

He got up, and ran into the kitchen, and stood there panting a little.

"Mama."

She was putting the cake carefully into the basket.

"*Ma*-ma. I didn't just go and tell on Margaret. *Didn't* you send me?"

He went over to her, smelling the lovely fresh frosting, feeling as if he had got back into the light from exile. "Yes, of course mama sent you." She whispered it. She put her arms around Carl, and they stood there in the kitchen together, his cheek pressed against her thin waist that smelled of ironing. They understood each other and felt as if they had both got back from somewhere else.

"Mama, I don't want to live anywhere else, with anybody but you, not even with Grandma and Grandpa."

He spoke, his voice muffled against the little frills of her yoke, that scratched his mouth with their fresh, comforting daintiness.

"Why, you don't have to. We wouldn't *let* you."

37

"I know it," Carl said happily after a moment. He drew a sigh. And now all at once he felt generous toward Margaret, and was happy, because he didn't have to hate anybody in the world.

4

The Fred Ferguson family filed into their regular pew. They were all here. Just once in a while, when there was going to be company for dinner, one of the children was allowed to skip church and go home after Sunday School. Carl was the one who had always been so good in church, ever since he was a baby. But he loved running into the empty house, fragrant with the chicken that mama had put in the oven before she left. It was his duty to keep up the fire and once in a while baste the chicken. He was sent home to do it more often than Margaret because he could be trusted to remember better. He was proud of keeping things going. Dinner on the table never tasted so good as the little brown pieces he broke off the chicken and ate so hot that tears came into his eyes. There was so much time that he couldn't decide what to do, and he got out his mechanical drawing board and let it stand while he lay on his stomach on the floor reading in his Sunday School paper the serial about boys going camping. But this morning there was no need to let any of the children off from church. They were all invited out to the farm for Sunday dinner.

Church was just the same as always. The old Fergusons sat up in front on account of Grandpa Ferguson's hearing. The grown folks couldn't get much more than the children out of Reverend Santley's long, theological discourses, but they listened with respect because he was the minister. The Presbyterian church was small in Belmond, but one of the oldest there, and had a few faithful members. Grandpa Ferguson wouldn't admit that any preacher they had in the Presbyterian church wasn't completely satisfactory, as long as he preached the gospel. He was jealous of the claims of the Methodist and Congregational preachers, and felt a hot rivalry toward the Baptist, since that church was in a class with the Presbyterian in regard to size. The United Brethren, which was across the tracks in the other part of town, he didn't count. The Catholic was beyond the pale altogether.

Certainly nobody could have guessed from Mrs. Ferguson's face what she was thinking. Since she was Fred's wife, she was of course a leading member. She brought cakes and made coffee for the church suppers, waited on table in a crisp fresh apron, took the fancy work booth at the bazaar and tried with flushed, anxious face to get people to buy the leftovers so that they could close with more money than the Baptist ladies had made. But she had never quite felt as if she belonged here, even in this nest of Fergusons and their relations, or felt as if her real place was among this congregation—Essie Bartlett and her mother, the Whites, Mrs. White and Lillian sitting subdued and colorless beside the old man with Howard placed meekly at the end of the pew, and Mrs. Dunn billowing under rusty black, and getting tearful and snuffling when she saw her boy Lloyd pass the wicker basket for the offering. The keys were streaked, like old finger nails, on the dark organ. The small choir sat, vacant and uncomfortable, on dining room chairs facing the congregation. Mrs. Ferguson liked to have everything nice. If she could have chosen, she knew secretly that she would have gone to the Congregational church, which was of brick on a pleasant shady corner, and where all the ladies she liked best belonged. She had been taken into the Monday Club last spring. She was the only Presbyterian among its members. But of course nobody would ever have any idea. The Fergusons and the Whites were all important here; they ordered the supplies and put up the stoves and revered and patronized the ministers; and Fred looked up to Old Man White, sitting bleak-faced and unmoving in front of the pulpit, really as to an elder. Her sister Louie was the only one she could have told.

She felt remorseful at her secret thoughts, and settled herself, spreading her black silk skirt. But she had felt a guilty sympathy with Margaret that time the child had come home from the first grade, crying, because Ada Rist was the only other girl in her room who went to the Presbyterian Sunday School.

The sermon was longer than ever. The church had to be satisfied with elderly ministers, since it couldn't offer much in the

39

way of salary. But the preacher was sure of getting all that was offered. Finally it was over. They got up to sing the last hymn, the voices sounding above the pumped-up loudness of the old organ. Mr. Santley raised a large, bony hand for the benediction. The organ broke out again into reluctant music. The audience broke up. The Fergusons moved out of their pew into the aisle among people. They greeted Essie and asked how her mother was. Mrs. Dunn, when she took anyone's hand, always held it squeezed between her fat thumb cushion and her fingers, denting it with the moist gold of her thick wedding ring, while she spoke in a commiserating tone. "Where's the other folks? Nobody sick out there?" "Oh, no. They're all right. Just didn't get in today, I guess." Mr. Santley stood holding out his bony hand at the open door.

Then they all moved outside, down the steps, out into the gold of the September air, where the trees stood faded and thick against the blue sky around the dingy red brick of the plain old church on its little piece of sunken lawn. Mrs. Ferguson looked around for the children.

Teams stood out in front of the church. Everyone knew the old Fergusons' buggy and the two-seated rig that belonged to them and Ben and Ella equally. The old folks had driven in to church in the rig today, since they were to bring Fred's folks back with them. Ella had stayed to get the dinner ready. The brown horses switched flies from shiny rumps, and one turned and craned its neck with a creaking stretch of leather harness. Carl was already outside waiting, bright and eager-eyed, on hand as usual when it was time to go out to the farm.

"I can fix your reins for you, Grandpa! Aren't they too tight? I can fix 'em!"

"Are they? Well, I don't know. I don't just trust these horses o' Ben's. Wouldn't monkey around 'em."

"You better let things alone," his father said.

"I can drive, though!"

"No, I guess I better do the driving. You kin sit by me, though, and see I don't turn off down the wrong road."

"Oh, gee!" Carl laughed kindly at Grandpa's joke.

Grandpa said, "Guess we better put the young folks all in front, heh, and let the old folks sit in the back?"

"I'd better hold Dorothy on my lap," Mrs. Ferguson said nervously.

"Well. It's kind o' crowded, but Ben he didn't seem able to get in, for some reason."

"Yes, he's got great reasons for not doing things!" Grandma Ferguson observed, with a little sniff.

Fred Ferguson said amiably, "Oh, well, we're not too crowded."

"No, not a bit," his wife said.

"Well, they missed a good service today, we can tell 'em!"

The buggy went jolting down the Sunday street, past the Methodist church that was just letting out, and then turned into the long wide road that led out to the farm.

They were all to eat at Ella's. It was a point of pride with her to have no help with the dinner. She had sent the others all into the front room.

"No, I've got it all ready. That's what I stayed home from church for. All I've got to do is put things on."

Mrs. Ferguson and the two old people were sitting in the parlor. Carl had gone off to help unhitch the horses. Margaret and Dorothy had run out to see if their playhouse out in the grove was still there. They had divided off the rooms with stones and furnished them with pine cones and an old blue salt cellar. The bright country air went all through the somewhat bare rooms of the house. Good smells came from the hot kitchen. The talk in the parlor would start and then die down. Everything had to be repeated to Grandpa. Fred Ferguson wandered around, into the house and then out again, and stood on the doorstep. He liked to look over the place. Somewhere back in his mind was the sense of the road out there, of early autumn, the dustiness that mingled with the fresh, yellow, polleny thickness of the goldenrod and got into his nostrils and made his eyes smart pleasantly, while the evergreens out in the grove dipped darkly into the blue silence of the sky.

"I guess we're ready now, folks."

Mrs. Ferguson had gone into the kitchen to see if she couldn't do something to help. Grandma got herself up from her chair and sharply repeated the call to Grandpa. There was a general shouting for Carl. Uncle Ben was washing his hands out in the kitchen where Aunt Ella spoke to him in a low, intimate scolding. "Why didn't you do that before? Now dinner's all on the table." "Well, I'll be there as soon as anybody else. You're always in a stew about me." "I guess with reason!" Fred Ferguson, feeling good, went out to the grove and called the little girls—"Come on now and get your dinner"—and then came back with Dorothy skipping along beside him, holding his hand, and Margaret reluctantly trailing. There was no place on the farm that Margaret liked so well as the grove.

"Sit down, folks," Ella said. "Don't wait for me."

There was a scraping back of chairs while the dinner steamed on the table. Ella came in with her face darkly flushed under a hanging loop of black hair, bringing the coffee.

"Don't wait. Ben, can't you start things going?"

But Grandpa wouldn't say the blessing until she sat down. She did it provisionally, thinking of things that she had left off —she hadn't put on the sweet pickles. Grandpa's voice sounded sonorous and slow, like a kind of chanting, in the still country air.

"Oh, Lord, Our Father, we thank Thee for all these good things which we are privileged to eat gathered together again in Thy sight."

Then the passing began. Fred Ferguson said, helping himself largely from the great thick dish of stewed chicken and dumplings: "Well, this is something like!"

At first, they had so much to attend to getting everything passed around, that they couldn't talk. Ella pressed things on them, scolding Uncle Ben for not watching, and insisted on going down cellar for the pickles although everybody told her they had enough without. Grandma didn't like the way Ella put up her pickles, anyway. She'd never got just the right knack to it. Margaret was carefully drawing out the white meat from the mess of stew on her plate.

"*You'll* never get fat," her grandmother warned her.

42

"I don't want to be fat!"

Grandma said, "You don't want to grow up into a skin and bones!"

"You're a great one to talk, mother! Guess there wouldn't be much picking on you. Mother gets smaller all the time."

"Well, if I do," Grandma retorted, "you get bigger!"

"That's right! Take that, Ella. Mother's always got a comeback."

They all laughed; and Grandma was pleased, even if she didn't want to show it. She was beginning to get old and silent, to "fail," but when one of her sons was here she could still summon up a little of her old smartness.

"Yes, she's getting such a heft," Uncle Ben said, "if there was to be a fire I don't believe I could pick her up to git her out of the house. She'd have to set here."

"I guess I *would* set for all of you. You'd be too slow even to get yourself out."

The talk went on, the regular Sunday dinner talk—about the roads, the crops, the prospects of rain, the sermon, the Whites, this person and that . . . it seemed to Carl, eating happily beside Grandma, who always put him next her and looked out slyly for the best pieces for him, that the talk of the grown folks drifted about him mingled with the warm smell of chicken from the table and the scent of apples and goldenrod in the brightness of the early autumn.

"Won't somebody have some more pie? Fred, what about you?"

"Nope, not for me."

"Annie?"

"Oh, goodness, Ella, I couldn't possibly. It's just fine," she added quickly.

"Gee," Carl said, "I wish I could hold another piece!"

"No, you've had enough."

"Well, Ella, I guess we've all come to the end."

They got up from the table, the menfolks with a good, replete, relaxing sense of Sunday afternoon leisure. The womenfolks began to gather up the dishes.

"Oh, you don't need to help, Annie," Ella protested weakly.

"Why, do you think I'm going to let you do all these dishes alone?"

"Ma, you don't need to help, anyway."

"No, Grandma, you go in and sit down."

"Oh, I guess I'm still as able as the rest of you!" Grandma retorted.

Ella shook her head at Annie. As soon as she had a chance, she whispered: "I don't like to have her do them. She forgets where things go. But you can't stop her!" Grandma eyed them suspiciously when she came back into the kitchen, and Annie began to talk hastily and cheerfully about the church social, and the lovely cakes some of them had brought. "Did you get any of Jennie White's?" She and Ella were united now in their attitude toward Grandma.

"That's all, ma. You better go over and get your nap now."

"I'll go when I get ready. You don't need to tell me," Grandma answered, as she peered into the cupboard to see where to put the platter.

"You can't say anything to her!" Ella whispered again.

But when they went into the front room, the men had already left. They tried to sit talking; but there was not really much in common between the two sisters-in-law. They had talked over about everything they could agree upon, out in the kitchen, in the intimacy of dishwashing. Grandma had gone over to her own house for her nap.

"She always has to go to sleep now after dinner," Ella commented. "She don't like to admit it, but it's so just the same."

"Well, I think old people need more sleep."

"Yes, but she's failing right along," Ella said, with a kind of satisfied pessimism.

Annie yawned. "I don't know why I should be so sleepy myself," she apologized.

"You can go in and lie down if you want to."

"Oh, no, I don't need to do that. I guess I'll get over it."

"The menfolks seem to have made themselves scarce!"

The two women sat and rocked for a while. Ella yawned too. "Guess I've caught it." When she finally got up, with a muttered excuse about attending to something, Mrs. Ferguson sat on for a moment and then went softly into the bedroom.

She put back the spread, and lay down. Then she got up again, stealthily closed the door, and came back. She felt a snuggling of lonely contentment. She and Ella really didn't have much to say to each other, although they kept on good terms. Ella discussed Grandma with her, but she knew that those two in turn discussed *her* when she wasn't around. She was always a little nervous about the children, Margaret especially. She had her way of doing things, and Ella and Grandma each had theirs, and the ways were growing farther and farther apart. "They're getting to do just like all the rest of them in town," Grandma said now of Fred and Annie; and Annie was "the one." The air came in darkened below the shade where the window was propped up with a slanted stick. Ella's dresses hung shapeless, dark and large from a board with hooks in the corner. The crockery bowl and pitcher were cold and white, but outside the faded leaves were thick, the golden-rod was yellow and rich, there was a surrounding humming in the afternoon sunshine.

She felt a tenderness and pity for Grandma. Of course Ella was good to her—much better than her talk sounded; and Grandma *was* terribly hard to do anything with. She had always been so smart and capable, and so proud of her quickness —she looked down upon Ella's clumsiness. But Grandma knew that her powers were failing, although it made her so mad if anyone suggested a thing of the kind. Annie used to have quite a fear of Grandma Ferguson's sharp watchfulness. Not a thing got past her! But now it hurt her to think that maybe she needn't fear that any more. Grandma had taken to asking her about her own folks, asking queer, intimate questions about the illness and the burial. Grandma's voice had a flat tone;— but the eyes, still dark and bright in their wrinkled lids, looked out from a secret gathering of fear within, when she heard of other old people dropping off, letting go. Annie felt ashamed of the old secret wish that she didn't have to have Grandma Ferguson over her all the time. When she thought of her own

45

parents, tears rose slowly into her eyes from some deep involuntary source.

Margaret came dark and shadowlike into the room, sat down on the bed, and then let her head droop onto the pillow beside her mother's. She said in a small, faint voice:

"When are we going home?"

Her mother stroked the shininess of the black braids. When they were out here at the farm, she and Margaret seemed to draw together.

"Can't you find something to do?" Margaret shook her head. "Where are the others?"

"I don't know."

"Well, we'll go home after while."

She went on stroking the braids. But then she seemed to drop asleep; and Margaret wriggled away from her relaxed hand.

When she woke up, she was alone again. The sunshine had passed its height. The leaves outside were shadowy, no longer brightly filtered with light. She got up quickly, smoothed her hair with a thick white comb at the mirror that held a shallow greenish light; and then she went back into the parlor asking cheerfully:

"Where is everyone?"

The place seemed to be deserted. Sunshine lay long across the yard and driveway, and the rock house stood yellow and cool and firm against the darkness of the evergreens. Shouts came faintly from somewhere. Fred was strolling around. He had been out to take a look at the corn that was standing green and dry gold out in the level field. Grandma and Grandpa were at home taking their naps in darkened rooms. Uncle Ben had gone off somewhere with the children. Ella was in the kitchen again.

But now they all began to gather. Cats of different sizes came to rattle with hungry tongues the empty tin pan beside the back door. The collie dog rose, stretching, from near the rock house. Carl had been out playing with the pups. "Well, I'll tell ye," Uncle Ben said, "If you can't have one at home, then you can have one out here. How'll that be?" Carl tried to get him to say that dogs counted more than cats. But Uncle

46

Ben wouldn't be caught. He was for all the children. He said, "Yeah, dogs are nice, but cats are pretty nice too." In the grove, the chickens were rising on stiff legs from their white, crouched-down fluffiness in the holes they had dug out of the soft dirt. "Did you have a good sleep, Annie?" Fred sounded contented, but he wanted to be with his wife as soon as he saw her. Now Uncle Ben came with the two girls from the orchard. They bit juicy chunks from hard, ripening apples, and threw the apples away, bumping along the ground through the dust.

"Here, Annie." Ben held out a fine, red-streaked apple. "Isn't that pretty good for this time of year?" He gave it to her. "Sweets to the sweet!"

She laughed, and flushed prettily, knowing that Ben had always admired her; and Carl came running and hugged his mother, and then faced them all.

Ella was getting things together out in the kitchen.

"Oh, Ella, you shouldn't be getting us supper too!"

"It's just what was left."

They all protested, but the thought of supper was good. Carl was sent over to get the old folks. Now it was a little cool in the house.

Carl went racing over. "Come on, Gran'ma and Gran'pa! Aunt Ella says to come to supper."

"Oh, I can't eat any supper."

"Yes, you can, Gran'ma. Come on."

They gathered around the big table, waiting again for Ella to come in. Then they sat down, in the coolness, to the warmed-up stew and big slices of bread, and big, nobbly, cold green pickles, and the strong brewed tea that Ella brought in the granite pot.

5

The club was to meet on Monday; but on Saturday, all the hard cleaning had to be done. "Now, Margaret—Dorothy— you must get up. You know you promised to help mama to-day." It was bright, almost springlike, now in February. Windows in the house were open, curtains pinned back or hanging knotted, chilly bright air was all through the rooms where the

47

radiators stood cold, frosted and silvery. Chairs were set out on the porch for Margaret and Dorothy to do the dusting. The parlor and sitting room looked big with wide, empty, hardwood floors. "I'm going to slide!" Margaret told Dorothy. She spread her arms and pretended she was going to take a long slide— but instead, took little dance steps, bending her arms, feeling graceful and light.

"Margaret! Are you just playing?"

Margaret flushed. She felt as if she had been caught in one of her most private delights. But her mother didn't seem to notice.

"Go on now, dear, and finish the dusting. Mama'll soon be ready to have the chairs brought in. Are you using the polish the way I showed you?"

"Of course!"

When Margaret and Dorothy knelt to polish the legs of the chairs, it was like being lost in a kind of furniture forest. They began to talk their "foolish talk," adding "bingo" to things. "I-a-bingo know-a-bingo where there's a package of cocoanut-a-bingo." From the back yard came the dulled bang-bang where Carl was beating the rugs hung out on the line.

At noon, Mr. Ferguson came home with dried beef and some bakery rolls for which Mrs. Ferguson had hastily telephoned.

"What's going on around here?"

The hastily put-together meal in the kitchen, the only warm room of the house, made it all seem a private family affair. Carl had come in heated and rosy from beating the rugs. They were all in their old clothes. Mrs. Ferguson's face was flushed, but with a happy anxiety. The air outside had a sudden, irrelevant joyousness on this bright morning. The occasion of the club meeting shone ahead of the children like Christmas.

On Monday, Mrs. Christianson came while they were still at breakfast. They heard her coming up the walk.

"Who is it, mama?" the children were clamoring.

They turned and stared wide-eyed at the back door. Their father had opened it and was saying, "Come in!" Mrs. Christianson was stopping to take off her rubbers on the back porch. She had her apron and cleaning cap in a bundle.

48

"Well, I guess I ain't late, am I?"

She wanted to know where to hang her wraps. Soon her old coat and battered velvet hat were in the entry. Margaret whispered joyously, "Oh, are we going to have Mrs. Christianson?" She felt as if her family had suddenly risen to heights that satisfied even her own requirements. Mama had never done any entertaining before grander than having just the Ladies Aid and the Missionary Society. All the leading matrons in Belmond, the ones who did the nicest entertaining—Mrs. Hoagland, Mrs. Bird—had Mrs. Christianson to help them. A feeling of richness and festivity seemed to come into the house with her.

"Pretty cold outside?" Mr. Ferguson asked.

"Yes, 'tis, kind of. I was thinking coming over here too bad Mis' Ferguson didn't have such a nice day for her club. Saturday was such a nice day."

"We haven't quite finished our breakfast yet," Mrs. Ferguson apologized. "Won't you have something with us, Mrs. Christianson?"

"Oh, no, thanks, I've et my breakfast."

Mrs. Christianson's gaunt, strong figure in the faded blue dress, with the gray hair, took away the hardest work of entertaining. Already the whole family felt a reliance upon her.

"What you want I should do first, Mis' Ferguson?" she asked, when the others had all gone.

Now that she did have a helper, Mrs. Ferguson hardly knew how to go about it to set her to work. She was so used to doing things herself.

"Want I should wash these dishes first?"

"Yes, I think that *will* be best."

Mrs. Ferguson went on into the other part of the house, leaving Mrs. Christianson safely and capably at work in the kitchen. The ladies in the Monday Club were the ones she would have chosen beyond all others. But they were all in other churches, and it was only this last year, since she had come into contact with Mrs. Bird at the Washington's Birthday bazaar, and had begun to get so neighborly with Mrs. Viele, that she had really felt as if she knew any of them. She had been delighted and surprised when they had taken her into their membership. She

49

felt as if this day marked her first real entrance into the social life of Belmond, and she wanted everything to be up to the occasion. She wanted to *enjoy* it. Of course, she couldn't expect Fred, a man, to know just how she felt about entertaining the club. Nevertheless, she had been wounded that he should have seemed so dubious and cautious when she had first spoken about having Mrs. Christianson. She was always craving to have him enter into the minutiæ and delicacy of her feelings.

"Don't you think you could get along without her?"

"Oh, I could get *along*."

How she detested that phrase "get along!" It was the Ferguson way of doing things—canny, careful, just enough, instead of doing everything in just the *nicest* way possible. She wanted the ladies to go away saying:

"That was the loveliest meeting we've had this year."

And she could do things that way, too. She had something of the same rich, lavish streak in her as her sister Louie, although she was always afraid to let it out, on account of what Fred's folks would say. But Louie belonged to *her* folks. Fred always seemed to forget that, in spite of the wonderful things Louie did for them; and that maybe she, Annie, was more like her own folks than like his! But then when Fred had come home for supper that night, after thinking it over, doubtless, all day, and had said offhand, shying away from any admission of coming over to her side, or of being thanked—

"Well, I stopped in to see Mrs. Christianson, Annie. I guess she can come over Monday morning—"

She had gone into the pantry, as if she were looking for something, and had stood there berating herself for the secret thoughts she had been indulging in about Fred and his family. She fussed around about all these little things—while she knew he was *there*, always, and that no woman had a better husband.

"Mis' Ferguson!"

"Yes!"

"They've brought your things."

She hurried down from upstairs, where she was getting the rooms ready, all of them, because one of the ladies might just happen to open one of the other doors. The warmth of Fred's indulgence and dependability was all around her, giving her a slightly shamed superiority over Mrs. Christianson, who was both stronger and less fortunate. Poor woman—she had been a widow for years, and "he" wasn't much when he was alive, according to reports!

"See the mess that boy made! But I don't know as there's any use cleaning up the kitchen yet, Mis' Ferguson, till I get through in here. Well, anyway I'm going to mop up that dirt. I can't stand the looks of it in your nice kitchen."

Mrs. Christianson had accepted her now as one of "her ladies." Anxiously, but with a gloating sense of richness, Mrs. Ferguson went over the packages in the big grocery box on the table. She had gone down to order the things herself, because she didn't care to have Fred know just all she was getting; and taking along her own purse to pay for a few of the most fancy things herself, in case they might seem to show up too extravagantly on the bill.

"Well, I expect you'd like me to be getting after that cake, wouldn't you? I think I can fix up the sandwiches too, just as well, this morning. I kin wrap 'em in a damp cloth and they'll stay nice. That's the way I done for Mis' Hoagland. Now if you'll jest tell me where things are, Mis' Ferguson. 'Twon't take me long to git the hang of your kitchen. Next time I kin find things for myself. Oh, my, ain't it lovely to have all them fresh eggs!"

"Yes, we get those from the farm," Mrs. Ferguson said, suddenly pleased and happy. "Mr. Ferguson's sister sends them to us."

"Git 'em right along? My, they do beat the store eggs! Well, folks is lucky that's got a farm to draw from. I expect you got the chickens from there, too. You done the roasting ahead, did you? They'll make lovely sandwiches. My, I think we're going to have real nice refreshments today, Mis' Ferguson."

Happy and warmed by Mrs. Christianson's approbation, Mrs. Ferguson went on into the other rooms to give the finishing touches. She opened the folding doors between parlor and sitting room. She had tried to keep the family out of these rooms since they were cleaned on Saturday, but of course she hadn't altogether succeeded. She went over them again, quickly but scrupulously, with the carpet sweeper and dust mop. Carl could bring down the chairs from upstairs when he came home at noon. He was always eager to help. But she set the other chairs in the order she wanted for the ladies. The curtains had been freshly laundered. She wanted the house to be her own background, shining with order, to welcome the ladies. Some of them had nicer things than she did. That old velvet rocker on a standard that had been Tom's and Edie's wedding present was just dreadful for anyone to sit in. But she couldn't dream of getting rid of it, because they would notice that the first thing when they came to visit. Fred always defended it because he had thought it a fine present when it was given. She pushed it back into a corner where she could take it herself, if anyone had to. She put her best embroidered doilies on the center tables, and got out the ornaments, the tall cut-glass vase and the two sweet little porcelain figures, that Louie had given her, and that ordinarily she kept in the compartment of the sideboard on account of the children—and because she didn't care to have Ella look at them and think she had such fine things, either.

There! Now let nobody touch a thing.

"Is it *noon?*"

"I'll git something together," Mrs. Christianson said comfortingly. "I see you've got some things in the ice box. Folks can't expect much on club days."

The beautiful cakes, all frosted, stood on the pantry shelf, scenting the room with warm, fresh-baked fragrance. The children came running in rosy from the outdoor air. Mrs. Ferguson couldn't tell whether Fred might be looking dubiously at the preparations.

He asked, "Well, how's she been?"

"Sh! Just simply fine. She's the best help."

Her eyes shone with gratitude and pleading.

At dinner the girls reminded her:

"Mama, you promised to write us excuses."

"Papa, will you write excuses for them?"

"Are they going to be excused?"

"Well, I thought they might come home a little early. They're going to pass the refreshments for me. I need them. Run up, girls," she added hastily, "just as soon as you get through, and put on your other dresses."

"Going to wear their best dresses to school?"

Oh, dear! If she hadn't said anything, just shooed them upstairs after dinner, he would never have noticed.

"Well, I don't want them to go in and spoil the room after the ladies are here."

"They ain't going to be in that room, are they?"

"Well, *Fred.*"

She was really put out, and looked for a moment as if she were going to cry. How could *he* understand? The rooms had to be all in order whether the ladies went into them or not. She looked quickly toward the stove to see whether Mrs. Christianson had been listening to this little altercation.

"Well, I don't care, have it the way you want it," Fred conceded generously.

"Well, I want everything to be nice!"

When they had all left, and the man was safely out of the house again, Mrs. Christianson said at once, confidentially:

"Now, I better git these dishes out of the way first of all. If it wasn't for the dishes, life ud be easy, wouldn't it? But I guess we can't eat without making dishes."

Mrs. Ferguson smiled at her gratefully, feeling the support and comfort of having another woman in the house. She hurried off. There were the dishes to get out now. She didn't have any nice cups to use, for she had no really nice set of dishes. Nearly all the ladies had their Haviland china. She hadn't really needed any before. She had thought of asking Mrs. Viele to bring over some cups with her, but she didn't like to do that, since she had belonged to the club such a little while. She could have asked Jennie White for anything, but of course Jennie wasn't a member. She wouldn't have fitted at all among these ladies. And Jennie had no china of her own, just what had belonged to the Old Lady White—and my, if she ever broke any of those dishes! But Mrs. Ferguson was proud to get out her dozen of lovely hand-painted plates, each one with a different design, that Louie had given her. Up until now, she had had so little opportunity to use them. And she did have nice silver, counting the little spoons that had been given the children for birthdays. Every time any child had a birthday, Louie (no matter what else she gave) sent one of these dear little spoons, and Henry sent a five dollar gold piece. Mrs. Ferguson got the spoons out of their case of dark red felt in the sideboard drawer, taking pleasure in each kind, the one with the gilt bowl engraved with the picture of the Capitol building at Washington, and the little one with the twisted green-gold handle that ended in a calla lily. That one belonged to Dorothy, and Margaret had never got over weeping about it. Poor Margaret!—it *did* seem as if Dorothy always got just the one Margaret would have chosen, although of course Louie never meant it that way. She got the dozen best, shiningly laundered napkins out of their folder, on which Margaret, for her Christmas present, had embroidered a top-heavy F in red. The child always chose red!

"Now, if you'll just pour some hot water over these plates, Mrs. Christianson. I don't think the spoons need much. But there's polish, right up there on that shelf, if you need a little."

"Oh, my, what cute little spoons!"

"Most of them are the children's. Oh, dear, I don't like the looks of these cups! Mrs. Viele would have brought some, but I didn't like to ask her. She has all such lovely things."

"Well, she can have," Mrs. Christianson said comfortingly. "She ain't got any children to provide for, or to break things either. She can put it all into her house."

"Yes. Well, that's the way with my sister in Kansas City, too."

"I tell you where I don't like to work so well," Mrs. Christianson confided. "I don't know as I ought to say this. But I was just thinking while I was making the sandwiches. Mis' Stark's. That's the only place I don't really like working. I'm always in fear there ain't going to be enough. I hate to put jest little dribs on the plates I send in, even if they ain't my own refreshments."

"Oh, dear, do you think *we're* going to have enough?" Mrs. Ferguson asked, suddenly worried.

"Oh, good land, yes! My, I should say!"

As she quickly wiped the steaming plates, Mrs. Christianson added: "My, I jest think you're lucky! I tell you, there ain't many ladies in this town that's got a husband like Mr. Ferguson!"

Mrs. Ferguson listened in delight and amazement.

"He's always so nice in the bank. Folks like to go in. They'd always rather have him come to the window than Mr. Spencer —the young one! They know they can count on what he says. I s'pose I shouldn't be telling that."

"Oh, yes, you should! To me!"

So *that* was the way he seemed to other people. Fred! People liked to go into the bank! Oh, *she* knew well enough what he was like, inside, but she was always afraid that he was showing just his small, literal, meagerly apportioning side to other people and that they were judging him by that. Her eyes felt moist with happiness.

But how could that woman do so much for other people— with three children to look after, and no husband to stand back of her?—and yet she was so comforting, and sustaining, and took such pleasure in doing things in other people's houses. Other women had no right to fuss!

"Well, I guess I'd better be getting myself ready!"

She got the new brown dress out of her closet and laid it on the bed. They could say what they wanted to. Fred thought it was all right, anyway, because he knew how Mrs. Rist needed the work. She washed hastily but thoroughly, anxiously feeling of the texture of her skin. She went into Carl's room to curl her hair, because the ladies were least likely to go in there, and the lamp might leave a smell. Then she hurried back into her own room.

She was anxious about her dress, because Mrs. Rist never got the fit right over the hips, and she had had to rip out the seams and do all that over herself. It seemed as if she hadn't really looked at herself for weeks, months, years. She didn't know what had happened to herself. The brown hair, that curled softly and easily, like Dorothy's, was threaded at the sides with gray. The skin, her pretty complexion—she and Louie always used to be "the two pretty Luers girls"—was still fair, but had lost its old transparent bloom. She had given up trying to bring back or keep her old beauty when Dorothy was born. Besides, married women weren't expected to be pretty.

All the same, when her hair was up, and she had carefully put on the brown dress, she couldn't help seeing that there was something she had gained these last years since the children had been going to school. She looked "nice," if never again pretty and young. The matronliness that had come upon her with her acceptance of maturity had something of its own that was better than a faded girlishness. Now she realized that ever since last fall, a year ago, when she had gone back to her father's funeral, her attitude had been changing and settling. When she and Louie had stood with their arms around each other, looking at that face, so dear and yet remote, the deep eyes closed, the silver hair thin across the quiet forehead, the hands, long and thin, folded upon the breast . . . and turning away, her warm face flushed with the effort to keep back the tears that suffused her eyes, Louie had said in a hushed voice—

"Well, Annie, I guess we're the ones now—"
that had been the time.

Now she felt as if this day marked her first effort to take her own rightful place in Belmond. She had got a kind of painful joy out of sinking deep, deep into the personal narrowness of her household, shutting herself away even from her own folks, forcing her girlhood self into what Fred seemed to want without regard for her own desires, casting it aside for the needs of her babies, proving herself as a wife and mother. But she had passed that now. She had used it up with the last of her babies, and grown out of it in these past few years when it had seemed as if maybe there weren't going to be any more. Another self, old and new both, was rousing in her. The old folks were gone. Fred's folks were too old to have the running. Here were she and Fred. In the bank lay her own fifteen hundred dollars. They were doing well. They had their own children to think about, their own household. *We're the ones now.* She wanted to spread out, take the whole place in hand, make what she wanted of her own home; and it seemed as if she could endure no longer any strictures from the outside upon the ample working out of this newly realized maturity.

She hurried in to give a last look at the guest room and be sure that it was ready. That was where the ladies were to put their wraps. The best white counterpane was spread in snowy amplitude upon the bed. The white curtains softened and hushed the wintry light. Then, after setting wide open that door and the one to the bathroom, she went downstairs, feeling voluptuously that all was in order behind her.

Now the whole house waited in shining stillness, ready for the ladies to come.

At a quarter past three, Margaret and Dorothy came home from school. Everyone had looked at them in their plaid dresses, presenting their excuses and leaving early. The girls had come around Margaret at recess; but she, proud and aloof, had said: "I'm going to pass refreshments at my mother's club. I could have asked one of you if I'd wanted to. But I'd rather just be with Dorothy." Lucille and Edna Mae had looked impressed. They were still officially "mad," all the girls. But they had almost forgotten why by now. Today they would have been ready to make up. Irene wasn't at school any more. Margaret didn't know whether she had just dropped out, or had gone away; and she wouldn't ask about her. She had never been with Irene since that day at the beginning of school. Once when she was going along the street, Irene had tagged after her, with that hateful little Squirrel-Eyes; and both of them had kept saying softly, and simpering:

"Now, you must come home, Marg'ret. Mama wants you. You mustn't play with such naughty little girls."

There had been no one left for her but Ada Rist; and Margaret had to try to let Ada's devotion make up for her thick hands and snuffly breathing. But the girls needn't think that she was so anxious to be friends that they could come around to her when they pleased! She was no more anxious than they were.

Margaret and Dorothy felt proud of their own house with something going on inside. They went around to the side door.

They could see the ladies through the windows; and as they opened the door with elaborate carefulness, they could hear someone reading a paper. The meeting was still going on. The house seemed full of the shine of best dresses.

They had promised to go straight upstairs, the back way, and to take off their wraps in their own room. They were to be very careful to hang up their towels when they used the bathroom, and not to disturb the beautiful shiny towels with scalloped embroidered edges that had been put there for the ladies.

"Sister! Come look here."

Dorothy had discovered the ladies' wraps in the guest room, piled in softness and thickness on the broad white counterpane. The little girls tiptoed about in awe. They stroked the thick, soft denseness of Mrs. Hoagland's beaver coat. Their finger tips left dark streaks in the light brown fur.

"I think this is her hat!" Dorothy whispered.

They could recognize Mrs. Viele's familiar things, and they could guess which were Mrs. Bird's. Among the other wraps, over at the edge of the bed, lay Aunt Ella's old plain black winter coat with its collar of cheap, faded fur, and the knitted, purple-black hood she always wore driving into town in winter.

"I should think Aunt Ella would wear a *hat*," Margaret whispered indignantly.

They went down the back stairs into the kitchen. Mrs. Christianson was busy there.

"I was looking for you two!"

"Is it time for us to pass the refreshments?"

"No, I guess they're still a-going it in there. But it's pretty near time for them to stop."

The big warm kitchen was full of the fragrance of cake and coffee. Now there were snowflakes falling thick as a veil outside the windows. Mrs. Christianson had all the things set out.

"Oh, goody, we're going to use the pretty plates!"

"Yes, sir. And look here. Ain't we got nice sandwiches?"

"I wish we could have one to taste, Mrs. Christianson."

"Well, mebbe you can," Mrs. Christianson said good-naturedly.

She had made up the crusts into little sandwiches for the

children. But when they made as if they were going to steal some of the beautiful angel cake, she shook the bread knife at them, and they giggled and scuttled. Margaret went to listen at the crack of the swinging door. Mrs. Stark was still reading her paper.

"My, that's a long one!" Mrs. Christianson commented.

At last the meeting was over. In the kitchen, beyond the closed door, they could hear the polite patter of the ladies' hands. Mrs. Ferguson came hurrying into the kitchen. She was flushed, and as if coming from some remote region. The children had never before seen her in her new brown dress. Her hair was curled, and she had on her best opal breast pin that Aunt Louie had sent her, gleaming in the dull brown silk of her yoke.

"Is everything dished out? I guess the children can come in now. The program is finished."

They were to pass the napkins first. It was almost like getting up on the platform at the Children's Day exercises—to push through the swinging door and go on through the empty dining room into the parlor where the ladies sat with a little overflow into the sitting room. Some of the ladies were asking Mrs. Stark further questions about her subject; others were in groups talking about personal things; but they all looked up, pleased and complacent, as they accepted their napkins from the little girls.

"You little girls must have got out early," Mrs. Hoagland said.

"Mama had us excused," Dorothy answered proudly.

The ladies all smiled.

Aunt Ella said uneasily, when Margaret came to her, with some idea that she was just one of the family, or that there might not be enough to go around, "Oh, you don't need to give me any napkin."

The napkins were all passed. The little girls ran back to the kitchen, elated, with bright eyes, with the same feeling as when they had successfully spoken their pieces and were ready to do it all over again.

"Did you give everybody one?"

"Um-hm, we passed to everybody."

"Mama, Aunt Ella wouldn't take one."

"Well, never mind."

"What shall we take in next?"

"Dorothy can take in the cups, and Margaret can take in the plates." That was safe, because Dorothy would be pleased to be entrusted with anything, she wouldn't notice that the plates were nicer than the cups. "Won't that be the best way, Mrs. Christianson?"

"Are you going to let us take in the coffee, mama?"

"No, I'd better do that. But you little girls can follow right along after me with the cream and sugar and spoons on the tray. Better let Margaret carry it. Then you can ask the ladies what they want, and let them each help themselves, and Dorothy can give everyone a spoon. . . . It has to be exactly equal!" she murmured to Mrs. Christianson, pursing her lips significantly.

The little procession solemnly entered the front room. Shyly and proudly the little girls bore the tray with the best flowered cream pitcher and sugar bowl and all the pretty spoons on the crisp, embroidered doily. The buzz of talk was broken while the ladies helped themselves to cream and sugar. They smiled graciously at the little girls, and the mother's heart was large with happy pride and tenderness when she saw them doing so nicely. They looked so sweet in their little plaid dresses. Margaret wouldn't have the blue that she had first bought, such a pretty blue, the sweetest color for little girls; but they were both lovely in the brown and gold for which she had exchanged the blue. Their mother loved to dress them both alike, although they were so different.

Everything had gone beautifully. Mrs. Bird made such a lovely leader. Her chair near the large front window still had a slightly official look, made gracious by her sweet elderly presence, in her nice dark gray winter dress, with her silvery-gray crimped hair, her watch chain, her breast pin that was a cluster of dark bright garnets, the rings on her worn, delicate hands. There was a rustle of satin from the chair where Mrs. Hoagland sat, opulent and smiling. Mrs. Stark always had such a fine paper. And she was very pleasant today, although some of the ladies felt a little stand-offish toward her, knowing how—coming from the East—she criticized Belmond. Mrs. Viele was always nice. These were the very ladies whom Mrs. Ferguson had always wanted to know and among whom she had felt that she ought to take her place. The only wrong note was Ella—the way she sat, mute and defiantly humble, with dull black eyes, in her old dark winter dress, not feeling at home among these town ladies. When Mrs. Viele, who was acting as secretary, had graciously included her in the roll call, to which the ladies were answering with their favorite quotations, there had been a long, uncomfortable silence until Ella had mumbled, blushing:

"I guess I'll have to be excused."

But it was interesting to hear what the other ladies had given. Mrs. Stark, everyone had wanted to hear what she would select! It was a long quotation from James Russell Lowell, recited impressively in her precise New England voice—

"Truth forever on the scaffold, wrong forever on the throne."

Mrs. Bird always gave something so nice, something that seemed to belong to her.

"Stay, stay at home, my heart, and rest.
Homekeeping hearts are happiest."

Mrs. Ferguson would have liked to copy that down. She herself had sat trembling, nervous, until Mrs. Viele had reached her name—"Anna Ferguson"—because she had done nothing like this since she had stopped teaching and got married; and then she had repeated, in a faint voice, feeling tears close to her eyes, those lines that she had remembered from her schooldays, and that had always seemed to her the prettiest lines in the world—

"Silently, one by one, in the infinite meadows of heaven,
Blossom the lovely stars, the forget-me-nots of the angels."

A little breath had gone up from all the listening ladies.

The ladies were still there when Mr. Ferguson came home, although they were beginning to talk about going. He heard them as he started up the walk, and he went around to the back door, feeling all out of place in that feminine atmosphere. Although it gave him pleasure to see the parlor full of ladies, with Annie among them. It gave him a tenderness toward his wife, and a kind of appreciation of her as a woman. He felt proud of seeing her nicely dressed among the other ladies, and of knowing that she could hold her own with any of them. He had never lost his pride in having married one of the two pretty Luers girls.

"Well, Mr. Ferguson, they's some refreshments left for you."

"That's right."

He kept well out of sight in the kitchen. Carl came banging into the room. He had been playing with Harry; but he couldn't bear to miss anything that was going on at home.

"Gee! Is there anything left?"

Now they could hear that the ladies were leaving. They were going in twos and threes down the walk, and the snowflakes made sparkles of wetness on the feathered hats and the beaver coats. The animated sound of voices died down. Mrs. Ferguson came into the kitchen, pretty and flushed.

"Are you all in here?" she cried.

There was still that glamor of remoteness upon her. Carl hugged her so that she had to beg him to be careful of her dress, although she was pleased. He hurt his cheek on the opal pin that left a flower-like pattern of points on the rosy flesh.

"You're too much fixed up, mama!" he cried.

Mrs. Christianson was setting the table for them in the dining room. There was a great plate piled up with sandwiches, another with the crumbly, delicate, white richness of the left-over angel cake. She refilled the coffeepot.

"Look at this! Is this for us? Looks like a banquet."

"It's just the left-overs."

Aunt Ella had to be urged to stay. Ben was going to call for her, with the team, and she wanted just to sit in her wraps and wait for him. But Mr. Ferguson wouldn't have that.

"Ben can have something too when he comes. I guess there's plenty for all of us, isn't there, Mrs. Christianson?"

"What's that? Gracious, yes. I kin fix more if they's any need."

Ella submitted to taking off her coat again—as she had meant to do from the first, Margaret thought scornfully—and sat down at the table with them. "I've et. I guess I've had my share," she was mumbling, as she took up her cup of coffee.

"Isn't mother in on any of this?" Mr. Ferguson asked, surveying the table.

"She wouldn't come in," Ella answered.

"I asked her," Mrs. Ferguson said hastily.

"What was the matter?"

"Well, she said she didn't have the clothes to come to parties like this. She wouldn't have felt right."

"Aw, nonsense! What sort of notion is that?" Fred was hurt.

"She thought it would be too fancy," Ella persisted. She took up the ordinary cup with relief. She had been afraid to pick up one of those thin little plates the girls had passed around at the meeting.

"I tried to get her to come," Mrs. Ferguson said again.

"Well, she don't like to go out much any more, anyway."

"I know how 'tis," Mrs. Christianson said. She had come in to see that they had plenty of sandwiches, although she refused to sit down with them, assuring them that she had had hers in the kitchen. "My mother was jest that same way. Old folks sometimes feels kind o' out of it these days, especially if they've always been hardworking."

"Yes, the folks are used to things plain."

"Well, I guess they won't find them too fancy here!" Mr. Ferguson said nettled. "I don't know that we've ever been so fancy."

Ella would not say. But she gave a glance at the sugar tongs and the lump sugar in the flowered bowl.

Ben came now. He had driven up in the old buggy, since it was snowing. Bewildered, not knowing just what might be going on, what he had run into, he let Annie lead him to the dining room, in his old brown pants and gray shirt and black overcoat.

"Well, I didn't know we were going to stay supper, Ellie, or I might have fixed up a little more."

"You're all right," Fred Ferguson insisted. His face was flushed, and he spoke very heartily. "The menfolks are out of this anyway. We're all just in our working regalia. Better take two of those sandwiches, Ben. They're pretty thin."

Ben was abashed—he and Ella both—by the daintiness of the sandwiches, the fine coffeepot, the best silver. Ella had felt out of place all afternoon, and she knew that Annie had just asked her because she thought she had to. Ella didn't like these fussy ways of doing things. She had no place among these town ladies, that rich Mrs. Hoagland who went to Chicago every winter just to hear a bunch of these opera singers get up and sing, and that Mrs. Stark from the East who thought she was so much above everybody because she didn't know how to sound her r's when she talked. She thought it was pretty extravagant of Annie to have this woman just to help her; and she asked, nodding toward the kitchen:

"Don't she charge pretty high?"

Mrs. Ferguson began to feel flustered and apologetic. She knew how Ella regarded things—how she thought they were pretentious, "putting on style," unless the refreshments were just as plain and common as she herself would have made them. And of course she would go home and tell Grandma all about it. Grandma had been asked. It wasn't any wonder that she didn't choose to come among all younger ladies. But the pleasure in the success of the meeting was dampened. And now it seemed as if Fred was with his family against her.

"Well, I guess I'm through now," Mrs. Christianson said.

Mrs. Ferguson hurried out to the kitchen so they wouldn't all see how much she paid.

"Fred!"

If only she needn't have called him! But he made no comment of any kind when Mrs. Christianson, a trifle shamefaced as always when it came to asking for her money, admitted how much it would be. He got out the familiar deep pocketbook with the nickel clasps, and carefully counted out the amount in quarters. "And a brand new dime!" he said. He liked to pay people in bright new coins from the bank.

But Mrs. Ferguson felt on the defensive. She turned her back so that Fred wouldn't notice how many sandwiches and pieces of cake she was putting into the box she meant to give Mrs. Christianson. Everything needn't go to Fred's family! She would have liked to take a plate over next door to the Morgans too. Fred wasn't really disapproving, but he was watching; and she couldn't help feeling guilty and caught when he said carefully:

"We better save some to send the folks too."

She turned away rebellious. Then Grandma might have come! The meeting had been so nice. She had enjoyed it so—enjoyed the success of her efforts, the sociability, and the companionship of the ladies. It was all too nice to be spoiled. She said she couldn't eat any more, and stayed in the kitchen to wrap up the cake and sandwiches for Grandma and Grandpa. Not that she wouldn't have sent them the things—but she might have had a little say about her own refreshments! There was no more reason why she should do things the way the rest of them did than that they should do things the way *she* did. *She* might not approve of the way Ella served refreshments—the great thick meat sandwiches, and the pickles, and coffee—but what if she should ever suggest that? Suppose she had served these ladies sandwiches like that!

Ben and Ella drove off in the old buggy, covered with a heavy brown robe, through the snow that was beginning to fall quite bitterly now.

The house was left in disorder.

Mrs. Ferguson was not aware of the look with which her husband was following her as she set the room to rights and got the children off to bed. He had already forgotten about Ella's complaints. When they were in their own bedroom he put his arms around her.

"Well, I guess your meeting went off pretty good, didn't it?" he said.

All at once her lips began to tremble. Tears came into her

eyes. She was shaky with weariness. She could barely force the words out of her lips . . . Ella had criticized everything, so had the others—they didn't like the way she did things . . . he didn't, either, he made fun of her sandwiches. . . . She turned her head aside from him and began to cry.

"Why, Annie, that isn't true!"

He felt deeply hurt. She hadn't realized at all, then, the lover-like fondness he had been feeling for her all evening, looking so nice in her new dress, so flushed and eager. He had been proud to have her the mistress of his house and to think of her that way. Of course he understood how Ella felt about it— he himself was abashed at finding everything so fine. But he didn't really criticize Annie for that. He was ashamed of his own cautious misgivings, felt their inferiority, even while he couldn't help them. It hurt him that she did not recognize his feelings almost as much as if she had rejected an offer of love.

And there was just enough truth in what she said to cut him too. When she had first spoken about Mrs. Christianson, he hadn't liked the idea of their setting themselves up to act as if they were the Spencers or the Hoaglands—as if he were trying to be better than his own folks. But how could Annie believe he would ever really begrudge her any help she needed if he was able to supply it? He remembered how he had felt in the bank that afternoon, after he had left the house. There was a dissatisfied feeling under all the work and hurry of Saturday afternoon, with farmers coming in with wet, muddy-smelling boots from the country, merchants coming in bareheaded from their stores to deposit money, women coming downtown to do the buying for over Sunday. Old Mrs. Kruse came in, a widow, one of those who always asked for Mr. Ferguson no matter who came to wait on her at the window; and he thought of how her husband had left her with nothing to live on but the tiny bit of uncertain rent from their old eighty-acre farm. Mrs. Richard Spencer came in, bright-eyed in furs and veil, to get Richard. She had everything. And then the teachers came in with their February salary cheques, girls just out of college who were careless and used all their money for clothes; and then poor Fannie Allison whose little affairs Mr. Ferguson knew only too well, with a compassionate knowledge, from A to Z. The sight of all these different women, with their different conditions, some of them with no man to look after them and one of them looked after too well, made him more tender toward Annie, more proud and satisfied with her, and anxious to protect her as his own. He thought of her again (and he often did) as she had been when he first fell in love with her, that pretty Annie Luers who had the Buck Township school, prettier than any of the girls around, whose basket all the fellows used to bid for at the basket socials, he among them, doggedly outraging his thrift for her sake with a painful gladness, and determined that he was going to be the one to get her, although she was so dainty and fine it didn't seem as if he could ever get up the courage to ask her to marry him.

Now she whispered, sobbing, "You don't like the way I do things" . . . all of them, she meant, all the Fergusons.

"Why, Annie, how can you say that?"

He held her pressed to him, at a loss, bewildered by her sensitiveness, unable to tell her how the shock of her different feelings about things had affected him again and again, sunk into him, and changed him . . . what richness and fineness she had added to the old plain bareness of his life. Didn't she understand how it was after all these years? He was always taking it for granted that she felt just as he did—she seemed to—and then all at once he discovered that he hadn't known what she was thinking at all. It wasn't that he begrudged her things—or any of them. But he was the one who had to look ahead, provide for them, and he couldn't just be taking the present at face value, he had to make the future secure for them. But how could she think he would have had her any different?

But she felt what he was thinking. She grew suddenly cheerful. She gave a sobbing breath, and tried to get at her eyes to wipe them. She let him unfasten her things, standing passive and acquiescent while he carefully and clumsily drew off the brown waist with its tight cuffs. Everything seemed to go very fast then, and breathlessly, quietly because of the children. This was the only way he had of telling her how he felt about her. At first she just accepted it. And then they were swept together in such an uprush of the old passionate appreciation of one for the other, as they had not felt since Dorothy was born—had scarcely expected to feel just that way again; and it was only when they were laid apart from each other, quiet and appeased, that all which the years had accumulated, the unanswered questions, the doubts, disappointments, small resentments, his failure to share her feelings, her lack of understanding of what was required of men, and the fact that she had never been quite one of the folks, filtered again darkly through their warmth of contentment like a minor strain of music under the major tune.

Part Two
The Good Son

I. THE YOUNG PEOPLE

THE assembly room of the high school was always restless at this last period in the afternoon. Whispers went about—a gust of laughter hastily suppressed as the teacher in charge began clearing her desk. The little grade children were out already, and their voices sounded high and clear from the other building, a block away, as they went running home.

The principal came into the room. He went softly up onto the platform, leaned over, with one hand flat on the desk, and spoke to Miss Larrabie. Then he straightened up and stood waiting. The gong sounded out in the hall. It was fifteen minutes early. Mr. Bellew stood smiling and complacent.

"You may put away your books," Miss Larrabie said.

Then they came tramping in from their classes, up the two broad stairways, into the assembly room through the two big doors that were hastily opened, and noisily took their seats. Mr. Bellew nodded at Miss Larrabie; she gathered up her papers and left the platform, opening one of the front seats and sitting down there just below the platform with the other teachers who were all coming in; and then Mr. Bellew stepped forward and tapped the bell. The excited uproar in the room calmed down, the eager faces were all turned toward him.

"Now, if you'll just give me your attention, school."

A few more shufflings of feet, a book dropped and a head hastily bent as someone leaned over the aisle to pick up the book —and then it was expectantly, rustlingly quiet. They could hear the running steps of the grade children out on the sidewalk.

"Well, I suppose you're all somewhat worried if you've happened to notice that classes are letting out a little early today."

Laughter—shrill from the girls, bursting out in sardonic noisiness from the boys; but an uneasy shifting of bodies and shuffling of feet.

"Then I'll try to set your minds at rest and make it up to those of you faithful students who are regretting the last fifteen minutes lost from your studies."

Laughter again, noisy and cynical, but easier, more in tune with the attitude of the principal as he stood smiling and paternal, in his glasses, with his light hair that was growing thinner, his slimmish youngish figure that was growing heavier.

"I thought it was time to bring to your notice the fact that we're going to have a football team in B.H.S. and some games in the near future."

Clapping followed, applause and relief.

"Well, there doesn't seem to be any lack of enthusiasm! That's fine. But I want to see if we can't raise a whole lot of it this afternoon to give our team a good start. Now I think I've said enough. You're too used to hearing *me* talk." Laughter. "So I'm going to put this meeting in the hands of—" he looked around the assembly room—"of Carl Ferguson!"

There was a great burst of clapping, sudden and surprised, feet stamped, there was whistling, high excited girls' laughter, and all heads turned toward the Senior rows; while through the midst of it Carl, his fresh face stained with a bright pink flush, his eyes shining and eager, went up the aisle, leaped the two steps to the platform, and stood there hastily shaking down one trouser leg.

It took some time for the applause to die down. Mr. Bellew sat back gratified and benevolent. The teachers clapped encouragingly. Carl Ferguson was a favorite with most of the teachers.

The applause marked a recognition. This was a new school year. The old crowd was gone. There were different Seniors. Mr. Bellew's choice picked out Carl Ferguson as the new leader. Last year as a Junior, Carl had been popular enough, but not one of the eminent ones. Now, as he waited up there on the platform, modestly grinning but at ease, his fair hair mussed, his face rosy above the orange and black sweater in which his shoulders looked very broad, he suddenly stood out before the whole school, a potential hero. Margaret, sitting back among the Freshmen, blushed to see a member of her family elevated to the platform, feeling partly proud and partly satirical. Lillian White, whom Carl had been taking home from the Young People's meetings, blushed too, and sat tightly clasping her hands, unable to look up—in a sort of fear, as if Carl's sudden glory threatened her shy ownership. One of the teachers leaned over to whisper to one of the others, "Isn't he the best-looking thing?"

Carl looked down at the applauding school, and then around at Mr. Bellew, with an ingenuous grin that came like an inspiration.

"Well, I guess you're not used to hearing *me* talk. I'm not used to hearing myself."

At this, the applause thundered. Mr. Bellew threw back his head and laughed. The teachers gave each other congratulatory glances. "Fergy!" some boy shouted. Emotional tears came into Lillian's downcast eyes, and she sat primly still, lest they should overflow and disgrace her. Other girls looked excited. Carl stood smiling, his hands in his pockets to keep them from trembling, feeling inwardly aroused but marvelously, gloriously at ease. Words came to him.

"But I can say this, fellow students and—and Mr. Bellew— and everybody." Laughter again. Carl's rosy face got suddenly intent and serious. "I guess I can speak for the new team and say that if there's anything we fellows ask for, why, it's for the rest of the school to get together and give us their support this fall. We've begun practising, and we're sure going to give the best we've got. We got Bob Yetter to coach us, an old B.H.S. star, and he's willing to take time off from his law business for—for the glory of old Alma Mater. And we're gona show we appreciate that. We're gona train and work for all that's in us. Why, I already heard Chuck Messenger turn down an invitation to a fudge party last night." More laughter, heads turned toward the blushing Chuck. "So we're counting on you girls not to tempt us till after Thanksgiving. That's the way you girls can do your part."

The girls giggled. Mr. Bellew nodded at them beneficently.

"But seriously now, folks." Carl's voice became earnest. Lillian trembled and looked down at her clasped hands. "I'm

73

gona ask every one of you to help make this a banner season and stand right back of the team. Now it isn't gona be so darned easy." The teachers smiled. "We've lost a lot of our fellows, in fact we've practic'ly got to get together a new team except for one or two that don't count much like myself and Chuck—" approving laughter—"and some of the towns, like Hanging Rock, for instance, have practic'ly got their old team. But I don't see why that need keep us from having the finest team we've *ever* had. And we're going to."

In the applause that followed, Carl stood breathing a little hard, his face hot, his neck beginning to perspire under the heavy ribbed wool of his sweater. But he felt a curious exaltation. He could look over the heads of the assembly and see, through the long windows at the back, the trees leafy and full against the warm blue sky of fall.

He turned to Mr. Bellew.

"I guess maybe we ought to have some cheers."

Mr. Bellew nodded.

"I don't know just who ought to come up here and lead 'em. This is where we sure miss Jake."

"Lead 'em yourself!" Again the pounding and stamping on the wooden floor that made hollow thunder.

"Well, come on then," Carl said grinning. "Only after this you'll have to appoint somebody not on the team. What'll we have first?"

"Slingo!" some voices shouted.

"All right! Let's go!"

Carl flung up his arm. His face flushed hotter and drops of sweat ran down his back under his sweater. He looked down into gleaming eyes in tense, shouting faces.

> "Slingo! Bingo!
> Any old thing-go!
> Belmond High School!
> YES by jingo!"

"Again!" Carl shouted hoarsely. He flung up his hand and felt inspiration come hotly upon him. "*Ev*'rybody this time.

That wasn't ev'rybody. Miss Boggs, you weren't yelling. We got to have the support of the teachers too."

And in the joyous roar that followed, his eyes shone, his body became a hot push of energy, and a shout followed his motions that seemed to shake all the long windows behind which stood those leafy trees . . .

"SLING-go! BING-go!"

The yell died in hoarse echoes. The big assembly room was full of flushed faces, of panting breath. Carl stood back now, mopping his face with a very dirty blue-bordered handkerchief. He felt blazing with ardor, big with love. He turned again to Mr. Bellew, who came tiptoeing up to the platform and spoke to him in a low tone.

"Mr. Bellew says we ought to have a little singing now, folks."

Mr. Bellew leaned forward, looked out over the room, and crooked his finger at Mildred Summers, who came forward, smiling slightly and demurely, walked softly up to the platform, seated herself on the piano bench, softly spread her skirts. Mr. Bellew nodded again at Carl.

"I guess we've got time to sing our high school song."

"One hundred five!" voices shouted.

"One hundred five. 'The Orange and the Black.' Now, folks, we've got the same tune as the Princeton song exactly, so there's no excuse for any of you not to sing, only remember, where the song says Princeton we substitute Belmond. That's all. Now come on. Mildred's going to play for us. Everybody sing!"

He frowned, holding up his hand again, but not so sure of the singing as of the yelling. Mildred had to give the opening chord twice. Then the music teacher's strong soprano voice led them. Carl hummed along earnestly, singing a word here and there as he remembered it, just to help keep the thing going and to do his part. In the midst of the singing, the bell rang. With an impulse, Carl raised his hand, kept them going until the verse ended. Then, nodding to Mr. Bellew, grinning at the school, he leaped down the two steps again and went quickly to his seat, perspiring, refusing to meet anyone's eyes, even his hands on the desk in front of him feeling glowing and hot, while Mr. Bellew dismissed the school.

Mr. Bellew held up his finger. The music books were pushed into the desks. The teachers took their places beside the two doors and out in the hall. Mildred sat with fingers poised above the keys until Mr. Bellew nodded at her, and she banged into the first chords of the closing march. The pupils rose and stood at their desks, and at the signal began marching down the aisles and pouring out into the hallway, clattering down the two flights of stairs and out into the autumn air. Carl marched with them in happy self-consciousness. A boy clapped him on the shoulder—"Good work, Fergy!"—and girls brushing past him breathed, "Oh, Fergy, you were just grand!" He grinned modestly at the compliments; but as soon as he reached the open air, something seemed to explode in him, he stood on the stone steps, leaped the low iron railing, leaped back again, shouted to Chuck Messenger "C'mon!" and went at a gallop around to the door of the gymnasium in the basement.

In the girls' cloakroom, Lillian stood at the mirror putting on her cap, a pinkish-pearl flush on her cheeks, her eyes still downcast, and her hands trembling so she could hardly put in the hat pins, feeling modestly, but with beating heart, the eyes of the other girls upon her.

The girls caught up with Margaret going down the stairway. When they got outside, they begged, "Wait for Mildred."

"I have to go home."

"Oh, no, wait, kid."

Margaret waited with them reluctantly. The quarrel that had begun away back in the grades had never really been made up; and now that they were in high school, and beginning to go with the boys, Margaret knew that there were little intimate parties, the kind that counted, and that the girls meant to leave her out of them.

Mildred came running out of the building. She smiled radiantly. Margaret couldn't help reluctantly receiving and admitting Mildred's prettiness in her dress of thin blue tissue gingham, with her fair hair parted on the side and clinging wavy and damp to her round smooth forehead. Margaret was friends off and on with Lucille and Edna Mae. But she couldn't bear Mildred.

"Kids, didn't I play awful?"

"No, you played grand!"

Mildred thrust herself between Margaret and Edna Mae and took an arm of each. Margaret felt unwillingly her soft charm. Her arms were round and warm below the elbow sleeves, and her little hand clung confidingly.

"Where shall we go?"

They stood in a cluster on the high school walk in animated discussion. Margaret saw Ada Rist linger and then go slowly down the street. Ada was too humble to wait for her when she was with the other girls. Margaret felt ashamed. She tried again to say that she must go home, but the girls insisted that she must stay with them, and they started off four abreast. As they passed the school yard, that lay open and wide in the autumn sunshine, the football boys came trotting across it, over the short, thick, faded grass, in their heavy tannish suits and their dusty black sweaters. A little halt from Mildred made the girls stop.

"You made a swell speech, Carl!" Mildred called out saucily.

Carl stopped and looked back, grinning. His face was flushed, and shreds of dry leaves clung to his heavy sweater.

"I didn't know you were such a grand speaker!"

"Thanks!"

"Weren't you scared to death up there? *I* was."

Lucille and Edna Mae giggled nervously at Mildred's boldness in stopping a Senior.

"Hey, you're holding up the team!" one of the boys shouted.

Carl hesitated, then waved, and the boys went trotting on, down the street under the big trees that were just turning yellow, scuffling through the drifts of dry leaves piled along the curbing, and then turning down a hilly, rutted, unpaved side road that led out across the railroad tracks and over to the fields near the fair grounds. The girls were still watching them.

"I thought Carl was just grand!"

"So did I."

"I think you've got the grandest brother."

Margaret said, *"Carl?"*

"Listen, Margaret," Mildred begged confidingly, squeezing Margaret's hand, "do you think he really likes Lillian White?"

"I don't know," Margaret answered. "You needn't ask me about Carl. I don't know who he likes."

"Well, I just asked you, that was all. Because I don't think she seems like the kind of girl he *would*, exactly. Do *you*, girls?"

Margaret pulled away from Mildred's hand. So this was why the girls were so friendly with her all of a sudden! On account of Carl! Well, they needn't think they could get anything out of her like that. She didn't care to be considered just as Carl Ferguson's sister.

"I have to go home," she said abruptly.

The girls clustered around her again. They wanted to know why.

"I have to go to a social tonight at our church."

But the girls wanted to know all about it. Where was it going to be? At the church? Did you have to be invited? Could anybody come?

"I suppose so. If they want to," Margaret said slightingly.

She broke away from them now. As if she couldn't see through that too! Well, let them come if they wanted to be so silly. But they needn't hang around her at the social and pretend that she had invited them. When they had always made fun of the Presbyterian church for having fewer members! Margaret wished now that she had gone off with Ada, and she felt darkly ashamed. If the girls left her to the church Young People, then she wouldn't let them know she didn't enjoy it.

But when she went into the house, it seemed quiet and stale, with the autumn air outside, and only her mother sitting in there sewing.

As soon as he could get away from the supper table, Carl made a dash for the church. He had stayed so long at football practice that he had forgotten to go and open up the building, and Essie Bartlett and Lillian had had to go and get dad. "So I had to leave the bank and go over and do it myself. . . .

Well, that's all right. I know all that. But if you undertake something, then it's up to you to carry it through, and not expect to fall back on me or anybody else to do it for you." Resentment of his father's accusations was boiling in him, mixed with pain and guilt. But running through the dusk of the streets, that smelled of smoke and fall leaves, Carl's pride returned and glowed warmly inside him. His face burned suddenly with the thought of Mildred Summers standing fair-haired and saucy among the girls on the sidewalk and telling him how grand his speech was. Carl felt the flattery of her deft implication that he and she had been sort of partners up there on the platform together. But he was ashamed of his pleasure. Mildred was just a kid—she was only in Margaret's class. Besides that, the fellows talked about her. Oh, nothing much. But she wasn't exactly what you'd call a real nice girl, if some of the things were true, and Carl was a little ashamed of being attracted by her.

He had reached the church by now. He saw it standing there in the dusk, the familiar brick building with the little wooden Gothic entrance painted yellow. There were lights in the Sunday School room. The doors were open. Dad had given Essie Bartlett the key. Carl went into the stale chill of the entry. He could hear the banging, empty sound of chairs being moved in the Sunday School room. He went on through the bleak darkness of the auditorium, sliding expertly between the rows of cold, shiny pews, and pounded on the big folding doors. "Hey, somebody, let me in!" A key was scraped into the lock. The doors were opened showing Lillian's faintly flushed face. She stood back. Carl was flushed too, but he tried to carry it off.

"Why are you locking me out?"

Lillian was too embarrassed to answer, but Essie said with great severity:

"Aha, sir! Here's our janitor at last! We thought you must have given up your job."

"Gee, you know, we started practising football tonight, and I just couldn't get through in time to come and open up the church."

"So we hear!"

"Say, you got it all swept! I sure meant to do that."

"Oh, we've got along very nicely without you! Haven't we, Lillian? We've taken your job away from you. Yes, a very nice gentleman came to our rescue, and let us in, or we would have been standing out on the steps yet."

"I know it. Dad said you came after him. He gave me the dickens," Carl admitted naïvely.

"Well, you deserved it for neglecting us like that!"

Carl looked sheepish. But he caught the archness in Essie's tone. Carl knew very well that he was her favorite. Severe as she was toward the young people who put other interests before the society, the rest of them were always complaining that when it was Carl Ferguson who did anything—forgot to look up his Bible reference or anything—then it was all right!

"If it had been someone else coming in," she told him, "we would have made them go around to the back door. We're keeping these folding doors locked. Last time, some of those younger ones ran wild in the auditorium, got up in the pulpit and played the organ and everything, and we just thought we'd put a stop to that this time. We're going to lock the front door too."

"I'll go back and lock it," Carl offered.

He ran out through the auditorium, taking a long slide through the back aisle to the entry, just in time to lock the front door in Margaret's face and shout:

"No entrance! Everybody's got to go around to the back!"

Margaret pounded furiously on the door. "Carl Ferguson, you let me in!" Carl suddenly flung it open.

"All right," he said condescendingly, "since you're my sister."

Margaret marched disdainfully past him.

Carl lingered. He jiggled the big key in the lock. In the dark chill of the entry, where the bell rope lay in hard, heavy coils on the floor, with the harsh brown fiber mat crushed by many feet on muddy Sundays, he felt a security. He had joked with Essie partly because he was flattered by her partiality for him, but more because of a queer embarrassment with Lillian. Last Sunday night, he had taken her home from the Young People's meeting, and said, standing at the end of her walk where he always left her, "Well, I expect I'll see you at the social Friday night." Now he felt uneasy at having seemed to commit himself.

But after a moment, grinning suddenly, he let himself out of the front door, locked it, sprinted around the church, and marched solemnly through the kitchen into the Sunday School room. Essie shrieked, "Why, Carl Ferguson! I didn't know who you *were*, coming in that way!" Carl saw the nervous flutter of Lillian's eyelids.

Lillian was chairman of the social committee. But Essie seemed to have taken charge as usual. Might as well not *name* any chairman, some of the young people said. Essie was the oldest member of the Young People's Society. Her dark brown dress trimmed with brown velvet, the velvet band around the waist wrinkled by the slight bulge of the stomach confined only in a maidenly Ferris waist, her brown hair threaded with gray and coiled into a great round on the top of her head, anchored by sidecombs but slipping a little, betrayed the period of her right to be included with "the young people." Her own companions, as they married, had one by one dropped out of the Society; but Essie, living with an invalid mother, never having married or come close to marriage, felt herself still too immature to take her place among the matrons in the missionary and aid societies. Well, she's always *been* in the Young People's Society, Mr. Ferguson said indulgently.

"Did you bring the spoons, Margaret? Oh, yes, I see your mother's blue thread. My, I wonder if this church will ever get dishes enough! At the last social, some of the boys had to drink out of old fruit jar covers. We seem to have fewer and fewer cups. For my part, I don't think we ought to let them go out of the church to the missionary and aid. They never all get returned.

"Isn't it nice and warm in here? You can thank your daddy for that!" Essie's manner was arch again. "He built us a little fire when he opened up the church. Just enough to take the chill off. What you ought to have been doing, Master Carl!"

"But you forgive me, don't you, Essie?"

"I don't know whether I do or not! Lillian, do we?"

81

Margaret flung down her wraps on one of the little red chairs in the primary room. She tried to see how her hair looked in the dim reflection in the frosted glass of the window. She hated the way Essie Bartlett talked, as if they were all just concerned with the church, while Lillian sat so acquiescent and still, with her fair hair drawn back from her pale rounded forehead and pushed out just the least bit, discreetly, over her ears. And she just couldn't bear the way Carl let himself be made a little tin god by all the girls here at the church!

"I wonder if Reverend Montgomery will be over."

"Nope," Carl said.

"Isn't that funny?" Essie acquiesced. "I expect you young children don't remember Reverend MacDonald. He was so different from anyone we've had since. He was fine with the young people. Just one of them. Well, I suppose Reverend Montgomery does the best he can, with his health the way it is. I wouldn't say anything against our minister, anyway."

"*I* would," Margaret said disdainfully, "if I felt like it!"

Essie gave a little shocked, pleased, trilling laugh.

Carl said, embarrassed, "Oh, shut up, Margaret!"

"Well, Margaret," Essie said with arch cheeriness, "I expect maybe you and I had better go out to the kitchen and get things going. We'll leave Carl and Lillianna to hold the fort in here!"

Margaret followed her reluctantly. At the kitchen mirror, she pulled out her dark hair wild and fluffy about her face so that it wouldn't look like Lillian's.

Lillian mutely assented to being left with Carl. She began to arrange the chairs in a circle around the room. Her face, pale and soft above the white lace collar on her dark blue dress, had the pinkish, tea-rose flush that seemed to glow with painful delicacy from within. But she felt a distance between herself and Carl—and she dared not try to bridge it, for she saw him still in the after-glow of the glory that had surrounded him on the platform at school this afternoon. The radiance of his face, stained with a bright pink boyish flush, deeper than wild rose, daunted her and made her feel pale and humble. Carl began to whistle as he opened the door of the stove. Finally Lillian said:

"You made a nice speech."

But her shy attempt fell flat, and she knew it in helpless pain. Carl blushed and felt awkward.

"Oh, I guess it wasn't so much. I felt like kind of a fool."

Lillian wanted to protest. Essie called from the kitchen— Lillian hesitated a moment, and then left.

Carl kept on whistling defiantly as he went around the room pushing back all the chairs. He hated Lillian's passivity, her meekness, that left him everything to do. The things that had once seemed to set her apart in fineness from the other girls now gave him a perverse repulsion. He resented the demands of the church itself. Did Essie Bartlett think he had nothing else to do but sweep and fix fires? Dad seemed to think he could just leave football practice any time he chose. Carl knew that Lillian had wanted to say more to him. But he thought angrily—well, if she wants to talk to me, why doesn't she do it? Other girls could do it.

There were poundings on the front door and then noisy scurries through the kitchen.

"Oh, dear, I expect we'll have to let them in that way," Essie moaned. "They'll drive us crazy coming through here."

She hurried into the Sunday School room to tell Carl to get them started playing something.

"Some nice game. We can't just have them running all over."

The noise settled into the occasional scurries and shrieks and hoarse laughter of Wink 'Em under Carl's supervision. Essie returned to the kitchen satisfied for the moment. My, she said, she didn't know what they'd do if Carl went away to school next year! "We'll all be lost." Lloyd Dunn, the only other boy on the committee, had come in with the wieners for which Essie had sent him. "Don't you want some help with that?" he asked Margaret, with an awkward giggle. Margaret was buttering the buns. She silently stood aside and let him take the other knife. As soon as she could, she slipped away into the Sunday School room. But Lloyd was after her.

"Hey, you ran away from me!"

She had to sit down ignominiously in the chair he placed for her in the circle. She stared straight ahead, and at the first chance twisted her shoulders to elude his amorous clutch and slid into the chair that little Addie Weyant was holding.

Now there was a slight commotion. Through the opening of the folding doors showed the faces of Mildred, Lucille and Edna Mae. Giggling, half afraid and half bold, in their pretty fall coats, they ran over to Margaret. "Kid, we stopped for you, and you were already gone. Is it all right for us to come?" She had to show them where to put their wraps in the primary room, and to wait for them while they fixed their hair. But she knew why they had come—why all at once they showed such an interest in the Presbyterian social!

Carl's eyes shone elated. His color was high. Margaret could see with great disgust how pleased and self-conscious he was although he tried to hide it.

"Oh, *don't* let us spoil the game!" Mildred wailed prettily.

Carl cried masterfully: "All right! Let's have a new beginning all round! Come on, everybody. Get up. All start over and change places."

There were loud groans, but they all obeyed. They didn't know just what to make of these three girls from the other churches. Margaret observed with scorn Carl's elated excitement, and Mildred sitting in his chair, smiling and demure, her little hands lying lightly in her lap. A big gawky boy winked at Mildred vociferously, but she stared blandly straight ahead with widely innocent blue eyes; and the boy, blushing, winked hastily at little Dorothy, who ran happily to anyone who summoned her. All the girls were staring brightly at Carl, perched on the edges of their chairs, ready to fly if he gave them a look. Lillian came to the door, but he acted as if he didn't see her.

It was just a game between Mildred and Carl. To the others it seemed to go on interminably. Whenever Mildred tried to get away, Carl's hands clamped down tightly on her shoulders, and she submitted with a graceful little cuddling movement and a giggle. There were never enough boys to go around at the socials, and some of the little girls had to act as boys. They made frantic grabs to hold their unwilling partners and winked hopefully at others who didn't want to see them. Margaret sat scornfully stiff in Ada Rist's chair, with Ada's large reddened hands—Ada's hands always looked as if she had just come in from the cold—poised heavily above her. But at least they protected her from Lloyd Dunn! The girls who belonged to the church looked resentfully at the three outsiders who were spoiling their good times. Carl Ferguson was theirs, and those girls might have stayed out of here.

When the game finally ended, they could not seem to get anything else started, although Essie came in anxiously from the kitchen and tried to rouse the leaders. The crowd broke up helplessly into little groups and couples. Lucille and Edna Mae had captured Lloyd Dunn and little Addie Weyant, the only male prizes available since Carl was already taken. They were all sitting together near the organ. Lloyd looked up at Margaret, half uneasy, half elated, as she went out scornfully past him to the kitchen. He made as if to follow her, and then stayed with a giggle when Edna Mae protested.

"Those three girls have got everybody demoralized," Essie sputtered.

Lillian had gone out into the kitchen too. She pretended to be busy and not to hear the comments on Mildred and Carl. A painful little smile had settled tightly on her lips.

"I never *saw* a social like this," Essie fretted. "I think we ought to make a ruling not to let anybody come but our own young people. We didn't buy these refreshments for everybody in town!"

Wieners were boiling in a big kettle on the cook stove. Essie was fussing because the boys didn't keep the fire going and she had to attend to it—"like everything else." "I'm just tired of being left with everything to do in this Society. Sometimes I think I'll get out and let them run it for themselves and see where they come out." Margaret gave Ada Rist a look, and Ada got red and smothered a snorting giggle. The kitchen was small and unhandy. It was crowded with children coming out to get a drink and trying to snatch a bun from the pile in the dishpan on the table. Essie declared she had never seen them act as they did at this social. "We used to have the nicest socials." She didn't know what was getting into the young people these days. She had such a time getting leaders for the meetings. You didn't seem to be able to count on anyone any more, not *any*one. Shouts of joy greeted the appearance of the paper napkins which the girls demurely accepted and the boys boisterously refused. The social had got entirely out of Essie's control.

Carl and Mildred came running back into the Sunday School room. They wouldn't say where they had been, in spite of all the teasing, but their faces were pink and cold from the outside air.

But Carl looked sober now. He stayed away from Mildred, who went smilingly to sit with the girls. He watched Lillian uneasily as she passed the buns, and tried to make a little joke when she came to him. Even Addie Weyant and Lloyd Dunn had trailed away from their captors. Little Addie was afraid of having to take a girl home for the first time; and Lloyd was now hanging about the kitchen trying to catch Margaret's eye. After they had finished the refreshments, Edna Mae and Lucille and Mildred stayed for a little while, all clustered together. Then they went out to the primary room to get their wraps. Carl sat very preoccupied with a paper boat that he was making from his napkin and refused to notice that they were leaving, although everybody was watching him.

But he was different after that. The three girls had lingered, laughing and talking conspicuously, just within the primary room—Carl knew what they wanted, but he made no move. All the smaller ones were leaving. Carl wandered around the place uneasily, and then went out to the kitchen. Essie was talking about these folks from outside the church who just came to the socials because they wanted to be going somewhere! "They're all after the boys, that's what *they're* after." The pink stain in Carl's cheeks deepened. The kitchen was all in a mess. Plates with pieces of wiener and apple were strewn over the table, just where people had brought them, among coffee cups stained with dark pools of cold coffee. Essie was washing dishes in the big dishpan on the stove, and Lillian was silently putting them away in the cupboard. Margaret had slipped out with Ada Rist, to get out of having Lloyd Dunn take her home, and Lloyd was standing disconsolate. Essie said they didn't need anybody else out here—people were just in the way *now*—they might have appeared a little earlier if they'd really wanted to help!

"Mightn't they, Lillian?"

Carl went back to the empty Sunday School room. He began soberly to put back the chairs and set the room in order. He could come over and sweep it tomorrow morning. Sometimes, the morning after a social, Lillian came over to the church too, to see that everything was all right in the kitchen and to take back whatever had been borrowed. Carl had fallen into a strange fog of unhappiness after the restless excitements and triumphs and failures of the day. He couldn't go tamely home with a bad taste in his mouth. His feelings smarted from Essie's treatment. And dad had scolded him before he left the house. He felt sickeningly that he had failed all round. Always before he had been the chief of the snug little company working in the kitchen together after the socials were over. The strength of his ties with the church, and with Lillian, seemed to rise up and oppress him now in the empty room where the familiar chairs, the familiar long windows, were reproaching him for the way he had acted with Mildred Summers, an outsider. He was the leader, the one shining light of the Young People; and in spite of his occasional failings as a janitor, he had never known what it was to be out of favor before. Now that Mildred was gone, he felt a revulsion and a compunction toward Lillian. He couldn't let things stay like this.

He had lost his earlier elated confidence. It disturbed him now to think about Mildred. It was as if he hadn't known what he was doing for a while. When they had slipped off and run outside—he didn't know just which one had suggested it, he or Mildred—they had gone tearing around the dark streets, shivering with excitement under the thick sky of stars; and Carl had caught Mildred just outside the church, and held her for a moment, panting and warm, her little soft wrists captive in his hard grasp—he had almost kissed her. His face had seemed to duck down of its own accord, close to hers with the bright eyes, his lips had brushed the fringes

87

of her hair. With a shock of fear, he had suddenly let her go. He had never kissed a girl. He didn't know to what solemn meaning it might commit him. The danger had seemed suddenly to bring him to himself. Coming back into the church, he felt cravenly that he had escaped some great peril; but under the spurious relief, there was disappointment and self-berating. He didn't know what Mildred thought of him. Maybe she had wanted him to kiss her. He couldn't tell from the remembrance of her glinting, unblinking eyes. His feelings were all in confusion. Things were all at once coming between him and the old easy certainties. He had never thought of going with any girl outside the church before. His heart was crying out and seeking for the old simplicity.

Lillian went into the primary room for her hat and coat, and Carl followed her. He stood beside the closed organ while she groped for her things on one of the red chairs. He said in a low voice:

"Are you going to let me take you home?"

Lillian didn't answer. She was hurt. Carl felt suddenly that he wanted her to lead him back and keep him in the old ways. And his pride could not bear the thought of losing his old standing with her. When she left the church he caught up with her and got in step; and they went down the long street dimly lighted by the street lamp at the corner.

"You aren't sore at me, are you?"

He couldn't get her to answer him. The folks would feel bad if anything should come between him and Lillian. How could he explain it?

"Gee," he said after a while, "I sure am tired. We practised pretty long for the first time. I got an awful tackle from Beany Lowe. Made me kind o' dopey for a while. I hardly knew what I was doing tonight. Guess I was so tired I was silly."

He could feel a softening in her, although she wouldn't answer even then. Carl's confidence quickly returned. And he *was* tired now. He could feel bruises all over. He had been sorry for Lillian a moment ago, but now he was resentful because she held out so long against him. What did she think?

She wasn't the only girl who liked him! Still, he couldn't bear not to set himself right with her.

"I sure am sorry I seemed to act kind of funny tonight. But I thought *you* did."

"When?" Lillian asked in a smothered voice. She looked at him.

"Well . . ." Carl improvised wildly. "Well, when I first came into the church and you were in there with Essie. You wouldn't hardly look at me."

Lillian didn't answer.

"I thought maybe you were sore at me because I didn't come and open up the church for you."

No answer still. But he could see, by her softening and agitation, that she would let herself accept his explanation. A quick, unreasoning disappointment and relief swept over him again. Now it was like always, going home with Lillian after something at the church, carrying the apples that were left over and that Essie had insisted Lillian should take home to her mother. They went up the walk to Lillian's house—a spare white house standing lonely and incongruously prim in the wide September darkness, with one white birch tree beside it. Carl gave Lillian the apples. He saw her small face turned toward him, looking pearly-pale in the spreading dark. A feeling of bold power and excitement took hold of him. There were only a few lights in houses. He took hold of her hand. It lay in his passively, but with an inner trembling.

"You aren't sore, are you?" he pleaded.

Lillian raised her head. She *had* been sore, but she couldn't maintain it. Her hand quivered. Carl grasped it more closely. Desire, confused and denied before, flared up in him with imperious ruthlessness. He saw the clear, utter innocence of Lillian's eyes. For a moment they both stood frozen. Then with an angry sort of laugh, breaking through the icy barrier of their old, decorous, boy-and-girl relationship, he thrust forward his head with a kiss that barely touched Lillian's frightened lips as she drew back. Carl gave another laugh. He was frightened but exultant.

"Well, good night!" he said.

He turned abruptly and went off home, walking very fast, his feet sounding crisply on the long, empty walk.

Lillian stood for a moment where he had left her. Then she very carefully opened the front door and stole into the dark, narrow hall, where she stood, pressing her hands against her chest, one over the other, and breathing unevenly. She had left the apples out on the porch.

2

The Whites had given the invitation for the Thanksgiving dinner this year. They were not great on entertaining. The house was opened up once a year for the missionary meeting, and once a year the minister and his wife were invited to supper. But now, with unusual generosity, they had come out and solved the problem of the first Thanksgiving since Grandma Ferguson's death. "I guess we better have all the folks come to our house this year." So the little inner church clan, the Fred Fergusons, Grandpa, Ella and Ben, Reverend and Mrs. Montgomery, were all gathered now in the spare neatness of the White house.

The parlor was opened up for the occasion, but they chose to be in the sitting room where the plush sofa, miscellaneous chairs, table and stand collected there for winter gave a slightly more homelike feeling. The heat of the stove spread only a little distance through the chill of the parlor air. The men were sitting in a group, old Abner White doing most of the talking, Mr. Montgomery putting in a nervous, precise word now and then; and Grandpa Ferguson was a little apart, looking down with brooding eyes at the harsh red and brown pattern of the carpet. The children always felt as if they must be quiet in this house. Dorothy had promised to keep little Bunny amused; and they were sitting on the floor spinning in turn the wavering, frail needle of the old bicycle game that Howard had dug out from somewhere, and that was the very same one Carl and Lillian used to play together. Margaret had gone instantly to look at the old magazines piled meagerly on the bottom shelf of the combination desk and bookcase; and now she was looking with remote, dreary interest at the pictures of missionaries standing among bands of Chinese girls in homely dresses, in those thin old religious magazines that were all the Whites took, still with the fold down the middle as when they had come through the mail. But anything was better than having to be out in the kitchen and hear mama and Aunt Ella and Aunt Jennie talk about just how to dish up all the food!

Carl sat for a while among the men, with his ingenuous, glowing face turned toward them. But the expression was just a copy of what he wanted them (and himself) to think he was feeling. Inside, he felt terribly insecure when a sudden remembrance of the game that afternoon made his breath drop and leave a horrified emptiness in his chest. There was the pride of the game too. He seemed to be chosen out, in his glowing youth, from among the older people.

But all the time he had the feeling of something underhanded and secretly amiss. There was so much that the folks didn't know about. He had caught just one glimpse of Lillian when they had first come in, and then she had slipped into the kitchen. They had not been alone together since the night of the social. After the Young People's meetings, Carl had lingered, talking loudly with the other boys, until Lillian had gone on with Essie Bartlett. But all the same, he knew that the kiss he had given her could not be ignored forever. The memory of it glowed in the consciousness of her face when he happened to meet her in the hall at school. He said to her "Hello," with loud, hollow cheeriness, and she said "Hello"; but they didn't know how to meet each other's eyes. And Carl was pierced by the sight of Lillian's shyness, thinking she didn't know just how he had come to give her that kiss, what had led up to it, his mixed feelings—and afraid that maybe she did know it!

Carl got up and went out of the house, and wandered around the yard in the bright November cold, kicking up leaves that lay half frozen under a crust of snow at the edge of the lawn. With all the folks in there in the house, that was warm and fragrant with Thanksgiving odors, all just naturally taking

91

it for granted that he and Lillian were the best of friends, Carl couldn't believe of himself that he had been fooling around with that little Mildred Summers. And yet he had, and since he had given Lillian that kiss. He had gone to the library in the evenings, not admitting that it was for any special reason, and had nearly always found Mildred there; and afterwards they had run about through the dark, chill, autumn night, wild and at large. They saw each other sometimes between classes at school. All the time, they kept up a personal, never-ending touch-and-go of dispute—she answered it only by laughter or provocative teasing: Would you have been sore at me if I had kissed you that night?—or did you think I was going to? He did not quite kiss her now, held back secretly by an unwavering image of the clear, frightened purity of Lillian's eyes. But he came close to it—pinched her shoulder, rubbed his hand against the textured floss of her hair, let his hand pass softly over the round, warm, mysterious delight of her thigh. It excited and troubled him that Mildred didn't seem to care. These times with her were only half pleasure. He never was sure about Mildred. Perhaps she *was* running after him because he played on the football team, as Margaret had once scornfully told him. She was going with other fellows too, all the time. It shamed Carl, and made him uneasy, the way Mildred seemed to be willing to meet him under cover, without Lillian's knowledge—the sly, teasing reference she kept making to Lillian, softly malicious. But he couldn't keep away from her. He made resolutions at night in bed, and then they seemed to melt under the allurement of any chance meeting with Mildred. "What am I?" Carl thought wildly. But now, such things as walking home with Lillian, each of them self-conscious and discreet, were not enough—he couldn't get along now without the sweetness of touching and fending and exploring on into the mysterious, entangled, breathing wilderness whose borders he had just begun to enter. But pretty soon, if he wasn't careful, all the kids in high school would begin to say that now he was going with Mildred Summers.

In the kitchen, the womenfolks were talking hastily, between inquiries of "Are you ready to have the potatoes dished, Jennie?" and "Where do you keep your big spoons?" But Aunt Ella had time to glance about with dull black eyes quickly shrewd, and see how Jennie managed things. The cupboards had that sparse, neat look associated with the Whites. But they were putting on a good dinner today, at any rate. Finally Mrs. White went to the door of the sitting room, hurriedly tying a fresh, white, glossy apron with a border of crocheted lace.

"Well, I guess our dinner is ready!"

Leaves had been added to the oblong dining table that was covered with a lace-trimmed cloth which Grandma Ferguson, had she been there, would have remembered not having seen in use since the Old Lady White died. The best dishes were on the table—chilly, shining white; and the spaces between the covered vegetable dishes and centerpiece of yellow pumpkin were set neatly with red bright jelly and dark green pickles in old dishes of frosty, spider-webby glass.

Abner White took the head of the table. He sat down at once and began tucking his napkin into his collar, with solemn care, beneath his beard, not waiting for Jennie to name the places.

"Come on. Come on, folks. No need to wait. Sit down."

Chairs were scraped back, Mrs. White and Lillian shaking their heads and standing dutifully near the door ready for flight into the kitchen.

"Reverend Montgomery, will you ask the blessing on this Thanksgiving meal?"

Mr. Montgomery bent forward his head, with the strands of reddish-gray hair brushed carefully over the dry skull, and rested it upon his hand with thin fingers spread to shade his closed eyes. Mrs. Montgomery, as always when Mr. Montgomery spoke, sat with faded lips self-consciously compressed but ready to quiver with sensitive awareness. Old Abner's white beard spread on his chest as he listened with forehead bowed and chin drawn back, drawing his breath with solemn noisiness. The precise, aging voice quavered into a thin sonorousness before it sounded a lingering:

"Ah-men!"

The heads lifted in relief. Mrs. White slipped out into the kitchen and came back with the great, roasted, golden-brown turkey on a platter, setting it down in front of old Abner with painstaking and flustered care.

"This is Brother Ferguson's contribution to our feast."

There were exclamations and murmurs of appreciation. But Grandpa Ferguson, roused from the apathy in which he had been sitting ever since the blessing began, said hastily, almost humbly:

"No, no. Thank Ella here. She raises the poultry."

"Well, it's your gift, father."

"No, no. Ella deserves the thanks."

"Well, I guess we won't any of us quarrel about that," Howard said, "as long as we've got such a bird as this waiting for us."

Everyone laughed, in relief.

Mrs. White began anxiously to pass the food. Old Abner carved the turkey with solemn deliberation, scrutinizing each piece and laying his carving tools carefully on the edge of the platter. "Annie, what piece can I serve you to? Ella, what will *you* have?" He did not ask the children—they had to wait for what came their way. But he could draw no preference from either Mr. or Mrs. Montgomery. "Any piece you give me, Brother White. No, I really have no choice."

In the midst of the flurry of passing, Grandpa Ferguson spoke out, in a slow, strange tone that seemed to come out of some remoteness of remembrance into which he alone had withdrawn:

"This is the first Thanksgiving meal I've set down to without mother in fifty-five years."

There was a hush. The children looked frightened, Mrs. White distressed; tears suffused Ella's black eyes as her face swelled and grew red, and Fred cleared his throat and then turned his head aside and gave his nose a trumpet blow. They had all been thinking of this but hoping that no one would speak of it.

"Longer than that for some of us. Longer than that," old Abner White pronounced with sonorous lugubriousness; while

Mr. Montgomery said, "These things come to us," and Mrs. Montgomery murmured distressfully.

Tears had come quickly into Carl's eyes at his grandfather's words; but in the flurry of recovery that followed, the attention to the old man, the falsely cheering words of the women, the tears seemed to dry without evidence, leaving his face, still rosy from the outdoor air, burning and queer. Now everybody hastened to talk cheerfully again so that Grandpa "wouldn't think about it" and the Thanksgiving dinner would not be spoiled. The warmth and intimacy of the gathering of friends surrounded Carl and glowed in his own heart. When he had first come in to dinner, he and Lillian had not been able to look at each other; but now the flitting glimpses that he had of her, in the crisp sheerness of the little dotted swiss apron tied neatly around the waist of her dark blue dress, as she silently and deftly waited on the table, made the old attraction begin to stir. Carl felt a rising flood of liking and appreciation for everybody, even old Mr. White, who still took his time and made Jennie wait embarrassed and anxious at his elbow. Grandpa's mention of Grandma, simple and emotional, seemed to bring back to Carl the affections of his childhood. These were the people among whom he belonged, before whom he could play his real part. Howard, his cadaverous face above the long thin neck sweet with humble good-nature, sat inconspicuously straddling a table leg. Uncle Ben chose out tidbits for Bunny and Dorothy, winked at them and cracked his little jokes, secretly joining in with the young ones beneath the more pretentious talk of the adults. Mr. and Mrs. Montgomery, strangers that they were in this environment, with the small plain church, the plain congregation, many of them from the country—they with their precision of diction, their no one knew just what mystery of early superior training and education—were still the minister's folks. They were being anxiously if ceremoniously friendly, grateful for their inclusion among the chief members of their little church, showing that they were not entirely out of favor although the congregations were dropping off a little—both trying to eat more heartily, in appreciation, than their frail, elderly digestions allowed, while a dry flush rose slowly in Mr. Montgomery's thin face.

The gathering here today was reminiscent of dozens of earlier ones, since Carl was a little bit of a fellow, since he and Lillian —he in tight little pants and ruffled blouse, and Lillian with pale gold braids tied at the ends with braided-in black ribbons—had stood, Carl smiling eagerly and she abashed, in front of their elders when a photograph was taken beside the old rock house out on the farm . . . with Margaret scowling and not wanting to be in the picture in a dress she didn't like, and Dorothy held in her father's arms. Carl felt all this warmly, even while he was alertly watching the carving, ready to cry out—as he did now:

"I guess I'll have to forego the turkey, Mr. White. Will you please put hardly anything on my plate?"

He had been expecting the consternation that followed, and sat modestly enjoying his heroic conspicuousness. But he insisted, shaking his head and smiling, while he explained to the respectfully listening women what Bob Yetter had said about a heavy meal before playing, and while his little brother watched him with hero-worshipping eyes.

"I don't know as I'd care to play a game that took away my appetite for a meal like this," Uncle Ben drawled. "Is that the truth, Lil'yan? If you sat down there beside him, 'stead of being up waiting on all us folks, couldn't you git him to eat?"

Lillian shook her head, smiling, the tea-rose flush glowing through the pearly paleness of her cheeks.

"What can you eat, Carl?" Mrs. White asked anxiously.

Carl, in spite of grumblings from his father, anxious murmurs from his mother, replied modestly, deprecating the trouble he was causing while he enjoyed it:

"Well, Bob said the best thing for us to eat was poached egg on toast. But I don't want you to have to get it for me, Aunt Jennie."

Aunt Ella laughed. "Land! That sounds as if you was Grandpa. He *has* to eat that, because he hasn't got any teeth."

"Well, I guess Carl's got his teeth, all right," Howard put

in sweetly. "After the game is when he can come in strong. That right, Carl?"

"Carl's got *lots* of teeth," Bunny said loyally. "You don't know about football."

Everyone laughed.

In the talk that followed, Carl sat happily the center of a little flurry among the womenfolks—his mother anxiously protesting that *she* could cook Carl's egg, Jennie was not to bother, Jennie protesting that it wasn't any bother, and pitying and admiring Carl. Uncle Ben settled it by declaring, *"Lil'*yan'll get it! Won't you, Lil'yan? That right, Carl?" And Carl felt the pleasure of having Lillian bring his plate in to him and place it silently before him. Then she slipped into the empty chair by his side.

All through the rest of the meal, Carl was aware of Lillian's delicate warmth beside him, gratified by her loyalty when the grown people talked about football—"But ain't it awful rough?" Aunt Ella said. "I think it's awful rough, from what I hear, I ain't ever seen one. Don't they get their arms broken and all like that?"—and sweetly stirred by a memory of the scarcely touched softness of her lips. Was she thinking about that too? The flush made her face flower-like. She seemed purely colored and lovely, in the contrast between the dark blue sheen of her dress and the pearly whiteness of her skin, with the housewifely crispness of the sheer little apron, and with pale gold showing in the loosened puffs of shiningly brushed hair that almost hid her small ears. Carl felt with emotion the benevolence of the older people toward them as they sat together. It was a kind of treachery even to think of another girl. And now, when he did think of Mildred Summers, she seemed to him bold and pert beside Lillian. He was ashamed. Lillian was like one of those pink and white shells—like the one Grandma used to have holding open her parlor door, chilly and pearly and flushed with pink, in the coolness of that deep-windowed room in the old rock house.

Finally they got up from the table, at ease, flushed with coffee and good food, old Abner White spreading with the magnificence of his hospitality, Aunt Ella declaring that she was

97

"full as a tick," and making appropriate sounds and gestures to prove it; and before the women began to clear off the table, and the men retired to the sitting room, they all had to gather in the front hall to wish Carl good luck. It was time for him to leave for the game. He tried to make all the folks promise to come. He felt now an exalted calm of excitement.

"Well, good-bye, everybody. Guess I've got to go."

"Good-bye, Carl!"

"Lick those Hanging Rock fellows. That's what they deserve," Uncle Ben said.

"Sure. You bet we will." He went back to the sitting room for a moment. "Good-bye, Grandpa."

"Good-bye, my boy," said Grandpa Ferguson.

The others were leaving the hall now. Carl waited a moment for a chance to speak to Lillian. He caught her fingers. He whispered, "You want to root for us!" Her gleaming eyes promised. Carl ran down the steps and off through the bright November air.

"Well, he certainly deserves to win," Jennie murmured with sympathy, "going without his Thanksgiving dinner!"

Already there was a crowd in the gray, weather-stained bleachers out at the fair grounds. The folks had decided they would have to go and see Carl play, in spite of the women's fear of the roughness of the game, and the old belief that it was things like football that took up the young people's time and gave them too many interests outside the church. Jennie had sent them all off, not permitting Annie and Ella to stay dutifully to help her with the dishes. Even the Montgomerys were incongruously but gratefully there. A football game seemed a trifle too secular an event for all of them. But Carl was going to play. That made it different. The Fergusons saw the Richard Spencers. Ethel Spencer's silvery-blue furs, and Richard's face fresh-colored beneath the jaunty tilt of his gray felt hat, seemed to lift the game at once into an event of local fashion. Lawrence Brattle had brought his daughter Virginia, and sat with his arm around her, strands of her shining, long, gold hair blown across the rough dark blue of his coat sleeve.

The voices and shouting and occasional tooting of horns, the best clothes, the furs, the colors, the November air—all were bright with excitement. Patches of snow flashed at the edge of the field, and away off down the road the rusty, clustered leaves of the oaks in Hoagland's Grove were brown and cold against the blue. Off at the side stood the gray, empty buildings of the fair grounds.

"Well, I think it's very nice we could come," Mrs. Montgomery murmured.

The football boys came running out on the field to limber up, clumsy in their brown suits and black sweaters and heavy leather helmets. Cheers went up from the bleachers. It made Margaret embarrassed to hear her mother's feeble little unaccustomed attempt at a cheer. Margaret looked discontentedly about until she saw the girls sitting bunched together in another part of the bleachers. She didn't want to be with them, but she hated to have to come with the folks. Now the folks had located Carl among the players. The girls were cheering and waving. Margaret felt with disdain how Lillian was sitting conscious and still. Burdette Finney was prancing along in front of the bleachers, leading the cheers; and now as Carl ran out with the ball, he shouted:

"Fergy! Now come on, folks. Everybody yell. FERGY!"

The girls were yelling so intensely that their eyes glittered moistly in their flushed faces. Lillian sat with hands strained tightly in her lap. Margaret was deeply chagrined to see her mother wiping her eyes and smiling, while her father sat very stiff as if he had no connection with the proceedings, and the Montgomerys feebly but enthusiastically waved. Carl, conspicuous in his glory, ran across the field.

But now they were going to begin! Bob Yetter, with his wild head of football hair, which he still wore as in the days of his high school glory although he was beginning to get gray, was running back to the sidelines. The teams were lining up. Burdette, thrashing his arms, gave a last cheer, and then subsided. The folks could all pick out Carl, standing bent over with his hands upon his padded knees. Dr. Redmond, handsome in a white sweater and windblown, thick, silvered hair, was out there with hand raised and a whistle at his lips. The teams were scattered in formation across the field, dark in the cold sunshine, snow here and there flashing from the trampled brown grass around it, the wire that kept back the small boys glittering at intervals against the blue. The waiting settled, intense. Curt and shrill the whistle blew. The leather ball shot up, curved through the air, and the girls stood up in the grandstand wildly cheering. Hanging Rock had the kick-off.

The Fergusons, in their innocence of all such secular amusements as football, could not make head or tail out of the game. It seemed to be nothing but a tumble of bodies, the sharp whistle, the meaningless separation and panting run into formation again, and the tense silence before the quarterback barked out the signals. The Montgomerys sat dimly smiling, a little cold, determined to be pleased since it was their parishioners who had brought them. When they heard the cheers, they tried—a little late—to join in and show their approbation; Mrs. Montgomery once smilingly and innocently clapping for the other side. Aunt Ella kept poking Uncle Ben and wanting to know, in an audible whisper, what they were up to now.

"Well, I don't know. How should I know any better'n you?"

"Well, you're a man."

But all that any of them really saw or tried to see—to Margaret's shame, it was so transparent, and her standards for her family's social conduct were so lofty—was Carl. When one of the wild tumbles began, Mrs. Ferguson gave a little gasp and weakly grabbed her husband's arm until she saw that Carl had come out of it and was trotting off with the others. When Chuck Messenger made a twenty-yard run with the ball, she cheered and waved wildly—and then cried, distraught, "Oh, wasn't that Carl?" When Belmond went over the line for their touchdown, and she learned that it *was* Carl this time, and heard the hoarse, exultant chant of "Fergy! Fergy! Fergy!" she had to sit back on the bleachers until she could surreptitiously wipe her eyes. She was trembling. Then the whistle suddenly blew, and the boys with the water pail came running, the players for the other side detached themselves and stood panting.

"Papa. It's Carl!"

She started to get up, but he made her sit down, while the Montgomerys gave sympathetic murmurs, and Aunt Ella wanted to know what it was all about. Lillian sat in trembling silence. Aunt Ella hadn't yet found out what the matter was. "What are they stopping for? What's Carl done? Ain't he going to play? Is it over?" Bunny was getting ready to cry. . . . And then in another moment the group on the field was dispersing, the boys with the water pail were running back, Carl was up and stamping about spitting and shaking off water, and Burdette was running along the sidelines again with face wildly screwed and yelling:

"All right, folks! Wind knocked out. All right. Now, three big rahs for Fergy!"

After that, Mrs. Ferguson could have no more peace. The game was just push and tumble, never quite reaching either goal, a hoarse, weary, forgetful chant going on from the sidelines as Burdette pranced up and down making weary motions in the last few minutes of play. The Fergusons understood so little of what had been happening that they weren't even sure Belmond had won the game, although they supposed that must be why everyone was cheering. The whistle blew, a last roar went up from the scattering crowd, as Dr. Redmond tossed the ball to Bob Yetter, clapped Carl and Chuck Messenger on the back, and struggled into his big dark overcoat that had been lying folded at the end of the bleachers. Mr. Bellew stood up, and looking down at the boys, held his hands above his head and clapped them. People were streaming down from the grandstand now—Mrs. Richard Spencer stepping lightly, drawing her silvery furs about her rosy face. The girls had caught sight of Margaret, and they all came up to her. Weak with happiness, hoarse with strain, they wandered off from the field with the smiling, drifting crowd, across the trampled grass and out to the road where the blackish branches of trees held up a few last leaves into the cold, failing light.

"Wasn't Carl grand? Wasn't he *grand?*" the girls were moaning.

The Ferguson party stood gathered out near the roadway

waiting for Carl. People as they passed smiled and spoke to the proud, waiting parents. "Expect you're pretty proud of that boy of yours!" They all had a smile at Bunny's innocently, eagerly lifted face, rosy in the circle of the blue sailor cap, standing with one little blue-mittened hand in the clasp of his father's large, reddened, bare hand. When he saw Richard Spencer, whom he knew at the bank, he called out happily:

"Carl made a touchdown!"

and all the people laughed.

At last Carl came toward them, looking strange and overgrown in his football paraphernalia, dangling his helmet, his hair rumpled and a big bruise beginning to darken on his cheek. They felt almost embarrassed before the hero of the day. Howard stood grinning and deferential, Carl's mother tremulously smiling in her pride and relief, even his father not knowing just how to greet him. Lillian was still and conscious again. Bunny ran up and Carl caught his hand. While Carl stood there, Bunny looked up at him with sober adoration.

Carl said, happy, tired and glowing, "Gee, folks, but I'm glad you all came."

But his eyes, as he spoke, were ranging the crowd. His windwhipped color deepened as he saw Mildred and the girls lingering just a little way from the folks. They had hung onto Margaret as long as they could. But now there was nothing that could keep them except the faint excuse of tying a shoestring. Carl caught a gleam from Mildred's eyes. His heart beat thickly for a moment. But he could not move, surrounded by the folks; and after a second of sharp chagrin—seeing the trustfulness of Lillian's eyes shining through her shyness, seeing the folks' proud happiness—he felt a virtuous uplifted glory mixed indistinguishably with relief. He looked away. But he saw the little flirt of Mildred's shoulders. He heard her say in a clear, high voice that had a sting of mockery—

"Come on, girls! I guess we're blocking up the way!"

Then the brown coat was lost among the other coats in the roadway. He knew Mildred was gone, and knew it was all over between them—the deft little meetings in the hall or on the high school steps, the wild happy chases through the cold autumn nights, all the subtle, clandestine excitement that had flickered up through study and practice and work that fall . . . in that moment when he had refused to look at Mildred, he had given it up. It was gone from him with the pert little swing of Mildred's brown coat as she went out into the crowd and left him standing there with the folks.

They were back at the Whites' again. The men were in the sitting room, except old Abner, who was upstairs sleeping. Grandpa Ferguson was just waking up from a long, dreary nap on the sofa. The women were in the kitchen again helping Jennie to get a bite of supper. By a sort of tacit consent, the Montgomerys had been allowed to return to the manse after the game, and now just the three families were there at the Whites' together in the relief of intimacy.

Carl had had to go back to the high school and take off his football togs. Now he came into the sitting room in his familiar blue serge suit, but with some of the glory of the afternoon still around him. The bruise was scraped dark across the pink of one cheek, and his hair was combed damp and shining.

"Well! How's the hero?" cried Uncle Ben.

Carl tried to grin in response, deprecating the fun while he relished it. His mother and Aunt Ella and Mrs. White all had to come into the sitting room to see how he was after the game. Sure, he told them, he was fine! No, he hadn't been hurt much. Not with all that bunch landing on top of him?—Aunt Ella said. She'd have thought it would have squeezed the insides right out of him! That bruise? Where? Oh, on his cheek? No, that wasn't anything. He held and pressed his mother's anxious fingers. He refused to lie down on the sofa, declaring stoutly that he was all right, as good as anybody—while the menfolks commended him, and the women, still hovering about him in sympathy, assured him that there would be a good supper for him soon.

"Well, sir, ye licked 'em, didn't ye?" Uncle Ben said happily.

"'Twas an awful good game," said Howard. "Jennie, I wished you'd been there."

"I wish I could have seen Carl play! But I didn't like to leave the two grandpas."

"Carl made the touchdown!" Bunny cried again.

"That's right, Bunny," the others said, laughing; while Bunny, going up to Carl and taking his hand, first looked around fiercely as if somebody might be going to deny his brother's glory, and then swung back to see if he could touch the floor while Carl held him.

"Yes, Carl played a very good game," his father said magnanimously. "He was all right."

Carl let Bunny gently down to the floor and pulled away his hand, and then turned away, pretending to hum. For dad to say that much meant more than if other people had loaded him with praises. It seemed now as if the whole day had been perfect. The folks had come at last to see him play, and he had made the touchdown before their eyes. Everything was complete. He had lived up to the expectations of everybody. He could still hear the hoarse chant of the cheering out on the cold November field. He could feel the weary, tumultuous triumph of the end of the game, the fellows crowding around him, and Bob Yetter hugging him and saying, with tears in his eyes, "Y'*did* it, Fergy old fellow, y'*did* it!" It was the last game he would ever play for B.H.S. and he had given them their score. There was nothing about the whole golden day to remain after the glory was gone to scourge him with some of his own secret guilt and humiliation. It had been easy to feel generous about Chuck Messenger's twenty-yard run with the ball and to insist on the other fellows giving Chuck credit. He had lived up to his best all the way through. And from now on, his whole life would be like that. Now, in his relaxed, weary glow of happiness, he felt the thankfulness of relief run all through him— that he had been able to keep away from Mildred Summers, and stay right with the folks and Lillian.

But he couldn't bear, in his own happiness, to see Grandpa Ferguson sitting apart and forlorn. He went over and leaned on his grandfather's chair.

"I wish *you'd* come to the game with the folks, Grandpa."

"What's that, my boy? No, no. I'm too old to be starting in

seeing football games. But I know you done well, without my being there."

"Gee, we thought at the first of the year we'd certainly get licked when we played Hanging Rock. They had all their old fellows."

"No," Grandpa said, shaking his head, "I'm too old for such things." And he turned, and complained to Carl, as if somehow the young folks could understand better than the older ones, who were so full of their own affairs, that now for him were over—"I don't enjoy going without your Grandma. I should have stayed home today. I can't go places and feel cheerful."

"Don't say that, Grandpa," Carl answered fondly, putting his hand on his grandfather's shoulder. "We want you anyway." What Grandpa said made him feel sad, but suddenly protecting and strong and young. The old man grasped the hand. But after a moment he drew his own away, took a big blue handkerchief out of his pocket, and turning his head aside, wiped his eyes and blew his nose, and then carefully wiped his mustache.

"Well, well. Never mind, my boy. You get your rest."

Carl wandered back to the sofa. Maybe he would lie down a while before they called him to supper. Now his body was beginning to blaze with weariness. His grandfather's words, the thought that Grandma was gone, so bitter to him at first, only touched his bright well-being with a sweet sadness, that was like the end of the day, the clear golden light getting distant and cold behind the bare black trees. He felt his grandfather's trust in him. Gee, he thought with emotion, he could never do anything that would make the folks disappointed in him. Nothing in the world, not even his success today, the cheering, Belmond winning the game, meant so much to him as their pride and faith. Today made up for the times he had been late for supper, had forgotten to rake the lawn, neglected to build the fires soon enough in the church. He saw Margaret sitting off in a corner with *Ben Hur*, the only thing that looked like a story that she had been able to dig out from the sparse supply of Sunday School quarterlies and Presbyterian hymn books in the shelves. Carl wasn't sure how much Margaret might know about himself and Mildred. But Margaret was too proud and disdainful to tell tales, Carl thought with the quivering shame he had never been able to lose, remembering childhood things she could bring up against him—that time he had told his mother that she had gone to play with Irene Jackson and the Gowan kid. (But it *had* been partly because he thought the folks ought to know—because he was responsible.) Carl hadn't seen Lillian since he had got back from the game. She was out in the kitchen helping to get his supper ready.

Jennie came to the door and called them out to the dining room again.

"Oh, my, see what these womenfolks have got for us!"

There was not much turkey left—just some scraps, Jennie said apologetically; but they had a nice plate saved for Carl.

"Better let Lil'yan bring it to him. Then it'll taste better," Uncle Ben said jovially. "That right, Carl?"

They were saved—Carl and Lillian both—from having to make any response by old Abner who had come down from upstairs, flushed with sleep, and pleased with the remembrance of the long talk in which he had told Brother Ferguson that these things were the Lord's will. He now launched a sonorous blessing without waiting to see whether the others were seated or not. Half of them were, half of them weren't. Lillian stood silent and demure, her head bent, just inside the room.

"Now, friends, make out. I guess Jennie's got a few things together for us. If there's anything you want you don't see, speak up, tell her to get it for ye."

"Tastes even better'n it did this noon, by golly," Uncle Ben said. "How's your plate, Carl? Worth waiting for? Wish now *I'd* played football."

"Yes, you wish it!" Aunt Ella taunted. "I'd like to see you play anything that made you get a hurry on you."

There was a more informal intimacy now without the ministerial restraint of the Montgomerys. They could talk about the Montgomerys themselves if they pleased. The menfolks relaxed. They ate as they wanted to. Aunt Ella again supervised and scolded Uncle Ben—she had been able to do it only by glances at noon.

Carl and Lillian sat together at the end of the table. There was not so much serving to do tonight. There was a pleasant indulgence in the attitude of the older people that enhanced the sweetness of their intimacy, that seemed to mark them out in their blooming youth, and still flatteringly to include them. Now Carl had time to eat. The turkey was better than it would have been this noon. Everybody was anxious to wait on him and to see that he got the best. The blaze of fatigue died down into a luxurious tiredness, suffused with relief from the earlier tension, with satisfaction, a pleasure in himself through which only the memory of that little flirt of Mildred's shoulders as she went away from the fair grounds smarted faintly. He felt a desire to lean his head against Lillian and close his eyes in the certainty of her devotion.

"What do you get for all this running with balls and going without your vittles and getting the stuffing knocked out of you?" Uncle Ben demanded.

"Well, I get a pin," Carl said with condescending kindness.

"A pin? That all? Your Aunt Ella could give you that. She's always got some sticking in front of her."

"It's an honor pin," Mrs. Ferguson said proudly.

"An *honor* pin! Well, I expect that's something different."

"What's that?" said Grandpa Ferguson, with difficulty.

"An honor pin, Gandpa. They give it to Carl for playing so good on the football team," Jennie explained, with a smile.

Grandpa said with slow satisfaction, "So that's it!"

Afterwards, when all the others had left, adjourning to easier chairs in the sitting room while they left the young ones to clear off the dishes, Carl and Lillian stayed on at the littered table. Lillian started to take up the plates.

"What's your hurry?" Carl asked. He put his hand on her arm.

She hesitated, and then sat down docilely beside him. Carl could hear his mother urging Margaret and Dorothy to get to work, but he knew from experience that it would take them a while. He felt himself resting in the beautifulness of his hour, still irradiated by the fading bright glow of effort and glory, made sweet and warm by the approval and affection, the attentions of all the women, the sense of coming back to his own.

He said to Lillian, "Are you going to wear my pin when I get it?"

She gave him a startled look.

"Right here," he whispered. He touched the silk above her breast. His hand lingered there, as he felt her trembling obedience. She had the stillness of a bird when a hand closes over it. Carl felt the faint rasp of ironed embroidery under the silk, and sensed with awe the immaculateness of her person. He was warmly aware of the favor he was conferring—Carl, Fergy, the hero of the school today, how the older people took pride in him, other girls ran after him. He gave himself up voluptuously to the sweet impulse that was carrying him.

"You know what that means. Don't you, Lillian?"

She whispered, "I guess so."

All at once his emotion felt the need of confession—the need of complete absolution from her purity.

"Lillian, listen, I want to ask you to forgive me for the way I've acted this fall. I've been out quite a lot of times with Mildred Summers. I don't mean there was anything wrong about it, only—I guess I knew I wasn't acting right. I knew I was making you feel bad." He felt Lillian quiver. "Gee, I was kind of crazy, I guess. That kind of girl, when they go after a fellow . . . I never really meant anything by it. I never really meant to go with her. I guess maybe I don't need to tell you that, do I? Lillian, are you going to forgive me?"

He pressed his hand down over hers, knowing that he had the advantage and that his self-abasement was a luxury—and yet suddenly anxious, all the same. The anxiety changed to confidence in swift secrecy when he heard her faint murmur of assent. But it had left behind it a strange enhancing of her value to him. Carl felt bathed in joyous cleanness—although Lillian now was crying, almost noiselessly, her head turned delicately aside, a nicely ironed white handkerchief pressed to her face. Carl begged her, awed at her feeling, with a strange, uplifted, shamed knowledge that it was deeper than his own:

"Don't cry. *Don't.* The folks will hear you. Lillian *dear.*"

He put his arm around her, feeling a new warm affection go out to her when he said that word "dear." He was whispering, so that they wouldn't hear him in the other room. Any minute the girls might come into the dining room. That made these minutes more precious.

"Now it's all right. Isn't it? Listen, Lillian. I'm not going with her any more. I never did want to. I don't know why . . . Gee, I feel better now I've told you about it, Lillian. Listen. You're going to wear my pin, aren't you? Because I want you to."

He felt the movement of her head against his cheek.

He whispered, "You didn't mind when I tried to kiss you that night, did you?"

He felt her stillness. Shame and happiness and tenderness together came flooding over him. It was all right now! Everything was. He felt Lillian's shy kiss return his own with a restrained, frightened fervor. It was all the sweeter being in here together, with the others so perilously close. But then voices seemed suddenly to be very loud and surrounding. Lillian gathered up some dishes blindly and went out to the kitchen with them. Carl waited a moment, dazzled by this new delight, ashamed to think where he had learned it first, feeling with awed wonder how his heart was beating. Then he smoothed back his hair quickly and went into the sitting room, trying to look natural and ingenuous, while his blood was racing and singing.

"Gee!" he said. "That was a good supper, folks."

II. COMMENCEMENT

As soon as the academic procession had passed out of the church into the openness of the hot noon sunlight, the Senior class began to scatter. The little group who had received honorary degrees (mostly Presbyterian ministers) had to be detained on the lawn for a final photograph for the church paper. But the Seniors were through. They were out in the world. That hoary promise of chapel orators had all at once informally come true. The boys began to get rid of their caps and gowns at once, according to manly tradition. The girls kept theirs on a little longer, not sure of how their hair might look if they took off their mortar boards. Now they all began to move about in a strange kind of let-down freedom.

Carl looked around for the folks. He had thought he might locate them somewhere in the audience when he had come down after taking his degree; but that had all been so brief, it had passed in a kind of high, hot daze. Then he caught sight of them over at the edge of the sidewalk—the folks and Bunny, the girls hadn't come. Carl hurried over with his gown flapping open.

"Hello, there! Been looking for you."

He kissed his mother, shook hands with his father—"How are you, dad?" Today he could feel a pleasant sense of patronage and protection toward them as he saw them here at the college in their middle-aged simplicity. He drew his little brother up to him in a cherishing hug. "How's the big kid?"

"Don't you see who else we've brought along?" his father asked.

"Well, I certainly do. How are you, Lillian?"

The fresh pink in Carl's cheeks flushed deeper. He still kept the rosy cheeks over which the old ladies in the church used to exclaim admiringly when he ushered on Sundays. He said, trying to laugh, "Excuse the damp paw." He was hot and perspiring. He felt awkward and funny, shaking hands with Lillian this way. For a long time now, they had kissed each other at meeting and parting. But they couldn't very well do that here in front of the folks and everyone. He had expected the folks to bring Lillian, of course; and yet he felt this embarrassment at seeing her here. In some way that he wasn't ready to go into, it made a complication. He could feel how all the fellows were looking at Lillian, and the girls giving her bright, curious glances. She was being appraised by everyone as "Carl's girl." Carl Ferguson's "girl at home" had been only a tantalizing rumor until now, explaining why, although he was so good-looking and popular, he never took out any girl more than three times running. Unless it had been Nina Cunningham this spring. It seemed to Carl as if his prospects, which, just a few moments before when he had marched out of the church with his diploma, had been as boundless as the sunlight, were all at once brought down within familiar limits at which he felt himself chafe.

But of course he couldn't let the folks see any of this.

"Did you have good seats?" he asked them. "Did you enjoy the speaker?"

"Fine!" his mother answered loyally.

"I didn't!" Bunny complained. "There was a woman had a great big hat on right in front of me, and she never took it off the whole time, and when I'd look on one side then she'd look that way too, and turn her old hat."

"Well, that was a shame, old kid. You ought to have asked her to take it off."

"I did say things about it. But she just acted as if she didn't hear me."

They all laughed. "Oh, well, you could hear the speaker, anyway," his mother consoled him.

"Gee!" Bunny said, with big, admiring eyes, "you got on your cap and gown."

"Yes, and it's darned hot," Carl said. He took off his cap now, and mopped his neck. His fair hair was mussed and the hard mortar board had left a peak of red on his forehead.

"Oh, why don't you leave them on?" his mother pleaded. "They look so nice!"

"Where did you get your gown?" his father asked him. "Have to buy it?"

"No, there's an old bird around here rents them. You can buy them if you want to, but hardly any of the fellows do."

"Then you aren't going to keep them?"

"Why, what would he want with these things after he's through with them here, mama?"

"He might want them some time. I should think it would be nice for him to keep the things he graduated in."

"How much did he charge you?" Mr. Ferguson asked.

"Five bucks."

"Quite a lot, isn't it, for just renting the things?"

"Well, we have 'em all spring. Had to wear 'em every Friday at chapel."

"That isn't so much. Not for that time," Mrs. Ferguson said hastily. It embarrassed her that dad always had to go into the cost of everything. It wasn't that he was close exactly. But he had to have everything figured up where he could see it. She didn't want Carl to feel his parents had begrudged him anything he needed.

"You've never put on all this style, have you, Lillian? Cap and gown and all this business," Mr. Ferguson said.

But the black robes set off the fresh pink-and-white of Carl's complexion and the eager shine of his eyes. His father had been more affected than he cared to admit when he had heard his own son's name from the platform—"Carl William Ferguson" —with the impressive addition of "Bachelor of Arts." He had cleared his throat and wiped his mustache. His boy had showed up pretty well among the rest of them. He was proud, after all, that he was in a position to give his children these opportunities; and it had seemed to him, with secret humility, watching that youthful bright procession, and remembering his own lacks and efforts, that Carl ought to go much farther than he had gone. Maybe Annie was right, after all, putting the value she did upon education. But of course Annie wanted for the children whatever they wanted for themselves. Carl had kept begging them to come to Geneva before, wanting them to hear lectures and concerts; and Mr. Ferguson knew that his wife would have gone in a minute if he hadn't held back. He said he didn't care about those classical concerts, there was no use going away when they had a good lecture course right at home that he was helping to support, the pipes would freeze and he couldn't trust the girls with the furnace. But he always had a humble, wary sense of being out of place at the college. Now he felt secretly ashamed of all that, and glad he hadn't had the courage to disappoint Annie by not coming today.

"Well," he said looking around, "got a pretty fine church here, haven't they? Do the students attend pretty well?"

The Fergusons looked at the red stone church with its heavy

arches, proud to think that they were Presbyterians, and wishing that the people in Belmond who didn't know how strong the Presbyterians were elsewhere could see *this*.

Carl was looking about with bright, restless eyes. The crowd was scattering, professors were going down the street with their gowns over their arms, townspeople were looking curiously at the college crowd as they went past on the other side of the street.

Carl put his hand on his mother's arm.

"Here, folks, I want you to meet Prexie."

They went up flustered and proud, but feeling their right as supporters of the college and good Presbyterians. They waited while Prexie finished talking with a group of prominent alumni and benefactors. He was not a great man so far as looks went—medium-sized, with grayish sparse hair and mustache and glasses, a little meager and dry in the full folds of his doctor's gown with the purple and velvet. But the Fergusons regarded him with deep respect. They would have drawn back, since Prexie seemed to be busy, but Carl spoke with quick, modest ease the moment he got a chance.

"President Fullerton, I want you to meet my mother and father."

Then they were gratified by Prexie's friendly greeting, and most of all by his praise of Carl.

"Well," he said to them affably, blinking into the sunshine with strained eyes behind his glasses, "have you any more young people like Carl to send us soon?"

"We have two daughters," Mrs. Ferguson answered happily. "The younger one finishes high school next year."

"Ah, that's fine! And is this one of them?" Prexie asked still more affably, shaking hands with Lillian.

Carl felt himself blush furiously. He stammered, "No, this is—Miss White, President Fullerton. A friend."

"Well," Prexie went on, "we shall miss you, Carl, in our various student activities. You plan to go into teaching?"

"I think so. To begin with, anyway."

"I guess he hasn't got a school yet," Mr. Ferguson felt that he must say.

"Oh, no hurry about that. The best positions often turn up later in the season." The Fergusons listened reverently. "I wrote him a good recommendation." Prexie smiled. "Well, I could do that with very real pleasure in this instance. Carl has made one of our fine records. They need young men like Carl in the teaching profession. Wilson takes pride in sending out that kind."

Carl stood back, his flushed face set in a smile, happy to have the folks hearing such things from Prexie. He was aware that this was one of his great, high hours—now, with the memory of his graduation in the crowded church still bright and living . . . he felt this exaltation, as the sun shone bright on the young ivy leaves on the great stalks against the bumpy red stone wall of the church, and the light dresses and dark suits and flapping black gowns were all around—he knew that he was having this hour, and that it would never be again. Everything was complete now that the folks were here.

As they walked away from Prexie, affably dismissed—"Well, I expect as fine a record from you some day, sir, as from your brother," with a hand on Bunny's shoulder—even while Carl was still in a glow from Prexie's praise, his restless eyes finally caught sight of what they had been searching for ever since he had stood talking with the folks. He saw Nina a little way off down the walk with her family, hurrying along in her white dress, with the sun bright on her hair and the tassel of her mortar board dangling with its own special jauntiness.

After the luncheon in the dining room of the girls' dormitory —cold sliced ham, potato salad, rolls and ice cream and coffee, served by a flutter of undergraduate girls in light dresses— Carl had to show the folks about the campus. They went along impressed by the familiar assurance with which Carl opened closed doors upon strange new summer silence and led them up hollow, echoing stairs. His father made few comments except to ask veritable questions—"How many do you expect to seat in your new chapel?" and "What supplies your heat?"; but Carl could feel dad's slightly stiff effort to be equal to the college atmosphere, and could feel his mother's eagerly loving admiration. The Wilson campus was not very large, and rather flat, and the conglomerate buildings, with little reason beneath their unimposing architecture except varied attempts to be in line with temporary fashions, gave an effect of being both higgledy-piggledy and crowded together. The growing town— Geneva was now reaching the impressive size of thirty thousand —already threatened to swallow up the school, with ordinary houses thick all around, and street cars and automobiles going past. But the Fergusons regarded it with the highest respect as the leading college of their denomination in the state, and the place where their children would receive their education. . . . And today a halcyon brightness lay over it, sifting down through the heavy leaves. Everything was transfigured by the feeling of Commencement, by the new summer freshness of the grass and the flowering shrubs, the drift of people across the walks and the lawns, people whose smiles when encountered admitted them to a happy community of feeling, because these were parents like themselves, here to see their own graduates. The Fergusons noticed with pride that everyone seemed to know Carl.

Lillian went about with them, walking at times with Carl, at times dropping back in silent assent with his father or mother or even Bunny.

"Lillian, what's become of you?" Mr. Ferguson asked now, as they all came out of the library building. "We aren't hearing much out of you."

Lillian smiled. Carl stopped hastily and waited for her, dropping his mother's arm. Lillian went on with him, but silently, with the pink flush burning delicately through her pale skin.

"I've been so busy showing everything to the folks, I guess I've sort of left you to yourself," Carl said to her.

Then he thought how that might sound! His face burned. As if it was just the folks whom he had wanted to have come! But he rushed on with explanations, trusting to her devotion to make it all right.

"You know, I've been trying all this time to get the folks to come over here. I knew dad would feel better about it if he once saw the place. I want him to send the girls here. It would be a grand place for them. I think it would do Margaret a world of good. Don't you think so?"

"Yes, I do," Lillian agreed.

But they knew, both of them, even after this little exchange of confidences, that things were not quite right. Carl had been strange and aloof all day. Now they walked on silently together.

Going around the corner of the music building, they almost collided with another group—a girl and two older people. There was a flurry of apologies, followed by somewhat breathless introductions.

"Hello, Nina!"

"Well, Carl Ferguson! We meet again! . . . Father and mother, I want you to meet Carl Ferguson. He's the shining light of our class." This was added somewhat maliciously.

"Oh!" Carl laughed and blushed, trying to turn it off, although of course it was true. "Nina thinks she's going to rattle me. This is *my* father and mother. This is Mr. and Mrs. Cunningham, and Miss Cunningham. And my young brother. And Miss White, Miss Cunningham."

"Oh, how do you do?"

The girl spoke in a bright, enthusiastic voice, with a dazzle of shining eyes and pretty teeth and smiling red lips. Lillian in one glance that was wary with sudden sharp pain and hostility, took in the sheer fine elegance of the graduation dress, the sun glinting on the black brightness of the patent leather slippers, and the very feminine way the tassel of the jauntily set mortar board—fastened with two short silver pins—dangled against the mesh of sunlit hair. A bunch of heavy, red, slightly drooping, rich roses was pinned against Nina's waist. Her father was carrying the black gown over his arm.

"Well, I suppose that you people are here for just about the same purpose that the rest of us are," Mr. Cunningham boomed cordially.

So these were Nina's parents, of whom he had heard so much! Mr. Cunningham was a trustee of Wilson, but they lived in Chicago. It was considered a triumph for the college that the daughter of the Cunninghams was sent there. Carl saw that

Nina's father was a large, prosperous, authoritative-looking man, and that there was a fashionable elegance about her mother's waved gray hair and pearl earrings, and her hand, veined and soft, carrying crumpled white gloves. He felt sensitively that beside Nina's parents his own had an ordinary small town look, his mother in her figured silk dress, and his father's innocently unpressed clothes. It made Carl nervous and chagrined. It had never occurred to him to be anything but proud of the folks before. But it intensified his protective affection for them here, and his sensitive hostility toward some of the things for which he felt that Nina "stood." Now he scarcely knew what to think of the romantic friendship with Nina that had blossomed so suddenly and incongruously and excitingly just this spring.

"Well, it's a fine class of young people," Mr. Cunningham was booming on, in large and kindly patronage. Quite naturally he assumed the center—and the folks humbly let him. "I was proud to see the little college graduating such a class."

"I think Wilson *is* the best of the small colleges in the West," Mrs. Cunningham said in dignified, ladylike appeal to Mrs. Ferguson.

Nina cried, "I *love* Wilson!"

She gave her father's arm a quick squeeze, and turned her shining, wide-open eyes upon the others. All at once Carl forgave her for everything. He felt warm and excited. They began to talk eagerly about the Commencement exercises, with the feeling that they had been waiting all day for just this, exchanging what had already become dear reminiscences since the morning. The parents listened, Mr. Cunningham heavy with amiability, Mr. Ferguson standing back a little and not quite liking the Cunninghams' tone of patronage toward the college, Mrs. Ferguson smiling at the young people and feeling what they felt, while Mrs. Cunningham took the opportunity to confide in a low, dignified tone, "Our daughter is going East next year. But we thought it was very nice she could have her first four years so near us."

Mr. Ferguson said, "Lillian, you don't have to go through all this saying good-bye."

Lillian smiled with difficulty. All this time she had been standing stiff and constrained, unable to take any part in the intimate and spirited exchange between Carl and Nina. She gave a grateful, shy look at Mr. Ferguson. Her cheeks felt hot, and her throat was tight and aching. She was conscious that beside this girl, with her wilful bright animation that almost unconsciously demanded the center, her graduation gown and her prettily tilted mortar board, and the rich effulgence of her roses, she herself was stiff and colorless. She was merely someone who had come with Carl's parents. Her clothes—even the large hat with the black velvet border that the other girls in the town where she was teaching had persuaded her to buy, and that she had been almost afraid to wear it felt so fashionable and unlike her—seemed prim and old-maidish beside the kind of things the college girls wore. She felt older than Carl and this girl, from her two years of teaching—almost as if she were someone like Fannie Allison or Miss Vanchie Darlington at home. She didn't belong here on the campus. She felt with a deep, hidden pain that Carl didn't look at her. He left her standing apart. It was only Mr. Ferguson who took care to include her.

"Well, daughter, don't you think we'd better be getting on?"

They were just on their way to Chicago, Mr. Cunningham explained to the Fergusons with booming kindliness. From there, they would go on to their vacation on a lake in Michigan. The Fergusons listened respectfully.

Nina turned to Carl, suddenly again. She put out her hand, small and soft, the little childishly formed fingers tipped with pink, while with the other hand she held the drooping roses against her. Her lips were pursed up pitiful and small, and her eyebrows delicately lifted.

"Well, Carl—I suppose we have to say good-bye!"

"Oh!" Carl had taken her hand, confused, and held it. "Aren't you going to Prexie's, then, tonight?"

"My family seem to think we must all press onwards!"

Her voice, laughing, slightly shaken, ignored Lillian. The older people were taking leave of each other now, with a great deal of satisfied amiability on the side of the Cunninghams, but Mr. Ferguson noncommittal. Nina now held out her little hand, with that dazzling smile, to both Mr. and Mrs. Ferguson, squeezed Bunny's hand with a quick downward glance as if they two shared a happy secret, and then smiled wistfully again at Lillian. Carl stood there not knowing what to say. The Cunninghams were leaving before he could seem to get his wits together. He started to go on with his own family. Then he stopped and turned back.

"Oh, Nina!"

She turned, with a dangle of her tassel, and her eyes wide-open and shining. Carl went up to her quickly. He spoke in a low voice.

"Does this have to be good-bye?"

Nina looked at him, blinking her eyelashes once or twice over her bright brown eyes. Almost absent-mindedly, she glanced over toward Lillian; and then she touched the drooping heavy heads of the roses at her waist. Carl's heart beat thickly. Then the "man from Chicago," the mysterious sender of those great bunches of fragrant violets with which Nina used to cause such a commotion when she came sauntering late to chapel—it seemed that he, too, although so long a legend, was as much a personal actuality as Lillian! They were both tied. This day, with its June heat, and its freshness of grass and leaves, was so acutely real . . . and yet it was heavy with a suddenly realized weight of memories, of what was already past, even before the day was over. Everything today seemed to have passed too quickly, dreamlike, over his head. And the spring had gone in the same way. Why should it be that not until now, when he came to look back on it, could he realize how happy he must have been? He saw this last spring standing above the whole four years, a kind of after-space of sunlit leisure. The strenuousness was over, and, full of honors, he had at last been able to throw off effort, confident, careless and rich in his achieved greatness, and to breathe in the final, crowning sweetness of springtime romance. But it seemed as if he and Nina had never come to know each other until just this moment when they were parting. And all at once, as Nina's eyelids drooped and then lifted, it seemed as if an elegiac sadness, romantic and beautiful, had come over them and their few hours together.

Their hands clasped and parted with amazed reluctance.

"Well, good-bye, Nina."

"Good-bye, Carl."

Carl stood for a moment in a dazed whirl of excited thoughts —of revelations beginning and then confusedly breaking off. He had looked suddenly into the dazzling radiance of another possibility, one that had been foreign to him until that moment. He scarcely knew what he was doing when he went back to the folks.

He felt that his face was flaming with a sudden sense of strained exhaustion. He was burningly restless to get off by himself. There was nothing to look forward to about the reception now. He stopped—said he ought to go home and do his packing, relying on his mother's quick, supporting acquiescence to help him get away. He knew that he was running away from the question of taking Lillian out to supper without the folks, as was probably expected of him. But he couldn't help it. Mama would make it all right somehow. He pointed out the house where he had taken rooms for them, just a block down the street, and then turned and went away across the campus. As he went, he heard Bunny's slow, judicial voice, as if he were just getting to this decision:

"Say, do you know it, those were the biggest roses I ever saw."

The folks were at the house with the car before Carl got back in the morning. He and Harry had run over to the corner restaurant for doughnuts and coffee. There they had to say good-bye. Harry was going to stay in Geneva this summer, with a contractor's gang, and he had to begin work this morning.

Carl found the folks in the parlor with Mrs. Biegler, his landlady, who had to tell them all about her grief at losing her two boys. "They was the two nicest boys we ever had here. Mister and me both said that. Always so nice around the house, they always took such good care of the ashes. The other boys, they'd just dump the ashes wherever they was a mind to. My, I told Mister, where am I ever going to get boys again that'll help me with the dishes, like Carl done that time I had the Aid, and had the toothache just something awful, Mrs. Ferguson, oh I did suffer so." She bent over toward Mrs. Ferguson, her voice getting intimate and sepulchral. "And they was always so nice in the bathroom. They left it so nice. You know how some men are. My, I'm going to miss 'em. I'd a'most let the room to Harry this summer for the price o' one, if Mister was willing, but Mister he thinks we ought to get the full price."

Mr. Ferguson asked, "Well, Carl, ready to load up?" Dad was always uneasy until they got started.

"I guess so."

They brought down the familiar possessions of the four years, the big box that contained framed pictures of debating teams and basketball squads carefully laid between cushions and pennants, the battered laundry case that had been going back and forth weekly between Geneva and Belmond until all the baggage men knew it by sight. Mrs. Ferguson had never sent it back without tucked-in presents of cake and nuts and fried chicken, carefully done up in her funny little amateur packages so that Carl's clean shirts wouldn't smell of food. Mrs. Biegler stood in the hall lamenting that Mister wasn't here, or he would have helped them—but he had to drive out to the farm this morning, the renter couldn't be trusted to look after things the way they should be. "Now I know why my boys was so nice," she confided again to Mrs. Ferguson. "They've got nice folks. That makes all the difference, don't it? Well, I tried to bring up my girl good too. I guess we done it. She's got a real nice home and an awful good husband. If you folks are ever in Delaware, you want to stop in and see them. Hackenschmidt, the name is. He runs a creamery there." Mrs. Biegler came out to the walk to watch them load up the car. She stood intermittently smiling and wiping her eyes and making more confidences. Mrs. Ferguson was pleased with the way in which Carl said good-bye to her, the way he kissed her and gently patted her fat back, telling her he would certainly be over to see her. He was always so nice to people! He was more thoughtful than either of the girls. Dorothy, of course, was lovely, but she went around wrapped up in her own softly smiling serenity. At the last minute Mrs. Biegler had whispered, "Is that his girl?" She had looked Lillian all over. "Well, she'll have to be a nice one!" she said severely. She had kind of thought that Carl was a little sweet on one of the college girls this spring, and she and Mister had tried to tease him; but evidently that didn't amount to anything, *this* was the real one, since his folks had brought her.

"How do we go, Carl?"

"Straight ahead, dad."

"You want to do the driving?"

"Sure, if you want me to."

"Yes, you'd better, Carl." His mother spoke quickly. "You know the way through town so much better than dad."

"I guess mother doesn't trust me to drive in the big city."

"Yes, I do. Why, dad! Only—"

"Well, you better drive, Carl. Spare mama her fears. Lillian, don't you want to get in there beside Carl?"

"Yes, come on, Lillian," Carl said with false heartiness.

Lillian climbed in silently beside him, while Mrs. Ferguson persuaded Bunny to be content in the back seat. Carl started the engine. He looked out to wave at Mrs. Biegler standing comfortably weeping, but pleased with the excitement, in front of the familiar house. The leafy shadows from the trees lay thick across the pavement.

"Aren't we going to pass the campus?" Mrs. Ferguson asked.

"It's too much out of the way."

Carl didn't want to see the campus. He had a vision of how it lay there this morning, the buildings empty and silent among the summer trees. He didn't want to see any of these places that had been so full of meaning: the church where just yesterday they were all sweltering in their caps and gowns, the dingy station where he had arrived eager each fall, the corner where he had turned when he was going to Nina's. The town already, after the glow of Commencement, had taken on its oblivious, summertime aspect, and the old campus ways were deserted except for the lonely whirr of an electric mower. Carl was in the aftermath of yesterday's exaltation. The bright fresh color had drained from his cheeks and his eyes looked dark.

But when they got out onto the country road, there was a

feeling of change and refreshment. Geneva and the college seemed now to be left behind. It was a beautiful day, the sky cloudless above the big fields, that were striped with bright green rows of young corn, and the telephone wires singing beside the road. Carl felt almost like a convalescent as he began to come slowly out of his preoccupation. There was a faint beginning of the old pleasure at the thought of going home.

"Looks pretty good, dad, doesn't it?" he asked, turning around.

"Yes, the country looks pretty good this year."

Lillian had been sitting beside him acquiescing in his silence. Carl was now uncomfortably aware of his aloofness toward her. Ever since she had been in Geneva, she had seemed like a stranger. He had secretly blamed her for the renunciations he had made during the four years. But now he began to know her again. He cast around for something to say that would make it right.

"Get through your teaching pretty well?" he asked her.

Carl didn't know just how it was, but now the stiffness between them seemed to be broken. Nina was still in Carl's thoughts, but she was far away. The Carl and Nina of that brief thrilling interview yesterday seemed like figures in a romantic story; and now he was going home, it was as if he had come back to earth again. Lillian answered him, at first with constraint, but gradually more easily as Carl talked with bright unawareness of anything wrong between them. He had the power to do that with Lillian. He felt stubbornly that he wasn't going to make any references or explanations. If Lillian wanted those, she could go without. Carl felt almost indignantly virtuous as he thought of all his careful sidestepping of girls during the four years. They drove down the long roads, up and down the mild slopes, always with that same picture of trees at the end, those on one side slightly overhanging those on the other—he remembered that about the trees even when he was driving out to his grandfather's years ago . . . past the open fields, past stretches of woodland scattered with sunlight, and with elderberry bushes growing intimately close to the road. Now Carl saw Lillian, not with the judging eyes of the college students, but as herself again. She seemed sweet and homelike sitting beside him on the leather seat warm with sun. Her face was warm and flushed from driving in the open car. His body struck hers secretly when the car jolted; and he felt the tenderness of her bare arms below the short sleeves of her summer dress—they were burned faintly pink with June sunshine. That big hat with the black border that he hadn't liked yesterday, it had seemed so self-conscious and dressed up for Commencement, now gave Lillian's face a different, almost mysterious look. They turned sometimes and talked to the older people in the back seat, and laughed at some wise remark of Bunny's. Now it seemed natural again, this family party, and yet with a fresh feeling of renewal. Carl thought with a shock of blind fear how far away from Nina he was. And he had never been at ease with her in this way, but always alert and self-conscious— as if he must struggle against being intimidated somehow by the provocative danger of her differences.

"Where'd you get the big hat?" he asked Lillian.

"This?" she said fearfully.

"I like it."

Her face grew pinker. Carl could see that she was pleased. But with her usual reserve, she did not tell him anything about the hat. The other teachers had persuaded, almost forced her into getting it, knowing that she was going to the Wilson Commencement, having ferreted out somehow that it was to see that "grand-looking man" whose photograph she kept on her dresser, and whose name they knew in spite of never being able to get a word out of Lillian.

"You look nice in a big hat like that," Carl said approvingly. "You ought to wear more such things."

But there was a slight flavor of discontent as he said it. Lillian wouldn't answer him—partly because she was pleased, partly because she knew in her cold shyness that Carl was comparing her with that girl on the campus, and it made her deeply resentful. But she felt Carl coming back to her. The frozen, tight pain inside her breast, above which she had had to smile and talk as usual to Mr. and Mrs. Ferguson, who had been so nice about bringing her, began happily to lessen. She could hold again to the small, firm pride that had kept her poised and self-contained among the other teachers with their chatter about men and dates and clothes, from which Lillian's nature and upbringing held her old-maidishly aloof. Talk as they might (and she a little despised them, although she felt the strain of her reserve) she knew that she had Carl, his letters, his picture, those brief but deeply felt exchanges of kisses, the exquisite secret of their "understanding" which was just the next thing to an engagement. None of the other girls could possibly have anyone like Carl. There *was* no one like him.

"Gee!" Carl said. "I begin to feel real again. There's so much been happening these last few weeks I didn't know whether I was going or coming."

Carl took a new easy hold on the wheel with a sense of relief that evaded the disappointment he knew was lurking somewhere. His face wore a look of bright and open innocence that convinced himself. He tried to talk to the folks again, although dad was very stern about the driver keeping his attention on the road. Carl saw himself as a returning hero of romance, far older than his innocent family, superior even to Margaret's mysterious exactions, melancholy and experienced underneath, with all the wisdom that his college life had given him. And yet he felt cheated, uneasy, restless too. He began to ask about everybody at home, and laughed at Bunny's solemn, careful recital of all that the girls had been doing. Corny Mc-Intosh was coming to see Dorothy now, and brought her candy —he was working in the drug store; and Margaret was sore because Addie Weyant tried to come along with Corny to see *her*.

"That little shrimp?"

"Oh, he's big now. He's as big as the girls are!"

"You don't say! How about the abbreviated trousers? Thought they were responsible for Margaret's scorn."

"Gee, he wears long ones now!"

They were getting into familiar territory. Carl saw with remembering eyes the country around Belmond, the little burg of Mertonville through which he drove at a funeral pace, ironically obeying the sign to "Slow down to Eight Miles an hour," over which his father was concerned, as over all laws and injunctions.

"All right, dad!" Carl called back. "We aren't going to get arrested."

How small the town looked as they drove into it! This was Belmond, home, the place so known to him that until now he had never even questioned its being just naturally the best place on earth to live. After he had gone away, he had still been ardently concerned about the football team and whether Belmond beat Parkersville in baseball, and he had wanted to go home for the Hallowe'en social of the Young People. Now how did he feel about it? They went chugging up the familiar hill that led into town from the west, bumping over the railroad tracks, past the feed store and the old decaying livery stable, with the yellowish tower of the courthouse rising above the trees.

"Want to go through town, dad?"

"Yes, I guess you better let me off at the bank."

"Oh, Fred! Now? Look up at the tower. It's almost twelve."

"Well, I guess I better look in for a few minutes."

Carl tolerantly slowed down the car. Dad thought the bank would go bust if he was away for more than an hour. Here was the old business street again, so small but thinking itself so busy, the summer awnings up, and old Dick, the factotum, sweeping off the sidewalk in front of the bank. Of course Dick had to come up to them. He was bent and decrepit, but with a certain grotesque dignity and self-esteem still lingering in his precise New Hampshire voice.

"Well, Carl, I heard ye'd finished your college."

"Yes, they decided to let me graduate."

"Went over to the school at Genevy, did ye? Well, I had my days of schooling too. What ye going to do now? Run for President?"

"Sure! You bet."

Dick bent over with laughter. He nodded at Mrs. Ferguson and Lillian. "Well, I'll vote for ye if I'm alive to do it!" he promised.

The streets looked fresh and green. Carl couldn't help feeling some emotion as they came up to their own house standing back on the nice lawn, so ample and good and comfortable, so just like home. The girls both came running out to meet them, seeming to Carl prettier and more grown up, eager to tell the folks that Aunt Jennie had invited everybody over for dinner.

Carl said that he must take his suitcase upstairs. He could do it while they were phoning dad. He ran up, feeling stiff from his drive, but fresh and eagerly at home in the familiar summertime atmosphere of the house—familiar, but subtly changed too, he had been away so long. The girls' housekeeping had consisted mostly of putting flowers in every possible place.

Mrs. Ferguson nodded discreetly up toward the bathroom, but Lillian primly refused. She went into the living room to wait for the others. It was brightened and significant and alive now that Carl was home. But for Lillian this was always the most wonderful room in town. She appreciated, with her shy deep reticence, its warmth and ease, after the stiff sparseness of her grandfather's sitting room at home. Here she could sit down and pick up a magazine without any sense of the guilt and stealth that sometimes made her heart beat hard when she was alone in her own sitting room, where she never could get away from the feeling that her grandfather might come in and look at her and ask what she was doing.

Carl opened his door. He plumped down the heavy suitcase. The room was just as he had left it, except that it had been newly cleaned, and the window curtains were stiff from fresh laundering. Margaret, who was great on all the fancy side of the housework, had put a little glass of short-stemmed yellow roses on the table. Carl was ashamed of every bad thought he had ever had, and determined that he would act altogether differently toward her this summer. This was a return, but not like the others. Just this summer—and then he might be leaving this old room, perhaps forever. He remembered what Prexie had said. He felt that he was going to do something—somehow make the world better! Not just take a job, like fellows who hadn't had the advantages of college, and weren't imbued with its ideals. Carl looked forward to the dinner at Lillian's, with all the renewed affection and approval it would bring, and his own importance as a graduate. With a quick glance at the door, hearing someone in the bathroom, he opened his suitcase, dug through the worn plaid lining of the pocket, and brought out an envelope thick with snapshots. He glanced through them, sitting on his heels, took one out and held it up to the light. Bud Carswell had snapped this one afternoon just a few days ago when Carl and Nina were sitting on the railing of the porch at the house where Nina roomed. Her eyes and her white teeth glinted in the bright scattering of sunlight through the leaves.

"Nina."

Carl whispered that. The touch of her silky little hand was fresh in his . . . yet gone. The radiant face smiled from the glossy little picture that was stiff and clean from the drug store. But still he could not bring her into the room with him. His own whisper had to be its own response.

2.

Carl had been at home for over a week now. He had got through the very first period of renewal, let-down, restlessness that came with the actual knowledge that college was over. He had been to church and seen everybody, gone over to call on Essie Bartlett and her mother, received the congratulations on his graduation and put away his presents—the last one, from his cousin Verne in Nebraska, a copy of *The Spell of the Yukon* with tell-tale erasures that suggested the bargain counter. Now he was back to his old job of mowing the lawn.

"Well, Carl—glad to get back?" That was what everyone asked him.

He wouldn't admit to himself that there was any conflict in his feelings. He would be quite happy out running the lawn mower, going fast down the rows according to an old boyish tradition—he and Harry used to time each row and hold themselves strictly to schedule; but the conflict was there, in the sharp sound of the cutter, and it rose up to him, when he stopped, in the moist, fresh smell of the shredded grass. He wasn't even sure about going into teaching. That didn't seem big enough to make use of his ideals. Then at other times he stewed and worried because he hadn't got a position. He was back again under the stress of his old necessity to excel, to do what (he thought) everyone expected of Carl Ferguson. At the same time, he had a blind new desire to strike out for himself, go away somewhere, start out new, work out his great glowing ideas without the cautious limitations that he felt somehow the folks imposed upon him, even while they demanded great things of him. And at times he caught himself looking again into the dazzling newness of that different possibility. He was beginning to look back upon those last spring weeks of sunlit and twilit strolling about the campus, he and Nina, as a halcyon dream that was fading out of his life. And he wanted somehow to keep hold of it!

"Papa phoned. He wants you to come down to the bank, Carl!"

"What does he want?"

"I don't know. He phoned."

His mother and the girls went back to their leisurely morning occupations in the sunny house where freshly baked cakes lay under a white cloth on the kitchen table, sending a nutty fragrance through the rooms. Birds twittered and shuffled in the green vines that shaded the back porch.

Carl went down the street through the bright sunlight and the shadows of the summer trees. It made him uneasy even now to have dad tell him to come to the bank. He searched into all his failings. What if dad meant to question him about Lillian— about his "intentions"? Dad had asked him about Nina—who she was, who her folks were. "That girl we met there," he called her. Mother spoke about her too, saying again and again how pretty Nina was, almost wistfully. "They didn't seem to think so well of the college," dad had commented. "Why, yes, they did, dad. Mr. Cunningham's a trustee." "Trustee, is he? Belongs to our church? Trustee . . . must be pretty well off, then." Dad always had to know what everyone in the family planned to do. Carl began to carry on a highly worked out argument in his mind. He went frowning past the green lawns until he reached the unshaded glare of Main Street where the sun flashed from the glass of the show windows and burned on the asphalt and the dark red brick. The bank stood next to the corner. Carl went into the long room, that temporarily seemed cool after the street, with its dark green window shade pulled to the sill where a fly was knocking clumsily about. Ray Seeley stopped the clatter of the big old Oliver typewriter and came toward the grating.

"Oh, hello, Carl! Didn't notice it was you."

"Hello, Ray! Is my father here?"

"He's out in the other room just now. Want to wait?"

"Guess so."

Carl wandered around, looking at the only thing *to* look at, a calendar with a highly colored sunset at sea.

"Not going to work with us this summer?" Ray asked pleasantly, pulling at his black sateen sleeve protectors that looked dull with heat.

"Guess not, Ray."

"Got enough, did you, that summer?" Ray smiled paternally. His fear was allayed that they might be going to take Carl into the bank now that Carl had finished school. *He* hadn't thought so. "I don't believe F. W. would do a thing like that." But his wife, Gladys, had worried him with her suspicions. Now Ray felt suddenly jovial. "You might as well sit down and take it easy. He may not be out for a while. Got a customer in there."

Carl sat down on the long wooden settee near the window. He watched the one big fly bumbling and another caught dry and dead in a corner triangle of dusty cobweb. The typewriter clattered again.

He got up when his father appeared in the inner doorway with a man in overalls whom Carl recognized as a farmer named Mert Shinstrom who lived out on the Buck Creek road. "Well, thanks, Mr. Ferguson," the man was saying; while Mr. Ferguson answered briefly, "That's all right, Mert—glad to be able to fix you up"—paying no attention to Carl until the man had left the bank. Then he said:

"Hello, Carl. Came down, did you? Got those reports, Ray?"

"Working on them now, F. W."

"All right. Better get 'em off your hands this morning, if you can. Mr. Spencer won't be back today, I guess. . . . Well, Carl. Want to step into the other room a minute?"

Carl followed his father into the inner room. When he was at school, he felt as if he had gone far beyond his parents, and was at the same time deeply affectionate toward them and indulgent in his wider knowledge and experience. But here in the bank, in the familiar, long, narrow, solidly put up brick building, his father had an uncommunicative authority that made Carl nervously realize his youth and dependence. He felt unwillingly respectful as he sat down in one of the heavy chairs at the big table in the center of the room and waited while his father looked over some papers through his glasses. It was unpleasantly sunny in the room.

"Hear from any of the schools this morning?"

"No, I didn't, dad," Carl admitted. He felt guilty. "But then it's pretty early yet. I'm not afraid of not getting one." He felt as if he had to talk confidently before dad.

"You don't want to take that one you had the offer of?"

"Gosh, no. Mertonville? That isn't much more than a country school!"

"Mertonville ain't such a bad town." Dad had property there.

"Yes, but I don't want to teach there. What are you worrying about, dad?" Carl said, quickly sensitive. "Don't you think I can pull a job?"

"Oh, yes, I think you're pretty sure to get one." The mild tone was soothing, but Carl didn't like that "pretty." It hurt him to think that dad wasn't completely confident of him, as mother was. "You've got a fine education now. I expect the president knew what he was talking about. Ought to, in his position. It's beginning to get along in the summer, that's all." Dad always saw a season ended as soon as it was begun! "I just wanted to know what you had in mind. It's all right, I guess, if you're just waiting for a good offer."

Carl didn't say anything. His face was rather hot. Then his father looked up shrewdly through his glasses.

"You're sure you want to *go* into teaching, are you?"

Carl made a quick, defensive assent.

"We might be able to find a place for you in town some- where. Don't know whether it could be right here in the bank. That'd be up to Richard and the old man. They're the ones that have the say-so," his father warned him—dad always gave the family this warning, as if to impress upon them that all things, even his place in the bank which to them was as secure as Gibraltar, might be dubious after all.

"Why, you know I don't want to go into the bank, dad."

Dad always somehow made him feel on the defensive. Carl sensed in this a smarting touch of his father's old accusation that he undertook things he didn't know how to finish. That was humiliating after the glory of Commencement. Dad might express a little more faith in him. Going into the bank! That was about the last thing that appealed to Carl. He wanted something that—well, looked more toward the future, gave more scope for his personal talents (which it hurt him that dad didn't seem to recognize) and was more in line with his college idealism.

"I feel as if I could do more in teaching," he said.

But it was hard to explain all this to dad. Dad was religious, but not exactly *idealistic*. And then teaching itself was just the first easy step into that shining future where he would be able to work out his ideals greatly and freely.

"You think you can make a good living teaching?"

"Why, dad, they pay fine salaries in the big schools now. Of course, right at the start . . ."

"You remember, though, you'll be dependent on other peo- ple."

"Well, you are more or less in everything, dad."

"Yes, but not so much so." But his father was unexpectedly mild. Commencement *had* impressed him. "Well, I'm willing to have you go into teaching. I've never insisted on your coming into the bank. Rather have you make your own way. Be kind of hard on Ray, too. I just wanted to be sure you had a future in mind when you took up teaching. You'll be thinking of getting settled one of these days."

Carl's face burned. He answered, "Yes, I suppose so." He knew that dad was thinking of Lillian.

"You have that in mind, do you?"

"Why . . . yes, I have."

His father made an approving sound. Carl sat with the palms of his hands wet and his cheeks burning. But he counted on his father's deep personal reticence to let it go at that. Mr. Ferguson seemed to be glancing through his papers again to find the one he wanted. He took out one, crisply folded, and silently handed it across to Carl. Carl looked up at him, startled —pretended hastily to be wisely looking it over.

"See what it is?"

"I don't know whether I just—"

"I've put a thousand dollars for you into a second mortgage. That'll yield you a good seven per cent and give you something to have back of you when you start in. Then if you can save a little of your own out of your salary, you'll have a nice start."

"Gee, dad—" Carl started to thank him; but his father went on:

"I intend to do the same for the girls when they're ready to marry, or—get settled," his father finished somewhat vaguely.

"And Bunny!" Carl said foolishly grinning.

"What's that?" His father didn't know that he was attempting a little joke. "Oh! Well, he's too young to think about that just now. We'll do plenty for him when the time comes."

"Sure. I know. I just meant he was such a kid."

Mr. Ferguson got up. Carl did too and stood somewhat awkwardly. He wanted to thank dad, but it seemed as if all kinds of things stood between them. They could both talk to mother, but they couldn't talk much to each other, not when they were alone.

"Well, dad," Carl began, "I certainly do appreciate this from you. I'll do my best, all right." He blushed to hear how boyish he sounded.

"Well, that's all right, Carl. I know that. You did very well at college, and mama and I appreciate it." Carl's eyes were moist. "I guess sometimes I've seemed to hold you back. Your mama's sort of felt that way about it. But I wanted you to be sure of what you were getting into."

"I know you did, dad," Carl said with quick, ardent repudiation of all past resentments.

"Well," Mr. Ferguson said, and he smiled a little, "you'll find out what it is some day to have a family on your hands and be responsible for them. You can't always do just as you'd like to, then. You have to look ahead. You have to bear a good deal in mind."

"I guess that's true all right, dad," Carl said humbly. "I've taken a lot from you as it is. Gosh!"

"Well, we won't speak of that. The way to repay me—and mama—" dad always brought in mama, with loyal conscientiousness—"is for you all to get well settled. Just so you have that in mind." He turned. "What is it, Ray? Guess I'll have to go back to the counter now, Carl."

"I sure do thank you, dad."

"Guess I better look after this, now I've put my money into it," his father said with a dry smile, turning to pick up the mortgage. That meant dad felt good—when he could make his kind of little jokes. He went on into the front room where he greeted the customer with curt, cautious reserve. "Just a moment," Carl heard him say; and saw him go into the vault with the paper to get it carefully and methodically stowed away.

Carl went out again into the glare of sunshine. His response to his father had been immediate and real, rising up eagerly out of his affection. But all the same, he had the feeling that he had committed himself.

He couldn't settle to anything at home. At noon, he asked his father if he could take the car.

"What do you want it for?" Mr. Ferguson asked, on principle—not that he wasn't willing to let Carl have it.

"I thought I might drive out to the farm."

"Oh, yes, that would be nice," Mrs. Ferguson said quickly. "Grandpa would like that. He gets so lonesome."

The drive out there did something of itself to quiet him. Carl liked this road. It was associated with his childhood. There were big cornfields on one side, and on the other a stretch of pasture land with oaks clustered about the winding, caved-out banks of Buck Creek that Carl used to follow back and back into green, wooded stillness. Then he would come out into a kind of open place—what they used to call a picnic ground—where the sunlight was motionless and golden, and he had seemed to be all by himself as nowhere else in the world. In this place, he felt himself believing in God, in a different way from the ardent, but unsure, and somehow guilty way that he felt inside himself when he got up to talk—quickly, warmly, persuasively—in the Young People's meeting, knowing that the leader always counted on Carl Ferguson to keep things going. Every once in a while, Carl got the hunger to drive out along this road again. After his grandmother had died, and while his grandfather was traveling about in a melancholy fashion trying to make a home with one or the other of his children, Carl hadn't cared to go out to the farm. Uncle Ben and Aunt Ella didn't mean so much out there as the old people. But after Grandpa had moved back to the rock house, Carl didn't mind going again. He accepted the latter era into which the place had passed—a kind of lingering era of evening, different from the old full days when they had all gathered about the long table, and made significant by the afterglow of childhood memories.

He saw the old place now—"the farm"—the rock house with its narrow frame porch standing back beyond the low green of the pasture in the level afternoon light. The white frame house across the driveway was closed. Aunt Ella and Uncle Ben had moved over and were keeping house for Grandpa. He had been too unhappy anywhere but in his own house. He had tried it for a winter at Tom's in Nebraska, and for a winter at Fred's in town. "Well, we better move our traps in across the way for the time your father needs us," Uncle Ben had finally told Aunt Ella.

As Carl drove up, Aunt Ella and Uncle Ben were just getting into the car to go to town. They were full of apologies for going off and leaving him, and tried to make him promise to stay to supper.

"Oh, never mind, Aunt Ella. I wouldn't want you to stay at home for me. Grandpa's in the house, isn't he?"

"Yes, your grandpa's in there. He didn't want to come with us. He hates to go more and more."

"I guess I'll go in and see him a while."

"You do that," said Uncle Ben. "That'll be fine. He gets pretty lonesome."

They drove off, and Carl went on into the empty quietness of the house. There was one fly buzzing in the kitchen, where a basket of ripe red and yellow tomatoes stood on the oilcloth-covered table, and the tin-lined wooden sink still smelled wet from Aunt Ella's dishwashing. Carl found his grandfather in the dining room sitting in a large rocker near the bay window with his hands spread on a paper open in his lap. There were still three or four plants set there, on the sill and on a little white-painted stool; but in Grandma's day the whole bay window had been massed with earthy-smelling, leafy-smelling green —Aunt Ella wasn't "a hand" with plants, she didn't like to be bothered with all those little fussy things to take care of.

"Did I wake you up, Grandpa?"

"What's that? Oh, I didn't see who it was come in! I s'posed it was Ben. It's you, is it, my boy? I guess the folks have gone somewhere."

"You're the one I came to see, Grandpa."

His grandfather was pleased. He showed Carl a kind of respectful formality now that Carl had grown up and finished school—almost as if his grandson were some highly honored stranger. In his age, Grandpa Ferguson had reverted to an earlier, more primitive self than that of his prime, and Carl had only a dimly flattering idea of what a prosperous and fashionable town-bred young fellow he seemed to the old man. Now he wanted to take Carl into the parlor. Nothing else would do—Carl had to follow him in there. Grandpa was complaining sadly that things didn't look the same as when Grandma was living. "Well, Ella does pretty good," he conceded. "She does the best she can." Carl had to smile at this estimate of his aunt's housekeeping abilities. But there was some truth in it. Chairs were set about clumsily. Aunt Ella was a worker, but she had no eye for the fierce and finished perfection of Grandma Ferguson's orderliness upon rigidly established personal lines—and that the folks often said was where Margaret "got it," although Margaret fiercely denied any resemblance to Grandma Ferguson, or to anyone but her own self.

The front room, Grandma's parlor, was kept piously as she had left it. An air, clean but faintly dusty, rose up from the ingrain carpet under which newspapers crackled. Two pale sprays of plumy grasses, the color of fluffs of dust, stood up from twisted glass vases on the little promontories of the organ. Dorothy always used to like to pretend that she could take a fairy drink and change into little-doll size, so that she could live somewhere in the organ and come out to walk on these little balconies. The cold pink seashell still lay in the corner to hold back the door.

"Well," Grandpa asked, "what are you doing?" He would forget, though, after he had been told.

"Not much of anything, Grandpa, this summer."

"The folks well?"

"Oh, yes."

"I haven't seen any of Howard's folks for a good while. All well, are they? Lily got back from her school-teaching?"

"Oh, yes."

"Well, she's a nice girl. She's a real good girl," Grandpa said, out of a heavy musing. He had never been able to say "Lillian"—that seemed too highfalutin; "Lily" was what girls had been called in his young days.

Carl was silent.

"So you think you'll go into school-teaching too, do ye, next fall?"

"I guess so. If they'll give me a job." Carl smiled.

"You don't want the schoolhouse out here at Buck Creek? I heard Ben say they were in need of a teacher."

"No, I guess not, Grandpa." Carl smiled again. Grandpa was several years behind the times, anyway. He had forgotten. All the little country schools around here had been closed when they built the consolidated school in Belmond.

137

"Well," Grandpa agreed, with reluctant admiration, "I expect town school is what you're after." He went on to say: "It's a good school, though. Always has been. Not so many scholars now as it used to have. Too many goes into town. Think they must do it. Yes, it's all town these days. Your mother taught out here at Buck Creek once. That was how your father come to meet her. Well, you've already picked out a nice girl, so you ain't looking around any more."

Carl tried to laugh. He felt a qualm.

"Yes, I expect town school pays better. If you can git one. I thought you was going to be a farmer."

"That was what *you* said, Grandpa. I didn't."

"Well, I guess that was the way of it. I always said you was going to be a farmer, and your grandma had you fixed up for a preacher. Now you're going back on both of us! . . . Well, I expect you want to make some use of your studies," Grandpa agreed. "I guess you'll do well no matter where they put ye," he said with satisfaction.

Carl sat smiling, glad to rest for a while from the effort to make the old man hear, and indulgently respectful while his grandfather wandered off into a recounting of the good lives of his various children. Carl liked such talk. It gave him, while he listened, a kind of warm, snug pride of family. It made him feel sorry for the old folks, and young and strong to go out and do something for them. In earlier days, Grandpa Ferguson had been severe enough, a hard worker, hard on his hired help, even hard on his sons, stern against any person who drank liquor or in any other way broke the laws of his country. But now, with Grandma gone, with the incentive of her fierce meager ambition and her clinging to life and authority lost, the old man seemed to have dropped the reins more easily than any of them could have imagined, and to have settled back into a proud and mournful contemplation of his family and his own life.

"Yes, your mother taught school out here a while. I guess she was the only one. Ella she never *taught* school. She helped us here at home until Ben Graham come courting. And a good while after that begun. They were slow getting to it, them two, for some reason, but after a while they come to the point. Well, they have their differences"—which was true!—"but I tell Ella Ben's made her a pretty good husband. Take it all in all." Grandpa was evidently carrying on an ancient dispute with Grandma. "Haven't any children, though," he admitted. "That's too bad. It's too bad. The boys they all went into business more or less, my boys did. Tom he went into the storekeeping business out there in Nebrasky, and then he got Rob to come out with him, and John he was in the storekeeping business too with the boys before he died. He died awful early. He didn't much more than live to manhood. An awful good boy too. Would have made a fine man. Will he moved out West there and went into business too. Fred he done this and that around Belmond until he got the chance to go into Spencer's bank. They all done well. I don't know but what your father's done about the best of them. None of them took to farming for some reason. None of my boys. So I expect it's Ben after all that goes on with the farm. . . . Well, I expect you want to get some good of your studies."

Carl said, suddenly restless:

"I don't know yet, Grandpa! Maybe I won't teach school. I might go to Chicago." He felt his face hot. "Or out West somewhere."

"What's that?" Grandpa thought he must mean "out West" in the state, where Uncle Will lived. Or out with Uncle Rob and Uncle Tom. That was about as far as Grandpa's thoughts could travel now.

"No, I mean clear out West. Lots farther than Nebraska."

Carl didn't know why he should say that all at once! But he was suddenly kindled with restlessness. Grandpa was only able to get the idea of distance.

"Well," he was saying, "my folks come a good ways to get here. They come from Ohio, and formerly York state. Your Grandma's folks come over from Scotland when she was just a year old." Grandpa offered this bit of familiar information as if it would be new and mournfully interesting to Carl. "Her sister Kittie was one year older, a little better'n that. Her sister

Jane must have been somewheres around nine or ten. That was your father's Aunt Jane. I guess you never seen her."

"Why, yes, I did, Grandpa. Lots of times."

Carl remembered Aunt Jane's funeral. His grandfather heard him, but remotely—as if he had sat for so long in this house that now it seemed too irrelevant to try to fix his mind on anything new. He broke in on Carl again. He seemed to be saying something that he had had in his mind for a long time.

"Well, my boy"—and in the pause, Carl heard the chickens outside, the slow farm noises, the gasoline engine pumping water—"well, my boy, wherever you go, let me tell you what you'll find is the best thing. I'm old and I know it. That's to have a good home and a good wife. That's the thing that matters. Your Grandma and me lived here together for fifty-five years. We had our troubles in those times, I don't say we didn't—" many a time Grandpa himself must have suffered from that sharp tongue of Grandma's!—"but they don't seem much account when you look back upon them. I done well with my farming. I done better than most. I can't complain that way. No, I'm not complaining. But we want a partner in our joys and sorrows. Now your Grandma's gone, seems like I don't care to attempt much without her. She was always there by my side. Howard's girl is a fine, good girl. She ain't like so many of the young people these days. She's been a helper in the church since she was little. She'll stand by ye. Whether you go into school-teaching or some other business, that's what I wish for ye, my boy."

Carl said soberly—the tears had almost come into his eyes at the emotional simplicity of his grandfather's language, spoken in the slow measure that Carl felt as the primitive rhythm of his own country, that suited the great slow roll of the land, and the level width of the fields, the somber glow of the prairie sunset:

"I guess there's a lot in that, Grandpa."

"Take to yourself a good wife, and don't drink nor smoke nor gamble your money at cards, and work hard at whatever your work is—then you'll get along, my boy," the old man repeated. "Those are the principles I've always stuck to. And uphold the Lord and His holy works."

When he got home, Carl found his mother and the girls greatly excited. There had been a telephone call from Lorraine—it must have come while he was driving home, for they hadn't been able to reach him at the farm. Grandpa never heard the telephone. Carl had applied for the principalship of the high school at Lorraine, because he had liked the thought of living so close to the Mississippi; but that was so long ago that he had given up expecting to hear from there.

"What did they say?"

"You're to call up a Mr. Long at eight."

Carl went upstairs whistling noisily.

"That settles it," he thought. "That settles it."

He wanted to shut himself into the privacy of his own room, this old room at the back of the house overlooking the apple tree. His emotional response to his grandfather's words was sobering down into conscious thought. But he felt how deep the impression had gone. To have a good wife, and not to smoke or drink or play cards—certainly Carl didn't put it as simply as Grandpa Ferguson did; but yet, what he thought of as those "ideals," which a girl like Nina didn't exactly share, were beliefs he had held with a pure and serious ardor. Besides, he had accepted that present from dad! The choice seemed to have been made for him. He felt almost superstitious and awed. With his grandfather's long family recounting in his mind, he felt eager all at once to take up the duties of an adult citizen of the United States.

And yet, as he sat there on the cot, breathing with relief in that familiar atmosphere, he was aware of something in himself crying out after that barely glimpsed new perilous delight, for striking out into what was unmapped and unknown, something that would have forced his life out of the clear daylight course he had set out on in his childhood.

Carl got up, and digging stealthily through his top dresser drawer, he took out a little heap of things that he had stowed away under a pile of handkerchiefs and bow ties. They were the remembrances of his brief romance: a few notes that Nina had scribbled and passed across to him in Major History, the snapshot, the postal card with her little round clear writing that she had sent him from Chicago. A springtime fragrance seemed to cling to these things. And another perfume—Nina's—slightly foreign, and disturbing. He saw the green leaves of the campus, and the cinder walks scattered with sunlight and shade. He felt the warmth of a May night, when he and Nina sat together in a corner of the porch at the Peabody House, in an intimate, soft excitement, Nina now and then tapping the floor with her slipper toe to keep the creaky old swing going. Carl looked at his mementoes a long while, started to put them back into the drawer, changed his mind and stuffed them hastily into his wastebasket, covering them with an old magazine—then, digging through them again, he rescued the snapshot of himself and Nina, and put it into his copy of Tennyson, beside the poem that he had always held dear, "The Dream of Fair Women."

Carl got away from the table as soon as he could that evening. His parents' eyes followed him significantly. He was going over to the Whites. Howard had just finished his supper and come out on the porch to read the paper. He greeted Carl with his slightly shy friendliness, never presuming to take the part of an elder.

"Where's Lillian?"

"Lillian? Why, I think she went off somewhere just now. Didn't she, Jennie?" Howard called in to Jennie, who had come to the screened door. "Didn't Lillian just go somewhere?"

"Yes, she started over to Essie Bartlett's to take a book. But she's just gone. You can catch up with her if you hurry, Carl."

"Thanks!"

He was already down the walk. He saw Lillian ahead of him.

"You seem to be in a hurry!"

"Oh! I didn't know you were behind me."

"I wasn't until just now. You don't have to take that book back right this minute, do you?" Carl took the book from Lillian, who yielded it to him, but hesitantly. "Can't you walk a little while? I've got to be back at the house before eight."

Lillian said, "Why, I guess so."

They turned down the walk that led past the high school building, a favorite way for all young people on summer evenings. Both went on in a slightly uncomfortable silence. Lillian had felt at once that there was something out of the ordinary. Carl could sense a kind of fear in her, but he was too absorbed to try to make it out.

"I've got something to tell you, Lillian."

Her face became suddenly rigid—her eyes waiting and bright. What did she think he was going to say?—Carl wondered for a second, with a slight shock of pity. She hesitated, and then walked on, with her head a trifle bent, as if to accept a blow. But Carl couldn't stop to think about this, to take it in, exactly.

"I was out to the farm this afternoon, and while I was coming home, there was a telephone call for me. It was from Lorraine. I don't know whether I told you I'd put in an application there."

Lillian murmured. The rigid look had melted in a suffusing blush. "Where is it?" she asked Carl softly, at random.

"Why, right on the Mississippi. Haven't you ever head of that place?"

"Yes, I think so. But I didn't just know . . ."

"They say there's awfully pretty country around there. Somebody left word I was to call up at eight o'clock. So I guess there's no doubt they'll offer me the position. Principal of the high school and charge of athletics. I thought it sounded pretty good."

She murmured, "Yes, it does."

She was looking straight ahead now. Both their faces were flushed. They were conscious of meaning more than they had said so far. But Carl could see the light thin voile of Lillian's waist stirred slightly by her breathing.

"Of course I don't know," he told her conscientiously, with a thought of dad, "until I've actually talked with them. Still, when they call you up long distance—! I think the folks would like to have me take it. Lillian, do you know dad called me into the bank this morning and gave me a second mortgage for a thousand dollars he'd made out to me. He said he was going to do it for all us kids."

"Oh, did he! Oh, I think your father's . . ."

She didn't know how to finish it. But Carl felt the delicate fervor that had come into her voice. It drew them together.

"Gee," Carl said, "but dad was nice this morning! I never appreciated him so much. I think the folks both want me to get this job. They'd like to know I was fixed for next year. And I feel as if I owe it to them. Gee! But they sure have been good to me."

Both of them walked slowly. Carl looked suddenly up and down the street. A car was coming along, and he waited until it had passed them. Then he came to a stop.

"Well—I might as well say what I came out to say. If this job does turn out—then I'd like your promise, Lillian, to marry me before I go there in the fall. I mean, so we could both of us start in together."

It was said. Carl felt exalted, good. But he saw Lillian give a frightened glance around. He hadn't chosen a very auspicious place to say this, maybe. Right out on the open street. Mrs. Bellew was sitting on her porch and nodded to them. But Carl felt suddenly outraged and stubborn. He didn't want Lillian to consider that! Lillian seemed to be trying to move on, in embarrassment. But Carl stood there.

"I wish you'd answer!"

"I don't know . . . can't we walk somewhere else?"

He was ashamed, for the moment, of his domination, when he heard her voice come breathless and almost unmanageable. And in a way, Carl knew guiltily that this meant more to Lillian than to him—although it meant so much to him, the decision that would affect his whole life! He let Lillian cross the street in her confusion, and followed her; and he did not say anything more until they were in the school yard and almost hidden by the honeysuckle bushes that grew along the side. Then—

"Why don't you know?" he demanded more tenderly.

She had let him pause again, but she had turned away and was gathering up some leaves of the honeysuckle bush in her hand. Carl heard her say something about her position—she had taken it for next year and signed the contract. . . .

144

"Well." Carl gave a laugh. "Contracts have been broken, haven't they? For *such* reasons."

Lillian was silent.

Carl felt a shock of angry hurt. That Lillian should put him off!—he hadn't bargained for that. He had looked forward to the shy, trembling gratitude of her response. She didn't know what he was giving up to make this offer now—and the possibilities he had let go all through the four years of college. He might have gone with almost any girl there. And he didn't know that Nina actually *was* engaged, after all. Maybe . . . Carl felt suddenly impatient at something meager, blind, provincial in Lillian. And then there was that disturbing sense of having gone through all this before at some time. Carl didn't exactly think of an old affair with Mildred Summers, years ago in high school, but its ghost was present between them. Maybe Lillian was thinking of it. But in spite of his hurt feelings, Carl was more or less aware now, shocked into awareness by Lillian's hesitancy, of the way he had been going about this tonight. He could feel that he had not put his questions in the most loverlike manner. He had a perception of some distress in the withheld quality of her silence—her head bent, and her fingers still playing with the leaves.

"Maybe you . . ."

"What's that? Lillian, I can't even hear you."

"Maybe it would be better if we didn't decide anything so soon . . ."

Lillian had turned away, and now she was leaning against the wall. Carl followed her.

"What makes you say that?" he asked in angry chagrin.

She couldn't give an answer.

But he knew—in his heart he knew—something of what was back of that difficult whisper that trailed off into summer silence. The birds twittered and fluttered about among the honeysuckle bushes. Shame came flushing over him again. He had thought, of course the doubt was all his; that Lillian would have no suspicion if he didn't say anything to her. And now it appeared that she had more instinct than he had given her credit for! She had sensed something out of the way in his preoccupation, his sudden announcements too early in the evening that he must go home and go to bed and get some sleep, his failure to urge her for those shy kisses that she had always seemed so reluctant and fearful to give—until they actually knew they were going to be married. Carl saw himself for a moment as he had the feeling that maybe dad saw him—too confident that everything would go just as he had planned it. Suddenly he was afraid of Lillian's scrupulousness. His desire was aroused to overcome it.

"I'll tell you this!" he cried, out of a hurt somewhere. "It hasn't always been easy to keep loyal to you the way I have, and not look at any other girl. Maybe you don't know that! But it's the truth!"

Well, it was good for her to hear that! Carl felt his own righteousness again now that *she* was the reluctant one. Of course that wasn't quite the truth—although, yes, it was the truth too. There was Nina. Lillian must be thinking of her too.

"Lillian!" Carl said. "Oh, gee, don't let's talk like this. We've been so much to each other so long. I didn't want to say that. You sort of made me. Gosh, you *know* how I feel."

He tried to get her away from the support of the wall, and to draw her toward him. They couldn't break off now. Everything would be thrown into confusion.

He had got her face turned toward him. He was making anxious assurances of his sincerity to her eyes blind with tears and her quivering lips. The intensity that he had been waiting for, to blot out that other dazzling possibility, came over him now, in pity and anxiety, and he was half crying too.

"Aren't you going to answer me?" he pleaded. "Lillian? Aren't you? I want you to so bad. I love you so well."

He felt with exultant triumph that he had broken through the chill fineness of her resistance. It had melted at that word. Carl felt awed. That was what she was waiting for! And he *did* love her . . . he felt more now than he had ever felt before. He was holding Lillian. Then he felt her face turn blindly and offer itself to him. He felt how helpless she was in his arms. He had forced the old virginal reluctance at last to give way. For this one moment in the dusk of the school yard—half frightened, both of them, that someone might pass—the pressure of Lillian's lips was moist, yielded and free; and holding her, Carl felt as if he drained from them the immaculate sweetness that had always been blooming, hidden and pure, like some cold spring flower, in the prim aloofness of her slender body.

Carl went home—it seemed as if he was running on air. It was right now. He had done the right thing. He felt noble and clean. And he was glad, glad all over—shocked, gladly surprised. He had learned the sweetness of Lillian. Learned her *truth*. She was new to him. Now he *did* love her. He held with exalted ardor the beauty and purity of her gift.

That night, after the folks had gone to bed—after all the excitement about the telephone call, looking up maps, finding out just where Lorraine was and how far away from Belmond—Carl knocked softly on the door of their room.

"Can I come in for a minute—mama and papa?"

He had scarcely ever been in their room when they were both in bed. But tonight his emotion lifted him above childish embarrassment. He couldn't keep it to himself. It seemed as if his love overflowed. He couldn't go to sleep until he had shared his news with the folks. He stood in the dim, summery light with the familiar furniture shadowy around him.

"I just wanted to tell you, mama and papa, before you went to sleep—I guess Lillian and I got everything fixed up tonight. We want to get married before I go over to Lorraine next fall. So I guess she'll go with me. Gee, I—I sure feel good about the whole thing."

III. *HOMECOMING*

Lillian had left the room softly so as not to disturb Carl, he had been so busy these last few weeks of school, and up so many nights. But he came down to breakfast soon after the others. He looked fresh and brushed this morning. The children were in their faded play suits—summer had begun; and Lillian wore a house dress and had her hair combed plainly. When Carl squeezed into the breakfast nook, beside Forrest

147

who must always sit next to his daddy, Lillian glanced at him with a shy, restrained consciousness.

"Hello," Carl said absent-mindedly, to all of them.

Then he took up the paper.

Lillian asked him after a moment, "Do you have to go to school this morning?"

"Yes. Lots to do still. Have to get the teachers' reports."

"Can I go along, daddy?"

"No, you can't go."

"Why can't I?"

"Because you'd be in the way there."

"No, I wouldn't," Forrest said hopefully.

Carl didn't answer. Lillian glanced at him again, but surreptitiously. A sensitive expression touched her face. Her eyes took on a rebuffed, disappointed look. But all in silence. They let the boys do the talking. When Lillian saw that Carl's cup was empty, she reached for it and poured him out some more coffee.

He looked up hastily. "Oh, thanks!"

He tried to rouse himself out of the mood he was in this morning. But when he so much as glanced at Lillian, he felt a cold averseness of which he was ashamed. What had become of that brief intensity of last night? It had gone more flat than if it had never been. It had left behind it just this bleak, flat disappointment. Carl didn't know how much of this Lillian realized; but her reticence always gave him leave to trust that he deceived her. He said now—"Well, I see the summer exodus has already begun"—with bright perfunctoriness, that seemed to him enough to convince her that everything was all right.

He handed her the paper, and started off; and then to convince her still further, went back to the kitchen and said, "I'll have to go now. Anything you want me to get in town?"

She said, "I guess not." But there was a withheld disappointment in her voice, that made Carl guiltily aware he ought to have given some recognition of last night. Well, he couldn't. His own disappointment filled him with cold anger. It seemed to him, anyway, that she had been to blame for their failure. She hadn't given him what he had been trying to wrest from her with his fierce love-making—nor had any understanding of it; she had just acted frightened, had struggled in a dim, shocked terror, and submitted because she couldn't help it. So it seemed, at least, to Carl.

But he felt curiously free, and able to drop the whole thing, just as soon as he got out into the early June morning. He knew there were a lot of things in his mind to be settled, but it seemed as if the new season would do that for him, somehow. A diamond spray was flashing over the colored freshness of the flowers in the Brinsleys' garden. The brightness made both the crisis and then the dead flat blackness of last night seem a long way in the past. Almost irrelevant. Carl went squeezing in between the rough wall and the car, in the cemented coolness of his garage. Forrest came running out of the house, but too late. Carl waved to him as he drove off, hardily ignoring the wail of "Daddy!" The poor little fellow had thought he would get to ride as far as the corner.

"Well, I can't spend *all* my life on my family!"

Carl pulled into his special parking place near the high school. That gave him the pleasant importance of being the head of the schools. "You can't park there. That's where Mr. Ferguson parks." He went up the long cement walk and the wide flight of steps into the sudden summery leisure of the big, many-windowed new high school building. Up and down the stairs fluttered girls smiling in release, with their schoolbooks under their arms. This morning, with school over, they had a pretty air of tossing boldness in greeting the superintendent.

Carl went on into the auditorium. The great sunny room was cool and echoing this morning. Carl felt a warm, expansive pride and ownership of the whole school system. This fine new building was due to his efforts. He went over to the group of teachers near the rostrum, and said with the suave, cheerful authoritativeness of the head:

"Well! The prisoners almost free?"

There were ripples of dutiful laughter around him. Some of the teachers were faded and schoolmistressy; but what Carl felt this morning was the warm youth and femininity of the group. Most of these girls were not long out of college. They came from "good homes," and spent the greater part of their salaries upon their clothes. Carl looked smilingly and impersonally at the whole group, careful not to glance directly at Gladys Gibbs or Marian Stuart, the two girls whom he had championed and who had caused the recent trouble.

Then, while he was talking, Carl saw that Miss Chisholm had withdrawn from the group. Her face had a tight expression. She would not look at him. This hurt Carl unreasonably, inordinately. He knew what Miss Chisholm was "like," as everybody else did. He knew that she was a cross to the other teachers. Poor thing, she had been here so long, she felt as if she ought to have authority with them; and yet she didn't have it. She was teaching Latin grammar just as when she had started in thirty-five years ago in the Salisbury schools, and her position was no different now than it had been then, except that it got more precarious instead of more assured year by year. Carl always felt a special compassion and comprehension for these aging spinsters. Miss Chisholm reminded him in some ways of Essie Bartlett at home. He had got along wonderfully with Miss Chisholm until this trouble had come up about the two girls. He was the only superintendent she hadn't kept in hot water for years. When Carl had made little jokes at the opening of a teachers' meeting, to get everyone in good humor for what was to follow, Miss Chisholm had always managed to squeeze a slight smile out of her dry, frozen bitterness of monotony and diminishment and disappointment. She had come to him with questions about management, and with suggestions of what ought to be done in these schools; and Carl had always listened kindly and tactfully, and even adopted one or two of the suggestions. She was no fool! Now what hurt Carl so dreadfully was the knowledge that in *her* eyes he had failed her. He had gone over to the side of the devil. She was disappointed in her good opinion. In spite of the years that he had been superintendent of schools, Carl couldn't take that kind of thing easily. Miss Chisholm's severe, faded eyes and her tight mouth gave her verdict: that those two girls had got around Mr. Ferguson with their wiles, that it was just because they were pretty young fools that he had taken their part. Oh, he was no better than other people! Just another disappointment.

Carl went through the empty, sunny glare of the outer office into his own sanctuary. Around him here were all the symbols of his position. Books and papers lay in neat piles on the polished expanse of his desk. Everything was hard and shining and modern and new. But all at once Carl was restless. When he had first asked for time before signing his new contract, it was because he was so terribly hurt and disillusioned at the criticism he had received for standing up for the two girls, and at the way his school board had at first failed to stand back of him. He realized that they would have allowed him to be ousted, if the sentiment of the town had seemed to demand it! Without any regard to the rights or the wrongs. He couldn't bring himself to make it up right away when the evidence of his general popularity with the teachers and pupils, petitions from various organizations, a sermon commending him by the new young pastor of the Methodist church, had shown them where he stood and had overwhelmed Mrs. Bondy and her crew. Then the board had backed down with deprecating, shamefaced, conciliatory attempts to smooth the whole thing over. They had swung over to his side so violently that they had given him until July fifteenth to make his signing of the contract final—an almost unheard-of concession! But they didn't want the town to be able to say that the school board had driven out Carl Ferguson and lost the schools the best man they had ever had.

Carl had a moment of realization of how absolutely ridiculous it would seem to Katherine Brinsley if she knew how upset he was because Miss Ida Chisholm disapproved of him. But he couldn't help it. Katherine had thought the whole business a huge joke—the school board and the entire town getting all wrought up because two of the high school teachers had been reported as smoking cigarettes in a hotel in another town! And this in the days when there were gangster shootings and hold-ups and kidnappings and things *to* get wrought up about! "Are these women fit to teach our children?" And so on. Katherine had come to one of the high school programs just to see the culprits. And what sinners! Two little girls, one of them so thin and homely she couldn't be any kind of a menace, and the other still with a milk-fed country look about her. Katherine booed with delighted scorn at the picture of that whole bunch of fat-faced Babbitts solemnly sitting there, all of them heavy smokers, all afraid to commit themselves on the awful subject of two little girls trying out two little cigarettes—for fear of being put down as "radicals"! All because one or two old busybodies like Mrs. Bondy, who were more of a nuisance to the business men than to anyone else—even!—had got themselves excited in the dearth of other public calamities. But to Carl! it hadn't been any joke. It couldn't be while he was involved. It was no joke to him, well-liked and popular as he had been in every town where he had taught, to have even Mrs. Bondy denouncing him as "the superintendent of our schools, who has the welfare of our own young people in charge, setting himself on the side of those who . . ." And so forth and so forth.

Oh, there was more mixed up in the silly business than anyone else knew! Here in the privacy of his own office Carl could let himself realize that. He had pleaded with the school board that smoking was being recognized in some of the best schools and universities. As if the children of all these men hadn't long been smoking! The thing shouldn't be made a public matter. The girls were otherwise unexceptionable in their conduct, good faithful teachers, and all that. But if the matter *had* come to a public meeting, as Mrs. Bondy had demanded and most of the school board so heartily wanted to escape, would he have had the courage to hold out for the girls? And if they hadn't come to him beforehand, Gladys crying and distressed—would he have sidestepped the issue and "quietly let them out"? Nearly all the school board, in their private conversations, admitted that they "wished this thing had never been started, wished that old Meddlesome Mattie had let it alone." And yet they had been cautiously willing to let Mrs. Bondy run them, if that was the way the cat was going to jump. It made Carl feel liberal and courageous. But how much part had it played, that he knew he would have burned with shame if Margaret had ever got hold of the news of such a rumpus in his town over two girls smoking—the town which he had praised so highly, with its nice wide streets, upholding its advantages of wholesome, "normal" living against the pernicious excitements of the metropolis! Carl, always eager to have his actions put in the best light before other people, himself must go frantically into his own motives, and had never, in anything he had done, escaped that slight tinge of secret guilt. How much was Miss Chisholm right, and how much did Gladys Gibbs have to do with it?

It was a pain to Carl that the stand he had taken had put him on the side of the flouters, the "radicals," the gay set—the Brinsleys, the antiprohibition crowd, the fierce young heavy-haired editor of the meager little socialistic paper—who occasionally, incongruously, all got classed in together in Salisbury. He had always been a good boy. He felt the whole satisfaction of the years he had spent here. He had come at a happy time when the town seemed to be growing and expanding. And he felt the same warm-blooded possibility of expanding powers in himself. The first bright collegiate youth was past, the insecurity and brief, struggling stagnation of later youth when he hadn't yet proved his powers; and now he was conscious of just coming to the full flush of his best years.

But it was just this very flush of success and real possibility of stability that suddenly seemed to be filling him with restlessness.

Maybe the friendship with the Brinsleys, that had developed over the humors of the cigarette battle, had something to do with it. Carl had always scoffed at Lillian's fears that those people "would have an influence on him." But now he was in favor with the other side, where it seemed as if he had always partly craved to be. At least he had been secretly sensitive over being excluded. He had felt it when that little tough Irene somebody and that little kid they called Squirrel-Eyes used to walk behind him coming from school and chant nastily:

> "Carl stuck in his thumb,
> And pulled out a plum,
> And said what a good boy am I."

Carl worried about that yet—how he had gone to Irene's and told Margaret that the folks wanted her to come home. It had left a scar. He had never ceased trying to justify himself in his own mind. He wanted to be good, he agonized over all his failings; and yet he agonized because the other, secular kind of people thought that he *was* good!

The air came in warm through the wide, raised windows. But now he was ready to change. There was almost a disappointment in having won out with the school board. He felt that only half his possibilities of life had been lived out. Terribly as all this criticism and opposition had hurt him at first (although he had kept that hidden from Katherine) it had given him a kind of new freedom . . . And yet, though he had come so far himself, had gone through the war period that seemed to have brought such a change over the country, he remembered the naïve innocence of his childhood when he had trustingly believed Grandpa Ferguson that men who smoked and used strong drink were bad. He couldn't be left behind, outmoded, he was impatient with Lillian—he felt life rushing on—somewhere . . . out of the innocent green pastures of his childhood. He had life and vigor in him. But sometimes he felt like a hurt, lost child in a strange world because things were no longer so simple as they had been when he was a little boy in Belmond.

Carl heard hesitating footsteps in the outer office. He looked up. Gladys Gibbs stood just outside his doorway. He said quickly:

"Oh, come in, Miss Gibbs!"

She looked frightened; but she came in with a determined, soft, sidling boldness. She *was* a bold little thing, in a purely feminine way, although she had such an air of almost rustic shyness. Carl felt the sweet flattery of that audacity, of her coming to seek him out, just as years ago he had felt it with Mildred Summers. But he knew that he would have been secretly embarrassed and impatient—although kind—if it had been the other girl, Marian Stuart, who was a thin, homely, dark little thing with big glasses.

"I'm leaving now, Mr. Ferguson."

Carl saw that she really was frightened. Her eyes looked dark and there was a little dew of anxiety on her round white forehead.

He said very kindly, "Well, that's too bad, Miss Gibbs. I hate to see you go. What do you have in mind for next year?" he asked her.

He had saved the girls from being dismissed, but of course that was as much as he could do. In his position, there always had to be a compromise. He felt embarrassed now, because he could say so little—impatient with the cramping, petty limits of that "position." The girls weren't coming back next year. For Marian, that was better. She was going to Chicago, where she would be happier than in Salisbury, was bound to be, no matter what she found to do. But it seemed to Carl that this soft little unoffending Gladys had been a victim.

Gladys said, "I'll probably stay at home next year with my folks. They want me to."

Carl said heartily, "Well, I think that'll be fine. Get a little rest from teaching." He asked her where her home was, and she said on a large dairy farm in western Wisconsin. She looked as if she had been brought up on Wisconsin strawberries and Jersey cream! Carl hadn't really known anything about Gladys, or cared anything, except for the warm physical attraction that she possessed. "But you mustn't feel that you can't go on with your teaching," he told her. "Whenever you or Miss Stuart want a recommendation from me—as teachers—I'll be glad to see that you get it." He didn't know whether he had meant to say that much.

Gladys murmured, "Oh, thanks!" She raised her eyes. They were dewy. Carl felt sure that her parents were simple good people, somewhat like his own, who would feel much more badly than there was any occasion for because their daughter had got into this kind of a scrape. She made a little movement and said with breathless, soft determination: "I certainly do want to thank you, Mr. Ferguson, for what you did for me and Marian—Miss Stuart. I think it was just fine. I just felt as if I couldn't bear to go away without telling you how I felt about it."

She turned her head aside. She was crying in little subdued, smothered, feminine sniffs. She felt disgraced at losing her position. And how silly the whole business was! Why couldn't they all just cut right through it? Carl took her hand. It was soft, plump, warm, unresisting, and seemed to confide itself to his. A delicate delight came thrilling that flattered him all through.

"Why, you mustn't feel so badly! All this will be forgotten in another year."

Gladys still had her head turned aside, and was standing with her hand left softly in his. Instinctively, Carl had placed himself between her and the outer office. Then she looked at him again, and he was ashamed of his uneasy caution. He felt with a shock the appeal of her warmth, her roundness, her living freshness with the slight dew of perspiration on her round white forehead just where the golden, stiffly-waved hair was brushed back—the humid brightness of her large eyes with the gray and golden irides in the almost super-healthy, pearly blueness of the eyeballs. The red freshness of her lips glistened through the lipstick. There was a slight trembling of her full red mouth.

"You mustn't feel so badly about this thing, Gladys!" he repeated—with more tenderness than he quite knew. "It's nothing in itself. Not worth bothering over! A lot of people haven't caught up with the times, that's all."

He was saying things to her that it amazed Carl to say. It amazed him to realize that he believed them. How could he stand any longer all the little tight, outgrown strictures that bound him in!

There came over him a sort of blinding, hot perception of this girl's warmth, softness, physical richness, pliability. He could have cried out in sharp agony over the bleak failure of his attempt last night to wrest from Lillian the kind of response he needed. He felt himself bound in on every side. Now he was ready to live his life to the full. He bent toward Gladys—he had almost kissed her . . . when he heard someone come into the outer office. Carl dropped her hand. Her humid eyes were still raised, her lips parted. He felt himself bathed in a sudden cold douse of caution. Hardly knowing what he was doing, he said loudly:

"Well, Miss Gibbs, I hope you have a good summer and a fine year."

He turned away from her to gather together the papers on his desk. His hands were sweating. Gladys stood hesitating. Carl did not turn around. After a moment, she was gone.

Then Carl was in a confusion of exquisite relief and humiliated self-beratement.

Oh, but he was sick of the whole thing! What an outcome of last night with its stars and warm, fragrant gusts of air! He got up again, hot all over, and walked about the room. It was Miss Winship, his secretary, who had come into the office. She had seated herself neatly at her typewriting table and was working. He must forever think of other people, at every step, as he had been doing all his life long! There were all sorts of desires and powers in himself that were confined, untried, almost to bursting. The superintendent in a town this size—or any size—was forever in the public spotlight. Even when he went over to the Brinsleys', he couldn't forget what people would say if they heard of his doing this or that. (And Katherine was very naughtily and embarrassingly aware of it!) Now at last he wanted to live. It wasn't that Gladys Gibbs herself meant anything so vital to him. He didn't know what or how much she meant. No, but it was . . . some part of his life, for which all at once he was ready, would be getting past him. And now it was here! He felt his full, warm-blooded strength still unused. It was as if he had suddenly veered around in mid-course and seen all the things he had been missing. Everything—the whole world—was changing.

What had been his life before had simply turned stale to him. He saw all of a sudden that there was nothing more to be done here in Salisbury. He had built the new schoolhouse. He had been going up—and now it would be simply standing still. He wanted to get away.

Carl lay on the davenport. The room was in early twilight. Ordinarily he helped Lillian with the dishes; but he made his tiredness an excuse for staying in here tonight. The telephone rang. He let Lillian answer it. Now she came to the living room door.

"It's Mrs. Brinsley, Carl. She wants to know if we'll go over there this evening."

"Katherine?" he said at once, with eagerness. "Sure! Why can't we?"

"I thought you were tired."

"Oh, well, I've been up so much now I might as well be up some more." He sat up on the davenport. "It's the last time we're likely to see them before we leave. I think we ought to go over. We can rest all we want to when we get to the folks!"

Carl felt suddenly animated. He saw Lillian's reluctance and heard the careful coolness of her voice over the telephone.

"Why, yes, I think perhaps we can come over for a little while."

Then came the clink of dishes again from the kitchen. He had no excuse now for not helping. But he stayed where he was. Finally she reappeared at the door.

"Are we going?"

"Why, yes. Sure. Didn't you tell her so?"

Lillian stood a moment, doubtful and reserved, and then turned away.

"You'd better change your dress, hadn't you?"

Lillian didn't answer him. "I'll have to get the boys to bed first." Carl didn't answer this time. She never forgot a single duty! Now that school was out, and in a day or two they would be starting for the folks', it did seem as if she might loosen up a little. He heard her sedate footsteps upstairs. He supposed she wouldn't go off and leave her room unless it was perfectly in order. Then she had to go and get the boys, who were playing outside, and see that they got into bed before eight o'clock. Carl thought the boys were big enough to look after themselves, especially when their parents wanted a little outing.

"Lillian! Aren't you about ready?"

Finally she came down. Carl's impatience melted treacherously when he saw the efforts she had made toward dressing for the Brinsleys. She had put on her blue-flowered chiffon, in which he had told her she looked the nicest of anything she owned, and she had touched her cheeks slightly with rouge. She had never done that until this winter! He could remember when she would have thought it absolutely wicked. These meager little evidences of her playing up to Katherine touched

Carl and made him feel defensive and warm toward her. It wasn't Katherine toward whom he was attracted, in the way that Lillian thought . . . and she knew nothing about Gladys Gibbs coming in to see him this morning. She was both suspicious and unsuspecting. This was the first warmth he had felt for her in the secret cold hostility he had been cherishing for a long time.

"You look nice," he told her. He patted her arm.

It was perfectly still under his touch. A sensitive look went across her face again. "Do you want to go over now?"

"Yes, I guess we'd better be going," Carl said in a careless tone. "We won't stay late. I don't want to, either."

They went together across their driveway. Carl noticed how wet the grass was, and took Lillian's arm to draw her out to the walk. The fragrant, beautiful, warm evening seemed to make some demand on them to which they couldn't rise. Carl knew how he had avoided Lillian all day, and he had a sensitive, guilty awareness of how she must have been feeling. That touch of rouge on her cheeks had made him realize the efforts she made—all so slight, and yet for her so terribly difficult and significant, with the almost nunlike purity of her upbringing in her grandfather's house—to be "liberal," and to try to loosen up a little in her ways and manners. It filled him with a disturbing mixture of impatience and compassion.

They went up the carefully rough flagstone walk to the timbered Tudor house and pulled the knocker on the heavy oak door. Katherine was there almost before they were through knocking.

"Wasn't it sweet of you to come? I just suddenly got the notion I might kill Joe in some horrible way, double him up in a trunk you know, if somebody didn't come over and save us this evening?"

Carl felt that he was laughing a little too heartily in the attempt to respond to that trail of upward inflection. Lillian smiled very slightly. Carl always felt, too, that he must be very hearty and friendly all the time in order to cover up Lillian's inward disapproval of Katherine and Joe, and the sort of sedate, wounded coolness that she opposed to Katherine's vivacities.

Katherine was leading them on into the studio-living room, very animated, with a flutter of chiffon and of thin little hands, all accentuated by the staccato trip of French heels on the tiled floor. Carl always felt flattered, flustered, awkward, and yet somehow warmed and elated. He was roused by the appreciation of how exquisite Katherine looked tonight—it almost shocked him at first glance—in this softened June twilight, with shaded golden pools around the two floor lamps. Her dress of bizarrely figured red chiffon fluttered around her minute thinness. There was a jangle of earrings below the fuzzed-up blackness of her short hair.

"She *is* beautiful," Carl thought, with that shock, and elation. And all at once Gladys seemed rustic and shapeless and remote—that encounter faded from his mind except for a faint, embarrassed shame.

Flitting through the big room, Katherine looked like some kind of exquisite black and red and green-gold insect. Carl and Lillian were just some sort of clumsy things trailing after her.

Joe came to meet them. "Here are your rescuers, Joey!" Katherine sang out. "If they hadn't been so nice, and come over to see us, you would have been in a lot of little pieces under the cellar floor by now. Darling. Did you know that?" Her voice went plaintively, cooingly soft. She gave Carl a wistful, wicked sort of little girl-elf look and then stood on tiptoe and kissed her husband.

He was being the good host. "How do you do, people? Glad to have you come in."

He took his cigar out of his mouth and held it between the fingers of one hand while he hospitably greeted them. "Trust you don't mind the cigar," he always said with heavy courtesy to Lillian. She could never understand how he could take the things his wife said about him so easily. Didn't he see through it? Lillian could not comprehend the demands of external social courtesies on people who had been brought up under them. To her, it just seemed like being insincere—she was bewildered and disapproving both.

Katherine was fluttering and flittering about getting comfortable nests arranged for them. "Joey, pull up the little armchair, won't you, precious? No, darling. The *other* one. Heavens, is that a *little* one?" She gave a funny twist and a glance at Carl. He was aware that Lillian had her lips firmly closed with distaste at Katherine's "darlings" and endearments. And then to have talked just before, even if she did pretend it was fun, of wanting to murder her husband! Lillian disapproved of the way that Katherine let the audience in on the joke of Joe's obtuseness, making herself seem tiny and pitiful—and then tried to make it up to him so obviously with one of those mock kisses before everybody. Lillian believed in the code that married couples should uphold each other before outsiders, "other people," under any circumstances—she remembered how her own parents had stood together surreptitiously and silently as one beneath her grandfather's rule. Her deep, secretive reticence recoiled from the endearments with severe distaste.

But even Lillian was mollified by the comfort Katherine always created. Katherine must have some kind of instinct that knew how this little, black-upholstered chair, with the quaint precision of its embroidery—a Valentine group of lady and gentleman and posies—pleased Lillian. She always gave it to Lillian as part of the ritual of their visits here. The great heavy couch was inordinately comfortable with the velvet cushions that Katherine piled extravagantly behind their backs. Carl didn't notice these things separately—as Lillian did, with acute minuteness—but he was conscious of an elated sense of general luxury.

"Let me give you the footstool," Katherine begged. "You're tired. I think anything that happens is about ten times as hard on a man's wife as on the man! I suppose Carl thinks *he* closed up the school today, doesn't he? How sweet you look tonight!" she whispered. Her hands left just a gossamer touch on Lillian's shoulder.

Lillian couldn't help feeling the fascination of Katherine's secret little touch of thin, fine hands, and the suggestion of personal flattery that rose like a subtle perfume from her words. But under the surface mollification, there was a wounded, hostile distrust. Katherine, after showing no more attention to Lillian than if Lillian hadn't existed, after she had first become amusedly and interestedly friendly with Carl after the cigarette episode, had suddenly seen her mistake and become flatteringly attentive. Lillian was too unsophisticated to know how to rebuff these attentions, and she felt bowed down under the obligation. It worried her, because when she was alone with Katherine, Katherine seemed so different, so quiet and simple and rather pathetic, so nice about the boys—Lillian would forget what she was "really" like until she came over here with Carl and saw that other side of Katherine again. But Lillian had her own wisdom. It was that first unconsciously neglectful attitude of Katherine's that showed how Katherine actually regarded her. And she was never quite sure that the perfume was not infused with a delicate, malicious poison.

Joe was passing the cigarettes. "Have one? Oh, I forgot—you don't care for smoking, do you?" he said with heavy, good-natured courtesy to Lillian. She had learned to accept smoking in other people, although she still refused it for herself. Since the war, she knew that everyone was smoking, and Lillian seemed to be dragged, reluctantly, bewilderingly, along with events. But she did secretly mind it over here. It fitted in with the flaunting of everything that she and Carl had been taught to believe was wrong. There must be *some*-thing wrong in the stand that Carl had taken, that it should throw them with people like this, instead of their own kind! How could Carl come over here and act as if all their early training and convictions were just wiped from his mind? To Lillian it seemed dreadful.

But even she couldn't help feeling a touch of delighted feminine interest in the queer little vermilion box, smooth and yet intricately carved, in which the cigarettes were passed. Everything that Katherine had was somehow different and striking. It gave an elated sense of well-being that Lillian recognized, with hostility, as a more delicate pleasure than just the warm, prosperous comfort she had always been used to in entertainment—the kind in which Carl's folks excelled.

This place was suited to the June evening. The big casement windows opened upon the warm dusk; and the sense of elation came again as they sat here in deep cushioned comfort and heard the sound of cars outside on the pavement. Katherine called this room "the studio." So Carl always took pains to call it that now too. Lillian once protested:

"*She* doesn't do any painting. I don't see why we should call it a studio."

The word smacked to Lillian of the vague but awful dangers of Greenwich Village—of her disapproving picture of Margaret Ferguson's rebellious career.

And now she saw why Katherine was so thoughtful and assiduous about giving her this favorite chair!—so that Katherine herself could go over and flutteringly nestle beside Carl on the couch, childishly folding her knees and drawing up her feet on the velvet, and leaning over to suck the fire from a wavering, soft, gold candle flame into her cigarette. She thought they would both accept that as perfectly casual! Lillian was cold with anger at what she perceived as Katherine's idea of their simplicity. She didn't see why she had to stay here and endure all this when she really hated it.

"Well!" Katherine said, blowing smoke and holding her cigarette between her fingers, "I suppose you've been weeping salt tears over the prospect of leaving Salisbury and all its excitements?"

Carl laughed—again too heartily; but it was the only way he had of meeting the delicate sarcasm of Katherine's tone. He was uneasy with people who used innuendo. He uncomfortably felt himself a rosy-cheeked lad beside Katherine.

"Hasn't this been the most desiccated spring? If you hadn't saved things by putting on your little show I could never have borne it."

Lillian looked very stiff. She didn't see why Carl laughed. Salisbury didn't seem that way to *them*. In fact, to Lillian, life here had been a whirl of upsetting modernity. She didn't like to hear Carl's trouble with the school board referred to as a "little show." It had been serious enough to her!

"I think we've had a good many nice things this year," she said stiffly. "I think people go too much nowadays instead of too little."

"Oh, but you're so much better at heart than I am," Katherine sighed. "Lillian my dear. You really like to do your duty. I'd probably enjoy things if it weren't my duty to go to them. But everybody in Salisbury's been so perfectly gorgeous to me, and so you see it's my duty to respond?"

Lillian flushed. She did not know what answer to make to show that these plaintively malicious words of Katherine's hadn't imposed upon her! But at least she could close her lips and keep still.

And then Carl laughed. He had liked that jibe about doing her duty! Lillian felt with a thrust of pain that he had been holding something like that against her, and was glad to have someone else say it for him. To have this other woman say it!

Katherine faced toward Carl again. She said very softly and plaintively, "Is she disgusted with me?"

"Of course not!" Carl laughed, reassuringly hearty. He leaned over and deliberately flicked an ash into the fireplace. He was wrought up inside over Lillian's display of prim provinciality. It had now become a matter of honor with him to prove that the superintendent of schools was as free as anybody else —that he well knew how absurd all this pother had been. Things like that didn't matter nowadays with any but the Mrs. Bondys. But then, Carl had always stood high with the Mrs. Bondys. They were like Mrs. Dunn, for instance, in the church at home. They had been Lillian's natural allies.

Katherine pleaded, "But I want you not to sign your contract?"

"Why not?" Carl was nettled—flattered—a little guilty because Lillian would perceive that he had told Katherine about the contract. Lillian would think that ought to be a highly private matter, just between themselves. And Carl was secretly hurt that Katherine made so light of his position, which to his own people had always sounded so impressive. It had to Carl himself. But he had to seek this—he was restless now, unstable, dissatisfied.

"Oh, just because . . . I'd like to see how you'd conduct yourself if you weren't a 'professor.'" Her hazel eyes shot a sparkle of mockery. Everybody in Salisbury called the superintendent of schools "professor."

The boyish stain that Carl still kept freshly on his cheeks burned to a pink as bright as paint.

"Oh, maybe you *have* been conducting?"

"You like to think you can bother me, don't you, Katherine?" Carl finally found to say.

"I think I *do* bother you!"

"Oh, no, you don't, not so much as you think."

When they got away from controversy onto just the man-and-woman plane, Carl felt a happy renewal of personal confidence. His attractiveness to women, little as his conscience had allowed him to make use of it, was one thing about himself that he had never had cause to doubt. He felt the warm, slightly tickled assurance that Katherine knew nothing about his encounter today with Gladys Gibbs, in spite of being such a little witch—and that she had long ago been thrown off the track in regard to the heroines of his "little show" by her laughing perception of their rusticity, and by Carl's dazzled response to herself. It might be a surprise to her to learn about that!

And besides, sitting this close to Katherine, Carl's elated consciousness of her beauty had changed, as often before, into disappointment. He had an uneasy remembrance of remarks of Lillian's, made with scornful feminine decision, and that Carl had indignantly denied. In Salisbury, where the Brinsleys had been living only a few years, Katherine was generally accepted as "much younger than her husband." Her fluttering, wheedling, little-girl actions with Joe, as if he were a nice big blind beast and she the little princess kept in pretty docile captivity, had carried out this assumption. Carl had put perfect trust in it. But he caught now, beneath the brilliancy of the make-up, the queer, sagged under-mask of Katherine's face with a pathetic withering under the chin—it was as if suddenly the brilliant little insect had grown brittle and faded and was almost at the end of its day. This gave Carl a shock. He felt as if he could understand why he had never been sure whether Katherine was beautiful—or whether she was physically attractive to him, in spite of her elegance. While the warm, confident, luscious ease of his feeling with Gladys fitted into the breath of warm summer air that came through the windows, flaring the candles, making them aware of flowers blooming in the night outside. . . . And then, just at this point, he didn't like being obliged to acknowledge this respect for the accuracy of Lillian's perception.

Lillian had been sitting conscientiously not listening to this brief, intimate exchange between Katherine and Carl, but stiff with unhappiness. Joe played the part of the good host and came over to her. Lillian couldn't feel toward Joe as toward Katherine, because of his simplicity, although she felt that she must distrust him on account of his drinking and spending so much of his time playing golf and shooting clay pigeons. He wasn't, somehow, quite the middlewestern type of business man. He had come from Philadelphia a few years ago to manage the insurance company located in Salisbury. He had a long heavy face like the face in the bowl of a spoon, with an incongruously small, clipped mustache. He was an "eastern type." Features of a distant English ancestry had been only partially made over into an American full-faced mold. This seemed to give him a queer, heavy touch of aristocracy. Whenever Carl and Katherine were talking together, Joe felt as if he must take pains to fill the breach. But in spite of his good intentions, he couldn't keep his eyes from getting preternaturally solemn whenever he looked at Lillian, he considered her so prim and out of his line.

Katherine cried dramatically, "Joe!" She had sprung up from the couch.

He laughed in good-humored appreciation of her feminine excitability. "What's the matter?"

"Why haven't we thought of Uncle Phin before?"

Joe looked blank but ready.

"Why, Carl Ferguson!" she told him sweepingly. She looked around as if amazed at all of them. "My beloved old Uncle Phineas getting apoplexy because he can't find anyone noble enough to look after his foundation, when Carl Ferguson might just as well be doing it!"

"That's right. Be fine," Joe said heartily.

Katherine sat back on the couch, sweeping her arms around her knees and hugging herself like a witch.

"Carl, you'd love living in Philadelphia," She laughed. Lillian was sitting flushed and hostilely bewildered. "No, but I think it would be lovely! The cradle of liberty? Why don't I talk to Uncle Phin when I go home next week? Oh, yes, I'm leaving, too! Do you think I could endure Salisbury without you? Never mind, darling Joey knows all about it! But I can cajole Uncle Phin. Joey, can't I cajole him?"

"Well, I guess you can get about what you want," Joe answered good-temperedly, with the heavy business man's indulgence of this high-handed method of disposing of positions.

"Oh, I know I could! Thanks, darling, for your belief in me. That's one of Uncle Phin's beliefs. He believes in 'the young man from the West.' He thinks they work so much harder! Oh, it's almost a religious conviction!"

Katherine swept them all into excited talk—whether or not she really meant it for more than the moment. "Then whenever I went back, I'd have someone to make life happy for me. *Two* people," she said with wide generosity, just faintly infused with malice. "I'd have an excuse for not dragging out Uncle Phin wherever I wanted to go. Poor darling, he thinks he must be *so* gallant. He has the idea, you know, of the ladies of the seventies, daintily lifting their skirts in a small gloved hand and pausing fearfully at the street crossings? He *couldn't* let a lady go unescorted." In between laughter and delighted prophecies of what the change would do to Carl, she gave what seemed—to Lillian's shocked, wary susceptibilities—a heartlessly frivolous description of Uncle Phineas. "Isn't his name too perfect? And, my dear, he's just like that! Just as incredible!" It seemed to Lillian that Katherine was only making fun of them —and yet she wasn't sure. She was afraid. Uncle Phineas was a philanthropist. "Oh, yes, it's his only profession! And just as eccentric as if he'd been made to order for a mystery story." Katherine added: "Of course I'd hate to take you from Mrs. Bondy and the P. T. A. But how wealthy he could make you! I wish Joe were noble enough to suit Uncle Phin—but he isn't! Uncle Phin can afford to pay a good fat salary. I'd love to inveigle one. Oh, but it would be a blessing to him, Lillian! Poor old dear, he's wearing away under his cares, too much money to give away. He's terribly old, you know."

"Maybe Ferguson wouldn't care for the job," Joe put in. "Doesn't sound any too lively."

"Oh, yes, he would! Carl Ferguson could manage anybody. Just see what he did to the school board! And he has the P.T.A. all loving each other. No, but really, it's quite interesting. The foundation has rather a reputation, you know. You'd meet all sorts of important people."

Katherine leaned back against the cushions.

"Oh, I think I'm just too lovely to have thought of this! And how unselfish, depriving myself of my own best neighbors, out of the sheer goodness of my heart! Joey, you ring for Stanley. We must all have something to eat!" The smiling colored servant came to the door, saying "Yes, Mistuh Brinsley!" as if in expectant delight; and Katherine cried coaxingly, "Oh, Stanley—can't you bring us in some awfully nice sandwiches?" He smilingly promised. Joe got up. They ought to have a little drink on this, hadn't they? "Oh!" He looked blank. "You people don't drink, do you?" Katherine said: "Why, Joey, are you asking our superintendent to break the laws of the country? You mustn't give away our iniquity." She whispered to Lillian, pausing near her as she went out to speak to Stanley, making a confidante of her, "I don't want him to have it, anyway." She gave a coaxing little smile.

They ate sandwiches and drank ginger ale. Carl was excited by all that Katherine had said—for the time being he believed she meant it. The rest of the evening seemed to go in a whirl.

The Brinsleys followed them to the door. In the light that Joe had turned on, Katherine again looked haggard and wispy. Her curls of black hair seemed fuzzy and dry. It seemed to Carl that she was making an effort, and for the moment he felt somehow depressed. But she had turned sweet and serious, disarming him with a tired pathos.

"I really do mean I'm going to speak to Uncle Phineas. You don't believe me, do you?"

"Oh, yes, I do," he said, confused.

"I really have good impulses! And you'd be a *blessing* to Uncle Phin. I mean you really would."

Carl and Lillian started back across the driveway. Carl was

excited. He didn't know what he thought of Katherine's idea, but its novelty excited a kind of restlessness that Lillian had always fearfully felt in him.

"She's a great Katherine!" he exclaimed, laughing. "Loves to engineer things. But you have to grant that she can do it!"

He felt this last as a concession to Lillian. Her silence made him uneasy—worse than uneasy, as he saw in the glow from the corner light that she was crying. Carl was angry. But he couldn't show it. He slowed down and put his hand on her arm. They had stopped at the edge of their own walk.

"Why, Lillian, what's the matter? I thought we had a good time."

Lillian stood, struggling to get out some words. She said in a strangled voice, "I don't see why we should go there, with people so different from us."

Carl felt outraged. The tone of her voice threatened all this new promise. "Did you see anything wrong?" he demanded. "Tell me a single thing you saw that you could call wrong."

Lillian couldn't answer that. But even if the Brinsleys wouldn't drink when she and Carl were over there, she and Carl both knew they *did* drink. Lillian was trembling with the fear of rupture from all her early convictions. She didn't see what Carl could find in such people! All evening she had had to endure the smarting hurt of knowing that Carl was accepted and made much of where she was out of her element. It seemed as if all this year they had been getting farther and farther apart. In her own mind, Lillian blamed it with fierce unreason upon Katherine Brinsley. She had changed Carl! But there was a dark, lurking, helpless fear in regard to Carl himself. It was as if she stood tied, weighted and helpless in some race, and had to see Carl running ahead beyond her. And now this black threat of the future—she held back from it with hysterical fear.

She said in a trembling voice, "Well, I don't *like* people like that. . . . It seems as if they're the only kind we know now."

Carl said after a moment, in the cold, biting voice Lillian dreaded, "Well, perhaps you'd rather have seen me false to my principles of teaching and let those two girls have their careers ruined for nothing!"

Lillian had to be silent. It was what she *did* wish—with all her heart, mutely, in deepest secret—but she had stood by Carl, acting as if she believed with him, and so she could say nothing. She began to cry again, feeling bitterly that she had been false to her own principles—because it was so hard to oppose Carl. Her head was bowed with the feeling that she deserved this.

They went up the shallow steps, and across their little rough brick porch pavement, and Carl switched on the lights in the house. After the Brinsleys' living room, their own seemed sparsely furnished and uninteresting, with the small, clean, carefully rough brick fireplace in which they felt as if they could go to the expense of having an extra fire only on holidays and when they entertained. Lillian had learned her principles of housekeeping in her grandfather's home where everything must be kept sparse and spotless, and her mother had kept hidden away in the bottom drawer of the cupboard the few doilies and table runners she had embroidered, because when it came to risking Grandfather's comment on them—"Is *that* what you've been spending your time on?"—she felt she would rather have them buried out of sight. Once when Lillian had protested, mildly indignant, just home from teaching and having been out of the home atmosphere for a while, "Mother, why don't you *use* your things?"—Jennie had answered, "Well, maybe, some time . . ." That was about as near as the mother and daughter ever had come to an acknowledgment of their secret feeling toward the grandfather.

Now Carl's anger died down momentarily when they stood together in their own house. He thought that he was in the right, and yet he felt a sense of shame. He knew something of what it had meant to Lillian to say nothing of her own feelings and hold to him, comfort him, express anger at Mrs. Bondy, when he was going through all that unpleasantness.

"Katherine would like you if you would just let her," he pleaded. He put his hands on Lillian's shoulders to draw off her light coat. It made him feel badly to think it was the same coat she had worn for spring and fall for three years—although that wasn't exactly to be blamed upon him, he would have liked

Lillian to buy more clothes than she did. But it seemed unjust for her to have to compete with Katherine.

Lillian drew away. "I wouldn't like *her*," she said bitterly. "You're the one *she* likes."

"Oh, Lillian!" That made Carl furious, for some reason—perhaps its truth. He flung away. "You want no new friends, ever," he accused her. "If it was just up to you, we'd go along in the very same old rut we've been going in for years. This isn't Greensville any longer. We can't live the way we did there. You'd like to tie me down to your own little principles and keep me there!"

Lillian was white. She couldn't answer. When Carl got angry at her, she was too hurt and overwhelmed to oppose him. But neither could she speak what she thought was untruth. She could only be dumb and suffering and stubborn.

They undressed in a cold burning silence. Carl informed her that he was going to sleep down on the davenport tonight. Her frightened, wet eyes stared back at him from the bed. But then she turned over and lay stubbornly mute. Carl exulted because she lay there like that, because she did nothing to stir up his sensitive compassion. He took his clothes over his arm, and took up his shoes, and went on downstairs.

There he had the feeling that it wasn't just the visit at the Brinsleys. This had been coming anyway, forced by last night. At first he lay in cold rejoicing because they were separate. There was a menace in the way Lillian had simply turned away from him and let him go. But if she thought she could keep him from accepting Katherine's offer—if it *was* an offer, he had a qualm about that, then she was wrong! Carl was too sensitive to every influence, and knew it, but he felt with cruel exultance that Lillian was the one person who had no power over him. She was his. She loved him too well. Yet he was afraid of her hard, small, narrow integrity. That hard certainty was something that he lacked.

He couldn't stand this way of living any longer! There had to be something more—somewhere. He let himself think of Gladys Gibbs and imagine what she could give him.

He turned restlessly. He had drowsed and then been awake

again. The mahogany clock on the mantel—a wedding present—ticked loudly in that dim light. He felt the accusing silence of the house. But he crushed down his treacherous compassion. He would not go upstairs. Something had to come of this. He could endure it, because so soon they would be going home—and then somehow he could make up his mind.

2

The drive home had been pretty unpleasant to begin with. It was always hard getting started anywhere with the boys. And then things weren't right between Carl and Lillian; and the children felt that in some unhappy, fractious, undefined way.

But a different feeling began to come over Carl when they got near home. The place always looked good to him. No other house seemed to him quite so comfortable. The trees seemed bigger and the grass greener every time he saw them. He felt the warm, relaxed sense of being at home.

"Well," Carl said brightly, resting his hands on the wheel a moment, "here we are!"

The boys tumbled out of the car, dazed but eager.

"There's grandma on the porch! Which of you can be the first to say hello to her?"

This was Forrest's chance. He began to run his fastest, crying "Hello, gran'ma, hello, gran'ma," with his little feet beating hard on the cement; while James had grown so much taller and older in the last year that he was ashamed to run, or to admit that he was glad to see anyone. Forrest stumbled up the steps, his breath panting and his eyes bright, and looked back at his big brother in innocent triumph as he clung to his grandmother.

"So here they are! I didn't know you'd come for a minute—I was busy out in the kitchen. Well, he knows his grandma, don't he? Oh, and see this *other* big boy!"

They were all on the porch now. Forrest was still hugging her and shouting, "I was first, gran'ma, I was first!" while she assured him that she had seen his triumph. James turned his face so that his grandmother could kiss only his cheek. Mrs.

Ferguson kissed Carl, and then quickly reached out her hand and drew Lillian close to her, remorseful and tender because her own first feelings were with her son.

"Did you expect us sooner, mama?"

"Oh, no. I wasn't expecting at all. I just thought you'd be here when you got here. Are you tired, all of you?"

"Oh, no," Carl said robustly. "We're not tired."

Mrs. Ferguson gave Lillian a little smile of apology and comprehension for the blindness of men. She could see that Lillian *was* tired. Lillian's looks shocked her a trifle. She was trying to make them all welcome, taking the boys' caps, looking for a place to set down their bags. But Carl took her by the shoulders and held her smiling and blushing in front of him.

"Well, mama, let's see how you look. I believe you look nicer than ever."

She tried to glance with laughing, shy apology over Carl's shoulder at Lillian, and not to show quite transparently how pleased she was.

Carl meant it when he told her she looked nicer to him than ever. He remembered how he always used to feel when he was at any church or family gathering with his mother—that there was something finer, *fancier* he called it, about her always than about any of the other women. He used to adore her when she came home from a club meeting, eager and sweet and radiant in feathers and silk and gleaming opal breastpin, the scent of powder from the crowded room that she had left still clinging about her. She herself would have said that all such prettiness as she had ever had was gone. The hair that waved across her forehead was a thick streak of gray over the faded and darkened brown that underlaid it, and her figure had set in a small, elderly massiveness. But her son caught the old delicate feminine aroma as the crispness of her company apron and the fineness of her dark blue chiffon were crushed against him. There was a kind of hunger and straining in his embrace that both moved and disturbed his mother. Her eyes grew humid in her flushed face.

"That's the way *daddy* hugs grandma," Carl said to the boys when he let her go.

173

She tried to smile now. With a pretty gesture that concealed an anxious generosity, she took Lillian's hand as they went toward the stairs.

"Yes, but everyone better not, or grandma won't have any apron left. Come on, Carl. Be good. I know Lillian wants to get upstairs and get rested and washed up a little, don't you, Lillian? I'll show you all your rooms."

She went cheerfully up ahead of them, feeling gay and exhilarated now.

"I thought I'd put you in here," she said tentatively, opening Dorothy's door. "We've been using this for our guest room. The boys are going to have their Uncle Bunny's room. Won't that be fun, Forrest? Your daddy's old room? But if you think this is too far away from them . . . Margaret's room is a little closer. It's a little larger, too. But there are so many of her things still in there, and I thought . . ."

She stopped, wishing she could pierce Lillian's scrupulous reserve, and anxious to make them comfortable.

"What do you think, Lillian?" Carl asked gently.

But of course Lillian wouldn't hear to any change. The front room was all ready for them, with the curtains freshly laundered, and a bouquet of summer flowers on the table.

Mrs. Ferguson left them to get unpacked and cleaned up, and hurried downstairs to finish with the dinner. The good smells of chicken and coffee and fresh biscuits came up to them. Carl felt the atmosphere of his mother's own daintiness; and felt again, with a happy expansion of the heart, the prosperous ease and amplitude of the household. He went whistling to the bathroom, pausing to look in at the boys and to share their proud delight in having Uncle Bun's tennis racket and golf clubs. But he couldn't help answering them with a slightly satirical tone. He had an emotional attachment to this room as his own, and didn't quite like to see it furnished with so much more collegiate elegance than in his day—remembering how his young brother had chosen to go to the state university instead of to Wilson.

"Yes, Uncle Bun has lots of things!"

He scrubbed lustily with the soap and hot water—smiling as

he recognized the soap! It was the kind the folks had bought for years and years, from a lame man, "not any too bright," whom they wanted to help out because his family belonged to the church. Carl went back to the front room, with his collar open, and his face shining and fresh-colored from scrubbing, feeling informal and at home.

Lillian was bending over one of the suitcases, getting out some of the boys' clothes. There was something lonely and dejected about her attitude. It made Carl remember that now she had no home but this to go to, here in Belmond. He was ashamed of his own satisfaction.

"Can't you leave the unpacking?" he asked her.

He couldn't stand that look. It was as if she felt herself in some lonely place all by herself. Of course she wasn't! The folks thought almost as much of her as they did of him. But maybe he had hurt Lillian by the way he had greeted his mother; reminded her . . . Here in the warm home atmosphere he felt differently about everything again. He couldn't stand to have her a stranger like this, no matter how much still lay unresolved between them. To break through her isolation, he pulled her away from that suitcase and held her in his arms. She was passive and unrevealing, until finally he felt a slight, involuntary trembling. Carl pressed her more closely, silent with the sustaining, pained desire to make it up to her in this embrace, and with the secret shame that he still couldn't endure it without the admission of her old docility and devotion. Lillian tried nervously to draw away, but Carl wouldn't let her, forcing her to believe that what he had given his mother he gave her—and himself to believe it too. They could hear the cheerful sounds from downstairs.

Mr. Ferguson was somewhat late this evening. "Oh, dad's in so many things these days," Mrs. Ferguson said. "I don't know how he did get into so many." But now they heard the car out in the driveway. Forrest had to run and say hello to his grandfather—be first again.

"Well! Got here after all, did you?"

175

"Didn't you think we would?" Carl demanded, laughing, but rather sensitive beneath it.

"Oh, I thought you'd get here some time," Mr. Ferguson said mildly. "How are you? Well, Lillian, how are *you*?"

He shook hands with Carl, but kissed Lillian—and it was only on great occasions of meeting and parting that he ever kissed his own girls. His voice was hearty when he spoke to her. She responded with shy sincerity. Lillian cared deeply for her father-in-law, with an admiration that perhaps tried to make up for her own father's adult deficiencies.

Mrs. Ferguson had come to the door to tell them that dinner was ready. The table was festive with the shine of cut glass and silver and flowers.

In this light, everyone seemed to look better. The little boys were washed and brushed and shining. Mrs. Ferguson saw with a quick glance that Lillian's blue-flowered chiffon was a very nice dress, much better than any she used to wear. Well, she *should* dress well, both for Carl's sake and her own, in their position! But tonight was she actually wearing rouge? *Lillian?* Well, why on earth must she be prim—any more than my *own* girls, Mrs. Ferguson thought impatiently. But then her tenderness reproached her, remembering the subduing influence of Lillian's grandfather—the way Jennie used to think she must dress Lillian, with those two blond braids so tight they looked as if they hurt the child's tender skin, and those stiffly starched white aprons. That petal touch of pink on each pale cheek gave the illusion, in this becoming light, of Lillian's old seashell delicacy . . . that had faded out, when and how none of them knew, not Lillian herself.

Carl, his mother thought anxiously, was not quite so heavy as he had been a year or so ago. Perhaps that trouble in his school had been more serious than he would let on! His mother knew how Carl worried. But his face still had its fresh color and seemed boyishly unmarked, making him youthful in spite of the receding of his light-brown hair—especially when he took off his professorial spectacles for a moment to rub his eyes, which showed eager and bright in the pink skin before Carl put the glasses on again.

176

Carl said boyishly, "Gosh, mama, this looks swell!"

"Oh, you've seen our new furniture before. 'Tisn't so new any more, anyway."

They used this room so seldom when they were by themselves that the big polished table and the new mahogany chairs with tapestry seats had a pleasingly formal air. The prosperity which the folks had attained seemed to give a solid backing to Carl's own life. They had the best chicken that Rolfe could send them in from the farm. There was such a homemade taste to everything—Carl didn't know how else to express it. His mother never achieved the scrupulous perfection of some of Lillian's best dishes. Mama's biscuits, even tonight, came to the table all different sizes. Her ideas of measurements had always been a family joke. Whenever they talked in figures—"How big do you want your bread board, Annie?" his father would ask. "About ten by eighteen inches?"—mama's eyes would take on a funny, scared look. But just because of her innocence of all science, the things she cooked seemed to *taste* better. Nothing according to rule, they seemed to be more—well, made by hand. They were the products of a woman's cooking; and there was something personal and—to Carl—endearing in the lopsided delicious loaves and the little dishes of this or that which she set on the table. "What's this spoonful of something, mama?" his father would ask indulgently. But the biscuits, some of them runts and one a fine overgrown mountain, melted in the mouth. They were mama's cooking and no one else's.

"So Bun decided he had to have some experience, did he, this summer?" Carl asked with adult tolerance.

"Yes, I guess that won't hurt him," his father said. "Might have got it as well working in the canning factory here at home, though, if that was what he wanted."

"Well, he and Joseph thought they wanted to see the West," Mrs. Ferguson apologized. "This gives them a nice chance."

"Where is Uncle Bun?"

"Why, you know, don't you? Haven't you heard us talk about it?"

Mrs. Ferguson said with some sentiment, "Forrest, he's away

out in Colorado in a factory where they make sugar from beets. Just think of that!"

"He and Joseph have any social science hobbies?" Carl asked, still keeping to his tone of easy indulgence. "Want to share the life of the workingman?"

"Oh, I guess he isn't Bolshevist," Mr. Ferguson answered.

Carl smiled. Dad's doctrine was almost as simple as Grandpa's had been. He was hurt by any dereliction from the Republican party or the Presbyterian church, the source on the one hand of national respectability and on the other of all moral good. Carl, who ever since he had been in college had considered himself a progressive, sometimes advanced a few cautious arguments—which had helped to make his father regard him as a little unsound. And yet dad didn't think that of Bunny! Carl felt angry with the others, and compassionate and protective toward the folks for their innocent acceptance of their children's motives. He was slightly shamed and disgruntled at the idea that his young brother might be more openly liberal than himself. While Margaret, Carl supposed, liked to consider him a regular, old-fashioned, middlewestern Babbitt! But Carl could never bear to disillusion the folks in regard to some of his ideas —partly out of a sensitive affection for them, partly because of that slightly humiliating fear of his father which he had secretly carried all his life.

Carl was in a queer medley of feelings this evening. He was happy to be back at home, resting in its comfort. And then all at once he would feel a kind of revulsion toward all his old affections—a restless excitement in regard to the future. He couldn't help overdoing consideration for Lillian, as if to reassure the folks that everything was well between them.

The dessert was a fine strawberry shortcake with whipped cream. They were still getting their nice cream and eggs from the farm. "Yes, and butter too. Dad won't let Vina off from churning butter." She didn't mind it, Mr. Ferguson said. Mrs. Ferguson lifted one shoulder expressively, and made a deprecating little face at Carl. But then she hastened to say:

"Oh, well, it doesn't hurt her, dad does a lot for them. He got Rolfe out of that pickle with that oil man. Just think of those fellows going around and getting money out of poor hardworking boys like Rolfe, who haven't any education! There ought to be a law about it."

"There are laws, mama."

"Well, then, men like that ought to be arrested." Mama was quite fierce.

"Oh, they always get it sooner or later," Mr. Ferguson said. He didn't like to admit any hitch in the working out of the country's laws, under the men he had helped to elect. "That sort of business don't pay in the long run."

"Got a pretty good renter, have you, on Grandpa's place?" Carl asked.

"Yes, pretty good as renters go," his father conceded.

"It doesn't seem right not to have some of our family out there, does it?"

"Then you better turn farmer yourself, like Grandpa wanted," his father suggested with dry humor.

"Oh, my!" his mother said, with a distressed pucker of the lips. "You *have* been away a long time. How long is it, dad, since Rolfe and Vina have been out there? It's time you were spending a summer here!"

"Well, this summer we can get up on all past history."

"Yes, there've been changes," Mr. Ferguson said rather heavily, as they all got up from the table. His voice had a kind of sad pride.

"Well, Lillian, ain't you coming in here with the rest of us?" he asked.

Lillian smiled, shyly pleased that he wanted her, but said that she was going to help Aunt Annie with the dishes. The "Aunt Annie," which still seemed more natural for Lillian to use than the now proper "Mother Ferguson," came from childhood days, when Mrs. Ferguson had been Aunt Annie to Lillian, and Mrs. White Aunt Jennie to Carl and Margaret and Dorothy.

"Oh, well, I guess mama's going to have some help with those. Aren't you, Annie?"

"Oh, yes," Mrs. Ferguson said, Mrs. Entwhistle was coming. Basking in their freedom from the old task of the dishes, the problem of which of the company should help, they went to the living room to sit down in blissful ease.

Then Mrs. Ferguson said, half apologetically, "I asked your father and his wife to come over this evening, Lillian. I thought you would want to see him."

Lillian said, "Oh, yes." Her face had flushed in distress at the mention of the marriage, but her eyes had a grateful gleam.

Reassured that she had done right, and forfeited her first evening with Carl to good purpose, Mrs. Ferguson went cheerfully out to the kitchen to put the food away. Carl followed her. He said boyishly, "I thought we'd be alone with you and dad tonight, mama."

She was pleased, but said anxiously, "Well, Carl, I felt as if I ought to. I know Lillian feels badly about it, and I wanted to show her we still think a lot of her father."

"Oh, it's all right, mama," Carl said kissing her. "It was nice of you."

Her eyes moistened with pleased gratitude. Carl was the one of her children who always appreciated her little efforts!

But then Mrs. Entwhistle arrived at the back door with her apron done up in a package. She was a small, chipper, middle-aged woman, with bobbed brown hair, just turning gray, and a hard little frame of masculine endurance. She wasn't in need, as Mrs. Ferguson explained, but she was ambitious, and did what work she could get to do outside to help along her children. She looked at Carl with bright-eyed but unobtrusive and self-respecting interest.

"This is my oldest son, Mrs. Entwhistle."

"Yes, I knew that must be who he was," Mrs. Entwhistle returned, and nodded her head briskly. "How do you do? I remember him when he used to play football, but I guess he don't remember me. My sister Violet was in his room."

"Oh, yes," Carl said heartily. He shook hands. But he said to his mother as they went out through the dining room, "What Violet?"

"Oh, didn't you remember Mrs. Entwhistle? Why, Mueller, I think their name was. This one was Myrtie. We've had her to help us so much, since Mrs. Christianson died."

"I didn't know she had died!"

"Oh, yes. Quite a while ago. And Nellie and her husband are living in Mertonville. I'm afraid she didn't do so well."

They went back to the living room happy and refreshed with those few moments together. Carl now dimly recalled a Violet Mueller as one of the more lowly high school maidens who had looked up to him from afar as one of the heroes.

They were all rather uncomfortable waiting for their guests. They couldn't help thinking how different this was from the early days of Carl's and Lillian's marriage when it had been an affectionate contest between Annie and Jennie to decide which should entertain the children first. The doorbell rang. "Now you be nice to her," Mrs. Ferguson whispered, with a little poke on the shoulder, as she passed dad on her way to the door.

She felt flustered too. But she couldn't hold a grudge against Howard, as Fred did. Maybe she just wasn't as loyal—the Fergusons were all so strictly loyal within their own clan. Fred said sternly that it was no more than Howard deserved, to lose his old friends, man making such a fool of himself at his time of life. His wife said, "Oh, well, Fred." Think what it must have been, living with old Abner White! But she couldn't tell that to Fred. He had always respected Abner White, or felt that he should respect him (about the same thing with Fred!) as one of the elders of the church.

Mrs. Ferguson tried to show some of this human indulgence, to reassure them, as she greeted them at the door.

"Come in!" she cried brightly. "They got here."

Her secret compassion and tolerance, which Fred would have regarded as sinful weakness, made her feel responsible for the strange couple as she took them into the living room, after the new Mrs. White with great dignity had taken off her silk coat and allowed it to be put in the hall closet.

And they were a strange couple! That couldn't help but be felt all over again, with renewed force, when Howard came shyly trailing after this mountain of a woman into the room where his own daughter sat at home. The Whites, Howard and Jennie and their one child, had been one of those devoted families that seemed to be all of a piece and inconceivable otherwise. People had nearly forgotten that old Abner White wasn't Jennie's father as well as Howard's! Both were equally devoted and subdued. Denied any adult freedom, the parents had centered on Lillian; while she, growing up as overshadowed as themselves, even more timid and silent than her mother, and more undemonstrative, had cherished deeply, almost rigidly, a silent, mature compassion for her father, and a secret, stubborn adherence to her mother. On the surface, all three were equally reverential of the noble Christian character of "grandfather." When her mother had died, soon after grandfather's by this time unlooked-for death, Lillian (except for duty) would almost have left her own household to care for her father. Howard seemed more truly and longer her child, in her secret heart, than Forrest and James. She went about her work, when Carl was out of the house, silently weeping to think of him in those lonely rooms—cheerfully unnoticed by Forrest, who was busy at his games, but with James following her, coming finally to stand beside her and painfully ask her, "Mother, what? Grandpa Howard?" She made no answer. But she let James hold her hand and stand silently beside her.

That house of the Whites! To think of it now with this stranger woman in it—arranging Jennie's meager ornaments, the one hand-painted vase and the few doilies, in the rooms that had been funereal and bleak all these years since grandfather had been left a widower. Setting up her bright new electric stove in the kitchen where Jennie had labored over the creaking old soft water pump in the wooden sink that grandfather had put in when grandmother was ailing—and that he had still considered an almost sinfully indulgent innovation! Howard was cheerfully putting in plumbing in those spare, bleak walls, and turning Jennie's big cold pantry into a bathroom—that pantry where a row of pies had invariably stood on the papered shelf in obedience to grandfather's New England notion, sacredly inherited, of what constituted a sound meal and a decent preparation for company.

"I declare," Mrs. Morgan had said, referring to the sale of the stove and the bathroom fixtures, "I don't care how much was paid for those things, I hated to have Loren let that woman have them. When it seemed like it ought to have been Jennie!"

The Whites' house! To think of such a change coming to that place of all places! That house of tall New England spareness standing on the wide middlewestern lawn—it had seemed more indissolubly itself than any other building in Belmond. Everything was in keeping—Lillian's cool pale blondness when, as a little girl, she came shyly to open the door; old Abner White's portentous voice and Gothic beard; his long blessing at the table when he referred to the dear departed in funereal tones that made the children shudder; and the grave in the cemetery as neat and prim as the house itself, near the snowball bush that grew beside the flashing broad surface of the granite stone that marked the family lot, and said "WHITE" in large, firm, undecorated letters.

But Mrs. Ferguson felt anxiously sorry for everyone concerned, as she ushered Howard and his wife into the living room. The new Mrs. White returned the greetings with suspicious affability. Although she kept her old feeling for Jennie, Mrs. Ferguson couldn't seem to hold it against this woman, as the rest of her family did. Her tender heart couldn't help divining how it had come about. The woman had appeared in town only a few years ago, to sell dresses in Horner's new ready-to-wear, and no one knew exactly what her history had been up to that time; but that it had been none too easy for her, her made-up middle-aged face, heavy and fat, with suspicious eyes, was evidence enough. Her hair was dyed dark brown, like that of a cheap doll, and parted like a doll's wig. That dry dyed hair, and the make-up, gave away the woman's fears during so much of her life, the humiliation, precariousness and isolation of a commonplace, unmarried woman with no provision for the future. And then unexpectedly (or at least, almost at the end of hope), had come this chance to get married! To live in equality with the solid matrons of Belmond! Well, she could understand it, Mrs. Ferguson knew she could—how it was that, finally blessed with a husband after all those hungry years, and yet no doubt feeling some misgivings because she had had to help Howard along to the point a little too much, she must wrest from him in every way the constant assurance that she was a desired wife. She was second with him, while he was first with her. It wasn't any wonder that she couldn't stand the evidence of the other wife, whom people in town still meant when they said "Mrs. White," and always would. She couldn't enter into Jennie's old place in the church. People wouldn't have let her if she had tried. So Howard, all his life one of the faithful, was seen no more at the meager evening services—which, in these latter days, had dwindled down to the Fergusons, Ella and Ben, Mrs. Dunn, and Essie Bartlett when she could leave her mother. Instead, Howard had become a member of the Odd Fellows, to fit in with the Rebeccahs, among whose somewhat lowly social company the new wife had found her only chance to shine as a matron. If the Old Man White could have beheld his son as the belated member of a lodge! "He who climbeth up by any other path than the great white way is a traitor and a thief." The old man used to quote that in thundering tones when anyone mentioned the lodges; and one poor minister, Mr. Corry, seeking his one secular chance with the Masons to be a man among men, had had to leave. The new wife must have everything new. Well, Mrs. Ferguson had to ask herself conscientiously, wouldn't I want it that way too? I can understand it. And then it doesn't seem as if Fred and I ought to talk, we can't have been perfect parents ourselves, if our daughter doesn't want to stay at home with us!

But she did feel Lillian's position. Glancing at Lillian, seeing the fineness of her face (so like both her father's and her mother's that it didn't seem possible to say which she resembled) Mrs. Ferguson's motherly feeling overflowed. She thought of Lillian again as Jennie's child. The two women, Annie and Jennie, had been thrown together largely by circumstances, but the long friendship between them was seasoned by so many kind acts on each side, that it had meant almost more to both of them than if they had been just naturally congenial. So, if she herself felt this way, what must Lillian be experiencing, having to see this alien woman as her father's mate? Lillian wore no ornament except a little locket, given to her when she was graduated from high school, and hung on a fine gold chain. She was like Jennie—she could not bring herself to more display than that. The few early white hairs in the blond smoothness above her temples were barely visible in the soft evening light. But they were unconcealed. There was just that faint, telltale tint of pink upon the cheeks to reveal that her appearance was a matter of concern to her, after all.

Mrs. Ferguson ached with the desire to defend Jennie. But what defence was there, after all, for the dead? Nothing but memory.

She knew that Howard still cared for his daughter, no matter what dad said. He showed it in the vacant, uneasy, rather silly smile with which he looked at Lillian. But he was too timid to presume, or to ask for understanding. People could never make out whether Howard used to be too much under the old man's domination to dare to resent it, or whether he was naturally so meek that he liked working as clerk and handy man in their small grocery store at the end of Main Street and going to call his father whenever a traveling man came in. The new wife was the first person in Belmond to speak of Howard, with invariable dignity, as "Mr. White." Well, perhaps that did Howard good! Howard was terribly ill at ease tonight. Dad, heeding her admonition, was talking about business conditions and the weather; but he had a stern air very different from his old good feeling toward Howard as the brother in the church. And, oh, dear, when dad wanted to look stern—! And yet Mrs. Ferguson couldn't get rid of the idea that Howard was inwardly proud of his mountainous bride, in her dark blue satin and red beads, with her heavy eyebrows black and masculine above her small suspicious eyes, showing a few stiff white hairs although there was not a one to be seen in that coarse, dark brown, doll's wig. Yes, and slyly proud of himself for winning such a woman! Little skinny men often were proud of having great fat wives. Mrs. Ferguson thought:

"I believe he's kind of enjoying it after all!"

But she was guilty over cherishing such tolerant, and to her, even ribald thoughts. Because, in some ways—keeping things straight, keeping the lines simple and clear—a strict, rigid loyalty like Fred's was better than her helpless compassion.

"Well, ain't you coming over to grampa?" Howard asked Forrest, weakly smiling. He scarcely knew how to greet the boys.

Mrs. White smiled with defensive, majestic dignity, half closing her eyes.

But the boys "wouldn't make up," as Mr. Ferguson afterwards observed, commending them. Forrest couldn't understand. He couldn't accept this almost strange man as "grandpa" too. He looked doubtfully at his Grandpa Ferguson. And James understood a little too much. He permitted his hand to be limply taken, and then went over and stood beside his mother and looked at the couple, severely forming his judgment from under level, frowning brows.

"I guess they don't remember me so well," Howard said, with a painful smile.

Mrs. White sat fat and heavy in the light mahogany and cane rocker, with one foot in a painful patent leather slipper slightly extended, and from time to time delicately touched her nose with an embroidered gift handkerchief with an air of great social majesty.

Carl was the only one who seemed able to talk. His mother smiled at him, thinking how nice it was of him to make an effort to keep them all entertained, he had the same sensitiveness toward other people's feelings as she did herself.

And she was proud of Carl's looks, even in this company. He had seemed a little tired when he first arrived; but tonight, in the home atmosphere, and after the good dinner, he seemed to be in the very flush of young manhood. The slight evidences of maturity, even of approaching middle age—the receding hair, a few lines about the eyes—only added to his look of vigor, which he had gained so far without losing bloom. His mother could not help comparing him silently and anxiously with Lillian, noting that slight haggardness of the neck, and the droop of the lips when their compression relaxed. She wondered if everything *was* all right. But there seemed to be a new fresh excitement about Carl that made his mother feel buoyant.

He had to keep on talking, for when he stopped the whole conversation seemed to fall heavily and leave a desert of silence.

All the same, as he sat on the piano bench lightly drumming the wood with his fingers, and leaned forward and smiled, he was aware of a perverse, contrary sympathy for the newly married couple. And it pleased him to conceal this, and to exercise it secretly, right here with the folks.

Cake and grape juice were passed, as a mild compensation for not having asked the Whites to dinner. Forrest, with very bright eyes, watched the way Mrs. White ate her cake, delicately crumbling it before she picked up the crumbs—as if there were a regal social superiority in this method of doing it which committed her to nothing. After the refreshments were eaten, she rose; and Howard then had to rise too. There was an awkward moment.

"Well," he said to Lillian, fond and abashed, but a little reassured by Carl's attitude during the evening, "when are you coming to see us?"

"Soon," Lillian said sedately. But her face was flushed again.

"Carl, you want to come too," Howard weakly invited.

"Had a very nice evening," Mrs. White murmured with immense sedateness that seemed to conceal some mysterious feeling of offence.

The Fergusons stood politely and hospitably in the hallway until the guests had left and they could hear the noise of Howard's car outside. Lillian had gone upstairs with the boys. Carl explained it cheerfully—it was past the kids' bedtime, but she'd hated to send them up before. But his mother's eyes were stricken and conscious, and his father's innocently perturbed. Carl went upstairs himself. He took a long time washing in the bathroom. If Lillian had been up there by herself long enough, so that he could get into bed carefully as if he thought she was asleep, she would keep up the pretence with him by lying rigid and still, and his sensitive tenderness would not have to be stirred, letting him in for he did not know what.

3

Mrs. Ferguson got up the next morning happy and excited in the thought of having the house full again. She could get her own and dad's breakfast out of the way before the children came down. She reset the table on the screened side porch, and then went out to the fresh, wet garden to gather the best of the roses.

"Well!" Mrs. Morgan called over to her. "I see somebody who looks pretty happy this morning!"

When she heard someone stirring upstairs, she hurried to put a fresh tin of muffins into the gas oven.

Carl was the only one who came down.

"The kids were asleep when I looked in," he explained. "Thought we'd better let them sleep it out now and have it over with. Lillian's pretty tired. I told her not to get up for a while."

Both tried to ignore their pleasure in this chance to be alone together. It was pleasant on the side porch. They could hear the morning sounds of the street. A bird was splashing in the bird bath, minutely busy, attending to its feathers and shaking off the bright drops. Mrs. Ferguson sat down provisionally. When she saw that Carl had nearly finished his strawberries, she hurried into the kitchen calling back, "I can hear just the same," and came out with the muffins and coffee. Her feelings hovered between the desire to do everything for her son, as when he was a little boy, and pride in him as a man. It melted her heart when he still called her "mama." He, the oldest, was the only one of her children still to cling to that childish word. It sounded deliciously flattering from this fine, grown-up man.

In the intervals of her anxious waiting upon him, she told him the news of the other children. Carl answered judiciously and patronizingly in his character of the oldest; and his mother listened with respect, almost with humility—both she and dad had a great intellectual respect for Carl in his position as a superintendent of schools. Carl always had the feeling of siding with the folks against the thoughtlessness and selfishness of the younger ones. They had always seemed to do exactly as they pleased without any consideration for the folks at all. But mixed with this now, along with the old pride of the oldest child, pressed down and hidden there was a touchy uneasiness in regard to what the younger ones thought of him. Carl still felt it with a shock of ingratitude that, in spite of all his advice and persuasions, Bunny had calmly and all by himself decided that he wanted to go to the state university instead of to Carl's old college. Bunny, who used to worship all that his big brother did!—now astoundingly grown up, and an individual not at all after Carl's pattern. The university had been regarded at Wilson with a mixture of moral superiority and social awe. But now Carl, as the graduate of a small denominational school, no longer felt quite sure of himself beside his younger brother's worldly experience. He was the one who had stayed closest home. He tried to be generous and Olympian in what he said about them to the folks, tried to control the quivering personal sensitiveness that longed to put the others slightly in the wrong.

Today, however, his attitude was strangely different. With the possibility of the position in Philadelphia glowing in his mind, he could be indulgent—yes, even toward Margaret, reassuring his mother's fears, and telling her that it was natural for young people to want some experience of the city.

"But with no fresh air, and no trees or anything—so noisy, and those awful subways—it seems to me such an unnatural life. What do they get out of it?"

"Oh, other things, mama. Music, plays—and then there's the feeling of being in the midst of what's going on, you know."

"I suppose so," she said reluctantly. But they had the radio and the victrola—they could have all the music they wanted, it seemed to her, right here at home. She would feel so much better, she sighed, if Margaret would just pay them a nice visit, so they could see for themselves that she was all right. That was all she and dad would ask.

"Why don't you and dad go there?"

"To New *York?*" She looked frightened. That seemed too metropolitan for her middlewestern humility to contemplate. She was always hoping to pry dad out for a visit to Dorothy in California. But the words "New York City" overwhelmed her.

"It isn't far," Carl told her, with affectionate indulgence.

"*Dad* would think so. Well," she sighed, "I'm glad you and Lillian have such a nice place to live in, anyway."

Carl felt a pang of guilt. But now, it seemed, was not the time to say anything. Later.

"Don't you want to come out and see what we've done with the yard?" his mother asked him brightly. "Unless you'll have something more to eat?"

"Nothing more, mama. It was all fine. Nobody makes such good things."

"Why, Carl! Lillian's a *much* better cook than I am. And so was Jennie."

She showed him her flowers, and Carl listened with affection-ate interest, although he didn't really know petunias from geraniums. She wanted him to appreciate all the landscape gardener had done. The Ferguson lawn, once casual and hetero-geneous, was now combed and arranged into a replica of all the other "landscaped" lawns in Belmond, with a rose trellis, a white seat dwarfed with a high back, and the inevitable bird bath. Little bird houses, that Uncle Ben spent his leisure mak-ing since he had moved in from the farm, were set up on white-painted poles. The ladies were all making studies of birds and gardens in their clubs now. Mrs. Ferguson told Carl proudly how many varieties she had counted around the bird bath this summer. He looked with attentive interest at the improvements in which the folks took such pride. With them, anything new was taken on anxious faith as an "improvement"—and with Carl himself, except here at home. Here, he seemed to be jealous of changes. His eyes were seeking out, almost unconsciously, the old landmarks of his childhood, the big maple tree where he used to have the swing, that old funereal urn which dad still considered "a fine piece" and which the landscape gardener hadn't dared touch.

He tried restlessly to turn away from his old attachment.

"Is anything the matter, Carl?"

"Why, no, mama. What makes you think so?"

"Well—you did have a little trouble with your school, didn't you?"

"Oh, that's all blown over! You know, mama, in school

work you have to expect some of that—can't always expect everyone to agree with you. . . . As a matter of fact, I do have something to talk to you about, though."

He saw consternation—confused fear—flash into his mother's face.

"Oh, it isn't anything bad!"

"Oh, no, of course I know it isn't," she replied quickly, trying to compose her face.

They were out near the side porch now, and they sat down on the steps. Mrs. Ferguson was nervously aware of that dog from next door rooting around the lawn. That dreadful Dolly, she must always make herself a part of any company she saw around here, in her own peculiar and not very gratifying way! But at that, Mrs. Ferguson almost preferred Dolly to her owners in the rented house. In spite of her quick response, Mrs. Ferguson's heart was taut with the fear of trouble. She had known there was something—known it before Carl and Lillian ever arrived!

But it did all sound quite glowing, as Carl told her about it in his ardent, persuasive way!

"Only I thought—"

"What, mama?"

"Only that you've done so well in teaching. I'm surprised, that's all."

"Yes, but that doesn't necessarily mean I must keep on with teaching all my life. I can better myself, as well as other people."

And he went on to paint the advantages of the new position. His mother made a few little faint protests. Until she had convinced dad, she couldn't be quite whole-hearted in the approval her tender sympathy was never able to withhold from her children. The Brinsleys? Weren't those the people who lived next door? "But I thought you didn't like them very well." From what Carl and Lillian had once told her, she had got the idea of the Brinsleys as quite fast people and not very desirable neighbors. Carl was impatient at any such notion now. And, of course, if the uncle was a philanthropist—certainly that was very fine.

191

"But where would you live then, Carl?"

"In Philadelphia."

"Away off there?"

She looked frightened. It seemed for a moment as if all her children were getting away from her. She had always counted on having Carl near her. But Carl silenced her again as he told her of the advantages. It seemed as if there was nothing he didn't know about Philadelphia. What a delightful city it was, with the historic Quaker atmosphere, "a city of homes"—not like New York, for instance!—and all the old historic places she and dad could see when they came to visit. "Do you know what state has the most wild game and deer within its borders of any in the Union? Well, it's Pennsylvania! And do you know what's the finest farming country in America? No, sir, it's not Iowa. It's Lancaster County, Pennsylvania." His mother, as a good Iowan, had to be silenced with that. It seemed as if her old faiths in regard to country districts had to be overturned —if Carl was going to live in an eastern city! And as a middle-western small-towner, in spite of her faith, she was too humble to maintain her claims.

Oh, yes, she did think it was fine. It was a wonderful opportunity! What worried her, although she couldn't say it, was Carl's talk about "pulling wires" and "grandees" and a "fat salary." It didn't sound like Carl. He had always been so idealistic. Both the parents, in their prosperous materialism mixed with religious faith, had often felt humble before their son's ideals. Still, charitable institutions—to maintain those was certainly a splendid work.

Lillian—how did she take the idea?

"It'd be better for Lillian than for any of us! Just think of the advantages she would have living there—and her time to herself, as it can't be in our position. Of course you know, mama, until Lillian gets used to the idea, well, she's something like dad."

Yes, she *did* know. And why should dad be so against any sudden change? Already Mrs. Ferguson was ranged on Carl's side. Both felt a sudden overflow of eager confidence. They felt intimate and at one sitting there together. Dolly, feeling this intimacy, tried to worm her way into it, lying down absurdly on her back, revealing shamelessly the blatant sex of her dragging teats, while she seemed to be pleading, with the dull humble darkness of her eyes, to be accepted as just dog.

"Mama, now don't you think it would be fine?"

"Yes, I do, Carl. The more I think of it—just fine!"

Carl now felt happy and buoyant. His mind, relieved of part of its burden, seemed for the moment, with a false lightness, to be relieved of the whole. He was safe in his mother's approval. He felt as if he must do something about the matter this very moment. The mail man had been around, but there was the chance that something had come in since.

Everything was clean and bright along the street at this hour of the day. There was a fresh smell and a dark shine from the sprinkled asphalt. The same bunch of old codgers were settling the affairs of the nation out in front of the Globe Hotel. Carl gave them a genial salute, which they doubtfully returned, wondering who *this* could be. "Ain't that a Ferguson? Yeah, I believe he's one o' Fred Ferguson's." Here in Belmond, Carl felt completely at ease with the knowledge of his own successful career and the background of the folks and their good standing. He wore no hat. The air was good, the alternation of sunshine and shade. Full summer heat hadn't arrived yet.

Carl stepped briskly into the post office. He felt a return of the old sense of pleasure and importance in working the combination of the big, official-looking lock box which his father and Richard Spencer rented in partnership.

"Well! Hello, Carl! Glad to see you with us again."

"Hello, Mr. Goodrich. Thanks. Don't happen to have any mail, do I?"

"Lessee. Nope, don't believe you do, Carl."

He hadn't really expected to hear from Katherine so soon.

Every local greeting gave him a slight pang of unreasonable remorse against which he had to harden himself. And yet, perversely, one of the pleasures in deciding not to go back to Salisbury was the knowledge of the shock it would give the people who were counting on him. "Oh, I'm not such a fixed quantity!" he muttered in his own mind—addressing Margaret, his bright young brother with all his brand-new ideas, perhaps Lillian. . . .

He believed he'd stop in at the bank a minute and say hello to the folks there.

He almost started to go into the *old* bank before he thought! He was not used to thinking of dad here in this new building in semi-classical style that occupied a whole corner. But it gave him the feeling that everything was going ahead, expanding, and he must keep up and go beyond the folks here. He went into the big light room, almost sultry in its sunniness, with the hard sound of feet on the tiled floor, the sharp tap of a woman's heels. Carl was proud of his new school building—but here was dad in this modern bank! Carl hadn't yet got accustomed to the idea of the old bank staff in this place. But he saw Richard just stepping through the low mahogany swinging door, natty and up-to-date and not much older, the same light figure and the jaunty face with the shiningly brushed hair and untrustworthy gray eyes. Richard fitted at once into this new building. Belonged here! He had always been a trifle incongruous in the old place, that narrow long room, the counter and the grilling and the woodwork all with an 1880 massiveness that somehow kept the sense of the heavy retail reliability of old Mr. Spencer.

"Well, well! We see you once again."

"Once again," Carl said lightly.

He felt a pleasant confidence with Richard now. He no longer had to think of dad as working for the Spencers. Dad had long got past that in reality, and now, as vice-president, with a little swinging door of his own, it was openly acknowledged. He was in a way more solidly well-to-do than Richard himself, for the "young Spencers," as they were still called, might always be called, were spenders. Dad had the confidence of more people. There were a good many, not just the old farmers any more and the church people, to say "they'd rather have their dealings with Fred." Dad had been gathering a kind of slow, solid, underground authority.

"Like the new building? Pretty big improvement, isn't it?"

Richard had now that jaunty, eye-to-eye, confidential

B.P.O.E. manner that he employed with customers and never used to waste on a kid like Carl. But the Ferguson family had come a long way since the old days when they had been the business but not the social associates of the Spencers, when mama had always maintained that she didn't care about going to Ethel Spencer's luncheons, they were too elaborate, but had taken note of them in the paper just the same. Richard respected the superintendent of schools in a Wisconsin town of twenty-five thousand—a "good town."

"Well, you'll find the old man somewhere around here."

Carl looked around and finally saw his father. The new glasses and the clean-shaven face did something to fit dad into the place, along with the heavy, indeterminate, business man's bulge that wrinkled his vest. For years, in spite of being in the bank, dad had kept his old farmerlike, hardworking leanness. He had the tall, rawboned, ancestral frame of a man who was "meant to be thin," as Grandma Ferguson, in justification of her cooking, used to say of Grandpa. There was a certain rusticity that he had never lost, just as he had kept a few homely turns of speech; but now it seemed to Carl that dad had come to look almost more like the other business men around town than like himself. Carl recognized this look as combining middlewestern wrinkled easy-goingness and prosperity.

"Hello there."

"Hello, dad."

"Well. What can I do for *you?*"

That used to be dad's chief joke when mama or any of the children came to the bank. But he said it now with a gratified respect for his son's affairs.

"Oh, nothing," Carl answered. "Just thought I'd stop in and see the place."

"Um. Well—think it's pretty nice?"

"Pretty nice, all right."

Mr. Ferguson looked around with strict noncommittalness. "Did you speak to Richard?"

"Yes, I saw him just now."

"Guess Ray's out just at the present. Well. Look around. Make yourself at home. Got any check you need cashed?"

"No, I guess I'm pretty well fixed for the present."

"Better wait a while and ride home with me."

"No, I guess I'll walk. See how the kids are coming along."

An old fellow who was laboriously turning over a packet of notes at the counter, wetting his thumb for each, looked around, frankly curious.

"This one of your boys, Fred?"

"Yes. He's my oldest. Don't you remember Carl?"

"Oh, Carl! *Oh*, yes. Ben away quite a while, ain't he? I know the young one better. *He's* a nice young felluh."

"Sure," Mr. Ferguson said, with a touch of his dry face-tiousness, "that's the only kind I'd have."

"That's right, that's right," the old fellow spluttered. He still stared with open interest at Carl.

Carl smiled and moved away. In the midst of his satisfaction in dad's new establishment, he felt a sad and shifting sense of transitoriness. Even Belmond didn't stay quite the same! There was no longer quite the old retail, small town familiarity of the other bank, with all its material disadvantages that furnished the staff with the intimacy of local jokes—the poison fly paper that they kept in the window and that one big old bumbling fly they could never catch; the primitive toilet facilities of the early days, the planks leading out to that tipsy old privy that Carl and Harry had set out to guard one Hallowe'en, armed with baseball bats. "A dollar a piece, boys," Richard told them magnificently, "if I find her standing in the morning." Ray used to say, "Wait a minute, Carl. Give you the change later." Screwing his face appropriately. "Got to walk the plank."

Dick was the one he missed! It wasn't "the bank" without Dick. He had died just in time, really. That was what Mrs. Ferguson had said with compassion. He never would have done for the new place. He couldn't have coped with such magnificence! Dick had been a figure for as long as they could remember in the lives of the Ferguson children. And yet he had a mystery about him! Other than that he held some sort of unrecognized relationship to the Spencers, people didn't know just who he was. It had pleased the Fergusons to try and figure out how close the relationship was, in the days when Ethel Spencer used to come smilingly, in her fragrance and furs, for her yearly ten-minute call on mama, graciously considering that sufficient condescension, leaving her engraved card— "Mrs. Richard Boardway Spencer"—in the hand-painted dish in the hall. "Well, I wouldn't get so stylish," dad used to declare, when he saw Richard jauntily stepping past with the only cane possessed by a young man, purely for ornament, in Belmond. "I wouldn't get so stylish that I couldn't acknowledge my own kin!" At another time—and this had greatly impressed the children with the mystery—dad had observed drily, nodding toward Dick who had just left, "Guess that's the reason Richard has to get up on his high horse when anybody calls *him* Dick!" The Fergusons had always been good to Dick, accepting him as a charge like the poor members of their own church. The children had always talked to him when they went to the bank. Dorothy, declaring that she liked Dick better than Richard Spencer, he was nicer, had once presented him for a Christmas gift with one of the little booklets tied with baby ribbon and adorned with water-color roses and noble sentiments from Longfellow that they had just been making in her room at school. Years afterwards, Dick had brought that out and showed it to Mrs. Ferguson, when she went to his room in the shabby old boarding house to see him in his last illness —he announcing proudly, with the failing breath that whistled through his remaining tusks of teeth, "You tell Dor'thy I still got her little book!" Now Carl missed old Dick's cackling welcome. "Well, I see you ain't President yet!" He had never let that old joke die. "Well, sir," he had promised, sputtering and cackling, "I'll cast *my* vote for ye!" . . . and now another election was coming, and the Grand Old Party would have to make out without Dick's vote! "Well, I guess I'll cast my vote for the G.O.P. same as always," Dick had invariably ended by saying, having weighed all the candidates. "We're all of us Republicans here in the bank."

Carl wanted the old things to hold him—he wanted to get away from their hold.

Now it was too hot on the street. He wished he had worn

his hat. The earlier pleasant fresh aspect seemed to have evaporated with the damp from the sprinkling, changing into the wide anonymous dreariness of noon heat. Where did all these young girls come from, that seemed to be parading the streets? Carl resented them because they weren't the ones he had known, they were since his day. Yet he felt a tingling of full-blooded pleasure at the sight of those fresh bare foreheads and round bare arms and legs in the full blaze of the sun.

Someone behind him was calling, "Hello, Carl Ferguson!"

He stopped. He didn't recognize this youngish woman. "Don't you know who this is?" She gave a dimpling smile. "Mildred Summers?"

"Why, of course!" But that wasn't her name now?

Oh, no, her name was Mrs. Allen. "I married Gardner Allen. You remember him?"

Of course he remembered her now. He remembered that little manner—that shrug toward him, almost a cuddle, with the sidelong look from the eyes. Pleased, he felt nevertheless a shock of disappointment. He didn't believe he had seen Mildred since she was a little girl in high school—she had stayed fixed in his memory at just that particular stage. Now, although he saw her as a young matron who seemed not by any means to have given up her pretensions to attractiveness, the girlish roundness by which he had once been so taken was in visible process of settling down into a fixed and rather broad-beamed heaviness. But in spite of Mildred's coarsening loss of early bloom (the dimples that were just on the verge of deteriorating into mere folds in dry, middle-aged skin, the general look of sloppy, let-down, spreading comfort of the woman who has made her marriage and considers her life work accomplished), there was a good deal of pleasant consciousness between them. It was flattering to perceive how well each had remembered the other. And all these little cuddling mannerisms, brought out and accentuated by this meeting with an early admirer, left Carl with a certain tingling of male affability!

Yes, he did remember Mildred Summers! And to meet her just at this moment had something almost like fate! A strange, dreamlike sense of repetition came over Carl. He used to see his life going straight ahead of him all in one direct line. But now he knew with excitement that it held more elements intertwined in its pattern than he had ever admitted. He saw these two kinds of women, repeated in his life, giving him a queer sense of destiny. He could put Mildred Summers and Gladys Gibbs together, as representing to him one kind of attraction, and then Katherine and Nina Cunningham (with whom he had been infatuated for those brief, heady days at the end of his Senior year in college) represented another. In both kinds he felt the tingling intoxication of danger. But there had always been—there still was—the firm, narrow, old-fashioned, central stability of Lillian in his life.

But now it seemed as if Carl understood better why he must get away and get out of all this. None of these other elements in him had ever been given full play. He had tried always to squeeze them into that fixed, straight line! He used to condemn Margaret for the way she simply went out for what she wanted, fierce and intent and absorbed in her own privacy, telling the folks nothing and then being angry with them because they didn't understand her! But he saw a good many things now that he hadn't seen. Oh, there was so much he wanted to strip off—that he had outgrown! And he never could do it here, in the old atmosphere. He cared too much for the folks. He must get away where they couldn't know, where he couldn't hurt them. It seemed as if Katherine's half-flattering mockery had left him smarting under his tortuous self-deceptions. And then Gladys . . . the lusciousness of the white neck and the helpless softness of the golden hair trained into a callow attempt at fashionable lacquered stiffness, in scallops above the round white forehead . . . he seemed to get a sudden blinding glimpse into the possibility of new delights—as once before, long ago. . . . Off there away from the folks, with all the ties cut, it seemed as if he could make a new start—at last could begin to find, could be, himself.

4

Carl had been keeping Katherine's letter in his pocket until his mother was safely out of the house. He had read it through once out on the porch beside the mail box; but he felt as if he couldn't say anything about it to the folks until he himself knew what he thought of Katherine's proposal. He smiled at his mother. But his heart was thumping. She was in her pretty dark blue chiffon, going to a meeting of the Garden Club.

"Want me to run you over?"

"Oh, no, it's over at Mrs. Viele's, just a step. I wish Lillian felt like coming," she said anxiously. "We have such nice meetings."

"Well, the rest'll be better for her."

When his mother had gone, Carl took out the letter again. Days had gone by, and it hadn't come, justifying the slight, reticent expression of scorn on Lillian's face, condemning Carl for his easy hopefulness and credulity, making him afraid that he had spoken to the folks too soon, and ashamed that he could never keep things safely to himself, like dad, and Lillian.

Now, as he read the letter through again, in the shaded afternoon quiet of the living room, he felt a jubilant recklessness rising. He saw on what a flimsy basis Katherine had made her suggestion, and how near Lillian was to being right; but a secret smile curled his lips at the perception that Katherine wanted him to be in Philadelphia, and was going to push it through somehow, no matter what wires she had to pull. Evidently she was determined that Uncle Phineas should give him something. Why? Caprice, maybe. Meddlesomeness, as Lillian had once said. A desire to try what she could do with a man so different from herself—to make some kind of bond between them. Carl's eyes had a sparkle. Well, let her try her game! He had always the protection of her lack of physical attraction for him. But the sight of that characteristic writing, dashing and fantastically looped, only a few words to a page, so easily and capriciously extravagant—cowed him slightly, and made him with a sort of inward blush accept Katherine's careless implication that of course he would do anything rather than go back to the absurd, petty limitations of his old position in a town like Salisbury.

He knew what objections Lillian could make to the letter,

and they simply hardened him. He felt as if he had to have it out with her at once.

He ran upstairs, stood outside the bedroom door for a moment of secret indecision, then turned the doorknob.

"Lillian? Asleep?"

She was lying down. Carl felt secretly impatient at the sight of her depressed pallor and her worn thinness. She didn't need to look like that! If there was something amiss in their situation, a good share of it was her fault, for always *being* like this. It made his decision still more stubborn.

"This came this afternoon."

He tossed the letter onto the bed, trying to act unconcerned, and angry because he couldn't keep a barely controlled excitement out of his voice. He was hardly ignoring the marked intimacy of the tone, as if anything that Katherine wrote him Lillian might read. While she was looking over the letter, Carl strolled to the window and stood with his hands in his pockets looking out at the green treetops.

He heard the crackle of the thick, stiff pages being smoothed out and turned—between, stillness.

"Well?" he said, when he couldn't stand it any longer. He came back to the bed.

Lillian was lying there now with the letter in her hands. Then she laid it carefully down on the bed.

"Sounds pretty good, doesn't it?" Carl said carelessly.

She made no answer.

"If I go," he went on, with that barely controlled excitement, "it'll have to be just as quickly as I can get away. It's better to get there while Katherine's still in Philadelphia." He said that hardily too. "There are only a few more days before I'll have to let them know in Salisbury."

As if Lillian didn't know that as well as he did! Carl felt an exultance at the thought of the shock that he was going to give Salisbury. He was fired with eagerness to start immediately—to throw everything else behind him. He had felt plenty of moments of cold doubt and retreat while he was waiting for the letter.

"Well, why don't you say something?" he asked Lillian impatiently. He accused her, "You thought Katherine didn't mean it, didn't you?"

Lillian wasn't able to answer that. She said after a moment, seeming to move her lips with difficulty, "I didn't . . . think it would turn out just this way."

Carl demanded indignantly: "How did you think it would turn out? You never would give them credit for being decent to us! They tried their best, both of them, to be nice to us, and you always held back. Not everyone would have taken the trouble Katherine has!"

Carl knew how much was being ignored when he said that, and he rejoiced in it.

Lillian again had no reply. Carl moved around restlessly. He pulled open the bureau drawer to see what clothes he would have to pack. Why didn't Lillian come back at him if she didn't like it? His heart was swelling with a hurt, stubborn indignation at her silence. Resentment against her was growing in him with invigorating warmth. He moved briskly because of it.

Then he saw Lillian lying with her eyes wide open, her face fixed in an expression of hopeless distress, the tears almost silently running down her cheeks.

"Well, *Lil* . . . lian!"

He was halted.

He protested, "What makes you take it like this?"

All these weeks she had known that this was possible. They had even spoken of it with the folks! Of course she had shown that she didn't like the idea; but never had she really said a word. Carl spoke in a tone of helpless exasperation. And as he stood there looking at her, suffering her queer pent-up agony in lonely silence, not making a move to keep him from doing what she hated, Carl felt rush over him the whole flood of his indignation against her. She was always holding him back, clinging to fixed ways—with the bowed head that seemed to express her devotion to him—and then, with all that, her physical unresponsiveness. It was simply too much. She had brought this on herself.

"Oh—good God!" The coat that he had taken up, Carl threw from him—it lit in a grotesque heap on Dorothy's small enameled chair. "I might have expected this. Whatever I want to do, that isn't just what I've always done before—there you are, pulling backwards! Did you ever do anything but pull backwards?" She was still mute. "Why don't you *say* something, then?"

He kicked a little shoe of Forrest's that was lying on the floor bang against the satiny, rosy-striped wood of the cedar chest, feeling a hot pleasure when it struck.

Lillian still lay with eyes open and staring at the wall. But at the sound of the shoe hitting the wood, she gave a start and a nervous shuddering. She flung back her head, as if to get rid of something, and then turned over and her hands clutched the pillow in straining appeal. Words struggled breathlessly at last through her frozen silence.

"Oh, I can't go there! I can't!"

She began to sob.

Carl stood with the heat of anger pulsing in waves inside him. But in spite of himself, he couldn't wholly withstand the appeal of her clutching hands. Although it wasn't to *him* they appealed,—Lillian would never so far forget herself as to do that! It was always to some lonely, secret aid outside somewhere.

"Oh, Lillian. What makes you take it like that?"

Carl came over to her. He wanted to take hold of her hands. Instantly she tried to be still, to crush and hide herself again, let her suffering escape only in shuddering quivers which she couldn't stop. Carl felt a mixture of exasperation, bafflement, pity. He knew guiltily that the tone of Katherine's letter was equal to a sweeping ignoring of Lillian; and that all the inducements she had given—with that delicate malice!—were the very things that would drive Lillian away. But Carl was halted and shocked. He had counted on Lillian's reserve and her silent docility, on her caring so much for him that she couldn't set up opposition.

Lillian tried to draw her hand away. She couldn't seem to yield herself to his comfort, ever! Carl felt that with a queerly mingled sense of hurt resentment and guilt. She wasn't satisfied until she had pulled herself away from him entirely and

203

was lying huddled by herself, her stockinged feet looking un-
clothed and helpless, and tears brimming from under her closed
eyelids. But she was tight and hard against him. The slight
warmth of reconciliation between them on their return to Belmond was now all gone and they were further at odds than
when they had left Salisbury—had really been going opposite
ways, Carl felt, all this time.

He tried to argue with her, knowing half-guiltily how many
times he had overcome her this way—it was so hard for her to
talk, to have any give-and-take. "Look here, Lillian, you have
the wrong idea about this. You know, you're like dad, afraid
to try anything just because it's new. It isn't the thing itself.
There isn't anything against that. What could there be? There's
everything for it. Even the folks think so!"

She had no answer for that.

"There's no power to say I must keep on in school work all
my life! You act as if I'm turning my back on all the decencies,
if I leave it." He saw her slowly flush. She *did* think he was
turning his back on the decencies—but not in just the way he
said. "Why, it's crazy!"

He had worked himself up to virtuous indignation. Lillian
finally managed to get out, through trembling lips, "I don't
want to go there."

"But you don't know anything about it until you've been
there. You wouldn't hold me back, would you, because you're
afraid to move a few miles away from the place where you
were born?"

Lillian couldn't say anything to that. How could she?—for
it was all pent up in her, smothered by her reticence, what Carl
knew and yet slid over with his fine-sounding reasons and
arguments, what her silence was begging him to understand
—begging not to be taken at its own value. The words said
themselves in her mind. But she couldn't make them be spoken.
They seemed to come to nothing on her tongue . . . I can't
go there, not among those people, I don't belong there, you
know it—we're getting apart as it is, oh, then we'd be farther
than ever . . . oh, don't you *see* . . .

"It . . . that isn't it . . ."

Carl said, his voice hurt, mocking and virtuous, "Yes, I know you don't like Katherine!" Lillian gave a shudder of protest. "You aren't willing to acknowledge she's friendly to us in this. It's because *she's* doing this for me. That's the trouble. I know it well enough. Isn't it?" he demanded.

Lillian cried in a strangled voice, "No, it isn't! If it was . . . if I thought I could do it . . ." I wouldn't let *her* stand in the way, was what she wanted to protest. Not her or anybody! The very word "Katherine" made a wound in Lillian's mind, but she would crush down jealousy for Carl's sake! She had done it before. She had seen the conscious manner in which teachers, for instance, went out of their way to speak to her on the street. And then there was a woman in the choir in Greensville who was always having errands at the house. It seemed to Lillian as if she had told it now, and Carl must understand and help her out. He wasn't admitting her side. He was making her seem smaller than she was, in order to make his point. That shamed her with its falsity.

"Oh, yes, it is! What makes you pretend? You've hated her right along."

It seemed to Lillian as if everything in her was strangled at that tone! It had a cold fire in it. She had never heard that from Carl. This battle was real! And she was bound, and couldn't fight.

Carl walked away. He felt himself innocent in regard to Katherine, and bitterly angry in that innocence. But down underneath it was the private, sweetly guilty knowledge of his feeling toward Gladys Gibbs, that no one had suspected—unless it was Miss Chisholm—Carl had a fleeting, worried memory of her tight, thin face. But Lillian knew nothing—nothing of her real enemy! She could only feel in him a change. All at once, that made Carl sorry for her. She was beaten, anyway, fighting the wrong battle. He felt, and yet with pleasure in the shame, his own secret tortuousness.

He began to protest about Katherine, in a reasonable, persuasive tone. There were things about her that he didn't care for, any more than Lillian. But why look at the matter so personally? It was the position itself, wasn't it? And he wasn't crazy about returning to Salisbury after all this rumpus. It would mean a constant fight, now, with Mrs. Bondy and her gang! And then the school was built. What more could he do there?

Lillian seemed to listen. She knew she *was* jealous of Katherine—although not just in the way Carl thought. How could she feel right toward the kind of influence that was pulling him away from their old life together, the feelings and convictions they had shared since they were children—abetting Carl's restlessness, "changing" him? Lillian had thought that coming back home to Belmond, being with Carl's father, would somehow steady Carl again!

And then . . . she just couldn't go there. All the words Carl said were thrown away beside that fact. Even in Salisbury she had come to the limits of possible change—had strained herself beyond the mold in which she was cast, trying to live up to the life *there,* which was already changing beyond her. Yes, she did still wish they were back in Greensville or Lorraine! In the depths of her reserve Lillian felt intuitively much of what Carl expected from the change, and she couldn't pretend to accept it. Her hard rectitude was ashamed of his own specious arguments sliding so brightly over the hidden yet deeply known truth—the arguments sounded so good, so unanswerable, that when she spoke they could make her disjointed, irrelevant-sounding bits of the truth unreasonable, unfounded, just sounding on the air with nothing to rest on and only her own feelings to back them up. It was an agony in every nerve to owe the new opportunity and the very money they must live on to the woman she felt about in such a way. And then she thought she saw what Carl didn't—that Katherine was only half in earnest, that it was an idle meddling in their affairs, an idle woman who called her living room a "studio" and had a husband who was better to her than she deserved. Katherine was amused and curious inside. It was a flirtation with Carl, an interest in his fresh-faced comeliness and personal attraction (which it seemed to Lillian no one could resist). Lillian felt herself both deeply scornful and deeply afraid. There was always something in Carl, something she feared, because she couldn't follow . . . there were those other times, long ago, when he used to go to the library at night to meet Mildred Summers, when they were in high school here in Belmond—he had thought Lillian didn't know about it, but all the time she was agonizedly aware. She had seen the little signs that gave him away and that he had no idea she could notice—a look exchanged between him and Mildred across rows of seats in the old assembly room. It had all been made up. But Lillian had kept the memory and the pain with others in her deeply hidden, small horde—the memory of a girl with glinting eyes and sunlit hair on the campus at Wilson. . . .

Besides, now . . . why couldn't she say it? It was killing her unsaid.

"I can't go there. I can't . . . get through with it."

Lillian panted and flung out her hands in strangled appeal.

Carl was alarmed and wouldn't admit it. He tried in a slight panic to calm her. "Why, Lillian, yes, you can." He tried to speak firmly, sensibly. "You take change too hard. You make it mean too much."

She wasn't even listening. Now Carl felt anger blaze up in him joyfully! If she wouldn't answer him, then he would tell her!

"I'd never get anywhere if you had *your* way! You didn't want to leave Greensville to go to Salisbury—or Lorraine to go to Greensville! Why shouldn't I be interested in Katherine? A woman with more than two fixed ideas! I don't care what little pattern she doesn't hold to. The world isn't like that any more—and you'd better find it out!" Now he was started and swept on with reckless, heady joy. If this took him from her —very well, it would have to be the parting of the ways. "You needn't think, Lillian, no matter what you do, you can hold me forever to one little mold! I've grown beyond that." He felt his spirit beating against her. "Long ago, if I'd admitted the truth. I've got to have a chance for change and I'm going to have it. The world isn't all of a piece. I'm not going to cramp myself forever inside your limitations! The way you want to make me. You want to keep me there." At that he was sobbing. Through sobs he shouted. "Like my friendship with Katherine or not like it! You can just get over some of your ideas. I'm not going to throw all this aside because you're afraid and years behind the times. Don't you think it. I'm not GOing to!"

Carl flung out of the bedroom and clattered down the stairs. Sobs still thickened his throat and he was breathing hard. He was glad, glad he had said it! He hadn't known how long all this had been accumulating! All her little cramping fears—he thought, I won't put up with them any more! He didn't care whether Lillian had said what she wanted to or not. He was aware of things unspoken. Still, he thought he knew what it all was, better than Lillian herself! Carl was seething with hot restlessness. He had the sense to know that he couldn't write to Katherine in that mood. And although he joyously let himself hate Lillian now, he still felt her too close to him to give her away to Katherine. But he had to do something for relief. He got into his car, which was standing near the alley, ignoring the two boys who immediately came running from their pup tent which the folks had let them put up in the back yard. "Dad, where you going? Can I go, dad?" He flung at them, "Tell grandma or grandpa if they ask—" it gave him a cold, burning joy to ignore Lillian—"I've gone over to Merton to see if my tire's ready."

It was a joy to drive at this hot, fierce, whizzing speed. Carl felt as if all the old limitations were off. He didn't care now. A few nights ago, when they were taking Essie Bartlett out for a drive, they had had a flat tire and he had left it at the garage in Mertonville, to go after it later.

He drove to that garage now, and waited as they put on the tire. As he walked about a little, he took a scornful pleasure in the flat, local bleakness of this burg, the garage with the litter of old car machinery on the vacant lot next it, the meager line-up of store buildings that constituted Main Street. Lillian might like him to come here! There would be no effort involved—she could have him safe—they could live as folks had done forty years ago!

He took the car and drove off, hunting out the unpaved side roads, brown and rutted and humped in the middle, so that the car drove tilted. He wasn't ready to go back. Let Lillian think about what he had said to her. Let the folks know that there was trouble. The kids—he didn't care. Something in him belonged to himself! As he kept on, the seething calmed down into a fixed heat of determination that was symbolized by his fierce, controlled, on-and-on driving of the car, turning abruptly into side roads when he felt like it.

He was not going to be held by her limitations. Now Carl felt that the limitations were all Lillian's. In himself, there seemed to be boundless possibilities. There was nothing fixed, nothing settled—there never had been. Was that the guilty secret he had always held? The source of his irony with Bun and Margaret? But now he had the courage of that lack of inner rectitude. And at last, by a drastic move, he would break out of an attitude of provinciality he no longer believed in, a dead letter he must still be upholding against the younger ones, who had gone their own ways. They seemed not to be held by the things that had held him—that were fixed and firm in his early childhood, but already changing in theirs. When Carl was a child, the old local spirit was still unmitigated. He had memories of himself, a little bright-cheeked boy in ruffled homemade shirt and tight pants, being dragged along hanging to his parents' hands to church meetings in the evening, when the church air was close and mingled chilly and hot, a smoky drowsy smell of wood from the big iron stove. Those early days had entered into his blood. The long drone of the Presbyterian hymns—

"The Lord is my Shepherd,
I—I shall not wa-ant"—

before all the Protestant hymnals began to be mixed and indistinguishable and Sunday Schooly—no other hymns had ever sounded quite right. He felt his head resting against his father's arm; he felt himself lying and playing with his mother's wrinkly kid gloves and folded handkerchief, felt the brown slickness of the mink muff Aunt Louie had sent her, so much nicer than any the other ladies wore. He thought of staying at the farm, driving out with Uncle Ben on Friday after school, sitting with Grandpa and Grandma in the dining room on

Saturday evening helping them to study their Sunday School lesson. Their pride in his brightness! "How do you find the verses so fast? Why, you beat Grandma and Grandpa all to pieces!" And then once sitting with all the folks in the parlor out at the farm, after Aunt Jane's funeral, where the close heated air struggled through the closed-up chill of months, the smell of woollen winter clothes, the interest of listening to the talk of the older people, drinking in their reiterations— "Yes, sir, I hope I'm as well prepared when it comes my time to go" . . . Things they said floated in the air, distant to the little boy, solemnly meaningless—death, age, religion, God— but the rhythm of them was deep in his blood where he couldn't get it out. He and Lillian sat together, and he felt the ribbed woollen thickness of their winter stockings, and the clumsiness of their buttoned shoes. These were days when Carl was inno- cent of all life outside his own family, when his own church was just "the church," when he simply couldn't believe in the reality of any other existence. Anything else was no more true than a storybook. It was he who knew these things earlier, more deeply, than any of the younger ones; and always he had felt bound by a jealous loyalty to what they had never compre- hended.

Part of him was closed in that early life. Yet had it ever been himself? Still listening, taking in, loyally repeating . . . had he ever done anything more?—unable to stand the severed pain of growing beyond the roots of his early affections. Some- times it seemed as if he clung more tightly than the folks themselves—because he saw beyond, and they didn't. He had lived in that innocence until he had come to Salisbury—making up by the closeness of his hold on the old ideals for the loosen- ing of the younger ones, always between the folks and them, feeling the pull of the one side, held by an old affection, half childish and half protective, to the other. What more had his marriage to Lillian been? And then the shock—to think one saw things so clearly, in right and wrong . . . and then, at another turn of the road, to look back, to see that old decision as mere confused and immature helplessness and pliability under the force of circumstance!

He wasn't going to be held back any more. The shell was broken now, except for old attachment. He knew there was a world outside—it wasn't a myth, to be laughed down, as he had actually supposed! Now he had to come to actual terms with it—trust himself at last to danger. All the things that he had held away from—luxury, secularity, money-making, splendor—had now suddenly become real to him in an overpowering vividness. No matter what the others thought of his seeming change of front—Margaret, her scornful laughter . . . Carl smarted in anticipatory sensitiveness. But if he cut the old ties he would no longer have to suffer that touchy fear regarding himself. He wouldn't need to be afraid of being left behind. He would lose that old guilty terror of worldliness. There were untouched powers in himself that the younger ones didn't give him credit for. He had more than any of them.

He passed a big farm. The buildings lay low and scattered, the rich land sloped, and the oak trees were full-foliaged. Carl thought of Gladys. He had always tried to sneer at what he roughly called "those Freudian ideas," fearful of their somehow touching upon himself, putting them off in the class of things that Margaret and her friends fell for. But now he felt some thrust of bitter truth. That old boyish affair with Mildred Summers, for instance, he all at once saw in a different light. He pitied himself, his own crude boyish confusion and blindness. So anxious to do right! Oughtn't something to be credited to him for that?—or did it simply make him out a fool? He richly pitied himself again. And he remembered how, when he was a very tiny child, he used to follow the folks about, pleading anxiously, "Carl good boy! Carl good boy!" But now life was what he wanted—all that he had put aside in his pliant ignorance. Life was what lay all around him! If Lillian couldn't give him that response, then she couldn't. But why should he be doomed to miss it?—and forever to crave what he had missed, thwarted, unfired, defrauded, left out in some cold sparse waste land.

There was a grove at the side of the road, and a gate a little open. He left the car tilted half in the ditch, and squeezed in through the fence and went along the scarcely marked old wagon road. Then he came to an opening, some old picnic place, with a few paper plates scattered through the long shiny grass. He ached all through with that half-sweet, piercing want of life. The summer day throbbed with a rich hot sensuality. Carl lay down on the grass. The sun burned his upturned face. He couldn't go to Gladys—that was impossible, he hadn't the courage—and anyway, she was too rustic, too innocent. It was only what she brought before him. He felt the living richness all around him, the dampness of the deep soil packed with the earthy life of worms and bugs, the smell of the grass, the heavy-leaved trees, the birds, and the teeming hum of insects in the hot air.

5

It was dinner time when Carl got home. Mrs. Morgan had evidently been on the lookout for him. Now she came over.

"Say, the folks have been waiting for you! They're all invited over to Mrs. Viele's for supper. I said I'd send you when you showed up."

Carl said quickly and effusively, "Oh, thanks!" It was a relief not to have to face them at home and explain things. And then he had been afraid of how he might find Lillian. But if she'd gone over there, it couldn't be so bad.

He hopped into the car again and drove over to the Vieles'. The familiar neat square porch, with its flower boxes, in the six o'clock light, brought back a comfortable sense of the commonplace, and helped to steel him to meet gaily the inevitable comments.

"Well! What became of *you?*" . . . "Almost thought you were going to lose out on these good things." . . . "About made up our minds you'd skipped the country, Carl."

Carl laughed, put his hand on Forrest's shoulder as the little fellow instantly made for his father, and explained about the tire. Lillian was sitting in a corner of the davenport. Carl's eyes tried to avoid her, while he was all keyed up to make the others think that everything was as usual. There had been such a small meeting, Mrs. Viele was saying, and so many of the refreshments left over, that she had thought "you Fergusons" might just as well come over and help eat up the sandwiches. It might not be much of a supper, probably not as good as they'd have had at home, but . . . Sure, Carl said. That was fine

"Well, now that we're all here, I'll go out and put things on the table."

Mrs. Viele disappeared into the dining room. A few minutes later she called to them:

"Now we're ready. Come on, everybody."

"Come on, folks," Mr. Viele echoed.

They started for the dining room. Carl stood back somewhat uneasily to let the others go ahead. All at once he had a startled sight of the pallor of Lillian's face. In spite of their quarrel, the tie of marriage drew them instantly together as allies against everyone else. Carl took her hand quickly. She turned a face of distress upon him, and said in a shaking voice:

"Carl, I can't stay."

He said quickly, "Do you want me to take you home?"

She mutely nodded. Forrest was looking up at them. Lillian blindly put out her hand to hold him away. She went back and sat down on the davenport again. Carl saw with terror that she looked as if she might be going to faint. But she wouldn't let him get her anything. She only wanted to go home.

Carl had to go into the dining room and make the explanations. In the midst of all that followed, the awkward consternation of the men, the women's sympathetic voices, the sight of James' frightened, glowering face and the heartless, blithe ignorance of that little villain Forrest—who always became talkative and gay when there was any trouble on hand, like a little elf who wouldn't admit trouble—Carl and Lillian seemed again to be allies, even in their quarrel. No one knew them so well as they knew each other. "She hasn't felt well all day," Carl heard his mother saying anxiously. Lillian tried to carry it off as well as possible, suppressing her illness while they were still in the house, and Carl tried to uphold her in his intimate knowledge of her state while he made light of it to the others. Mother and Mrs. Viele both sympathetically agreed that what she needed was to be quiet and lie down. Carl cheerfully answered his father's inevitable, "Maybe you better have the doctor," and agreed with the two women that Lillian was a little upset and shouldn't have tried to go out. Carl and Lillian both refused to let the folks go home with them. It wasn't anything serious! Carl kept his arm around Lillian, anxiously, and felt her clinging to him, as he got her away from everybody and out to the car, sensing that she was almost at some breaking-point.

But when they did get away from the Vieles', when they were alone together, it seemed as if all that momentary unity was gone. Once more they were hostile, apart, wary of each other. Their quarrel couldn't be ignored. While Carl started the engine —having trouble, of course, because he was in a hurry—Lillian sat silent and trembling, her hands clasped and her face turned away. Carl asked, "How do you feel?" She moved her lips. "I don't know." A kind of physical tenderness remained, from the long habit of bodily cherishing; but when she answered like that, Carl felt his heart drawing away from her again.

He put his attention on his driving. Although he didn't want to feel like this, and was ashamed of it, his sympathy wouldn't act. Everything in him seemed to be drawing to a hard center of resentment. It was unjust of her to go and be sick. He hated her for it. It seemed to throw all the fault upon him. All through that short, ghastly drive home, he was aware of some crisis of distress in her; but his anger was unmalleable, and couldn't yet change into pity. It clamored its own demands. Carl felt bitterly hurt and aggrieved by this new turn. When they reached home, and he tried to help her out of the car, he couldn't make his help anything but perfunctory. Yet he was enraged when Lillian shook off his hand with a slight gesture, and went silent and trembling up the walk. They entered the house as enemies.

Carl forced himself to say, "Do you want me to call the doctor?"

Lillian shook her head.

"What can I do for you?"

She whispered on the breath of a sob, "Nothing."

He was aware of her standing for a moment in a kind of helplessness. At first the weakening of pity went through Carl.

She looked so lonely. He put out his hand, ashamed now of his hostility, and able to get above it. But Lillian ignored him. She had her face turned away from him, and was going slowly up the stairs in a blind solitude. Carl was left down there in a horrible uncertainty. The shock that he had felt at the sight of her face when they were going out to the dining room came over him again—again he was forced to believe in her illness as illness, not just as part of the game. The mute force of her distress began to enter him and shake that hard core of resentment. But it hurt him—as it always did—that she had refused his sympathy when he had been able to give it. The moment that he had drawn away from her, she had felt it—she had drawn away too, in that instant overresponse of sensitiveness, asking nothing from him that he didn't offer . . . and in his own aggrieved state he felt that tenderness had to be drawn from him. Lillian let him act worse than he wanted to act! He didn't want to stand here like this, seeming cruel. But if she wouldn't tell him what the trouble was, wouldn't accept anything from him—! She was always able to keep things to herself, and he wasn't.

All at once he heard a burst of sobs from the bedroom above him. The sound shook him. His heart stood still. He heard her go faltering through the hall.

"Lillian!"

Carl rushed upstairs. He didn't know what he feared. He seemed to be rushing blindly through fear and confusion and some deep enragement.

"Where are you?"

He hurried to the bathroom. He yanked open the door and saw Lillian standing there. She had a queer dumb look as she cringed back from him. Everything happened in an instant. Carl snatched the Lysol bottle out of her hand, believing and disbelieving.

"Did you get any of that? Why, you're crazy. You're crazy!"

He snatched it away in an utter black fury. He had never even imagined such anger as this. He stood glaring at Lillian. Then he felt himself shaking. He could scarcely get out a word.

"What on earth? Did you *know* what you were doing?"

He didn't know whether he was shaking with fury or fear. Lillian stood there with her hands empty—she just looked silly . . . the familiar everyday scene, the nice big Turkish towels, the talcum powder cans and the shaving things—where something like this they were living through just couldn't happen . . . Lillian had a queer, bereft look as if he had done the one final thing to her. Her mouth opened as if she were going to cry, but no tears came. She suddenly spoke in a thin little strangled voice that didn't belong to her.

"Oh, I can't . . . Why didn't you let me?"

She slipped down onto the floor and huddled there with her arms weakly propped on the rim of the bathtub and laid her face against them. Carl got down beside her, shaking and half crying. He took hold of her, and she let him. Her eyes seemed not to look at him. They seemed to hold a kind of death beyond agony. But now words came out faintly, in a wail.

"I can't go through it. I can't help it."

"What do you mean? What can't you go through? Lillian. Tell me!"

He shook her desperately.

"I didn't come this month. Oh, I can't go through it. I don't *want* to!"

Lillian rolled her head away from him until it was hidden on her arms. She began to cry in a kind of beaten desolation.

A shock had gone all through Carl as the meaning of what she said came to him.

"Lillian. Why, if it was *that* . . ."

He felt suddenly almost a singing and shouting of relief. Through his confusion of terror he seemed to touch something tangible. He bent over Lillian, fumbling to get his arms around her, and he made her let him help her up—feeling her weak and sobbing against him, both of them now in a sudden trembling weakness of relief; and Carl guided Lillian through the hall, stumbling in his arms. There was a queer unity again between them. He made her lie down. But why had she done this? Why hadn't she told him? It seemed as if he couldn't take any answer now. He was still too sore, too weak, too shaken, the precipice from which he had snatched her was still too close. Suddenly he was sweating in a new terror, even while he was soothing her. It seemed as if he could no longer picture that scene and couldn't be sure that he had got the thing away from her in time.

"It's all right. I'm going to call the doctor now. Don't be afraid. Now just wait."

He kissed her. He ran blindly downstairs to the telephone. As he picked up the receiver, he felt how his hand was shaking. He recognized that his whole world was undermined. A dizzy whirl of sickness enveloped him and he had to reach trembling for a chair and sit down. He hadn't the strength to remember the name of any doctor. He called the folks instead.

"Mrs. Viele?" He tried quickly to make his shaken voice sound commonplace. But he heard his own breathlessness. "I think maybe the folks had better come home. Will you tell them to hurry?"

Carl sat on the bed beside Lillian, holding her wrist with trembling fingers. He was in a cold sweat of panic. It seemed as if he couldn't stand it without some kind of help—if the folks didn't come soon, he would run over and get Mrs. Morgan, hail someone on the street—anyone. But when he heard the folks coming into the house, it seemed all at once as if he could live again.

They were coming straight upstairs as fast as they could. Carl went out in the hall to meet them. "Gosh, but I'm glad you got here. She took the wrong thing. I don't think she got any of it. But I've been just about crazy. I couldn't think of any doctor . . ."

He felt an hysteria of relief. In spite of their startled faces . . . But someone knew. It was off his hands. He would have help. The folks were here. It seemed as if he had never appreciated them so much before. As if he had gone back to the utter dependence of childhood! A deep sob broke from him. But he didn't care. His pride in himself was all shaken.

They took things at once into their hands. Dad would get the doctor. They would have someone here soon. Everything was going to be all right. A moment ago, he had been sure that

Lillian was dying. But as soon as mama was there with her, he felt that nothing could happen. Mama would do the right thing. When dad came back upstairs looking frightened, saying that he couldn't get Purcell, she wasn't upset, but told him firmly to get somebody else then—any doctor. Her small, veined, womanly hands, worn, utterly capable, the hands that had so often tended her children, had charge of everything. Carl fixed his eyes on them in desperate trust. Dad came upstairs again—"I had to get Redmond, only one I could reach"— awkward, alarmed, profoundly out of his element, but a final rock of dependence. Carl felt weak and childish.

Finally the doctor came. The folks didn't like Dr. Redmond, but their innocent disapproval of his character was swallowed up in their reliance upon him. He seemed now a good man, noble, a higher being, a kind of savior, as he listened with grave sobriety—she was sick, took the wrong thing, didn't know what she was doing, was the way the folks told it; and it seemed to be the story now. He stood holding Lillian's wrist in the listening silence of the room. Carl's eyes felt blind, although he saw the whole scene with agonizing acuteness. It seemed to be time itself that was being counted, pulsing inside his own brain. When Dr. Redmond finished, everything would stop. But he gently laid down Lillian's wrist. "I think this is just the shock." Carl heard that—knew that with the words he had fallen from that agony of tension to some lower plane of suffering that was almost relief, except that now again there was the painful need for hope.

The hospital in Belmond was an old-fashioned brick building looking something like a house. It might be better to take Lillian there for a day or two, Dr. Redmond had said. It would give her a rest, and they could make sure that nothing serious was going to develop.

The doctor's hand had rested on Carl's arm as he spoke, addressing his words to the folks, and there was a slight tightening of the fingers. Carl felt an hysterical appreciation of the doctor's worldly knowledge. The strong fingers holding his arm admitted a comprehension that could not be spoken. It was with people like this that he belonged now—with the sinners! No one else could understand. He was grateful for the battered eyes with the discolored puffs of dissipation below them. This seemed to him a man like himself, who knew without confession. He couldn't have stood the dry, neat, professional uprightness of the folks' doctor. He felt in a flow of gratitude that this was another man who had been through the humiliation of a sinner. The evidence of some kind of native superiority was in his portly dignity of figure that showed even through the slovenly slackness that had grown upon him. There was something distinguished in the brown of the eyes and the thickness of the hair, although its shining premature white, set off by the light suits that had made Dr. Redmond a noticeable figure on the streets of Belmond, was now getting rough and dead-looking and old. But he was a defeated small town doctor with a vaguely shady reputation, who had lived unhappily with his wife, and let his talents go to seed through a kind of indulgent, cynical, thwarted indolence. He knew that there could be misery. And the folks didn't know.

Still, Carl was grateful for their innocence. They had accepted, it seemed, without question the explanation that Lillian "had taken the wrong thing." Suicide was something too melodramatic for them to contemplate in their own family. The very innocence of their kindness had saved Carl from the wild impulse for confession in his first abasement. He had told them everything but the heart of his fear. At first he had heard with guilt dad's explanations to the people who stopped to inquire. "She was feeling sick and went home and pretty near got hold of the wrong medicine. It didn't hurt her, but I guess the shock was pretty bad." Carl had heard that reiterated until he wasn't sure but that it was the true story. He had got rid of part of his burden by telling his mother about Lillian's pregnancy. He saw her quick relief, and knew from the spontaneity of the comfort she gave him that she had accepted this explanation of any "trouble" she might have sensed. "She might be mistaken, you know. There could be other causes. Still, it would explain . . ." And in the inability of the folks to believe the worst, it seemed to Carl wrong and foolish that he should believe it himself.

"Maybe you'd better let me go alone," he told the folks, however, when he went to the hospital to see Lillian the next day.

At the door of Lillian's room, the nurse smiled at him, recognizing his right to be there, and disappeared.

That smile brought Carl's spirits up to a relieved buoyancy. In this interim he had grown used to the thought of the child that might be coming. Any readjustment that such news required was overshadowed now by his anxiety for Lillian. In his abasement he had accepted the fear of changes it made in his future, because of the relief it brought.

The door was a little open. Carl softly pushed it farther. Fear came into his mind when he saw the long, slender outline of his Lillian's body under the white spread. He still kept his carefully gathered buoyancy. But as he stood looking down at her, he felt a strange physical sensation of pain in his heart.

He said tenderly, "Lillian . . ." somewhat doubtfully—and put out his hand.

Lillian's head turned slowly toward him. She had not moved until then. Carl felt with a shock, that once again undermined him, the deep, dull suffering that looked out at him from the very depths of her eyes. There was no concealment. Her eyes seemed dark.

Instantly, in shame, all the false, easy consolation that Carl had gathered was gone, and he was down on a bedrock of pain. He could not bear the dull, beaten, helpless darkness of Lillian's eyes. All his concealments and consolations were swept away. They mattered no more than at the moment of acutest fear, when he had seen Lillian standing there with that thing in her hands. He was thrown back onto the reality of suffering again.

"Oh, Lillian, why did you do that?" Carl pleaded. His lips shook. A sob broke from him. He realized now how much he had been suffering all this time, beneath all his false assuagement. He saw now how false that had been.

He took hold of her lax hand. Lillian looked up at him with a stare of dumb, beseeching pain that he could only partly fathom. But he knew that it was truer than any of his own suffering. Last night he had been enraged when he thought of what she had done to him—the cruelty, the injustice, and selfishness. That was gone when he saw the depth of her misery.

"Can't you tell me?"

Lillian's lips moved, but she did not speak. She lay struggling in the bonds of her old silence. She wanted to answer the pain in Carl's voice and in the tight grasp of his hand. But how could she tell him? There seemed to be no way to break through the long habit of incommunication. . . . And then there was so much—it went back so far—when she tried to speak, her voice seemed to be lost and powerless in the tangle of confusion. She had always wanted Carl to understand her, had suffered under his easy interpretations of her wishes, her actions, and her silence, because she loved him. But it *was* that love—when he misinterpreted her, or when he neglected her, she was powerless to do anything because of the very suffering it caused, which seemed to strike at the power of activity itself and turn it helpless . . . because he *could* misunderstand her, he *could* ignore her, and not care as she cared. She had suffered within her own limitations, and she knew that she had always been waiting for the one she loved, for Carl, to set her free. But now it was as if, while she lay bound in this helpless silence, the years opened up visibly behind her. She could see herself, as she had been at home; and see how the old need for creeping about unnoticed by her grandfather, the tacit reserve between herself and her parents, putting aside and keeping in silence their own concerns, so close there was no need of speech among the three —had built this habit of reserve under suffering out of which now she could not break. She could never break out of it now! She felt that fatal certainty. And she seemed to be helpless, because she could not communicate anything that she saw revealed—because Carl could not see the life and heart of that little, quiet, pale child from whom she had grown. It had frozen her words forever. Carl had never loved her well enough to understand that old necessity of going silently through her duties, to escape those awful, sonorous rebukes that had numbed her with childish terror. That fear had put her in a world by herself. And now she was there alone—she was in a universe alone. Carl had not saved her, no matter how she loved him.

He had failed to set her free. The words he had said to her had entered indelibly into her, not with resentment, but with a deep dreariness of conviction, confirming her own hopelessness about herself. With a shy, secretive, deeply hidden hope, Lillian had always looked forward to the time when her grandfather would be out of her life. While he was alive, it seemed, no matter how far away she was, he had forced her to keep on being what she had always seemed to be. She dared not come out into the open. The sense of his eye upon her had gradually grown into some great, undefined, stern watchfulness, so that she was guilty whenever she stepped from the strict path, or showed any desire beyond what he had permitted—when she bought a new hat, spent a few cents of money foolishly, caught herself talking or laughing too freely. But after he was gone, when her mother had died, and her father was no longer hers—the two who had known, with whom her secret being could live—then she saw herself being carried farther away from Carl than ever, alone in the great blind cold. There was no one but James. And then she was afraid that she was binding James to her by her suffering, as she had been bound in mute loyalty to her parents —it was better she should be taken from him soon, that he should be left to grow. She had felt that she could not stand it, could not go to that new place with Carl only to see him getting farther and farther away from her. She could not go through with bearing a child again when she did not feel that he cared for her. She had realized the weakness in herself—she could not do all that again, and this time with no hope and for no reason.

Her lips opened again. But what she was able to say was only the faintest part of all this that was held bound and aching within her. Her head gave a faint, spasmodic movement.

"I couldn't come through it."

Carl was holding both her hands. He looked down at her baffled and imploring.

"But, Lillian—didn't you think I'd want it?" he begged.

The ending of that last desperate effort at reunion! But he *did* want it now.

Lillian's lips parted again. It seemed as if she was about to speak.

But there was too much involved and entangled—she did not know how to answer him. Not unless she said everything, and she did not know where to start. She felt the resentful struggle of her helplessness against Katherine. Didn't Carl see? How could he ask her to fix herself in that agony? And she could not change. The power was not in her. She couldn't live up to that strange new life. It would be better for him to go there without her—be free of her. . . . Lillian remembered now the very stamp of the smile on her lips when she had lain with Forrest a baby, and Carl's delight and eagerness, his vital love for children, so much easier and more natural than hers, his pride in the new baby's strength—a faint, weak smile had been the most that she could manage. Carl was so happy that she had felt she could never tell him—she had hidden her deep, secret perception of the cost to her vitality. She hadn't enough, that was all. But she had blamed herself for her own inability. She couldn't spoil—she must pretend to live up to—Carl's ardor as a father, householder, family man, in those early married days, full of hidden difficulties, when she had still been so much happier than ever since. She had strained herself beyond her slight strength. . . . And yet it had all been false! She had failed after all. Falseness was always failure. Lillian felt that in her deep secretiveness she had been nothing but false all her life! She must try to come up to what Carl wanted. Always, always, she had deeply loved him. He was the only boy, the only man she had ever loved or could imagine herself loving. And yet she had never been able to come up to him! She should never have tried. Now she felt herself slipping into some deep abyss, where she could lie gratefully, beatenly helpless. She could keep it up no longer, she had to let it fall from her hands. Marriage with Carl was the sum of all the happiness she had ever dreamed of. When she was a girl, she had never dared let herself be certain. Carl must always make the first moves. She had felt that it would be a happiness almost beyond her. But when she had it, she could not rise to it after all. She was a closed flower, that had grown in too chill a shelter. Shadow was her habitat, and she could never open out under such sunlight. She had only wilted beneath it without opening. Now she could never say any of these things to him! They were too deeply buried. She had too long held the habit of secret familiarity with them only in herself.

She looked up at Carl, struggling to show him her inability. The warmth of his hands made her feel the pain of all she had relinquished. Without her volition, the most deeply hidden of all her secrets came out, painfully whispered, her lips barely moving, as if it said itself. It was the completeness of her wretchedness that let it be finally spoken.

"I should never, never have married you."

"Oh, Lillian . . ."

Carl felt as if he had never had a hurt like this. In spite of all the past weeks, he could feel nothing but a sense of amazed cruelty that Lillian could speak so to him.

"What makes you say that?"

He sat down now on the edge of the high hospital bed, still holding her hands, squeezing them to wring some response out of their laxness. He could not think about anything now—he could only suffer with himself and her. He was half crying, although he didn't realize it. He felt himself wicked and a failure. He bent toward her, his eyes on her, as she whispered, in that fatality of stillness, her eyes wide open with suffering, and a tear slowly running down her cheek—

"I married you when I knew you didn't really love me. Because I . . ."

She couldn't finish that.

"How can you say that?" Carl begged.

She shook her head slightly, her hands left slack in Carl's, but not looking at him. "I forfeited my soul."

Carl was crying now. He did not attempt to answer her. The moments drifted away from her words in a flat uselessness. The words had gone into the very center of Carl's mind. He cried because he could not make them unsaid, and because Lillian had had to say them—because of their truth, his shame . . . and yet their falseness that he couldn't make her see. He did love her now, more truly, he felt, than he ever had, with an awful pity. Her admission had swept away all his resentments on this flood of pity. He realized, now that he had come so close to losing her, the length of the attachment that had so nearly ended in disaster. It couldn't be. She was still Lillian. Her life had been twined with his from the start. How could he have imagined he could have broken that attachment off so drastically? Some people might—but how could he have imagined himself to be one of them? All the force of his life was against that. It was worse, because he knew he was crying, too, over all that he was losing from the future—that what Lillian had said was partly true, because some horrible, discredited part of himself had considered how it would be if she should die. His words were false to that. But all the same they were true. They came out of something true in him, that was down underneath all the rest.

"Don't. Lillian, don't. Why, how can you say that? You don't know how much you make me suffer."

And the boys? Had she forgotten them? What would they do without her? A tremor that he could not make out passed over her face. This was a new start!—Carl tried to tell her. It was he who had done this to her. He felt as if he must comfort her, as he would comfort a child whom he had struck, a child who could get comfort only from the person who had given the hurt. He felt as if he saw, with grinding pain, the whole of what Lillian had passed through, and he couldn't bear to have been the cause.

But now he felt himself completely shaken. Before the completeness of Lillian's misery, as she lay there not caring what she admitted, he felt a kind of awe. Until she had somehow responded to him, she seemed to be far away from him. It was almost the same as if she were dead. That terrified Carl. He had a blinding perception of how it would have been if she *had* died. He couldn't have stood it. The depth of his appreciation of her caught him like a stab of pain. He didn't know whether it was exactly love, but it held him in its power. He sobbed, with his head lying against Lillian's shoulder. Carl knew in humiliation, open at least to himself, that he could never have spoken the truth as she had done. It wasn't in him—didn't seem to be in him. All last night, with the folks, he had skirted truth. He had taken refuge in the doctor's comprehending, perhaps half-cynical silence. Even now he could not admit to Lillian how much truth he felt in what she had said. He must cover it up, hide its pain in his heart, persuade her of some kind of love. Such an admission brought him up terrified. Lillian was better than he was. He was ashamed of himself beside her. Yet he couldn't refute her. Truth had that much stubbornness. The words wouldn't be spoken.

He had thought he was as wretched as he could be last night and live. But now, here with Lillian, he fell to lower, more hopeless depths of yielded misery. He half lay on the bed beside Lillian, forgetting about the nurses, and cried. They heard hospital sounds, a chair being wheeled down the corridor, nurses' voices. Carl tried to muffle his sobbing. Even now he could not let himself go. Some little part of himself was alert remembering that he was Carl Ferguson and no one must suspect any disaster in regard to him. Yet his sorrow was more real, more selfless, than any he had thought he could feel. He could not believe that he had come to such unhappiness—that he had brought Lillian to it—and that part of it neither of them could help. It seemed to be not within their power at all.

He wanted reassurance from Lillian, and felt himself so low that he couldn't ask anything from her. He moved his hand slightly on the bed without touching her.

Lillian faintly moved her hand and touched his. Carl seized the hand with quick gratitude. He had not realized how he would want that touch when it was withdrawn from him—how he had counted upon it. The hospital sounds went on, but now seemed to bring them together as they both listened. Carl felt, as he clung to Lillian's hand, out of his abasement a deep joy of sacrifice. He wanted to tell Lillian—what she had said was the truth, and yet it was *not* true. He moved and put his cheek against Lillian's. He was remembering their first months of marriage, his fresh happiness in the new estate, how new and warm and bright the world had seemed about him—his almost sacred joy in her immaculate body the first night he had seen and possessed it . . . his easy, bright conviction that all the little things in which she did not suit him could be done away with by his influence. . . . He had imagined that! He remembered with anguish, as if it were a marked stone that stood there huge in their path forever, the night when this new child, the life only started (and that perhaps would flicker out through this disaster) had been conceived—his desperate attempt, cruel and ruthless as he hadn't known he could be, to force Lillian to the heat of response he had dreamed of in the still unadmitted attraction of Gladys and all that she suggested to him of the rich delight of sensual life . . . he ached with the thought that this little jeopardized life was the fruit of that. Yet it had not been wicked—in a deep and vital sense he had been right in craving that response.

Oh, yes, he knew that what Lillian had said was the truth! He wondered more at her saying it. Both of them knew it was true as they lay here together. Carl saw his whole immaturity now in a wonder of clarity. He could remember the night when he had really asked Lillian to marry him, out beside the wall of the high school building in the dusk—he remembered her kiss, given entirely to him, all she was . . . and he was never really given to her, not even then, when he had been in love with her. But now he hated himself for that. He saw as something lesser his restlessness, inner promiscuousness, light attachment, selfish concern—beside the small, simple completeness of her integrity.

He put his arm around her, feeling the depth of their attachment, unsatisfying as it was. No other could ever be the same. Part of him was buried in his marriage, as part of him was buried in the atmosphere of his childhood. Now he felt as if he could never do anything else, or be anything else, with conviction. The break was too great after all. He never could leave Lillian. He suffered helplessly with her. It was himself who had barely escaped this death—and yet himself who had driven her to it. He must protect her from that. They seemed to be small and together. He loved Lillian with humble, wounded respect, and with protectiveness.

"You mustn't think that. You mustn't think it," he whispered. He drew her face close against his. He did not care now whether he was speaking the truth or not. His pity was larger and overflowed the truth.

He had a sense that the awfulness of her act had cleansed

them—a cleansing of disaster, after which the hard purity of the bare essentials showed again with grateful and inescapable force.

The knowledge of all this was like something weeping within him. It seemed as if it had suddenly struck his youth, like a wind that scatters all the leaves and denudes the trees at a stroke. It was this very untruth that he was hiding, their inequality, his and hers, which welded them indissolubly in marriage.

"I'm going home now," Carl whispered. He got up, went over to the lavatory and washed his face, drying it with Lillian's towel. He came back to the bed feeling light and dizzy, and as if too much had been revealed—he had to look away for a while. "Shall I bring the boys?"

Lillian was looking at the wall. She smiled slightly. Carl saw that her lax hands had a look of rest.

6

Carl had almost forgotten what the world outside was like. The streets were deep in summer. August rains had freshened the green. It was greener now than it had been in July. Layers seemed to have been added to the heaviness of the leaves.

For the first time Carl could leave the house free of anxiety for Lillian. It felt to him as if he had been walking bent, and now could begin to straighten again and go upright. Lillian's agony had reached its peak on that dreadful night. Since the day when she had talked to him in the hospital, she had been strangely acquiescent and at peace. It seemed to Carl that the burden of the situation had shifted over to him instead. Lillian, all through her weakness, and the catastrophe that had finally followed, had lain acceptant. She had been willing, now, to bear the new child. She had even looked forward to it in a way she had never done before; with a shy eagerness, a first pure stirring of joy, smiling when she talked with mother; not quite ready to join in plans for the future, but smiling all the same. She had only just come out from the sheer facing of death, and in that one brief hour of blackness she had grown used to the thought that she might be lost. Before, she had held back secretly, stiff and frightened, feeling how close were the limits of her power.

Even when the baby was lost, although she cried, she was acquiescent. Perhaps, in her humility, she had felt that it was deserved—that she, who had tried to destroy herself, could ask for nothing else. It was a different kind of sorrow, from the hand of God, not from human cruelty.

But it seemed as if tragedy had swept her clean. The loss of this child that she had wanted had cleared her eyes; and now Carl could see that she looked in a different way at the boys. It was as if, until now, the old fears and restrictions of her childhood had still darkened and straitened her view. She had loved them, had sacrificed for them, but she had seemed to regard motherhood as a deep duty laid upon her, to the demands of which she must rise sternly, keep herself up, never let herself waver. She could not conceive of *pleasure* with her children. But this time she had looked forward to motherhood as something almost new, to which at last she had learned how to yield herself. Losing this new promise, she turned back and loved what she had all the more. She appreciated James' fierce, childish devotion, accepting the wonder of its consolation. Carl felt that the center of her love had silently moved from himself to the children; Lillian no longer seemed to make a personal claim upon him; and he didn't know which he felt more, relief or an obscure, ironic disappointment. At any rate, he was the one who was left to realize the catastrophe of the new mysterious life, begun in defeat and sacrificed to the dissension of the parents —abortive from the start, and ended. The claim of the lost child was stronger upon him than if it had become a living claim, forcing him to a hidden, perhaps futile expiation which concerned only himself and his own secret integrity.

He could leave Lillian with the folks. It seemed as if his mother had never cared so much for Lillian, been so really close to her. Carl only dimly realized a secret impatience his mother had long cherished, believing that her son deserved a woman more equal—Mrs. Ferguson had always remembered with a kind of longing the pretty girl with the radiant smile whom she had seen for a few minutes with Carl on the college campus. *That* was the kind of girl she would have liked to have for a daughter-in-law! But the loss of a baby was the kind of sorrow that Mrs. Ferguson could understand. It brought Lillian closer to her as a woman. Both the folks were very tender to Lillian. They were both ready to do things for her and Carl! It seemed now that Lillian had begun to enjoy with shy openness her mother-in-law's sweet, frank, maternal demonstrativeness. She kept the memory of her own mother loyally in her heart; but this being openly petted and made so much of was a new kind of daughterhood. At first Lillian had brooded with secret, painful remorse over what she had almost done. Perhaps, if they had known, they would have condemned her, and she had no right to accept their innocent care. But on these summer days, after the rains, as she lay in Dorothy's bed tended and loved, Lillian felt as if that memory was being softly washed away out of her being. She listened in a new way, almost as if it were a new gospel, to Aunt Annie's soft bright hopefulness. The folks in their goodness and kindness and ease did not know in what place of agony she had been. But it seemed as if they had drawn her into their kind of life at last, and for this little while at least she rested in it.

Carl felt as if he had been waiting for this time to get alone. Claims had been so thick upon him, and his heart was so sore and tender, that nothing could be cleared and decided. He had acted, but simply because circumstances were stronger than he was. As he went out to get his car, he avoided Mrs. Morgan, who would be sure to ask, with her brusque kindness and her appraising look, "Well, how's the lady today?" He couldn't endure to meet Aunt Ella's prying that was shrewd just because it was so primitive. Carl's old feeling of being somehow secretly guilty had now become truth. He wanted to drive out where he needn't see a human being. Even his fellow feeling with Dr. Redmond had not come to anything. The doctor, in spite of his comprehension, was a dissipated, middle-aged blade, too lazy to bother deeply any more with anybody else's troubles.

Carl drove out past the cemetery, that was so well-kept and

230

well-populated, with its bushes and smooth mounds, the mown grass laid in fresh heaps, the tall white Spencer monument in the center—it looked almost as prosperous and comfortable as the town . . . he was thinking into what a strange turn of events he had come. At the beginning of the summer—such a brief time past, and yet now at a distance as irrevocable as his childhood!—all had seemed to be at the flush, with new life opening up before him. It was true that everything had changed (but the actual working out of events, as always, had been unpredictable and eccentric)! Now, even in this late August green, there was a sense, a sort of darkening sense, of autumn. It was true that the ropes were cut. They didn't know what was before them.

That now they wouldn't go to Philadelphia had been one of the things that had flashed through Carl's confusion at the very start of all this trouble. He knew that that was given up! His own mind had turned away from it in revulsion, even if Lillian had been willing. Now he couldn't have risen to that change. It had faded like some flush of a dream, in which he had never really believed.

"Well, it might not be so good anyway. These rich men are sometimes kind of hard to work for."

He was grateful for that mild statement of dad's. But of course it didn't touch the truth of the matter. He could no longer tell the folks how things actually were. He accepted the soothing of their innocence and forbore to break it.

But he couldn't simply go back to what he had left. His mind had turned away from that too. Again he was almost hysterically grateful to the folks for their inveterate need to put the best construction upon everything. Dad did suggest that maybe "people would think it was funny, Carl staying here and giving up such a good place." But mother had declared loyally, and with her invincible trust in everyone's good feelings: "No, they won't! They know that Lillian is sick. It's perfectly natural that we should keep them here with us for a while." The folks understood that something more had happened than appeared on the surface; but Carl relied on their goodness and simplicity, their desire to avoid hard issues and see all for the best, not to divine how much there had been.

Salisbury was dead. Gladys would not be there. If he could only have blundered into some fulfillment before he had come to this blightingly clear knowledge of himself! He didn't want to see Katherine again. When he had come to the realization of how deep his attachment to Lillian lay, it had seemed as if he had taken on himself the feelings Lillian used to have toward Katherine. Fundamentally she didn't matter—not Katherine herself. Carl saw her as trivial, and hid as something shameful his compassionate perception of her withering vivacity. Yet he had forfeited something. To match himself with such a woman, whose fascination was worldly and opposed to his own make-up, seemed to be a need of his life. Again and again—as in college, with Nina—he had approached it. He was somehow incomplete without it. Some part of him as a man would be left humbled and unused—would shrink into uncertainty, with the knowledge that each time he had failed. And yet there was some deviousness and audacity in him that might have answered Katherine and shown itself her match!

As he drove out along the country road, he seemed to be entering into a strange freedom. It was hard, stony, bare. It was not that flush of opening life that had come with the first intimation of maturity. But he could not have gone back to that feeling now. Beside this, somehow, it seemed false. Carl felt a strange, defeated and yet cleansed relief in having come down at last to the truth with Lillian. It was a sort of painful bedrock. It was more final than the other hope.

But he wanted truth all through! He was sickened by the compromises and half-tones of his life. That feeling of having been brought by one stroke to maturity . . . was right. But it was only now that the realization was sinking into him of what that actually was. The night of crisis had scored into him the knowledge of his limitations.

Carl was driving out along the road to the farm. He had taken it so often that there just seemed to be no other one to choose. The farm was a place where he could be alone for a while.

He drove in, circling the windmill. He left the car at the rock house. The place lay in August stillness, and Carl felt again as something healing its plain simplicity. The best of his childhood was connected with this place. He had always been happy and loved and appreciated with Grandma and Grandpa. He felt that he had been at his best. What had happened in these last few weeks seemed impossible in this remote, but deeply familiar atmosphere, and he could feel everything becoming simple again, in spite of the wounds that still pained him. To the old folks, Carl had always been chief among their grandchildren, the pick of the flock. It seemed as if until this summer, in spite of a frequent smarting discontent, he had never really questioned that verdict. He still felt more at home here, in a way, than in his own house.

Of course the place was changed now, like everything else. There were renters in the frame house, and the rock house was closed. The renter's wife had preferred the other house because it was newer, "more up-to-date." Besides, the rock house was too palatial for renters. The family kept it closed. The frame house belonged to Aunt Ella and Uncle Ben, but the rock house belonged to the folks.

Yet everything was just as usual. The gasoline engine was slowly pumping, with long steely gasps. White chickens shone in the sunshine, crouched against the wall of the frame house. The evergreens in the grove were dark against the blue with a silent, country somberness.

Carl went up the back path toward the rock house. The green shades gave a blindness to the deep-set windows. Carl walked past the house toward the grove. A few beehives stood out there, discolored and neglected. Grandpa had "fooled a little with bees" after Uncle Ben had taken over the heavy work, but the renter didn't have time. Grandpa had raised just enough so that they could have a little honey themselves and bring in a few cakes so the folks—"wouldn't have to buy it at the store." The grass on the lawn was high, with spreading yellow rose and syringa bushes. Uncle Ben came out sometimes and gave it a cutting. Couldn't expect the renter to do that, he said— although Aunt Ella always declared, "He don't do enough to hurt him! Why do we give him the land if he don't keep the place up for us?" Carl could go all through the altercation in his mind. "Well, now, Ellie, I guess it don't hurt me to do that." "No! You're a good deal more ready to go out there and work over that big place with nobody living there than keep our little yard here looking nice the way it ought to!" Carl smiled a little at his fancy. But he felt sad. He remembered Bunny's innocent, "When Uncle Ben says one thing, Aunt Ella always says it isn't, don't she?" He felt the dreariness of that loveless, fruitless marriage. It enveloped him in the air of the ground, among the empty beehives, where the trees were getting to look shaggy, not neat and upright as the pointed windows of the Presbyterian church, as in Grandpa's time. He didn't know whether the dissatisfaction began with Aunt Ella or Uncle Ben. Maybe they just didn't match. He shuddered to think of how long they had been together. Aunt Ella was a stout, tough, dully conceited woman, it would take strong handling to bring her to time!—and he could see Uncle Ben's tolerant smile that brought out the deep seams in his weather-worn face. Maybe it all came down to the fact that it was *her* folks who owned the place they lived on and not his. Why couldn't she have been kinder to him? . . . But that thought brought out with painful sharpness the inequalities and dissatisfactions in his own marriage, into which no one else could really penetrate. To the folks, to his grandparents, to all his relatives, his marriage with Lillian had been the most natural one he could make. No one else could realize the dissatisfactions. Carl thought of the German singer they had heard in Milwaukee, when they had driven over from Salisbury—the ample spread of her great bosom from which the voice came out easy, deep and full, the rich emotional longing unimpeded . . . "O füll' es ganz" . . . He heard that great word—"ganz" . . . And score his own shortcomings, bring down his own bright unfounded egotism as he might, that was what he would never have. "O füll' es ganz." It was a strange sorrow to him, standing here in this place with all its associations, that he should still be moving within the fate that had been his over and over—he had done again, at the point of agony, what had seemed to be right . . . and yet he saw at this moment that it would have been braver, in some primal way truer, to have let Lillian go to her disaster, taken his own way, shattered his marriage. He couldn't do it. It wasn't in him. Carl never before had made such an admission. He felt it with wonder. That something simply, actually *wasn't in him*. Always before he had thought of it as circumstance. The knowledge shook him with a sense of profound insignificance. In a way, ruthlessness was grand. It forged paths, it cut entanglements, it made the great bold stroke. And yet Carl felt that he hated it. He shrank from it— but he hated it too. He could never make any way of his own, no matter if it was all in all to him, seem right, with a simplicity of conviction, if it hurt the people he cared for. He always must have within him their feelings about what he did as well as his own. To disregard them was like trampling on himself. Lillian was the only one to whom he had once been able to have a semblance of that egotistic ruthlessness—because she was closest to him, he felt her weight, and she had loved him too much. There was something in Margaret's fierce pursuit of her own way that Carl knew stealthily that he admired; he felt uncertain before it, aggrieved in the thought of his own defeats and compromises, for which, in her innocent self-absorption, Margaret simply did not see the need. But he despised her for it too. His disapproval was no mere defensive pretense, as Margaret thought—she had said once, "Carl just wants to do what I do and hasn't the nerve." He despised the callowness of Margaret's way. She was enclosed in her own identity, could not see or feel outside herself—all that was not as *she* wanted it was wrong! She had the complete conviction of her own desires and prejudices, and that was what gave her her strength. But Carl was thinking now—there was a callowness in all ruthlessness. It was bound up with power. If such people—people like Napoleon, for instance—once *saw*, then the concentration of their power would be gone . . . and yet it was only when they did see that they could have wisdom. *He* had seen to what he had brought Lillian's life—had been forced to look down into it, with a cruel, blasting sharpness . . . and now he could not go on his own way.

235

He had thought time after time that he had plumbed the suffering of that moment, that now he had met it and finished with it . . . that moment when he had seen Lillian standing there beside the bathroom window and had rushed to snatch the stuff away from her. And yet it was as if just now, all over again with a terrible blighting newness, he was actually realizing its effect. Yes, it had happened!—actually happened. It could not be washed out. It still kept dragging on its consequences. Perhaps even yet he hadn't seen the last of them. The last faint ripple would wash out with the end of his life. The blow had been direct. Carl recognized in wonder that he was not the same. The brightness of his easy, superficial confidence had been turned into an essential caution that came from a deep wound. He could look back at his old self as eager, youthful, hopeful, radiantly blind. Now he must forever skirt the actions which would call for more certainty than he could give them. It was his *certainty* that was beaten. That moment and the way he had met it had suddenly marked out his limitations with blinding clarity and enclosed him within them. They were set—for confidence and desire could no longer push them aside.

Carl felt the heat of the summer sun. The tall scraggy evergreens stood dusky against the blue. The chickens were drowsily squawking. He saw the glisten of the grass. His shirt clung to his back and shoulders. He felt the wet heat of sweat. Carl leaned against the fence. The sensual joy of life was all around him and yet he was apart from it. It seemed to him now that it would have been enough just to have had a woman like Gladys and to have lived in the hot, everyday, richness of ordinary life. But the need for Gladys was as if beaten out of him. He had aged beyond that at a stroke. His youth was gone. He looked back to the troubled, magical spring as to a miracle which he could never again attain. He felt a nostalgia for it, but not a desire. He was with Lillian. Her suffering had sunk into him too deeply. It had beaten down and sponged out all that was not connected with her. Now he couldn't think of leaving her, or even playing her false, because he couldn't face the pain of his own compunctions.

The past agony came back. Carl walked around through the

grove not knowing what he was doing, moaning under his breath. After a while he went and stood on the wooden porch of the rock house, with its faded, loosened fancy scrollwork. Someone was calling to him.

"Carl!"

A woman was coming toward him smiling—Vina, the renter's wife. He saw her coming through the sunshine. She was blushing.

"I 'spect I oughtn't to call you that, but I always call your father 'Mr. Ferguson.' "

"Oh, that's all right."

A little boy came tagging after her. Carl was able to smile to him, with a renewal of love for childhood—a sharp, piercing hurt at the thought of the unknown life he and Lillian had lost. But existence had too many mishaps, people were too much bound in, harassed . . . he couldn't feel remorse for that too.

"I wondered if you wanted to go into the rock house. I brought you the key."

"Oh, thank you. Maybe I will."

He was assuaged by this little attention. It seemed to denote the warm feeling of respect for the Ferguson family that all the community held.

Vina turned back rather shyly. "How's your wife getting along?"

"Oh, pretty well now, thanks."

"That's good. . . . It's the back door key. Mrs. Graham keeps the front."

She didn't ask anything more. Carl felt the gratitude of the wounded. Most of the inquiries seemed to him to be poisoned with a lurking curiosity.

He fitted the large old key, silvery and darkly tarnished, into the back door. The lock was painted over with the same dark brown as the door. This seemed to be an action that he had long known. He went into the silent house.

It was stale and stuffy on this summer day, and yet there seemed to be an empty chill lingering somewhere. Carl went on into the dining room. The table stood bare. The relationship hadn't yet decided what to do with the furniture. How strange

237

to see the bay window without its array of plants! A big fly blundered in the blank emptiness. The shades pulled down made a grateful dimness. Carl felt the rest and quiet of the room. It was changed, and yet its very proportions were something he had known and felt at home with since the beginning of his life. He had some part of his being here. He almost felt the presence of the two old people—could smell the woolen cloth of their winter clothes, could hear the dry rasp of his grandmother's worn hand across her skirt, hear the wooden creak of the rocker as his grandfather moved. He could be the Carl that he had been then. But they were not here. They were gone. It was this summer day. Things were as they were now. His life had moved on so naturally from its start—and yet in the very naturalness there was something awry.

He wandered through the house. There was a homesick choke in his throat, but his eyes were dry. He went up the narrow, wooden stairway painted brown, enclosed in walls that were badly papered, with the homemade unevenness of pioneer days. All the heat was held in these empty rooms. Carl stood in his own little low-ceilinged bedroom from which he used to hear the chorus of the frogs.

The only thing that he wanted was to get back into that lost simplicity. It seemed to lie like a hidden treasure in the empty air of this house. He wanted to hide himself here with Lillian and the boys. If he were here, he could work things out for himself. At home, he must consider the folks. While he accepted their kindness, he was bound to them. But here, in the country loneliness, away from the influence of other people, he could have the simple, bare, hard chance to work out his own salvation. Dad had suggested that, if he wanted to give up his school, he might go off and take a year of study—dad would lend him the means. But then he would be bound again. He would have to feel himself preparing for something. He and Lillian had enough to stake themselves to a winter here. It would be good for all of them. He could help Rolfe on the farm. The use of his muscles would be a compensation. He was homesick for the summer heat of the hayfield—for hard, natural things, the ring of the axe in the woods on a smoky winter day, his old task of driving the big horses in from the field, even the stream of yellow animal urine beating down into the trampled muddy ground around the tank and sending up its sensual ammonia smell. He wanted the boys to know this place that he loved. He was jealous, like all people with a country background, of wholly urban experience for his children, of the thing that they would always have lost, not knowing they had lost it. There seemed to be nothing he wanted but the bare simplicity of this life. He could work with Rolfe in the day-times, and in the evenings he could sit and soberly read in his grandfather's wooden rocker in the stove-heated dining room. Then one hard thread of difficult truth would make itself clear —if he had only that. He would bind his life within the life of his family, while his mind worked slowly, soberly, veraciously by itself.

After a while he went downstairs and turned the knob of the parlor door. He knew that too—the dab of brown paint on the bald white. This room was different now from the days when he had trustingly believed in the sacredness of his grand-mother's parlor. The relatives had taken such furniture as they wanted and divided it among themselves. Even the carpet had been taken up, leaving the bare, pale, soft-looking boards. But a few things were left. The old organ stood in the corner. On the floor still lay his grandmother's seashell. It gleamed in the musty dimness of the room. It brought back a faint return of his old feeling for Lillian. It lay cool and smooth and chill and pink-flushed white, an entity, small and what it was, enclosing itself. Limited as she might be, her truth was deeper and simpler than his, and he still needed it. He hadn't really got away from it. She still fitted into his grandfather's words—"A good home, and a good wife, a partner in your joys and sorrows." He himself was bright and confident on the outside, but inside he was all uncertainty. He could never have said what she had said to him—if he saw the hard truth, he could only hold to it in his secret self. He felt, far away, the memory of that night when she had given him her yielded lips, and he felt that he had reached her. With a gasping, difficult, dim vision he could see, from his different place, the meaning of the mute bowed

head, the timidity of her approach, the passiveness of her response. The flower of their love had never really gone on to
bloom. How much of it was his fault? Not fault—it just was.
He had never admitted, would not admit, that he had not loved
her enough to marry her. Where did one kind of love leave
off and the other begin? He didn't know anything. And now
Lillian seemed to have left the answer to her admission in his
hands. He felt once more that profoundly startled appreciation
of the intuition hidden in her reticence. All these years he had
thought she accepted what he gave her—and all the time she
had known! She could strike the very center of truth, and he
spilled wordily all around it. He felt how he had grown away
from her; but how he still had need of that hard, essential,
Puritan rectitude enclosed in her pallor, her provincial primness. Oh, he was a liar . . . he was shifting sand. . . . But
living here, caring nothing for other people, for standing well
with them, bending down all his treacherous superficial talents
(that did not represent himself!) to the hard, single line of
primitive labor—he might find some true salvation. Lillian's
act had shaken him all through. Yet its very finality had set
them free—broken the old easy-sounding shams, put them
down on a low hard level, where it was better to be.

7.

Sunday morning was just as Carl remembered it; everybody
getting ready for church, taking turns at the bathroom, the
smell of dinner being started, the sound of water running. The
late summer light all through the house was colored by the
green leaves outside. Carl went down the stairs shining in the
light from the open door. Big bouquets of flowers were set in
the hall and the living room. That would be her job, Mrs. Ferguson had told Lillian, smiling—the girls always arranged the
flowers. But there was none of the old stern hurry to get to
church on time. Only those were going who cared to go. The
folks were taking things easier now. Carl felt the mellowing
atmosphere of the household.

"I'm going with daddy!" Forrest shouted.

He ran and grabbed his father's hand, turning his face and looking with wicked, round bright eyes at the others.

"Have you got time to get him ready?" Mr. Ferguson asked uneasily.

"Oh, I can get him ready in plenty of time. Come on then, old kid, hep to it."

They went up the stairs, Forrest holding Carl's hand. "No time for monkeyshines if you're going to get ready for church," Carl warned. Forrest had started jumping with feet together from step to step. Now he climbed with his father, solemnly imitating Carl's steps. He held up his face and then his hands obediently to have them scrubbed. James was going to stay with his mother. He had slowly come to the silent conclusion that he could forgive his father, sensing a new feeling between his parents; he no longer stood aside and scowled. Carl had been fearfully hurt by his son's stand-offishness, but he had accepted it almost with humility. He felt it right that he and Lillian should each have their child. There was no such fierce protectiveness in Forrest's partiality for his father. It was just a plain heathen liking for the parent who was strong and well.

Mr. Ferguson said mildly, as they started out, "Seems to be the menfolks who attend church now!" But he accepted it that mother should remain at home when they had company coming. The folks had been very gentle about urging the children to come to church these last years. Carl could see that they had been much chastened by Margaret's rebellion.

It was almost September, but everything was still very green. Carl remembered the days when the family had all walked in procession, the children's shoes solemnly squeaking down the cement. "Afraid there won't be many at church," Mr. Ferguson observed. "Too nice a day." But he stated it as a fact, long ago accepted. A few cars were parked outside the brick church. Their own was the most splendid.

"Guess we're late," Mr. Ferguson said. The doxology was already being sung when they stepped into the entry. But he made no other comment.

They went into the small auditorium. Addie Weyant, who was ushering, tiptoed up to them, but seeing Mr. Ferguson, smiled and nodded. Carl followed his father to their old pew, keeping hold of Forrest. Addie resumed his seat on a folding chair near the door. In these latter days the church was glad to get anyone to usher. It no longer tried to bring the young people in on that task. Addie could be counted upon always to be there. And Addie, in spite of having been for some time husband and father and householder, seemed not much more grown-up than in the old days when Margaret and Dorothy hadn't wanted him to take them home from the Young People's meetings because he wore short pants. With his gentle bright eyes, and his thin little narrow-shouldered figure, he was more like an aging child than a man. He hadn't grown up enough, Carl thought, to get away from the church. The young business men of Belmond, such as Gardner Allen and Chuck Messenger, were out playing golf on a day like this. The congregation in this small, chilly-smelling auditorium formed a little backwater of the aged and left-behind in the changing life of the town.

"Hymn one-fifty-six. Number one-fifty-six. Now I'll ask all the congregation to do their best," Mr. Lowrie announced cheerfully, "as we seem to be without a choir this morning."

Necks were craned and people smiled. The only choir member who was present blushed. It was too nice a day, as dad had said. Bertha Williams, called "the organist" although she had only a piano to play, was pretty faithful, since she had no car. The church had long since given up trying to make up a choir of the young people. They took thankfully whoever would sing.

Still, when they all stood up, it seemed a fairly good gathering for such a fine day as this. Nearly all the old stand-bys were here, at least . . . although some of them, of course, like Grandma and Grandpa Ferguson, were gone. The congregation seemed not much changed. There were only three or four whom Carl didn't know. The Fergusons were almost alone in the desert of empty front pews. Dad still felt his responsibility. He would "help fill up the front," in spite of his general dislike of any conspicuousness. Carl didn't mind standing up here in full view, except for a slight uneasiness in regard to Forrest's behavior. It brought back the old pleasant feeling of belonging to the chief family of the little flock. Without the more assured voices of the choir, the singing degenerated into an uncertain quavering. Mr. Lowrie had made the mistake of not choosing one of the old hymns. Carl had to subdue his voice to keep Forrest from an imitative bellowing.

They sat down again and the hymn books were shoved into the holders. Carl settled down to an attempt to keep Forrest occupied during the sermon. But he didn't mind the smiling glances that followed the little rascal's restless antics. He was sure of his acceptance here. There was a comfortable atmosphere of old Sunday, meager as the congregation was. The pointed windows lowered from the top showed the green of the trees outside. It pleased Carl to top dad's dollar in the velvet-lined offering plate with one of his own. He had always looked forward to and enjoyed this feeling of return. He could feel at ease again, as he hadn't been since the beginning of the summer. He knew what he was going to do. He need no longer make explanations. He felt bathed in a warmth of relief.

Then after the service, there were all the greetings—which for Carl were good-byes as well.

"Well! I hear you're about to leave us."

He stood smiling as he replied, still keeping hold of Forrest, who danced and plunged at anchor.

"Yes, leaving tomorrow morning."

He felt again that warmth of relief as he answered the questions. And he knew now, with a knowledge edged with cynicism, that he never could have gone through with it if he had kept to his plan of staying out on the farm. He couldn't have endured the certainty that all these people, who had known him so long and expected so much from him, were thinking of him as queer and a failure. No one would have had the slightest understanding of why he should want to stay out there. Carl himself looked back at the idea as a romantic dream from which he had been saved. He was glad that he had kept it secret. Even the folks wouldn't have understood. At the moment when the telephone call had come from Geneva, Carl had felt an almost craven relief. Now he could stand up before people—he felt like Carl Ferguson again. The world was going on, not very much changed after all in spite of the crisis he had passed through; and he was disappointed and rehabilitated at the same time. Now he needn't fear anybody's questions. Geneva had even a few thousand more population than Salisbury! People didn't wonder now at his not returning. The acceptance of the new position made his explanation of "their plans being uncertain while Lillian was ill" seem credible.

"Well, so I hear we're going to have you real close to us next winter!" Mrs. Dunn exclaimed.

"Isn't that just wonderful!" Essie Bartlett trilled.

Carl stood and smiled. Mrs. Dunn, standing heavy and billowing in the dark silk dress with its rusty look, was smiling and a friend, but if he had appeared before her a failure, she would have been someone to be feared. She was firm in complacency over the splendid success of her own son. Lloyd, after the war, had remained in the regular army. His mother believed that he dazzled Belmond when he came home in uniform. Carl writhed at the idea of being counted less successful than Lloyd Dunn! Essie Bartlett looked at him with shining, haggard admiration. Carl knew now, with furtive guilt, how much it meant to him to receive the praise and approbation of this little flock. The memory of the Brinsleys—all his later allies in Salisbury—faded out before them. These were the people before whom his primary rôle was still enacted.

He stood waiting for his father near the open door in the summer light. Dad had been counting the collection. Now he came out with the minister. Mr. Lowrie's thick gray hair was brightened by the sunshine.

"Well, Reverend Lowrie, we'll see you and Mrs. Lowrie over with us for dinner."

"Yes, oh, yes, we'll be there," Reverend Lowrie said, laughing heartily. "Oh, yes, you know what they say about preachers!" But there was a gratified tone in his voice.

"You might as well drive with us now, hadn't you?" Mr. Ferguson asked.

"Well, thanks, Brother Ferguson. That's fine. But I have to see Addie about the quarterlies, it'll take me just a little while."

"Perhaps Mr. Ferguson had better go on," Mrs. Lowrie said anxiously.

"Yes, yes. We'll drive over ourselves. Guess the old bus can make it."

"Well, all right. Be glad to have you come with us."

"Yes, glad to have you!" Forrest repeated importantly. His naughty eyes gleamed at the laughter; and he tugged at his father's hand, wanting to make a grand leap down all the steps at once.

"Now, just calm down," Carl told him.

But he was proud of the rosy-cheeked, tanned rascal among all these people. Of James, silent and withdrawn, Carl was not so proud—and yet he longed for James' approval much as he used to crave his father's, when he was a child. He felt that he and Forrest were confederates.

"Well, so you're going to leave us," Howard said. He had come up quite shyly. He made a weak motion toward Forrest, who dodged behind his father impishly. Howard tried to smile. "Lillian all right, is she?"

"Pretty good," Carl said cheerfully. "Just thought she wouldn't come today."

The new Mrs. White waited apart in majesty.

Mr. Ferguson said, "Well, Ben and Ella, expect you're coming along."

"Yes, we'll follow along," Uncle Ben replied.

They set out in the two cars. The streets were bright with noon and other cars passed on their way home from church. It was pleasant to have the old group coming for dinner. But as Carl sat silent beside his father, keeping a restraining hand on Forrest, he had a kind of vision of the farm . . . of the evergreens standing motionless in the sunshine, and the closed windows of the old rock house. He felt a silent dignity of reproach in the plain strong outline of the barn as he remembered it against the country sky.

245

Dinner was a party for Carl. Mrs. Ferguson had said that she wanted to have all the folks here before he left. It was too bad they couldn't have Essie. But Essie couldn't leave her mother at all now, except just to get to church.

"No," Mr. Lowrie said, comfortably eating, "it's a miracle how that old lady clings on."

"Well, some of these old folks do," Aunt Ella said.

This was a real Sunday dinner. There was the usual fine big platter of golden-brown fried chicken from the farm. Mother was using the best thin Haviland dishes with their pretty pattern of faint green leaves. Aunt Ella had long ago got used to the best dishes. In fact, she now had a set of her own. In the last few years, Aunt Ella at least, if not Uncle Ben, had become a satisfied town dweller. She kept herself busy with church and house work and very hideous embroidery. There was the sound of the cars going past outside on Sunday excursions. Mother in her pretty thin dress was flushed from cooking. She sat ready to get up and wait upon them all. She had excused herself for not attending church. Mr. Lowrie said graciously, "We'll have to excuse you when you give us a dinner like this." But he had his little joke, pretending that she was a backslider. It worried her a little, although she knew it was a joke. Now she was explaining in a low tone to Mrs. Lowrie about Lillian and the children, why she was having the company, Carl leaving so soon . . . to which Mrs. Lowrie was replying in sympathetic murmurs. When it came time to take out the plates and bring in the dessert, Lillian got up to help. Mrs. Ferguson demurred, but Lillian insisted. It seemed to Carl that he saw Lillian in a different way since she had got up from her illness. She was fragile and white. She had definitely lost her youth. But today, in her blue-and-white chiffon, her skin slightly flushed with returning health, he felt some faint renewal of her old delicate charm.

Carl found himself pretty largely the center of conversation. They all had to talk about his going to Geneva.

"It couldn't have turned out better, could it," Mr. Lowrie said exulting, "to have him so close? Carl, I already have my eye upon you to come over and lead my men's class some Sunday."

"Carl, I guess you must have been waiting for this," Aunt Ella said.

"Isn't it wonderful to think they're going to be so close?" his mother cried. Her anxious, fond glance took in the boys and Lillian.

And they went on, excusing, explaining and commending. Well, the other place was too far away. Carl had been right to let it go. He oughtn't to go out of his own state, Uncle Ben said. Old Ioway was good enough. Carl smiled to notice how his mother took pains to let them all know that he had been wanted back at Salisbury! "He didn't feel at that time like promising. Lillian not being well, and all . . . and he had thought of studying next year." The folks made no mention of the offer from Philadelphia. Explanations would have been too difficult there. But this was just as it should be. Belmond looked up to Geneva as Mertonville looked up to Belmond.

"Well," Uncle Ben said humorously, "that superintendent at Geneva ought to know how well pleased a lot of folks here were when he got sick and give up his job."

"Not wishing him any ill luck," Mr. Lowrie added virtuously, attacking his chicken.

The frozen dessert made in the electric refrigerator was eaten. Only little pools of the excellent coffee remained in the Haviland cups. Replete and comfortable, they all got up from the table. Mrs. Entwhistle would come and do the dishes. They all went into the living room. Carl perched himself fondly on the arm of his mother's chair. Aunt Ella, although she had changed considerably in the last few years, sat heavy and unyielding as always. Mrs. Lowrie was a neat woman, but her dry skin with its faint light fuzz and something prim about her hair made Carl think of a missionary. His mother was always the prettiest. She had something that the other women didn't.

But Lillian had a touch of it too. Something finer, Carl thought it was. He was feeling a sweet, half-painful affection for Lillian today, mixed with the undercurrent of submerged resentment. He remembered how Howard and Jennie always

247

used to be of this group. He heard Lillian moving softly about in the dining room. She had slipped out there so that she could have the food all put away by the time "Aunt Annie" came out from the living room. Carl went to her and gently took hold of her arm.

"Go in and sit down," he said. "Will you?"

She stood passive, but Carl felt as if he understood the slight quiver that went through her. Then she raised her face. Her lips trembled.

"Carl," she said, "do you want to take this school?"

"Sure, I do! Don't you want to?" He was aware that he was partly lying.

Lillian's head was turned away, and her lips moved. Carl realized that she wanted to give him the right to his real judgment. But what was it? Carl felt a cynical doubt even through his gratitude. He didn't want to have to think about it any more. He squeezed Lillian's arm. She cried a little, out of sight of the other room. But she accepted it. She went into the living room obediently.

The Lowries had gone home in the afternoon, but Aunt Ella and Uncle Ben had stayed for Sunday night lunch. Now they were discussing who should attend the evening service. The other churches had nearly all dropped the pretense of a Sunday night meeting; but the Presbyterian flock was so small that it feared to let go. Carl could see that now they regarded it frankly as a duty. If one out of the family was there to "represent" them, that was all that could be asked. Even Mr. Lowrie didn't try to increase the attendance at the evening meeting any longer. He accepted the congregation as it was and dismissed it as soon as possible.

"Well, I expect we ought to go," Aunt Ella said, "as long as Reverend Lowrie was here."

"I'll go too," Carl said. "Don't you want to come along, Lillian?"

The others demurred. He needn't go again, especially since he had to get up so early tomorrow morning. But Carl insisted.

The service would be short. And Lillian thought she would like to go along.

"Well, then, if you're both going, I believe I won't go," Mrs. Ferguson said with relief. "I'll stay at home with the boys."

"Yes, you do that, mama," Carl said smiling, with a hand on her shoulder.

Carl had an almost tender feeling about the smallness and intimacy of the evening service. There was something precious in it—the core of the old life, the old beliefs, the old lost simplicities. Only the faithful were there: dad, Aunt Ella and Uncle Ben who went to sleep, Mrs. Dunn, the Rists. Mrs. Lowrie played the piano. Carl's strong fresh voice led the wavering voices of the scattering of elderly people. He no longer sang these familiar hymns with the innocent, bright fervor of the little boy who used to visit his grandparents; but with a reminiscent, deep affection, both nostalgic and protective, with a desire to lend the strength of his voice to the failing voices of the older people. And yet all the time it was only half real, half true.

They lingered on the church steps for a few minutes after the service. Everyone told Carl good-bye.

"But you aren't going away so far this time. We'll see you oftener after this. We feel as if we've almost got you back."

Uncle Ben and Aunt Ella got into their car, and the Fergusons into theirs. They were going to take Mrs. Dunn home. The Lowries crossed the lawn to the manse, Mr. Lowrie with his Bible and sermon under his arm.

They found Mrs. Ferguson still reading when they got home, and the boys not yet in bed. She had to undergo a little teasing. But everything seemed upset tonight, since Carl was leaving in the morning. The boys wouldn't be awake to tell him good-bye. Lillian went up to bed now. But the boys were hungry again, and their grandmother was going to get them a little lunch. Now that they had stayed up this long, a little longer wouldn't matter.

"Well, kids," Carl said, "what are you going to do without your dad?"

He felt curiously happy and reunited with his family.

"Aren't we going to live in Geneva too, dad?"

"Oh, sure you're going to live in Geneva. But your dad has to go first and find you a place."

Carl felt no particular anxiety about that. Looking for a house was part of the business. He was an old hand now. After he had got settled, and got the school business well started, the others would come. He could do that more easily by himself; and he didn't want Lillian to lose what she had won. But he felt as if he were going to be separated from his family for a long time.

"Let's go out a minute and take a look at the weather," he said to the boys.

"Why, daddy? What kind of weather is it?"

"Oh, it's fine weather. But I just thought we'd take a look."

Each of the boys held a hand as they all went out of the house together. The boys liked to go anywhere with their father. Carl held Forrest's little paw easily. But he squeezed James' thin hand in his, mutely testifying to their reconciliation. There was a shy lack of response, which Carl felt he understood.

Cars passed swiftly along the pavement. But Carl felt still the old-fashioned, fading smallness of the evening meeting.

The boys were excited over the idea of going to a new town, a new school. Carl smiled as he answered their questions. He had nothing really new ahead of him. A certain hope, expectancy, feeling of boundlessness was gone from his work. He felt sure—he thought—of his competence, but he expected only to do what he could. The old innocent "ideals" of his college days were like a tale that had been told. And yet he felt a kind of firmness—not wholly cynical—underlying the future.

"Daddy, can we go swimming in Geneva?"

"Oh, yes, I expect you can go swimming there just the same as anywhere else."

Carl wondered what dazzling mystery the word "Geneva" signified to Forrest. Once he himself would have considered it a great thing to be asked to teach there, in his old college town. Now he seemed to have no particular feeling about it, except relief to know where his bread and butter was coming from, and a tender satisfaction at the folks' pride and pleasure. He frowned, hardening his sensitiveness to meet the irksome things that belonged to teaching.

"Gee, I hope they got a monkey in the park there!"

The garden hose was lying in the grass, and Carl stiffened his arms obligingly so that the boys could jump over it. As he felt their small hands depending upon his clasp, he realized that he had crossed the entrance to middle age. That sense of expectancy had imperceptibly passed out of his own life into the lives of his children. If he, Carl, had actually failed as a husband and father! . . . that was what he was at bottom, he knew. He could no longer hold up Lillian's lacks when he felt so deeply his own defects and inconsistencies.

He stopped out on the lawn to let the boys watch a bird. The street looked green and pleasant in the deepening twilight. It had lost its newness, though. There was a kind of fading pathos about the frame houses, as with a woman who has only just begun to lose her youth. The boys were excited by the cool evening air. They thought it was grand to be staying up beyond their bedtime.

Oh, right and wrong were no longer simple! Carl didn't pretend to unravel them. He felt with a certain wonder and loss that his pride as an individual was gone. Out here in the evening, on the familiar street, he knew himself to be just one of many. What seemed fine to his family and the little old provincial circle no longer really meant much to him. He missed his old bright confidence. He scarcely felt he was himself without it. And yet he couldn't go back to certainties. There was a kind of freedom and enlargement in the very sense of his insignificance that made his old youthful self-confidence seem childish and tawdry. A little portion of his mind could be skeptical and free, belonging to himself alone, in secret. But Carl felt in that, too, a sort of defeat; a quiet humiliation that yet left him with self-respect. Anyone was a child, he thought, who had never learned for how little he counted. That was what led people to religion, to resting on Jesus. He had grown up in the church, and yet he had never understood that before! When a man felt himself so small, he *had* to feel something greater. But what? Carl felt a more complete and devastating sense of nothing—nothing, at any rate, for himself—than Margaret with her fiercely-held personal values. All that he had was a furtive, hurt, protective affection for what he had once seemed to possess, which he dared not, could not and would not let go. He would always be removed from the great ones of the earth. And yet there was a certain truth they didn't possess in his own hard-learned, beaten smallness.

"What is man that thou art mindful of him, or the son of man that thou visitest him?"

The stars were beginning to come out thickly in this sky that had a local look to him above the familiar houses and trees. He had at least that text in which he could humbly believe!

He felt himself suddenly close to the edge of that abyss of cynicism that had secretly lain in wait for him ever since he had given up the thought of staying out at the farm at the first offer of the job at Geneva. He felt that he was dignifying himself by calling himself a sinner. What had he ever done? His actual peccadilloes had amounted to so little that they were a joke. The series of abortive love affairs: Mildred Summers from whom he had taken far less than she was ready to offer; Nina whom he had scarcely had the courage to touch; Gladys whom he hadn't dared to kiss; Katherine whom he hadn't even come near. His "ideals" to which he had held—yes, he really did hold and cling to them, but never enough to keep them against more imposing claims. When it had come to the point, Carl had been ready to crumble and surrender so easily that it was just a joke. His whole career had been so feeble and minor that the thought of it choked him with satiric disgust. And part of this was because he had really, truly, ingenuously tried and desired to be good.

The boys were speaking to him. Their voices brought him away from the edge of the abyss and back into the atmosphere of half-reminiscent contentment in which he had been dwelling all day.

"I want a swing, dad, before we go in."

Carl obediently hoisted Forrest into the seat and took the ropes in his hands. The boys' grandfather had put up a swing for them in the maple tree where Margaret and Dorothy used to have theirs. Carl's thoughts went on as he gave Forrest a turn and then James. The swing cut back and forth through the evening air. The undefeated have power. But it seemed to Carl that only the defeated could have wisdom.

"Now you've both had turns."

He stopped, getting his breath, while James sat feeling ecstatically the last faint back and forth of the swing, not ready to jump out until the old cat had died completely. That ugly dog from the rented house next door came running over to them.

"Daddy, isn't she funny-looking?" Forrest said.

James said with disdain, "Gee, I wouldn't want such a homely one."

Carl patted the dog's head. Her dull eyes, yearning and humble, with some inner hurt that couldn't be reassured through all her efforts at establishing friendliness, looked up at him.

"Oh, she isn't such a bad dog," he said.

Part Three
The Loveliest Time of the Year

DOROTHY was just waking up. She was under orders to sleep as long as she could. First of all, she recognized the quality of the sunlight—this summer sunlight, flecked by the leafy green of the trees outside, lying in a square, pulled slightly out of shape, on the polished floor; and then the air, scented with grass cut early in the morning, and with peonies open in the sun, smelling of coffee and breakfast and of Margaret's Red Rose bath soap.

She turned her head on the smooth pillow and spread out her hair to watch the sunshine gild the roughened curling ends of light brown with wiry auburn, wondering whether she liked her new permanent. She was in a blissful state of new perception of her body.

Her eyes wandered from herself and took in the sweet familiarity of the room. The curly-haired doll, in its foam of lace over French-blue taffeta, sat among the lacy cushions piled in pretty disarray on the chest. The folks had let both the girls get new furniture when Margaret had left this room at the front, that had always been hers and Dorothy's together, and had taken the old guest room on the north. But now Dorothy could scarcely remember how it had looked before that. She lazily draped one arm over the blue coverlet and watched the sun bring out its frosty whiteness . . .

She made a restless movement. Now she felt too excited to stay in bed.

She stood and stretched herself in the square of sunshine. The lace strap of her flesh-pink nightgown slipped down from one round shoulder. Dorothy contemplated the smoothness of her arm down to the pink finger nails that she had sat up to manicure last night. Her eyes, veiled by the lovely lids with their feathery spray of golden-brown lashes, had an ecstatic glint.

Jesse was coming at half past eleven. She sang "Half past eleven" just under her breath, not knowing whether she was more thrilled or frightened.

She heard the battering sound of Nellie's dust mop as it hit a foot board. "My room be empty in a jiff, Nellie!" she cried. She flung her old blue crêpe de chine negligee around her like a cape and ran pattering in her blue mules down the narrow hallway to the bathroom—pausing a moment to peep into Margaret's room, empty and shaded, on the darker side of the house, with the furniture painted (not all of it successfully) in black and green and Chinese red. Margaret couldn't find any ready-bought furniture around here to suit her ideas. Dorothy looked into the room just for the confirming sight of Aunt Louie's things in there. A wonderful negligee of fruity-colored crêpe de chine and yellow cobwebby lace lay across the bed. Dorothy thought of trying it on—Aunt Louie wouldn't care; but the powder and perfume-scented stillness of the darkened room, where one of the shades blew in and out a little, was somehow mysteriously private.

Margaret had put out a cake of her own blue bath soap for her. Choosing bath soaps to match their auras was one of the secrets Dorothy and Margaret still had together. How grand to have all the towels she wanted, after rooming all last year! The shelves of the white-painted cupboard were thickly piled with the rough white softness of Turkish towels. Dorothy relished every little circumstance of these last few days at home. The folks all remarked on how calmly Dorothy accepted the fortune that came to her. She did, and in a way, could, because she had always felt a sort of certainty inside herself. And yet she knew how happy she was; she felt it in a trembling wonder. She heard Nellie's mop, voices somewhere in the house, and she felt herself strangely, yet rightfully, naturally, the center of all this luxurious commotion. She had always known that it would happen just like this some day. Now that it actually *was* happening, it seemed at the same time dreamily familiar and utterly fresh.

She dressed and started down the back stairs to the kitchen, standing for a moment on the little, inconvenient, three-cornered landing, alone with the broom and the dustpan and the long-known, shut-in odor. She squeezed her hands together and shut her eyes, and smiled all to herself, before going down to the others. When she opened the door, she saw that someone else was there besides her mother and Aunt Louie, and the shy knowledge of her own shining conspicuousness as a bride made her want to say something irrelevant.

"Oh, you've got one of those new dish-racks! You villains, you never wrote me. The folks are getting just too spiffy! Something new every time I come home!"

"Don't you see Mrs. Morgan, Dorothy?"

"Oh, excuse me, Mrs. Morgan! I just came rushing in."

"Oh, I guess we can excuse anything these days, can't we?"

Dorothy's smile had a shy, subtle radiance. Every reference touched some chord of happiness with a thrilling bliss. The morning seemed marvelously fresh. Aunt Louie sat there large, warm and opulent, like a full-blown rose in her pale pink summer silk, with a flash of rings as she sewed. Mother was dear in her fresh print dress. Even Mrs. Morgan, with her harsh skin and frizzled hair, looked summery and nice in one of those lawn housedresses ("porch dresses," they called them) that were advertised in catalogues. Sunshine came into the room across the white sink and the table, and centered in the dark bright ruby of the glass of jelly Mrs. Morgan had brought over.

"For your breakfast," she said. "Dorothy was the one, wasn't she, that always wanted the cherry, when I used to spread bread and butter and jelly for children? 'Cherry, please, if you have any,'" she mimicked. And the others laughed affectionately, recognizing the imitation of Dorothy's soft little-girl speech.

"Oh, wasn't I a little simp? *Thank* you."

Margaret came in from the back kitchen with her glass of orange juice. "Want me to scramble your eggs, kiddo?" she asked.

"Oh, thanks, you're a jewel. Oh, Megs!" Dorothy made a coaxing face. "Put in little pieces of bacon?"

Mrs. Morgan said in a simpering tone:

"Won't be home much longer to have sister get her breakfast, will she?"

Left alone in the dining room, Dorothy ate with slow, dreamy relish. The bowl of rose-colored peonies, shedding large silken petals on the cloth, was so familiar to her that it seemed she must be still the same Dorothy at home from school or teaching. She heard them talking about the presents out in the kitchen, and her mother asking Mrs. Morgan if she would like to go in and see them.

"Better hustle, Mademoiselle Bride," came Margaret's slightly satirical voice, "if you want me to prepare the table for your gent."

"I'm through!"

Dorothy went out to the screened porch and sat down in the ancient slatted swing that creaked on its iron chains. Some day she and Margaret threatened the folks with new porch furniture. But now Dorothy was secretly glad that everything was as it was. There was a cool green light all through the porch from the leaves outside, except for one shifting bar of sunshine. Some pink crêpe de chine was crumpled on the table. Through the shininess of the black screening she could see the lawn mower standing at the edge of a mowed sweep just where Bunny had left it when he had run off on an errand.

Dorothy heard the voices in the sewing room, where the presents were displayed. She didn't want to be called in there. When she had to talk to people, it broke into her blissful preoccupation. But when she remembered that Jesse was coming, in just a little while she would have to go to the station and meet him, fear undid her. She seemed to die away inside.

She went out to wander over the lawn. The back yard lay open and bright in the early June morning. When she had first come home from Crown Point, fresh from being with him, it had seemed to Dorothy she was just waiting until Jesse got here so that she could show him everything. Things had no value any more when she looked at them by herself. But now she had this queer fear. Almost averseness. It was as if she had suddenly gone back to her little-girl self. Lonely and strange, as sometimes when there used to be no one around to play with her, and Margaret was reading and wouldn't tell her what, Dorothy wanted to seek out the consolation of her favorite haunts. She went over and smelled the yellow roses on "Grandma's bush," as they always called it, because it had been transplanted from the farm. Then she leaned with her arm around the low bough of the apple tree, staring up through thick leaves and branches studded with small green apples at the far-away blue sky. She thought of all the games they used to play out here, trimming doll hats with pink and white phlox blossoms,

260

when she hadn't known there was such a person as Jesse. She felt as if she were hiding from him here.

She walked dreamily about among the flower beds, lonely for him, and yet dreading to have him come. The rich grass was so green that it glistened. Geraniums were red in that old cemetery piece—the folks' pride. Dad wouldn't dislodge that urn from the front lawn. He had set the bird bath out here in the back. Everything smelled so good! She could smell the roots in the rich earth, and the blossoms hot in the sun. Shadows of leaves flecked over the cream-colored wall of the freshly painted house. The car stood big and green and glistening in the graveled driveway, with sun flashing silver from the hooded lights, and shade scattered across it from the evergreens.

Maybe this was the last time she would ever see it all alone—just as her own self. When she was married, it would not be the same. She didn't know how she would see things then, but differently. She wouldn't be Dorothy Ferguson any longer. A cardinal hovered and settled on the hot white rim of the bird bath; and then in a splash of red, sent up a shower of drops that fell dark on the white stone and bright onto the grass below.

Dorothy looked in at the kitchen door.

"Can I do anything, mother?"

Her face was flushed from the sun outside. In her thin pink housedress, with her arms bare, her skin seemed to have taken on some of the warm tints of the flowers among which she had been wandering.

"I don't think so, dear. You'd better get ready to go to the train. You aren't going to wear that dress, are you?"

"I guess not."

Dorothy looked over the new clothes in her closet. She had never had so many before—although, since she had been teaching, she had spent quite a lot of her money on clothes. She had gone to Geneva with mother a week ago to get her permanent and to buy dresses. And then Aunt Louie had brought just scads of things besides. It was like a dream to have so many things to wear. It was like that game she and Margaret used to play, sitting out under the fir trees in the grove at Grandma's, when they had pretended that they had different dresses for every kind of occasion in the world—and shoes and hats and jewelry to match. And what they had called their "nationality game," having a dress from every kind of nationality. And she remembered how they used to steal two of their little cups and little tiny spoons from the dining room, and some cookies from the kitchen, and come up here and put on their kimonos and light two sticks of ten-cent-store incense and sit on the floor having what they called "a Japanese tea."

Nellie was lingering in the hall outside, and Dorothy remembered that she hadn't shown Nellie her things.

"Don't you want to come in and look at my duds, Nellie?"

Nellie came in with suspicious readiness. She had already peeped into Dorothy's closet while she was cleaning the room, and so now she blushed. She left her mop outside and rubbed her hands against the sides of her soiled bungalow apron.

"I guess I'm kind of dirty."

"Oh, pooh, who cares."

Dorothy opened her closet door again. She heard Nellie's eager and slightly adenoidal breathing.

"Do you like this? It's what I'm going to travel in."

"I should say!"

Nellie kept her hands close to her sides as Dorothy held up the dresses. The lovely pastel colors of the soft little slips of dresses—orchid and pink and blue—almost made her feel like crying. Dorothy Ferguson had always been her secret adoration, her ideal image of what it meant to be "a pretty girl." When Nellie imagined herself in the future, she always saw herself as looking somehow or other like Dorothy Ferguson.

"Wait a minute," Dorothy said.

She ran into Margaret's cool, shaded room and brought out a long, shrouded package from the roomy closet where they had always kept all their special things—evening wraps in flowered coverings, and graduation dresses, and furs. She unpinned the soft cloth wrappings.

"Oh, gee!" Nellie said. The dress was like those lacy patches of shining thaw on top of the snow late in winter. "Is that the one you're going to be married in?"

"Do you like it?"

"Oh, I never saw such a pretty dress."

Margaret was standing in the doorway. In her passion for clothes, she couldn't resist looking at Dorothy's things whenever Dorothy was showing them. She watched Dorothy try to put the dress back into its wrappings.

"Here, let me do it! You aren't doing it right."

Dorothy gave a slow, droll wink at Nellie, while Margaret, with fierce exactitude, pinned the soft veiling about the delicate froth.

"What are you going to wear to the train?" she demanded. "Oh, don't wear that blue. You're going to wear so much blue. Wear the rose-beige. That'll look different. I'll get it. Now stand still. I'm going to put it on you right. You always get things hiked up somewhere."

Dorothy stood with eyes childishly big and meek while Margaret settled the fit of the dress—aware, however, of something very pleasing in the mirror, of flushed cheeks and round white arms in a setting of delicate silk. Margaret pushed Dorothy's hair severely into its correct waves.

"You shouldn't get a permanent, Dot. You hair has too much curl of its own. You should get a water wave."

"Why didn't you say that, then?"

"Oh, well, you and mother already had the appointment."

"Don't I look all right?"

"Oh, yes, you look all *right*."

Dorothy made a face.

"Now, please, ma'am, may I go?"

"You may when I get through with you."

"But I'm going to be la-ate!"

She was dancing up and down in impatience—finally she broke loose and ran for the stairs. Margaret's satirical voice called after her, "Better stop in somewhere, kid. You know what you look like, dancing that way." Nellie snickered. Then she tried to look very sober. They heard Dorothy starting the car outside. Nellie wanted to ask a lot of questions about Jesse.

But she didn't feel so much at ease with Margaret as with Dorothy. She retired to her cleaning.

Margaret went to hang the wedding dress in the closet. In spite of her deep disgust for regulation weddings—regulation *every*thing—she felt somehow exalted and emotional when she thought of her little sister Dot being married in that lovely gown. It was only for moments of outraged chagrin, to assert and make everybody acknowledge her feminine equality with Dorothy and Mildred Summers and the rest, that she herself ever thought of getting married. They needn't think, all these women, that she was really envying Dorothy getting married at twenty-three with nothing strange and adventurous to look forward to after this! Dot and Jesse would be married exactly a year, and then the folks would get word of the first infant, and just about eighteen months later the second would arrive. The first would be sure to be a boy, either named after dad or called Jesse Junior, and the second would be sure to be a girl. Dorothy always did everything exactly right.

The car was gone now. Jesse would be here in a little while. Margaret felt as if she would have liked to stay here in this closet, faintly scented with mothballs, one of the familiar refuges of her childhood. She was sure that Jesse would be just the regulation type of young man whom she couldn't like and who would see nothing in her. And in spite of her scorn of weddings—unless there was something different and off-color about them like Sybil's and Frank's—she couldn't help feeling the humiliation of being the one left.

Fragrance was all about her as she went out to cut the roses for the table. She felt emotional again. Dot was closer to her than anyone else in the family, in spite of resentments and jealousies—her ally, her pet, her doll, her little sister. Margaret's own distantly glittering and much more romantic future, of which she was convinced through no matter what periods of bitterly realistic dissatisfaction and angry hopelessness, receded even from her dreams. Now, out here in the yard where they used to play, she felt a homesickness for their childhood. But there was a kind of dramatic delight in seeing how all things conspired together for the perfection of Dorothy's wedding.

Jesse had come.

Now they were all out in the hall to meet him, the folks flustered in their attempt to be cordial, Bunny shaking hands in silent, youthful awkwardness. Dorothy's face was flushed. He was so handsome! That was all they could think of at first. They had known that he was good-looking, but not that he was so handsome as this! He looked like the polo pictures of sunburned, smiling young scions in *Town and Country*. Even Margaret was reluctantly impressed. Jesse was so tall, and he wore exactly the kind of thick, soft, gray summer suit that she approved of. The family pride was flatteringly enhanced. And of course today, meeting his bride's family for the first time, excited and conscious of the eyes upon him, with a deep red color under the elegantly smooth brown of his sunburn in taking contrast to the shiny black of his hair, he was at his very handsomest.

Behind them, through the open doorway, the table was visible set for luncheon in a glitter of the best glass and silverware, Margaret's bowl of roses in the center, very artistically arranged with bending stems; and Nellie in a crisp fresh dress trying to see as much of the new arrival as she could while she filled the cut-glass goblets.

Luncheon, in spite of its elements of embarrassment, went off excitingly well. Then they must all go in to look at the presents.

Mrs. Ferguson and Aunt Louie were even more delighted with Jesse then. He exhibited none of the traditional masculine embarrassment and disgust at the fuss of a wedding. He was interested in everything; impressed with the mahogany clock with chimes from the Richard Spencers, which represented the gift of the bank, and delighted with the chest of silver for the magnificence of which Aunt Louie would take no credit. It was "just a little remembrance," she said. The most splendid gift of all was to come from Jesse's family, from the wealthy old grandfather in Michigan who represented all the family he had. Tomorrow Jesse and Dorothy were to pick out the roadster in which they were to make their wedding journey.

"Well," Mr. Ferguson said, "this ought to help load up that covered wagon."

Jesse laughed heartily, showing his handsome white teeth.

Mr. Ferguson went back to the bank pleased with the little secret that he himself was keeping. He had said nothing about it yet, and he wouldn't until the right time. But everything wasn't to come from this young fellow's rich grandfather! He could do a little bit himself.

In talking over what was to be done with the day, it had long ago been decided that Dorothy was to take Jesse out with her to make a few calls. There were people, like Essie Bartlett's mother, who would want to see him and who couldn't get out to the wedding. Better stop in and make arrangements with Reverend Lowrie too, Mr. Ferguson had added. Besides, this would give Jesse a chance to see a little of the town.

"Marvelous sight!" Margaret put in.

"What's the matter with it?" Jesse asked her, with his brilliantly disarming smile. He gave Margaret's arm a brotherly squeeze that flattered her while she resented it. He had adopted toward her an intimate and affectionate yet slightly patronizing attitude, as if she willingly and gracefully stood in Dorothy's shade. "I've been hearing about Belmond for the last year."

"Dot must have been hard up for subjects."

Jesse laughed heartily.

Now, while he ran upstairs for a moment, they had a chance to express their satisfaction. They had gone in to help Nellie clear the table and set away the food.

"Goodness! Why, Annie, he might have stepped right out of the rotogravure."

"I think he looks kind of like Douglas Fairbanks," Nellie said eagerly.

"Well, do you know, he does a little?"

"Douglas Fairbanks has a mustache. And anyway!" Margaret said in scorn. "You're behind the times. You aren't on to the new raves. But he *is* just almost too handsome to be real."

"He's just as nice as he can be, though," Mrs. Ferguson said. "He takes such an interest in everything."

"Oh, yes, he *is* nice, Annie. Can you imagine a more perfect couple?"

Dorothy came lightly tapping down the stairs in her beige kid slippers. The large picture hat that Aunt Louie had brought her drooped shadily about her face and gave a mysterious new effect to her prettiness. She went out on the porch and waited. Now, after the earlier excitement of the day, she felt queer and flat. She was afraid to be alone with Jesse. She called in to Margaret:

"Don't you want to go along with us, kiddo?"

"And be a third party? No, thank you!"

"You're mean," Dorothy whimpered faintly.

She felt an awful qualm when she heard Jesse come downstairs.

"Come in, Dorothy. I was just telling Jesse," her mother said, with a radiant face, "it would be so nice if you were to stop in to see Mrs. Bird, too, while you're out. I know she'd appreciate it."

"Be fine!" Jesse agreed.

"All right, I guess we can," Dorothy murmured.

They had to set out before the eyes of the assembled household. Dorothy felt that all down the street everyone was looking and saying, "There goes Dorothy Ferguson and the man she's going to marry!" She had dreamed of just this moment. But the pride that quivered in her was kept back by this new queer embarrassment with Jesse. She couldn't think of anything to say to him that wouldn't sound forced and affected. So tall and black-haired, in his gray suit, he seemed like a stranger in Belmond. Their footsteps rang loudly on the cement.

Finally he asked, "Who is this lady your mother wants us to see?"

"Mrs. Bird? Oh, she's a friend of mother's. She's a nice old lady. But maybe you wouldn't care about calling on her."

"Sure, I'd like to," Jesse said, half hurt.

"Well, I mean she's just an old lady."

They walked along silently. It seemed to Jesse that Dorothy might have realized he was as interested in Belmond as she was.

He had never lived long in any one place. His parents had died when he was small, and he had gone from school to school and from relative to relative in his childhood. He had taken over this little town for his own.

"Well, let's go to see Mrs. Bird first," Dorothy said quickly.

She had always childishly loved going down this street. She wanted Jesse to share her feeling for it, but she couldn't tell him so. Maybe it wouldn't seem like anything to him. It had a retired, old-fashioned look—completed. Mrs. Bird's was the last house. After that, there was a shady ravine through which the "crick" ran that had to serve Belmond as its only body of water. Dorothy had always liked it when her mother had sent her with club records or programs to Mrs. Bird's. But now, in a hurt, childish loneliness, it seemed to her that Jesse was so grand and remote he couldn't understand how she felt about a little place like this.

Mrs. Bird's house, although it had a second story, gave the effect of a cottage. Its white paint had always a New England snowiness, and the siding ran up and down in the wide perpendicular stripes called "boards and battins." This was one of Dorothy's reasons for liking the place. Another was its lowness, the deep green of the ferns around it, brought long ago from the woods, the wooden lace trimmings neat as tatting on a handkerchief made by an old lady . . . the wideness of the lawn and the bigness of the trees, the clean aging look of the old white barn which years ago had housed a shiny brown horse and a one-seated buggy. Somehow it expressed for Dorothy a side of Belmond that was only here and there discernible in the composite of all its aspects—an old-fashioned, faintly literary, leisured side with a remote New England flavor, that was connected in Dorothy's mind with such things as the family surrey the old Spencers used to drive, its fringe gently flapping, and with the cool odor of a high-ceilinged room in which there were books and a chilly globe map in pale colors beside a black marble fireplace, and with the pure blue and pink tints of the transplanted wildflowers growing near the ferns along Mrs. Bird's house wall. It had something to do with an interest in the birds, and in the Latin names of wildflowers, with curiosities from abroad seen through the crystal of a cabinet, and with Shakespeare. People like Mrs. Bird and the old Spencers were part of it. Not Mrs. Stark. She was a stiff, alien New England. It had always had a slightly foreign flavor to Dorothy, when she was a little girl, because it had nothing to do with the folks or the Presbyterian church.

Dorothy turned the handle of the funny old bell, with its chipped white button that always made her think of the eye of a doll. They heard the faint jangle die away into the aging quietness of the place. The vines, and the overhanging heaviness of summer foliage, gave a darkness to the narrow porch. Now, in their youth, Dorothy and Jesse drew together.

They heard Mrs. Bird coming to the door. All these years she had been slowly aging, but it seemed to Dorothy that she had always looked exactly the same. And the figure of this old lady, with her delicate wrinkled face on whose cheeks the finely broken veins made a pinkish-lilac semblance of rosiness, with the yellow-silver hair curled and neatly held by pearly-gray shell combs, the indoor old-fashioned summeriness of the figured thin dress with its feminine softnesses of lace, and yet the padding, flat, sensible, old-lady shoes—somehow was the very substance of that aspect of home that Dorothy felt, and wanted Jesse to feel, but that she never could have described to him.

"Why, it's Dorothy, isn't it? Come in, my dear. How glad I am to see you."

"Mrs. Bird, I want to present Mr. Woodward."

Mrs. Bird bent her head slightly forward, to be courteously sure of hearing. She took Jesse's hand in her hand, frail, shell-like, brown and lilac with age, and she kept hold of it while she turned to Dorothy. "Not . . . ? Why, my dear! How nice of you to bring him to see me. Well, I *am* glad to see you now." She pressed Jesse's hand.

The estrangement between Dorothy and Jesse had somehow melted at Mrs. Bird's greeting. Now, as they followed her into the parlor, they were shy but together. This was what Dorothy had dreamed of doing—taking Jesse to her own places here in Belmond, letting him share in her unspoken love for her home, in all she had had clear back to her childhood. She could not have told why it was that she loved this room so much. It was a small room, without special distinction except for the light glitter of the maple wood floor across which fell lengths of sunlight from the long shuttered windows that came almost to the ground. But there was something—the cool shine of an old walnut-framed mirror below which, on a little dark stand, was a small marble bust of Pallas Athena—the gleams of gold from the leather-bound sets of Emerson and Shakespeare in the bookcase—the green of the ferns outside.

Mrs. Bird always gave her a fan too—this time it was one made of straw-like palm with a purple ribbon run through it. When Dorothy waved the fan, it gave out a faintly grassy, old-fashioned odor.

"And I suppose I can't offer you a fan!" Mrs. Bird said, smiling at Jesse. "There are penalties attached to being a man."

"It's so cool in here, though," Dorothy said softly.

"Yes, it's a cool house, I think."

There was something—not coquettish; you couldn't associate coquetry with Mrs. Bird's dignity!—but delicately, flatteringly feminine in the way the old lady talked to Jesse. He felt it, and answered smiling, while Dorothy sat in a silence of happiness. Now it no longer seemed to her in secret that she was mysteriously betraying Belmond by marrying this handsome stranger instead of Corny (as she thought the folks had hoped). Everything was perfect again. She felt as if Jesse had to know how happy she was, and how she adored him at this moment; and she slowly raised her eyes that had now a liquid brightness.

Everything, the wedding on the lawn, the romance of the honeymoon journey wherever they wanted to go in the new car, seemed delicately perfected by the sweet warmth of Mrs. Bird's appreciation. She made them feel happily young, beautifully cherished, as they sat in the cool, shaded parlor with the ferns outside, where Dorothy had loved to sit when she was a little girl.

"I'm afraid we must go, though, Mrs. Bird."

"Yes, my dear, I know you have other places you must visit. But it was so sweet of you to stop in to see me! I would have been very much disappointed if I hadn't been permitted to see this young man."

Jesse smiled. He was slightly flushed, but Dorothy felt as if she had never adored his beautiful manners so much as she did now—not even in Crown Point, where the other girls were all crazy about him. Suddenly she knew again in a piercing happiness, how much more wonderful it was to be marrying *him*— she knew that she could never have married Corny. This— Jesse's gray eyes light and bright in his sunburned face, his smooth hands, his slightly alien splendor—was romance.

They walked toward the door. But there they waited a moment. Mrs. Bird had gone into the dining room. Now she came back, and they saw that she was bringing a package not very well wrapped in white tissue paper.

"Dorothy, I have this little remembrance for you. I wondered just how I was going to get it to you. You don't mind carrying it home?"

"Oh, Mrs. Bird! Of course not, but—"

"It's just something I thought you'd like to have to remember an old friend by. Oh! I'm afraid I didn't wrap it very well, did I? I'm so poor with packages."

Jesse took off the tissue paper to try his skill with the package. Dorothy's eyes shone with that liquid brightness. She recognized the present. It was that dear little old-fashioned square soup dish with the cover, in which Mrs. Bird had given her her ice cream, once when she and Lucille had passed the napkins when Mrs. Bird had entertained the club. Mrs. Bird remembered how she had loved it! She loved the delicate fadedness of the decorations, traced finely in brown, like the faint print of autumn leaves—cool, like the feeling of this house.

She thanked Mrs. Bird, standing with lifted, shining eyes. Jesse looked down at her, feeling her as enchantingly small and young at that moment, a little girl. He could scarcely keep from touching her. He felt a slight trembling of his brown hands.

"It's very old. Well, I say 'old'! It's one of a set my mother got when she first went to housekeeping. That *is* a good while ago."

She was so happy to have met Mr. Woodward, Mrs. Bird added. "Or Jesse, I have to call you that. I can't think of little Dorothy's husband as Mr. anything." She was glad the weather was so beautiful—to show Jesse how nice their little town could be.

"I didn't need to be shown. I was ready to believe it."

Mrs. Bird took his hand again.

"Well, now that I've seen you, I can feel all the happier about Dorothy. You know, she's one of the very nicest girls we have!"

"Yes, I *do* know it," Jesse said. Now he laid his hand on Dorothy's shoulder, and she leaned toward him a little. His bright gray eyes in their thickets of shiny black lashes had grown moist.

"Well, my dear, how can I tell you that I wish you a happy journey? But it can't be otherwise, can it?"

Mrs. Bird stood in the doorway as Jesse and Dorothy went down the walk under the shady trees.

Jesse said soberly, when they regained the street, "She certainly is a sweet old lady. You didn't ever tell me about her, did you, Dot?"

"Well, she doesn't belong to our church."

That made Jesse laugh. It was hard for him to imagine such a tight little existence. But because it was Dorothy's, it seemed to him a tender joke, and it pleased him to think he belonged to it. He wanted to get hold of her again, but he was carrying the rewrapped china with great care, and both his hands were occupied.

"What is this thing, anyway? A soap dish?"

"Jesse Woodward! It's for soup."

"Must not be going to get us very hefty meals, if this has to be the family tureen."

"It's just one person's dish. Idiot," Dorothy said softly.

"Oh, *I* see. *You're* going to have the soup."

She slapped him lightly, and then giggled. Any joke that they had together now seemed too delicious. She could still feel the touch of his hand on her shoulder as they stood together telling Mrs. Bird good-bye. At the station when they met, there had been a lot of curious people, and at home there had been all the folks.

"Didn't you love Mrs. Bird, though?" Dorothy asked happily. She gave a little skip, as she used to do when she and Margaret were walking together. "That was one of the places I wanted to take you to, Mrs. Bird's house."

"Bird house, hm?"

"Idiot!"

"You weren't so enthusiastic when your mother mentioned it!"

"Oh, well, I felt funny then," Dorothy said humbly.

She gave Jesse a look, and then her eyelids drooped, and he saw the fringe of her lashes on her pink cheek. For a moment his fingers closed over hers, while he carefully balanced the soup dish in one hand. They both laughed—and then they went on happily, in a delicious secret accord, under the shadows of the green leaves.

Jesse said, "Well, I expect the next thing on the program is to go over and make our peace with the parson."

That was spared them, however, for just as they came up to the church they met Mr. Lowrie. He greeted them with beaming ardor. "Well, well, well! Whom have we here?" They all stopped. But Dorothy let Jesse do most of the talking. She stood feeling dreamily the familiarity of the place, with the shabby brick wall of the church, and the walk slightly sunken and grass-grown—under this same tree, that used to look huge to her but now seemed only about as big as other trees, where she used to stand in her starched summer dress waiting for the folks to get through talking to everybody and come on home to dinner.

The church had had Mr. Lowrie only for a little while. He was one of the modern-style ministers, heartily secular, wearing business men's glasses, brought here at an increased salary in a last attempt to build up the dwindling Presbyterian flock, in this spurt of prosperity that followed the war; but something about his shoes, and the iron-gray thickness of his mop of hair with the cowlick in front, gave away his calling. His tone was appropriately jovial as he talked to Jesse about the particulars of the ceremony.

"Just have a ring, that's all. Everything else is up to the preacher. He's the one that keeps the ball rolling. Don't care for a rehearsal, folks? Well, I guess it isn't necessary. Too much of a good thing, hm? I'll just drop over between now and the great time and let you point out to me where the party is to take place. Don't want to get into the wrong pew at such a time, do we? Well—I'll see you on another occasion! Better take good care of Dorothy between now and then. She's a pretty popular young lady!"

He lifted his sunburned straw hat, carried over from last summer and cleaned by his wife, with high joviality. Dorothy and Jesse were both flushed with the sense of their conspicuousness as a bridal couple.

"Seems a jolly gentleman of the cloth," Jesse observed.

"Yes, he's kind of a Rotarian." Dorothy added, "He's nice, though," for he was the folks' minister, and her heart was too tender to make fun of him, or of anything connected with the folks.

"Oh, sure!"

"See our crazy old church," Dorothy said. "Do you want to look in?"

"You bet. I want to see everything in Belmond."

They went up the shabby steps. The brown-painted wooden door gave with a loud, alarming hollow sound. They stepped softly, almost guiltily, into the shaded silence of the auditorium. Dorothy looked around her. How little it all seemed! Until she had gone away to college, she had never thought of questioning the folks' church. A sense of pity and loss came over her when she saw how bare and hard the pews really were, how bleak were the pointed tops of the windows, most of them frosted, only a few colored, the memorial window for old Mrs. McIntosh, Corny's grandmother, and the one that the relationship had put in for Grandma and Grandpa Ferguson. The upright piano stood chilly and closed beside the platform. Yet there was a worn, homely dignity in the shabbiness of the little church. It had been built by true believers. Believers, at any rate, in the sanctity of their own denomination. Dorothy knew now that, although she had felt herself shocked and hurt sometimes by Jesse's teasing, she had long ago grown out of the folks' belief and could never go back to it. Maybe it was better that she was going away. The place and the people were intertwined in her affections.

"Is this where the little girl sat? In one of these little red chairs?"

Jesse pinched her ear. He was looking into the Sunday School room. The colored picture chart and the artificial birthday cake set with tipsy pink rosebuds and candles, seemed to him touchingly primitive. There was a tender glow over all the things that were connected with Dorothy. Dorothy, half lost in a melancholy dreaminess of reminiscence, lifted innocently troubled eyes. Jesse liked to think of her as devout and simple.

He felt an almost sensuous tenderness for this plainness and simplicity. He kissed her. The kiss was prolonged . . . in the churchly stillness, a wasp buzzing somewhere. Dorothy broke away with flushed cheeks. They went out into the sudden brilliance of sunlight. Dorothy was tingling with new, fresh happiness and wonder. It seemed as if Jesse had obliterated her tender remorse and old affections with the confident insistence of his kiss. She could never again think of Corny. And yet it was as if they had shared some sort of worship together.

Essie Bartlett's house was on the way home.

Dorothy said, "I sort of hate to make you stop there."

"Why? Can't I stop where you do?"

"Oh, well . . . Essie makes quite a fuss. You just have to take it the best you can. And old Mrs. Bartlett has been sick quite a while. She looks kind of awful, if you aren't used to her. Still, I ought to go in. Do you want to?"

"Do they belong to our church?" Jesse teased her.

She blushed. "The folks kind of look after them. So I guess . . ."

"Come on. Sure."

Jesse's hands were occupied with the soup dish, so he brushed her arm with his elbow, grinning down at her. Every evidence of Dorothy's attachment to this little town pleased him, and gave him the feeling of at last having roots somewhere. Under the summer green of the trees, smelling the freshness of the sprinkled asphalt, he almost wished they had been going to stay in Belmond.

There was a happy sense of trust between them as he solemnly followed her into the little old house. He had set down his package in a corner of the porch, and was carrying his hat in his left hand. He felt glowingly generous toward everyone who knew Dorothy; and as if each visit gave him a deeper share in her childhood. Otherwise he might have been shocked by the sight of the old woman wrapped in a quilt beside the one window. Jesse had never come so close to the hard and inalienable elements of poverty and sickness and age as he did now, in this tiny bedroom, sunken and old, where the worn, thin rug only partially covered the sagging floor. But a glow of tender feeling and of bridal exaltation overlaid his outraged, young, plutocratic resentment at having to see and acknowledge the existence of suffering and poverty. He had a romantic feeling of Dorothy as the squire's daughter visiting her father's ancient retainers.

The old woman leaned forward from her quilt, putting out a shaking hand that Jesse took almost too quickly, and forming a few difficult words with her toothless mouth, from which a little saliva helplessly dribbled, to the embarrassment of the two young people.

"Ha-ha . . . ha-do-yuh . . . d-do?"

"Oh, very well, thank you," Jesse answered in a loud bright tone. He had an idea that anyone so old was a kind of foreigner, and that he must speak loudly.

"So you're thuh—thuh . . . Dorothy . . . the one," she managed at last.

"I guess I am," Jesse answered with the same loud brightness.

He gave her a brilliant smile, which her eyes, straining through their cloudy film, were almost too dim to see. It seemed to Dorothy that Jesse, in his thick gray suit, looked almost impossibly big and young and handsome in this little room.

They tried to carry on the difficult conversation, which had to consist largely of repetitions from Dorothy, accompanied by vigorous nods. Yes, they saw that Essie wasn't here, yes, they would wait a little while, yes, the wedding was Friday, *Friday*. Jesse kept his brilliant smile of reassurance. The illusion of being actually one of a close family circle made him eager to adopt all Dorothy's connections, no matter how alien. That Dorothy came from a small town, and a rooted family life, had been one of her charms for Jesse, against those of more "stunning" girls whom he had known at the university. He felt something natural and stable in Dorothy, to which he was almost pathetically eager to attach himself. His handsome nostrils quivered a little at the strange odor of carpet and medicine and age, made even thicker by the darkening of vines outside the window.

Steps sounded quickly from outside, and Essie came rushing it. She threw up her hands at the sight of the glorious visitors.

"Oh! And I almost missed you! I had the feeling I just ought to hurry home. Isn't this a glorious visitation! Aren't we honored! Mother!" She nodded exaggeratedly at Jesse. "You know who *this* is, don't you?"

She made motions that to Jesse seemed almost crazily fantastic. And her appearance was almost as weird as her manner. Essie made her own clothes, and she still wore a modification of the waists and skirts of her girlhood. In her own feeling about herself, she could never permit herself to get really beyond that time. There was a fantastic, superannuated youthfulness now about her whole appearance. Gray had gradually encroached upon the whole mass of her hair, but she still wore the brown sidecombs and the great bone hairpins to match its remnants of faded color. Her old archness had changed from a mere slight silliness, at which "the young people" secretly laughed, into a weird exaggeration that to Jesse, in the clean youthfulness of his vision, was almost horrible in its contrast to the kind of starved, shining, fearful valiance he discerned in her eyes. But to Dorothy, although it was "sort of funny," and she was a little troubled, this was just Essie Bartlett. This manner was only the gradually developed, provincial accentuation of Essie's "way."

"So this is the young man, is it? Oh, but you don't know

277

what a famous figure you are in Belmond! The man for whom our Dorothy is deserting all our home boys! Aren't you afraid we're going to dislike you *ter*-ribly? Taking our nicest girl away off nobody knows where?"

Jesse smiled brightly—the only answer he could give to this dreadful arch gleefulness.

"And what is the *church* going to do?" Essie's voice had now become a singing wail. "We just get her back for the summer, and then you come and take her away from us!"

"It's pretty bad, all right," Jesse managed to say.

"But such a *hand*-some bridegroom!" she made big eyes. Jesse blushed and tried to laugh. Essie turned to Dorothy. "I see we have to forgive you for breaking Corny's heart and going away from us." Jesse kept his smile, but the bright red color glowed under his sunburn. "Mother! Did you see how wonderful they look together? Stand up. I want mother to see you."

Laughing, they stood up together, enduring in their pity the extravagances of praise.

Essie put her hand on Jesse's arm. "I hope you're going to be as good to her as she deserves." Her voice quivered. "You don't know what a wonderful family you're marrying into! We think there's no one in town quite like the Fergusons! So we can't bear to lose any of them. Carl and Lillian live away off in Wisconsin—that's bad enough—and now you're going to take Dorothy still farther! But then, it's just wonderful to think of the position Carl has. And we all want Dorothy to be happy."

Dorothy's softly smiling calm was disturbed a little at the sight of Essie's tears.

"Oh, but it's just ideal!" She recovered her archly valiant smile, that tried to create a social atmosphere above the visible misery of the little house. "I think it's just *I*-deal. Having Dorothy's wedding, I told Mrs. Ferguson, out on that beautiful lawn—if only the weather—oh, but it will. Everything turns out right for Dorothy, doesn't it? She was just born in good fortune. And she looks so sweet. Doesn't she? I never saw her look so sweet. It's the loveliest wedding I ever heard of!"

There was a trembling liquid brightness in Dorothy's eyes.

She was still smiling. Jesse put his arm around her shoulders. All at once, his feeling about Essie's absurdity had changed, and kindness for all the rest of the world overflowed his heart. Standing there, Jesse and Dorothy had an awareness of what they signified to the two women impaled in this little house on the bleak implacability of their small, minor tragedy. Jesse had never felt so proud of his bride. The dark little aged-smelling room became the center of their happiness. Here Dorothy was appreciated as nowhere else. Here she stood as the acknowledged and adored princess of the little, local circle of the faithful of the church. Her loveliness in her delicately tinted silks bloomed in a radiance of bridal freshness in the close darkness of the room. Jesse was proud to be thought of as only the bridegroom, as he stood with his arm about Dorothy. He felt the other sister dark and shadowed beside her. Dorothy—the chosen maiden, the bride, the rose—stood out from them all. But in the loveliness of her silks, crowned by the shady hat, her handsome bridegroom beside her in the stunning splendor of his masculinity, these adoring ones knew that she was too wonderful for them to keep. They accepted the right of this stranger prince who had come to bear away their princess to a distant land. The happiness of the bridal couple had never been so poignant as now.

Old Mrs. Bartlett groped with a painful hand toward Dorothy's, that sweetly enclosed it, flowerlike and soft; and she managed a few words out of the dimness of her fading comprehension and the still enduring struggle of her effort to hang on to life.

"A nice . . . a nice . . . time—wedding . . ."

A tear trickled out and wet the channels of wrinkles driven hopelessly deep into her withered face.

3

That evening the house was full of company. What had started out as a dinner for the relationship—Uncle Ben and Aunt Ella and the Whites, all of them rather shy before such a resplendent bridegroom—had changed into a gay young people's gathering.

But not the church young people! Quite a different set. Corny, of course, was not here. He was working this summer with a road survey gang in another part of the state—"had to get away where he wouldn't need to see Dorothy marry someone else," Aunt Ella had stated with that shrewd, primitive bluntness the girl disliked so. During the last two or three summers, although so gradually and naturally that the folks themselves had hardly noticed it, Dorothy had been getting into another crowd. Margaret was aware, if the folks weren't, that these young people who had dropped in so casually tonight, to see Dot and the man she was going to marry, were the élite of Belmond's younger set, the rather anomalous but most glorious crowd between the high school gang and the young married people. Virginia Brattle was the leader; and tonight, ranging like a princess through the social possibilities of the town, she had picked up and brought along a girl who was visiting the Hoaglands, and three youths, two native and one imported, whom she had gathered from Belmond's scanty supply of eligible young men beyond high school age.

Margaret didn't want to stay with the other young people. She went upstairs to put on some powder, and remained for a long time shut in her own room, that was consolingly fragant with the loveliness of Aunt Louie's toilet things. Margaret felt at the same time gratified by the social glory that Dorothy's marriage was bringing upon the household, and more lonely and aloof than ever. She exaggerated the two years' difference in age between herself and Dorothy and Virginia. The radiant bloom of their success made her feel shelved and old. It humiliated her, made her feel that she had nothing ahead of her but being assistant forever in the home town library, an old maid's job, while Dorothy was getting married to a man the girls were all crazy about, and Virginia, in a day or two, was leaving for Spain, where she had a year's scholarship for travel and study— for *Spain*, one of Margaret's own countries! Still, Margaret felt fiercely that this was not her real rôle. Some day everybody would have to acknowledge it.

She came downstairs, knowing that if she stayed up there alone her mother and Aunt Louie would be after her, urging her, with mistaken kindness, to have a good time with the other young people.

The victrola was going full blast. *Dancing.* They were actually dancing! And the folks were letting them!

"Come on in, Sister Anne," Jesse called out gaily, dancing past with the new girl, who looked at Margaret coolly and appraisingly over Jesse's shoulder.

Margaret shook her head. She would not answer her mother's quickly pleading look. She felt dark with resentment. She knew that Dorothy, the little villain, must have been dancing all the time she was in Crown Point, and probably long before. But trust her to say nothing to the folks about it until exactly the right moment! Margaret remembered how she had begged and stormed all through one period of her girlhood to be allowed to dance—and then, of course, the folks couldn't hear of it! Now they would have been glad enough to have her go to dances if that could have kept her contented here—now, when it was too late, and nobody would think of asking her! And then Dorothy, as always, had just easily and naturally held out her hand, and the fruit of all Margaret's stormy and useless rebellion had dropped softly into it.

Aunt Louie beckoned and Margaret went over to her.

"Why don't *you* go in with them?" Aunt Louie coaxed. She squeezed Margaret's hand, and Margaret felt the pressure of her rings.

"I don't know how to dance," Margaret said curtly. She drew her hand away from Aunt Louie's, without deigning to look at her mother.

"I'm going out and help Nellie."

This was probably her rôle in Belmond, helping Dot's crowd to have a good time! That was what Jesse supposed. He accepted her with naïve simplicity as just a natural-born second fiddle. If she could have made any little gesture that would have forced him, just for one moment, to take her on her own grounds, that would have satisfied her! But she had to go on fuming darkly under Jesse's radiantly kindly patronage.

"I didn't know you girls danced," Nellie said shyly.

"We never have. The folks never let us before. I've done it, however," Margaret couldn't help saying.

"Gee, isn't he—isn't Dorothy's—Mr. Woodward—isn't he grand-looking?"

Margaret brooded as she cut the chocolate cake. This gang probably had liquor at Virginia's, but the folks would think they were being quite gay with grape juice. Margaret could remember when she had looked with awe at the tall, narrow, much towered and balconied house where the Brattles lived. And she remembered how Virginia had seemed to her like a storybook heroine, sitting with her father's arm around her on the bleachers at the football game. Virginia's father "adored" her like the fathers of only daughters in books—except that Virginia's mother was alive, and that Mr. and Mrs. Brattle did nothing but fight, except when Virginia was with them.

But Margaret couldn't feel romantic about anyone in Belmond any more. Her thoughts were all away. And she was disdainful because Virginia, in spite of her great reputation for intellectuality and her scholarship in Spain, took out all the Kathleen Norris novels from the library just like other people, even if she could chatter a little about the new poetry.

This made Margaret feel her disdainful aloofness from Belmond again. She was fortified by it when she went back with Nellie to pass the cake and grape juice, contemptuously acting the part that Jesse thought was so lovely for her. She wished that Aunt Ella had stayed to see them dancing! But anger at Uncle Ben for beginning to snore had routed Aunt Ella at last—she wanted to get him where she could wrangle with him about it as openly as she pleased. And probably, since it was Dorothy dancing, even Aunt Ella wouldn't say anything! Aunt Louie, warm and smiling, looked upon this as just the natural good times for the young people. She did not know that it marked an epoch, that it showed that the Ferguson family had finally broken out from the tight little provincial circle of church and relationship and taken its place among the leading modern households of Belmond. Dorothy's wedding had brought that about just naturally. But it was too late for it to matter to Margaret.

She was elated, all the same, and felt a certain victory over the folks. Virginia, tall and stylistically thin, in her white summer silk with a hanging heavy rope of dark green beads, her golden hair combed in a shining wing across her forehead, a long narrow foot in an elegantly heeled and pointed white slipper dangling, was perched with angular grace on the arm of Dorothy's chair, from which she dominated the room with her vibrant voice and long-armed gestures. Margaret fastidiously approved of Virginia's "distinction." She noted, with hungry acuteness for all such points, how Virginia parted her hair far over at one side and brought it down over her ears to be gathered into a sort of loop at the back. But Dorothy, sitting between Virginia leaning protectively over her and Jesse hunched on a cushion at the floor on the other side, kept her softly smiling, womanly poise. Margaret felt a hot wave of her old big-sister, proud, critical, emotional love for Dorothy. She was fiercely pleased that in spite of Virginia's dominance, Dorothy was really the center. The boys really liked Dorothy better. That was it. They were a little afraid of Virginia. Margaret despised the boys, too, for this, for their touchy masculine pride and conventionality; but the family pride that existed along with intense criticism and disdain, blazed up in exultation. Dorothy's pastel-blue frock made her eyes really like forget-me-nots under the fluffy brown of the new permanent. Virginia's angular style was more modern; but Dorothy's softness, her pretty feminine compactness, with the tapering wrists and ankles, had a more ancient charm. Yet Margaret felt, as she went about with the cake on the best silver dish, that she herself belonged more to Virginia's kind of girl than to Dorothy's; and anger was tangled up in her feelings.

Virginia and Dorothy had a moment to themselves in the hall as the crowd was leaving. Virginia's hands, narrow, white, long-fingered, angularly distinguished, clasped Dorothy's, that were small and yielding, but with capable little feminine fingers. The two girls felt a thrilling equality in their destinies, in the radiance of the future for both of them. Virginia was leaving for Spain in two days—on the very day when Dorothy was to be married.

"Dorothy, I think he's simply grand—absolutely marvelous!" Virginia said in a low, vibrant tone. She squeezed Dorothy's hands. Both girls swayed a little. "Aren't you the lucky child?"

Dorothy smiled. She stood pliant and soft, letting Virginia swing their clasped hands. But there was a subtle certainty in the dimpling corners of her pretty lips. Her friendship with Virginia had really begun a summer or two ago, when they had found themselves the only two girls of their particular age in Belmond, who were of a complementary degree of attractiveness, and who could both play tennis. At first Virginia had chosen Dorothy with regal nonchalance as her new little lady-in-waiting. But tonight they had suddenly become equals. No, with Jesse here, as Dorothy's own—the most marvelously handsome male creature who had ever struck Belmond!—it was Dorothy who wore the crown; this was Dorothy's evening; and Virginia was generously admitting it now.

"Dorothy, you sweet little creature, I simply have to kiss you!"

They embraced, both laughing exultantly, Dorothy casting a glance back toward the other room. All at once it seemed as if they were destined friends—as if they couldn't bear to part. Yet this parting just when their friendship had reached its height was one of the sweetest events of this whole wonderful week.

Everyone else came into the hall now, to say good-bye to Virginia, and to ask about her journey. She held center for the moment. But Dorothy stood back, one hand still in Virginia's, smiling and secure.

"I think it's so wonderful for both you girls!" Aunt Louie said with warm generosity.

Dorothy and Virginia were smiling. Helen, the other girl, smiled too. She was going to Vassar in the fall for her final year of college work. After that she meant to do—something. It seemed to the older people that never had there been such a fortunate set of young people. Everything was before them, everything in their favor, nothing dimmed the radiance of the untouched future. They would have all that had been lacking for the older generations.

"Margaret, you'll have to go away too," Virginia said graciously.

Margaret glanced toward her mother and shrugged her shoulders.

"Oh, no, we have to keep Margaret for a while, if you others are going to leave us," Aunt Louie said. She put her arm around Margaret. She would never allow herself to show any partiality with the two girls. "I can't let her go before I do, anyway. Can I, Margaret?"

Margaret flushed.

"Bun, aren't *you* going somewhere?" one of the boys demanded in mock drama of Bunny, who was standing grinning.

"Yes, I'm going to the baseball game between Belmond and Parkersville next Wednesday in the fair grounds."

Everyone laughed.

Jesse and Dorothy had walked down to the car with their guests, and stood talking. Now, as they went slowly back up the walk toward the house, they saw that already some of the lights had been turned off. Bunny was scooting off toward the alley, making for the pup tent where he was sleeping with his friend Joseph, so that Jesse could have his room. All the other houses in the block were dark. The noise of the car was dying away down the street. The moist, sweet darkness of the June evening surrounded the house, shut in by trees. Jesse had his arm around Dorothy. For the first time they seemed to be really alone together. Jesse's arm tightened, he felt the quivering, soft response of Dorothy's body. They still kept the elation and excitement of the successful evening—the admiration of the other people made each appreciate the other to the utmost. But now, out here in the evening, this feeling was touched with awe. They walked slowly.

"Don't you want to stay out a little while?" Jesse murmured.

Dorothy let herself be led across the wet lawn. She let her steps be guided by Jesse's. She began to feel that she had no motion of her own. It was a strangely blissful sensation, not as if she were weak, but as if she had surrendered herself to some greater element within which they were both moving enchanted.

They had never been so much in love with each other as now in this secret interval of dewy darkness. And they felt, as with each further opening up of their love—this was new!

They stopped for a moment under the big maple tree.

"Shall we have our rehearsal?" Jesse whispered.

Dorothy lifted her face to smile back at him. But Jesse's face almost frightened her. She felt it, with the dark, dilated eyes, coming closer to her own. She could not get away. She had been a little innocent fool, moving blissfully along in that dream of surrender. For a moment, she wanted wildly to struggle. Then she was as much a part of it as he was. That first touch at the station had been all awkward, awry. It was almost an alienation. But it had broken the way for others—the quick exquisite touches, the clasp of hands on the shady street coming home from Mrs. Bird's, and then the kiss in the silent church—broken off—coming out into the brilliant sunshine . . . this moment had grown out of those brief, snatched-off touches. All day it had been mounting to this sudden, glorious completion. They seemed to melt into one being, to be in only one dimension that was a point of center; and everything else fled away from them, leaving them dizzy and together. They could not separate. A helpless, long, ecstatic sigh, almost a sob, breathed from Dorothy's lips as Jesse's pressed harder and harder against them.

"Dorothy—sweetheart—" she heard Jesse whisper—"you'd better not stay out here any longer."

She said in wonder, "No, I guess not."

She drew herself away from Jesse. Something in her obedience to him did it for her. She had no power of her own. Dorothy went back across the lawn and into the silent house.

She had never known *this*. That was what she felt, as she went quickly and softly up the stairs. She felt with wonder how she was trembling. The world seemed shaken, broken apart, by a shining, wonderful amazement. The features of her small, happy, known world had not really been changed for Dorothy by her "falling in love," or by the excitement of her engagement. They had been confirmed. But now she felt the ground move under her feet—she had even a sight of depths beneath it. Falling in love with somebody, engagement, marriage—these old terms, that she had always accepted, had a new meaning now. Terms, outlines, had suddenly become luminous. She had experienced a miracle. She felt as if she must tell someone—and yet she didn't want anybody to see her. She wondered if anybody else in the world really knew what she did now. And it seemed as if they couldn't—or they wouldn't just go on calmly living. Margaret didn't know it. Dorothy felt a warm, great rush of pity for Margaret's ignorance. She felt infinitely older now than her sister—almost maternal. She felt sorry for everybody in the world, who didn't know . . . that there was something beyond people, something that was greater than they were, that in love there was an absolute center of joy. And yet it seemed to be something that only she and Jesse *could* know in the world.

Dorothy got into bed beside Margaret and lay there as quietly as she could. But her body was pulsating in a new, shining restlessness. When she heard Jesse come up the stairs, after quietly closing the front door, and go tiptoeing down the hall, it was almost too blissful a torture to know that he was only as far away as Bun's room, sleeping in the same house with her. It was all she could do not to get up and go to him, softly, in her bare feet, with the little lace straps of her nightgown slipping from her bare shoulders. But she was glad. For now it was all to be kept for that first night of their own that would follow the lovely, long-dreamed-of ritual of the wedding.

4

The perfect sequence of events went on rolling out smoothly, one after another thing happened—like Dorothy's old dream of what it would be, and yet colored and made real by the local home setting, making it not just a wedding, but her *own* wedding. Dorothy seemed to herself to be passing through it all in a dream; and yet inside she felt herself quiveringly, exquisitely alive to all that happened.

There was a delicious crowding of events. It seemed almost impossible to get them all in! The day of Jesse's arrival had been filled with calls and the party in the evening. The next day they had decided on the new car, which dad had tentatively selected for them at the dealer's, after long weighing of the advantages of this and that. Dorothy and Jesse would rather have gone to Geneva; but dad would have been hurt if they hadn't patronized the local dealer. And then they had to drive out to see Uncle Ben and Aunt Ella, and to show Jesse the farm. All this time mother was anxiously mourning over how tired Dorothy was getting! Mother and Aunt Louie both treated her like some precious, cherished doll. They had to get back in time to go to Ethel Spencer's for luncheon—the cool, high-ceilinged dining room of the Spencer house, the grand house of Dorothy's childhood, all so cool and darkened and fresh, the fruity, tingling summer drink in tall glasses frosted with moisture, the salads on the dark green grape leaves, the memory left of all that—and then she must take the rest mother and Aunt Louie insisted on in the afternoon, and then go down to the Beauty Shoppe to get her nails done, and then they must all go to supper at the Whites'. Carl and Lillian and the kids were there now. Carl and Jesse got along splendidly together. All the folks liked Jesse! Aunt Ella had commented, "I thought maybe he'd be stuck up, at first, he kind o' looked like it, but he ain't a bit, he's just real common." That was terribly high praise from Aunt Ella!

Everything went so swiftly, so relentlessly. Yet there were little moments to herself. Dorothy went into the sewing room again to see her presents, not so much for the richness of all these possessions, as for the associations. The other teachers in Crown Point had clubbed together and bought her and Jesse a marvelous silk-and-down coverlet. And there was the lovely little silky, Japanese negligee, from old Mrs. Spencer out in California, and the note that said in a tremulous, slanting handwriting: "A blue-flowered robe for a blue-eyed maiden." And she hadn't seen old Mrs. Spencer since she was a child! People were too good to her—and yet, somehow, it was right. And there were times not marked that stayed now in her memory.

Driving back from town with Jesse in the new roadster, having the family come out to see—the delicious, thrilling, shaking conspicuousness of that moment when she and Jesse sat there smiling in the beautiful little shining dark blue car, waiting to be seen. Now it stood out in front. Through the windows, from the open front door, she could catch thrilling glimpses of it, shining and elegant and new, drawn up under the patterned shade of the trees, the silver gleam of high lights from the smoothly hooded lamps and from the little dashing winged radiator cap. Dorothy knew—but she couldn't stop to think about it—that she was going away in that car. And then the times when people came to the house . . . Essie Bartlett came to see the presents, repeating that it was "*i*-deal," and telling Jesse he never could have rightly appreciated Dorothy unless he had seen her here in her own home; Mrs. Viele came, so kind, an old friend and family neighbor; and Ethel Spencer, linking her smooth arm in Dorothy's, telling her with that flattering personal effusiveness that Jesse was the handsomest bridegroom ever seen in Belmond, and that he and Dorothy made a couple too stunning for words. Dorothy had to forgive Ethel, in the perfection of her happiness, for the way Ethel and Richard used to ignore the folks.

In the late afternoon, when maple tree shadows lay long across the green grass, across the pavement, Dorothy was upstairs cleaning her face with cold cream and changing from her silk suit to her little orchid pastel silk to go to Aunt Jennie's for dinner—when they called her down again.

"Dorothy, come here! Something for you!"

She ran lightly clattering down the polished stairs and through the hallway where the great bunch of daisies that Margaret and Aunt Louie had arranged in the jardinière filled all one corner with starry white.

"See what you got!"

They were all laughing—and yet moved. Old Dick had given dad this present to take home to her. He was so lame he couldn't have hobbled over with it himself. It was one of the gift books from Stark's drug store—they all recognized it, part of a stock that had been brought out at Christmas and Commencement from time immemorial—*The Perfect Tribute,* in fat shiny green leather binding, already a little broken at the back. "I expect the title took him," Mrs. Ferguson said in a low voice. While they all talked about it, Dorothy looked at it, her lips in a lovely line of pathos; and when Jesse came in she gave it to him, with a little-girl pleading for him to like it, to pretend with her that it was lovely, saying—

"Look, Jesse! From old Dick, at the bank"—in a soft voice.

All this for her, for Dorothy! For her, everyone was here, Carl and Lillian, Mrs. Christianson and Nellie helping in the house, Aunt Louie, Uncle Henry coming late tonight. And yet it was right—amazing, but right. This was her time. All the secret undercurrents were flowing toward her. In her happiness she could accept it.

"Isn't she looking lovely?" Someone would murmur that to someone else. Dorothy would half hear it. "I never saw her look so lovely!" She knew it, in a trembling, beautiful daze. A face, strangely brightened and aroused, looked back at her from the mirror—that liquid brightness in the eyes . . . and yet somehow, in a soft flutter of the hands, in a soft curve of the lips, there was something waiting, trembling on the very verge of awakening, and yet still in its dream.

Best of all, interspersed with marvelous haphazardness among the marked events, were those moments alone with Jesse—the touch, the kisses—exquisite in pain.

And then tomorrow—the wedding.

Dorothy thought of that, its utter incredibility, its utter inevitability, as if she had never thought of it before—thought of it when she came home from the Whites' in the evening, and she and Margaret were undressing together in her room. Having to sleep together again brought back the old sisterly bond. And because they were both thinking that this was the last night they would be here like this, the two daughters of the house, they talked frivolously and giggled inordinately about things that had happened at dinner. Their mother came in. "Aren't you two silly girls going to stop laughing tonight?" Her face was a little hurt; yearning for some acknowledgment that Dorothy understood what the event was, that she realized this was her last night among them as their little girl. But Dorothy veered away from any sign of emotion, and she kept on being silly as she kissed her mother good night. She and Jesse had only brushed each other's lips with a kiss on the porch, before Dorothy fled upstairs to her room. The family had carefully gone inside to leave them out there together.

The lights were out at last. Dorothy and Margaret were in bed. The night passed, dark and cool and enveloping, a little breeze rising toward morning, in the first darkness a flutter of moths and insects outside, the faint motion of the leaves, the familiar night sounds of the town, cars passing, the whistle of an engine off on the tracks. Margaret and Dorothy were both awake at intervals. Dorothy knew that this night was passing, but she seemed not capable of realization—knew in the same strange yet ineffaceable way that this was her last night at home—tomorrow night she would be with Jesse—somewhere . . . there her thoughts stopped in a breathless dazzle, that yet was softened by her inability actually to imagine that it was going to be. When she awakened in the darkness, she knew again that Jesse was here in this same house, lying in Bun's bed, in Carl's old room, his window open upon the darkness just as hers was, upon her own familiar back yard. Once again she was awake, in that secret darkness—barely awake—and Margaret was turning toward her, feeling for her with her hand. The two girls were both silent, neither acknowledging that she was not asleep, and neither fully awake although cognizant. They snuggled into each other's arms. Then after a while, sighing, each turned away again and drifted into sleep. They knew that each must have been thinking something, but there had been nothing but that mute drawing together, in Margaret's clasp a protective affection, in Dorothy's an affirming of the old bond.

Then at dawn she wakened again—heard the morning chatter of the birds through the damp, unearthly grayness that held the town so strangely silent—until the swooping past of the cars came more steadily and noisily, some voices shouted somewhere . . . Dorothy was all at once irritated and querulous. It seemed to her that she had been awake all night. She would look awful at the ceremony. "I am going to be married this morning." Fear clutched at her heart. It seemed to stop beating —the world seemed to stop living . . . until the high sound of the cars became soothing, she went to sleep and this time slept soundly.

In the morning Dorothy was calmer than she had dreamed that she could be. The event brought its own strange calmness. It was a queer breakfast, hurried and yet ceremonious, as if it didn't belong to their family, but was a sort of public affair. Aunt Louie, with social tact and affability, kept everyone talking and saying the right things; with that kindness that raised platitudes to a ceremonious charm. Yet her smile lovingly acknowledged the bridal pair. Dad would break in with naïve references, not understanding the social etiquette of a wedding that Aunt Louie was trying to maintain, asking Jesse if he had any trouble in driving the new car, if they knew where they were going to stay tonight, had maps, had the trip all in mind.

"You mustn't ask them that, dad," Mrs. Ferguson pleaded.

"What?"

"They're just going where they please. You mustn't map it all out for them."

"Well, I don't want them to get lost."

"They won't mind that!" Aunt Louie said.

They all laughed. Jesse's brown skin was brightly flushed. Margaret looked dark and constrained. Bunny's eyes were excited, but he was reserving his comments for Joseph.

Nothing she ate had any taste for Dorothy. The talk passed over her head, although she sat there smiling. She felt a queer coldness inside. Her hands were cold. It seemed as if she were no longer an individual with any movement of her own, but a little marionette going through with something that had been started outside her volition and couldn't be stopped. Jesse was the other marionette. But she had no feeling for Jesse.

Yet she was acutely conscious of things around her. She knew that she would never forget the feeling of this day, the brightness of the morning, the glass bowl of ruffled pink roses on the shining best damask of the breakfast table, the smell of toast and bacon in the summer air, and Nellie silently passing around the table with the silver coffeepot. When she went out on the porch for a moment, she was aware of the mowed greenness of the lawn, saw the dappled shadows under the big maple tree, and knew—although she would not believe it—that that was where she was going to stand in a little while. She had an interval of being able to talk quite naturally with Aunt Louie out on the porch—and then knowledge caught her up again. She had to go into the sewing room and give last minute directions about the presents. Mother and dad were to keep them here, and send them along when she and Jesse wanted them. It seemed as if the whole stock of shining new gifts had always been laid out just like this in the sewing room. But now Dorothy had none of the feeling about them with which she had stolen into the room—that here lay the nucleus of the home that was to be all new, all hers and Jesse's, yet carrying on the tradition and the life of the old household, of which she was the daughter. Going back into the living room, she realized the shining, spaced, formal cleanliness of the house. She felt the controlled excitement. All at once it seemed silly, incredible, that this was happening, that everybody was making such a fuss. It seemed as if dad ought to go back to the bank. He always looked so helpless and at large when he had nothing to do. It was an absurdity that she, little Dorothy Ferguson, was the center of all this great to-do. Didn't everybody else see that? No, they were all quite solemn. They believed that it was real. But it wasn't—none of it. Jesse was simply a strange young man with shining black hair trying to work off his excited constraint by talking with Bunny about aeroplanes.

But the thing went on, and she couldn't help it. People began to arrive. Aunt Ella and Uncle Ben came in early. Dorothy felt stricken by the momentousness of the occasion when she saw Uncle Ben in the thick blackness of his best clothes, and Aunt Ella in her dark brown silk with her hair actually curled under one of her awful stiff hats. Aunt Ella always got those stiff hats! She said that soft ones didn't seem new, and she wanted to know she had a new hat when she had one. Dorothy caught Margaret's eye; and they had to dive into the sewing room and stand there giggling, hugging each other, almost as silly as they had been last night. Her sister, for the moment, was much closer to her than her lover. But they had to go back into the living room. Aunt Ella and Uncle Ben were asking solemnly how she was, as if she were sick. Uncle Ben, when she smiled at him, had a timid look, almost as if she had become a stranger. She wasn't allowed to keep the naturalness of that interval on the porch.

"You'd better go upstairs now and get dressed, Dorothy."

She tried to take leave easily and naturally. But she could make no headway against the atmosphere of the house. Now her nervousness began to overcome her, like a sickness kept at bay but finally overwhelming her and taking control. She felt how strange it all was—the brightness of sunshine across her polished bedroom floor, the doll sitting up straight and stiff, as Nellie had placed her, among the lacy cushions. Dorothy wanted childishly to kiss the doll. But even the doll was staringly significant of a new secret. Now all her attempts at naturalness had given way to a height of excitement, through which her mother, smilingly tearful, and Aunt Louie in her lovely consoling poise, were moving about her. It was all so solemn, and yet so cluttered up and familiar too. She ran into Jesse as she was leaving the bathroom, with Aunt Louie's negligee (her own beautiful new forget-me-not one was packed) thrown over her shoulders, and her arms still damp and cool from her bath. She felt a queer shock of intimacy when she met Jesse in his white shirt, with no collar, the shining black hair brushed.

"Where are *you* going, kid?"

He put his hands on her elbows and squeezed them tight against her; and she saw the bright excitement in his eyes with their shining black lashes.

Dorothy hurried smiling back to her room. She couldn't get her right breathing. So this was what a wedding was like! It was her own wedding.

"Aunt Louie, you look after me," she whispered. "If mama does, I'll cry."

Aunt Louie pressed her hand.

In spite of the intimacy of dressing, there was that exciting, foolish, alien formality. Dorothy was the bride. She had her room all to herself now. Margaret was dressing in her own room, where Nellie, with fingers careful from awe, had stiffly arranged Aunt Louie's lovely, fragrant toilet things. The house was all given over to the wedding.

Dorothy felt herself less and less a person, more and more a kind of puppet—a precious one. Aunt Louie had dressed quickly, her mother still more quickly, so that they could come in and help her. It was exciting, like a home talent play, like the first sight of familiar people in their costumes, to see everyone dressed for the occasion. Her mother had hurried so that Aunt Louie, laughing, had to fasten up the hooks, at the side of her light silk dress, which she had forgotten. Dorothy felt that Aunt Louie, in the peach-pink exquisiteness of her georgette gown, the flat yellowish lace softly curved by the abundance of her lovely bosom, gave a beautiful sumptuousness to the day. Some of the relatives were coming in to see the bride. Lillian came. Dorothy, sitting on her dressing table bench, her legs in their shimmering pale silk stockings held out for her mother to fasten the new white slippers with their elegant heels, smiled at Lillian with pale lips in a pale face. Aunt Ella had come up too, asking, "Anything I can do to help?" She had to watch with dull black eyes and comment on all Dorothy's things, sitting heavily on the little enameled cream-white chair. On the bed lay the wedding dress, and the three-piece ensemble of blue shantung in which the bride was to "go away." Dorothy felt the wonder of the delicate, new, silken underthings touch her body.

"My! Going to be fine all over!" Aunt Ella said.

"She has to be now, if she's ever going to be," Aunt Louie said fondly.

Dorothy stood and lifted her white arms to have the bridal slip of elegantly heavy crêpe-de-chine put over her head. She saw herself in the mirror—but the image was strange. While her mother and Aunt Louie were gently fussing with the wedding dress on the bed, letting Lillian see it before it was put on the bride, Margaret came into the room.

"Well, look here!" Aunt Ella commented. "Look at the other one, would you!"

Margaret had come in excited and strange; and the older women stood away a moment from the bride to appreciate her and exclaim over her, slim and changed by her bridesmaid's dress of pale green chiffon with roses, in a rustle and fragrance. "You look good in green. Look almost as pretty as the bride!" Aunt Ella said in frank amazement. Margaret scowled. But she looked prettier than the bride—she knew it—whether anyone noticed it or not. She was elated by her sudden keen sparkle of beauty in the fragile pink and green. Aunt Ella could put a damper on anything!

"Hasn't Dot got her dress on yet?"

"We don't want to put it on her before we're ready to go down. She can't sit down after she has that on!" Aunt Louie said.

But they lifted it now, carefully, the frosty white silk and laciness; and still more carefully, with soft skillful touches of Aunt Louie's hands, its beautifulness was put upon the bride and shaped to her. Dorothy stood with lightly outstretched hands. There were murmurs and exclamations. The others were all surrounding her, and she in her whiteness seemed scarcely visible among them. Dorothy, strangely enough, at this highest moment, was small, and queerly sad, too colorless, subdued, in the utter whiteness of her bridal array. It was as if she had shrunk from an individual to a symbol, and had no life or beauty of her own.

"I look *awful*," she cried with sudden despair, seeing herself in the glass.

Her mother and Aunt Louie indignantly denied it. She was a little pale. She couldn't help that. But her beauty in the white was strangely impersonal; while Margaret, flashing and dark in her fresh light colors, was an individuality. Nevertheless, Dorothy was the center.

Mrs. Christianson had come to the door. She said in a mysterious, loud whisper, "I wanted to see Dorothy!" The others dispersed, and Dorothy stood to be viewed, smiling through the exclamations, not feeling real.

"Oh, my! Isn't that just too beautiful. Nellie told me about it. Well, I just wanted to see how she looked before it was too late! While we could still call her Dorothy Ferguson."

Mrs. Christianson clasped Dorothy's fingers in her large, veined, bony, work-worn hand. She said to her in secret, "Well, you're going to have a nice lunch to take away with you, anyway." And then to the others, "My, it don't seem like she kin be going off, does it? I don't know what we'll all do."

"Everybody likes Dorothy," Mrs. Ferguson said emotionally to Aunt Louie, who quickly squeezed her hand. She felt the comfort of having her own sister here.

Mrs. Christianson added, also amazed, "Margaret looks awful nice, too! Say, I never saw you look so nice."

"Better look out, Margaret, or you'll be getting married yourself," Aunt Ella said, "if you're going to get so good-looking."

Cars were parked around the house now. They could hear the sound of people below them. Reverend and Mrs. Lowrie had come. Aunt Louie went for the two glorious bridal bouquets with which Uncle Henry was presenting the bride and the bridesmaid.

"Did you ever see anything so wonderful in your life! I bet those didn't come from here."

"No, Henry got them in Chicago."

"Well, I thought!"

And now was the moment. It could not be avoided. They must go through with it. Everyone was here now, waiting. Hurried word was sent up to know if Dorothy was ready. It was time for all the others to go down, leaving Dorothy and Margaret for a moment alone. Mrs. Ferguson now was crying as she hurried out to the lawn. Aunt Ella looked solemn and abashed.

In a high strange dream, Dorothy came out of her bedroom, in her white. Only Margaret was left to follow her down the stairs, that lay shining and still in the hush of all but music, where Della Fessel, the church organist, was playing the piano beside the open parlor window. Jesse, solemn, incredibly handsome in his white summer suit, waited at the foot of the stairs.

Bunny, his best man, pale and very young, stood beside him. Mr. Lowrie waited easily, but with a look of gratification on his face. His thick gray mane was damply brushed. Dorothy, small and white, went down the stairs.

They went out onto the porch and down the steps, across the green lawn in the summery brightness of early noon, only half aware of scents and sights and movement that would always stay with them—seeing with startled fear the people gathered there, all so strange and formal in the best clothes put on for this occasion, the little group of the immediate family, Carl standing with a hand on the shoulder of each of his little boys. Mr. Lowrie preceded them. They took their stand near the maple tree. Jesse and Dorothy were together; yet each was lost in a cold desert of self. They managed to form their group, with Dorothy and Jesse in the center, Margaret and Bunny on either side. They stood trembling but still. Mr. Lowrie faced them. He had his black church manual open in his hand. The music from the house stopped. The words began that Dorothy had heard in her own mind many times, in secret—but that now were being spoken for her.

"Dearly beloved, we are gathered together in the presence of God and these witnesses."

At that "dearly beloved," in the sudden solemnity of Mr. Lowrie's voice, tears that had been waiting sprang to the bright surface of Dorothy's eyes.

Now, Dorothy seemed to have only a cold, acute perception of things about her, the breeze in the maple leaves, the people facing her, the soft blowing back of her lacy skirt. She knew that she stood before them all, being married . . . but she realized nothing more than that her voice gave the responses, and the other voice was Jesse's.

But to the other people gathered there, the small white figure held their eyes. It formed the center of the sunlit, green, June day, with the leaves and the roses. Margaret stood with eyes dark and strained, and yet elated. This was Dorothy's time and place, and there was a sumptuous delight in feeling that everything was perfect. Uncle Ben had to get out his folded white handkerchief and wipe his eyes. Dorothy had always been his little favorite. The parents felt blinded. But Mrs. Ferguson kept smiling to show that it was all as it should be. Mr. Ferguson stood in great constraint, concentrated on his determination not to show the faintest sign of breaking down. He hated all occasions. Aunt Louie, though, was crying. She stood large and opulent beside the small, dry figure of Uncle Henry. Tears kept welling up, and she had to wipe them away with a lace-edged, delicately stiff handkerchief. She was going to excuse herself afterwards to everyone by saying that it was because Dorothy made such a lovely bride. But under that feeling was an awareness of the subtle disappointment and fading aridity of her own marriage—happy enough, because she knew that Henry loved and valued her, there was never anything wrong between them—and yet she knew that her girlhood hopes were somehow unanswered, would always be unanswered.

She was being married now, before them all—the folks, Essie, all the familiar church circle. This was the moment. She, Dorothy.

Then it *was* over. That great moment had passed. The hushed, sunlit solemnity was all broken up by the flutter, exclamations, movement, embraces, tears of this stage of the wedding. Now Dorothy felt suddenly that she was present, the dream had lifted, she was going through with this. The color came back into her pale face. A bright rose-pink burned on her cheeks, her eyes, dark still from the strain, were bright as after a shower. Her soft, smiling passivity was heightened into radiance. She submitted in bright excitement to all the embraces, turning from one to another, begging at one moment, "Mama, don't cry—*don't* cry"—turning radiantly to lift her face for Uncle Ben's kiss, not caring about the tears still on her face, lifted above caring. She felt so deeply her love for all the people here. Every contact was strangely heightened after that free, deeply and silently fervent kiss between herself and Jesse, when they had turned their faces toward each other in a beautiful spontaneous movement after Mr. Lowrie had "pronounced" them "husband and wife." She had never had such understanding and sympathy for people—for everybody. She felt humble in her happiness, beneath her pride. Everybody seemed at his best, everyone to be appreciated for what he was as friend or relative. Cars went past obliviously on the shade-dappled pavement beyond the trees. But a few passers-by, some women, unknown to the family, who lived over stores downtown in a few rooms, and had timed it to walk past here when the wedding was going on—and one or two people coming along by chance—slowed up to have a look at the company out on the stretch of lawn between the Ferguson house and the little rented house next door; and to catch a glimpse of the bride and groom.

There were all the jokes about first calling Dorothy "Mrs. Woodward."

But after that, the occasion slipped away from the bride and belonged to the guests, to everybody. The luncheon was for them—the carefully planned plate luncheon, talked over so long with Aunt Louie, shaped by Margaret's fastidious exactions, served in the house by Nellie Christianson with Lillian and Jennie helping, and Mrs. Christianson in the kitchen.

The bride came back into her own for a little while, however, before she left. She came downstairs in her little blue silk suit and hat, with Jesse just behind her. Then everybody had to go out on the porch to see the start. It was a mixed company, but all drawn together by some long connection with the Fergusons—Essie, the Lowries, Ada Rist, Vanchie Darlington because of Margaret, Ethel and Richard Spencer in smiling graciousness, the Morgans, some more of the church people, and of course all the relationship. Margaret, hating demonstrations with a fierce, aristocratic averseness, would not go to the front of the group although Essie tried to push her forward. Other neighbors were at their windows.

The two ran down the walk and got into the new car which Bunny had just driven resplendently to the curbing. It took a few moments for them to get seated, while Mr. Ferguson made sure that all the baggage was safely in the back of the car. Then their faces turned back toward the house. Dorothy had said good-bye to her mother upstairs. But now she bent forward to find her mother's face among the others. It was still full daylight. Everything was flooded with light. The familiar lawn, the cream-colored house standing there, were transfigured. It seemed as if the whole earth, at this most beautiful time of the year, was in bloom for the wedding. And by this symbol, the dark, alien dream of the war had finally lifted from this small inland place among great cornfields. For this hour, their world had gone back to its old innocence, and everything was prosperous and fresh and sunlit again. The two young people in the shining car, with their journey ahead of them, their marvelously fortunate prospect of settling wherever they chose, had come into the free inheritance of all the years that had gone before them.

The engine was started. There was a quick wave of the hand from Jesse. Dorothy looked back a moment, then was looking ahead. They had one smiling glimpse of her face in the little blue hat.

"Well, sir, there they go!"

Part Four
The Other Girl

I. THE HIDDEN TIME

MARGARET had locked her door again. At least she had a door that would lock. That was her one consolation in this house. It gave her a savage pleasure to shut herself in with her own misery and to keep the folks outside. She lay on the floor—the bed was too soft for her wretchedness—and her head rolled from side to side. This was the culmination of all her unhappiness at home. Let mother plead now. Let dad break the door if he wanted to. He had shaken it once until the whole upstairs seemed to shake. She would never forgive them again. She felt her heart as hard as a stone inside her—imagined hands tearing apart that frozen stone . . . The folks had not believed her. They had believed that old—Margaret couldn't think of anything bad enough to call her—of a Dean of Women. She had never really belonged to her own family, and now she wasn't going to pretend at all any more.

Lying there on the floor, on the harshness of the rug, feeling the stealthy drafts that managed to get through the storm windows, Margaret went back through the whole story. She felt as if she were looking back into the seductive shine of Sybil's eyes—but remote, with a sense of hopeless estrangement, almost as if Sybil were dead. She couldn't exactly wish for the old—it wasn't exactly friendship; more fascination—back. The folks had spoiled it for her. They had believed just what the Dean of Women had told them. Well, it was true, Sybil *was* deceiving her father and the faculty, and she *was* in love with a man who was getting a divorce, and meeting him "outside." Yes, and Margaret *was* helping her to deceive. But none of it in the way that the folks thought. She felt again the futile, struggling pain of not being able to make them understand her side.

But then, she had never been able to explain anything to them. Her real life had always been lived inside herself, in secret. The others were the kind of children that mother and dad really wanted. She had always been the off one.

"Where does she get it?" Margaret could hear Aunt Ella saying that, in her flat, naïvely wondering voice. Sometimes mother said it too, in despair.

Margaret remembered how she used to brood over being adopted. She had always felt like an aristocrat in disguise. "Margaret always thinks she must have the best of everything." That had long been an accusation against her. She used to imagine the kind of parents it seemed to her she must really have had instead of just the folks. She wanted her father to have distinguished gray hair and black-rimmed eyeglasses with a very broad black ribbon. And she wanted a father who adored her, like those artist fathers in books—the mother had conveniently died at the birth of the child, who was so exactly like her that the father would turn pale. Virginia Brattle's father was a little like that, so that Virginia had always seemed to Margaret something like a girl in a story—except that Mrs. Brattle was very much alive, and she and Mr. Brattle spoiled the story by squabbling over Virginia. The things that dad had said to her when he came to the Normal after her were cut deep into Margaret's memory in a bleeding pain. She felt that she could never have a father again. But she was frightened of being in the world without one. She imagined herself leaning her head against a big strong chest, smelling of harsh expensive wool like Frank's, a deep voice telling her indulgently that he would look after her . . . Frank Gesell was more her father, in her heart, than dad was.

Margaret began to cry again, but drearily, rolling her head on the harsh nap of the rug. How could she stand never to see Sybil again, to lose all the luxury and loveliness and brightness, Sybil's white arms in sleeveless dresses, the square-cut bottles with ribbons from which Sybil dabbed little dampnesses of perfume on Margaret's hair, so that she went stepping down to dinner in a dreamy, scented luxury. . . .

She moved with restless impatience, away from the soothing

heat of the radiator, and in the chill from the north window the wretchedness of the whole winter enveloped her. She could never get back to that day in Geneva. The folks believed that she had disgraced herself forever by going there. Margaret didn't care. It was always the "bad" things that she did that gave her any happiness—like skipping school, or playing with the wrong crowd, or slipping up to dance in the Odd Fellows Hall with that red-haired kid on the basketball team from Hanging Rock. If she were to die right now, she would choose that day with Sybil and Frank as her one day to remember. That was Margaret's chief fear: that she might die without having had one perfect day. Even the day in Geneva wasn't enough her own for that. But if it hadn't been for Sybil and Frank, she would have thought it was just in books that people were ever really happy. She never thought of any other people she had known as being actually *lovers*. They just went together, or were silly over each other, or something like that. Regular marriage meant being like the folks, presenting a united front to the world, neither one doing as he or she wanted to do. Or like Aunt Ella and Uncle Ben, stuck together and forever bickering. Or like Grandma and Grandpa, who had always seemed to think that young people when they reached a certain age must just naturally get married unless there was "something the matter with them," and then the next step was to begin raising a family. "What's the matter with him?" Grandma would always demand, when she heard of any single young man past twenty-five. Marriage, Margaret had always thought of as just the end.

She didn't regret a single thing about that whole day. She was glad she had lied to the Dean of Women—the Dean deserved it. Dad had tried to make her apologize. He couldn't see that it was because she scorned to lie that she wouldn't say she was sorry; and he hadn't known what awful, shaken, painful courage it had taken to hold out against both of them. Margaret felt as if she could have stood it if the Dean had asked her straightforwardly, when she got back from Geneva that night, if she had been with Sybil. But not a word! Margaret remembered how sweetly the Dean had greeted her going in to dinner, walking beside her and asking her if she had had a nice day and had found her sister—while all the time she knew everything about it, knew that Sybil had gone with Margaret to Geneva, and was writing the folks.

And the folks thought it was all right for the Dean to deceive *her* like that. It was the Dean's "business," they thought —they actually thought that!—to sneak and spy. It was papa, her own father, who had taken the Dean's part against her. He had told her that he and mother were both ashamed of her. She had given them more trouble than their other children put together. They would rather have their boys at war, he said, fighting for their country, than to have a daughter acting as she had done when they made sacrifices to let her go away to school. And then he threw it up to her that she hadn't stuck it out at Wilson, either—she was just restless, didn't know her own mind. . . . Her own family, her own folks. That was the worst of all. She wouldn't have cared about being suspended if they had felt some sympathy. Oh, mother did, in a way—but they both acted as if she had done all this on purpose to make more trouble for them just at this time! *She* couldn't help it if the country had gone to war, and if even Carl might have to go. They just didn't understand that she had felt that she was doing the real, hard, underneath kind of right in helping the lovers.

Mother laid it all on Sybil. Sybil had corrupted her. Margaret had planned it just as much as Sybil! She had asked the Dean for a day's leave of absence in Geneva to meet her sister —of course she hadn't any intention of seeing Dorothy. Margaret had put some of Sybil's things in her own bag; and Sybil had pretended to be going over to the campus, but had stopped in at the little drug store and telephoned for one of the two town taxis—Sybil was the only one of the girls who dealt boldly with things like taxis. She had stayed hidden in the ladies' toilet, because people from the Normal might be on the train; and then at the Junction, she and Margaret had got off, and Frank had met them with the car. . . . That long, smooth, purring ride through the misty rain that clouded the windows and shut them all three in together in the luxurious warmth of the richly upholstered car—now it was a dream. And a still brighter dream was the dining room of the hotel—their secluded corner table, with the rosy light casting a circle of shade on the glittering tablecloth, the spiciness of the roses intermingled with the good smell of food, and the dark little waiter bowing and running. It didn't seem as if it could have been just Geneva. It had seemed like a city somewhere else. Margaret, in spite of her last year's coat which she hated, had felt that she and Sybil were fêted beauties. Sybil and Frank had made her almost more the heroine of the occasion than Sybil herself! Now she could get a sad exultance remembering the things Frank had said to her. "We don't need any lights with those eyes at the table." "Some lucky man's going to get a big kick out of that hair some day." They were compliments about the very things she had always wanted praised. They seemed to make her over into the kind of person she ought to be. And all the time they were eating, the rain was making splintered streaks of brightness on the dark windowpane. . . .

Sybil and Frank hadn't dared take her to the courthouse. The wedding was to be absolutely secret. That was part of their loving protection of her. "If they ask you if we were married, you weren't there, see—you don't know anything about it." Frank had got a taxi for her, and a magnificent violet-colored box of candy sheathed in glittery tissue paper—Sybil wouldn't let him get flowers, because the girls in the dorm would be sure to ask about them . . . and then they had both kissed her—she was pressed to the glowing softness of Sybil's face in the midst of the wet gray fur of her big coat collar, and she felt the exciting male pressure of Frank's big lips and smelled the wet wool of his expensive coat with shining mist caught in the harsh weave . . . and she was in the taxi, back in the familiar, overheated train. . . .

And now she was just at home. That was over. She was going to visit Frank and Sybil in Chicago, and they were going to take her to dine at the Drake, and Frank was going to let her and Sybil—"both my girls"—go to Marshall Field's and each pick out an evening dress. A new life had been opening before her in a dazzle of radiance. And here she was back at home, with only the folks and Bunny. How awful home had looked to her when she had come back to it! The wind struck icy along the brick platform where Margaret stood dumbly waiting and staring at the red-and-black water tank on black cinders flooded with ice. They rode home in the town taxi, where she was squeezed in between her father and a traveling man, on the broken-down seat of black leather worn to the weave on the folds. The cold got in around the flapping side curtains. The traveling man coughed, and she thought they were all going to get the flu. They had to keep silent because they couldn't let Bob Wessel know that she had been sent home. Bob Wessel, who had got his foot cut off in an accident when he was drunk, and wasn't fit to do anything but drive this old taxi! Margaret couldn't see much of the streets through the dirty panes in the side curtains; but she knew how they were, icy and lonely, the trees looking scrubby and bare, old vines frozen against the streaked side walls of houses. Dad fumbled around to get just the right change out of his purse. Margaret thought of Frank Gesell's opulent roll of bills in a smooth brown leather folder that he carelessly shoved down into his pocket after he had paid for everything. She saw the house standing in its winter ugliness, dark streaks down the light-painted walls from the bent-over pipe at the eaves, patches of ice on the withered brown grass, that horrible old urn with a few brown stems sticking up brittle and thin from the caked, frozen, flower-pot earth.

And of course by this time everybody in Belmond knew that she had been suspended from the Normal! Margaret thrashed about, beating the rug softly with her fist. Still, in a hard way she was glad. It put her really apart from the rest. The Dean in her letter, trying to smooth things over, had pretended that Sybil was "a bad influence" and "not the sort of girl"—that was the worst of all, that suave implication that Margaret really was "the sort"! Her eyes sparkled with fury. But the folks didn't even know it was an insult.

Sybil and Frank had seen. They had treated her as the only girl in the Normal worth their attention. They took it for granted that she was a person to whom wonderful, out-of-the-ordinary things would naturally happen as soon as she got out of the wrong pew. Mother and dad, at best, thought her someone to be pitied, because she wasn't popular like Dorothy and Carl. Margaret wanted to do something desperate to show them!

No, they were on the other side. She classed them in with the Dean of Women. Dad had written that terrible letter—but mother had let him write it, and instead of taking it back, just cried. Mother wanted to be on all sides at once. That was like all married women! Nothing—no worry over her being thin, no shamefaced suggestion from dad that it might be nice to visit Aunt Louie next summer—could ever make her forget. She remembered the horrible pain of that trip home when the coldness of the November cornfields outside the window had seemed to cast her out, because she was suspended from the Normal, and her own folks were against her.

The hideous winter seemed to have lasted for years. The town was worse than it had ever been. The dark cloud of the war and the epidemic hung over it. Now even the movies were closed. And, thank heaven, so was church! How could the folks still pretend to believe the Bible and then think a whole nation ought to be killed! Now they would never get her to church again. She wouldn't go through the misery, if *that* was all the good it did. Fighting with the folks, and then rushing up to lock herself into her room! But in a way, Margaret reveled in these quarrels. They gave her a chance, when she got thoroughly wrought up and off her guard, to tell the folks things she had hidden and brooded over since she was a child. She had accused them of not caring for her. That hurt them. They tried to deny it.

"But you never would open up to us the way the others did."

"Because you never understand or believe me. You don't believe me this time."

"Yes, darling, I do believe you didn't mean—"

"I did mean. Oh, you just don't see!"

They might talk about loving her!—loving *all* their children. But Margaret had heard mama, years ago, saying how she was so dark and Dorothy was so fair—she had heard that and never forgotten it. That had given her some reason for thinking she might be adopted. But anyway, Shakespeare had fallen in love with a "dark lady"! The discovery of the "dark lady" was the one thing she had got out of that dreadful old Shakespeare class where all they ever did was read the different speeches and then "tell the meaning in their own words."

The folks had tried to make friends with her. Mother had even suggested that she have some of the girls over and play cards. Once, what wouldn't she have given to be allowed to play cards like other people! But then the folks had been too religious. Now even Bunny played.

Lately they had been trying another tack. They were letting her stay in her room, "not noticing" and not trying to force her to open the door. Nothing more was said about her returning to the Normal. Dad had gone back to the bank. The warm, steam-heated house was flooded with its silent afternoon leisure.

But Margaret would not sink back into that leisure. She was hard against her childish desire to break and cry in mama's arms, away from this awry aloofness, folded warmly into harmony. At night she thought wildly of running away and breaking with the folks. But her inexperience terrified her. Darkness and danger and sickness were everywhere. Now she couldn't even teach. She had only gone to the Normal because it wasn't Wilson—and then teaching had seemed a sure way of getting away from home, buying her own clothes, not going to church, saving enough money to go off on her own.

Anyway, she wouldn't stay in this house!

She got up, stealthily tiptoeing as she dressed, expecting every minute that her mother would come to the door.

The sense of loneliness rose bitterly in her throat as she walked down the street.

All the same, if the inside of her life hadn't been so empty and miserable—if she had been having some romantic affair, with a married man, like Sybil and the heroines in modern books—she could have got a dark kind of pleasure out of this lonely walk down the long street past frame houses with ice crusting the roots of the pine trees in the yards.

Margaret thought about Dr. Redmond. He was the only

possible person for such a rôle in Belmond—he had prematurely white hair and wore Palm Beach suits; and he belonged to that fast young married set—still called "young married set" although they were all middle-aged—that the folks thought were so dreadful. Richard Spencer was cute-looking and a good dresser. But he was in the bank with dad. Sometimes Margaret's dreams reached through darkness into bright future, and then the man with whom she was having the great love affair was a stranger, in New York, or even Europe—an artist, so that she would be known to history. But sometimes, even in a dream, she couldn't wait that long. She had to imagine something that could happen right the next minute and make living possible—make her have a great tragic experience behind her when she left—and then it was Dr. Redmond. But he always loved her more than she did him, and she always left him. She couldn't contemplate staying in Belmond. That was why she had never really been interested in any of the boys in high school, although she had wanted them to admire *her*—they seemed to bind her to Belmond. How could she make all this begin to happen? She had to *know*. Her innocence was a humiliation. Then she could be equal to Sybil, not just hungrily admiring. She could deal with men like Frank Gesell with no more timid fear. Then she could read poetry with a satisfied feeling that it had all happened to her, instead of with that baffled, shamed, hungry wonder. She could write poetry. It was a love affair, of course, that she wanted, not to settle down and get married, like Lillian and Carl.

One of those side streets, a block or so long, led off from this street. Margaret felt again its shoddy, unnamed quality that seemed in some queer minor way native to her. It was here where she used to sneak off after school and play with Irene.

Irene Jackson! What had become of her? And that mean little Gowan kid whom they used to call "Squirrel-Eyes"! Margaret suffered still from the way her clandestine friendship with Irene had been broken off. She had never forgiven Carl. What was that dark, different wisdom that girls like Irene possessed, that made them mockingly superior to the people who talked about them? Just as, in a way, Lucifer was superior to God. He *knew* more. Afterwards, though, Margaret had been so ashamed of not being able to ask Irene to her house that she had gone through agonized maneuvers to avoid Irene at school. Even now it hurt her to remember her cowardly perfidy. Lucille and Edna Mae had never been interesting again—and of course she detested Mildred!

When she looked back into her life, there were just two people in this town with whom she had not been friendly from force of circumstances, or from her own frozen fear of coming out before disapproving eyes in her own colors. Irene was one. And the other was that woman from New York who had visited Mrs. Richard Spencer.

"Grimmie," Mrs. Spencer called her. She and Ethel Spencer had been schoolmates. Miss Grimm was the first woman Margaret had ever seen who was really what she thought of as "different," "distinguished," who had a style of her own. Of course, mother and the other ladies called that queer-looking. "But isn't she *queer*-looking?" She wasn't pretty like Ethel Spencer. Margaret had not yet fully decided whether she liked odd, distinguished looks the best, or whether she wanted the most completely impeccable Parisian elegance. At any rate, Miss Grimm didn't look like anybody in Belmond. Ethel was beginning to pay more social attention to the Fergusons now that dad had become more important in the bank. She had invited mother to the reception she gave for Miss Grimm; and Margaret and Dorothy had very graciously been asked, with Virginia Brattle, to pass the refreshments. Margaret, bringing in the handsome silver cake basket that Ethel had resurrected from the old Spencer house, had walked softly with her lashes drooped in awe, but lifting them once for a look of adoration at the eagle profile and the fuzzy black hair drawn in straight bands down each side of the face to a knot at the back. Miss Grimm had worn a big rope of beads and queer earrings, and there was a sort of Russian embroidery on her flowing sleeves. Afterwards, when the girls had gone to get their wraps, Ethel Spencer, flitting gracefully to thank them, had taken Margaret's hands in her soft little fingers and murmured, with that luminously flattering look she could give—"Grimmie asked me, Who was that child with the marvelous eyes?" She had seen. People who were different did see.

Now if she could get to New York, where people like Ethel Spencer's friend might like the queer things about her looks, then she, too, might have a chance to become a person with a style of her own! But it was too tragically distant. On a day like this, with a bleak watery feeling in the air, the trees motionless against the gray sky, she seemed to have no power of getting anywhere. She dreamed of writing to Miss Grimm and asking if she couldn't get a position in a bookstore.

But she was afraid. Margaret thought of New York as filled entirely by "different" people, all sophisticated in a glittering way, and knowing strange secrets of art and life. She would be a coward if some time she didn't try to find out those things.

The walk ended here. Margaret's final dream, no matter how she started out, was of herself in marvelous clothes and long earrings coming back to Belmond—not to stay, of course!—but interesting and a little weary, after a life of passionate, tragic and glorious experience, such as no one could have here at home. Now she had finished her new variation of that. To go on into the country would be a kind of lonely triumph. But then she could never stop thinking until her mind was screwed up into a painful whirl.

She turned, and walked hurriedly to her old haunt the library, although a feeling of dreary stuffiness came over her the instant she went up those whitish stone steps, traced now with wintry footprints, and on into the hushed, overheated stack room. She ranged forlornly among the rows of books. There were only those rebound copies of *Lazarre* and the Red Pepper Burns novels in the little cart. The librarian came tiptoeing into the stacks and whispered, "Finding what you want?" She had always been interested in Margaret, she had once told the folks, Margaret was such a reader! But the favor of Miss Vanchie Darlington hurt almost more than it pleased Margaret's vanity, for Vanchie approved only nice quiet children and sent the kids who came for dates out of the library. Margaret writhed under the ignominy of being thought "quiet."

She sat down in the rocker near the magazine rack. The

unbecomingness of her old coat and brown hat that looked so shabby at the tail-end of winter would not let her have the superiority that her pride demanded over Vanchie Darlington's thin, sallow, sweetly smiling face and two pathetic loops of fading brown hair. Margaret reveled in dark satisfaction at having been suspended from the Normal.

"Oh, here you are!"

Her mother had come into the library. She was smiling brightly and ignoring the last quarrel in that way she and dad must have agreed to try now. Her gray velvet hat was a little crooked, and Margaret disapproved severely of the way her skirt hung.

"What are you reading, dear?"

They never liked the things she read, so why pretend to answer?

"Let's go downtown now. I want you to help me choose things for supper. What would you like?" her mother asked cheerily.

"Nothing."

It was all the worse to have mother so sprightly and pretending they were such good companions—she had acted that way ever since Margaret had told her she was always more friendly with Dorothy.

Just outside the library, they met Mrs. Viele.

"Well! Doesn't this look nice? These two pretty young ladies in their nice warm furs going about together!"

Margaret saw her mother beam at that. How could she? But the folks didn't seem to care anything for the truth. While the two ladies talked, Margaret stood aside. The things Mrs. Viele said were always worse, because she saw everything in a rosy light and never knew the facts of the case. Margaret dug with her oxford toe into the hard crust of snow while she had to listen to, "And how is Carl? And Lillian and the little ones? But it's so lovely that you can have Margaret this winter!"

"She's so nice!" Mrs. Ferguson said gratefully, as they went on.

"I can't bear her."

"Oh, Margaret!"

"Well, she just gushes. She knows I got sent home from the Normal and that you and dad don't want to have me here."

She was savagely pleased to have brought tears to her mother's eyes. They went on down the street silently.

2

Margaret had put two big kettles of soft water on the oil stove for her bath. She lay full-length across her bed while the water was heating, with her blue crêpe kimono open across her chest which she contemplated with frowning absorption. Her skin tinted with brunette was smooth. But she was so skinny. Her collar bones showed. Her breasts looked small and unripe. She thought of Mildred's breasts, how softly white they were in the glimpses she had caught of them when they undressed for gym, and of how they swelled, adequate and womanly, beneath her silk blouse. Mildred Summers had been more popular with the boys than any other girl in high school. Nasty little snip!—pretending to be so sweet, and just working her schemes all the time, wanting nothing else in the world but to get married. Dorothy, even when the two girls had started to college, was what their mother called "developed"; and that had always made Margaret, with her little long thin arms, and her scrawnily unfledged neck with its brunette darkness, feel herself at a resentful disadvantage. She had always felt that Dorothy, with her easy-going good times, was really the daughter of the household.

Their bedroom was almost all Dorothy's. She was the one who had the photographs of smiling college girls with marcelled hair and youths with hair combed wavily or slickly back from their open foreheads. Sybil's picture was lovelier than that of any of these girly-girly regulation friends of Dot's. But of course Margaret couldn't put that up!

There was just one thing in this room that was really hers. That was her desk.

She got up and padded over to it, barefooted. It had been promised to her once when she was getting well from pleurisy, and she had been allowed to pick it out for herself at the furniture store. The cheap little varnished affair with curlicue ornaments and rickety legs was still precious to her. Every few weeks, Margaret went over her books, to rearrange them according to some strictly personal plan. At one side, she kept only "new" books, the newest and most dangerous, that she thought no one else in Belmond would read. Between brass book-ends she had set her own personal, intimate favorites— Marie Bashkirtseff, and *Wuthering Heights,* and Mrs. Gaskell's *Charlotte Brontë,* because in the seclusion and stormy emotions of the Yorkshire sisters she felt some of her own loneliness and rebellion. And then, most preciously kept of all, the small notebook with shiny red covers in which she copied with exquisite care, in the blackest India ink, all the poems that seemed to fit into her own existence. She had just copied, when she found time at the library, some of the *Sonnets from the Portuguese.* She hated those that talked about God and the angels. But she got a dark joy out of reading to herself—

"I lift my heavy heart up solemnly . . ."

Standing there now in her bare feet, curling the toes of one narrow foot over the other, Margaret whispered it to herself.

"Behold and see
What a great heap of grief lay hid in me,
And how the red wild sparkles—"

Her cheeks burned, and she felt a sweet, fiery thrill . . .

"Margaret! Your water *must* be hot!"

Oh, dear, she couldn't even take a bath without the whole family getting excited! In angry haste, Margaret rushed into the bathroom, and got some of the black off the bottoms of the kettles onto the white rim of the tub when she dumped in the water. Why didn't the folks put in a water heater, like other people? Dad always had to be so careful. He would do it some day, when the children were all gone, and he and mother were too old to enjoy it. "Two?" her mother always said. "Do you have to have *two* kettles every time? You know what dad said about the cistern." But Margaret had decided not to care if the family did run out of soft water before the next rain, because of the importance to her of indulging in these wonderful steamy baths in which she had a mysterious hope that the delicious amber softness of the water would make the dark places around her collar bones white and perfect in preparation for going somewhere and beginning her real life.

But she avoided the sight of the mirror because of the scrawny, sallow look she feared she would have until the bath had flushed and freshened her skin. When she finished, however —in spite of her dissatisfaction with the family's plain white soap, which they always bought from that crippled man—she rubbed away the silvery mist from the glass. She looked at the thin little naked image, shrinking with sensitive consciousness of its defects, beseeching it to know if she dared take hope from elusive intimations of a different kind of attraction from Dorothy's blooming prettiness, and Mildred's blond softness— even from Sybil's charm, with the warm ripe body, and those shining, seductive, greenish eyes under the fluff of sandy hair. Her eyes glowed darkly with the memory of Frank Gesell's praise. She was sensitive and unsure about them even yet, thinking of how Carl and Harry Santley used to tease her and call her "Pop-Eyes." "Where did that child get those great black eyes?" How often she had heard that! There always seemed to be a kind of reproach in it. Margaret had the trick of letting the lashes droop, partly because of the boys' teasing, but even more to veil the ardor that she felt would give her away if people really looked into her eyes. But Frank Gesell was a real man, who had a business of his own, and had been married and divorced, and could order taxis and flowers and send waiters on the run. What did innocent, goody-goody boys like Carl and Harry matter beside him—boys who felt important ushering in church?

Margaret had always known that there was something romantic in store for her. Frank—an admitted connoisseur of women—had recognized it. Her own confidence in it made a burning core of pride in the empty blackness of her heart.

She spread out her long black hair all around her, and turned, with a dancing motion, until she had the very best light on the image in the mirror. The dark eyes flashed back at her from between black draperies of hair, and for a single moment she was as she wanted to be. Passionately she yearned to overcome all her awkward and scrawny defects so that she could be worthy of that strange delight of which poetry was full, and for which she felt that fate had marked her out. She saw the secret triangle of black hair curling softly below the white belly with its subtle brunette tints. She felt rare and precious.

But she heard steps outside the bathroom door, and halted, poised in her secret dance, startled and wildly shy. Hastily she put on the detested blue kimono and twisted her hair up into a top-knot—perversely glad to look just as plain and hideous as she could. Now if mama saw her, she ought to be satisfied!

"Wait a few minutes, dear, and I'll go with you."

Margaret heard that as she was putting on her hat.

"I have to hurry. Vanchie wants to leave."

She didn't intend the folks to think that because she was working in the library now, and Vanchie liked her, she was going to be satisfied to stay in Belmond! "How lovely for Margaret to be in the library!" She made a face. It helped her pride to be able to walk down the street in lofty solitude and not to have succumbed to the weak craving for having her mother with her—to keep on the bad terms that her pride and integrity demanded, instead of slipping down into false, easy good terms. She couldn't help cringing a little when she had to meet and speak to people, because she knew how they regarded her having been suspended from school. Vanchie thought she had been a victim! The library was tedious, when hour after hour passed and no interesting stranger came in to discover her reading good books. But it was a refuge.

Vanchie was alone.

"What pink cheeks our lady has!"

"My cheeks are never pink."

"Oh! Just look in that glass!"

Vanchie put on her coat and rubbers—the drab-brown coat that Margaret knew as well as her own—and the wide black hat trimmed with the ribbon bows of a past era. "Where does she *get* those hats?" people always marveled.

"Listen, Vanchie!" Margaret suddenly cried. "Tell my folks

that I'm such a good librarian I ought to go away and take a course."

Vanchie took it very seriously, although Margaret didn't know whether she'd thought of saying it until just this minute.

"Where have you thought of going, dear?"

"I don't know. I just want to go somewhere."

Margaret looked up at Vanchie with eyes fiercely tearless. She drew into herself, hard and untouchable, because she didn't want Vanchie to get too near her. There was something too pathetic and personal about Vanchie's affection, although it helped Margaret's vanity. Vanchie had fallen under Margaret's domination with meek gladness. It was almost the way that Ada Rist used to be. Vanchie had a wistful, older woman's faith in the radiance of Margaret's future. She was nervous now about Margaret's judgment on books. Margaret liked to come out with wild, bold statements. They flustered and pleased Vanchie—Vanchie who, to so many people in town, seemed patrician and aloof!

Vanchie was reluctant and afraid to lose her, but too dreadfully and sweetly unselfish to give in to that.

"Oh, I do wish you could go to Boston!"

There was a faded shine in Vanchie's colorless eyes. Her big hat was crooked and fine short hairs strayed from the two loops.

"Did I ever tell you about my trip East? It was the most wonderful . . . Wait. I think I have the pictures."

Vanchie went into the sacred inner room about which—Margaret remembered guiltily—the girls used to have jokes, pretending that Vanchie retired there to pen love letters to Lawrence Brattle who was supposed to be the most cultured man in town. How mean they all used to be! The little room was neat and intimate, with a framed photograph of Vanchie's parents, and a couch with faded college cushions where Vanchie made Margaret lie when she had a cold.

"Here they are!"

Vanchie came out looking eager but a little embarrassed.

"It was one summer—oh, I'd hate to say how long ago! You wouldn't even remember. There were three of us, Amy

Sanderson, and Julia Viele, and I. Can you find me?" Vanchie gave a little trill of embarrassed laughter. "Look at the hats!"

The picture was taken with one of those old-fashioned cameras and mounted on gray cardboard. Of course she could find Vanchie. She wore her hair in just the same loops, and her wide sailor hat—which Vanchie thought so funny!—wasn't very different from those awful hats she wore now. What did surprise Margaret was that Vanchie looked young! There was an evanescent softness, a rounding of her prim slenderness, a radiance in the too-sweet smile that lingered only in that wistfulness now.

"Where were you?"

"Where was it taken, you mean? In front of Longfellow's home in Cambridge. There, you can just see the house. I *loved* New England. It's so full of interesting, quaint old places. Just look at us! Don't we look like three gypsies? What a time we had to make our parents consent to let us go gallivanting off that way—three young girls by their lonesomes! It was the most wonderful time I ever had."

Margaret gave the photograph back to Vanchie. While Vanchie put it reverently away, Margaret sat staring at the bust of Longfellow once presented by old Mrs. Spencer. She supposed in Vanchie's day it *had* been adventurous for those three girls to make a trip East and visit historical places. But did Vanchie think anything like that would satisfy *her*?

"This bean jar came from Boston. We got it in the funniest little place down in a basement—I remember Amy wouldn't go down, and she thought Julia and I were terribly bold!" Vanchie touched the bean jar with loving remembrance. There were some pussy willows in it now. "Well," she said, "good-bye, dear. I'm so glad you spoke to me. If you really do want me to have a talk with your mother and father . . . I know you're wasted working here in this little library. But I shall hate . . . oh, I have that new book of poems you wanted, dear. I slipped it into the list."

She left. Margaret sat wrapped in the heated, silent air. Her hands were clasped lightly on the shiny desk. The new volume of poems was by a woman. Margaret had seen the title in the catalogue which she always searched hungrily. Maybe the book would yield her—if it was any good—more of those tantalizing hints of the way love seemed and the way it had turned out in another person's life. That was why Margaret had to devour books of poetry and memoirs by women, even those titled British women who only wrote gossip about other "important" people and tried to make themselves sound ravishing and smart.

She couldn't actually make herself intend to be a librarian. But after the things that Sybil had said about the girls who wanted to be teachers, she couldn't bear to think of teaching. Besides, being a teacher always made Margaret afraid that she would get to be like Fannie Allison, who had taught the third grade ever since anyone in Belmond could remember, who stuck little net yokes into her collarless dresses, and who lived with her brother and his wife and took care of the children when they went to card parties. There was a cloistered but more æsthetic atmosphere about Vanchie, with her love for "the best in literature," and the nice old chairs and dishes from the Darlington home in her room at Mrs. Keppler's . . . Yes, but if she was going to get away, there was the long, awful time of forcing her own way against the folks—who didn't believe in her, didn't think she was capable of getting on by herself, or of keeping on with what she had started. "You know the other times," they would say.

3

They had to call Margaret two or three times to get her to the supper table. Mr. Ferguson wanted to be angry, but Mrs. Ferguson gave him a warning look.

"Come, dear, now. Put on your kimono. Don't dress until after supper. We want to get through in time to all go to the concert."

They were taking it for granted that she would go with them.

Margaret tried not to give in the least bit to the homelike pleasantness of the dining room at this hour. She tried not to see the evening light across the table and the bright red jelly in the cut-glass dish—or to see the funny little sawed-off bouquet that was the kind her mother always picked, cosmos and nasturtiums mixed up together, with some little scraps of sweet alyssum.

"I wanted you to arrange the flowers. But I couldn't find you. You can make so much prettier bouquets than I can."

Margaret wouldn't answer that, nor be diverted by praise of her taste in arranging flowers from the issue that must be settled if there was to be any real friendliness between them. It was like a hard transparent wall between her and the folks. Mother tried brightly to ignore it, when it wasn't just absolutely visible. But she needn't try to make out that they were a loving family party sitting here at the pleasant supper table ready to go to the concert together, as Mrs. Viele would picture them.

"Why, no, Fred!" mother was saying. "You mustn't go over to the church now, there isn't time."

"Why not?"

"Why, the concert!"

"Oh!"

Dad looked ashamed, and naïvely uncertain. He followed mother into the kitchen. Margaret was left sitting alone at the supper table finishing her raspberries, with thick cream from the farm that turned a faded pink as she stirred it. It made her almost ashamed herself that dad failed with such awkward honesty to play up to mother's little schemes. Mother was trying to show how, when none of the others were here, she and dad and Margaret could have such good times together! But now that the wedding was over and all the company gone—everyone away that could get away, even Bunny escaped on a camping party—all that mother had to fall back upon was an ancient, resurrected band concert! Margaret put down the souvenir spoon—mother was using the pretty silver, and the best china, trying to make her contented . . . oh, it was all such an entanglement!

"We won't stop to do the dishes, dear. We want to get nice seats. What are you going to put on?"

Margaret wanted to say, "Nothing. I'm not going." But that

bright little hopefulness of mother's overcame her. She could only be sullen and unresponsive. They were pretending that now that Dorothy was married, and she was "the only girl they had left," they could all be sweet and happy here at home. They were counting upon Margaret to stay at home and "comfort" them when Bun went away to college.

"I've ironed your yellow dress. You can wear that."

What a tremendous concession! It was the dress that mother hated, because she said it made Margaret look "so dark"; and that made Margaret think again, just as when she was a little girl, that the family really thought her dark and hideous.

Margaret sat down on her bed and took off her old slippers. But then she couldn't seem to get any farther. The house was awful again. For a little while it had been filled with the excitement and éclat of the wedding. But now the household seemed to have slipped back into the dreariness of an earlier day. Margaret was the only one left. Carl and Lillian were grown-up married people. Dorothy was married and gone. Even Bunny, before long, would be a college boy. And Margaret could see herself, getting older and older, a spinster daughter and a fixture in the house—as bad as Essie Bartlett! That seemed to be what the folks wanted. They were afraid to let her go. For a little while, they had kept her contented, by letting her furnish her own room and go to Geneva to do her shopping. Vanchie had told them that "Margaret was doing so well in the library, it would be lovely if she could take up the work"; and they had gone so far as to talk about "some time." This summer, after her brief bridesmaid's radiance, she was getting thin and sallow. Everyone noticed it. Aunt Ella had said cheerfully, "Maybe she's getting consumption." Dad's brother John had died of consumption, and *he* had been thin and dark. She would get thinner, take revenge on them, die if they didn't send her away —get rid of all scruples, all compunctions. But they were afraid to let her go!—for mother knew that if she went, it would be forever.

"Here's your dress, Margaret." Mother had come to the door. "Oh, haven't you even begun to get ready? Never mind—" she went on hurriedly—"there's time if you start right away. We'll be out on the porch."

Anything was better than staying in this room. Now that it had lost the fragrant luxury of Aunt Louie's things, it seemed bleak and ordinary; and Margaret couldn't be consoled any longer by having her own furniture in her own colors. The pleasant light was in the bathroom, too, and the clean-smelling towels and the cool tingle of the water wouldn't let her hold to her hardness. Her big eyes looked back at her from the mirror dark with remembrance of Frank's praise. She couldn't be hideous. Not if Frank and Sybil didn't think so. There must still be hope for her in this world.

But when she started to put on the yellow dress, perversity made her take it off again. What was the use of trying to look decent when everything else was wrong! She would wear as unbecoming things as she could, to please the folks, and then when she got away she would dress exactly as she wanted to.

"Oh, here she is!" Then mother noticed. "But why didn't you—"

Margaret answered proudly, "I didn't want to."

They had to ignore it. They were afraid of a storm from her, knowing that now their vague promises would have to be fulfilled. Mother had wanted to drive, but dad didn't want to use the car until the brake-bands were fixed. "All right, let's walk!" mother said brightly. But at least she didn't take hold of their arms, an arm of each, to show how friendly they all were, when they weren't.

"How lovely Mrs. Viele's flowers are!"

Margaret wouldn't be interested in anything in Belmond. Dad looked vaguely over at the Viele lawn, but he never even pretended interest in such feminine things as flowers.

"How do you do? Yes, isn't it?"

Mother nodded and spoke brightly to people.

They reached the little town park where the band concert was to be held. Not many people were there. They needn't have hurried. "Do you want to sit close, or at a distance?" "Oh, this'll be all right," dad said. They took one of the straight, green-painted benches with the seats sawed off slant-wise at the ends.

Mother sat down, smiling, nodding to an acquaintance here and there. How silly to pretend that this was fun, when almost nobody cared that they were trying to revive the old band concerts again. Cars stopped now and then for a little while, and then drove away. Margaret sat disdainfully silent.

Mr. Ferguson said, "I don't call this much of a crowd."

"Well, they haven't begun yet. You know everything is always late." But Margaret saw that even mother realized the entertainment wasn't turning out very well. "There's Mrs. Dunn! Shall we go over and sit with her?"

"What's that? What do we have to move for?"

"Why, dad, I thought it would be nice to sit near Mrs. Dunn. But if you don't want to—"

"Oh, that's it. No, I don't mind."

Margaret silently followed the folks. As if she cared about sitting with Mrs. Dunn! If the folks thought *that* was any entertainment—! Now they would have to hear all about the sorrow of having Lloyd so far away, and Mrs. Dunn's pride in having her son a soldier. It *would* be someone like Lloyd Dunn, Margaret thought disdainfully, who didn't have brains enough to do anything for himself, who would stay and get into the regular army! Mrs. Dunn laid it on thick about Lloyd, giving Margaret sharp little glances of mingled resentment and satisfaction, meaning that she had now forfeited forever the glorious chance of Lloyd's attentions. Margaret looked coldly at Mrs. Dunn's fat, creased neck, with the gray and brown hairs straggling below the brownish coil, and the thick fat of the shoulders above the corset and under the cottony texture of the figured voile.

"Yes, isn't it nice they're starting again. I think every town ought to have a band. It brings people together."

Rains had made the grass in the park thick and dark green, and the leaves thicker and even darker, so that in the sultry heat of the middlewestern summer night the trees overhung the little frame band stand with an ominous heaviness. Margaret moved her feet uneasily as she felt the mosquitoes at her ankles. She intended to stick it through grimly, though—show mother, when it was over, how much there was for her here in this town.

"Do you think we want to hear all of this?" dad asked at last. "These mosquitoes seem to be after me."

"Some folks they bother," Mrs. Dunn said.

"Well, unless Margaret—"

"I don't care," Margaret answered with disdain.

Mrs. Dunn accepted complacently the offer to go with them. Finally they were back on the sidewalk. Margaret could see that her mother's face was troubled, and wondered, with a mixture of scorn and compunction, if mother was thinking of her own young days when the band concerts had been great occasions. She tried to picture dad bringing mother into town and buying her a sack of popcorn. But she could only see the folks at the age they were now.

"I thought perhaps some of the girls might be here," mother said.

"What girls?" Margaret coldly demanded.

On their way out of the park, through the blare of band music, she could see that mother was nudging and making signs to dad. When they reached the walk, he said, in that shamefaced tone in which he followed mother's lead:

"Well, shall we stop and have some *ice*-cream?"

Margaret went upstairs ahead of the folks, when she got home, and into the refuge of her bedroom. It was a refuge, even in the breathless thickness of the heat. She got into bed quickly, so that she wouldn't have to talk any more to the folks.

After a while she could hear them getting ready for bed in their room. So fixed—so dumpish—such a united front to the world, and then mother was always lying inside and acting as if she agreed with dad when she didn't. It made her disgusted and impatient—that flat, bare sound of heavy, middle-aged feet on the floor.

"I'm never going to get like that!"

But she simply couldn't endure it to stay at home any longer. She couldn't stand it any longer when mother and Aunt Ella and the rest got started on marriage. Somehow she had to escape from that humiliating superiority of married women, the wise "You'll know some day!"—the humiliating admonitions at the wedding, "Margaret, you oughtn't to let your little sister get ahead of you this way!" Mildred Summers had married Gardner Allen right out of high school. Not that Margaret considered *that* much of a triumph any more! Still, it had been a triumph at the time—"the first of the girls to be married." And Mildred greeted her with smiling patronage, saying, "Hello, Margaret —what are *you* doing these days?" Now even little Dorothy was admitted to the wise, whispering company of the matrons, who could look down upon the uninitiated, and put them slightingly aside. To marry anybody in this town would be to forfeit the real story of her life. What she wanted was to look *down* upon this town—to know something wild, rapturous, free. . . .

But it was different since Dorothy was married. The memory of the bridal kiss on the lawn seemed to open up a new world with a presage of piercing delight. As once, the male touch of Frank's big lips had given her just a fleeting, hungry suggestion of joys more hotly actual than those of the pure passion between the characters in *Wuthering Heights*—until then, her ideal. That, she didn't have to experience to understand. But what was bodily must be experienced. Imagination only brought a frustrated, aching pain. It used to be her dream—to find the perfect complement, the other self, who thought and felt exactly as she did. She had thrilled with passionate sympathy when Catherine said, "I *am* Heathcliffe." But now, seeing Jesse's face with the dark line of the brows bent toward Dorothy's tenderly feminine face, Margaret felt instead the portending excitement of difference. That was the thing she craved to break the narrow, intense, self-bound world in which she was imprisoned, and to make her complete. Not marriage, though—the kiss of marriage was consecrated and made docile and pure before it was even experienced!

> "And for one hour of ecstasy
> Give all you have been and could be—"

one of the things she had copied in her red notebook. What did it matter if you dragged through a whole lifetime without *that*—without the very most rapturous thing there was to know?

Margaret kicked off the sheet impatiently. She looked down the length of her body in hard disdain. She knew all her deficiencies better than anyone else could—with a searing knowledge, after the hours, secret and agonized and lit with hope, that she had spent in front of the glass! But she had never felt that *this* was really herself. There was something pent up and concealed within this hard little body, if only it could have the chance to get free. There had been just a sparkling glimpse of it at times—with her powdered hair, in her Martha Washington costume, in the rose-and-green sheerness of her bridesmaid dress. She would have to endure and go through anything for the sake of that—and soon, for she couldn't stand the humiliation of her innocence any more.

That made her afraid. Here at least, hidden and dreaming, she had herself—her little hard, untouched self. She exulted in that knowledge. The life of last winter, now that it had passed, seemed to have a lonely romance about it. That was always the way when she looked back upon things! Margaret could see that aloof little self, guarding its secrets, writing in the red notebook, crouching hungrily on the outskirts of passion. The glamour of her books had seemed to make a kind of starlight inside the room. The folks couldn't stop her. It was because she had feared, inside herself, to break away from that dim, cold, starlit security, bounded by frosty darkness, in which she had her secret being untouched.

Yes, but if she was ever to know what the splendid, reckless kind of people in books and history know—Cathy and Heathcliffe, and the mistresses of kings—and that was the only kind of life she cared about having!—then she couldn't keep herself hidden and intact any more. No matter what it did to her, she would have to break through her self-distrust and fastidiousness and pride. It was a kind of consecration to ecstasy.

In the hot secret darkness—a dog barking outside, a car going past with the grinding of the clutch—her thin body uncovered on the bed was quivering into a dream of blossoming . . . not just her body, her whole self. Sybil's choice of her, and Frank's praises, the devotion she had always drawn from people like Vanchie, and like Ada Rist, her old satellite in high school days —she had these things to go on, besides the queer absolute certainty that she had always felt, like a tiny glowing core of fire, under the blighting coldness of fear and disapproval and misunderstanding. Out at the farm, she used to run into the grove, feeling that the dark fir trees standing there were on her side.

That was what she wanted more than anything else—to come to herself. But until a man whom she could love had recognized and confirmed its special kind of beauty, her body would have to stay thin and cold in its alien sheath of self-distrust—and her whole self stay, tight and unripened, within her body.

II. BASEMENT APARTMENT

MARGARET sat in the train, in the green velvet seclusion of her Pullman section. She looked out at the stations between the wide stretches of country. But somewhere in her mind, beneath these actual sights, was the memory of the car drawn up beside the station platform; and she could still see the folks as they stood there together, looking up at her, while the train was pulling out.

All her life she had meant to get away from them. And now, finally, she had got her way. There was a dreadful wrench of loneliness in the onward-rushing noise of the train, in the rattle of the couplings, when at noon she went unsteadily through the Pullman coaches to the dining car. The coffee joggled in her cup, and not even the silver shine of the cover that the colored waiter lifted with a cherishing flourish from her platter of sweetbreads could take away the solemn finality of the backward rush of country she was leaving. All the little towns they were passing made her think of home. She kept seeing people who looked like the folks, and cars that were just like their own car. The train stopped, and she stared out at another brown-

and-yellow depot, another town that—with its vacant lots across the track, and its asphalted street under shady trees leading to the business section past a dingy old frame house with a shingled tower—might just as well have been Belmond. The innocent sameness of these towns made her queerly guilty and remorseful, and harassed her with a sense of failure.

But she wanted to get away from these places that kept the the sense of failure alive in her—that made her as she had always been, and yet knew she *wasn't*. The country itself was shadowed over with the feeling that she could find no acceptance in it. It belonged to the folks and the folks' ideas . . . the great rolling country, where the rough stubble was getting brown in the fields, and autumn was drying the rich pastures. She had always felt more at home in the landscapes in books than anywhere here . . . in the picture of some old palace garden in the bound magazine copies in the library . . . in the fairytale house with the green door that stood in the midst of the forest. . . .

All the distasteful phases of her meager little history in Belmond were smarting in her. If only she had something romantic behind her!—if she were leaving someone like Dr. Redmond a sad and broken man. No boys had ever kissed her, except Harry and Carl for meanness—and she had scratched and fought back and given them as good as they gave her. She had had her little triumphs, but they had all been the wrong ones. It was Mildred who had won the Gardner Allens!—while Margaret, by some dreadful fatality, had attracted only the Lloyd Dunns. Oh, yes, her horrid little triumphs—but always on the wrong grounds—always with a fatal flaw. Worse than anything else— far worse—was the smarting sense of her own unsatisfactoriness. But she had never *been* herself. Only at moments—when she had jumped off the highest pile of shingles in the lumber yard, and won the admiration of even Carl and Harry for her daring. As long as she stayed with the folks in Belmond, she could be nothing but a kind of shadow, creeping resentfully about the edges of things, or staying apart in frozen agony—never able to get into the open.

Oh, the folks had their grievances, too. They told her she thought more of anybody else than of her own father and mother. She had forced them to take in that tramp dog one night last winter—the dog that was around town everywhere, and that dad said ought to be shot for his own good. And look what had happened! Right on the best rug. And then after they had chased the dog out of the house in righteous wrath, Margaret had gone out to the alley and petted the poor old uncouth, homeless creature to make up for their cruelty. She could always make excuses for cats and dogs, they told her. But she didn't care how she hurt *them*.

But Margaret knew with secret shame and torture that she did care. She had to go about the house wrapped in her air of scornful dissatisfaction, or she might have given in to her mother's hurt, uncomprehending eyes, and piteous, sprightly little efforts at cajolery. Only she couldn't, mustn't care about hurting the folks—they were too close, she had to keep her purpose secure against them. Just because dad had worked hard when he was a little boy, and because mother's arms had a pleading touch, she couldn't let herself forget that they had never acknowledged, never even perceived, a single one of their wrongs against her. Her way of doing things was always queer, and they cared more for their other children than they did for her . . . oh, that conviction was at the very center of her count against them, so that she couldn't give in to them no matter how she ached with loneliness. "What makes you do that? We don't understand you. You're the queerest child we ever saw." So she couldn't admit *them*, either. No matter how good everyone thought them, how everyone trusted dad in the bank, how Mrs. Morgan and Essie Bartlett and everyone said that mother and dad were the salt of the earth. Her life wouldn't fit in with theirs.

The strange, long, broken night passed, in the swaying darkness of the Pullman berth.

Now, at last, the landscape was beginning to get different! A station of an unknown, unexpected town—an old brick station, of a between-stage in architecture, with an arcade and fancy posts stained dingily by the weather. But at least it was not just like the station at home. The ground was getting thicker, more turfy, older, darker. There were great brown rocks with ancient water streaks painted blackly down their sides, and houses of discolored red brick with shutters that made Margaret think of the Revolution.

Oblivion came over her as she stared through the window—but the oblivion of restless expectation. The country was visibly different now, and that, while it frightened her, seemed to set her free. When something had happened to her—when she *knew* —Margaret had always thought she would write great poetry. A series of love sonnets, maybe. She could almost see their vast, shining outlines in her mind.

Margaret took her bag, and trying to look haughtily traveled and impersonal and experienced, she went to the dressing room. No one else was there. The mirrors shone with intimate secrecy. The thin, dark, secretive face looked back at her from carefully veiled eyes. Was that herself? The complexion wore the sallow tinge it always had when she was a little upset. She could see now, against her will, that she really *did* look a little like Grandma Ferguson—and the thought made her furious. She didn't want to look like anyone in the family. She cherished the thought of being just herself. Grandma's hair, when she was a girl, had been long and black. But Margaret's large dark eyes with the full eyelids were not like Grandma's sharp black eyes, or Aunt Ella's dull ones. They were her own. No one knew where they "came from."

She went back to her section, around the smooth turn from the dressing room. The trip was almost over, and there had been no exciting and gratifying adventure. None of the men were distinguished-looking; and Margaret had frozen out those two fussy women who were always calling the porter. She settled back into the almost unendurable brightness of her visions—because she didn't have much time for them, soon she would be put to the perilous test of making them come true.

They were going through miles and miles of dingy suburbs that seemed to be left out of any real scheme of architecture—to be on the desolate, nameless outskirts of any recognizable way of existence. But any place that was strange held romantic possibilities for Margaret. She scorned to be too eager to put on her wraps, like those two elderly women, who were calling to the porter again to know how soon they would be in New York. Margaret's hands were trembling. But her inner excitement held her tense and darkly scornful in the midst of a stirring, large excitement that threatened to dissolve the boundaries of all she knew of life.

The darkness and sudden static feeling of a great railway terminal had come over the train. Now Margaret was glad to have the ladies ask and the porter confirm it. They were there. It gave a sense of queer let-down and of trembling, vast expectancy. Through this darkness, people were moving toward the door—halting—step by step they were getting out of the train. Margaret felt the strangeness of firm ground.

People and people and people poured into the open doors of the great station. And she was here in the midst of them, one separate little person arriving in the multitude—not looking, in her tan coat and small felt hat, the kind of person she really felt herself to be. Margaret felt crushed. Her breath wouldn't come right. She was arriving with nothing but humiliation and emptiness behind her, and she was too uncertain now to think ahead. Her feet were just following the nonchalant, accustomed footsteps of the redcap who had her bags.

Light poured down in great slants from somewhere above them . . . and there was the floor hard and actual and interminably wide under her feet.

Margaret had a confused, exciting, unhappy awareness of the crowds. There was only time for a glimpse of foreign black moustaches, a scarlet hat with just the dashing tilt that made her envious . . . and they were past, the crowd had shifted. She paid the redcap and stood alone. The cathedral light of the station filled her with such awe that her knees were trembling. Margaret did not know why she had dismissed her redcap, or where she wanted to go. She picked up her bags herself, staggering a little, although she scorned unaristocratic behavior; and she tried to feel as if she were hurrying too—somewhere. . . . She went past shining windows of little shops, stirred by the sight of books, a red dress, a silken medley of tinted stockings—making her think desperately of all the things she wanted and didn't have—and how was she going to get them? Everything that she saw was hallowed by an irrefutable distinction because this was New York. Still trembling, Margaret came out into the brilliant sunshine of the city, blue sky above, horns snarling through the confusion of traffic. She felt a thrill of rejoicing, tentative, painful, and yet so sharp she could hardly bear it.

But at the same time she was breathless, small, insignificant, and lost. She was glad to get into the refuge of a taxi—although she could have walked and walked, walked forever. . . . She sat rigid through the hurried, swinging drive that seemed to blind her with the confusion of all she didn't have time to see.

She had another moment of breathless, stopped bewilderment when she got out of the taxi into a street that seemed high and rocky with the towering apartment houses. It was like being in some giant graveyard, among titanic tombstones, the buildings were all so high and stony and dull white. In a secret torture of fear that she might have mistaken the number, Margaret went up to the desk in the apartment house and asked for Mr. Bellew.

"Are you Miss Ferguson?"

"Yes."

The man handed her a note. Mr. and Mrs. Bellew had gone out of town for the day. They would be back early in the evening. She was to go into the apartment and make herself perfectly at home; and there was a nice little tearoom just five doors down the street. She would find the door of her room open. She was not to be worried. They would be back before nine o'clock.

Margaret was ashamed of her own craven weakness in wanting someone to welcome her first, without plunging straight into unknown, exhilarating danger. She must enter cautiously, feeling her way, clinging at first to what she knew even though she despised it. Mr. Bellew had been superintendent of schools in Belmond. Now he was taking a course at the Columbia Teachers College. To think of being a student with Mr. Bellew!—it showed how exciting and jumbled up the old pattern of existence was here in New York. Margaret felt a distant respect for the Bellews, going off on some adventure and leaving just a note, instead of being here to look after her, as people at home would have thought was their duty with company. She was glad to have her first few hours alone, even if she was afraid.

The colored boy carried her bags out of the elevator and down a stony corridor that made Margaret think of either an office building or a prison. He fitted the key into a heavy door that opened upon darkened, empty air.

"Anything else, miss?"

The imaginary picture of her room in New York—something both artistic and distinguished, drawn from novels and magazine pictures—had to change into the actuality of a plain room with miscellaneous furniture. The folks had believed that she would be "safe" with the Bellews. That was one reason why they had finally agreed to let her come to Columbia, instead of going somewhere near home. But what was she to do with herself? The emptiness of the rest of the day was frightening. Margaret's expectations seemed silly. She missed the motion of the train, the crowding excitement of the Grand Central.

It was stuffy. She managed to put up the heavy window, with an instant's slanting glimpse of the stony street far below her. Ethel Spencer, before she left Belmond, had told Margaret that she must go to see Miss Grimm. Somewhere among the jumbled towers was that distinguished figure, surrounded by "interesting people," and promising an initiation into all that meant New York. But now she seemed farther away and harder to reach than when Margaret was in Belmond. Margaret felt at once tired and restless. Even in the narrow, shut-in, old-fashioned bathroom, where she had to turn on the electric light, she was aware of the city outside. Her eyes, although tired from two nights on the train, had their glowing look, not their shadowed, dull look. Nothing was in the least as Margaret had imagined it, and yet she could feel, even here, the surrounding stir of immensity.

She couldn't just stay shut up in this apartment! It seemed wildly adventurous to go into that stony street alone. Margaret didn't know what she was afraid of—having her purse stolen, or losing her way, or just being inadequate to a street in New York. There was a strange freedom in wandering about where no one knew her at all. The air was fresh in the shade and the sky still brilliantly blue. She caught a sparkle of water. She went on and on, wild to see taxis and well-dressed people and the kind of buildings she had read about. She was in New York. She was drunk with exhilaration.

But then the sun got lower. The brightness was gone from the streets. Margaret felt the stony chill. Suddenly her eyes were aching, and her new magic vitality, that had seemed to lift her into another kind of being, was gone. Afraid either to ask or find the way, she cravenly took a taxi back to the apartment house, knowing what the folks would think of the extravagance. She had the depressed feeling of still being just the same Margaret Ferguson stealing into this alien place.

She sat down beside the window and leaned her elbows on the sill. But even up here, she could get the feeling of being in New York. The quiet of her stuffy little room existed within the great tangle of noises. The white buildings of the university would shelter her for a while until she could find her own kind of existence. But after once having been in these streets, she could never just go off to some little town and be a librarian. She wanted her own kind of things, the things that were more real to her intimate self than the furniture at home—fireplaces, candles (even to light a twisted penny candle left over from the Christmas tree had given her a feeling of festival), and always, somewhere in the scene, a distinguished-looking man and a beautiful dark woman seated in low chairs, and their faces just turning toward each other in passionate surrender. . . .

The noise continued, made up of infinite variations, and yet with an enveloping sense of sameness. Lights were on now, glittering in triumphant constellations. Margaret felt as if she were caught and whirled away in the jangled symphony.

2

Margaret got off the bus in Washington Square. She had wanted to come down here by herself, without Mrs. Bellew.

"Some day we must go down and explore the Village," Mrs. Bellew had told her with a laughing, apologetic, and yet daring, eager air. But then they would have been two people from Belmond out to see the sights. The cold wind, with its bleak watery feeling, whipped against Margaret, so that it was only through aching, tear-filled eyes that for a moment she saw the Square with the empty fountain and the arch stony against the colorless sky. She couldn't just stand here. She walked off at random, with what tried to be a purposeful air, along one of the paths between empty benches.

She was at a disadvantage because she didn't know where she was going, but on the alert because any of the people she met might be artists. A fat shoddy woman in a shawl passed her, and then two young Jews with their eager, chilled, spectacled faces thrust forward. They made Margaret angry, because they acted as if they were out for intellectual, radical things that ordinary bourgeois people like herself, from the Middlewest, couldn't understand. But Margaret never got tired of seeing "different-looking" people in New York. They seemed to contradict, thrillingly, all that the folks thought and said, all their comfortable certainties. Once Mr. Bellew had taken Margaret and Mrs. Bellew to the East Side. "Oh, you must see the East Side! See how the other half lives." With a gratified, information-seeking air, the Bellews had gone about among these "queer, foreign people." Margaret had followed with a hang-dog look, acutely conscious of the provincial flaws in her own party, and wanting to apologize for the Bellews' self-satisfaction.

It was just the same with all their excursions. When they went to the theater, Mrs. Bellew pointed out interesting-looking people and whispered about them. "That man looks like some kind of a count, doesn't he? Look! Those must be real society people—the four hundred. What do you suppose that girl is? An artist of some kind? Probably a *would*-be artist. My, but don't you see a lot of funny-looking people!" She always seemed to be ingenuously admitting that *they* had no part in such an interesting scene—and yet keeping a small, provincial, complacent superiority. But Margaret still went about with the

Bellews. New York overpowered her—the idea of it, because it *was* New York. She had the feeling that if she started out alone her real life would have to begin. And she still wasn't ready. She wasn't actually ready to start in today. She had her old feeling of being invisible, a kind of ghost wandering hungrily through these streets to find her habitation.

She saw the old houses along the north side of the Square, and turned and walked all the way past them, reveling in their early eighteenth century elegance. Sometimes it seemed to Margaret that her real home was in one age, sometimes in another. She used to think she might have lived in a Spanish castle, dark on the inside and burning white on the outside. But now she felt almost as if fate had turned her out of one of these houses. Perhaps elegance was what she liked most of all.

"*I* live here, you're *my* house," she said rebelliously to a white doorway.

An old childish, romantic part of her mind still connected real stories with things like white doorways and velvet hangings and the glow of a sea coal fire on a stormy night.

She came to a little alley, that she recognized with an obscure thrill as a real Village place. She walked to the end and back, with a feeling of stealthy intrusion and of almost incredible recognition at the sight of lanterns above doorways and odd little windows with the frames painted a hard Italian blue— things that she seemed to know with a kind of personal inner knowledge in an altogether different category from her actual, ground-in knowledge of plain windows at home with curtains and draperies. Artists lived here. Margaret was humble and excited. She felt that they would not accept her—a thin girl in a commonplace coat, uncertain of herself because she had had no experience, and with her eyes stinging from the cold. Yet under her cringing diffidence—the external image of herself from which she couldn't get away—she had a fiery inner certainty and resentment.

Little shops. Little odd, *different* things. They were what Margaret had always wanted and had felt belonged to her personally, as distinguished from herself having to live mixed up with other people. The bleak wind made her eyes water, and her legs in silk stockings were bitterly chilled. But she kept walking on in a cold, uncomfortable daze of happiness. Candles, in waxy colors, at last her fill of candles—little foreign things, bizarre jewelry, little bookshops with queer names where they sold the kind of books she had always supposed she was the only person in town to read, perhaps the only person in the world. . . .

Margaret made herself break through her cold glaze of self-distrust. She always tried to recall Frank Gesell to her mind, to hear his deep, flattering voice. But Frank didn't fit in here. She went unfortified down several steps and into a bookshop. A *little* bookshop, from which the books always seemed more æsthetic and daring. The warm air made her slightly dizzy. A girl with bright black hair laid in careful flat curves (Margaret was always hungrily collecting data about haircuts) and with lips painted an American-beauty red, was sitting at a desk and talking to a pretty young man in knickers. Margaret was dashed by the superior sophistication of the painted mouth. She felt an instant predatory jealousy. But she wouldn't submit to this cool, supercilious neglect of herself as a patently uninteresting customer. She asked for a new book of poems, savagely glad to interrupt the conversation. The slim volume with its purple-and-pink striped cover would add to her vicarious store. The girl negligently tied up the package in smoke-gray paper and purple string and then went back to the pretty youth. The two young people had an intimate air of knowing the place and not caring to bother with just anyone who happened to come in. It seemed to Margaret that they acted as if they were initiates of the inner secrets of art of which she, in her tan coat, was ignorant. But at any rate she had made some assertion and not gone meekly out of the place. She imagined Miss Grimm getting a place for her in a little bookshop—and then she saw herself, in a miraculously becoming haircut, talking not to a pretty boy like this but to a tall, lean artist with keen eyes and face worn by the world's sorrow. . . .

By the time she went out into the street, she could feel her spirits soaring toward that pitch of heady exhilaration where she could forget her deficiencies and commit some piece of reckless daring. It was the feeling she used to have just before she jumped from the shingle pile.

But there couldn't be anything interesting on a street that had an elevated. It was too shoddy and commercial. Margaret walked back to the Square to get her bearings; and then somehow, with another thrill of recognition, she got into the very sort of street she must see—very crooked and narrow, with the painted doors and colored curtains giving her the necessary feeling of art and oldness and oddness. But there was a shoddy actuality about the dirty, uneven painting, and about the iron grating in front of a basement window—a crudeness about the blue-green paint with its hard lumps. She had never counted on that. She had never imagined, either, big dented-in garbage cans filled with the dingy bleakness of old ashes, and poor skinny cats nosing among the scraps spilled from a broken paper bag. Down in a little basement shop, with "Ann's place" daubed in childish letters across the glass, a stubby old candle and a blue vase stood on the window sill. If she was going to be a bohemian, would she have to put up with an unheated room, cockroaches, and the awful feeling that hair and skin could have when you washed in a little cold water on a winter morning? Margaret hated the memory of the white crockery wash basin out at Grandma Ferguson's. She could picture the splintery wooden floor of Ann's place. It made her hands feel blue and swollen with grimy cold, the way they used to feel when she looked through old piles of things in the attic on a winter day.

Now the demand for luxury, so strong in her—"Margaret always must have the best!"—was frightening. Because she would have to break through that, too, unless she was just ready to give up and accept the regulation things. Margaret was afraid that she was not a real artist in spite of her dream of writing love sonnets after a great experience. She was ashamed of all those old free verse ravings, in India ink on very white paper, about "my grief" and "my sorrow" and "you." Who *was* "You"? Just a very dimly remembered Gardner Allen when he was the pretty boy in the grades, or the red-headed kid with whom she had danced in the Odd Fellows Hall, or Sybil, or

342

Frank Gesell at the moment when he had kissed her. Or just someone imaginary.

> "You did not see
> The hands I flung."

That was about Dr. Redmond, more or less. But he ought to have recognized her through the dark little disguise of her lonely shyness! Margaret had never dared send any of these exquisitely written and carefully cherished verses to a magazine. To herself they were significant and precious, commemorating her own life and imagination, but out among real poetry they would have no meaning.

Little houses opening right on the street aroused Margaret's old craving for some place that could be the setting of her own story. More and more she hated to go back to that stuffy old apartment with Mr. and Mrs. Bellew. It wasn't for *that* she had made the folks send her to New York. But she had been a little unsure even with the Bellews at first, because they had been in New York all summer. They knew how to use the subways. She was gratified, too, by seeing how they had changed and become more modern. They spoke with pride of having taken cocktails at a party, and then said, "Well, you know, you have to do some things so you won't be conspicuous." Mrs. Bellew had worried for fear that Margaret would be shocked! Of course the folks were for Prohibition. The Bellews were themselves, at home. In a restaurant, Mr. Bellew had lighted a cigarette and said jauntily, "When in Rome, do as the Romans do." He had offered one to Margaret and Mrs. Bellew, but only in a jocular way—that would be going a little *too* far. At first the Bellews had dazzled Margaret with their talk of the new plays she mustn't miss seeing, and of the interesting places where they had eaten. She was impressed when she saw their progress from the way she remembered them in Belmond, living in that little rented house with the bay window, doing all the regulation things, both of them singing in the Methodist choir, and Mr. Bellew on the committee for the Chautauqua. But she soon saw that they were only jaunty and excited with their year off, and were just the same people, really—no more interesting than

Carl and Lillian. She, with her youth and the boldness of her secret intentions, belonged in New York. But of course the Bellews were nice to her; and one part of herself liked them and was soft to them, as just other people.

Margaret looked into the windows of all the little shops with uneven doorways, at Russian smocks with red embroidery on coarse-woven linen, and silky scarves of peacock-blue with batik patterns like brown cobwebs, like patterns formed from the smoke of cigars, or like the faded prints of great, brown, skeleton tobacco leaves . . . cringing a little at the shoddiness all around her, the cold wet smell of fish from a shop with a wet floor, the dark little children with dirty noses—and yet gratified in some secret place because everything was different, intimate, small . . . silver jewelry with handicraft unevenness, and the bizarre dark goldiness of gipsy earrings . . . with a rising excitement that burned through the pain of craving for nearly everything she saw.

Well, why shouldn't she go into a tearoom if she felt like it? What if she was late getting back to the apartment? Why did she have to be so terribly scrupulous? Because she had inherited it from the folks. The whole Ferguson tribe was like that. Dad always did business on time, and if mother had to help at the church, she must be there even before the minute and do even more than was expected of her. The Fergusons were always to be relied upon. Well, that was a good reason for beginning to practice bohemian haphazardness. . . . And why did she have to feel so afraid? Even if she didn't look the way she wanted to, couldn't she just submit herself to the new experience? Why must she go through this silly, secret torture before she showed herself to any new people? She used to go around the block rather than meet people at home. Did she honestly think she wasn't as good as other people? Then kill herself and be done with it!

Only she didn't think it. And if they supposed so, just because of her diffidence, then they were fooled!

Angrily, her eyes in a dark set blaze, and her face rigidly expressionless, Margaret turned and went back to the tearoom.

She wanted to go into one of the most Villagey of all. One in a basement. Something in her, something that she scoffed at, romantically craved it—just as, when she was a child, and they were all playing, she had to go back and tiptoe alone into the darkest, most creaking corner of the barn. She had noticed "Marta's" painted in fat blue letters and a candle tipsily burning between chintz curtains. She went down stone steps and through a cold, shabby hallway. With an inward shrinking for which she scornfully berated herself, she opened the blue-painted door with an old-fashioned latch, the sort people had on sheds and chickenhouses at home.

Once again the reaction from the cold made her tingling and dizzy. Margaret didn't know whether to be disappointed or relieved because there were no artists in the tearoom. But she was saved again—to her shame, her secret relief—from the great encounter that was going to change her whole life.

She sat down on a blue-painted bench. There was one of those horrid floors. But there were candles, and a feebly burning old chair leg in a straggling soft mass of dingy gray ashes in a fireplace painted the same blue as the walls. Margaret's lids drooped over her telltale, ardent eyes. The candles and the fire deeply pleased her—although she couldn't help being a little squeamish over the way the candle had dripped blobs of cold white tallow on the wooden table. But she was going to get over things like that.

She still ached with cold, and a draft from under the poorly fitting door chilled her feet. The old familiar bitterness of not belonging rose in her throat. Margaret wanted to run before anyone saw her. But she forced herself to stay on the hard cold bench, trying to get hold of the shining audacity that was hidden somewhere in her cold dullness. She had been in New York almost two months now, and she hadn't, in spite of her little excursions into tearooms and art galleries, and buying caviar and pâté de foies gras and eating them on crackers at night in her room to learn expensive tastes—hadn't stepped immediately into an utterly different existence. She was still taking her library course, and going around with Mr. and Mrs. Bellew.

345

To the people who would eat in a place like this, she supposed she would seem just a regulation Village tourist.

A tall thin girl with queer hazel eyes, wild and bright, and a curly childish mass of chestnut hair, came now to take Margaret's order. "But I couldn't wear *my* hair that way," Margaret thought enviously. She did not look at the girl directly, as she ordered cinnamon toast and tea, but tried again, by drooping her eyelids, to make herself invisible. She felt all at once dreadfully commonplace beside this girl's slightly dingy, yet charming, elfin oddity. Later, she saw the girl staring at her from the kitchen door. What was it about those eyes? They were a little too close together, and one of them was set slightly slanting—but they were attractive. Margaret stared haughtily at the wall. She supposed her clothes, or something, were dreadful. Margaret never permitted herself to think of any pleasing reason why people should look at her. Those eyes! There was something not quite human about them. Maybe the girl was a genius or something. She had disappeared into the kitchen, to Margaret's relief, but now she came in with two little fat brown teapots and a flowered cup with a chipped saucer. Margaret noticed her thin hand, attractive also but none too clean, with a very large silver ring.

"You aren't Margaret Ferguson, are you?"

Margaret couldn't believe she had heard that!

"I *thought* I recognized you!" The girl spoke in a breathless rush. Her queer hazel eyes had a bright stare. "I don't suppose you remember me. Jane Gowan?"

Margaret was excited but disappointed. She had thought this girl was some odd genius—not anyone she knew!

"I don't suppose you do remember. I was in the B class and you were in the A class. I was terribly dumb. I lived in Belmond once—until my dad had to leave town. You used to go home from school with Irene Jackson. You were playing being Lady Phyllista and Countess Dorinda. I was terribly impressed!"

The A class and the B class—Irene Jackson and the Lady Phyllista—Margaret couldn't believe such words were being spoken, in this little basement room with the candles, where she had expected to find some unknown genius writing immortal poetry on the back of an envelope!

Then she did remember. That bright hazel stare, wild, and yet disarming! Only no wonder *Jane* Gowan had meant nothing! Those Gowans—that awful family, who had lived next door to Irene Jackson, in that horrid little house with tin cans in the yard . . . that Mr. Gowan who had had a fight and almost killed a man on Main Street, right in front of the bank, and people had said he oughtn't to be allowed to stay in town! There *had* been a skinny little kid named Jennie Gowan. She didn't pass in school. She was the one who had hung around, bothering Irene and Margaret, when they were all dressed in their imaginary ball gowns, about ready to enter their coach. In the midst of her amazement, burrowing back into the darkness of memory, Margaret could realize what it was now about those hazel eyes. "Squirrel-Eyes" was what the kids at school had all called little Jennie Gowan!

They were suddenly excitedly glad to see each other.

"I didn't know you were in New York!" Jane said with childish eagerness. "What are you doing?"

"I'm taking some work."

Not for worlds would Margaret have confessed that she was taking a library course! It made her feel like Vanchie or someone. Anyone who had known Irene Jackson!—had known that little off side of Margaret's childhood history instead of the everyday side! There was a queer, somewhat shoddy halo about the memory of Irene even yet. Margaret tried not to show how much she admired Jane's tall childish thinness in her odd, tight-fitting, torn black dress, and the mussed prettiness of the tousled curls.

"What are you—"

"Oh, I'm just helping Marta right now. She took me in out of charity. I'm out of a job," Jane confided blithely. "Marta!" she shouted. "Come here!" A buxom older girl in a blue smock came in from the kitchen. "Here's someone I used to admire *ter*-ribly. Margaret Ferguson, this is Marta. I don't know her last name. Guess she hasn't got any."

"Little rat," Marta said amiably.

"Margaret Ferguson lives in Belmond, where my dad had a fight and had to leave town."

"Well, sit here and curse your native village together! Excuse me, Margaret. I'm making a cake. Isn't that wonderful?"

Margaret felt the aching chill go from her hands and feet and the warm brightness come into her blood. To think of finding that little Squirrel-Eyes, of *all* people, here in New York! The unlikeliness of that made the place even more jumbled-up and exciting. Jane brought herself some tea, and sat and asked questions about Belmond, and Margaret replied with ironical answers. There was a secret defiance of the folks in this alliance with a girl who came from the wrong part of town and whose father had had a fight on Main Street. There was the exciting realization that under their ironical quips they were both working off their grudges against the town.

"I haven't heard of Irene Jackson for years!"

"Oh, didn't you know about her? It's marvelous. She married a clerk in a little hotel—and then one day she ups and offs with a rich old customer, and he died and left her all his money, and she's living in Paris in perfect grandeur. Oh, yes, didn't you know that?"

Jane snuggled down beside Margaret and squeezed her hand.

"Listen, some night I'll give a party, and you must come! I'm crazy about having you here. You're the only person in Belmond I ever wanted to see again!"

3

If little Squirrel-Eyes Gowan could change as much as that, why couldn't Margaret herself? It was a miracle! But the world was getting to be full of miracles. It seemed sometimes as if the earth was shooting off on some dizzy orbit, like a rocket, and that the past didn't count any more.

Margaret walked boldly into a barber shop and had her hair cut. The barber held up the long, shorn, black locks, and asked: "Shall I wrap up your hair for you, miss?" Panic came over Margaret. Mother used to comfort her, when people praised Dorothy's curls, by saying how long her hair was. But mother had really mourned over her straight black hair. Its length had

been her only pride. . . . No. She wouldn't take it. She wanted
to be rid of the stuff altogether. She walked out of the barber
shop with her hat too big for her and resting on her nose, and
the back of her neck naked and cold.

"Why, Margaret FER-guson!"

Mr. Bellew thought, of course, that he must be facetious.
But Mrs. Bellew was wistful, and talked about cutting her own
hair—wispish, drab-colored hair, faded and dry; it seemed
cruel to think of it in comparison with Margaret's new crop of
shining black.

The hair cut made Margaret feel different altogether. She
couldn't quite trust her own elation at the view, in her hand
mirror, of the bold outline of her cropped head that seemed
to make her neck more softly girlish. She was filling out a little,
too, and beginning to look slim instead of scrawny. Now, when
she glanced at the mirror in the drug store where she ate her
lunch—obliquely, always, for she had never quite dared risk a
full view of herself—she thought she caught the sparkling look
of her eyes instead of the dull veiled look. Of course she had
always intended to become beautiful.

Margaret did her library work with meticulous competence,
just as she had done her school work. Her pride, and her Ferguson inheritance, demanded that. But Mr. and Mrs. Bellew, who
had thought of her at first as the kind of girl who would make
a good librarian, were beginning to be a little doubtful about
her now.

All the time, Margaret was tentatively, thrillingly, occupied
with herself; with the changes that even the Bellews noticed,
the whitening and filling out of her unfledged neck, the shininess
of her hair that had glints and gleams of brownish red in the
black when it was washed. It all seemed to be a preparation.
When she walked down Fifth Avenue, she felt an aching, rasp-
ing envy of the beautiful things in windows. After she had
taken her bath at night, she went through a scrupulous ritual
of tending herself, a secret, devout preparation . . . stealthily,
so that the Bellews wouldn't wonder why she was still up and
what she was doing.

She wouldn't admit to herself how much she counted upon

Jane Gowan's party. It had taken the place of the hope that some day she would gather courage to go and see Miss Grimm. It wouldn't be the passport to the world of "interesting" people —but to a kind of secret, dark, haphazard basement world through which she must pass before she could really be rid of what she used to be. She let the Bellews suppose that the invitation was from some girl in her library course. How shocked they would be if they knew she was going down to the Village to see that little Jennie Gowan! She almost wished she had told them. They called after her:

"Remember what we told you about those Villagers!"

But there was uneasiness under their determined facetiousness. They weren't quite sure of a girl who lived in the Village, even if she *was* going to Columbia. They had seen Margaret changing and getting away from them. Mr. Bellew thought he must be funny about the books she brought home. "Are you going in for these free versifiers and Russian novelists?" He thought there was something immoral about free verse and modern painting, and yet he was a little bit afraid because he didn't understand it. The Bellews had both agreed that Margaret was getting to think too much about her clothes.

It was glorious to be away from that stuffy apartment and out alone in the rainy darkness. There were just the misty ghosts of the tall buildings, but their outlines held a distant power.

Margaret got off the bus in the Square.

Fearfully she carried out Jane's haphazard instructions, going quickly through the exciting little secret streets until she came to a row of small, dark-red brick houses. The iron basement railings were coldly misted with rain. The street excited her in some minor way, just like that rutty little off-street where Irene used to live. She pressed a dubious-looking bell above a card lettered girlishly in purple ink:

Gowan-Rindemiller . . .

while she waited, shivering with nervous expectancy.

The door clicked feebly. Margaret pushed it open and stepped into a chilly narrow hall carpeted with linoleum.

"Here we are!"

Looking up from the stairs, she could just see Jane's face looking down at her from over the top railing. Margaret climbed the narrow stairway that leaned perilously to the side, refusing to let her fastidiousness take alarm at any dinginess—because she wasn't going to be shocked by anything in New York. She wanted to know the worst. She had had enough of the best, of "the bright side of things." Jane's eyes stared glittering down at her from the hanging tousle of curls.

Jane squeezed her hand.

"I was scared to death you wouldn't come!"

"Why not?"

"Oh, I was such a little perp when you knew me."

"What do you think *I* was?"

"Oh, I thought you were grand!"

She took Margaret into a funny little anteroom. On one side stood a wabbly dresser painted that same hard shade of blue, on the other a very dirty kitchen table with a gas plate. Margaret had to pretend that nothing seemed strange to her. Jane was wearing that funny little scant black dress and dangling earrings. Margaret wished that she had dared to buy the flaming red chiffon that she had really wanted, instead of the innocuous beige that Mrs. Bellew had encouraged her to get because it would "do for any occasion." But the red dress would have given her away. When she had started to try it on, a sort of uprising of her old self-distrust and longing to be hidden had overwhelmed the faint new audacity. Jane looked so odd and different that it was exciting to feel this queer, homelike kinship with her. As they powdered their noses at the shaky dresser, Jane with an old powder puff that was soggy pink, they felt that they were both New Yorkers and secure in their superiority to Belmond.

"You've cut your hair! It's swell. But I remember those great long braids you used to have. You could sit on your hair. All the girls used to talk about that. 'Margaret Ferguson can sit on her braids.' "

"Makes me sound like a hen or goose or something!"

"Oh, I thought they were grand! I used to stare at them in

school and wish I could have hair as long as that. You had the ribbon braided into the ends—a red ribbon."

"Do you remember *that?*"

"Oh, you don't know how I used to adore you!"

Jane's eyes were staring and hazel-bright as she said all this in her breathless little voice that seemed always just about to break into some gloriously exciting news.

"I always hated my hair, and my folks did too, because it wasn't curly like Dorothy's."

"Who was Dorothy?"

"Oh, don't you remember? My pretty little sister?"

"Did you have a sister? I don't remember anyone but you."

"Goodness! Nobody else would say that."

"Oh, I've never forgotten your eyes or your hair. I always thought, if I could just have eyes like Margaret Ferguson's, instead of crazy ones like mine, I wouldn't ask for anything more. Don't you remember how I used to stick around, awful little brat, when Irene tried to chase me away, because I just couldn't stop looking at you!"

"How disappointed you must be now."

"Oh!"

Jane made a horrified round of her lips.

"JANE!"

Jane said hastily, "We've got to go back to the party." She squeezed Margaret's hand again. "I invited Dr. Finkbein because of you. He's got a wonderful mind! Stella isn't here— my roommate. They sent her to Trenton. She's got a job. We've had an awful fight. I don't want you to like Stella!" She pressed Margaret's arm childishly. "They're all just crazy to meet you. I told them how grand you are."

Margaret's cheeks were stained with the clear rose-red that came only when she was excited; and she could feel, in a vivid rush, the same dashing boldness that once in a while used to make the other children in awe of her, and that she had always felt was really herself, breaking through the cold restraint of her self-distrust and thorny, fastidious reserve.

"Here's Margaret Ferguson!"

Jane made the announcement with naïve triumph. Her thin

352

hand with its childishly cold finger tips was still clinging to Margaret's. The small room was dense with smoke. The men were standing, and the girls, seated, were looking up with an instant, cold, feminine appraisal scarcely veiled in their eyes. One of the men had a beard. Margaret supposed he must be the "wonderful" Dr. Somebody.

A youth said nonchalantly, "Hello, Margaret Ferguson." He was sitting on the floor with his head against a girl's knees. He had silky side-burns and a petulant small mouth, and he wore an orange silk shirt.

"Get up, Rod," Jane begged. "I won't let you meet Margaret if you don't!"

"Well, I know who she is already. She's Margaret Ferguson, isn't she? I like your eyes, Margaret!"

The others laughed scornfully at Rod, and yet they seemed to approve his debonair insolence. He closed his eyes languidly, and settled his head against the girl's knees. His long lashes curled like flowers beneath the childish purity of the white lids.

But all these people were different. The girl who supported Rod wore a red peasant dress with bright embroidery. Margaret always felt jealous of any girl who wore red. Her beige dress seemed commonplace and girly-girly. Another girl had on a black evening dress. She had blond hair, and looked like Mildred Summers, and Margaret instantly hated her. It disappointed Margaret that the men seemed to be inferior in looks to the girls.

At first Margaret was mute. The couch was so wide that her feet felt funny and stiff sticking out beyond it. The furniture was disarmingly childish, like Jane herself, in its foolish pretty cheapness and inadequacy. Most of the people sat on the floor. There were two wicker chairs, one painted in streaky black and one in green, that squeaked when anyone moved. A dormer window, opening like a casement, was set in under two slopes of ceiling like those modern paintings done in geometric blocks. The room was at the top of the house. Margaret imagined herself crouching at such a window at twilight, looking across the dark, narrow, little tucked-in street, and thinking of a love affair that had ended in sorrow.

A little man with fluffy hair was bringing drinks. Margaret accepted hers with the air of cold immobility that she adopted to cover her excitement and uncertainty. Once Frank had given Sybil a bottle of port, to "give her strength" when she was getting over a cold; and every night before they went to bed, the two girls had made a deliciously private rite of solemnly clinking and sipping from two small ten-cent-store glasses. "I drink to Frank Gesell." "I drink to Red McGafferty." He was that boy on the Hanging Rock football team—the only male interest that Margaret had been able to dig up. But anyway, that was better than never having tasted liquor before.

Secretly fearful, Margaret sipped the stinging, bad, orange-colored concoction. The people all joked about the drinks and made a great deal of them. One man was a little stewed. Margaret remembered the disgraceful fact that Grandpa Ferguson had been a Prohibitionist. He had voted with the party for years, saying "they'd get a man in the White House yet." Margaret felt a burning tingle in her throat. Then her finger tips tingled. Her cold diffidence was being submerged under a heady gaiety. The apartment looked beautiful. All at once she could talk to people.

The little fluffy-haired man had come up with Jane. "So you two damsels used to know each other in earlier days?"

Jane was plaintive. "Just sort of knew each other, Daggie! I used to admire Margaret Ferguson in the distance. She lived in the right part of town and I lived in the wrong part."

"You lived in the wrong part?" Daggie repeated with gently mocking commiseration. He put his arm around Jane and rocked her consolingly. Jane laid her curly head against his shoulder and snuggled to him. The tousle of curls almost hid her eyes while her lips took on the pout of a petted woman. "How grievous that our little Jane had such a humble origin!"

"But she's among the aristocrats now!"

Lee, the thin light-haired one, who was sitting beside the light-haired girl, said that with a scornful inflection.

Dr. Finkbein waited, alert and serious.

"I want to know what sort of native village produced these two interesting young women!"

Margaret said darkly, in a rush of angry daring:

"The worst place on earth!"

She had triumphed! She was accepted. All had laughed. She had proved her right to be included in this aristocracy of exile. Margaret was dazzled by Jane's candor about her social deficiencies. She had always jealously hidden her own defects. Uplifted dizzily, she began to say things she had never dreamed of admitting except in the painful secrecy of her own mind.

"Oh, she lived in a grand house!" Jane sighed.

"*Grand house.* Why, you little liar. I despise our house. It's just absolutely ordinary. That *urn.* You thought that was grand! You mean that hideous old affair in our front yard? My dad's one idea of a work of art!"

This was the way, then, of dealing with all her guilty secrets! Margaret heard the approving laughter. Only that horrid little blond Louise looked superior and was still. The wonderful Dr. Finkbein had got up from his cushion on the floor and sat down very close to her on the couch. Margaret was afraid that she would give away her innocence and inexperience. She was impressed but not attracted by his dark Jewish looks. Still, she wasn't going to be judged any more by Harry and Carl. They would be out of place among people who lived in New York, and talked about music, and sex, and perversion. The wonderful Dr. Finkbein was interested—she could see it in the alertness of his eyes, and feel it in his body as he pressed close to her, breathing too near her face. Now it seemed that all the old values were overturned. The things that had been held against her were her assets. When she told them that she had been fired from the Normal, she achieved her greatest success.

She detested Belmond. She had *hated* the Normal. She loathed her name—Margaret! It had been her grandmother's name, and she couldn't bear her grandmother. It made her think of one of those horrid "womanly" women who were such liars and tried to please everybody at once.

"Then why not change it?" Daggie asked, with his gently quizzical smile of amusement. All these girls had changed their names to suit their features or the dictates of the numerologists. Little Jane had some sort of cast-off appellation. "I am not a member of the worthy brotherhood of numerologists, and I must confess that my arithmetic is faulty, but I see no reason why you should not answer, hereafter, to the far more suitable and decorative title of—say, Margot."

Jane shrieked ecstatically. "Christen her, Daggie! Go on, you're good, you're just lovely, you're better than any priest." Daggie solemnly sprinkled a few remaining drops of gin upon Margaret's head.

But she never, never could go back to the Bellews' apartment. Now the gin was gone and they were all eating hot dogs and drinking coffee out of chipped Italian pottery cups. Jane embraced Margaret, and hid her head, wailing. There was Lossie's apartment! Daggie had the key. Lossie had left it with him when she had got a chance to go abroad as secretary to that woman with the sandals and fillets who was going to revive the ancient arts of Greece.

It was perfectly crazy! Simply mad. Mr. and Mrs. Bellew would think that she was a criminal. She had no money and she couldn't take an apartment. The folks would never send her another cent if she dropped her library course. They had enough against her already. . . . Well, then, why shouldn't they have everything? It was a dare in which she couldn't back down, unless she were to fail in everything from this time on. There was no use in asking the folks. They would never let her do it. Library course!—Lee said. Did she want to live and die a holy virgin? Money! Dear me, Daggie said mildly, what was money to hold one back from the heart's desire?

It was like those terrible, glorious moments when she had stood—all alone in the whole air—on the highest shingle pile in the lumber yard, and all the other children down below her, shouting, "You dassent do it!" Margaret felt almost that old, backward, thrilling rush of air and the hard, welcome shock of the ground. The eyes of the other people were shining with the same startled, pleased, reluctant admiration she used to see in the faces of those children. Now was her moment. She couldn't stop for what the folks would say. It was more important—breaking out of her old bonds, asserting herself, *starting*—than any right or wrong.

But there was so much more to it than just impressing anyone! Margaret realized that when the others had left, and she was alone in her apartment. It meant that now she had cut loose from her whole unsatisfactory past. When she thought of what was ahead of her, the very floor seemed to dissolve. She would have to write to the folks, go to the Bellews' and get her things, find a job. She had just forty dollars left, and she couldn't ask the folks for more—even if they would send it to her, after this.

But forty dollars—Jane would consider that an immense amount! It seemed pretty large to Margaret herself. She would soon be making money at some interesting job, in a bookshop or a tearoom. And even if she went on the rocks—actually on the rocks!—she had at least reached out to seize the kind of life that belonged to her.

Now it was almost morning. Jane's crowd had stayed to get the room warm for her, with all the rubbish they could scrape together for the fireplace. It had all seemed to be wild fun at the time, the most fun she had ever had, but now Margaret could scarcely remember any of it. Only that Lee had gone to Tony's for a bottle of wine, and they had all drunk from the bottle to celebrate Margot's emancipation from the career of librarian, and then taken hands and danced around the room. She could see Dr. Finkbein prancing with a serious intentness to be pagan and jolly. Everyone had seemed transformed—and it was so much gayer because they belonged only to this night, she didn't know who most of them were or where they had come from, except that, like herself, they were outlaws.

Now she was Margot. This was her own apartment. Margaret went softly about the room, looking at her possessions, not yet able to believe that they were hers. A crazy little laugh seemed struggling in her throat.

She didn't have the complete elegance that she ultimately demanded. But these were the things that she wanted now. She had the floor, with its wide old boards roughly painted.

357

She had the little green table with the two candlesticks and the tipsy candles. She had the creaky wicker chairs. The low open shelves on which to accumulate her chosen books. The big old kitchen fireplace, with the soft sooty blackness, the straggle of gray ashes on top, a few warm gleams of red still softly winking. When Margot came and stood before the fireplace, in her tiptoe wandering, the crazy laugh burst from her throat and she beat her hands lightly together in a solitary ecstasy.

First she lighted the two candles with the matches Daggie had left. Then she twisted some paper, as she had seen Jane do, and made the first solitary, romantic fire in her own fireplace. She felt dark and bright and wild and free! She curved her arms in a secret dance and saw their shadows on the low wall— whirled—and then stood still and gave a queer, happy moan.

But dearer even than her fireplace, dearer than the candles, were the two deep basement windows set snugly, excitingly, mysteriously below the jangling noises of the narrow street.

4

There had been rain during the night. But when Margaret finally woke up, there was only a fresh chill air blowing in through the open windows.

It was still quite dark in the basement apartment. For a long time the roar of the trucks had been making the windows shiver. The noise enveloped her in strangeness and made her feel that she was in the very midst. Margaret thought of all the dreadful things that were ahead of her. Last night's cold gray ashes lay scattered in the fireplace, and now she had nothing else to burn. She lay huddled under someone else's half-soiled blankets in the little chemise she had worn all night, and she felt herself shivering in a dark ebb of fear.

A narrow shaft of sunshine came suddenly through the upright iron bars of the farther window. It brightened up the wide green window sill and a space of dark painted floor. Margaret knew then that she would go through anything rather than give up this place.

She didn't dare to look in the glass as she shiveringly dressed.

She felt too dreadful in her beige georgette in the morning. Everything that she owned was at the Bellews' apartment. What were they thinking now? Maybe calling up the police! Margaret thrust on her hat with only the barest glance at the mirror, for fear she would hate herself.

Outside, she suddenly felt different. The narrow streets were streaked with rain. But sunshine kept breaking through, and then the dark streaks of wet glistened. Margaret began to feel queerly happy. She had a share now in the narrow, noisy streets —the hurrying people, the dark Italians in the doorways of chilly little shops with sausages hanging in the windows, the bookshop with dirty copies of *Beulah* and of ancient textbooks on the shelf outside, the smooth handicraft tea tables in another window, the taxi skidding and pulling up in front of the small brick house with the window boxes, while all the little kids went scattering. . . .

This was the first day of her real life. From now on, she would be Margot, never Margaret any more. Breakfast had to be a kind of beautiful rite. She went hastily past the common cafés and the wagon lunches, the corner Coffee Pot with men sitting around the counter and bending down to gulp pale coffee from thick cups, the drug stores where people with jobs snatched hasty breakfasts. From now on, she was going to do what she *wanted* to do, not what was sensible. She chose an expensive restaurant with heavy, cream-colored, French-looking curtains. With an air of cool immobility, in spite of her hatred of her clothes, Margaret followed the dark stout waiter to an upholstered seat.

She felt a solemn, luxurious joy in the ceremony of her late breakfast in this leisurely, upholstered place. How did she know? This might be the last day of her life. Holding the large menu card between her hands, she languidly scanned it. Her old Ferguson thriftiness quailed. But another side of her—her own side, the *real* side—seemed to come alive and bright and gay at this extravagance. The blood came into her chilled hands and feet and she felt her movements growing graceful and slow to fit in with the hushed atmosphere. She could live in a basement, without conveniences—but when she went out to eat, she

had to do it in the proper style. The folks were just the opposite! When they drove to Geneva, they took along a lunch and
ate it in the park, saving the price of a meal. Margaret felt
above them. She felt *richer*. There was no one else in the place
except a good-looking man with a clipped moustache absent-
mindedly pouring amber-brown coffee from his silver pot as he
read the *Times*.

The sun was out, brilliant, shining on the dark wet. Taxis
darted under the long, sweeping, clanging roar of the elevated.
Margaret felt that she couldn't go and see the Bellews today.
It was *her* day. This was her own secret celebration. Without
stopping for any decision, she turned and fled toward Washington Square, where she paused in the sunshine, among the bare
wet trees, in the freshened air. Without thinking again, she
climbed to the top of one of the green busses that after a moment began to lumber up the bright width of Fifth Avenue.
The blue sky was narrowed by the tall buildings, and she looked
down on the sauntering people with mazed eyes, as if she were
fulfilling some dream. She felt crazy with happiness.

Hastily she rang the bell and went down the perilous steps.
She knew that she had to buy some new clothes to suit this
feeling, no matter how she used up her money. The windows
of the fine shops brought back the guilty shame of her poverty. It was a physical hurt—this craving for the tinted exquisiteness of the sheer silk stockings, the beautifully done up
jars of cosmetics in their expensive colors of pink and lilac and
cream. With shame, Margaret hung about the racks of reduced
dresses, hating the supercilious knowledge in the eyes of salesgirls. A saleswoman came toward her, with the pretense of refined speech and of obsequious enthusiasm trying to belie the
open secrets of her hennaed hair, white at the roots, and the
deep sagging lines and under-eye puffs beneath the dry pink-
and-white of make-up. The sight drove Margaret to grasp
her youth. She was twenty-seven—old enough!—and if she
didn't have things pretty soon they would do her no good.
Driven, unsatisfied, her money burning in her purse, Margaret
could not stop until she had bought a black silk dress with unusual sleeves, and a red hat from a bargain counter. Even

then, the fever was not spent—not until, sick with audacity, feeling the floor drop away from her at the fatal dwindling of the bills in her handbag, she had bought rouge, geranium-red lipstick in a silver case, a package of scented cigarettes, two little wine glasses in an antique shop, and a heavy supply of ten-cent-store candles.

Her feet were noiseless on the carpeted softness of the Rest Room in the department store. She managed triumphantly to change into the new black dress in the cramped space of one of the toilet booths. Then she stood before the long shining mirror, detesting the critical eyes of the other women, and made up her face with the new rouge and lipstick. Everything about her seemed changed, and yet more than ever her own. Her eyes sparkled darkly under the red of the hat. She seemed to have come into possession of a light, sauntering step, and she felt that now she truly was "Margot."

She went out into the bright street. Instead of feeling poor because of her extravagance, she felt much richer.

She chose a French restaurant for luncheon because it was foreign. This meal was another secret celebration. Margot slowly relished each course that she ate in her free solitude—the rich soup, the asparagus, the chicken. All seemed sanctified because they were French; although the table-d'hôte luncheon was not particularly good. She was aware of two men with foreign moustaches, and their presence made her hands seem whiter and her movements more graceful and significant; although she felt the disgrace of never having had a romance in her life, and the difficulty of working up her feeling for Dr. Redmond into anything that would do. She smoked one of her new scented cigarettes, idly and gracefully she felt, one elbow on the table, as she ate the small pink-and-white slab of ice cream and drank the bitter coffee from the small thick cup. The meal was sumptuously complete.

Still she was not ready to go back to her cold apartment and the consideration of her problems. Some part of her exuberance had not yet been given vent. She had spent all the money that she dared. There was nothing to do but go into a church.

Margot felt that this was like entering religion in a book: to open a gate, and go past a small fountain chilly with thaw, and into the silent dusky charm, heavy with the accumulated silence of old beliefs, of the low, irregular rooms of the little Anglican church on the side street. Margot had long ago decided that she didn't believe in religion. But the high church atmosphere had a romantic attraction for her, as a child of Puritan upbringing. She felt that she was treading on the edges of a mystic feeling that she couldn't quite accept. She was all the more intrigued because this feeling was slightly spurious. Things irregular, off the set pattern, little steps up or down, odd windows, hidden window seats, balconies, unexpected corners—these were the kind of things that made Margot feel as if she were just on the verge of being in a story. Nothing was irregular at home except the cupola on the old Spencer house. Margot walked softly down the aisle, hungrily feeding her appetite for color and difference with the sight of the white-and-gold altar, the woody smell, the cushion and candle smell, the thick silence. She solemnly knelt on a prayer bench . . . but nothing came, no answer, no more than when she looked into a glass on Halloween; and she left the church feeling surreptitious and unsatisfied.

The sun was clouded over again. It was colder, and the noonday brilliance was gone from the streets. Margot took the bus to Washington Square. She was tired now, but only partly appeased.

She didn't know just what to do. She stood on a corner, chilled and jostled, confused by the overhead roar of the elevated. Someone was coming toward her. She recognized the little beard—it was the wonderful Dr. Finkbein! Margot saw guiltily that in the daylight he looked like a poor professor. There was the wrinkled dreariness about him of a man who lived in a small rented room. But they greeted each other with enthusiasm.

"Just the young woman I was thinking about! Won't you come in somewhere for tea? Then we can continue our very interesting conversation."

The smoke-filled room where candles flickered was like the inside of some dark shell. They took their place among the heterogeneous couples sitting on hard benches and leaning their elbows on unsteady tables. Margot felt some unsatisfactory romantic pleasure in the spurious charm of the "quaint" little tearoom made over from a stable. She played with the pretense that Dr. Finkbein might be that "older man" who had come into her imagination in so many guises, and who could form and direct her. There was a sweet, insidious flattery in the thought of being led, adored and guided—like Charlotte Brontë's heroines. It was a little difficult to sustain the idea of Dr. Finkbein in that rôle; but she felt defiantly that she had to begin to live right now, with what was around her. She tried not to meet Dr. Finkbein's earnest, empty eyes.

He was nervously responsive and delighted when she asked him boldly to go back with her to her apartment. He had already clapped the admiring label of "hedonist" upon her. All day Margot had scarcely dared believe in the existence of her basement room. But there it was—her own—below the noise and the passing, with the barred windows and the little grated door down two stone steps.

"I haven't any lights," Margot said nervously. "I'll have to unwrap my candles."

She felt Dr. Finkbein breathing too close to her. He was fumbling helplessly for the candle. Then she felt the awkward, timid earnestness of his hand on her arm. There was a moment of embarrassing hesitation. Trembling inwardly, disgusted with her inexperience, Margot tried deliberately to smile. She saw his bright spectacles—and then his kiss fell, clumsy and fervid, on her lips.

Margot pulled herself away. But at any rate she had dared! She had made her first day end with a kiss.

Why did she have to suffer humiliation just because she wanted to stay in New York and do some interesting kind of work instead of just the ordinary kind?

There was a bookshop that Margot had seen on just the kind of street that charmed her most, a piece of street that went zig-zag, like going down the Crooked Street in *Old Witch*. On one side of the shop was an Italian grocery with funny cheeses in the window, and on the other a gift shop with Czechoslovakian toys. Margot had gone in trembling and humble, scarcely able to raise her lashes. A cadaverous young man in black-rimmed glasses was leaning against the table and talking with a stout young Jew with fuzzy hair. The cadaverous one, the owner, had come up negligently. She had to swallow before she could speak. "I just wanted to ask you if you needed anyone here to help you." Her timidity had amused them highly. "Well," the man had said, lifting one eyebrow, while the other silently shook with laughter, "what kind of help do you offer?" Margot said haughtily, "To sell books!" "Why, my dear, I'd love it if I ever sold any!" And they both had laughed and laughed, thinking that because she looked shy and young, and had a middlewestern accent, they could be as funny as they pleased and she wouldn't really understand it. "If I could support myself," the cadaverous young man repeated, in his gently supercilious tone, "I'd love to support you too!"

The bookshops, the tearooms and gift shops she had entered, stopping outside blindly to fortify herself with the memory of all the praise she had ever had—every one had been a humiliation! The antique shop where the tall woman had come toward her from out of a tantalizing disarray of glass decanters and clocks and andirons, lifting her insolent threads of eyebrows, judging and discarding Margot as a customer not worth while. The bookshop in the Grand Central, in an entirely different New York, a kind of giant place that seemed to belong to the teeming present and not to the romantic past that lingered about the painted doorways and the iron railings down in the narrow streets. The crowded little shop had best sellers on all the shelves. There was a crisp noon smell of coffee from the tiny, nickel-bright eating place next door where all the people were catching trains. The proprietor, efficient, fresh-skinned, large-bosomed, like a clubwoman at home, had turned Margot out tolerantly but in quick order. "My goodness, I believe every girl in this country comes to New York wanting to clerk in a bookstore! If one-thousandth of them got jobs, the town would be swamped." And then the fading, literary, spinster woman with graying hair done in a braid around her head, looking like Vanchie, who had taken Margot's name and address. "Margot!

What a charming name! Are you French? I thought so, with those great dark eyes! Do you write? Oh, I don't believe that! You must come to one of our poetry readings some night. And bring some verses of your own!" She was only another example of Margot's fatal ability to attract the wrong kind of people.

Now Margot lay huddled up on her cot. A trickle of tears had dried on her cold cheeks. She still had some of the rubbish the gang had left her, scraps of kindling gathered from the sidewalks, crates thrown out beside wholesale houses. But her matches were gone. And while she didn't have a job or any money, she was ashamed to see any of the crowd.

She would tramp about answering ads as long as her shoes lasted. She wouldn't let the Bellews into her apartment if they came with a final effort to bring her back to the fold. She would never read another letter from the folks. She would stand crushed with little sawed-off Jewesses and fat Italian girls in gaudy make-up before the dirty windows of dark factories until a short dark man appeared upon the steps and shooed them off. But she would never be a teacher or librarian! Then she would die. There would be the consolation of the cold bright fantasy shed around her last moments by the poem she had copied into her red book and that now was her favorite.

> "In the dark, I shall rise, I shall bathe
> In waters of ice, myself
> Shall shiver and shrive myself
> Alone in the dark . . ."

She would leave a note asking for a pauper's burial so that even after she was dead she wouldn't be indebted to the folks!

"Margot! Let us in!"

Somebody pounded, laughing, on the window. Then there was a prolonged peal of the bell. Margot kept perfectly still. They shook the grilled door.

"Margot Ferguson!"

Her fierce sense of privacy broke down. She ran, with trembling hands opened the door, and then plunged down on her cot and buried her head in the blankets.

"Go away! I didn't tell anybody to come here. I want to die!"

Jane, who had been laughing, now suddenly burst into tears. "Oh, Daggie! Oh, don't let her!" She tried to clutch Margot through the blankets. Daggie lit a match, glanced mildly about the room, and settled his eyeglasses. He stood smiling down at them with that gently admiring and quizzical air with which he regarded all womankind. Why, assuredly, he said—while Jane wailed—Margot might have the privilege of dying. It was a privilege which he believed in extending—among many others —to all the human race. But he must remark that she would then pass to the great beyond with the honor of being the first hungry damsel who had ever turned down the offer of a meal from him.

"Jane, here, comes and suggests them herself!"

Jane made a face at him, and rubbed her cheek against his arm. He sat down on the couch beside her.

"Being a philosopher," he remarked, "you must permit a few philosophical observations. Even in the presence of contemplated death." Jane moaned and buried her curly head against his shoulder. He patted the curls. "Which," he added gently, "is dubious of action, after all is said and done."

Margot kept her face determinedly buried. With one hand Daggie stroked Jane's curls, with the other held Margot's wrist. His soft voice flowed on, never varying its mildly philosophical tone, and in the dim light from the basement windows his fluffy aureole of hair was comfortingly visible.

In the first place, he gathered, without too great a strain upon original observation, that the damsel who now chose to be called Margot Ferguson (having been gifted by Christian parents with the rather too well-worn name of Margaret) found herself in a situation far more common to members of the human race than she imagined. The circumstances, briefly, were these: no heat, no food, no lights. And to judge from the wrist which he was now holding (not entirely without pleasure to himself) the situation had been of some duration. His first suggestion was dinner—again, not without some reference to himself. A slight plumpening increase would make the wrist even more pleasurable to hold. The proposal, however, had not been well received. Strange! For in innumerable instances, some of them close at hand—Jane slapped him, and then hugged Margot—it had been used to meeting with instantaneous approval. The reason for this was—*pride*. An estimable quality, but in the present instance, misplaced. For pride in regard to "what ye shall eat and what ye shall drink" was according to scripture a characteristic of the Philistine. Consider, not the lilies of the field which were not available, but little Jane! Did she take heed as to what she should eat and what she should drink? Nay! And it was given unto her.

Jane struck him with her small fist. Daggie captured the fist gently.

The trouble with Margot Ferguson was that she was still acting the part of the no doubt far more estimable but far less interesting Margaret!

"Let me," said Daggie, offering cigarettes, "paint a word-picture of the Ferguson household of Belmond, Kansas or thereabouts. According to our authority, Jane, it is a prosperous household, even grand! Upon the spacious lawn stands a dignified urn of some cemeterial plaster resembling marble, from which vines trail in a graceful manner."

Margot gave a smothered sound of tremulous laughter.

"Say it is noon. The whistle—town has a whistle, of course? —has blown. From the kitchen where Mrs. Ferguson, a respectable lady of gracious proportions, is bustling, comes an enticing odor of beefsteak to procure which many also graciously proportioned creatures are annually slaughtered in Kansas. Potatoes are boiling merrily in the kettle, while the garden— where Mr. Ferguson takes his evening recreation with the hoe— displays a highly vitamized array of peas, beans, squash and rutabaga. This is the meal to which Mr. Ferguson, a fine old gentleman with the moustaches usually described by the term 'walrus,' is wont daily to sit down, after due attention to the blessing, with an excellent appetite."

"Dad doesn't have walrus moustaches!"

"Ah! Smooth-shaven. . . . But I'm only proving that up to this time Margot Ferguson has not known the meaning of the phrase 'to be hungry.' She invests it therefore with far more significance than the term deserves."

A little help? Why should she mind it? Consider the youth Bobbie, or the youth Rod—lilies truly. Bobbie, who held that plaid knickers marked the artist, and so attired was sharing the excellent bed and board of the ever-generous Marta, ousting —Daggie was sorry to remark—the little female Jane. Unless he, Daggie, was misinformed, Margot herself had accepted an invitation to tea from a learned and serious-minded gentleman of his acquaintance.

"Oh!" Jane breathed. "Dr. Finkbein thinks you're *won*-der-ful!"

No job? Jobs came and went. Little Jane could tell her that. It was the private life that mattered. And she, with her interesting conquest of a learned gentleman, was just beginning her private life.

Margot let herself be dislodged from the blankets. Jane, still with moans of sympathy, washed the tearstains from Margot's face, intently, as if she were tending her doll. Daggie, smiling, watched them, and flicked the ashes from his cigarette. He had found and lit the stump of a candle. The others, he said admiringly, she must have consumed, like the lost children in *Tom Sawyer*. But tallow as a diet, although its literary backing might be excellent, was hardly sufficient. Tony would supply more plumpening fare.

"So let us on to Tony's."

Daggie and Jane marched her down the street between them. Margot felt strangely weak and cleansed. It was as if the winter rain that was falling had swept away the old accumulation of grievances, leaving only this wet blackness that sent up fragrance into her heart. All the lights had rainbow haloes. They went down into another basement and rang the bell at another grilled door. The deliciousness of the steamy smell of food and tobacco that came through the noisy chatter made her head swim with hungry ecstasy. It was like coming back to life. There were red tissue paper roses on the white mantel. They were more beautiful than if they had been real. The thick brown soup sent up an intoxicating steam. The crusty Italian bread and the unsalted butter were more delicious than the image of the bread and jug of wine beneath the bough which she had once thought so enticing in the *Rubaiyat*. The bright, noisy, basement room was a refuge for difference, a sanctuary for the exiles from homes both too good and too bad. It *was* home, now.

Even after Jane and Daggie had left her, Margot couldn't go straight to bed. She crouched beside her beautiful fire on a little red-painted stool. How lovely her room was now, how changed and mysterious!—the softly flaming tips of the red candles that Daggie had bought her, the big unsteady shadows on the walls. "Here today and gone tomorrow." The words whispered themselves with a mysterious consolation. The red wine, the firelight, the candles . . . Margot sprang up to get her red book because she couldn't sleep unless she had tried to keep this happiness from slipping away.

Coming home radiant, amazed, Margot couldn't believe what had happened! And just as casually! She had seen a funny little tearoom, in a crazy little place not much bigger than a passage-way; thought, "Shall I?"—and walked boldly in; said "Do you need anyone to help you?"—and the woman in the pink smock, looking up with mildly distracted, wide-apart, gray eyes, had answered, with a trail of Southern inflection: "Yes, I reckon I might!"

Now the story of herself was beginning to come true. She was in her own basement apartment, and she was going to work in a Village tearoom.

5

Margot stepped lightly about the room washing off the black-painted tabletops, feeling gay and artistic in her yellow smock, humming as she worked. She went into the kitchen to get the lunch cloths out of the tipsy black-painted chest of drawers. She loved even the kitchen in this crazy place. The most delicious kind of cozy heat spread out from the ancient range where they had things cooking in big kettles that might have come out of a folk tale. She simply adored their huge old coffeepot.

She spread the yellow cloths on the black tabletops. They were of cotton crêpe with fringed edges. They had been her own idea. Mary Lou had let her paint the furniture black.

"Mary Lou!"

"What, honey?"

"I just had a swell idea!"

Mary Lou came to the kitchen door with her hands floury.

"Oh, no—I don't know—maybe it isn't. Go on back."

Mary Lou went back into the kitchen obediently. How queer it was! Margot thought—this sort of power she seemed to have over worshiping older women. They seemed to belong mysteriously to her guiding star. Mary Lou's fondness was half childish and half maternal. It was even worse than Vanchie— the utter round-eyed, trustful admiration with which she accepted all of Margot's ideas!

"I can't help it. It's my destiny."

Now came something that every day she simply loved to do. It was to go to their big old crooked cupboard in the kitchen and get out the dishes. They didn't match. She didn't want them to match. Margot and Mary Lou had picked out every one separately. She saved until the last, with sensuous pleasure, the two thick yellowish plates and cups of Spanish pottery. She was going to keep them for the little table where she and Lee would sit. If Lee came in today!

Never would she get over her joy in this tiny, tucked-in, unexpected, folk-tale place! Daggie said it had been a hang-out for a bunch of Italian gamblers. Margot hoped that was true. The kitchen floor was crooked. You went down one little step. Nobody but Mary Lou could have done such cooking on the ancient range.

She hugged Mary Lou.

"What's the mattuh?"

"Nothing! I just thought about our breakfast."

"Honey, tomorrow I'm going to get us some little sausages."

Daggie laughed at them with his gently philosophical pessimism. One wild woman and one addle-pated!—he said. But all the crowd were reveling in Mary Lou's expansive maternal care. Bobbie had driven them away from Marta's. Mary Lou had the money from the estate back home. All her life she had wanted a tearoom. Now she *had* a tearoom. Why think beyond that?

Every morning, they both got up late and came over to The Hole, and Mary Lou cooked a leisurely, luxurious breakfast which they ate at the kitchen table beside the warm stove. They had their own little special granite coffeepot. They used the Spanish pottery.

"Honey, what shall we have for dinner?"

"Oh, anything good."

"I might have another ham with cloves. Jane likes that. I want to put some flesh on that child's bones. Her little hands make me think of the canary bird's claws my old Aunt Nancy had. She was a little bit queer—well, *right* queer—and she didn't love anything but that skinny old canary."

An atmosphere of Southern laxity and warmth and ease seemed to emanate from Mary Lou plump and flushed at the kitchen range. She had a helpless maternal softness. Yet in the clarity of her round gray eyes there was something virginal. All those years when she had been keeping house for "papa," she had been dreaming of a tearoom of her own. If she had thought about men, it was only shyly, as a little girl might think while she played with her tea set and dolls. But she had taken the crowd for her children.

"Oh, my only precious! Where is he? How could his mother forget him?"

With her voice drenched in pity, eyes wide in compassionate horror, Margot swooped down upon the scrap of kitten asleep beneath the stove. Its black fur was brown with dust. Margot brushed it rigorously. She held the little creature up against her cheek to feel its ecstatic purr. She had found it in the alleyway—little black, mistreated thing! Starving and crouching on the edges, just as she herself used to do. It was as if her own little lost cat, the one that Carl's dog had killed years ago, had been given back to her. She was finding all that she had lost. It was a kind of symbol. A little black cat!—to wind in and out among the black table legs with lifted tail, to sleep curled up on a yellow cushion, to lap its milk while they drank their coffee—a kitten's lapping and purring, the final sounds of luxury! Now Margot could close her eyes to the other frozen, skinny felines nosing the sorry garbage cans of the Village.

"*You* aren't going to starve, you little black one," she told it passionately. "Margot has you. You're *my* kitty. You're saved."

With a glance of defiance at Mary Lou's back, she poured out a bit of coffee cream into her yellow saucer and screened the kitten while it drank with little black paws on the table and little furry neck outstretched.

"Now, little blackest, you can go to sleep."

They didn't have many people for lunch. Mary Lou didn't want many. She didn't like to work her head off for strangers, she said. The crowd all came for dinner. But it was an excitement every day to see what people might drift in. Once a Village sightseeing party had come. "Isn't this quaint! Isn't it the *quaintest* place." Margot, as she went out to the kitchen with orders, made whispered reports of the diners to Mary Lou. Those they didn't like the looks of, they gave the homeliest dishes and the poorest pieces of meat.

"That old buzzard again? Here's this piece of fat. It'll be good enough for *her*. Honey, I like that boy with the glasses. Poor boy! He looks so thin. If he comes in again, you can ask him if he wants a second cup. He looks like he needs more to sustain him."

"Hello, Princess of Darkness!"

Lee had come in again. He dropped in nearly every day for lunch now. Louise didn't know it. He was sitting at their own little corner table.

"Come on and sit down, and let's have our grouch out on the world."

Margot sat down, propped her elbows on the table, accepted a cigarette.

"This is Princess's black cat?"

"Oh, Lee! If you aren't nice to him you can't stay here.

Mary Lou's afraid of him. She thinks he's going to bring bad fortune."

"Sure. We Southerners are all afraid of signs. All sunk in superstition. I'm scared myself."

"My precious!" Margot moaned. She took the little cat.

"You don't want to let Louise see this cat here!"

"Why not?" Margot belligerently demanded.

"She yells if she sees one. Got one of those complexes."

"You needn't think I'm going to chase out my kitten just to suit her complexes!" Margot buried her face in the softness of brown-black fur. "My little dark angel, little blackness, I adore you. I don't care, I do!" she said, coming up, and glaring defiantly at Lee.

"I don't doubt it. You give every evidence. Doesn't Mary Lou think you're a witch?"

"No. She thinks I'm just lovely."

"Hasn't heard you go on about your grouches. Margot: Prejudices: Seventy-seventh Volume. It'd be Louise's grouch today if she knew where I was!"

"Oh, I wish you wouldn't everlastingly keep bringing in Louise!"

"You two girls don't like each other very well, do you?" Lee asked, curious and excited. "What's the trouble? Been quarreling over my attentions?"

"*Your* attentions! I've never had any of your attentions."

Lee said meaningly, "That's what you're getting today."

Margot looked at him witheringly. But she felt the exciting pleasure of sitting here with him talking inanities, beneath which there seemed always to be hidden significance. His knee pressed hers under the table. His thin hand, with the fore-finger stained deep orange, strayed, as if by accident, towards hers. There was an attraction between them, half reluctant and jeering, but more than she had felt for any man since Frank Gesell. Daggie was nicer than Lee. But she didn't count Daggie or Dr. Finkbein as men exactly, since she couldn't have fallen in love with either of them. She didn't know whether she liked Lee, but there was a give-and-take between them. Besides, she liked to beat out Louise. Louise *would* be the one to grab the best-looking man in the crowd!

"Margot, tell me, what has been your love life? Ever have any fellow but me?"

"*You*," Margot said witheringly.

"What did you do back there in Belmond, in the old days?"

"Oh—went home with boys from the Young People's meeting."

"Was there a line-up outside the church? God, don't I remember those line-ups! The church stag line. I was raised in the Baptist faith. Somebody always got away with the best girls, left me walking home alone. No wonder I took to the pool room. I never had any luck in love. Don't have any more. Unless you're going to be good to me?"

"I suppose you were in love with someone like Louise!"

Lee settled himself with relish.

"Why don't you like Louise?"

Margot refused to answer.

"If she knew where I was at this moment! She hates you. She's afraid of you. You two girls are the great antithesis, aren't you? That's why I have to seek you out. You're my only antidote. Darkness and light. Tempest and sunshine. I told Louise to go and hear your friend Doc Finkbein's lecture on Frigidity in Women. And well he ought to know! Must have been favored with plenty of it. Until Margot was kind. You don't need any lecture, Margot, beyond what I could give you. Want to hear mine?"

"I don't care to be an antidote!"

"They cure," Lee told her meaningly.

"No, merely neutralize."

"God! Even that would be something. I never could make a hit with a girl like Louise. That's why I always run after them. One of those who always love what they can't have. Look here, if you want to see what a fool I am."

"I know anyway, but I'd just as soon have the confirmation."

He emptied out his pocket on the table. Margot laughed at

the litter. But she felt a little thrill of excitement when she touched the things, all bitter-scented from the squashed package of cigarettes. Lee rooted about until he brought out a soiled, folded paper.

"Read that, if you want to know the worst."

Margot read incredulously. She felt a jealous fury at the thought of such words being applied to Louise.

> "She is all so slight
> And tender and white—"

"Louise isn't—if you mean her. I'd call her quite fat." Margot scornfully thrust out her own slender dark arm. Lee took it, and bent back the slim, smooth, flexible thumbs. His hand crept up the wrist. Margot felt the stealthy pressure of his fingers. She jerked her arm away. "I just don't see the application," she said disdainfully.

> "She is as gold
> Lovely, and far more cold.

That's the truth, too!

> For if I win grace
> To kiss twice her face—

And that's about all I've got for two years' straight devotion! Well, not much more than that, when you come down to essentials."

He stared at the litter on the table, then swept it back into his pocket.

" 'And far more cold,' " he repeated. "That applies anyway. Well, that's the only difference there is between girls. Some get hot and messy and some stay always cool. That girl's body is always fresh and cool. Not that I ever had much chance with Louise's body! She looks to that. She's the only virgin in the crowd. Unless you're one. Are you, Margot?"

She refused haughtily to answer.

"I wouldn't answer for you. I don't know, though."

He reached out and turned her face up toward his, with his finger under her chin.

"God, but you've got beautiful eyes," he said intensely. "I could fall in love with you right now. You could get me if you wanted to, Margot. Look how those lashes curve." He described the curve with his finger. "They're immense. They're bigger than Louise's. Hers are gray, though—cool."

"The color of cool dishwater," Margot said spitefully.

Lee laughed exultantly.

"No wonder she's afraid of you! She's jealous. Do you know that? You've made her jealous already. Margot. Would you love me the way you do that cat? Daggie's going to take his protégés on a jaunt tonight. Margot. Will you be my girl?"

"No!" Margot said furiously.

She swept up the dishes and carried them out to the kitchen.

First, Margot thought that she would luxuriate in the hot bath—no matter how many people wanted to get into the bathroom . . . and then all at once she was so eager to read and write in her red notebook that she had to jump shivering out of the tub and wipe herself in a hurry. The bathroom was a funny little sawed-off room at the end of the long dark hall.

But before she opened the notebook, she had to arrange everything to her complete satisfaction. She had a ritual for these two luxurious hours at home. When it was raining, she lit candles. She would light the red candles today. Her cot was drawn up in front of the crackling fire. She had plenty of fuel now. All the gang knew about her not being able to pay for gas and electricity. The fireplace smoked, but she liked the bitter smell. She liked the noise outside her windows. Margot herself, warm from her bath and fragrant with Woolworth talcum, sat wrapped in blankets, her hair soft and damp about her neck, and all her paraphernalia around her—little cake she had brought from The Hole, her red notebook, cigarettes.

With infinite relish, eager but slow, she went over the later entries in her red book, written in hastily between exquisitely copied pieces of poetry. She was just entering upon her own youth—held back, delayed, like flowers in a cold spring.

"I tell you beauty wears an ultra fringe."

376

Let Dorothy, and Mildred, and the other girls have the ordinary things! It was that "ultra" which *she* demanded. Margot's red notebook was beginning to brim over with the poems of Edna St. Vincent Millay.

Her friends weren't just the ordinary kind. They were exiles, outlaws from home, who had found their refuge in the smoke-filled rooms in these narrow streets. They warmed themselves at the fireplaces of the past. They all had "histories." Dr. Finkbein had been born in Europe. He had suffered awful things when he was a child. Daggie had been the odd one in a New England family. He didn't consider a Dagget necessarily superior enough to the human race to be entitled to live on the labors of others, nor could he feel a spiritual alliance with the making of cheap shoes. Music being a boon to humanity, he would clerk in a music store. Mary Phipps had a sister whom she hated. And think of even Mary Lou!—soft, maternal, child-like—but suddenly, at thirty-seven, deciding that she wasn't going to be another old maid in a Southern town. Now Margot thought that perhaps her great work would be a picaresque record of a modern woman's life, enriched by the histories of her friends.

But life . . . she stopped . . . she was still upon the outskirts. For herself, she would have nothing to put in—nothing beyond her quarrel with the folks. She was a virgin. When they talked about "virgins," she blushed all over with secret shame. Jane had lived with men. She was like a thin little cuddly kitten, with half-wild eyes, snuggling down for a moment with anyone who was good to her, and then suddenly running off upon her own queer little concerns. But Jane had started with the advantage of a disreputable family! "Virgin" was the greatest term of obloquy. Margot couldn't stand it, to be shut out in her innocence, not to be free of the world. She was as innocent as Mary Lou—as Vanchie! *More* innocent than Dorothy. She was ashamed to live when her only real experience with men was confined to those awkward, overgratified kisses that Dr. Finkbein had felt himself privileged to bestow upon her ever since she had kissed him that first night. But she had accepted them, because she wasn't going to hide away any longer from *any* kind of experience.

Margot threw her red notebook against the wall in disgust.

The crowd came to The Hole for dinner.

Of course Louise had to be here!—sitting beside Lee, silky and cool, scarcely glancing at the other girls. Jane and Mary Phipps and Lenore hated Louise because she was only playing at living in the Village. Her folks supported her, and she let everyone know that she came from a wealthy family. Louise let out a scream. The little cat, perking up spirit to be playful, had touched her shoe with its paw.

"Lee—somebody—take it away! Oh, I hate the damned things! Scat!"

Margot swooped down furiously upon the little cat and bore it off to the kitchen.

"Lee doesn't hate it." Margot's voice was hard. "He held it on his lap this noon."

She saw with triumph the look that shot from Louise's eyes. Well, let her know that Lee had been here without her! Louise thought she needn't bother to be a rival to a little bit of riffraff like Jane. But she had to reckon with Margot, and she knew it! And Margot felt with malicious triumph that this was her place. The black tables and chairs, the color of the dishes, even the darkness of the night were on her side.

"I know I shan't come to this tearoom again if I have to have *alley* cats crawling over my feet, as well as—" Louise gave an expressive glance at Lenore and Jane across the table. "It's rather hard on Mary Lou!"

Jane hopped joyously into the fray.

"I think the little cat's *darling*. Bring it in, Margot. I'm going to let it eat off my plate."

Daggie spread a gentle, deterring hand. "I'll protect you from the beast, Louise." He lifted the kitten from Jane's plate.

"Oh, never mind," Louise said with cutting distaste. "No doubt they're accustomed to keeping the pig in the parlor."

"Oh, yes, we were!" Jane cried, in ingenuous delight. "I had the *dearest* little pig—"

"Sh, sh!"

"With a little curly tail—"

Daggie put his hand over her mouth. She struggled, wildly laughing.

"And the sweetest *rat!*" she shrieked.

Louise got up from the table with dignity. Well, let her sit like an outraged queen, saying her dinner was completely spoiled! *This* was the night when it got nothing for her. She still kept the notions of the petted small town beauty, who expected that things would be *done* for her, not that she would ever *do* anything. Now the tables were turned.

"Children, children," Daggie expostulated. "Don't spoil the party."

When they left the subway and came out into Wall Street, Margot tore her arm away from Dr. Finkbein's and ran off alone down the empty street. She didn't want to hear about capital and labor and the class struggle tonight. In his awkward, earnest fatuousness, he would never forget the promise of that kiss! Well, it was everyone for himself. It had to be. The tall buildings narrowed and towered on each side, filling Margot with a hard, exultant sense of power. The voices echoed weirdly in the cold, dark canyon of the street. How little they all looked between these towering walls! There was a ruthless power here that cared nothing for them and would crush their tiny lives out of them without mercy. But at night-time they could play about these stony fortresses. There was some kind of gleeful revenge in that! They could have their own lives while the world was going ponderously on—in the interstices of time and place, here in this uncharted hour of night-time. They were the outlaws.

Margot dashed up into a stony doorway and stood for a moment, panting, feeling queerly alone and sorrowful. She pressed her cheek against a cold stone pillar. She had got away from Dr. Finkbein at last.

Footsteps beat lightly up the stone steps. Margot stood in rigid wariness. Now her heart began to beat thickly. Lee pulled her out roughly from behind the pillar.

379

"Here, none of that! You ran off to be chased, didn't you?"

The likeness between his thin, bitter hardness and her taut rebellion quivered in their hands, with a strange, unsatisfying thrill of hostile attraction.

"And their lips met!" Lee said dramatically.

Now the others had discovered that they were missing. They heard the jeering voices from the street.

"It's the moonlight!" Daggie said.

But with his usual philosophic air of a quizzically and affectionately amused onlooker, Daggie would do nothing to check the catastrophe that was overtaking his walking party. He watched it come, as he might have stood at a window to watch a cyclone approaching.

"I want Margot to walk with *us*," Jane whimpered.

"Don't check the mating fever. Be content with your loving Daggie."

In this cold canyon between the huge buildings, where the moonlight made sharp cubes of white among the shadows, it was natural to be cruel and fierce. The fight was on between Margot and Louise. Margot felt that it was something that had been ordained since the beginning of time. The figure of Louise, in the soft gray coat with the soft gray fur, the little gray hat pulled down over her golden hair, had drawn into itself everything that was hostile. Margot fantastically piled her hatreds upon it. It was the gray and white kitten that Dorothy had chosen, that all the girls had cuddled because it was so soft, leaving out the little black one . . . all the smooth Eve women, masking their shrewd maneuvers beneath their softness . . . for the first time Margot gave herself up with wild joy to the white blaze of her jealousy.

Daggie led his flock into a corner shack for hot dogs and coffee. Louise was walking close to Lee again, silently, demurely. A pang of hot anger shot through Margot. It brought the power of her insolence, sharp and bright. She pushed past Louise, and grabbed Lee's arm; and then, from her perch on the stool at the counter, looked back with hard triumph at Louise's furious, defeated face. "Lee asked me to be his girl tonight!" Louise

380

couldn't take defeat straight. She was outraged. She thought somebody else ought to do something about it *for* her.

"Let 'em alone," Daggie said. He threw up his hands.

Margot's legs were trembling. She felt a wild desire to cry, in the perilous remorse of victory. But the smooth Eves weren't going to have everything forever! They had their weapons—their selfish deftness, their yielding softness that masked as sympathy and flattery—but they had nothing to match her insolence. Because she dared! She would give everything she had for what she wanted. Louise sat baffled and crying in her inability to go the whole way. Her care for what she would gain was less than her fear of what she might lose. Well, they got the soft places, the fearful ones! But Louise couldn't have this cold, bright moonlight.

The rest of the night was a kind of hectic scattering. They all stood shivering near the cold harbor. Then there was the hollow, softened thudding of their feet on the wooden platform as they hurried onto the ferry. The breath of the cold water had a wild, fresh touch of spring. A mist of spray touched their faces as the boat swung out, carrying them across the dark swell of water.

Now Louise was trying for consolation and support against Margot. She was making the others pity and surround her. But Margot was the one who was in league with this night. Beneath the necessity for her triumph, Margot felt a darkness, a queer fatality. Here at the ferry railing, with the heaving black brightness all around them, the hostility between herself and Lee was yielding to the perverse thrill of their likeness. They were standing against Louise together. The fascination each felt for each—thin, sharp, too personal—was straining to defeat, by its own assertion, all that made up their bitterness and loneliness, from long, long ago.

They were off the boat and all crowding into the taxi. Jane was wickedly glad that Margot was winning. She burst into wild fits of giggles that Daggie tried mildly to subdue. Louise sat in stony silence. Margot had beaten Louise tonight. Lee was hers, they felt alike. She had made him admit her, assert that likeness, admit that here *she* was the choice—not

Louise, stealthily invading even this place where she didn't belong and that she couldn't live up to.

"I'm going home with you. Do you know it?" Lee challenged her. "Louise'll never forgive me for this."

"Never forgive you!" Margot said scornfully. "She'll love you."

They stood shivering on the dark pavement while Lee paid his share of the taxi. It seemed to Margot that she was trembling on the very edge of the world. But she wasn't afraid—she wouldn't turn back now. This had to be. She fitted her key into the lock of the grilled basement door. They went into the cold room.

"You know I haven't any lights."

She heard Lee laugh. "You girls are all alike, aren't you?"

"I'm not alike!"

She felt hard and alone. The others saw her as insolent, predatory, triumphant. They didn't know that inside she was frightened and trembling, wildly at bay before all the established canons of the world. What she felt was a kind of dedication. Yes, a dedication to her own way of life! Lee put his arms around her, and the unlighted candle fell bumping to the floor. "You little mad Indian." There was a note of hard, admiring hatred in his voice. But the hatred was joy. Or almost joy. Again she felt that it *had* to be like this. Something within her was weeping, was helplessly protesting. But she fought blindly against the protest, to force out of their bitter likeness rapture enough to hold against Louise—against the world.

Margot went out into the street. The world ought to be made new. She was changed now. She was a woman of experience.

Christopher Street roared with its narrow confusion. It was dark in the rainy morning. Margot felt that she was walking through the very center of the noise, the traffic, the people, the skidding cars and lumbering old truck wagons with the heavy feet of horses slipping on the gleaming wet. Battered tin ash cans stood out in front of tenement houses. The same poor skinny cats were nosing. She was on an equality now with the heavy Italian women with the dark shawls over their heads. She need no longer bow to what mother and Aunt Louie and Aunt Ella and all the others said.

It seemed to her that a mysterious ripening had come over her slight body. Lying in the cot, alone this morning, just wakening out of a final deep oblivion, she had felt a curious upper sense of fulfillment and ripening—with underneath, something crying, fatal and lost. But it was done. At last she was entirely at home in her basement room.

She went into The Hole. Through the crooked doorway of the kitchen, she saw Mary Lou's unconscious figure.

"Honey, what happened to you? You're late. I ate my breakfast. You don't mind? I saved some things for you."

Did Mary Lou know that she was changed? There was no knowledge in the round, innocent clarity of those virginal gray eyes. Margot felt a shiver of loneliness. It would never be the same again, eating breakfast here with Mary Lou. She would never again have quite the old, unconscious wholeness. She held the little cat with its whiskers and fur pressed up against her cheek. "Little black one. You're my little black one." Her eyelashes were wet.

"Honey, I'm goin' out to buy a few things."

Under her calm, now, there was a restlessness. It was rising and taking possession of her. Margot got up from her breakfast. She stared into the wavy little mirror beside the cupboard. The coaly brightness of the pupils widened and made her eyes all black. She thought, with a fierce defiant joy, she was really an outlaw. The folks would repudiate her forever. She had gone outside and made herself a free lance, wrecked her "virtue," set herself beyond the pale. She was glad! She caught up the little cat again. They were both black ones. It was a queer, solitary, exhilarating feeling—as if she were some kind of dark, bright meteor shooting dangerously across the safe, settled, complacent orbits of the fixed stars. . . .

People began to come in for lunch. Margot felt a curious lack of interest. They were people, that was all. There was one of those parties of sightseers. Margot went in to serve them with a cool, contemptuous assurance. But she had the dramatic feeling of herself, slim and different in her yellow smock, with a dangle of gypsy earrings beneath her short black hair.

"Do you suppose she's foreign?" one of the women whispered, half shocked and half admiring.

There was no reason to be diffident with the large, handsome married woman, dressed in inconspicuous expensiveness, with the old-fashioned diamond solitaire and the thick, plain gold wedding ring pushed together on her plump left hand. Her kind of self-assurance came from having known only the tame, admitted things. In a place like this, she was superior but uneasy. Margot could recognize the high, hungry animation, the restless, shut-out ignorance in the seeking eyes of the thin, unattractive, well-dressed woman, just getting to the point when her unclaimed solitude began to seem hopeless to her. She was the kind of woman who felt exhilarated and flattered in Rod's little shop, up one flight of dark stairs, on the narrowest street, watching him handle with delicate fingers some little blue Chinese vase, while he explained its beauties, with a glint of callow, cold, dark disdain in his almond eyes. Ladies who thought Rod was such a *beautiful* boy! The thin woman giggled with nervous delight at having dared to come to such a dangerous place as this.

Lee didn't come in to lunch today. Margot was glad. But it left everything flat. The rasped, angry solitude that engulfed her made her afraid.

"I've got a headache," she told Mary Lou. "I'm going home."

It was the same as all other days, only more so, as she fitted her key into the lock of the grilled door, sidestepping the scattering of rubbish the garbage collectors had left when they emptied their cans with noisy carelessness. The cold stale silence of her room surrounded her. The memory of the night before lingered in it like the events of a dream, so vivid that—unreal all the same!—it lasts over into the morning.

What was there to do with herself? What use to light the candles—gloat over the fire, alone?

> "There was a time when I was sad and lonely,
> And stood in strange forgetfulness apart."

Was *she* "lonely for her loneliness" now? She could never go back. The torn-in-two, crying ache of this new solitude had to be assuaged—but never again by that old, rapt solitude. The icy glaze of the shell that had surrounded her was broken. Whether she loved Lee or hated him—whether it was happiness or misery—it was nothing to be here without him now.

Slowly a strange depression came up from depths below all her other feelings and settled darkly over her. She didn't take it back. She *wanted* to want him—in spite of the trembling, new humiliation of finding that another human being might be necessary to her. She felt that she had to go on to the end that she could almost see. But in everything that she did, there was always a flaw, something fragmentary and broken. It seemed as if she had only used herself to triumph over herself. She wanted to cry. But there weren't any tears. Perfection was still beyond her. She was furious at her own desires, hurting herself upon the memory of imperfection, but wanting even that more than the old enclosed unreality of a dream.

6

Grimmie asked, "Do you really mind if I go off, Margot precious?"

"Of course not—you crazy thing."

"Well, I hate to leave you alone. With those big dark eyes!" Margot hooted.

But as she sat tucked among the velvet cushions, with the book of H. D.'s poems, the Armenian cigarettes beside her, candied violets in the Chinese bowl on the lacquered stand, she felt lapped in the warmth of Grimmie's generosity; and the dark misery that still stayed, like a cold spring flowing underground, made the contrast of her comfort all the more dramatic.

"Sweetheart, are you warm enough? There's plenty of coal in that sack in the do-diddy. Don't warm up that old stuff in the kitchenette. Go out and get a good dinner when you're hungry. I want to fill out those thin little cheeks. H. D.! Oh, isn't she glorious? She simply made Greek poetry *live* for me. 'Then swam a new planet into my ken'—or anyway . . . you know. Good-bye, dearest, I have to *fly*."

Grimmie rattled more coal onto the fire from the little brass hod, looked around for cigarettes, kissed Margot—she was finally gone, with the orange wool hat that she had bought enthusiastically in a new Czechoslovakian shop (it was going to bring the æsthetic element into modern dress) tilted wildly over one ear, and a streamer of fuzzy hair flying. The way Grimmie always made her departures!

Coal slipped in the fireplace. A few sparks scattered. Black satin mules had been kicked idly under a chair. The wintergreen branches in the big black bowl had dripped red berries on the white mantel. Books lay all around behind cushions and sticking out from chair backs. The luxury of books, more books than she could ever read! Ash trays everywhere. The ash trays at Grimmie's were always full. From the signed photographs of Grimmie's friends, hanging crooked on the white-paneled walls—writers with pipes, artists with and without beards, strike leaders with tossed tumultuous hair, the "interesting people" of whom Margot used to dream—she drew again an exhilarating sense of the variety of existence. The dark, shut-in life in the basements of the Village was far away. Her room stayed as she had left it, chill and stale with old fires and cigarette smoke, when she had walked out blind with misery. The paintings that Grimmie had bought from future geniuses were striking, some of them, and some of them just crazy; but it was nice to look at them from half-closed eyes whenever she stopped reading for a moment. The one of the cypress tree on the Pacific coast, battered and twisted by the winds into a shape that had a meaning—none of Grimmie's friends got excited about that one, but Margot didn't care, for it was *hers*. It justified her own way of existence. And then the faded old brownish photograph of Grimmie's home, somewhere in Missouri, with all the family drawn up in front of a white frame house with pillars, remotely colonial, under big trees . . . in that was the comforting sense of old ties, distant but unbroken, among the colorful clutter of foreign things. From the Greek atmosphere of the verses, a faint timeless scent of hyacinths drifted through the pleasantly smoky atmosphere of the white-paneled room with its glowing fire, up above the small seclusion of Bank Street, with the noise coming muffled from Seventh Avenue.

Here she was under the adoring protection of an older woman again! This was another way-station of her destiny. But she had to rest a while in the luxury of this feminine lavishness. The desperate impulse had been right that had sent her out at last to find Grimmie's address. Grimmie was more her mother than her *own* mother, than mama, was—just as once she had felt that Frank Gesell was more her father than dad. Grimmie's headlong kindness and understanding had slowly soothed the rankling wound of Mary Lou's defection. Yet Margot felt that she would never forget that, nor the shock of its surprise. Even now she had to go back and live again in that moment when Mary Lou had come into the tearoom to face her with flushed cheeks and round, glassy eyes. "Honey, I can't keep it back any longer. I've got to tell you. I don't guess we can work together any more. I don't believe in what you're doin'. I think it's wrong." But didn't Mary Lou know me? Didn't she care about *myself?* To me, her *in*experience was just as wrong as my experience was to her. But I loved her for what she was behind her life. Why couldn't she have seen *me* behind my life? Mary Lou had wept. She couldn't explain it. She wouldn't keep The Hole any longer. She had gone back on the crowd. Her little spurt of adventure was over. She had retreated into the innocence which was, after all, her only possession. Yes, perhaps it was her quality. And without it she would be commonplace.

But Grimmie was better than Mary Lou! All people who had made mistakes and put themselves on the other side were truly better than the ones inside the strict circle—although Grimmie's mistakes were only carelessness, and generosity, and that sort of "unfeminine" awkwardness that had worried her family and made her an exile, having a dangle of petticoat trailing, her things all pinned together. Her being on the other side was just a passionate, haphazard espousing of the cause of anything unfortunate. Margot adored Grimmie for the recklessness of her generosity. Maybe it was foolish, and solved nothing, and laid up trouble for other people in the end, as Katherine

Griswold said. But it was *better*, all the same, than prudence, and she would always, always say that it was!

There was comfort, also, in the false security of the folks' approval. Grimmie had written Ethel Spencer that "Margaret" was living with her. Margot had to try and keep Grimmie from writing to the folks themselves, ashamed because they would never be able to credit or comprehend the reckless innocence of Grimmie's views. Grimmie backed Margot up in refusing to do the regulation things that had nothing inside them, that were just jobs. She had enthusiastic plans in the offing. She was sure that her friend Hjelmer Jonsen could find a place for Margot on an archæological expedition; or that one of the rich women she had known off and on from her excursions into philanthropy, some of those women who had "favorite charities" and sold their best photographs to advertise cold creams, would set Margot up in an art shop.

Meanwhile, Margot had to try and calm what Daggie called "the middle-class scruples of the estimable Ferguson family," and Dr. Finkbein her "inhibitions," by accepting Grimmie's generosity. But then, Grimmie had to have an object for her enthusiasm. Katherine Griswold had said that. "Don't mind taking a few pence, child. Grimmie has to see the hope of the world somewhere. At present, you're the hope." There was something brisk and lucid about Katherine, that Margot felt as tonic, even while she resented Katherine's whole way of looking at things. Not thinking about herself in any personal way, and with men set resolutely out of her life, did leave her mind free and cool to pick out just the sensible side—kind enough, but with what Katherine called "rational" kindness, with an untouchable superiority that hurt.

"I'd never want to have to take anything from Katherine!"

At night, Margot and Grimmie talked for hours before the fire. Grimmie sat wrapped in a patchwork quilt that an old Kentucky mountain woman had given her, looking hunched and thin like a kindly witch. Grimmie had taught for six months in an experimental school in the Kentucky mountains. Grimmie's eyes, unworldly, innocently mad, took everything that Margot told her into herself and out of her warm lavishness gave it back touched with the fire of her enthusiasm. She declared that Margot's generation of girls was wonderful. They had learned a secret of life that her own generation had missed. They went out to *meet* life, that was it! They *sought*. Margot said that all the women she had met at Katherine Griswold's tea seemed bare inside.

"Now, what do you mean?" Grimmie cried with shining interest.

"Well, I mean they all go into things, but just into *things*, all outside, they haven't worked out *themselves*. I mean, personally."

"I see, I see!" Grimmie chanted joyously.

And she went around preaching the doctrine of the personal life to all her friends, until—Margot thought—they must hate me.

Grimmie appreciated Jane too. "She takes life as it happens. She takes it lightly."

"I don't want to take it lightly," Margot said rebelliously, switching away from her championship of Jane, now that it wasn't needed. "I want to take it *hard* and have everything matter."

Even now, because of what had happened to her—painful and broken as it was—Margot felt a sense of inner superiority to these women. She had felt it that day at Katherine's tea, despite the comfort of returning to that atmosphere of feminine elegance. In the room with the white bookshelves and the white fireplace, her allegiance had gone back fiercely to the chilly, sooty-smelling darkness of her old basement apartment. Nearly all the women had wide bosoms and hips, but they were briskly spinsterish. They didn't believe in using make-up, and they were interested in outside questions. Running home through the cold autumn rains, leaping the puddles at the corners of the narrow streets, Margot had felt a rush of wild, defiant exuberance and kinship with the dark.

A delicate thread of smoke went twirling up from her Armenian cigarette. Margot watched it, as she lay among the cushions. She had torn herself away from her torturing, unsatisfying absorption in Lee. But there was something still aching and unappeased in the desolate darkness—somewhere far away from this fine, gray, upward twirl of smoke.

All the time, it had been real (rackingly, acutely real!) and yet, in some deeper way, not real at all. Their brief glorying in likeness could not disentangle the hidden twists. Their hatred of each other had always been lurking, a kind of belittlement, just because they *were* alike. The knowledge that behind each of them was the guilty secret of unhappiness and early failure had only made them despise each other. But she had taken him away from Louise!—that was her triumph—that, and her superior boldness in escaping from Lee before he could escape from her. At the time, she had believed that nothing could ever again hurt her so much. But now it seemed to Margot that she was crying because it hadn't hurt her *enough*. She felt a hardy, fierce zest in the new knowledge that gleamed brokenly through her failure. She had wanted to shatter her nice-girl fastidiousness—to learn what innocent, beloved women like mother and Dorothy would never know; a knowledge that would triumph darkly forever over the deft subtleties of the Mildreds and Louises who were after their own security. No boundaries, no limits, to feel herself out in open water.

Margot heard with a secret delight the ticking of the little traveling clock on the red lacquered desk in the littered warmth of the room.

And then all at once she was beset by the feeling of the cold November outside the windows—the smoky fires behind tattered shields of rusty iron where children played in the small, dark canyons of the narrow streets—and she had to get out into the midst of it!

The dinner at Romany Marie's was the first meal that Margot had enjoyed for itself since the breakfast in the French restaurant on the first day of her new existence. There was a fresh pleasure, subtly malicious, in being all alone. An assertion of herself, and defiance of all entanglements, and of what they could do to her. A piano was banging in the other room. But she no longer felt hungry and apart at the sound of other people having a good time together. She could live up to the requirements of life in this place. Beneath her sensuous pleasure in the spiced richness of the South European food, there seemed to run a strain of low, dark music that was an echo of her personal life. Margot sat with her head on her hand, as she dreamily took her last sip of the thick sweet coffee, that she enjoyed as being *Turkish* coffee, although she didn't like it. She stubbed out the light of Grimmie's Armenian cigarette that she had brought along to match the food. The piano kept banging; and the harsh music, reckless and discordant, seemed to follow out, like the accompaniment to a dance, the entangled lives of all the people in these narrow streets, Jane with her wilding, mongrel prettiness, Rod with his perverse delicacy, Marta's fatal kindness—the reckless, fragmentary lives, and the bitter, broken childhoods that lay behind them . . .

But she would escape! As she had escaped from the motley little group of "others" at home in Belmond.

Margot ran out alone into the windy darkness of the Square. Bare trees, dark sky, dark buildings, a few stars, and winter coming. She could breathe in the scent of change!

She had *herself* again—changed, disrupted, broken into, but herself! Well, at any rate, she felt that she was forever superior to anyone like Lucille! Margot had met Lucille on Fifth Avenue one day. Although they hadn't really been good friends at home, Lucille was delighted to see her—with that provincial delight, Margot thought disdainfully, at meeting anyone who happened to come from the same place. They "must have tea together," Lucille had said. Lucille's greatest New York adventure was still to have tea with another girl at an Alice Foote MacDougall tearoom. Never, never would she have to suffer now the fate of Vanchie's withering innocence! In the cold night, in the windy November darkness big and portentous coming down upon the earth, Margot felt aching deep within her the hurt and guilty shame of all that had been cruel and unscrupulous in her history—deceiving and breaking with the folks, the way she had treated the Bellews, her triumphant escape from Lee after she had taken what he could give her . . . yes, more than anything, the secret, half-realized selfishness in her brief, discordant affair with Lee . . . It had been—

Margot recognized now, and had somehow recognized even then —just a dark, nameless, necessary prelude to her own story.

How different it was tonight from the first time she had come to creep hungrily about the edges of the Village! It was worth having gone through everything to have all this added to her. It had been for the sake of adding to that completed self which she saw standing like a figurehead at her ultimate destination. Before she had a past, she wasn't even ready to begin. The night wind was blowing her clean. Then what was coming?

On the other side of the Square, Margot saw the old houses standing dignified and withdrawn.

III. AND IT HAD A GREEN DOOR

WHAT was it that gave this queer sense of familiarity? Then Margot remembered. She used to live on this street! She used to pass this small Italian bakery every day. Over there on the corner was the pet shop before which she used to stand looking at the smoky ears and jewel eyes of the Siamese cats. Her own little cat. The little black cat. She and Grimmie had gone night after night to search for it around Mary Lou's old tearoom. But it had never come. . . . Here, in this very next house, was her first apartment! Lord, how many since? A feeling of dingy chilliness came over her with the memory of the sunless windows and the smoky fireplace. A strange distance separated her from all that had happened here. It was as if she were just beginning life again, and this time in her own real person. The days of the basement apartment had become a legend.

What had happened to the people who used to live in this house? Margot had gone only a few streets away; and yet they, too, were legends. That little wisp of a man with the beautiful, bright, dark eyes—"a hack writer with a hacking cough," he used to call himself—who earned a sort of living writing for the confession magazines. "I was an only child. I know that I had beauty of a sort, and that more dangerous thing called charm." He kept a scrapbook full of what he thought were his real works of genius, wistful little lyrics printed now and again in Sunday School papers or the lesser known household magazines.

"Through the pale evening
Comes a song . . ."

Some of them did have a kind of dim, appealing, girlish charm. How Lee used to despise the little fellow! Lee. It was more than a year since she had even heard Lee's name.

Margot didn't believe she had actually realized until this moment how much Bruce had affected her life. It was true, as Daggie reproached her, that she didn't see the old crowd now. Almost unconsciously, Bruce's attitude had influenced her. They were "Villagers" in his eyes—play boys and girls who didn't know how to deal with the actual, solid things. And it wasn't just the Villagers that Bruce disliked and depreciated. There was a need in him to disparage her whole way of life. Because her recklessness fascinated him and shamed his own solid prudence—the prudence that had got him into the dry rut of existence in which she had found him! Nevertheless, it was that sense of solidity about Bruce that made Margot look back at the time in the basement apartment as shoddy and precarious. She repudiated the image of a little thin, dark Margot in bizarre earrings and a peasant dress, crouching over a fire of twisted papers in the smoky fireplace and getting a sense of romantic festivity over the burning of two five-cent candles. It was as if she were just coming up at last from the shadow into the real sunlight.

And yet she pitied the little dark image. Underneath, she clung to it with stubborn pity. She was the only person on earth who would ever entirely know the painful, rapturous, inner secrets of its history. She knew how different this history really was, to her, from the version that Daggie, for instance, loved to give of it, smiling and licking his nice little chops.

"When Margot Ferguson first came down to these parts, she was a scared little virgin from the hinterland, who had yet to taste her first strong drink." Dr. Finkbein saw it as the bold stroke for freedom of a kind of Shaw female. Margot alone could know the secret of the grim resolution to conquer her fiercely shy virginity, to break the frozen glaze of self-distrust enclosing her. But now all her earlier affairs with men seemed nothing but a preparation for the meeting with Bruce.

She turned and walked back to look at the house again. Deep down, there still lay a hurt loyalty to the old crowd, although she had forsaken them. There was something more than Bruce knew—not just "affectation"—in their refusal to admit the importance of any but intangible things. They were all lost children—Peter Pan's Lost Boys afraid to grow up— and partly because (she told Bruce fiercely in her mind) most grown-up people were so awful! His world didn't *deserve* to be fitted into. Anyone who could fit into it entirely was just a fool.

And Bruce himself—as if he fitted! Then he would never have come down to the Village, superior and curious, "just to look around," and have found her in Marta's tearoom. That day she still held in her memory as the beginning—with the darkness, the shine and smell of rain, the flicker of the in-adequate fire, the muted, yearning sound of foghorns through the soft thickness of the air. Bruce had come into the room shaking himself slightly. He looked big and competent and excitingly out of place, as he took off and folded his heavy coat. His hands came cold and fresh out of his leather gloves, as he rubbed them together, and then took up the foolish little menu card. It was written in purple India ink, in Margot's arrogantly girlish letters, with curly tails to the y's and the g's. The corners of his lips drew down as he stared at the card through tortoise-rimmed glasses he put on and then imme-diately took off again and stowed away in a soft leather case. But she had interested him, standing and waiting in her Rus-sian smock, in spite of the superior, distrustful, uptown amuse-ment in his eyes! In that soft lull of between-time, with the foghorns sounding in the rainy air, her real life had begun to flower.

She couldn't stay here. This street was the past. She couldn't admit her own inclusion among the Lost Boys and the Lost Girls—as she had refused to stay in Belmond and admit herself to be one of the company of local outlaws: Dr. Redmond, because he "went with other women," and was vaguely tarnished with the rumor of illegal operations; Louella Allen who had written letters to herself and declared they came from the good-looking young Methodist minister; and that queer little shy-animal man, who had left his family and gone to live in an abandoned country schoolhouse, to be free to complete a great invention.

Margot ran, leaping in front of an outraged taxi driver, fiercely determined to be done with the old life, that had never been more than partly hers . . . although a lonely loyalty to it was crying somewhere in her heart.

There was always a lingering, fairy-tale enchantment in opening a green door. The brick house, with its two dormer windows, looked private and small between the taller houses on each side.

Then there was the beautiful, sumptuous knowledge that Bruce had found this place for her. He had gone with Margot and Frances one bright Sunday afternoon to look for apartments. He wouldn't have the girls living in a gas-heated house. "Margot might take out the plug some day when it happened to be raining and she'd drunk a little too much the night before." Margot tossed her head rebelliously at the memory of Bruce's satirical tone. But at the same time a secret smile seemed to come from deep within and curve her lips. (It was the same smile that Mildred Summers used to wear, lurking and subtle, when she came into the assembly room with the knowledge that Gardner Allen had asked her to go to the football banquet.) Margot had got her job through Bruce too. He had sent her to a friend of his who ran an advertising agency. "I can't have you living from hand to mouth this way." The sense of Bruce's protection pervaded Margot's whole existence with a flattering, velvet warmth. She was the Fair Rosamund—the Dark Rosaleen—whom the king really loved and kept apart for his delight in this little house of enchantment.

She ran up the painted staircase to her room.

She stood for a moment in the warm air feeling her joy in coming out of the chilly street into the midst of beloved, significant possessions. Bruce had had something to do with nearly everything in this room. When he gave Margot her big armchair for Christmas, he had given Frances a chair, too, a dear little old-fashioned, oval-backed rocker—out of his dreadful prudence! Margot's was upholstered in rose and Frances' in blue. He had lent her the *Grammar of Science*, with a wine-stained menu card stuck between pages seven and eight, disgusted with her "totally feminine" reading. A nice big pair of shiny rubbers stood in full view near the fireplace, revealing the obtuse masculine simplicity that went along with his prudence and competence, making her laugh at him and love him.

But she must hurry! She would get a scolding for being "extravagant with time." She dashed into the little bathroom and turned on the water full-tilt.

The door of Frances' room was open—the neat, trim room, all in cool blue and white, precise as a spinster's. Margot liked having Frances this close and no closer. Frances' own continuous, although never tumultuous, love affairs added to the secret warm richness of feminine life in the crowded little apartment. Margot's history had had more exciting episodes. But Frances was upheld in her cool poise by the constancy of the "older man" at home in Cincinnati to whom she could always turn. Bruce approved of Frances. "I want someone who'll remember to pay the rent if you don't." He insisted on his view of Margot as a "night moth." Jane, the real "night moth," he abhorred. Margot told Bruce she hated thrift. She had had enough of that at home, with Grandma Ferguson and Aunt Ella roused for weeks because once mother had let them, the two girls, wear their best dresses to school! She was going to *use* her things, and not take care of them, and spend her money for what she wanted, not what she needed—with only one life to live and that "no longer than the sandpeep's cry." . . .

But the tub must be full to running over!

The bathroom was steamy from the hot water greenish and bright in the porcelain tub. Thank heaven she was living with someone who liked to keep the bathtub clean—after those awful two months with Jane in the room with the peasant bed! Margot poured in the powdery remains of her bath crystals. They were like pale, ground-up emeralds. Little white receptacles that she and Frances couldn't resist when they went to the ten-cent store were more or less filled with cakes of scented soap in various stages of jellied dissolution. The blue, of course, belonged to Frances. The rose-red was Margot's. Once more, blue and rose-red, just as it had been at home! Margot wallowed luxuriously in the bath, thinking of the awful bathrooms that she had known in her varied life in the Village. Just at this moment, nearly everything was right! She even liked the kind of advertising—perfumes, and draperies, and cosmetics—that they were giving her to do. Bruce was coming to take her out to dinner. She thought of her crazy old dream about Dr. Redmond. Perhaps it had been a sort of prevision—because now she really was having a love affair with a married man. Margot felt borne up lightly into fragrant luxury, above the fundamental precariousness of her life. The things that she had ached to possess, through all these years, were being slowly collected around her.

She ran tapping back to her room in her black satin mules. Again the warm, intimate air surrounded her. Gossamer stockings were strewn over the back of a wicker chair. On the table was her red leather handbag, alive with its soft creases, just as she had tossed it down. There was the inevitable, untidy gray sprinkle of last night's ashes in the grate.

The mirror hung above the polished chest of drawers between two tall, crimson candles. Margot saw her face stained with a rose-red flush and her throat white above the negligee of rose-colored silk. Her short hair was strewn in locks, glossy, damp and black. At last she had that miraculously "right" haircut, of which every woman dreamed. The glossy

397

wave, shaped like the chiseled hair in sculpture, fell low across her forehead, but left the tips of her ears chastely exposed and glowing now with a faint rose-red. It gave just the touch of personal distinction to her features, and her great dark eyes, and the fine bold outline of the back of her head. The liquid powder she had learned how to use, when for three months she had done publicity for that awful French singer, whitened the brunette darkness of her skin. The rouge was laid on like the pressure of two rose petals. The painted mouth was a deeper rose. In the white face between the glossy black of the hair and the rose of the silken gown, the lashes of the two great eyes were like the upturned petals of some gorgeous flower. All the angles of her body had subtly filled with smooth white flesh; and her arms, when she lifted them up from the loose rosy sleeves, were small and white and round—like the woman's arms in that poem in the *Oxford Book,* that Daggie had once read to her, smiling.

> "When her loose gown did from her shoulders fall,
> And she me caught in her arms long and small."

(But she hadn't caught him in her arms—dear, dear little Daggie!—whom she would love, no matter what Bruce said.) Yes, at this very moment, she was on the thrilling, exquisite edge of becoming the very sort of person she had always meant to be—and she liked her name, her hair was exactly right at last, she had experience instead of ignorance behind her, and there was a man—a married man!—in her life. It had taken her all these years to struggle up fiercely from diffidence and innocence and provincialism. Now—when she was over thirty —she was coming into her blooming.

> "There came a day entirely for me."

She drew the rose-colored gown closely about her, and then opened it in a soft, flushed effulgence of revealment.

All around her in the warm air of the sweetly crowded room there breathed a kind of sumptuousness of excitement, happiness, rich expectation, that was like the final ineffability of fragrance hovering over flowers.

Bruce sat in the armchair smoking while Margot put on her wraps.

"It's getting cold as the devil outside," he warned her. "What kind of shoes have you got on?"

With a sensuous delight in obedience, Margot thrust out her foot, that felt beautifully slender in its satin slipper.

"You'll freeze to death in those things, you silly kid. Haven't you got some overshoes around somewhere?"

"*Overshoes.* Galoshes! Don't make them sound worse than they are."

"Well, put 'em on, whatever you call 'em."

"You aren't planning to make me walk all the way to Carlo's, I hope?"

Margot shrugged her shoulders. Rubbers and even galoshes made her think of winters at home and being called back to the house protesting. But when Bruce told her to wear such things, she felt again that subtle, sensuous pleasure—that female pleasure in obeying, when she knew, *half* knew, that she could rule. She brought out the galoshes with exaggerated meekness and sat dreamily still while Bruce's large white fingers were fastening the clasps.

Bruce said, "Let's see you." He put his hand on her shoulder and turned her toward him. "What's different about you? Have I ever seen this dress?"

"About a million times!"

He frowned, and Margot laughed tantalizingly. She knew what the difference was that Bruce, in his large masculine obtuseness, could not name. But there was a breathlessness in her laughter. For mingled with the blooming of her power, she had a feeling of shyness, almost of flight—just what maidens were supposed to feel. She! After the "experiences" that now lay satisfyingly thick behind her. She had felt it, with a delicious surprise, when she had heard Bruce's footsteps on the painted stairs.

Bruce flipped the book on the table.

"Let's see how you're getting along with Pearson. Eighth page! Is *that* the extent of your progress?"

Margot lightly shrugged her shoulders, realizing obscurely

that his sardonic tone was partly a tribute to her—he wanted to pick some flaw, assert his masculine superiority, because he felt that she had power tonight.

"I'll get it read sooner or later—when I have time."

"Hmp!"

"I know what you're going to say! I'm 'subjective,' and just interested in what has a 'personal application,' and what 'titillates the senses'—"

She did a little dance step in front of Bruce before she took the book away from him. He couldn't hurt her by criticizing her tonight. It gave her pleasure, since she thought she could discern in it a defense that he was putting up. And anyway, it was a delicately perverse delight to feel that she had power to fascinate him while he disapproved of her. Or thought he did! Because men didn't know what they really felt—they always thought they felt according to their theories.

"I don't want to talk about science while I'm starving. I don't even want to talk about myself."

"It's the first time, then!"

Margot danced softly while he tried to button her heavy coat. Bruce put his hands down firmly on her shoulders and made her stand still. But she looked away sidewise, with a secret delight, thinking how all these poems and novels and biographies and memoirs that Bruce derided had their own purpose for her, all helping to make the very thing that troubled him tonight. She felt as if all her books were like a great bouquet of chosen flowers surrounding her with their fragrance; and she smiled, lightly scorning Bruce's "science" that didn't dare believe anything was said unless it was said in black and white.

"Here—come on, you young Pavlowa. Get some of that food you're starving for, and then you won't feel so airy."

Margot ran downstairs ahead of Bruce, drawing on her gloves as she went. Bruce was always very solemn and discreet, except when they were in her own apartment—probably trying to create the impression that his interest was equally divided between Frances and Margot. But at least he didn't prudently suggest, any more, that they ask Frances when they went out together! The people who owned the house, a youngish couple named Allison, he an editor of some sort and she an interior decorator, lived on the first floor. When Bruce chanced to meet either of them, he quite unnecessarily froze into his character of heavily respectable business man. "Trying to look like an uncle!" Margot thought in rebellious scorn. But there was no one in the hall tonight; and Frances was working overtime and hadn't come home.

"Where are we going?"

"Why, to Carlo's, aren't we?"

"That where you want to go?"

Margot felt almost foolishly hurt. Bruce knew it was their own special place, where they could feel hidden and alone; and he oughtn't even to suggest going anywhere else when she felt so happy. But he was so fearful of making the slightest admission that there was any understanding between them! As they stood on the cold street corner, Margot's power seemed to drop away from her, and she felt shivering and alone. Bruce's heavy figure in the expensive overcoat was like a monument of all the settled solidities that menaced everything she cared for. He looked like a family man.

"Oh, of course we'll go somewhere else if you'd rather!"

Bruce smiled at the pride in her tone. "We'll go where the little girl pleases."

"I don't please any more than you do."

"Well, I please, then."

But she had to like him again for the curt, masculine gesture with which he signaled a carefully slowing taxi, and for the sound of his voice giving Carlo's address. She tried to gather to her for protection all that she disliked: his blindness, obtuseness, terrible bulky stubbornness, the tone of amusement he used toward her friends,—as if his country club friends from whom he was running away were better!—the rubber-stamp words he used like "radicals," his insistence that the only good stories were in the *Saturday Evening Post*, and that he only read Conrad because it was "adventure stuff" . . . and yet all the while she was feeling the fine, perverse—yes, "ultra"—delight in forcing this very kind of man to admit her fascination. She was somehow incomplete with any other.

But the joy with which Carlo greeted them—greeted them *together,* as a couple: "Oh, Mees Ferguson, Meester Weeliams, come in, good evening!"—seemed to renew their intimacy magically.

"There's our table all ready!" Margot cried joyously.

She sat down in her own special chair close to the warmth of the big stove where she loved to see the red cinders as they fell into the tray. Carlo's was their secret place. No one they had ever heard of came here. Margot felt a childlike, blissful contentment.

"I think maybe Mees Ferguson and Meester Weeliams come tonight!"

"Why?" Margot asked eagerly.

"Oh, I do' know why, I look for them all day."

She laughed out joyously. Bruce went to hang up their coats with the serious care he bestowed on all material things of good quality, horrified at Margot's habit of hanging things jauntily askew. He wouldn't believe her when she told him that once she had been even more pernickety than he. None of the family could do anything to suit her. Now, to cure herself of impossible fastidiousness, she had run to the opposite extreme. But then, Bruce demanded that things must *have* quality. In his eyes—gray, shrewdly appraising, with a surface of regulation business man's look—there was something baffled, hurt and defensive, obscurely misled, and unlit.

Margot leaned her elbows luxuriously on the table. There was no one else here except a dark, silent Italian gobbling spaghetti at a corner table. She loved Carlo's funny Italian ornaments on the mantel—a toy lamb, a little wineglass, and valentinish things made out of red and green tissue paper. She *adored* his old-fashioned gramophone, with its far-away sound, as if the music were coming from the just perceptibly out-of-date era of fifteen or twenty years ago—funny and touching, and sentimentally melancholy, like an old summer hat with its faded gaiety of flowers suddenly unearthed from a bent pasteboard box on a top closet shelf.

"Play my waltz thing," she begged Bruce.

He smiled at her with his expression of indulgence—the nice

expression, not the false one that tried to belittle her. This was the way that she liked Bruce to be, just the way he was now. She loved the feeling that against the background of his strength and large indulgence she could play airily with even her whims in a willful refinement of her individuality.

"You're a funny girl."

Feeling the smiling fondness of his tone, she could sit back for a moment secretly with her enjoyment. The faded melody seemed to put her back into the undefinable time when Carlo's rooms had been the parlor and back parlor of a distinguished mansion. Now the ornate carving of the ceiling was broken and the marble fireplaces were closed. Margot liked to think herself sensuously back into the times of those old scenes in magazine illustrations she used to pore over on rainy days in the back room in the library where they kept the bound volumes of *Harper's*. One of those scenes where there was always a sort of small, insignificant man with a curly moustache, overshadowed by the great bare shoulders and rounded hips and satiny train of a Gibson Girl. At the side stood a potted palm, just partly drawn into the picture. Any scene of the past was always romantic to Margot. And here was she, Margaret Ferguson become Margot, actually *in* such a room . . . but in her scant black crêpe de chine post-war modern dress, her little pulled-down black hat, with a dangle of earrings beneath it—and she was here with a man who was handsomer than any storybook hero, and she was beginning to live out her own thrilling, half-known, half-unknown drama . . .

Bruce was asking, "What can you give us tonight, Carlo?"

Carlo, happy in the stiff, torn white jacket he had run into his kitchen to put on,—Margot adored his punctiliousness, here in this faded room—was eagerly repeating:

"I have scalopini, I have broil' chicken . . ."

"I believe we'll have the scalopini. Does that suit you, Margot?"

"And cheese!" Margot put in eagerly. "My kind!"

"All right, then, Carlo, the scalopini, and a bottle of the red, and bring the girl her kind of cheese."

Margot sat back with a contented murmur. Carlo went off

smiling. The faint music of the waltz had trailed into dying discords.

"Do you want it on again, Margot?"

She shook her head decisively.

Bruce laughed at her. "Little 'my, my, my,' " he said. He shook her slightly. "Always knows what's 'mine,' doesn't she?"

"Well, I have to! Nobody else does."

"Nobody else does, hm? Don't you think I have a little glimmering by this time?" She shook her head. "You don't? I only wish I knew my own as well!" He got up, and touched her hair. "I'm going out to discuss the subject of the wine more at length. Can you amuse yourself while I'm gone?"

"Of course not!"

She wouldn't admit that Bruce, that *any*-one, really knew a thing about her. But it was only with Bruce that she had this feeling of sumptuous excess. It was his bigness, the kind of clothes he wore, his presents, his flowers, the way he scolded her, and looked after her, the little extra delicacies of food and wine. She seemed always to be moving in velvet surrounded warmly by his care. Bruce was the only one who could give her the right to be the princess of her own fairy tale.

Margot rested her chin upon her hands and waited. The dark Italian slithered up the rest of his spaghetti and left. Even though Bruce was in the other room, she felt close to him. She could sense that his first resolve to stand out against the fascination she had for him—pretending it was all amused friendship on his part—was melting into that complete indulgence in which they were most in harmony with each other. This strange, thrilling, discordant harmony! Her time was coming. The day "entirely for her," that she must have before she was willing to die. That was what she had realized, with that feeling of delicious flight, when she had heard Bruce's feet coming up the stairs.

"All right. Got it fixed."

A shock of tenderness went through her at the familiar, mannish satisfaction of the tone, mingled with a kind of underlying heaviness of responsibility long borne. She knew what it was that Bruce had really missed and wanted, although he couldn't name it or even perceive it. He had confessed to her once, as they sat before the fire, fulfilling her old vision of the man and the woman in the two low chairs—with bashful difficulty, almost like a schoolboy—that she "stood for something he had missed." She wanted passionately to fill the blind emptiness in his life. She had never felt like this toward anyone before—not as if she wanted to *give* things. It was as if her little glazed sheath of self-absorption had suddenly cracked, letting in a kind of light she had never known existed.

Carlo came in, consciously and decorously reticent, but triumphant, with the hot dishes.

"Oh, our beautiful food!" Margot cried ecstatically.

Bruce looked at her, smiling at her eager voice. The lines of bleak dissatisfaction seemed to have faded from about his mouth. Warmth had suffused the assured, hard gray of his eyes, under which lay that lost, dark bafflement. He had to admit *her,* as she had admitted him—not just smile indulgently at her highly personal tastes, really *admit* them.

"Wait!" Carlo cried in delight.

And in a moment, he came running back from the kitchen with three of his dear, funny, squat little glasses, into which he poured the rich red port, with its hidden sparkle.

"We mus'n' have jus' common glasses. Mees Ferguson she look so pretty tonight!"

Bruce flushed. "That's right," he said heavily. "Join me, Carlo. We'll have to drink to Miss Ferguson."

"Thank you, Meester Weeliams! Tha's nice."

They both raised their glasses. Bruce touched Carlo's almost solemnly. Margot's face slowly grew hot up to the sculptured black wave of hair. She wanted to say something; but she sat mute, helpless, open, in a shyness that made her eyes burn through a mist of tears. Carlo seemed to know with them that there was something significant about the little ceremony, and to be giving them his blessing.

The flush slowly died. Carlo had left the room again. There didn't seem to be any way to keep him. They heard the homely sound of the embers falling down into the tray of the stove.

Bruce put his hand over hers. Margot sat looking down at the

405

large white hand with its plain gold ring. Who had given that to him? His wife? Margot had always disdainfully and airily skirted the thought of Bruce's wife. But all at once she hated the woman with a blinding hatred. Bruce never mentioned her directly. Only once or twice, as if inadvertently, he had referred to his family—and once at the first, conscientiously, to let Margot know that they existed. But Margot was scornfully sure that she could imagine what the woman was like!—one of the kind who had always been her enemies. Louise, Mildred, yes, clear back to Eve—the fair, smooth, sly, complacent, deft "womanly" women, who were nothing on their own, made out of a rib of man, or pretending that they were so made to keep the man happily conceited. Even mother was one of them. Even Dorothy. Nearly every woman in Belmond! When all that they were after was to line the nest for themselves, and, by lining it so softly, to blind their mates to the wild, rapturous freedom outside. And the man plugged away, and read travel and adventure stories. But this was *her* day. She was the dark other one. Hers was the secret of the "ultra." And she felt fiercely exultant because her hand beneath Bruce's, narrow and satiny white, lay significantly ringless.

Bruce drew away his hand and pretended to be absorbed in his dinner. But from the slight rigidity of his shoulders, the way he looked away and cleared his throat, Margot could tell that he, too, realized that their "friendship" had imperceptibly, involuntarily reached another stage. Impatient as she had been at Bruce's prudence and his ostrich blindness, a kind of painful, suffering reluctance that she discerned in him, and closed her mind against—yet Margot herself relished the slowness, almost sumptuous slowness, with which this relationship had passed inevitably into phase after phase, leaving the last one behind in an epoch utterly past. She wanted to dwell in each stage by itself, experiencing its final essence, knowing that when it was gone it was irrevocable. It seemed that she had known beforehand—from the day of her birth, almost—every stage as she reached it. And yet each one was utterly new when it came, with the blinding shock of a revelation.

But now the time had arrived when both of them must see

and acknowledge where they were moving. Carlo's quaint little compliment had torn away the veil. Why should she care about that woman in the background, any more than the woman would care for *her*? The Eves had all the soft places. Everybody was on their side.

But she couldn't make a single move toward Bruce. She felt amazed, terrified at her helplessness. Not even to grasp what she fiercely felt belonged to her! It was as if she had to sit just trembling and waiting—because this was what she had been waiting for all her life. For this she had broken ruthlessly through her old bonds of fastidiousness and fear, so that she could be free whenever it came, ready for it, equal to whatever it demanded. She had lost the bold, wild aggressiveness with which she had torn Lee away from Louise. That wouldn't count now. She couldn't make a single move. Because this was the test! All the womanhood that she had acquired would go for nothing unless he proved to her that it was nothing she did, but herself, that was desired.

Bruce was looking at her, and Margot looked back at him with her eyes open in a suffering, dark, exquisite humility. He could take her or leave her. That was the truth. Nothing counted if she had to take *him*.

"It's a pretty funny thing, isn't it, that a man can go along for forty years not knowing that he wants something? He must be pretty much of a dub, don't you think?"

"Maybe it's an acquired taste!" Margot said bitterly, falling quickly into her old self-distrust.

"Anyway, I'm getting to see it's something it would be damned hard to get along without. What am I going to do about it?"

Margot would not answer.

Bruce asked her suddenly, "Where did you get those great dark eyes?"

It was a silly question. It sounded like Red Riding-hood. It was what she had heard in her childhood until she was sick of the words. "Where did that child get those eyes?" But then it had always seemed to be in a tone of reproach, marking her off from the rest of them. When Bruce said it, he marked her off too—but as someone special, unique, chosen. She had been waiting all her life to hear this said to her in just this way. It blotted out the other voices with a miraculous comfort—as if Bruce had known. It was too perfect to be true. But it *was* true. It was something she could never lack again.

A strange, almost mystical sense of enlargement came over her, in another of those blinding sweeps of revelation. It seemed as if she knew herself, and, through herself, something more. It wasn't just Margot Ferguson whom Bruce was choosing— but all that she stood for, the one precious thing that had gone so long neglected, useless and yet absolutely necessary above a dead level of existence . . . the enhancement, the "ultra" . . . finally given its right to be, through her, if Bruce, with his solid masculine authority, could see and choose it.

"Margot. You haven't answered my question."

She struggled blindly to say something.

"I can't now."

Because she felt wildly that this time it must be perfect, not flawed and broken. Perfect, if it lasted for only an hour! This was part of her own story, in which every event must be true and real, and follow out her dream. It had to be as much to Bruce as to her. She knew the creed of all her friends—to snatch at happiness wherever it offered, and not think beyond: there was little enough of it in this world. But this time—the great time—must be all beautiful. Her after-life would have to feed upon it. Whatever was wrong and unbeautiful could never be made up for. It would hurt her forever. This wasn't just a "Village affair."

Some more embers dropped into the tray. Taxis passed in the street, below the windows, and an old street car went bumping and banging down there, the trolley scraping out a momentary fire.

"When are you going to answer it?"

"Some time."

Margot got up. She wasn't conscious of planning any action. There was something outside herself that did it for her. Maybe astrologists were right, and her guiding star was in power.

She wandered about in a soft restlessness while Bruce paid the bill. She stood a moment at the long window. Beyond the empty streets, and the narrow edge of the island, the whole Atlantic lay. In the wideness of the night, she was conscious again of that mystic enlargement. She felt her part in the universe. Her own line in history and tradition. All the powers were in league with her, everything she wanted was coming to her. But this time it must go slowly, like music—not hasty, broken, snatched, and jangled!—until it reached its perfect consummation. She went over and petted the toy lamb, feeling childishly that it was allied with her, in her feminine world, against all the ways of men.

"You like your supper, Meester Weeliams?"

"Everything was fine, Carlo!"

"You like it, Mees Ferguson?"

"It was the best I ever tasted."

Carlo opened the door for them, with a beneficent flourish of courtesy.

"Good night, Mees Ferguson, Meester Weeliams, come again!"

2

As she undressed, sitting on her day-bed, Margot let herself have one quick glance out of the window and down at the little back garden. It belonged to the people downstairs. It was nothing but a square of earth not quite covered with thin-rooted, yellow-green city grass. At home, the folks wouldn't have called it a garden.

But the jonquils were enough. When she saw the flutter of petals on the long single stems, pale green and tender in the strip of damp black at the foot of the high board wall (where a neighborhood of cats promenaded) she could feel the spring hovering around them, wild and secret and sweet. Windows were open in the brick houses of varying heights that faced each other across this pleasant side street. It gave a mingled feeling of intimacy and variety to see the warm flutter of all the curtains—white, rosy net, bright cretonne, and some long draperies of golden silk that blew softly out and then clung for a moment, like butterflies, to the snowy window sills in the third story of that tall brick house. The curtains meant that all the different, unknown people were having *their* experience of spring. Margot felt that she loved New York until she wanted to leap and run and break into shouts and singing! She loved to sit on the swaying top of the green bus that lumbered down the Avenue in the early twilight toward the arch standing small, but with a hardy dignity, among the budding trees. That was when she reëxperienced the triumphant feeling she could never get over . . . I'm in *New York!* She loved the blue-gray twilights when the buildings near Central Park had the quality of old-fashioned paintings of the Whistler period, that made her think of pretty ladies in victorias, with gleaming eyes behind tiny veils, breathing the perfume of the violets that brought memories of their lovers. She loved the fragrance —the sudden whiff of heliotrope—that came from the massed bunches of yellow and white and lavender flowers for sale on the warm street corners; and to hear, on an idle Saturday afternoon, sitting on her day-bed with books of poetry scattered luxuriously around her, flicking ashes into the beloved little dish of flowered red pottery Grimmie's friend Jonsen had brought her from Mexico, and knowing that she was going out to dinner with her beloved—to hear the long-drawn-out cry of the bearded old man hunched over on the seat of his small wagon crammed with pots of pansies delicate and living in their damp earth, the wagon slowly passing down the street, the wheels creaking, the old horse stopping . . .

The folks pitied her, no doubt, for being shut up in New York! But Margot had become a city child. It was more exciting, not to see, but to feel all the bloom that was centered in one row of jonquils; the relaxed warmth of the evenings when she and Bruce walked back from Carlo's, stopping at the window of the little antique shop, and Bruce carried her jacket over his arm.

"Pastures that call from a leaf."

Because intimations were all that she could stand! And even now, she could scarcely endure the delight that she was always

410

pressing, pressing down, in her heart . . . she would have to run out shouting—or do *some*-thing. . . . She buried her head in her black satin cushion.

But now the first beautiful time was over, almost over—the time when it seemed that her love was more precious to her for the quickening sense it brought to every tiny thing she did: putting away her clothes clean and crisp from the laundry, eating in her French restaurant at noon—even more precious than being with Bruce himself. That had suddenly become perilous. Such bliss poured through her when he even touched her hand that it left her nerveless and shattered. She was afraid. They were both afraid. Because they must wait until they were alone, just she and her lover together, in a time stolen out from ordinary existence to be their secret treasure forever. She had put off a little glaze of sophistication to learn this new thing step by step, exactly as it happened. Now, with her eyes closed tight and the cushion pressed against her ears, she could go back into it from the very beginning. The rainy day in Marta's tearoom, with the foghorns weaving their muted music, like the prelude to a great event. The dinner at Carlo's when he had greeted them together, knowing that they would come, and they had kissed, and she had had the courage to send Bruce home. The blank, awful hours when she jumped into a taxi and rode and rode because she couldn't stand it to be anywhere without him. The night when Bruce had come solemnly to talk to her, and they had seen that they must make their mighty decision, like people in a play. Only the play was real.

"Margot, you know I'm married. I don't see how this thing is going to end."

"I don't *want* to be married. I want to be perfectly happy."

"And you think I can make you perfectly happy?"

He was the only person in the world who could. Well, he could take a little time off for that!—for the gift of everything that he had missed. It didn't matter where they went, only so it was away from here, nowhere they had ever been, a place that would belong to them alone. Then when it was over, it would be over.

Margot got up, breathing quickly.

It was time to take her bath. But first she must dance around her room, bare feet softly thudding on the painted floor, to experience the naked joy of her own body, the movements of her arms "long and small," the rosy flowering of her breasts. Alone for the last time. No sunshine in her cool back room. She felt herself cringe away from the imperfections of earlier experience. Now she understood why a bride should be virginal. But there were always forerunners. Even Juliet had had some dim predecessor with Romeo. That was the rôle of the others, in the secret continuity of her life story, whose destiny had been to shatter her fear and make her ripe for the season of true love for which at last she was fully ready.

There was a sense of queer reluctance in having the time come. She wanted to hold it back, to stay a little longer in this cool shadow, before she must step into the open light. She could never have this time again. When it had reached its fullness, it would be over. Again she had the old sense of something irrevocable—an undertone of her own low music that made tears from a secret, lonely depth come slowly to her eyes.

But this was her own time! The day "entirely for her."

With that knowledge, she seemed to enter again into that sense of mystic enlargement. She huddled down among the cushions. Her own body was small and white at the center of a spreading darkness that was fluttering and alive with intimations she could barely touch. It was as if suddenly she could see that everything in existence was bound together.

Yes, in books, in poetry, it was beginning to be *her* kind of heroine. This was her day! It was *her* kind of clothes that women were wearing; not the girly-girly things she used to storm at; but things that were rakish, dashing, brief and colorful, eyes mysterious and dark under the pulled-down softness of the little hat brim, earrings dangling. The clothes she had had to wear when she was a girl were just a disguise. These were her self-assertion. Now shocked elderly authors felt it incumbent to write about "the modern girl"—usually landing her back in the home, of course, well chastened, but sometimes actually permitting her to triumph at the end! It had seeped even into the movies. The Mary Pickford curls had given way to the sleek darkness of the "vamps" and the naughtiness of the flappers. Bringing it down, of course, to its lowest terms! The other day she had met Lucille. With her open middlewestern face, soft and featureless as a prairie landscape, her pretty-girl clothes, and the wrong kind of lipstick, Lucille was placed and dated. It was about time for her to give up her career and enter into the duties of wife and mother, looking back on the one romantic day when an actor had taken her to tea. It was the dark, vivid, naughty heroines of the Restoration who were in favor now with the intelligentsia. They were reviving Congreve in the Village little theaters. Poetry was doing homage to Lilith instead of Eve—*Eve,* whom Margot always pictured as an opulent nude, standing in a modest position, and looking up from under fair tresses with the sly, self-satisfied glint of Mildred Summers' eyes. Even that little Harvard professor, a friend of Grimmie's, had read a ponderous sonnet to Lilith.

> "When I look into the darkness of thine eyes,
> Where dwell those sparks of infinite dangerousness."

As if any real "dangerousness" wouldn't scare him to death! Katherine Griswold, pretending to seek an ash tray, had leaned over Margot to whisper, "Child, beware!" But then, it showed! Now the triteness of the old fairy tales was being reversed; and it was Rose Red who was coming out into the sunshine, and Snow White who was banished to the shady side of the story. Dorothy had had her time. She was married, and had babies, and was living in a bungalow in southern California. Rose Red could no longer be shunted off with the prince's brother . . . because she, Margot, had been given the personal crown of Bruce's true love.

Now it was she who was getting the roses. Bruce had sent them to her last night. They were the deep crimson ones, her own kind; not the pinky-white ones that Dorothy had carried at her wedding; but roses, and not the off-flowers that were lovely, but at the side. Now she could claim the rose, the center of bloom. She looked at the red glow of her roses in the midst of the deep green leaves. Exultance spread all through her from some exquisite center of joy. "These are for you." But even in those words, a premonitory sadness came over her, beautiful and dark. The undertone to her happiness sounded its own low music—the knowledge, at the very height of the moment, of its briefness, and its irrevocability.

She went to take her bath. The drumming of bright hot water into the porcelain whiteness of the tub, the reckless scattering of crystals from which a powdery fragrance rose, the peeling of thin white paper from the smooth cake of Red Rose soap—all these made up the sumptuous beauty of a feminine ritual. Care of her body was a secret religion. All this spring, buying clothes with a magnificent extravagance, Margot had told herself, "It's now!" And afterwards—who knew, who cared? Everything—she thought, as she splashed the sudsy water —everything contributed to make this her springtime. She could see something symbolic even in the weather. First, the cold; but even then, with a wild sweetness in the air. The dark March, when rain dashed against the windows, and she and Bruce sat together in front of her fire. Those days were like the first fragmentary, stormy intimations of love. The clouds were darkened and then white above tall buildings, suddenly breaking in the wind to show a cold blue April sky. And now the wonder, the warm amazement, of a May all soft and ineffable, coming with the marvelous blessing of fulfillment after the spring storms!

Margot dashed back into her room. She was warm and glowing. With the same high sense of secret ritual, she began to put on her new clothes. She must have everything new to correspond with her new existence. The silk stockings were still creased and shimmery. The little bodice and knickers of crêpe de chine clothed her in silken softness.

Everything was contributing! It was as if she stood at the center and all things converged by some natural law. Other people felt it. Men looked with blank eyes at the vacant seat in the bus and sat down by her. The old man at the corner paid her gallant compliments when she bought the morning paper. She no longer had to endure shrewd, deflating looks from salesgirls. They brought out their nicest things as if she wouldn't deign to consider any others. Even that stiff at the office began to show signs of interest! Suddenly all her old friendships opened new intimacies. People whom she hadn't seen for months began to seek her out again. She and Grimmie had talked until two, sitting on the floor in front of Grimmie's fire, with sherry gleaming in the little cut-glass tumblers; and Margot had let herself go in the luxury of telling Grimmie all about herself and Bruce. Grimmie had begged her solemnly not to let this pass without fulfillment. "No matter what's in the way. Don't you let go of it. Margot. It will never come again." She saw Grimmie's face with its fuzz of graying hair, the profile that was like a kind Indian's, with a queer, mad touch of nobility; and she felt how other life histories were woven about her own in her secret, picaresque record. Years ago, Grimmie, too, had been in love with a married man. But they had parted with a single kiss. It was as if the imprint of that kiss could still be traced on Grimmie's lips, full and dark and faded, marking her out for renunciations and throwing her into vicarious generosities. The man had stayed in the Missouri town, getting fat outside and hollow inside, like all people who let the perilous, real thing go. Margot felt, with the deepened poignancy that even the slightest things awakened in her now, the sense of underlying kinship with women. Not with the smooth, safe, complacent ones, who worked underneath for security!—but with the others. "You and Bruce take your holiday. Don't pay any attention to what may happen afterwards. Everything has an afterwards." It was true that love was fatal, no matter how silly that might sound in all the little verses that repeated the same thing over and over; thousands of little voices murmuring words that someone was always finding to be true. It seemed to Margot that what had come to her was something she had always foreseen, although it was so utterly surprising in its actuality; and the unreal, shattered remnants of the old existence she had lived through just because she couldn't help it, were being cast behind her forever. Now that she had entered upon her own story!

She heard Frances' discreet little knock.

"Margot! May I come in?"

"Oh! I supposed you were at the office."

"I skipped out. I wanted to say good-bye."

"Oh, Frannie! You darling."

Frances came on into the room. She had on her little dark blue silk dress, and her face had its office sallowness, dramatizing the radiance of Margot. Frances conceded that generously.

"You're all ready! Where did you get the beautiful bag?"

"Grimmie's. She let me take it. No, not what you think!"

Frances sat down on the day-bed while Margot put on her tan felt hat at the mirror between the two red candles in the silver sticks. Margot hadn't told Frances much about the journey. But of course Frances knew that she was going somewhere with Bruce.

"You look grand in your new suit!"

"Do you like it?"

Margot turned around from the glass. Frances came up to her. She said in a softened, moved tone: "You look beautiful. I hope you'll be happy, darling." And kissed her.

Tears sprang into Margot's eyes. And as she looked at Frances' small face pale between the bands of smooth brown hair, she felt again that deep sense of kinship. Frances, Marta, Jane, Lenore . . . All women in the world wanted to be made happy once. Then they could afford to die.

"I want you to take these roses!"

"Oh, *no,* Margot!"

"Yes, I do. I can't take them with me."

"Goodness!" Frances tried to laugh. "I'll be buried in splendor."

She stood pale and small with her arms around the great bouquet. Margot saw her little face looking down from the head of the painted staircase. The door of Margot's own room was closed. She didn't know when she would open it again. She was leaving everything—the red-and-gold Chinese tea set, the fireplace, the rose-red chair, the books in the low white shelves, the poetry that she had been reading all over again, seeking affirmation now instead of the old hungry knowledge. But she was going away from other people's stories. In her bag, beneath the pale silk nightgown, lay the only book that she wanted to take—the little red notebook in which, on beautifully smooth new pages, she would inscribe every flutter of ecstasy so that nothing, nothing, of this time could ever be lost.

She felt that she was opening the green door into her fairy tale.

It was warm and sunny in the street. One of the golden curtains hung over the window sill of the tall brick house. The roar came loud from over on Sixth Avenue. Now it seemed to Margot that all this part of the huge, thrilling city was secretly packed with her own memories—every little news stand and tearoom and shop on the narrow streets. But she was going away to some enchanted place that had never really existed before and would never really exist afterwards.

"Margot! Catch!"

One big red rose plumped down at her feet. She bent to pick it up, to wave at Frances—

"Here, taxi!"

In the taxi, with its smell of leather and stale tobacco, its scrunched-up, empty cigarette package on the floor, she had all at once a small, ordinary, empty calm.

"Where to, miss?"

"The Grand Central."

Again she crossed the interminable width of floor, with the great slants of cathedral light pouring down from the hugeness above her—she, Margaret Ferguson, who had come here such a few years ago, in that old tan coat and hateful hat she had bought at home, to enter upon her destiny.

3

They stopped at a filling station, and Bruce got out to ask about the roads.

"Better get out too. Not good for you to sit too long."

He helped Margot out of the car, and they stood for a moment in exquisite unity. It seemed impossible to part for even this tiny while.

"Be good while I'm gone," Bruce whispered.

He went into the office of the filling station, and Margot wandered off in the clear, dry sunshine.

But she would never again be really alone. She was doing as Bruce had told her, keeping the memory of his touch. There were some nameless white flowers growing in the rough soil. As Margot bent down to touch them, the old sensation of existing within herself came over her like the shadow of a memory. But yesterday stood forever between her and the old narrow groove of personal intensity. In the miracle of perfect union, the enclosing sheath of individuality had been finally dissolved. She was reborn into a region of pure happiness in which she seemed to move with a divine unconsciousness.

This was the region she had always known that she would find. But now that she had actually entered it, every feature of the sunlit landscape held the shock of a magic newness. Every step of the way, long traced in a dream, was a divine discovery. She had known what it was to be perfectly happy. She had had the day that was entirely her own. But instead of making her ready to die, as Margot had always supposed in a dazzled way, it had opened up further whole regions of discovery—like this cloudless sky above the plains, which, as she looked, went into depths on depths of blue.

But now she felt too happy. She wanted to seek some shelter. Besides, she was too far away from Bruce.

The car stood in the dazzling sunshine. Now it seemed years and years ago that Margot had first seen it standing—stiff, embarrassing and new—beside the platform of the suburban station where she and Bruce had agreed to meet, on that first awful day when they had started out afraid to be with each other, cold and stage-struck at the beginning of their venture, feeling as if they were asking too much of an uncomprehending and grudging world. Margot got into the car and slammed the door after her. The sound had an intimacy so deep that it filled her with unbelievable contentment, shutting her in with memories that were all alive within the small, warm silence. Yesterday. Now it had become "yesterday." But it had been. And she still possessed it. She could see the rushing, cold stream where they had bathed, the space under the pine trees where they had lain together. The brown butterfly still hovered above the red mountain flower. Margot moved restlessly on the warm, velvet seat, feeling the difficulties before her if she was to keep her memory of perfection forever secure and undiminished.

A strapping young fellow in coveralls came toward the car, with his blond hair glinting rough in the sun. He hesitated, and grinned.

"Oh, you folks are together!"

He nodded toward the oil station. His grin, with the flash of white teeth in the tanned, grease-smudged face, had an easy, friendly understanding and acceptance. Margot saw Bruce's firm, large figure, as he leaned with one elbow on the counter having an earnest masculine confabulation with the oil station man over a spread-out map; and the pride of their being together was almost more than she could endure.

The young fellow thumped a tire. He was sticking around because he admired her. But admiration came easy now that she no longer needed it.

"Not had this car very long, have you?"

Margot smiled and shook her head. In her brown tweed suit and light felt hat, and the scuffed, comfortable, easy grace of her laced Prince of Wales shoes, she had a flattering consciousness of herself as an impressively urban figure out here in the anonymous countryside.

"I saw it was a new car. It sure is a good-looking model. Going to give you a lot of service too." He nodded, and tapped the hood in appreciation. "New York! Looks like you folks are a good ways from home! Going out to the coast?"

"Just driving."

"Sure! Well, that's the way to do it."

He grinned at her again, and went off.

Margot could see the gestures of the two men inside the building. Their movements had a pleasant, earthy slowness behind the sunny glare of the large front window. With a subtle smile of feminine contentment, Margot sat back to wait and let them settle the question of the roads between themselves. Now, with her head resting against the soft upholstery, and her bare hands folded, she could feel the sense of anonymous country leisure widening around her in the sunshine. "A good ways from home," the young fellow had said. New York seemed more incredibly far away to Margot than it must seem to him. Only that speeding stream of noisily high-pitched cars on the highway connected this little wayside jumping-off place with any memory of the city; and even the cars were more widely spaced than they had been. She thought of New York standing incredibly on its island, like some separate walled city, tall and feudal and feverishly modern, existing in and for itself, a crazy pattern of streets and buildings and rushing people caught in the thundering network of trains above and below. The life was a fevered, half-mad, half-splendid dream. Existing within the dream, on its own terms of terrible immediacy, people had to believe in it to the exclusion of all other existence. Get outside—and it was incredible! Margot felt the slow, beginning sweetness of a kind of reconciliation to the land. The rough dry ground smelled good. A tuneless music thrilled along the telephone wires. Now it seemed that a great space, that was more than just miles of country, lay between her and all the life she had known up until now.

She looked at Bruce, standing big, easy and absorbed, with one arm resting on the counter. She felt all over again the wonder of the richness with which his love had endowed her, adding to her what he was, filling out the empty places of her own being. All that had been rudimentary and fragmentary in her experience was miraculously fulfilled . . . even her silly old notions about Dr. Redmond at home, about having an affair with a married man . . . the need for someone big and competent in a worldly way that perhaps she had got from her old admiration of Frank and Sybil, and her dissatisfaction with the folks . . . the desire for the shock and delight of what was different from herself that had first been aroused when she had seen Jesse and Dorothy exchanging their bridal kiss. . . . At this moment Margot's life seemed to her an illuminated landscape in which all the lines were in perfect focus.

Bruce reached out and put his forefinger on a spot on the map. There was something personal in that little gesture— something that she recognized as *Bruce*—something dominating, accurate, but slow. Margot felt a sense of hot possession. It frightened her, threatening her ideal conception of love, which dictated that it must end when it was over. Her fear seemed suddenly to strike her with a distant, vicious hatred of the shadowy figure of the wife, who must have seen that very movement, who knew the brief, accurately judging squint with which Bruce "sized up" a hill before they came to it, the way in which he accomplished everything with that satisfyingly competent minimum of movement. She wanted to blast the woman into forgetfulness—to scorn her out of existence! With a piercing overflow of jealousy, Margot seized Bruce's heavy driving glove, that he had thrust into a pocket of the upholstery, and pressed it up against her face.

But an hour of yesterday was something that only she herself and Bruce would ever know. Margot felt that it had annulled everything that went before it. The men whom she had known before she knew Bruce seemed to have been washed out of existence. Life had all been pitched into the present. It was now. It was this moment, sunny and still, in the great slow drift of time, and she was living in it.

Bruce came out still looking thoughtfully at the map. He spread it open against the wheel. Margot fidgeted in her seat. She felt a qualm of the minutely vigilant fear which still had to keep its strained hold beneath the surface of her happiness. She sat scarcely breathing. If they had already had the best of their love, and Bruce was beginning to forget about her, then it had to be, and to try to do anything would be only a violation. Bruce's right hand slipped down from the wheel and groped softly and blindly for hers. She felt the even clasp. Everything swung into focus again, the sky was brilliant, and now to sit here while Bruce made out the way was only a delicious waiting.

Margot felt the rapturous triumph of her power, of having torn Bruce out of his fixed orbit and brought him over to her side, making him admit and care for her own kind of things— the out-of-the-way things, and out-of-the-way places, that had always been discredited. Through his love for her, she had triumphed finally over Eve immemorial—as somehow she had always felt that it was in her destiny to do. The magic balm had soothed and satisfied all the ancient wounds in her vanity. Bruce was the kind of man who, until now, had always belonged to the enemy. But it was more than satisfied vanity. It was lifted far, far beyond that—so far, that she could only realize, with a distant wonder, that the old cuts no longer hurt. Margot bent swiftly down to Bruce's hand and kissed it.

Then she settled happily into her place. She heard the familiar, exciting, mounting sound of the engine. The youth in coveralls, who was tinkering with a car, grinned and lifted his hand in a farewell salute. Margot waved back at him. As they drove away from the filling station, it seemed to her that she and Bruce were two free beings who had got outside all the small involvements of ordinary local existence.

"Want to drive?"

Margot shook her head. With Carl at home, she used to have tremendous battles over the car, treating all his directions with the highest scorn. But with Bruce she felt a soft, pampered and pampering feminine luxury in sitting back and letting him have the wheel. It seemed to her now as if any action of her own, anything that she did simply on her own account, would rouse up the separate individual being that was now submerged in love. Being in love was an element as far beyond control as the May weather. They were both lost in this element, and actions of their own could only distort the miraculous truth and rightness of love's unfoldment. Everything must be accepted as it came—even the moments when Margot felt herself drop into sudden bleak torture at the perception that she and Bruce were awry . . . when his way annulled her way, so that she lost her bearings, lost her being . . . when the shimmering texture of happiness was endangered. Now if an ending was in their minds, they kept it cannily hidden from themselves and each other, closing their minds to a decision that loomed somewhere ahead of them, far beyond this limitless sunshine.

Bruce was sitting in the lobby. The moment Margot stepped out of the elevator, he dropped his paper and went over to her. She saw at a single glance, with an exquisite relief and triumph, that he had been sitting and watching the elevator. His face broke into a smile that was a confession, as he stepped quickly forward and touched Margot's arm.

"Have a good sleep? I didn't either."

He grinned down at her. They could not kiss before these people. But this mute acknowledgment of their need for each other, with hands just touching, was better than a kiss. For a moment, as they stood together before going toward the dining room, they felt the marvel of being reunited. The morning became instantly radiant. Last night, lying for the first time alone, it had seemed to Margot, taut with the strain of that vigilant watchfulness, that perhaps the best was gone, and that she must speak quickly if she was to be the one to say when the parting was to be. But this morning they were happier than ever to be together. Reunion was another miraculous discovery. And only now that she had escaped it, could Margot really see into what a black pit she had been staring. But the danger was already incredible and forgotten.

"Well, we'll make it up on breakfast," Bruce said.

They went into the dining room. The head waiter instantly withdrew his hand from the chair of the table at which he had stopped, when he saw Bruce's slight frown, and led them toward the window. Several women sitting together were looking at them with impressed curiosity, and Margot had the delightful sense of their seeming a handsome and interesting couple.

It was cool and quiet in this hotel on the side street, giving the sense of a retreat. Bruce wouldn't admit it, but Margot knew that he had been afraid to take her to the more fashionable hotel. Out in the lobby, an Indian with a darkly classic face pattered over the tiled floor with baskets which he silently offered for sale. The other people in the dining room—an elderly fat man at a solitary table, and one of those inevitable parties of school-teachery women—seemed to offer almost a surfeit of safety. But there was always, even here, a slight tingle of danger in coming among people. Bruce feared this, but Margot loved it.

"How grand the food looks!"

"Does look pretty nice."

The smiles they exchanged were an admission. The magic still held, brighter, more radiant than ever, since they had learned how lost and empty it was to be apart. The fresh roses on the table, the grapefruit with their red cherries, the silver covers over the buttered toast, all seemed festive. The pleasures of civilization were new again. Last night it had been horrid and confusing coming into the hotel. Even on this side street, the noise had been hideous, after the room in the adobe house where they had slept the night before, in a small sanctuary of Spanish domesticity made up of stiff lace pillow shams, artificial flowers, family photographs, and rosaries, in beautiful incongruity with the great, pure, surrounding silence of the desert. Margot had felt as if she were bidding some kind of mournful, significant farewell when she had taken off the scuffed Prince of Wales shoes that had gone along so many beloved trails through mountain forests and meadows, leading her to the edges of silent lakes, and to hidden clumps of tall, blue columbines; and the tweed suit that kept in its rough meshes the dust of the roads and the smoke of their campfires. But this morning she felt washed and fresh and gay in her light silk suit and her shady hat. Now the noises in the narrow street had a cheerful sound. The cool room was brightened by the clear sunshine of the early summertime.

Margot looked out of the large window and felt with new delight the exotic strangeness of the place. Indian women in bright-colored dresses were passing; and she saw two men in ten-gallon hats, one of them wearing a red velvet jacket with Navajo silver belt. It was the kind of place that she could love, *her* kind. She felt with mystic certainty that they had reached a goal. After breakfast, she would make Bruce walk with her through the narrow streets looking at the silver bracelets and the Indian baskets, which enchanted her, while her ingenuous delight at the "foreignness" enchanted him, making him smilingly and teasingly indulgent, as she adored him to be.

"I *love* it here," she said.

She loved all the West. Now she had found her own country. Margot felt that all over again, when they took the car, that had been newly washed and greased, and drove out along the desert road. She remembered how it had been coming through the Middlewest, where the very sidewalks seemed to hold reminders of her lonely, dissatisfied girlhood, and she felt every minute that the big front windows of familiar-looking frame

424

houses in all the little towns were glaring at her with the same old humdrum, settled, family disapproval she was sure everyone at home would feel if they knew about this journey—and they would stop her if they could! But at the first sight of mountains, lying blue beyond the plains, she had felt that she was out of the houses' reach. It was the West, where everything was different—the land of outlaws, and bright colors, and bad women, and high-stepping horses. The soil yielded gold and silver and turquoise, instead of just everlasting "crops." It was hard and unmanageable and magnificent—*her* country—not the fertile soil the folks called "good land," moist and obedient to the plow, settling down tamely and patiently to the tasks that people exacted of it. She thought of the old country roads, as they were printed on her memory, with their rural, local look, where the marks of wagon wheels and horseshoes and of the aimless struttings and scurryings of chickens patterned the soft warm dust under a fringe of willow trees. It pleased Margot to think that Grandpa Ferguson would have said this land was "good for nothing," because it couldn't be "harnessed to the plow."

"You are useless, oh grave, oh beautiful . . ."

How she had hated "useful things" from her childhood up!— shoes that were bought "to give good service," those awful dresses, the kind Mrs. Bellew had wanted her to buy, that would be "appropriate for any occasion," houses that were supposed to be "nice" because they had regulation comforts, and the kind of dismal burgs that dad called "nice little towns" because they had the usual set-up of brick bank building and stores and churches and vile little movie house. Margot rebelled joyously against all that the folks had ever called "good"; and now, in this country, where the hills were tossed and swirled in magnificent madness, she had her justification.

At last she was in her own land. At home, it had always seemed as if everything really belonged to Dorothy and not to her. Dorothy's girlish loveliness was the only kind that counted. But Margot had always known that somewhere was the place where *she* belonged. Here, even the flowers were *her* flowers. The red and yellow cactus blossoms wore her own colors; and she felt that something in herself went with their frail, silken delicacy and wildness. And there was something in her, too, that could match and live up to the fierce splendor of these mountains—something that none of the folks possessed. She was the only one who had the recklessness to take her own way. They answered some secret she had always known. It was different from that hidden sense of personal knowledge with which she had gone creeping about the narrow streets, drinking in her first sight of queer little places and foreign things on that cold, bleak, long-ago day in the Village. That had been a kind of recognition, so private it was almost shameful—as if all that were something to which she belonged, and yet never could belong; for when she came to it, it was past. But here was something so ancient and deep and true that it went far back beyond personal recognition. It was so ancient that she felt it was eternal—the revelation of an ancient truth.

"Oh, Bruce, I *love* it here!" She clutched him, and laid her head against his arm. She gave a long, rapturous sigh.

Why couldn't they stay here where they had found the place they loved? Because it was wrong to the *real* reality, the only one she could truly own—a denial of this revelation of beauty, a cowardly failure to live up to the greatest thing they could feel—if they let themselves be governed by what other people had built around them, and succumbed to that.

The whole morning world lay before them. There was something deeply pending between them, that some day must be faced; but the gold of the sunshine dazzled it out of existence. In this strange, beloved land they were free again, with the illusion of belonging only to each other.

They turned down a long narrow road beside a bright little running stream with the tender green of poplar leaves above it. They seemed to have left all involvements behind them and to be driving into a world so old that it was all freshness. Margot thought of spring at home—herself and Dorothy gathering wildflowers in the woods near the farm—after a rain, the red maple buds on the wet, dark sidewalks. But that kind of weather had always left her aching and dissatisfied. Somehow, she had wanted to push the soft, lowering heaviness of the clouds aside, as if they were getting between her and some essence of the season. This was what she really loved! She watched a dry swirl of dust across a waste of desert. These were only the pale rudiments of the early summertime, archaic and classic both—the selected elements of eternal freshness in a world older than any of which she had ever dreamed.

Beyond the stream and the line of poplar trees lay the pueblo. An Indian was out working in the field. He did not look up as they drove past, with the familiar curiosity of the farmers at home, a little dubious of strangers but ready to be friendly, to raise the hand in a salute a little slower than the one given them. His back, in its red-checked shirt, was bent with a stern ease; and his long black bob swung forward under the red band about his head. Margot admired his indifferent reserve, too natural and poised to suggest surliness. The earth showed straight patterns of bright young corn, like the earth at home; but because this was far away, and the farmer an Indian, it seemed beautiful to Margot here. Far in the dreamy distance, the mesas reared their cut-off tops at different levels, giving a romantic isolation to the small fertile space of the young cornfield.

They drove into the open square of the plaza. There had never been such stillness—such utter, sunny, ancient peace. The earth-colored houses, with their softly rounded contours, the ladders bleached hard and firm in the dry pure air, clustered around the sunburned space. A dog the color of the tan dust was lying in a doorway. Women with twig brooms were sweeping the dry earth. The far-off, dim-blue mesas, the mountains still more dim and far away, and dark with cedars, seemed to endow the movements of the women with a rudimentary human grandeur and significance.

They left the car beside the little Spanish church behind white palings. The white wooden crosses in the burying ground just beyond were thrust up thick and crookedly with a primitive starkness. Margot and Bruce walked slowly across the plaza in its enchantment of morning stillness.

427

An old woman was standing in an open doorway looking at them with small, dark, unrevealing eyes. As they started to go past, she said in a level, emotionless voice:

"Come in. Buy pot'ry."

Margot looked eagerly and beseechingly at Bruce. He smiled at her, indulging her feminine weakness for looking and buying. But it was really more to see the way the place looked inside than to purchase anything that she wanted to accept the invitation. She stepped through the low doorway, looking about her in enchanted wonder. Bruce followed her and stood smilingly aside. She turned to him with an expression of delight, with a deep, rapturous sparkle in her dark eyes.

This was the room of which she had always dreamed, so exactly as she had always seen it that she could not believe she was actually here: the low room, with its dry still air, the place dark on the inside with the burning sun outside. She hadn't seen just what would be here, but now she knew that everything was completely as it must be. It was simple in an elemental way, but with a sense of true selection in the few furnishings—no clutter of what was irrelevant, impersonal, unchosen. She loved the whitewashed gypsum walls, and the hard earthen floor. The round vigas overhead gave a scent of wood and bark. The white fireplace in the corner was deeply burned inside to a sooty blackness. There were only women in this place—the old woman who had called them in, one middle-aged, and two younger. One of these held a baby with black square-cut hair and soft, black, gleaming almond eyes.

"It's a *doll!*" Margot cried in rapture. She felt that she adored dark little babies—they had none of the milkiness of the fat white ones with their light little wisps of hair. She turned to make Bruce look, turning back eagerly to the woman who held the baby, innocently unaware of the constraint of Bruce's smile.

The women looked at each other in stealthy pleasure, and broke into bubbling laughter. The sound was as soft as doeskin. Everything was soft about them—their broad faces, the gleam of their dark eyes, their almost soundless steps on the earthen floor. And yet they were powerful, more candidly strong than

428

the women at home. Nobody could deny that! They were all secret, all together. This was a woman's hidden stronghold. The intimacy of glances told enough, no words were needed. The youngest one was silently placing various-sized pieces of pottery on the floor, earth-colored, with great flower patterns. Margot bent to pick up a bowl, adoring its earthen coolness, its lovely, hand-made unevenness.

"Do you want it?" Bruce asked her.

"Of course I want it! I want everything."

He was already asking "How much?" The women turned to each other, laughing again, a half-abashed laughter that seemed to share a secret.

"Fifty cent'," the old woman said.

The soft, spontaneous laughter bubbled up again as if out of some hidden spring of peaceful, secret, deep harmony. They all exchanged glances from under their black eyelashes.

"What will I do with it?" Margot asked.

"Well, you have it," Bruce told her.

"Yes, I have it," Margot repeated blissfully.

They walked slowly past the houses.

"Oh, Bruce, I want to live here!" Margot moaned.

He smiled at her, and let her clasp his large firm hand.

She cried passionately, "I *do*."

How could she tell him? He was pleased and smiling, enjoying the strangeness, but be*cause* it was strange, and had no connection with the life that he called real. Was that the way he thought of her too? Margot looked quickly up at him in fright. But his face had a tender look, although its lines were stern. She clung more tightly to his hand. What *she* felt was, that she had found her home. These were houses that belonged to women, houses they themselves had made, not places that had been made for them: soft, uneven, standing as they had grown, not built to carefully calculated specifications. And they had stood longer than any other houses in the whole land! Maybe would stand longer still. Margot felt a sudden fear of the metal hardness that was coming into the world. She knew that she had always been afraid of it; the great iron of machinery that was overwhelming all the small, intimate, irrelevant things. If it were to be all calculation instead of spontaneity! Then she wouldn't care to live any longer. Now she thought back with horror to the great skyscrapers with their metal doors, their hard shining spaces on which her heels made sharp, resistant sound, the intricate muffled mechanism that was beneath their towering magnificence. It seemed as if women were being driven back to a place like this; and again she thought with longing of the bubbling spontaneity of the Indian laughter in the intimate darkness of that room.

"I want to live here," she repeated.

"*You* do!" Bruce gently mocked her. They were going along hand in hand.

"I do, I want to dress the way they do, and eat from bowls that I love, not just *dishes* you go and buy. I want to be an Indian woman."

Bruce was still gently mocking. He swung her hand.

"This is the way women can live."

"Women depend on the luxuries men get for them," Bruce told her sententiously. "Wait until you see your hair get straight and your teeth drop out. Then you wouldn't be so contented. What's all this grousing I've been hearing about the beauty parlors along the way, that didn't know how to cut a woman's hair—"

"That was in the Middle-*west*," Margot said with scorn.

"Maybe you can start up a beauty parlor in the pueblo!"

Margot was silent. He thought it was a joke, because these people were Indians, and so he, as a good American, had to be facetious about them. He couldn't see. No, it wasn't a joke! Bruce was within the enchantment too. She could feel the sense of happiness that was mounting, mounting . . . Bruce pretended to tease her to hold back that sense a little. Now he had withdrawn his hand and he was tightly clasping hers.

She wanted this—she *wanted* it. It was like something that had always been hers and that was lost until today. It was far more hers than home. In this enveloping stillness and peace, movements, impulses, seemed to come from the inside. At home, Margot thought rebelliously, everything was put on from the outside. Even in New York. In New York worse than anywhere! She had loved it when she went there first; but now she felt that she could never bear to go back.

"But you *like* it?" she said wistfully to Bruce, feeling how different his ideas were from hers, liking them and hating them because they were so much the regulation American-man kind.

"It's nice, all right," Bruce admitted.

He gave a sidelong, appraising look about the place. There was a kind of pain in his voice. His hand tightened on Margot's. The silent, singing happiness mounted, mounted, carrying them with it—until she drew away her hand.

"Want something else?" Bruce asked her. His voice held a breathlessness. He loved to make her gifts. No doubt it was partly a sense of reparation—a desire to heap on her all he could in their brief time together . . . if it was to be brief. But she loved it just the same. The way, up in the mountains, he had stuck first a red flower and then a yellow flower into her hair—as if he could never get enough of the sight of her in different aspects, different colors. "Maybe we can find some of this silver jewelry to deck you out. A fellow told me you could run across better things in these pueblos than you can in town."

Bruce was looking around. Margot loved the air of masculine authority with which he did it, although she knew it was alien to the place, and gave them the air of foreign conquerors. She had exclaimed over the first piece of heavy silver jewelry that she had seen, feeling that it was what she had always been meant to wear; and Bruce had noted it, and been cannily turning over possibilities in his mind. A young woman was standing in front of one of the houses. Bruce went over to her, and then beckoned to Margot, as she stood waiting in the sunshine.

"This girl says she has a few rings. Want to look at them?"

The young Indian woman went through the open doorway and came back with a handful of silver rings and a necklace of turquoise which she held out in soft, questioning silence. Bruce examined the things with his usual appraising thoroughness. He held up one of the rings, squinting at it, and then took Margot's hand and slipped it on her finger. She loved its heavy feeling on her hand.

"Like it?" Bruce asked. "I don't know much about these things, but I believe it's pretty good. How much?" he asked the Indian woman.

A thin, hard, brown young man had come softly out after her and was now standing behind her. She turned to him. He said something in a guttural, unrecognizable language. The young woman said obediently, in stolid shyness, "Four dollar." The young man had made her ask more than she would have had the courage to ask for herself. Margot felt that she loved the Indian woman, and hated all the white race, and all its hard acquisitiveness, always wanting to get, not to enjoy and savor. . . . All but Bruce. He had all the qualities she had said she hated; and she loved him.

"Well, now you're an Indian woman," Bruce said. He gave a quick smile at her, admitting the happiness, still holding it off. "I didn't want to risk the turquoises—rather ask somebody who can advise me about the value. Like your ring?"

"Of course."

Bruce took her hand and held it up, looking at it, looking at the ring with its lumps of turquoise. The satiny white of the slim hand was tanned now to a smooth brown. It quivered slightly, and Bruce let it go.

"So now you have a ring," he said softly to her.

Margot looked away. She felt another astounding, sudden access of shyness, of fear. She chanted: "I want to live in one of these houses, all dark inside, and then come outside into the sunshine, *this* kind of sunshine. Don't you?" She looked quickly up at him.

"If that's where you're going to live," Bruce said.

He caught her hand again, and held it closely. The open light in the square was dazzling with sunshine. This moment of happiness was beyond any that she had known before. Margot looked at the silent enclosure of low houses. Of all the places where she had dreamed of living—the Spanish castle, the old houses on Washington Square, the eighteenth century French rooms, like the replicas in the Metropolitan—this was

432

most her home. It was not past and foreign. It was somehow real. When she looked through the open doorways into the interior of summer darkness, she could feel something like an old memory of a faraway dream just stirring. She saw before her, like a revelation, the beauty of living with Bruce. Just the simple beauty of *living*. Of course. That was always the end of the fairy tale. "And they lived happily forever after." And it was the line that she had skipped! But now she had come to it, and she knew its meaning.

They went slowly over to the car, which stood tilted a little on the rough ground, with the white church wall behind it. White walls, and sharp dark shadows. It seemed as if, for this moment, they had walked straight into the center of the morning peace. A kind of love she had never known for Bruce before, even in the wildly happy hours that she had reaped, softly flooded over Margot. It was peace. They two moved within it.

As they got into the car, Bruce drew her over to him, and held her against him.

"Margot, we *have* to be together," he said. "We can't separate—not now. I just can't let you go."

Margot felt with wonder that Bruce was trembling. His face was set in a grimace of pain. There were actually tears in his eyes. She softly, wonderingly touched his face. His hand was cold. She didn't understand, for it all seemed to her so natural. That was the only thing she could feel. It was the most natural thing on earth or in heaven; and that was what made it beautiful. It was the thing that came next.

4

Margot had found the tearoom in an inner court off the plaza, pulling Bruce through the dark little alleyway between the bookstore and the old museum, and exclaiming at the cool retreat in the shade of the piazza roofs. There were orange and blue tables looking out on the areaway paved with uneven flagstones, blinding white in the dry sun, with a center bed of cactus. But a shadowy coolness lay against the thick, damp-feeling old adobe walls in the piazza with its columns carefully carved in Mission style.

"Looks kind of Greenwich Villagey to me," Bruce said. He looked dubiously at the waitresses in crisp, light-green smocks, carrying trays of tall, misted glasses of iced tea with cuts of lemon perched on the edges.

"Oh, no, Bruce!" Margot said.

She liked the Indian chair with its thong seat which Bruce held for her, and the horehound-brown Mexican glassware and the yellow sugar bowl with its childish, painted flowers. She stared avidly around the court, seeing first the groups of people around the tables, and envying the woman with the sharply cut profile who could pull back her gray hair that way, and so stunningly wore the scarlet velvet jacket and the enormous belt of round silver Indian discs. If they stayed here much longer, she *must* have one of those jackets and one of those belts, to go with the ring and bracelet and heavy silver earrings that Bruce had bought her. It was the kind of dress that fitted this country and fitted her, and she could already feel herself, like that woman, boldly making her own the brilliant color and the heavy ornament.

Margot's eyes roved to little shops around the court, in the windows of which she saw the Indian and Mexican handicraft, etchings, drawings, paintings, and all the various loot of the region. She felt the group of people as intimates of the country, who made this a meeting place; and she was confirmed in this when a young Indian in a square bob and orange shirt padded across the court, and they began talking to him familiarly in a mixture of Spanish and English.

"When will there be the Eagle Dance, Juan?"

"Mebbe Buffalo."

"Quando?"

"Mebbe next week. You come Thursday," the Indian said with calm friendliness.

They were standing about him, examining his strings of turquoise and bracelets as he stood stolidly impervious to their patronizing remarks.

"No, Juan, not good," drawled a thin youth in a béret and a red sash. He negligently handed back the string of beads.

Margot was looking at the youth when his eyes lazily met hers. He detached himself from the group and came toward Margot's table.

"Margot Ferguson!" His large eyes examined her familiarly, and there was no mistaking the curling lashes. "It's time you were coming here, Margot," he drawled.

"Hello, Rod! I didn't know you'd come out here. This is Mr. Williams—Mr. Pingrey," Margot said a little coolly. She had no desire to meet Rod here. Somehow it put the wrong kind of color on the group from which he came, about which she had been weaving an exotic and envious interest.

She heard Bruce's chilly "How do you do," as Rod, with an insolent familiarity, turned his large eyes from one to the other of them.

"Margot, how charming you look. There is that *je ne sais quoi* about you, as of a properly cherished woman. I congratulate you—both."

Margot saw the way Bruce stiffened as Rod rolled his eyes toward him. Rod's silky black side-burns, coming down from under his béret, were lower than ever, and his blue velvet trousers were gashed with red at the bottoms. He had gone artily Spanish.

"What are you doing here, Rod?" Margot said quickly, to cover up the stiffness she knew Bruce was feeling. "I haven't seen you for ages."

Rod negligently picked up Margot's hand from the table. "Not bad, the ring," he drawled. "It's an old pattern. But you got hooked on the bracelet. Factory. Me?" he asked. "I'm quite established." He made a wan motion of his hand toward one of the shops. "Mexican things. The best in Santa Fé. You want to be careful of the stuff around the hotels. You should meet Everett—most valuable person to know here. Look, he's the man in the linen trousers. Knows when every dance is going on in the pueblos. One of the few people who have really seen the Penitentes."

Margot saw the short, fat man with the gray mop of hair,

like an old actor's, and the hanging pouches under his large eyes, sloppily dressed in an old velvet coat and thin white trousers. Poor Vernon, what a successor! But he could probably support Rod more thoroughly than she had done.

Rod said, with an intimate smirk and roll of his eyes, "Everett and I are very good friends, you know. He owns all this place. Listen, why don't you come and meet these people? Going to be here long? Everybody stays longer than they expect to. It gets you, you know. You ought to know some of the real people."

Margot looked at Bruce. He was sternly cutting his salad with his fork, with an air of heavy distaste which she could recognize.

"Oh, I guess not, Rod," she said quickly. "We're just staying quietly here, not seeing anyone."

Rod's eyebrows arched. "Oh, of course. Pardon me. Just one of those things—I understand. Well, you'll probably be dropping into the shop some day. I cannot know you from Adam —and Eve, if you want," he said, with a roll of his eyes. He languidly walked away.

"Margot, let's get out of here," Bruce said from a tight mouth.

"Oh, Bruce, before I finish my salad?"

But she saw the determined set of his jaw and knew when it didn't do to oppose him. She folded her napkin, trying to look nonchalant, while Bruce paid the thin, very refined woman at the desk.

"Bruce, I'm terribly sorry," she begged, when they got outside. "That awful little squirt of a Rod!—who ever dreamed he'd turn up?"

"Just the kind of place you'd expect to find him in," Bruce said. "With that gang of would-be artists. I didn't like it from the first."

"Well, we won't go there again. I'll do the cooking myself."

"Yes," Bruce said, mocking her. "On the good old-fashioned range!"

"I don't have to use the range. And anyway, this is different."

436

It did seem different. When they had driven back through the narrow winding street, that looked as if it had grown from an old Indian trail, and had climbed the sandy arroyo to the place where their low-lying adobe house sat into the hill under the poplar trees, with the piñon like a dark fuzz beyond, and beyond that the blue mountains which seemed so intimate, and yet were twenty miles away: Margot felt a secret little ecstatic sense that this was their home. She almost resented the fact that it belonged to a wealthy artist, and not to them. He was away for the summer, and they had rented the place a month ago through a real estate man. She had come to love the white interior, that was like the pueblo rooms, with the rounded fireplace in the corner, the woody vigas in the ceiling, and beautiful furniture which the artist had made himself. Even Bruce approved it, and said it was not so arty as the painter's house with the blue wooden gate and the old Mission bell above it. They were both affectionate toward the tiny stream that flowed in front of the house between its little thrown-up banks, and which was now a dry trickle, and again a miniature flood of pale brown water—depending on how much of the flow the irrigation farms up the valley turned aside, Bruce said.

The kitchen was warm from the slowly burning range and fragrant with the beans which had been cooking since yesterday. Margot went to the olla that hung from thongs, and was cool and dewy with the water in it, and poured herself a drink into a little pottery mug. She loved the faintly earthen taste of the cool water, and the porous feel of the cup at her lips. She loved to get a drink from the olla—just as water seemed to taste better when she got it from some out-of-the-way place, such as the spring in Stumpf's pasture, next to the Ferguson farm at home, where the clean sand bubbled in the bottom of the spring. Then she went to the range and lifted the lid from the kettle of beans, which had now turned a rich brown. She poured them into the big, irregular Indian cooking pot, with its zigzag design, added water, and set them in the oven to bake. Maria, the young Spanish-American girl who came in to clean, had taught her how to make the beans and chile. She had got to love the sensation of the fiery red sauce, which reminded her of peppery and reckless Spanish qualities. Maria brought in the flat, round tortillas, about which Bruce joked, calling them stacks of cardboard, and declaring that Margot would disdain them if they were served in American restaurants. But he liked them too. He had learned to scoop up his beans with them, the way they had seen a family of Spanish-Americans doing, all solemnly seated under a cottonwood tree near a stream, with their ancient, high-pockets of a Ford parked near-by.

There was an electric stove, beside the range, on which Margot made their breakfast. She loved the intimacy of the long breakfast hour, Bruce pouring himself three cups of coffee as they lingered; the lucid freshness of the blue southwestern morning, with the mountains dim and dreamy beyond the long windows. She even liked to give Bruce the best half of the Albuquerque paper, which Bruce always bought, with a somewhat shamefaced look, saying "it was more of a real town than this tourist's dump"—there were better baseball items in the paper. In fact, Margot was getting quite a housewifely feeling. Mother and Dorothy would never have believed it! But she felt that it was different, because this was Bruce. And it wasn't a stodgy marriage. They were to get what there was in it, and then let it go. Only there was so much in it—so much more than she had dreamed. Margot was a little fearful of the attachment that was growing. Yet she was fiercely resolved *to* get what there was in it. It had come, now, to the very heart of something sweet, and she realized that it needed this daily life together to bring it to full flower.

As she worked in the kitchen, it seemed to her to have a flavor and simple dignity of something fundamental, with the scrubbed, unpainted pine-board table upon which a loaf of bread ought to stand—a jug, a loaf, and thou. She felt the same revulsion as Bruce at the sort of arty, "atmospheric" tearooms and bizarre eating places for which she had had a girlish weakness until now. But she seemed to have outgrown all that. She was disgusted at the thought of Rod and his whole gang —that awful Everett in the sloppy pants!—and she meant to stay far, far away from the Mexican shoppe. Why did Rod, of all people, have to turn up here, with his beautiful insolent eyes, reminding her of her past, of Lee, and the smoky basement room—here in this sunshine? She gave a little shudder.

She heard Bruce moving about in the other room, and looking up, she saw him standing at the door with an amused, fond look.

"Well! What a charming little hausfrau."

"That doesn't bother me a bit!"

"Doesn't?"

"No." She came over to him and gave him an ecstatic little hug. "I *like* it. For you." She pulled him possessively into the other room and seated him on the low couch, with its old Navajo blanket of faded rose and white and black. "You do think our place is lovely—*per*-fect, don't you?"

She could never get Bruce to uncover the real depths of his feelings, and she didn't expect it. She knew how he liked to keep a masculine playfulness on the surface, as he let his lavish care for her stand for profession, imply his feeling underneath. She was content with the half-playful, half-painful look that came into his eyes as he squeezed her arm and then stared through the window.

"We won't go to that goofy little place again. I don't like it any better than you do. I just want to stay *here*, Bruce. I'd like to cook all our meals—honestly, I would. We can get Maria to come in when we want her. And then we wouldn't have to run into people, but we could drive to the pueblos—I just haven't *begun* to get enough of the country. Have you? Bruce, answer!" She shook his arm. "Oh, Bruce," she said, with a sudden sweet overflow of feeling, "did you ever think it would come to as much as *this*? I didn't know anything could."

Bruce shook his head.

Margot felt her eyes swimming as she looked intently at his face, the structural lines of which had become so familiar and necessary to her. She felt the imprint of his features like something bred into her. There was a sudden strange yearning inside of her, quite different from simple desire. She said in a wondering voice, "I can even see why women want children

439

—of someone they really love." She held to his arm and searched his face with her eyes.

Bruce was silent. Margot quickly felt that it had struck a wrong note. She was angry suddenly, and frightened. The silence throbbed between them. Bruce got up, drawing away his arm, and walked gravely about the room.

He stopped and looked down at her with a tightened face. "Margot," he said with difficulty, "look here. We've got to . . . decide some things pretty soon."

"Oh, Bruce! Why did you have to say that right now?" The tears in her eyes overflowed. She felt a willful anger at the thought of making decisions. She hated them. They seemed wrong. She wanted events to decide things of themselves.

"Well, I've got to say it some time."

"Bruce—it was just that little bastard Rod!—You've been rattled!" She couldn't believe that this was touching the thing she dreaded!

Margot sat silent. She looked at the wicker wastebasket and saw the corners of water-color paper sticking out of it.

"Bruce, you haven't thrown them *away!*"

She ran to the basket and retrieved the pictures with a little moan. Bruce's painting had been one of the reasons they had given for their stay here, for their taking the house. He had always wanted a free space in which to do the things for which he had never had time. Margot had been happy seeing him set his small easel on the terrace, and she had watched with little cries of appreciation as his tentative brushes labored at reproducing the look of the mountains or the rambling Spanish farms across the valley. But now, as she looked up, and saw the faintly cynical look he bent down on her, she checked her lamentation.

"They're junk," Bruce said. "It's too late for me to go in for that sort of thing. Even your friend Rod could do better. Earlier I might have—I don't know. But now it's just make-believe."

He took the water-color sheets and tore them across, and threw them at the wastebasket.

Margot couldn't say anything. They weren't good. She knew

it as well as Bruce. But he might do something good if he kept on—she felt now as if Bruce could do anything. Anyway, she had been happy feeling that Bruce was having this period when everything that he had missed in his too-early taking on of responsibilities would come to a perfect flowering—and through her. She felt a crushed sense at Bruce's turning on it, and she couldn't protest. Tears overflowed again in her great, staring eyes.

Bruce made an uneasy movement. "There's too much make-believe around here, anyway. It's beginning to get under my skin."

Now she looked up at him tragically. Yet she knew that she held power over him, and she said, daring him to deny it, "But what we have together isn't make-believe. Is it?"

Bruce winced a little and his face turned color. "No," he said, "I'm afraid it isn't."

"*Afraid?*"

"Margot, look here—"

"I don't want to look here. I don't want to see you tear up pictures and tell me I'm nothing but make-believe. Like Rod, I suppose. I suppose you think I really belong with him!"

"Margot—"

"Oh, please don't say anything." She clung to him again, and he held and kissed her remorsefully. "Not today, not today—not when everything's so beautiful. Not unless you don't love me any more. I don't care *what* you say then."

Bruce admitted, after a rueful moment, "Then I guess I'll have to keep still." She looked up at him. He was smiling. They kissed again, in a long, silent reunion. But the vigilant fear, which had been lulled for a while by their happiness in this place, was all awake again, strained and quivering inside her.

When Margot heard Bruce walking around she knew that she was not surprised. Neither of them had slept. For a little while, they seemed to have made up, to have been happy together. But it was not true, and both of them knew it. Their supper of beans and chile, which she had meant to be such a success, was a failure. Bruce had been indrawn, with a far-away look in his eyes. And afterwards, when she had told him that he needn't help her with the dishes, he had said, "All right"—with relief, it seemed to Margot. When she had gone into the studio, he was reading his mail, of which he had got a great batch forwarded this afternoon. He was thinking of either his business or his family, she didn't know or care which. But anyway, it had come between them, and she hated him.

She felt him coming toward her.

"Margot, are you awake?"

"Yes," she answered curtly.

The room was almost dark. Bruce, in his robe, sat huddled on a chair by her bed. Margot's heart began to beat heavily. It choked her, so that she was afraid she couldn't speak. She didn't want to hear—she wouldn't listen . . . but in horror, she couldn't help it.

Bruce took a deep breath. "Listen here, Margot—we've got to break it up." They were the words that she had dreaded. She was hearing them now. "We . . . we can't trust ourselves any further."

Those monstrous words had been spoken—and by Bruce. Margot lay like a black living coal of resentment. Once she had meant to speak them—if they were to be spoken. But now it seemed wrong that they should be said at all. When Bruce tried to touch her, she drew away bitterly. They felt so utterly different about this, as about other things; there could be no mutual understanding.

But in spite of herself, she was touched when Bruce, sensitive to her angry withdrawal, said brokenly, "You think I don't love you, because I'm saying this. If you knew what this takes!"

Yet her resentment flamed again, as she dwelt sullenly, broodingly, on what he had said. He couldn't love her, as she knew love. He couldn't feel that it could be put aside this way, after what there had been between them. It mattered to her more than *anything*. It wasn't love if it didn't. He couldn't understand as she understood what it meant to "give all to love." Bruce was talking, and she felt the suffering in his voice,

442

but she was set against him inside, and hardly heard what he was saying. She felt sealed up. There was no use talking or trying to explain. She gave a little moan and buried her head in the pillow.

"Christ, if it was only that I didn't love you! I'm crazy about you. You pulled me clear out of my orbit. I don't know myself any more—that's the truth. You needn't think this is just a business man's pastime!" Bruce said accusingly. "I never was the kind who went in for pastimes. You know that, don't you? Yes, you know it well enough! You made me feel from the start it was something different. That was why it meant so much to me. It was something I never expected to find in this life."

"*Was* something," Margot said bitterly. She didn't care whether she was fair or not. Her heart was too sore. "You just want to put it away, get it over with now. You *can't* love me. Because I'm willing for it to go on, and you aren't."

"But, Margot. There is some difference between us—in circumstances. Don't you see?—I feel all the responsibility."

"You're no more responsible than I am!" Oh, those were Bruce's old notions—still between them. "Don't you suppose a woman takes a chance?" She felt her fierce recklessness, the thing that had made her rebel against all the Ferguson cautiousness. "I take *every* chance, I'm glad to! It doesn't mean anything to me if it isn't *every*-thing. But you . . . when I said that to you—this afternoon . . . you were scared."

Margot sobbed, as if she had been holding her breath too long. Only now she saw—she began to see—of what he was depriving her. It could never, never come to the perfect final flowering. Not now.

Bruce sat humbly. "Well, call it that," he said after a moment, very quietly. "You see, I have a wife and two children, Margot. You have to know what that means, what it lets a man in for."

"It couldn't stop me, if there was something else I wanted more!" Margot said fiercely. But she was stiff with anger at the mention of his wife. The word made her hate him.

There was a beseeching note in Bruce's voice—and a little of

443

hurt resentment too. "Margot," he told her, "you've got to see it a little from my side. I don't think you realize how little you go outside your own feelings. You hold up love as if it were something apart from people. That's all right for you. You can do as you please. You haven't anyone else to think of. It *can't* be just the same for me. You've never been willing to look at my situation. Or what it meant to me, what I was doing. I've tried to do what would make you happy—what you said you wanted. You said you didn't want marriage."

"I don't! It isn't that I'm talking about. It's just . . . after what we've had, we ought to stay together—not let other things come between."

But Margot felt the hurt of what Bruce had said to her. The folks had said it too. "Margaret thinks her tastes are sacred." She could set herself against them, and disregard what they said. But when Bruce said it, it jarred her with a shock of truth. It was as if she were all tender and vulnerable where he was concerned.

"It was all for you," Bruce repeated. "Every bit of it. And ever since I knew you. You knocked me clear off my base, I tell you." His voice rose in suffering. "I've gone with you as far as I could. Now you won't see how it is with me." He stood up abruptly. "You've never looked at me," he accused her. "Just at the man who could make you happy."

Margot cried furiously that it wasn't true. But, in torture, she felt the fear of its truth breaking into her, leaving her without resources. She fought blindly against it.

Bruce had been walking about. Now he went out of the room. Margot felt herself alone in a pit of raw suffering. Without Bruce, she simply did not see how she could live. Everything was gone out in blackness. She could bear the sight of nothing, now that she had seen all the living world illuminated by his love for her. She felt wildly that it *was* something truly beyond her—not in glory now, but in a paralyzing fear. She didn't know what she could do. She would rush out to him—change him, make him accept her feelings as his. But she couldn't move, no more than in a dream. She lay trying to subdue her torture to the mere possibility of existing from moment to moment.

After a while, Bruce came back. He tried to lie down beside her and take hold of her. She felt his wet face against hers.

"Margot," he pleaded, "we can't keep on like this. We're fooling ourselves. It's going to get beyond us."

By now, she hated him too much. She felt again of what he was depriving her. Even *Lillian* could have children! Bruce didn't want a child by her.

"Because I know all about this," he whispered. He tried to stroke her hair. "Don't you see, Margot? We can't just go into things like that. You made me remember that I have children. I can't go back on them. I'm their father. They trust me. I can't tell you what that means. Not if you can't see it. And I don't suppose you can."

Margot was silent.

"Well, I had to have this much of you," he said brokenly again. "Whether I did wrong or not. I don't know. I can't help it. Haven't I given you some of the happiness you wanted?"

But she was still stiff and silent against him. After a while she whispered, turning away from him, "But you told me you loved me better than anything in the world, you'd never known what love could be."

"That's true."

It couldn't be true, Margot felt wildly, through a torture of whirling darkness. To speak of parting now was a betrayal of the revelation of their love. The only right there could be was to go on and follow it through to the end. She didn't care if they died together! She would rather die with Bruce. She began to sob.

"If it had meant to you what it did to me, you *couldn't* go," she tried to tell him.

"All right." Bruce was crying too. "Think it doesn't mean the same to me."

Margot muttered sullenly: "It can't mean the same to a man. They don't know what it is."

"I knew enough to risk breaking my whole life to pieces

to give you what you wanted most. My business—and everything else."

Margot was silent, feeling again the fear of admitting that as truth.

Bruce got up. She was listening to him with a terrible acuteness. He seemed to be talking to himself.

"But I can't go on with it. I can't go back on them. Maybe I don't put love as high as you do. I know I can't go back on my children, for another child. And that's what it would come to—would have to. Don't you see, I couldn't be anything afterwards, no good to you or anyone . . ."

"You said we could live together."

She saw the sunshine on the earth-colored pueblos . . . the peace in the plaza square.

"Well, I meant it. God knows! But, Margot—"

"Now if you go I'll *die*."

It wasn't a threat. It had said itself out of her anguish. She couldn't look into that blackness with Bruce gone. It made her scream out in fear.

"Margot, don't torture me that way!" Bruce was crying again. "You don't want me if I'm all broken to pieces. I couldn't undertake to be anything to you—not if I . . . I'm afraid of what it would do to me. I couldn't stand up under it, Margot, if I lost all my self-respect—and trustworthiness . . . I can't just do it for my own happiness."

But for her, happiness was the criterion! It was the only thing that was right. And *she* was to count less, just because she had given him happiness—had let him into that heaven they had shared together in the mountain stillness! He was against her. He was not hers. He belonged with other people. He was walking around the room now, blindly.

"Go *now*, then!" Margot screamed. "I just can't see you any more."

"I will." He stopped that blind walking. She had made him do that, anyway. She could hear his heavy breathing. "I've got to go now. I may not be able to do it. I've got to. You see that, don't you, Margot? I'm just myself. I'm what I am. I can't help it."

"Oh, go away. Don't talk. Not a single thing matters."

Bruce went. Even while she was driving him away, she hadn't believed that he could go. Margot sank back into that pit of suffering. She believed, quite truly, that she was dying. She did nothing to stem the tide of her suffering, and there was nowhere else that it could bear her. But still she lived on from moment to moment.

Then the din of her own inner pain seemed to fade out and leave her in an acuteness of listening. She heard Bruce packing in the other room. Margot rose up in her shock of resentment at that impossible actuality. She could almost feel the feverish trembling of his haste. A shoe dropped, and she heard him curse. His clothes—*hers,* the things she loved, the dark green tie that gave a sea-green tinge to his eyes, the rough tweed coat—how could they be the property of a woman he loved less than he did her? Why was the one most loved the one who must suffer? Bruce could actually leave her. Margot felt alone and hideously insignificant in the great blackness that was left all around her. The blackness surged over her, in helpless waves of agony. She had meant to "know suffering"—but not suffering like this. Not raw and actual, piercing to her marrow, turning her bones to water and her flesh to agony. Then she leaned on her arm again in that hideous acuteness of listening. Every tiny, actual sound she seemed to have to hear. And yet she couldn't hear enough! When finally Bruce came toward her room again, toward her, she felt as if her hands were beating the air and she was shrieking "Don't come near me!" although the whole time she was lying fiercely still.

Bruce came in and stood beside her in the semi-darkness. "Margot." She heard the strangled suffering in his voice. Was glad to hear it!—and then suffered herself because she couldn't comfort him. He sat down on the bed and tried to take her hand. He had something of his old protective, responsible manner back. He was telling her what he had thought of for her. "I want you to keep on this house. Stay here just as long as you want to—just as long as you can. You said you loved the country. If you want to stay out here altogether . . . why, I guess I can manage that." She made a movement of denial.

447

"I'm leaving some money for you. It'll see you through for some time. Now, listen, Margot, while I tell you where it is."

"I won't listen!"

"You've got to. I won't go away and leave you flat. You can't ask it of me. I won't do it." She had to hear, although she tried to hold her hands against her ears. "And I'm going to leave you the car too."

"You can't. I won't have it. I don't want to *see* it."

"All right," he said, after a while. "I'll take it away then."

"If you don't I'll take it out and wreck it!"

"Margot. Margot, *please!* Don't torture me more than you have to. By God, I don't think I deserve this!"

She feebly beat at him. "Go away!"

But he stayed, and tried to make her promise—she would write him if she needed anything, she wouldn't be cruel, would look after herself. He trusted her. She thought *that* much of him. And they both had this time to remember—just as she had said. Margot tried to be deaf. She hated his care—hated him to think of these little things, when he could do the final cruelty to her. At the last minute, she took hold of him. He had to break away from her. She heard, in horrified amazement, the sound of his great, broken sobs.

"I have to do it. Oh God, I can't if I stay any longer. Margot, let me go. I can't."

He got up, went blindly to the door. She heard him still crying—a man's fearful crying, that rocked the universe. She listened to it with her eyes open in horrified amazement. After a long time, she heard the sound of the car.

She got up, and struggled after him. Bruce was gone. She would stop him, throw herself at his feet and beg him to stay . . . anything . . . she couldn't stand it alone, that was all. . . .

She ran along the road a little way, slipping on the ruts in the darkness. After a while, she couldn't hear the car any more —nothing but the little stream, and the night-time rustling of the cottonwood leaves. She stood in horrified loneliness, listening to those sounds.

Then she felt her drained weakness. She couldn't get back to the house. She couldn't even throw herself into the stream and let the shallow water cover her. Bruce's words stopped her—the sick remembrance of the suffering in his voice. That was more to her than her own impulse. But she didn't care what she did. She was beyond that. It seemed to her truly that the end of the world had come. She lay flat down on the rough ground in the chill mountain night while her suffering seemed to bear her somewhere—she didn't know where. . . . She dug her fingers into the earth.

There was a tinge of light over the mountains now. Cars were going past. Someone would look over and see her—perhaps try to come to her aid, ask her what was the matter. She felt dragged out now, not alive. But if she were going to die, she didn't want to be found here. She got up, sauntering as if she had just come into the garden for some flowers, went into the house and stealthily closed the door, and lay down on the bed.

IV. AFTER THE END OF THE STORY

MARGOT woke up with a sense of rest. It was like a dream to be back in her old room. Her own curtains were at the window, carefully laundered; and the rickety little desk stood locked as she had left it. The folks had kept everything for her exactly as it had been before—hoping, she supposed, that she would finally come home. She felt the blessed ease of lying in her bed and letting things go. The shaded room, with its closed door, now seemed a refuge.

But this half-pleasant sensation lasted for only a few seconds. Now she was awake, and already the sharp grind of pain was beginning—in her mind, in her breast . . . somewhere. She felt the empty horror of lying here alone. Hunger for Bruce consumed her. She would have screamed out if she could —only it was too sharp and absorbing for her to make a cry. It took all the life she had just to lie and feel and contemplate its completeness. There was an interval when again it seemed to Margot that she simply could not live on from moment to moment. It passed—more or less.

Suddenly she got out of bed. She had heard sounds downstairs. Bun dashed into the house and out again with a slam of the front door. The sound hurt Margot, wounded her with its careless ease. It said that to Bun this place was home. And to her it wasn't. No place could be. She sat hunched in pain on the edge of the bed seeing the white walls of the adobe house that no longer belonged to her—not the house, nor the dreamy mountains, nor the little shallow stream. There was no use in dressing, in doing anything, with Bruce gone from her life. It had lost both center and background. Every time that Margot looked at her existence she realized more the extent of the devastation.

But another sound made her get up quickly again and act to herself as if she had been dressing all this time. If she didn't hurry, mother would come up to see what was the matter. Anything was better than breaking down before the folks. That painful, hard determination was all that kept her up now. It was all that was left of her pride. She knew that her mother didn't entirely believe in her account of the trip, although mother tried and pretended, resolved to have everything beautiful between them this time. She had told mother that she had gone West with some friends of Grimmie's. "How nice!" mother had dutifully said. If she could have seen this last crowd—! Hec, her gallant suitor, who had expected to spend his nights with her, thinking that of course he could do as he pleased with a girl from New York who was running around alone out West. Rod, no doubt, had told him about Bruce, and put his own sweet interpretation upon the story. And no doubt about Lee, too, and a few other things . . . Ugh! When Margot had been with strangers she had longed for someone of her own; but here at home, meeting all these eyes, she wanted strangers again.

She dressed as quickly as she could, shuddering away from her memories of this room. She had thought that now she was forever superior to those memories. But she wasn't. It seemed

to her that she had gone back into the old chill, shaded loneliness. She felt too hideous for any but her oldest dress.

And of course she had to find Aunt Ella downstairs with
mother!

"Well! You must have been having quite a sleep."

Aunt Ella's dull black eyes were looking at her curiously.
Since Margot had come home this time, Aunt Ella seemed to
regard her partly as a stranger. Half the time Aunt Ella was
formal, the rest of the time too familiar.

"That's just what I want her to do," mother said, with a
quick, anxious, conciliatory smile.

"Well! Let's see how you look by daylight. I ain't had a
peek at you yet except by night. I want to see if you look as
stylish as you did over at our house. I was afraid to speak to
you! Well, you look a little older," Aunt Ella observed with
satisfaction. "I don't know how all the girls manage to hide
their age these days. But it's beginning to show a little round
your eyes."

"She'll look better when she's rested," mother said again.
quickly, smiling.

"Haven't got much more flesh than when you left. What's
the matter? Run it all off? You ought to have quite a lot more
heft to you by this time. You ought to see Edna Mae Fawcett.
Wasn't she one of those girls you used to play with? My, she's
getting an awful behinder on her! I was just noticing that
when I saw her going down the street."

"I don't care for a behinder, thank you!"

"Oh, well," mother said, anxiously smiling again, "she'll have
several more pounds before we let her go."

Margot went on into the dining room. Mother had a woman
out on the screened porch, ironing, and so her place had been
set in here. Any walls were better than to be left to the awful
vacancy of the outdoor light. On her first day at home, there
had been a sort of freshness of renewal. It had seemed as if
here she could hide and rest. It had been grateful to her to
get away from that awful crowd, whose belated antics she had
long ago outgrown, with the very beginning of her love for
Bruce. She remembered her dry despair at the idea of returning

451

to *that*. Hec, with his gin and his hang-overs and his pumped-up hilarity, the unwelcome zeal of his disappointed love-making! For a few sweet hours, she had felt at home in this place and renewed by its innocent charm. But now it was just another restless sojourn. It was too late to make up the old quarrel. Too much had happened between. For a moment she almost pitied the folks and their transparent efforts, mother's anxious kindness, dad trying to make up with her and pretend that nothing was ever wrong. She felt as if she could have cried over their innocence.

Margot sat down and stared at her glass of orange juice. The perception that mother was using the prettiest dishes for her only made her feel worse; the pathos of these little conciliatory efforts, as if she, Margot, were still a child. It was useless, if she had to go on without Bruce, to do so much as lift her hand to her mouth. She drank the orange juice quickly, with aversion, so that mother would see that the glass was empty. But she couldn't get farther with the breakfast than slightly to move her spoon back and forth in the bowl of cornflakes and rich cream. Thank God, Aunt Ella was still there so that mother wouldn't come out and offer to cook her an egg! She saw that mother had given her, for her coffee, the little spoon with the calla lily handle. Her dry eyes ached with the effort for tears. Margot pushed the spoon aside. It belonged to Dorothy. Yes, she thought bitterly, she had come to admit it: Dorothy was the one who had everything.

Margot sat staring into dreariness. The crazy trip with that lousy crowd had dazed her, kept her in motion, held at bay the actuality of her pain. But now it only sickened her to remember the falsity of the whole thing. It made her angry with herself that she couldn't be worse than she was. But she had proved one thing that she thought fiercely she would like to tell a few of these people who were writing books: when a woman had really had the man she loved, if she did *love* him, she needn't think she could work it off with a bunch of others. No wonder women in the old days had become nuns! She wished she could hate Bruce—oh, she wished she could *hate* him. But when she dreamed of forgetting him, the world seemed to revolve dizzily and leave an abyss. She clung with both hands to the edge of the table. She could have nothing else while she remembered—but there would be still more nothing if it all were gone.

She heard mother and Aunt Ella talking in the living room, and it made her detest them. It made her feel wild and at bay. If they really knew about her, they would put her out of the house. It seemed cruel, simply too cruel, that Aunt Ella should be able to keep Uncle Ben, when they were bickering all the time, just because she wore a wedding ring!—while she herself and Bruce, who loved each other, had to be apart. The folks would call it "too bad"—the eternal bickering—but they would think it perfectly right for Aunt Ella and Uncle Ben to be together.

The front doorbell rang with sharp carelessness. Margot's heart literally did stand still. Her hope, discredited even while she felt it, hurt so that she began to hum loudly, in order not to be able to listen. But there was no sound of Bruce's voice. She heard Aunt Ella's exclamations of wonder; and then her mother called, "Margaret!" When she had first come home, it had been good to be greeted as "Margaret" and to drop back for a little while into her girlhood. But now when she heard mother call her that, she hated it, for it seemed to ignore and annul all her life as "Margot." And she hated the folks because she couldn't tell them about Bruce.

But there was still a little grain of sick hope left. When she went into the living room, and saw the long flower box, the hope grew suddenly so immense that it choked her. The boy who had brought the flowers read out loudly:

" 'Mar-gott Ferguson!' "

Margot saw their bewilderment. Aunt Ella said, "Here, we can't make this out. Seems to be for somebody we never heard of! Still, they ain't any other Fergusons in town."

The boy said the flowers had come "by telegraph."

"Hurry up, Margaret, open 'em up," Aunt Ella said. She was all eyes. And mother was just as eager although she was trying to subdue it.

Margot opened the long box. Her hands were cold and she

felt that she was trembling. She tried angrily to beat back her expectation. But she was sick all the same when she took the card from the shiny green tissue paper and glanced at it. She had known even before she looked! Yet the disappointment was so terrible—and so absurd!—that the whole room was swimming around her. She threw down the card.

"Aren't you going to open it up?" her mother asked.

"Maybe she don't want us to see it," Aunt Ella suggested. "Must be pretty serious when it comes by telegraph."

Margot saw how excited they both were.

She languidly laid open the green paper and took out the huge bunch of bright pink roses. Bright baby pink!—the very shade she hated. She had a wild impulse to laugh. This was such a perfect offering from Hec! But she remembered the deep red roses in her room—her *own* roses—Frances standing with them at the head of the painted stairs. . . . The world was too awful to endure. All that was gone.

Margot could scarcely bring herself to glance at these hideous flowers; or even to hide her pain from her mother and Aunt Ella. Mrs. Entwhistle had come into the room, doubtless hearing the commotion, and she was staring too in admiration.

"My—but aren't they pretty!"

"Do you remember Margaret, Mrs. Entwhistle?"

"Oh, yes, I remember *her*." Mrs. Entwhistle nodded briskly. "She's the one that used to be in the library!"

Margot tried to smile, to make them think she was properly delighted—to hide herself from them. It seemed as if the room was filled with women. But there was a dreary solace in their excitement. She could see that now they looked at her with increased respect. Even mother! To mother, Dorothy was still her colleague, and Margot was still the spinster daughter.

"Aren't you going to tell us who these came from?" Aunt Ella demanded. "What about that card? Don't you think she ought to pass it over to us? You know anything about this, Annie?"

"Not a thing." Mother looked at her half timidly, but smiling.

"You can see it," Margot said carelessly.

She flipped the card onto Aunt Ella's lap. Let Aunt Ella make what she could out of it!

"Oh, no, I guess we better not," Aunt Ella protested, somewhat scandalized.

"Go ahead!"

Aunt Ella read aloud ponderously, " 'Bee-reaved without you. All nature mourns. Hec.' Is that right? That's what it says. Is that a name?"

"Kind of a one," Margot said disdainfully.

"Sounds funny."

"The real name is Hector."

"*Hector?* Is that a man's name? I thought it was a dog's. Why, Roy Hatch has got a dog named Hector."

"Well, there isn't much difference," Margot said, with acid pleasure. But she was remorseful, seeing mother give her a confused, anxious look.

Aunt Ella repeated, "Well, anyway, it must be pretty serious when he telegraphs, whatever his name is. Annie, we want to look out. Margaret may surprise us by getting married yet." She frankly surveyed Margot.

Margot shrugged her shoulders.

Mother was still puzzled. "But how do you suppose they got your name like that?" she asked.

Aunt Ella chimed in again. "Yes, ain't that funny! 'Margott.' Whoever heard of a name like that? It's worse than the other. I should think the greenhouse would have known who you are."

"Well, I expect maybe the telegram—"

"Yes, but the greenhouse ought to have known who she was. Cliff Taylor ought to have lived long enough in this town for that."

Margot said impatiently, "That *is* my name. That's what people call me!"

" 'Margot'? Who calls you that?"

"It isn't 'Margott.' Mar-*got.*"

"Well, it's got a *t* on it!"

"Yes, but that's the way it's pronounced. It's French."

455

"What you got a French name for?" Aunt Ella demanded, very humorously.

Margot shrugged her shoulders again.

"I think it's a very pretty nickname," mother said.

She had to endure the excitement of all the three females over getting the flowers put into water. Margot hated these roses as she had the geraniums that little red-eared Eddie Whitby had given her once at school, in the days when she was making up romantic stories about the beautiful Gardner Allen. But she felt again that dreary solace in the uproar that the whole thing caused. It had raised her status quite definitely, she saw. Aunt Ella was trying to get her to explain, mother wanting to be told, and hurt because she wasn't.

Margot said, "Well, I'm going back to my breakfast."

"I should think you'd want your flowers with you in there!—where you could see them. I would, if anybody sent me a bouquet like that."

"You can look at them," Margot said pointedly.

"Well, she takes it coolly," Aunt Ella observed as Margot left them. "Must be used to getting flowers." She stared again.

Margot stayed in the dining room until she was sure that Aunt Ella was gone. Then she wandered back into the living room. There was the same quivering dreariness everywhere, without Bruce. His absence seemed to stop all action at the center. Margot sat down to the piano, played a few bars, and stopped.

"Oh, go on and play," her mother begged her.

"I don't know anything any more."

"Didn't you ever play in New York?"

"I didn't have any piano."

She got up restlessly, wanting to stave off questions about New York. Mother was hurt because Margot told her so little. But it couldn't be helped. Margot turned on the radio, getting bursts of sound from various stations, as she moved the indicator carelessly. A woman's hard, bossy voice blared out, disguised under a specious sweetness.

"And of course you will want the recipe for the ice box cookies, if you do not have it already. I know that each and every one of you swears by her *own* ice box cookies. But even so . . ."

Margot snapped off the radio.

"Horrors, what a female! How can you stand it?"

"She gives very good recipes sometimes. I don't like her voice very well, either," mother admitted. "But they all talk that way. It isn't so good in the mornings, but in the evenings we get lovely concerts. Dad likes the Eskimo Band."

Margot flopped into a big chair. It was a pain to be spoken to, a pain to be forced to give her attention. But when she was alone she couldn't stand the leaden dreariness.

Her mother said, "I wish we could have some of the girls over while you're here."

"What girls?"

"Why, Margaret, the girls you used to play with. Your old crowd."

"I never had any crowd."

"Why, yes, you did," mother said, pained. "You used to play with Edna Mae and Lucille. You've seen Lucille in New York. It's too bad she isn't here this summer. Of course the other girls are both married."

"Can't they get out?" Margot asked ironically.

"Well, I just meant, they're busy with their children. And Edna Mae hasn't been very well." She went on quite unconsciously to talk about Mildred. "She has three *very* sweet little children. Of course I don't see much of her. That young crowd don't do much but play bridge. But we'll probably see her at the picnic tonight."

"Is Gardner Allen in the Rotary?" Good heavens!

"Oh, yes, he's been in some time. He took his father's place."

He would be!—Margot thought sardonically. But she couldn't, even now, avoid a twinge of jealousy. Mildred was no doubt the perfect small matron, and had everything she wanted!

She got up restlessly, saying that she was going out on the porch.

"All right," her mother called after her, happily, "I'll come out with you after I've looked at my cake."

Margot sat down in the swing. The slight motion sickened her. She couldn't bear to look out on the lawn—to see the tree under which Dorothy had stood to be married. Mother was constantly lamenting, "It's too bad you couldn't have seen Dorothy while you were out West." "Well, mother, I couldn't say where to go." "No, of course not, if you were with other people." For a little while, she *had* thought of going to Dorothy's. They had always been different, and yet allies. Dorothy's house had seemed to her her refuge. But after all, Dorothy was married, she was one of the enemies—Margot could feel Dorothy judging her in advance. She couldn't bear to be "Auntie Margaret" and palaver over the children. And she couldn't endure to show herself to such an attractive man as Jesse in any light but that of being radiantly successful. To Jesse, she would still be only the unmarried sister—a kind of Sister Anne! There wasn't any refuge. Not anywhere. New York—but the old crowd had none of them liked Bruce, they would welcome her back in glee as one who had learned her lesson.

She heard Bun go tearing into the house again. "Where'd you get the flowers? Gee! She must have a boy friend." He said it carelessly, and tore out again, wrapped up in his own concerns. It made Margot feel old.

There was nothing she could bear to do, nowhere she wanted to go. She dreaded getting outside the confines of her own lot. Here, Mrs. Morgan was always nice to her, in her funny dry way, because she was a Ferguson—although Mrs. Morgan liked Dorothy best. And Mrs. Viele was sweet to everyone! The people in the rented house next door didn't matter. But Margot had met Vanchie one day on the street, had stopped—and Vanchie had scarcely greeted her. Vanchie had never forgiven her for deserting the Bellews and not going on with her library course. Why should she have cared so much about Vanchie? But she did. She had felt stripped and ashamed, losing that old fond adoration. Just as when Mary Lou had gone back on her! She felt that she could show herself to Vanchie only as careless and successful—not maimed and marred. Everywhere, now, she had to go unsupported by the knowledge of Bruce's care. She felt a shameful dependence on those silly flowers, which would get her by with the family. The morning sunshine was pleasant on the lawn, that was fresh and green after the late summer rains. The asphalt was dappled with leaf shadows. But she was out of tune with it. She had never been in tune.

Margot was dressing for the Rotary-Ann picnic. What a dreary joke! But nearly everything now was a dreary, sardonic joke—on her. Her reluctance of the morning had changed to a hard, cynical determination to show people in Belmond that she wasn't just Margaret Ferguson any more. She heard her mother busy about the house; and she felt, with an envy that was both painful and contemptuous, that she would put romantic ideas of love out of her life—that was the way to be successful—she would charm some roaming widower at the picnic and settle down in a home in Belmond. She would be what the folks wanted. It irked her that all these women still spoke in guarded tones about married life before her: Mrs. Viele, the other day, saying archly, "I don't know whether we ought to be letting Margaret hear these things!" Margot didn't believe in her resolve even while she was making it. All the same, she wanted to show people. She put on the white silk sports suit with the yellow hat, yellow stockings and white sandals. Yes, earrings, whether they suited this costume or not! She remembered, with an ironic twist of her mouth, how she had always meant to come back to Belmond in long earrings. Her Indian jewelry, though, she would never wear again. Never the ring which Bruce had put on her hand! *She* had a ring, as well as all these ladies, and far more exciting than theirs—but of course they wouldn't see it! She made up only her eyes and lips. She supposed it would kill the folks if she smoked out there! They accepted smoking now, as long as she didn't do it before other people. Bun had broken them in to all such things.

"Margaret! There's someone to see you."

Mother's voice was pleased and excited. At last someone had called on her! Mother had been hurt by Vanchie's coolness. It couldn't be Bruce—or mother's voice wouldn't sound that way; so it couldn't possibly be anyone she wanted to see.

Margot went slowly down the stairs. This morning she had had to fight against reluctance to see a soul, and to tear herself out of her painful absorption. She knew Aunt Ella had gone away saying, "Well, she ain't any better-natured than she used to be, even if she *is* better looking." Aunt Ella couldn't get over it that she was better-looking, Aunt Ella's expectations had been so low. But this afternoon, Margot felt hard, bitter and easy, competent to deal with anything in a sort of contempt of its lack of significance to her.

"You have a caller," her mother said, pleased.

A tall, rawboned girl in a badly hung dress was standing just inside the hallway, with her mouth open.

"Do you know me?" She gave an eager, awkward laugh. "I guess you remember Ada Rist."

As she heard the excited, foolish pleasure of the tone, Margot was ashamed because she couldn't feel anything better than relief that it wasn't somebody worse. For a moment she had had an awful vision of Hec following her here. But it was too easy to impress Ada! She saw the glisten of admiration in Ada's vacant eyes.

"Well, I should say I do," Margot said easily.

Ada laughed again, abruptly, too pleased, when Margot shook hands. She gave another laugh, and then moistly kissed Margot's cheek. She seemed delighted because Margot hadn't ordered her away.

"I wouldn't hardly have known you," she said now; and added with naïve enthusiasm, "You certainly do look great. I guess it agrees with you there in New York."

Ada's eyes glistened still more. For a moment Margot felt a cynical happiness, as she thought that here was one person with whom she wouldn't change places even to get rid of her misery! She used to endure Ada hanging around, see her only as a satellite, as if Ada were actually non-existent except in relation to herself; but now her own pain opened up to her a vision of Ada's life as it was in itself, with its meager personal pleasures and its vicarious excitements. Evidently Ada still adored her. She stood holding Margot's hand, fumbling it in her clumsy fingers. Margot heard the foolish eagerness of her laugh. What a mess the world was! This was only another instance of the way she attracted a person who could mean nothing to her. Anger at the craziness of existence forced her to smother her impatience, and smile. But she couldn't really think of a thing to say, the encounter was so meaningless to her.

She asked at random, "What are you doing now?"

"Oh, I keep the books at the implement works now," Ada said proudly. "It's a lot nicer being at home here where you know folks and have someone to go around with than being off there where I was." Apparently Ada took it for granted that Margot had been keeping up with her history. Margot hadn't the faintest idea where "off there" might be. "Aren't you ever coming back here?"

"Doesn't look like it," Margot answered.

"You must like it there in New York," Ada said with her foolish laugh, staring with admiration.

Margot smiled. But again she had a troubling vision of Ada's life, making her interest out of the events of the town from the outskirts, going with "the girls" to the movies and afterwards gorging themselves on chocolate sundaes at the less popular drug store where they could hide the shame of their aging solitude from the blithe callousness of the high school chits, excited by their adoration of their favorite female stars and hiding their crushes on the male stars, buying the movie magazines to read about "the love affairs of the stars." Margot perceived, with a good deal more irony and less pleasure than she had once expected to feel, that to Ada she herself was what Ada doubtless had learned to call "glamorous" from the movie magazines. But it did give her a slight revenge for Vanchie's flustered ability to hold to her disapproval and stay unmoved by the fascination Margot used to exert. Margot felt almost warm toward Ada—as warm as she could feel toward anyone, when her heart was so dry. She felt the irony of being appreciated at just the value she had wanted to give herself.

"Why do we stand out here?" she said with vague cordiality.

But Ada wouldn't go into the living room. She answered

461

with awe, "Oh, no, I don't want to make you late for the picnic."

Evidently Ada regarded the Rotary picnic as too lofty a social event to aspire to. It made Margot think of the old days when Ada would stand waiting in mute, awkward adoration, after school, until she saw whether Margot was going off with "the girls" among whom Ada was too humble ever to think of including herself.

"You must come again, Ada," Mrs. Ferguson said now.

"Yes," Margot repeated somewhat vaguely.

She pitied Ada as much as she could anyone when she herself was so sore. But did mother actually think she could be excited by a call from Ada Rist? Well, she would show the folks this afternoon. She would do *that* much.

Bun was out in front now with the car, honking loudly. Dad, as usual, was afraid they wouldn't be on time, and mother was afraid they would forget the baskets. It seemed to Margot she had known all this from the beginning of time. She went out and got into the car beside Bun.

"You the driver?"

"Yeah, if I can get dad into the back seat. I can make half an hour better time than dad and he won't know it. It's a trick." Bun grinned. "You want to drive?" he generously offered.

Margot shook her head. The words struck on a very tender spot in her memory. She felt the pain of being in any car but their own roadster, hers and Bruce's, driving through the sunshine toward the blue mountains. What if she should startle the folks by telling them that a man had bought a car for her! But they wouldn't believe her, probably. They still thought of Carl and Dorothy as "popular" and Margaret as "unpopular."

Bunny, however, as they got out of the car at the picnic grounds, showed a certain pride. Margot felt that mother was rather uneasy about her looks, about what people would think. Maybe she was a little too exotically "smart." Bun took her arm and led her forward, and Margot could feel that, even if she was his sister, he was half shyly pleased to appear with her before a crowd. It helped her vanity greatly and made her feel suddenly a sort of barren gaiety that would prove capable of anything she chose to do.

Oh Lord, but how familiar was this picnic grove!—the long tables under the heavy trees. What would the old crowd say if they knew she was attending a Rotarian picnic?—and looking forward to it with some excitement? Margot felt her old impatience at the familiarity of the middlewestern atmosphere, the dark green leaves, the concentration upon food, the fat men already licking their chops, and the matrons stooping broad-beamed over the well-filled baskets. The Rotary Anns were entertaining the Rotary boys. But at least Margot was pleased that the foks had got this much more secular. They were worldly, in fact, compared to what they used to be! Yet she had an outraged disbelief. How could she be here? For a moment she struggled with it as if it were a nightmare. She seemed to see, beyond these heavy oak trees, the sunny peace of the pueblo on a cloudless day.

There was the first slight embarrassment of facing the group. But she saw instantly that she was the best-dressed woman there, the most striking. It gave her a rather pleasant feeling of cool world-weariness above her pain. Her mother was saying nervously, with a little laugh, not quite knowing whether she dared to be proud of this daughter, "Of course you know Margaret!"

There was some consolation in seeing the surprised, interested eyes, the calculating glances of the women, no doubt wondering "what she had done to herself." Most of them hadn't known her well, thank God. Dad had become a Rotarian since her day in Belmond. It showed how the folks' prestige had increased that the club had made a pretext of dad's handling of estates to bring him in as well as Richard, two from the same bank. But Ethel Spencer greeted Margot with effusion, taking both her hands.

"Why, Margaret Ferguson! I've been hearing about you from Grimmie. She's wild about you. Isn't she a dear old thing?"

Ethel's bright eyes had taken her all in and approved. Margot had a subtle feeling of being accepted as a confederate in the great business of man-charming. She saw with mixed dismay and satisfaction that even Ethel was not so pretty as she used to be. The gray in her hair was pretty, like the powdering for a fancy dress ball, but the lines in her face were deeper, and the muscles of her throat sagged. "Oh God, does everybody have to get old?" Margot remembered what Aunt Ella had said this morning, that had caused her bitter moments before her mirror. She felt a cold breath of fear. It was not so much satisfaction, after all, to find that she was prettier now than Ethel Spencer.

However, she approved of Ethel's blithe forgetfulness of the duties of women. Ethel had set out the things for herself and Richard, and now she left the other females to decide on which end of the table to place her cake. She thrust her little hand through Margot's arm and went off with her, saying:

"Have you seen everybody? Let's get away from those tables. Aren't these things deadly? My dear, you've saved my life by coming! You look absolutely grand."

Ethel was walking her cleverly nearer the men who were grouped together, loudly jesting, and making sport of being pampered sultans. Mr. Viele was calling out loudly, "Let the women do the work!" Someone else was saying that this was his idea of feminism. "Say, if it is, let's have it every day in the week!"

Ethel murmured, "Have you seen Richard?"

Now he came up to them with alacrity. Margot felt a slight, sardonic smile on her lips. Richard had been eyeing her from a distance.

Ethel said with a subtle intonation, "You remember Margaret, don't you, Richard?"

"Margaret?"

"Margaret Ferguson."

"Well! For the love of—Little Margaret Ferguson! Why, I thought you were just a small child."

"Oh, no, I grew up before I left town."

"You did? Well, where were you hiding? I never saw anything like this!"

She said pointedly, "You never saw me at all!"

464

"What's that?" Richard seized her arm. "Well, I'm going to make up for that right now. Hear that, Ethel?"

Ethel smiled sweetly and ambiguously. Her eyes were wandering, but Margot wasn't interested enough to follow where. They were calling everyone now to come and eat. Some man with glasses and a fat face was getting up and bawling in stentorian tones. Some of the old notables of the town were here—the Vieles, the Hoaglands—but the club was at least half made up of what the folks used to call "the younger married set." It was funny to see the folks among them! Margot herself, when she was a child, used to think of them as almost unholily "fast." But now they looked staid enough.

"Ethel, is this our table?" Richard said significantly.

He drew Margot down beside him. Margot saw that she had been placed in a select group. Mother was looking a little anxious at Richard's attentions. But it must be all right with Ethel there! Ethel did not seem disturbed. Margot didn't know, or remember, who all these people at the table were. It was the "gay table," obviously. But looking down it a little way, she saw a head of white hair that disturbed her with its familiarity. All at once she knew who it was. It was Dr. Redmond! The hero of her dreams. But Richard was keeping up such a barrage of compliment and jaunty innuendo that she hardly had time to look around her.

"Does everybody know Margaret Ferguson?" Ethel asked sweetly and inclusively.

"Sure, everybody does!" Richard answered.

"They don't. Or I don't," Margot said to him in a low voice.

"Don't tell me you want to be introduced to anyone. I couldn't stand it."

"I don't. But I do want to know, where's Gardner Allen?"

"Gardner Allen? Hah? What's the heart interest there? I don't believe I'll show you. Well, there he is. I trust you, Margaret. The gentleman at the next table beside the chocolate cake."

Margot looked. *"No."*

"No, she says! What does that mean? Want an introduction?"

465

"I'll kill you if you attempt one. There's no heart interest. None at all. But he used to be the prettiest boy in our room at school."

"Is that a fact?" Richard asked with vague geniality.

Then he put several sandwiches on her plate, telling her that she was his partner's daughter, and he must look after her.

Gardner Allen! That fat slob! Margot knew that it had lain stealthily in her mind all day, hardening her and making it possible for her to stand things enough to go to the picnic— the thought of carrying off Gardner Allen before the eyes of Mildred. That was the reason for the mysterious eye-shadow, and the yellow silk stockings, and the yellow hat. But when she looked at him now, it seemed too much of a punishment. Yes, he had turned into a sloppy small town slob, with receding hair and rimless glasses, and a deflated, bewildered look. Mildred, of course, was too much for him. Margot remembered that mother had said Gardner wasn't doing so well with the store. Evidently he was not accepted among the élite of the Rotarians. But all the same, she bet it *was* because Mildred was too much for him! There was Mildred herself. And she was just a youngish small town matron. She, who had long been to Margot a symbol for a type of femininity, spurring Margot on to greater efforts! Nevertheless, Margot saw from her eyes, from a certain uneasiness and animation in her glances, that she was still capable of cutting up and was far from resigned to being no longer very pretty. She didn't like it very well, having to sit beside poor Gardner. He was quite out of the hilarity of the "gay table." Margot was confused between feeling sorry for him and still feeling jealously that it was his own fault. Mildred was sore because they had been placed where they were! If she watched, Margot thought, she could no doubt see with whom Mildred was having an affair or whom she was after. She could forgive and even approve that in Ethel Spencer. But not in Mildred Summers! Mildred was up to her old tricks! Margot thought she hated these women most of all who played both sides. But again it was not interesting enough to seem worth while to put herself to the trouble of watching.

Dinner was good, of course. You could count on food at

home, if nothing else. All were loud in their praises of the Rotary Anns. Margot was excited, after all, by Ethel's subtle implication that they two were banded together to have a little feminine delight apart from the housewifely herd. It was pleasing to have Richard's attentions, even while she discounted them. He was jaunty as of old, when she had stared after him, highly impressed, as he went down the street swinging the only walking stick in town. And she had always liked him, in spite of what she knew was the folks' unspoken disapproval, because he had said that she would "work havoc." Well, she hoped that now she was working it!

When they got up, Ethel again thrust her hand through Margot's arm and drew her away. "Tell me about Grimmie," she begged. They went off toward the creek. Ethel said ingenuously, "I love to wander in the woods, don't you?" Margot was amused at the dreamy look of absence with which she contemplated the other women getting to work at the tables. But Margot defiantly approved of it. She felt a savage hostility toward the housewives, and imagined that they were all regarding her with stern condemnation. As a matter of fact little Mrs. Cummings was saying wistfully that she wished *she* could wear yellow; and Mrs. Ferguson was flushed with praises from Mrs. Viele and Mrs. Hoagland in regard to Margaret's improved appearance.

"I always thought Dorothy was a lovely little thing. But I didn't know you had *two* such beautiful daughters! Somehow, I didn't seem to know Margaret so well."

But the men soon drifted near, as always when Ethel was around. Margot thought she saw now that Ethel was tightening the reins on Richard in a subtle manner. Her effusiveness toward Margot had not decreased, but now it was imbued with a certain defensive alertness. No, Ethel never gave herself away, either! She never really got in wrong. When four of them went strolling beside the creek, it turned out to be Ethel and Richard and Margot and Dr. Redmond. And then Ethel thought of something that she wanted in the car and Margot and Dr. Redmond were left together. To be regarded in Belmond as a dangerous woman! She supposed it was a triumph. It

467

afforded her no particular pleasure; but all the same, she wouldn't have been without it. For a moment, she contemplated going out for Richard and giving Ethel a genuine scare, feeling slightly angry at the sense of Ethel's maneuver. But it didn't seem any more worth while than to pretend to the folks that Hec was someone she might marry. Where had he ever got the money to send her those roses? He must have done it when he was drunk. She hated Bruce, because he hadn't even left her the poor satisfactions of her vanity.

Still, there was an ironic pleasure in contemplating the fact that she was in what had once appeared to her as a romantic position, strolling on the river bank (or at any rate, along the edge of the creek) with her old hero Dr. Redmond, while his wife was left laboring among the housewives. Dr. Redmond pretended that he remembered her perfectly. But Margot knew he didn't at all. They made conversation out of this. And she had thought that he would be a romantic lover! Probably because of the ice cream pants, she now thought sorrowfully. There was a curious embarrassment in his manner, which Margot only partly realized came from his uncertainty with her. She seemed to him too young and too well-dressed to consider him very seriously. He felt himself old and shabby beside her. It made Margot angry. She didn't want the person who had once represented all the romance that Belmond had to offer, now to be showing himself such easy prey as this. He laughed nervously at all that she said; and he was only too anxious and pleased when she suggested that she was in need of a drink.

"Come on," he urged her, seizing upon this. "I've got a flask in the car. Probably not so good as what you get there in New York, but it's guaranteed bourbon."

"No. I don't think so. It would be too much of a blow to my folks."

"They won't see us. There are lots of woods around here, aren't there?" He gave a foolish laugh.

"No, I can't be such an undutiful daughter."

"Come, now, don't tell me you're always so dutiful. I've heard about these girls who live in New York!"

"Yes, but haven't you heard you shouldn't believe all you hear?"

"Oh, come now, you've raised a thirst, don't go back on me."

"I may have raised it, but I can't satisfy it."

"Oh, yes, I think you could," he said significantly.

Margot suddenly felt angry, disgusted, and she wanted to laugh. He was a sickening old owl, at that! But it was simply too tiresome for her to go on with it. She would almost rather be back with the Rotary Anns than go on with this. Sorry to dash the good doctor's hopes, but—

"Listen! There must be something going on."

He was reluctant in none too delightful a fashion, but Margot insisted brightly that she must see what it was. "Of course I must!" She was interested in *any*-thing that could happen at a Rotary Ann picnic. Not anything, the doctor reminded her with significance. But she walked quickly out of the woods as if she were a prim virgin disgusted with "advances." Anything to get away from this sorry anticlimax of disillusionment! As she saw the crowd of wives settled to watch the men pack up the baskets, as had evidently been hilariously agreed upon, she thought all at once of her own little kitchen where she had puttered around during the sunny hours of the morning while Bruce painted on the terrace. Her pain was too great for hatred. But it seemed to her that she was shut out from everywhere.

And the villain still pursued her! She told him pointedly that he ought to be packing his basket. He refused to do it unless she helped.

"I help?"

"Well, you're not one of the Rotary Anns."

"No, but I'm exempt. I'm only a daughter."

"Daughters have to work."

"Oh, no, they don't. You must pack your basket, or I'll think you're not a good husband."

Well, it served him right! He had turned all colors. She was disgusted with him, anyway. She saw his wife, suddenly remembering her, a thin, embittered woman with dead eyes; and suddenly Margot wanted to be on her side. Yet she couldn't be on her side, either. Oh, everything was a mess! Margot sat

469

down on the bench beside her mother, glad all at once of mother's soft, bright innocence.

Mildred was there too. Suddenly she caught a glint of nervous hatred from Mildred's eyes. Mildred was sitting and loudly joining in the women's mockery of the men's basket packing. But if Mildred happened to glance at Gardner, her face grew vacant and she looked away. Life was turning out to be even crazier than Margot had supposed it could be! That one little look had told her that Dr. Redmond was now Mildred's Great Moment! That explained his extra gallant and reckless air. So she had now beaten out Mildred after all! Well, she was going to enjoy it. She *would* enjoy it, although her flesh crept with disgust, exactly as if she had been one of the worthy matrons. Oh, yes, Mildred was still in the running! Now coarseness made up for the loss of subtler attractions. It was a poor triumph! A mess all round.

Mrs. Viele said archly, "Margaret, how does it happen you haven't anyone to pack a basket?"

"Oh, we don't know what Margaret has up her sleeve," Mrs. Hoagland said.

She could see that mother hadn't been able to refrain from telling them about the roses! There was a kindly, interested look in the women's eyes, as if they thought they scented a wedding.

Dr. Redmond sat down near her again. Margot ignored him. But he was uneasy about Mildred too. He didn't want to lose out there. He had long ago ceased even the pretense of thinking about his wife. Margot hadn't heard, but she had seen—with a shudder, she could imagine—the dry little colloquy between them when he had gone belatedly to pack the basket.

There were shouts a little way off. They were getting up some races. Bun was at the head of them. He had constituted himself the leader of the crowd of youthful daughters, high school girls, and even younger.

"Oh, I guess the younger set are up to something," Mrs. Hoagland said, settling her bulk contentedly.

Margot watched idly. She felt a sudden searing jealousy. In the light of it, she hated the whole crowd with whom she had been eating and playing, who ought long ago to have forfeited their threadbare title of "younger married set." She saw Dr. Redmond's dissipated middle-age in heartless clarity. Even Richard's jauntiness was affected by a brilliant display of bridge work when he smiled. And she fancied he was using stuff on his hair. She remembered again what Aunt Ella had said to her that morning. Trust Aunt Ella for such sweet remarks! Margot had a cold, senseless fear that life was over. And as she watched Bun, she was acutely jealous of his easy youth, that had come into all the best of things; of his nice, ingenuous face, with the thick mussed brown hair and the freckles, the sleeves rolled up on his arms brown from swimming. The little girls standing taut and set for the race looked unbelievably slim and fresh, in their brief dresses, with their sunburned legs and casual socks. Margot felt all at once marked and dissolute. She looked in cold disgust at her slender, stained forefinger. She felt as if she had played out her part, and another show was beginning.

"Ready! Get set! GO!"

One little girl sprang ahead of the rest and won. Bun brought her up to get her prize from Mr. Viele. Bun was brotherly to all these girls, although slightly patronizing as a college youth. Margot felt again, as she looked at him, the happier auspices under which he had grown up—the kid brother—taking all the privileges she used to crave without suspecting anyone had ever had to fight for them. She saw that the eyes of the matrons had turned from her now and were fixed with smiling admiration upon this little girl. She was a hard little thing, athletic, in socks and sunburn, with her hair pushed carelessly back. Margot remembered how she herself had adored Grimmie, the person from away. But this child was cool and competent, she didn't even see the exotic stranger.

"Who is she?" Margot asked her mother.

"Why, that's Frankie Weyant. Addie's cousin. She goes to our church."

"Goes to our church!" That made it all the worse. Frankie Weyant had sat down with Bun, and was scratching a mosquito bite. As Margot stared at them, and at the next races, she had a strange feeling, like that old feeling of mystic enlargement, and yet different . . . as if the world, while she was not watching, had made another mysterious revolution, and was already turning from her own kind of girl—she was no longer standing at the center—but the light was shining prophetically, like the long light of morning, upon this fresh little hard figure with the tossed-back hair.

The light got dimmer in the grove. It took the folks ages to pack up. Bun was going swimming with the other kids, and then to the movies. Although he had been proud to make his appearance with Margot, she was too aged to be even considered. She would have to go home with mother and dad. As she waited in the thick twilight, she felt as if all the crowd around her were marred and scarred and past anything new. The heavy leaves shut out the sky, and now the mosquitoes were beginning. She had had what she wanted. Nothing could ever take it away from her, but nothing could bring back the wish. Now, at this restless moment of impending dusk, she would have wanted something new if she could . . . only she was impaled on the old, she couldn't . . . She saw ahead of her another night to be got through without Bruce. She had everything, even the belated admiration of Dr. Redmond—with Richard's attentions thrown in for largess—all because she didn't need them now, she supposed, and no longer cared for them. What forces had she set moving, down what mysterious pathways, when she had wished those wishes long ago? Now it seemed worst of all to remember that once she had had "the time and the place and the loved one all together" and could never have them in the same way again. Her fatal faculty for flawed experience—she had dropped back into it again. Those hidden forces, so cruel and so sweet and so hideously just, were no longer working for her. She tried to imagine a time when Bruce would come to her and she would no longer want him. She had to imagine something for the future—find some oasis in that dreary waste. But this wouldn't do, for it would poison, obliterate, make meaningless the happiness she had possessed. She would rather go on wanting him forever. Was that all that lay ahead of her? She thought of the thin, dark, hungry girl who had lived in this place hidden and alone. She felt that girl avenged. And after all—all the happiness, all Bruce's love—that seemed to be the only satisfaction she could really feel . . . and that, so faintly! She remembered the admiring glisten of Ada's eyes. She saw that she had become, more or less, what once she used to dream of being, in those stuffy afternoons at the library, reading other women's poetry—she was returning home after what she used to think of as a great, tragic experience, knowing how she wanted to dress, wearing long earrings. . . . But this was how it really felt. Margot bent down and killed a mosquito viciously. Why didn't the folks hurry? She had pictured herself sitting somewhere, beautiful and torn by life, dressed in filmy black, and writing sonnets that recorded the great experience of her life. She couldn't write of this grinding reality. It possessed her too completely. What was written about had to be held away . . . and if she *could* hold it away, that in itself was a kind of defeat.

The voices sounded like voices on the stage. And yet everything seemed local and small and actual. Margot stared at the women talking together, at the Hoaglands climbing into their big car. All her old ideas, so long, so intensely and jealously cherished, seemed suddenly to go to pot. She admitted to herself, in deflated bitterness, that she wanted nothing but to be with Bruce, and on any terms—she could even have been a Rotary Ann if *he* had been packing her basket. Was that what it came to?—being completely in love with someone? No, she didn't admit that. She still believed that she had had something beyond what these women had experienced. She had taken her love for what it was—anyway, for a time. She shuddered at the perception of the long, bitter, pitched, marital battles, and pressed to herself the sweet, painful knowledge of her love. She felt herself obliterated by it. That had been an exaltation. But if it left her to this blackness . . .

"Well, Margaret, ready to go home? You got sort of left out," Mrs. Hoagland said, coming back for a spoon dropped in the grass. "Whew!" She straightened her back. "I guess all of us wish we were young enough to run races. But I don't think even a prize could tempt *me*."

It was very different—the feeling of reaching New York this time. No one knew that she was coming back. Margot didn't know why she was, herself, except that she couldn't stand it at home any longer. The atmosphere had begun to get strained. Mother couldn't understand the telegrams and special deliveries from Hec—silly ass!—when Margot assured her that she cared nothing about him. She had tried to tell mother carelessly that he was a man she had met on her trip. But mother saw further than that—although not as far as the truth. "But do you think you ought to hear from him so much if you don't care about him?" The folks had pretended they wanted to keep her in Belmond; but actually, if they had ever told the truth, they didn't very well like the prospect of having a grown-up daughter on their hands. The folks had a social life of their own now. They no longer seemed to exist solely for the sake of their children. The folks had accepted it now that Margot had cut away from them. They actually liked her better for it! Dad, now, when he spoke to her, took an entirely different tone. But of course nothing could really bring up her stock with the folks except getting married.

Margot looked drearily around at the other people. A fat woman in a wrinkleless black crêpe (so well corseted that she probably didn't acknowledge she was fat) was now putting on her fur coat. Margot felt set apart in her brown tweed suit. She was returning to New York in the same suit and hat she had worn when she came away. She had gone with her mother and Mrs. Viele on one of the shopping trips to Geneva which were part of the weekly schedule now in Belmond; but long, long past were the days when she had considered buying a dress at Schauffler's Department Store as having attained the heights of fashion. The brown tweed seemed to keep woven within its rough texture the dust of the roads and the smoke of the campfire and the pure sunlit air of the desert. She wore it like a hair shirt. It kept reminding her of all that was past.

There was no interest, only a shuddering aversion, in getting back to New York. The recognitions that she couldn't help making hurt her. The train was passing through the great Jersey marshes, and soon it would reach those awful miles of suburbs. Margot couldn't bear to look. The waste, empty marshes were too symbolic of her own life. She had got past the first stage of acute suffering, and now she seemed to be entering this phase of emptiness. She looked at her love affair from outside, noting all its stages, as if it were a long-drawn-out disease. But when she thought of the cure, everything in her protested. She could not imagine life with no thought of Bruce at all. She tried to tell herself that she had no hope, and she knew disdainfully that her fairy tale was shot to pieces; but she was aware still of a little living, smothered thread of interest because Bruce was in the world.

She picked up her bag and went into the dressing room. Her face in the glass had a darkened, sallow look. Frowning, she took out her cold cream and her cleansing tissues, and then slapped her skin revengefully with a cloth dipped in astringent, according to the best beauty advice. But her face didn't come out all new, as the advice promised. There were dark places still under her eyes. And now for the first time she noted a faint hollow under her chin. No—it wasn't just that she wasn't feeling her best, that she was tired. These things were marked to stay. What Aunt Ella had said was true. She didn't look so young as she used to! She had begun to lose her looks. In a struggle of wild revolt, Margot thought in horror of what this would mean: no longer to rejoice in the tingling smoothness of her body when she rubbed it dry with a great Turkish towel, nor to feel that every change of color in a hat or scarf brought out another aspect of her dark charm. . . . She had thought that everyone could get old but herself. That it was something they could help! Now she felt the dry terror of that inescapable encroachment. The signs had begun. She fell into a hideous recounting of all the marks and ruins of age that she had noted— the way Mrs. Viele's hair had turned white underneath with rusty streaks of red on top; Vanchie's withered, long, delicate throat, yellow and pathetic; the mole with the stiff black hairs and the other hair patches on Ada Rist's heavy chin; the harsh, colorless fuzz on Mrs. Morgan's bleak face; Aunt Ella's hang-

475

ing jowls . . . Mrs. Lowrie's lumpy figure. . . . All these horrors seemed to be lying in wait for her. She saw just how they went. No! She would be an exception. . . . But even now, she wouldn't have dared to toss back her hair carelessly like that child Frankie. She would never look any better than now—and even now she didn't look as well as she had a while ago. She could only hope to stave off, not to improve.

Margot could scarcely bear to look at the mirror as she renewed her make-up. This face didn't represent her any more than had the dark little unfledged face she had seen in just such a glass as this the first time she had come to New York.

She went back to her section to endure the rest of the journey. That dreadful session with the mirror seemed to have killed even the one little spark of feminine interest she had felt that morning when she had noticed that the somewhat good-looking dark man had halted at the entrance to the dining car and at just the slightest look from her would have come to her table. She knew that he was looking at her now. And for a moment she was able to recover a slight, romantic consciousness of herself, dark-eyed and somber, a mysteriously experienced woman sitting alone. But she felt perversely that the doom she had seen for herself was already upon her. Margot felt a queer sense of almost hysterical gratitude at his interest in her, mixed with scorn, as if he didn't have the sense to know that she had begun to lose her beauty. "You ought to see Frankie Weyant!" she had a crazy desire to tell him. Why couldn't she have given him that look? She perceived him as a married man temporarily on the loose. Or why couldn't she have seen him on her first trip when she was dying to create interest in somebody? She felt again that she hated Bruce. She wanted to hurt him by developing an interest in someone else. But because other men weren't Bruce she wasn't able to trump up even that much interest in them.

No, she couldn't stand it, she couldn't live. . . . Before, even when she was miserable, she had always seen the shining outlines of some great experience ahead of her. Her misery was because she had despaired ever of reaching it. There had always been expectation. On her first lonely journey, everything had been before her. Now it was all behind. She couldn't think of anything in the world she wanted, because it wouldn't be equal to what she had had. She could only play out the same story over and over in more and more debased versions, like an old artist repeating himself. That was all, now, that any love affair could be. And when she thought of one so entirely different that it would create experience, the wrench from what she had known was too great. Even her wishes couldn't encompass it. She had wanted to love to the height of her ability, and now she did, and she was bound within those brutal limitations. She could feel nothing beyond a savagely bleak desire to act on necessity. She seemed to see things only for what they were—a flat vision, like that of all the middle-aged, ordinary people she had always despised. Either she must keep this hurt forever chafing, and live with it, or accept the flat emptiness if she tore the image of Bruce out of her heart where it was embedded.

She couldn't bear to look at the other people, who were now closing their bags and putting on coats and hats. She didn't want to have to think of them—her own pain was enough. She felt herself too well informed of the various signs of frustration and contentment.

The train reached the station. Margot stood up in the aisle with the other travelers. If she could be sure that Bruce still loved her, she could feel herself dark and sad and marked out with tragic experience from among them; but if he didn't, then she seemed to be nothing, not even alive. The fat woman in the fur coat was crowded up behind her, eyeing her with curiosity. Margot's eyes, grown hideously sharp, had spotted the drooping lines superficially erased by massage. She believed the other woman was noting with the same bleak, shameful fellowship the marks under her eyes and the new faint hollow under her chin.

Now they were leaving the train. She was coming back all alone, as she had come the first time. But it seemed now as if that had been the romantic entrance—not this. Whom did she want to see? Hope and interest was gone from every encounter. Yet as she stepped down, with the aid of the porter she felt a dizziness of excitement, a sickening alertness, because she was again in the same city with Bruce. She followed the redcap along

477

the noisy platform, unsteady and strange from the long journey. The sense of Bruce was all about her . . . and yet hopeless, almost as if he were someone who had died. She was walking alone and blindly. She had a panic sense of not knowing where she was going.

Margot came into the great light station. The noises of the footsteps dinned in her ears, and the voices surged around her, an indistinguishable uproar. She was here! She was back in New York.

But she couldn't think of anywhere to go. And there was a queer sense of change. She had not yet followed it to its source; but it was as if the light had shifted from morning to afternoon. Her apartment was no longer there. Or at least it was no longer hers. Frances had decided to marry the faithful lover in Cincinnati. Queerly enough, it was Margot's journey that had brought Frances to that! Margot's furniture was in storage. Once again she was a bird of flight. She couldn't have endured to go back to that house and open its green door—to see the chair that Bruce had given her, the bowls that had held his flowers, the books of poetry that had all taken on meaning from his love.

In a sudden fever of impatience, she paid the redcap—just as she had done once before. She sat down on a bench with her bag at her feet, trying to make up her mind where to go. She felt herself dark and alone in the midst of the crowd. Alone, and she could not call on Bruce. Tears were coming to her eyes . . . as they used to come at odd moments, on that hideous after-journey, whenever the noise subsided. Margot touched her eyes with her handkerchief. She remembered that she used to get pleasure even from the choice of a handkerchief in the morning! It seemed to her now that these were the things it was hardest to lose—all the little, irrelevant things, that once had been in-fused with happiness, that now were only tedious necessities, if Bruce was out of her life. It was this emptiness that was the worst! She seemed actually to realize it for what it was, as she sat alone in the great station, knowing that she was in New York but that Bruce was nowhere near. Even the acuteness of suffering, when Bruce had left her, the hours of agony when she had lain alone under the cottonwood trees, had been something to fight against. Then, at least, she could hope for alleviation. What was there to hope for or fight against now . . . in emptiness?

Yet she knew guiltily, deep within her, that she had stared into the emptiness, but not yet entered it. Not truly. It was the sight that appalled her. It was disappointment that made tears keep coming to her eyes. She knew the source of this sweet, sickening excitement, from which her limbs were trembling. She was back . . . she might see Bruce. . . . Wherever she looked it was with the unreasonable hope of seeing him. And she felt bitterly torn between the desire for him and for the recovered sense of life it gave her, and the need to wrench her thoughts and her love away from him entirely and submit to that great emptiness that might slowly bring change and renewal. After all, her life was set in a narrow groove, and not in the wide freedom of eternity—as she had felt after the first fulfillment of love . . . that which had seemed the beginning, and had already been the best. That was where she should have stopped, if her love was to be classic, a perfect memory. But now she cared more for imperfection.

Her heart was beating in a heavy expectancy. She opened her handbag and took out her thin silver compact. She remembered the day she had bought this, before setting out with Bruce—the counter at Best's, the heavy crystal through which the silken scarves, the ribbon corsages of satiny green and orchid, had seemed so magically springlike—and then the crowds, the sunshine, the mingled eagerness and warm languor, the blue sky above Fifth Avenue . . . if she lost Bruce and his love for her, she lost all of these. Having love, you were *part* of things, had the right to walk the earth anywhere. Another memory came over her of a moment when she had taken this same compact out of this same brown bag. It was on top of the pueblo at Tesuque, where they had gone to see the Eagle Dance. Margot could feel again the dry golden heat of the southwestern sun, an Indian sun, burning down on the dusty desert that surrounded the low square of flat-topped Indian dwellings. She remembered the very feeling of opening her purse and taking out the compact—as if the shiny leather were alive with warmth, *belonging* to her. It seemed as if nothing could ever belong to her again— for all things were marred, spoiled, meaningless, if she was not in love. Reality was still in those places where she had lived with Bruce. Margot seemed to herself like a superannuated actress, living in early triumphs, disdainful of aftermath.

She wouldn't be that way! Bruce couldn't have that triumph over her. Not when he had been able to leave her! She would avenge herself by living afterward!

Suddenly she felt how tacky she was in her brown tweeds. In the interval, everything had changed, even the fashions. She perceived with horror the women around her, as if a new race had appeared and preëmpted the city, a race to which she didn't belong. They *were* wearing longer skirts. Almost the hated skirts of her girlhood. It was true! She had seen the dreadful things even on the simpering wax models in the windows at Geneva, but she had refused to believe in them. As she noticed the decorous hang of these smoothly molded skirts, with their reactionary primness, Margot struggled with rebellious fury. They were not *her* clothes any longer. She was horrified at the new make-up, the faces smooth and bald as eggs, with sun-tan powder and purple lips. It made her feel both contemptuous and dated. She clung fiercely to her own individuality.

But all the same, the deep rose-red of her lipstick seemed wrong beside this obnoxious purple. Her legs looked awful to her helplessly displayed beneath her short tweed suit. She saw Frankie Weyant's face again, under the tossed hair, as Frankie turned away after receiving her prize, flushed with running, but hard in structure, like her firm little spine and legs and arms. She saw the cool way in which Frankie ran off with Bun, untouched by her triumph, taking it as a matter of course. It made Margot feel herself by contrast battered, marred, vulnerable. She had had her time. Frankie had the future. But she couldn't even find solace in hating Frankie as she used to rejoice in her hatred of Mildred Summers!

Margot stood up. She must go somewhere. She couldn't stand this inaction. In a bitterness of impatience, she thrust her compact and handkerchief back into her brown bag. There seemed to be a hard, competent insolence in the way these new women passed her, never glancing at her, leaving her out. What she would have given for one of those sharp, appraising glances, perceiving her at once as a rival, someone to be reckoned with—! Now she needed her lover in a new way—his love to make for her a refuge against this strange hateful world in which she no longer belonged. Yet she knew, with a sickening shame and helplessness, that she dreaded to leave the station and go into a room and shut the door, into a place where she would have to be sure that there was no chance of Bruce's seeing her.

A redcap cruising alertly held up his hand and came toward her on a slide. Margot let him take her bag and started to follow him. Suddenly she knew that she could never stand to see that compact again. It belonged to the past. The touch of it was poisoned. She took it hastily out of her purse and hid it behind a crumpled copy of the *Times* near her on the seat.

"Taxi, miss?"

"Yes."

As she followed her redcap, going along with such nonchalant competence, Margot seemed to be walking into panic. Where should she go? Her green door was forever closed to her. She had to follow the boy just as if she were not crazy. They came out into the noise of Forty-second Street. Margot experienced a moment of intense homesickness for the sunny silence of the desert. It was not brilliant today, only cold, with a dead gray sky, people going along shivering, a day that meant nothing.

The taxi driver swung open the door and looked back at her. She had to think of something to say. The only place where she could go was to Grimmie's. She felt the irony of her return to that often-used retreat.

"Bank Street. Do you know where to find it?"

"*Yes*, ma'am. Ain't that over by Seventh Avenue?"

"Yes."

She supposed he *didn't* know where to find it. Taxi drivers always said they knew. Anyway, he was driving her in the right direction. She would make him take her straight to Grimmie's door. She could not bear to walk through any of those familiar streets.

Margot stared out with hard eyes as they drove down Fifth Avenue. She felt a bitter hatred of the noise and the hugeness around the station, making her think of how she was to earn a living. She couldn't go back to her old place. She had stayed away too long. She was unable to look ahead now. She seemed to have lost the thread of her own story.

The taxi went along with jerks and impatient halts. Everywhere, Margot seemed to see these smooth, metallic girls whom she hated. They were like the modern buildings, not individualized, but stylized—with their small smooth heads and necks, like those of the figurines with the gilded or silvered hair in the shop windows. She bitterly pictured Frankie Weyant among them, groomed into urban smoothness. They were the culmination of the metropolitan era. She herself was an individual. "Different," "strange," were words that she had always loved. She could never belong.

It was New York, her city, but all seemed changed. It was full of the noise of tearing down and putting up, the dust of plaster flying. Margot saw with helpless indignation against "business" and "progress" that one after another of the old beloved landmarks was going. They "needed the space" was what people said—the men with brutal mouths and shrewd slits of eyes pictured in the rotogravure section of the *Herald Tribune.* A great wooden framework was built all around the old Waldorf. The interminable noise of feet on the wooden walk under the temporary roof seemed to exterminate the fragrance of violets worn on mink coats that had risen like an emanation of the nineties whenever Margot had walked lingeringly by this place. She felt lost in the mighty steel and metal implacability of this commercial world that cared nothing for her own sacredly held feminine values of beauty and romance and association. She would go back to the pueblo and live with the Indian women. She felt a grinding homesickness again for the uneven, handmade softness of the adobe walls with their rounded corners and their crooked doorways grateful to the hands and the feet. But she couldn't be there without Bruce. Each of those soft-voiced women had her mate. Then where could she go? The expatriates were returning from Europe, driven out by the bitter breath of strange, approaching storms. She was a Middlewesterner. New York had been *her* coast of Bohemia. She seemed to see her little cluster of confederates scattered and put to rout among these stony towers. Jane—where was she?—with her wild, little-girl face faded and brutalized. Frances—turning back to prudence and stability. Marta—defeated by her own generosity. And she could see even Grimmie getting older, a nuisance to these hard young people in the new causes, with her enthusiasms . . . She could have wept over them, in fear and rebellion, the lost children of this ruthless, blind, stony world, who for a few brief years had found among the narrow streets of a left-behind village a kind of tawdry make-believe of the sort of world *they* would have chosen.

Margot felt a wild impatience for the small retreat of Bank Street. She directed the taxi man brusquely. That, at least, kept a kind of twilit dignity. She wanted to see the house where the "original owners," or their descendants, still lived, those almost mythical beings—where every day, behind the clear glass of the front door, stood a great basket of formal flowers. But she felt at bay, in a wild fury, when even here she came upon the noise of riveters and the dust of tearing down and building. It was the old apartment house on the corner with its square, dignified windows, where people said that Willa Cather had lived, and that always made Margot think of the cool clarity of Willa Cather's prose. She shut her eyes. She couldn't bear it. In a tone of suppressed anguish, she told the driver to stop at Grimmie's door. She got out blindly, went up the steps, and rang the bell beside the beautiful tall white door with its carving and its rounded panels. She rang again. There was no click in answer. She felt in despair. Then she heard footsteps in the hall. The door opened. Margot started eagerly to speak, thinking that it was Herbert, the smiling colored janitor. She had a feeling of almost hysterical gladness, that changed into shock, when she saw that it was not Herbert, but a small hard-bitten white man with suspicious eyes.

"Do you know if Miss Grimm is here?"

"Grimm? She don't live here."

"Yes, she does," Margot retorted, with angry impatience. "Don't you see her name on the bell?"

The man came out and looked at the bell.

"Yeah, I see the name. But that apartment's empty."

Margot went down the steps and stood idly for a while on the sidewalk, then walked blindly toward Seventh Avenue.

3

For a little while, the musty retreat of this small room in the old-fashioned hotel on Twenty-third Street seemed to be a refuge which Margot could accept. The long windows had white inner shutters and there was a dark red carpet on the floor. The decorous dignity of the elderly clerk seemed to hold away and make of small account the noise of the riveters all over the city; and the faintly British atmosphere with its deflating coolness, its refusal to perceive what it didn't wish to perceive.

Margot lay across the bed. She had closed the blinds and shut herself into the half-provincial air of the room. She had a sense of bitter triumph over Bruce, since she would never see him in a place like this. She pictured herself living in one of these superannuated streets, in one of the houses with dilapidated bow windows, going to a small, left-behind church with a beautiful ritual, and being noticed by the rector. But even daydreams were no consolation if they did not somewhere contain the figure of Bruce—and hurt too much if they did. She could have stayed where she pleased. She had the thousand dollars with interest that dad had solemnly handed over to her, no doubt having given up the hope of her getting married. He had given the same to Carl and Dorothy at their weddings. The folks seemed to emphasize the fact that they were treating her the same as the other children, if she *had* disappointed them. Margot remembered the forty dollars with which she had first set out to "live her own life" in New York. Now she knew that even a thousand dollars wouldn't last. She still had something left from the money order that Bruce had sent back to her in Santa Fé, and that she had cashed because she couldn't help it; but this she didn't want to spend; she only wanted to keep it and look at it mournfully now and then, hurting herself in various ways by the thoughts derived from its possession.

The sense of loss was too acute! Margot felt she had to get out of this place as out of all the other places since she had left the adobe house by the stream—their home. She put on her felt hat, that now looked unbelievably out of date compared to the sort of winged skullcaps she saw other women wearing. In spite of the cleanly quiet given by the long windows, she could not bear to stay in this silence that quivered and hummed with her restlessness.

Margot felt too confused and disheartened to do anything but sit in the lobby. She had been grateful at first for this old-fashioned atmosphere in which she didn't feel herself such a relic. But now she was aware of the dreary people all around her; old ladies of a past vintage, their white hair done up with shell pins on top of their heads, wearing dark dresses with lace collars, looking like old Englishwomen, narrow, dried-up, old-fashioned, and assured. She felt stifled by age, and she wouldn't accept it. It was like an actual, physical smell of corruption that made her sick. She went out blindly into the open air. For a moment, she was grateful for the noise of the taxis and the street car on Twenty-third Street.

But now it seemed to her that she couldn't bear to stay among *any* people. She felt a wild beast need of solitude. She would find a place where she could be "alone with her memories," she used to picture herself. She would seek her own way of living— she wouldn't submit to new conditions.

The seminary always gave a feeling of seclusion to Twenty-first Street. One of Grimmie's friends used to live on this street, and Margot had dropped into her apartment occasionally for tea—a woman who was following Gurdgieff after having out-lived a stormy affair. Margot felt slightly better. She began to see the faint outline of an after-career for herself. In this street with the seminary chimes, a sort of hiding-place, she could live out the tail-end of experience writing her sonnet series before an 1820 open fire. These houses were not pretend-old, as most of the Village houses seemed now, on streets the names of which

485

had once shimmered in a romantic haze, but now brought only dreariness, visions of little fruit stands with the refuse thrown out beside them, of the poor skinny cats around the garbage cans—Barrow Street, Commerce Street, Grove Street, now she hated all of them. But the numbers by which *these* streets were called seemed to make them anonymous.

The place, however, was *so* genuine that it was depressing and impossible. Margot's fastidious nostrils curled at the ancient smell of frayed linoleum and horrible curtains and bad cooking. The fat, regulation landlady, who snuffled and asked if she was "a single woman," humiliated her by even supposing that she would consider living in that hideous room with the round dining table and the felt cloth and the folding bed. Margot thought sadly, as she left, that she must want the pseudo after all. She turned with a sense of guilty relief at a place with all the familiar marks of inner shutters, arty curtains, and tearoom below.

"Ring Bartholomew for Apartment."

Margot rang. How often had she done this? She was back in the old feeling of being a New York woman on her own. It was what she had always wanted to be. But now she felt horror at its iron grip of familiarity.

A woman—Bartholomew, doubtless—leaned over the dark banisters and called:

"Do you want to see the apartment?"

"Why else would I ring?" Margot wanted to ask.

She went up the sloping, slightly perilous stairs, fighting down and refusing to recognize another of those uprisings of the sensation that she had done this before.

Bartholomew was waiting for her. She wore a faded green smock and drill riding breeches.

"You want to see the apartment? Right-o!"

Margot had to say yes, since she had come this far. But she felt an instant outraged repulsion at the dry, cynical sound of Bartholomew's voice, with its false, bright, valiant cheer, trying to make "the apartment" sound attractive. She hated the whole affair, as in mute derision she followed Bartholomew into the all-too-familiar large front room, with the long windows

486

and the white inner shutters, the white fireplace, the floor with its wide boards painted a dark shiny brown. Too well she knew this woman's gay, sensible, "free" suggestions with their careful note of casualness. "Yes, I know all about it, old girl, you might just as well drop it, we're just buddies together." The smiles which they could not help exchanging revealed with dreadful embarrassment that both were all too experienced in the matter of New York apartments and that each understood too well what the other was up to. Still, they went on with the silly business, Bartholomew brightly overriding Margot's cynical objections, as if the idea of Margot's taking the place was already settled.

"Now it has this little kitchen."

Bartholomew opened the well-known closet door revealing the two-burner electric stove on the shelf, with a crumpled, half-used breakfast food box and a coffee can on the shelf above it. It was apparent that the usual burner was out of commission.

"It's rilly all that one person can use—if you're alone. There's an *aw*-fully good tearoom downstairs. I know the woman who runs it and she *does* have very good food. This is all we need for two, and we have even cooked chicken on our stove!" Now Bartholomew was trying to put over the advantage of *not* having a real kitchen, knowing well that neither of them believed it. "Gas is rilly unsafe in these old houses. And we do all insist on our old houses!" Margot gave a loathsome, answering smirk. "Electricity is so much cleaner, and we like it *so* much better. It's awfully jolly to cook this way, everything within reach, you know?"

And seeing a protest coming, she added quickly, cheerily, "And I must say the fireplace does work!"

Why make a protest, anyway? The poor female had saddled herself with this house, thinking doubtless she would have "freedom to write" or something of the sort, and now her living depended on finding all its disadvantages enticing. And what was the use of a kitchen when Bruce would not come for dinner on a rainy night, folding his thick coat smelling woolly of moisture, and drawing off his heavy gloves as he had done that first afternoon in Marta's tearoom, smiling at Margot's little card table in front of the fire with the red and black fringed cloth and the black candles? Margot mutely let the demerits of the place be shown to her, although she disliked it more and more bitterly.

Bartholomew admitted with wistful archness, "Now, there isn't a private bawth. But there are only three of us to use it. It's rilly the same thing, you see. We do try to be coöperative."

The carefully hasty glimpse which she was vouchsafed of the littered "bawthroom," with the copper blossom of the electric heater about the ineffectiveness of which she could be told nothing, finally enabled Margot to find a handle for refusal. It was apparent that in spite of the "coöperativeness" of Bartholomew and her partner, Bartholomew was all too used to having a refusal on these grounds. She had a fatalistic, although martyred, smile, suggesting that Margot had done her great injustice. The door of the room which "we" evidently occupied was open, adding to the sum of Margot's distaste, with its sight of a feminine domestic life in the midst of wabbly painted furniture, unwashed teacups, and India prints.

At last Margot was able to flee this place also—to get away from her unadulterated understanding of the life of the two women, with whom, thank God, she wasn't going to coöperate! This one, in her drill breeches and her synthetic accent who was taking Margot's "I don't believe it's what I want, I don't care to share the bath" with that martyred smile, was valiantly upholding the part of the man. Margot refused to admit the sense of Bartholomew's pathos in that rôle, her unripened body in the smock and the riding pants, her thin little hands with the skin darkened, the deep orange stain on her delicate forefinger, the hair chopped off straight across the forehead in a Dutch cut too young for the faded face beneath it, with dark circles of perverse dissipation beneath eyes that embarrassed Margot with their look of suffering intelligence—like the eyes, somehow, of that awful dog at home, that kept coming over from next door, and that mother detested and pitied too much to drive away, with the eyes begging you not to observe the femaleness wished upon her all too generously by an unkind God . . . except that the dog's eyes were dull and mute and Bartholomew's were so bright with painful intelligence. Margot fled down the stairs, away from even the memory of the crêpy thinness of the delicate throat above the mannish collar of the smock, the small, distended cords that made Margot ache with a sense of strain—as if the love which infused this person was too rarefied, too thin, felt on the naked nerves. She was only less awful than the sight, for a moment, of her "coöperator" in the doorway of "their" room—full, soft, discontented, babyish and faded, with cheeks that had once been a blooming high school pink and were now cushions of tiny red veins intertwined in a minutely intricate leaf-veining, the fuzz of fair hair pushed back in the girlish dishevelment of 1910 which had set the type for this girl . . . as a later time, Margot felt with horror, had set it for herself.

"O God, I couldn't live there!"

To live in a place like that, and no longer to have Bruce! Now she was oppressed by the seedy quality of Twenty-third which used to make it romantic. Those windows with diamond panes in shoddy rooms, with each a large bed with dubious covers, a gummy gas-plate set on an old commode, inhabited by broken-down actors!

Margot felt damp with horror at the thought of all these places. Their familiarity was not a refuge but a kind of disgraceful admission. That aging atmosphere, the wide boards so hard to sweep, in which fluffy strands from the rugs were always dingily caught, the gritty dust collecting in the panels of the shutters, the drift of cold ashes under the grate—she had felt that she was getting away from all these things (which vexed the fiercely orderly instinct inherited from Grandma Ferguson) when she had left with Bruce.

And yet there was nowhere to go. She was lost. She didn't seem able to think of anywhere else to look, and she couldn't bear the idea of the hotel—that was shot. To find new life!—in this cold, bright air. But she seemed too dull to seek for it. There was only Twenty-fourth Street left, a final hope. Perhaps she could stand a lonely life in one of the little brick houses with iron-lace balconies. There was a small dark green one that she remembered. Margot trudged over to Twenty-fourth Street, although she was tired and cold, and her head ached. But when she got there, the cupboard—no, the whole block was a gaping hole!

Margot went back on the run. But she had the sight of a hag on a street corner, and although she went quickly past the old woman, she had seen with horrible acuteness the marks of hopeless, shifty age and failure, as the poor creature wheedlingly held out pencils that she knew no one wanted to buy. Margot could feel already the end of her thousand dollars. She saw herself in varied hideous form in all the superannuated women she passed. And Chelsea was full of them! With face set, she took her key from the dignified clerk. She went up to her room and threw herself again on the bed. She thought of the people who had been for a brief time her companions in rebellion—all the Lost Children—like pigeons ousted from the old buildings where they had built their dubious nests and felt for a little while at home. Now she saw Bruce as belonging to the brutality of the money-making side, and she felt that he was a stranger.

She couldn't live in one of those old places, anyway. That was outlived. There would be no more romantic joy nor meaning in making one of them her own. Margot felt a desperate need for something new and selfishly satisfying to blot out of the faces she saw the stamp of unfulfillment, that she recognized, and would not share.

She lay quiet on her hotel bed. But now she loathed Bruce's wife with a deadlier hatred than she had ever known. She started up, damp and trembling—almost with the sense of having committed a crime. She would never give Bruce children. He didn't want children from her. She was something else to him. She was just what she had wanted to be. The fragrance, the disturbing gleam, the thing that was "different." Why must these things come back upon her, when she had lived through them once with so much pain? But she felt now, far more bitterly than before, the depth of the wound which Bruce's reluctance had given her. . . . She craved something new, something that had none of herself in it. She had given herself away and she didn't care for the thing back. She understood why women wanted children, when their own beauty was going, their own lives were lived out. She could have endured Frankie Weyant, if Frankie had been her own, succeeding to the throne which she had vacated willingly, because the time had come.

No, she wanted nothing. She hated all feeling. And what good had *she* ever done mother?

Margot sat up on the bed. She looked around the room with eyes of hatred. She was fooling herself with this atmosphere of preserved decorum. She was one of the outlaws.

She hated herself too much to be alone. And it would be an anticlimax to make way with herself, now that she had outlived the night when Bruce had left . . . after all her fine feelings then, that now she seemed to have forgotten! But whom was she to call, when she couldn't bear the sound of any voice but one —and not that? It was a queer fate she had suffered so far, to be defeated by having every wish come true! If Bruce came back to her, would *that* turn out to be defeat? Anyway, it was too late for victory. She felt too far away from all the old crowd. But those whom she had known later, when she and Frances used occasionally to step out together, seemed too easy and successful—the Yale boys who were Frances' friends, who all had good jobs, and wore the right kind of neckties. They would be in favor of the "progress" that was ruining *her* city. Or, if not exactly in favor, they would run easily along with it, too well-bred to care.

Margot sat down gloomily before the telephone. Suddenly she thought with longing of Daggie's little apartment where she had spent other wretched hours. She sat a long time in front of the telephone until she was afraid that she could never take down the receiver. It was like calling a dead letter office, almost. But the number suddenly said itself from somewhere in her mind. And then, she heard Daggie's mild voice answering her.

"Daggie! This is Margot."

"*Margot?*"

"Yes, I don't blame you if you've forgotten me." Her lips trembled.

"Why, my darling, to forget you is beyond my powers. Where shall I find you after all these barren years? *Where?* No, sweetheart, I don't ask how you got there. That you call me again is the important point. Well, be as hideous as you like." Tears overflowed her eyes as she listened to his comforting tone. "I'll put on my worst tie. We'll be hideous together. Anyway, I love you for your beautiful soul. Sit in the lobby among the old ladies, and await your escort, who is overjoyed. You will recognize me by the red carnation in the buttonhole."

They got out of the taxi in front of the house where Daggie lived. So much in New York had changed—but there it was, just the same as always, the decrepit old red brick house.

Margot cried, "Oh, Daggie, I'm so glad you still exist!"

The times that she had done this before were around her like a dream—when she had stood, just as she was doing now, shivering a little, and waiting while Daggie fitted his key into the heavy door. "Hurry, Daggie," she begged childishly. "I'm freezing." She was eager to get up to his apartment. Now it seemed that *there* was her true refuge. She had always come to Daggie when she was downhearted or out of a job. After a party, in those ancient days of Christopher Street, she had come and roused Daggie, because she wasn't ready to settle down yet, had made him get out of bed and listen to her experiences with his amused, gentle, Olympian tolerance. She was returning to her old haunts. It made her think of that queer little nest of elderly people that she and Mary Phipps and Rube had turned up once in a basement on Fourth Street when they were out to make a "tower" of the Village.

Margot followed Daggie up the rickety stairs at which she had always fastidiously wrinkled her nose.

"Well," Daggie said, looking back at her, "the old place still hangs together."

"I think it's enchanted. It was ready to fall to pieces when I left, and it's at exactly the same stage now."

"Thank you, my dear, for suggesting that I exercise the spell —as I trust you *are* suggesting. Or perhaps you are likening me to a Sleeping Beauty? These rooms have sheltered many a sleeping beauty in distress. Sometimes, I do admit, the soundness of the sleep helped on a bit, by sundry potions."

Daggie opened his own door, the ugly, brown-painted door with its horrid little paintless scars. They stepped into the dark little hole between the living room and the kitchen that Daggie called "the antechamber."

"Welcome back."

He turned and put his arms around Margot. She lifted her face gratefully. As she felt the touch of Daggie's lips, tender, appreciative, with the reserve that came from the wide, unassuming knowledge that he could not step out of his fatherly rôle—something sadly humorous about it—she broke into crying and hid her face on his shoulder. Daggie was the one person on earth whom she didn't mind knowing how miserable she was. How *any*thing she was. They stood for a long time in the antechamber. Daggie took off Margot's hat and gently stroked her hair. She could confess everything in her tears—her loneliness, the predatory solitude in which she lived, what she hated and feared in herself and yet stubbornly clung to and defended, her happiness and her disillusions. Here was the one touch of continuity with what she had left. She felt—for the moment—that she had come home.

"You mustn't go away again," Daggie chided her gently.

She shook her head against his coat. She had wet his flowing tie with her tears. But Daggie wouldn't mind. He would lend coat, tie, anything, to the needs of distressed damsels. Margot was ashamed to speak. But she was confessing in silence her knowledge of Bruce's influence over her, of how she had forsaken Daggie. It was all that Daggie would ask for. The red carnation that he had worn when he came into the lobby of the hotel—handing her its mate—was the one little humorous touch of rebuke, delicately suggesting that it was so long since they had met she might not otherwise recognize him.

"Not entirely away," Daggie added.

He gently lifted Margot's head. She sought blindly for her handkerchief and he gave her his.

"I always have a fresh handkerchief for my lady friends. Never can tell when it may be needed."

Margot gave a shaky laugh. Daggie turned on his light,

shaded with the same foolish pink silk scarf, which he said he had put there to give a softening glow to tear-stained faces.

"I'm going to use your powder, Daggie. I see you still have some."

"The supply is from time to time replenished."

Margot combed her hair and powdered her face, remembering, with loneliness and remorse, the silver compact she had left at the Grand Central.

"Now, while the lady is repairing the ravages caused by emotion at greeting her long-lost friend, I, according to promise, will investigate the cellar."

Daggie came back, after a few moments, with a gilt-tipped handsome bottle, saying that the occasion demanded his best. Margot turned away from the mirror with quick, defensive self-distrust.

"I look like a hag!"

"Oh—no, no."

"What is it then?" she tragically demanded.

Daggie put his small fingers under her chin and tilted up her face, which he slowly considered.

He admitted, "You're changed a little."

"I told you I looked like a hag!"

Daggie set down the bottle. He put his arms around her again. He had less of his humorously dispassionate manner than Margot had ever seen. She felt closer to him.

"You do look changed. You aren't the little thin, dark, intense damsel who used to climb these stairs. You always seemed to have a fiery coal hidden somewhere, ready to burst into flame. Well—now it's burst! And a few things have succumbed to the fire."

Margot looked down, brooding. Her sullen lips quivered. She felt gratitude for his understanding, along with the old rebellious sense that no one but herself *could* understand.

"Why, Margot," Daggie said, chiding. He shook her slightly. "You were a girl—now you aren't. It's what you asked for."

She shook her head, thinking of that hard little untouched face of Frankie Weyant's. The old rebelliousness flared up.

She said in sudden bitter jeering, "*Men* don't think so. They

494

want girls to take experience, so long as it's with them, but never to show any sign of it in their looks! Why do you suppose those awful women talk over the radio, telling how to keep *every line* off the face—to be just as smooth as a piece of paper —the way girls' faces have to look in those awful hats they're wearing this year! No. Men want to *give* a girl experience, and then cast her off for a new one if she shows any of the results!" Margot stopped, confused—because *she* had been the new one. But all the same . . .

Daggie shook his head, making a face. "Why hit me? I'm on your side. Scratch any girl these days and you'll find a feminist."

"Scratch Louise and you won't find one—you'll find what men really like!"

"Tut, tut!" He gave her a little shake again. "That was long ago."

After an angry, shamed moment, Margot reached for the handkerchief again.

"Wasn't it what you wanted, my dear?" Daggie asked her gently, commiseratingly.

She said fiercely, "Yes, it *was*. That's just the trouble! I know what you want to think of Bruce, and you're wrong. But the Louises are the ones who always get men in the end! You can't beat their game.—And I'm not thinking of Lee, either, with any tender remembering passion, so you needn't think that!"

"Well," Daggie said, "they haven't got your old Daggie. He belongs to the other hussies."

Margot turned and hugged him fiercely. He gently put her arms aside.

"Never mind, Margot. I don't count myself. You are safe with me," he added, taking his old tone. "Come." He gave her a little push. "We will have our liqueurs in the drawing room."

They went into the shabby old living room. As Daggie made the fire with neat care, Margot wandered around emptying ash trays and shaking up pillows.

"I never can see," she scolded, "why, when you can mix drinks perfectly and make such a beautiful fire, you can let your house get into such a mess."

"Ah," Daggie said. "That's where it needs a woman's care."

"But you *do* make a lovely fire," she said luxuriously.

"Yes, I'm real handy," Daggie admitted, as he sat crouched on his heels. "That's why my family's ashamed of me. I take after the ne'er-do-well uncle who became the village handy man."

"Did you really live in New England, Daggie?" she marveled. "I can't believe you *ever* lived anywhere but here."

"Thank you, sweetheart. But some day, no doubt, you can ponder the dates of my entrance and exit in a New Hampshire burying ground. The tallest stone in the cemetery is marked 'Daggett'! I fear I shall attain to the family dignity in death."

Margot was staring at him soberly. Would *she* end up in the family lot at home?

"But let us not think of my demise," Daggie said. "Let us be cozy."

Margot waited while Daggie drew up his old couch in front of the fire—that old couch with its faded blue velvet cover, on which so many rebellious girls had sat, had wept so many tears, had received the comforting clasp of Daggie's small, neat hand. This place was just the same, yes, just the same. Margot felt a sad rejoicing to see the old chairs with their hollowed seats, the books overflowing the shelves and piled up on the floor, the ancient battered ash trays. And yet there was a queer, New Englandish sense of order about it too. The dilapidated, tumble-down house was a little center of stability and security in the shifting Village world.

"Come. Let us seat ourselves and be Romans," Daggie said.

He forced Margot gently down on the couch, and again put his arm around her. The blue cover was pitted all over with tiny brown cigarette holes. The ashes ground into the velvet were turning it to gray. But this room, and wherever Grimmie lived, Margot thought mournfully, were the only retreats to which she could come. At home she was a visitor on good behavior. The firelight flickered over the couch, seeming to hush even the noises of the cars in the street outside. Daggie ripped the gilded tip off the bottle of cointreau and filled the two small glasses. Margot felt the bliss of the first keen, orange-flavored sip. Daggie set the little glasses and the bottle comfortably on the table beside them. The thin blue smoke rose from their cigarettes. Margot gave a sigh. She stretched out and lay with her head in Daggie's lap. She felt that in that first embrace her wretchedness had been confessed. Daggie stroked back her glossy hair. He might come upon that first white hair for which she was always looking, Margot thought with an inward shudder. But she didn't care. There must be one place where she could be simply what she was. Daggie told her to make the sign when she wanted more cointreau. He would hold the glass to her lips.

She murmured at last, "Where are people? What's become of everybody? I don't feel as if anything in New York is the same." She stared tragically up at Daggie; and he smiled, partly at the tragedy, partly at a pleasure of his own in following the petal curl of her lashes.

Daggie said, "It is one of those periods in the course of human events when the elements order a scattering. Something is upon us. I know not what, I'm too old to know. I have decided to settle down quietly in my superannuation and hope for a visit from Margot now and then."

"But isn't anybody around?"

"Nobody. You were the disrupting force, Margot. When you left, the crowd broke up."

"Where's Mary?" she asked. She let her hand hang over the couch, watching idly the smoke of her cigarette, listening dreamily to Daggie's account—upon which he was very ready to start—told with the kindly, enjoying pessimism with which he treated all mortal affairs.

"Mary? Mary," he said, "has gone, so to speak, the way of all flesh. She has joined the great company of American matrons. In short, Mary is married."

"Not Rube?" Margot said, with big eyes, "Not the pro-*fes*-sor?"

"*Not* Rube. The professor is the man. After youth's fitful fever, Mary will find her solace in faculty teas."

"I don't blame her," Margot said bitterly. "Rube thought she could dangle around him forever."

"Is this our upholder of anti-matrimony?" Daggie marveled.

497

"I'm not an upholder of *mat*rimony. I hate it. Only . . . I like to see *one* man get the wrong side. But I can't bear Mary," Margot said, in quick revulsion. "I know just what she's like by now."

"Tut, tut," Daggie said again, and stroked her hair.

"Well, go on," Margot said grimly. "I want to hear all the worst."

"The affairs of our friends out in Croton," Daggie said, with a slight effort, "are, I regret to state, in one of those tangles that can only be described as a mess. Hammie—you have never known Hammie?"

"I know Bobbie."

"Then you more or less know Hammie. And you can guess the rest. I trust I may even be excused, by your inference and intuition, from going into the details of the great new venture by means of which Hammie is to nurse his genius in a secluded room on the proceeds of the tearoom which Marta has instituted in Croton? New place, new man, new art—in this case, the genius is a musician. But the tearoom remains. Hammie, it is doubtless unnecessary to remark by this time, being the central figure of what I referred to as the mess."

"And if you want me to, I can imagine the mess!"

"But wait. Others of our friends come into it."

"*Others?*"

"Several others. *I* came into it at one time, although not, of course, as a principal. I am never a principal," Daggie said reflectively, with a smile. "That may be why I look forward to my funeral. And even then, I shall be only one of the Daggetts —the one who hasn't been at home for a long while. Well, that will be my distinction. . . . But our friend, Marta, with another of her generous impulses which, as ever, proved ill-advised, suggested that little Jane come out to add to the upkeep of the tearoom—and the musician—Marta being overcome by the fact that Jane had fallen out of her one hundred and fiftieth job. Needless to say, Jane went! It was then with great expedition discovered by Hammie that music needed inspiration as well as mortal sustenance. Jane proved compliant. The matter was then discovered by Marta. Shall I add, with the most intense surprise?

Tears, tempests—in fact, many things followed, including a very unfortunate infant, which—I have not yet unraveled the sex, and what matter, since it is born to trouble, whether or not —but which appeared to me, while I was still acting a minor character part in the mess, to be brought up entirely on cigarette smoke and dubious milk."

"But Daggie, Marta's infant?"

"I believe, Jane's."

"Don't you know? Didn't *any*-body know?"

"I believe I took it as part of the mess. At any rate, the little child brought another generous impulse out of Marta's all too capacious bosom. When I withdrew—more firmly than has often been my wont—the household in Croton was composed in some involved fashion of what appeared to be the following: Marta, Jane, Hammie, the infant, an unfortunate but none too savory damsel named Vi, a sad kitten, a hungry police dog, and in some way better not to be examined—and I believe, at a little distance—Bobbie! At that point I withdrew. Music and poetry must fight it out."

"But you'll have Jane back on your hands!"

"No doubt. I may even have the infant. Little Jane has a great capacity for lighting upon her feet."

"Until she begins to get older!"

"Oh, if you're going to think about what happens when damsels begin to get older, you should never have left Belmond, Iowa."

"Poor Marta," Margot said, brooding. She gave a little shiver. "I suppose she supports the crowd."

"To the point that they *are* supported," Daggie said judicially, "yes."

"People ought always to set a price on everything they do, I suppose!"

"Well, love is its own reward, like virtue."

Margot shuddered. She threw her cigarette into the fire.

"And a mess," Daggie continued thoughtfully, "is all too frequently the reward of freedom." He had his small, Olympian smile.

"Can't you tell me something more encouraging, Daggie?"

"What!" He looked down at her. "Has Margot come to ask for the happy ending? Is *that* the outcome of experience?" She moved restlessly. "Oh, yes, I can tell you many a happy thing. Your old friend Lee, for example, I recently heard by roundabout methods, is out in Hollywood, waxing—and probably waning—rich. He writes that stuff in the gossip sheets."

" 'Is Garbo's Seclusion a Hoax?' " Margot asked satirically.

"That's the stuff. Tells how Jean Harlow in real life is a flower with the gold dust still intact. Meanwhile, it gives him a chance to dine with lovely ladies and hear how their marriages are going on the rocks. A very fine life for Lee! There's your happy ending."

"Well—" Margot muttered, staring at the fire, "Louise didn't get him, anyway!"

"You vicious little hound!" Daggie said with pleasure.

"Well, I can't help it."

Margot lay looking back at that old unresolved discord. She was surprised to feel that it still faintly rankled. Lee had always despised himself for not being the American big business man he loudly derided and that the sensitiveness in him hated. And he had wanted Louise because she was the business man's prize—wanted her, and groveled to her, and despised her . . . and now it was easy to imagine him in Hollywood growing fat upon his surrender to cynicism.

Daggie repeated, "Come, come, that was long ago." He tried again to look into her face. "If you don't like that happy ending, I can give you another. You have not forgotten the good Dr. Finkbein? Then you will be glad to hear that the worthy gentleman is flourishing. The old house in Thirteenth Street was finally sacrificed to the path of progress, and the Doctor —of Philosophy—forced to seek another home. At that time, with the proceeds of an amazingly successful book having to do remotely with the subject of the sexes, the Doctor suddenly decided to take an apartment, and—although without the customary female aid—discovered within himself an unsuspected taste for domestic life. I hear that he purchased his domestic tools in the ten cent store, so many that he had to convey them home in a taxi, thereby reducing economy. Now, I believe

—although I have evaded bringing it to the test—the Doctor is occupied in asking his friends to dinner. It would be worth your while to go, if well fortified before you start. If for no other reason than to see the apartment! It is beautifully, even magnificently furnished—in spots. The principal adornment, for no reason that I have ever discovered, is a pier glass belonging to the Astors. Imagine our Doctor arranging tie and beard before the pier glass in the morning. I never saw a bed in the place. I don't know where, or if, the man sleeps. He is writing a book, of course! Now, isn't that a pleasant story?"

Daggie looked down. He said tenderly, "Margot, you're sleepy."

She shuddered and grabbed hold of him. "Oh, Daggie, I can't bear to go back to that hotel!"

"Don't go back, darling." He rocked her. "Many a damsel has sheltered here in distress. I do have a bed—even if no pier glass—and I will go even now to prepare it for you."

"I don't want the bed," Margot protested childishly. "I want to stay here on the couch. Can't I?"

"Certainly, my dear. But I will wake you up when I go through in the morning. Remember, I am a business man, and up with the clock."

"I don't care. This is the only room I can stand."

Daggie embraced her gently. She saw that he looked pleased. His cheeks were even a little flushed. He laid his face against her smooth hair.

"I'm glad to have my little Margot back. All my other damsels have forsaken me. I was beginning to look forward to a lonely age. Are you going to stay now?"

She leaned against him, but didn't answer.

Daggie had gone to bed in his little room that contained just a cot, a chest of drawers, and an improvised closet. He had given Margot a pair of his pyjamas, with surprising lavender stripes, and left the bottle of cointreau near her "for consolation in the morning hours." Margot lay on the couch watching the last of the fire. The firelight played on the piles of books, on the cointreau bottle, on the unexplained picture of an austere New England woman that hung, framed, on the wall. Was that what had given Daggie his wistful, humorous tenderness for all the rebellious girls, for Jane with her wild, tawdry prettiness . . . the firm, sharp, unrelenting outline of that face? Daggie's own history was shyly hidden within the placid incongruities of this room, with inherited reticence, only a gleam of it shining here and there. The paintings done by Daggie's friends were all bad. About all his friends—even herself!—there was that chosen touch of tawdriness. Yet the room itself was somehow cool and clear. There was a mysterious consolation in the place.

But all the same, she was restless. The feeling of having come home was leaving her. She felt torn apart from Bruce. The physical need for him stamped the night with anguish. Daggie thought that her affair with Bruce was over. But it was never over. Any more than Daggie would ever really extricate himself from Jane's messes! His secret had shone for a moment in the strangely shy tone of his voice when he had hardened himself to bring in Jane's name—a secret that he himself looked at with quizzical dubiousness queerly infused with reticent pain. Margot looked again at the austere New England face in the dark oval frame. Perhaps Daggie needed Jane to complete himself, as she needed Bruce.

She turned from side to side—picked up a book, read a little—impatiently put it down, bitterly recognizing something grotesque in her suffering. She hadn't provided for this—and had thought herself so darkly wise! The early gray light came in on the battered ash trays, the aged couch cover, the chairs with their deep hollows, the dingy floor. Daggie was a thread with the past. But the thread was frayed, the past itself discredited; and now only the central pattern mattered. Daggie had won, by his philosophy and restraint, an eternal place on the margins. This was no refuge, either. Margot left a note for Daggie, and went out into the flat, mysterious chill of the early morning air.

4

Margot went straight on through the living room and into the bedroom, dropped her packages on the dressing-table bench, and flopped into the easy chair. She closed her eyes for a moment with a feeling of rest. She could shut herself in from that tormenting alertness she felt whenever she was out on the street and had to fight, angrily and yet fearfully, against the hope and expectation of seeing Bruce. Now she felt a sullen, deep pleasure in being up here hidden and alone.

Last night, it had seemed as if she couldn't bear it here in K's apartment. She felt as if she had thrown the die and thrown it against herself. Coming here seemed to mean that she had accepted all Katherine Griswold had said, the day when they had luncheon together—not in one of the old candlelit tearooms run by romantically ambitious women, but in the dining room of a Madison Avenue hotel. Naturally—K's treat.

"Well, Margot," Katherine said, with what sounded like satisfaction—funny how many people seemed to feel satisfaction about it!—"you're back. I heard something about it from Grimmie. Well, my dear, you don't expect those things not to get out. We all know everything about each other." K gave a hasty sweep of the hand.

"Take it as that," she went on. Katherine did always have to be didactic, but with such crisp assurance that her friends sat mute, impressed at least for the time being. "You've tried it once and got it over." Margot's eyes shifted. Her sulky lips trembled slightly. "Let me tell you, Margot—" K took a fat English cigarette, moderately expensive but plain, out of her smooth leather case, and tapped it efficiently. "I've been through it all once. It's a good thing to have done, and then—that's that." Margot's dark red lips took on a sulkier curve, as K leaned on her elbow and calmly blew smoke. But she couldn't help listening, with a kind of resentful fascination, while K went on with the trenchant platitudes that were her stock in trade. "Better to have learned now than later that we all have to depend on ourselves ultimately."

When it came to "the sweet," as K had learned to call it, after various vacations abroad, each one making her more disgusted with the way things were done "over here"—K had looked and refused, making Margot feel still more guilty. Katherine was thinking now of her figure. After years of brisk altruism, and early excursions into social work, K had now decided to become strictly commercial, rationalizing the decision, of course, in her usual convincing way. She grew confidential—for Margot's good—as she drank her coffee and smoked another of her well-packed, firm cigarettes.

"I'll tell you, my dear, I went through a very difficult time last spring. Of course, it was a transition period. But I came to several new conclusions. And I hope you perceive the result."

The chief conclusion being—platitudinous as all the others, but just as crisply and convincingly uttered—that we live while we live.

"I think Grimmie helped me to it."

"Grimmie?"

"Yes, in effect. I mean I have an aged parent too. I am also the unmarried daughter. I made up my mind right then and there, when Grimmie toddled home, that when the call came for me, I was going to be in such circumstances that *I* could dictate to my brothers. I'd send more than they did to mother, so they could have no kick coming, but as for going back to the little gray home in Michigan, it wouldn't do. Just one argument would work with them, and I was going to have it. I was going to be able to say to them: Look here. You boys earn so much? Well, *I* earn *so* much. And it would be enough more to shut those boys' mouths and make their eyes bug out. Let me tell you right here, Margot—that's the only talking-point that counts."

And then K went on with some more of her original wisdom, under which again Margot sat recalcitrant but dumb. We were living in a mechanical age. All right, quit hugging old fireplaces, and have the benefit of it. Her friends could keep their India prints and their rickety four-posters. But as for her, she was going modern. She was going to reduce her hips and never be caught in a peasant dress again. Suddenly she had waked up to the fact that she wanted an electric refrigerator, not a box outside the windows, and plumbing that could work without gasping out a whole symphony of tunes. First she had thought she would be psyched, when she had begun to get dissatisfied. Then she had found that a modern apartment and beauty culture were a lot more fun and no more expensive. She had set out to beat the game.

"You see what's happened to Grimmie. Come back? Pooh!" Katherine snubbed out her cigarette. "Her mother will outlive her. I don't care how old she is. She'll live to be a hundred and fifty if need be. After successfully getting rid of her ugly duckling, by pecking at everything Grimmie did, she now plays the one trump card to draw her back in the end. If Grimmie'd had a real job, she wouldn't have gone. She could have laid down terms. Oh, yes, there are half a dozen others, all living nearer by. But they're married, my dear, and 'have their homes.' The old lady would have to knuckle to *them*, not they to her, and well she knows it. That's the only job of the single woman of the family! She's always lying around loose, supposedly, to take care of those who've already had full lives. No. Each man has to go out for himself *some*-how. You're none too young to get onto that, my dear; and my advice to *you* is, to start right in. This is the psychological time."

"I did go out for myself when I went away with Bruce."

"Pooh!" Katherine pushed back her coffee cup. "*That's* not what I mean."

Margot slowly opened her eyes. Her feeling of refuge was shot through with the irony that gleamed, now, through everything. The inevitable older woman had appeared ready to shelter her in one of her transitions—most strangely, this time, in the form of K Griswold. God moves in most mysterious ways His wonders to perform. Margot had met Katherine, just as once, years ago, she had met Grimmie—and here she was, dwelling in luxury in K's apartment, and all fitted out with a new costume and a new job, and—supposedly—a bright new set of convictions. Because, of course, K wouldn't bother with her if she didn't think *that*.

It was light in Katherine's apartment high up above the street. For a moment, as she saw its chaste, hard, modern simplicity (which she had now presumably accepted) Margot felt that same old grinding, romantic nostalgia for the dark interior of the pueblo with the pattering feet and intimate, soft, bubbling laughter of the Indian women. She wished she was back in Grimmie's room with the candlesticks and clutter of "little foreign things," the helter-skelter of cigarette boxes and used wineglasses on the table, and the paneled walls with the paintings all hung a little tipsy. She couldn't go back to Daggie's. It made her sore and guilty when she thought that she hadn't called him and told him she was here, thus evading his gentle belief that she had returned to the old rebel fold. But she had to keep hold of this brittle new promise that had half dragged her out of her pain. She suddenly felt with panic that she had entered this modern hardness. She felt of her new sleek haircut. She already had a job! The first craven relief had begun to die, but Margot took a desperate clutch on it. She had gone to see Sarah Rosen, as Katherine had suggested— had done *all* Katherine had suggested, as if K's latest sermon had her hypnotized. K had called up and made the date—after that of course it was up to Margot. Sarah, a large, brilliant, black-and-white-effect person, was all for business, kind, but hard as nails. Still, she showed her femininity by the decorative and intimate nature of her small advertising business, specializing in commodities that appealed to women; by some providential chance, the very thing that Margot had done. All the time that she was giving a creditable imitation of a crisp young woman who knew what she was about, Margot had had a guilty feeling that Sarah Rosen *must* be sharp enough to see through its falseness. But she seemed to have taken Margot on her own terms.

Katherine had told her to go and get some new clothes first.

"And spare no expense, my child. A ladylike shabbiness will not appeal to Sarah."

So now she had gone in for "success." From this time on, she would have to blot out the thought of Bruce in which she lived—this sense of quivering readiness that would not permit her to pin herself down, even to ambition.

She felt that sick flutter again. She got up impatiently.

She stood and looked at herself in K's grand mirror. K, deciding to go in for clothes and looks, *after* she had decided to cut out men! Margot's big dark eyes grew hard as she stared at the somewhat unfamiliar figure in the glass. Aunt Ella ought to be satisfied, she thought. In this close-fitting dress she seemed to have developed all kinds of new protuberances. However, some of the same hard exultance came back to her that she had first felt when she had seen herself in the svelte new dress that changed her from the Margot of the brown tweed suit, of the scant black satin dress she used to wear—with red earrings—to Carlo's. After making her purchases and spending too much for them, she had felt the usual exhilaration. In the "modernistic" shop, with its glass and angles, and sleek metallic figurines, one pair of red shoes and gloves laid beside them "effectively" displayed in the expensive simplicity of a long counter, Margot had sat and smoked with arrogant carelessness, her knees crossed like those of the other women, one narrow foot dangling. These were the women of a period of hard drinks and strong manly cigarettes—no longer the epicurean liqueurs procured in fusty back rooms and the scented girlish cigarettes voluptuously smoked in candlelight before an open fire. Margot saw herself now as a kind of feminine misogynist, making use of men when she wanted them, but no more romantic about sex than about liquor.

She took off her clothes. At least she had the luxury of this glorious little bathroom, stocked with smooth fat cakes of soap and brushes from the kind of glittering little shops that were called "Chemists" instead of drug stores. But she knew that this was not like her old stay at Grimmie's. She could have it all and welcome while K was in Bermuda. But K would expect her to have found a place of her own by the time K got back. The thought seemed to harden her, to bring before her the conditions on which she lived now, a glittering ease mixed with an alert danger, hard, metallic and cold. This was symbolized by the shock of the shower in place of the old soaking, luxurious bath.

Margot went back into the bedroom refreshed, stimulated, with a feeling of cold freedom.

As she dropped the negligee from about her, and felt her own body, an arid bitterness went through her at the thought of going unloved. Never to have one kiss on the white space between her breasts, nor a hand cupping the breast in joy, delight like the taste of sweet sharp liquor burning through her—while she looked on in wonder, contented yet amazed, outside as if apart from herself. She couldn't be alone, like K and Sarah Rosen. She *would* not be alone. She felt a black desire to rush out and degrade what had been beautiful, throw it all to the winds, and harden herself to this degradation in contemptuous triumph.

"I shall be treading these grapes—"

She shook back her loosened hair in anger. She would have no more poetry. She didn't know what was ahead of her. She didn't care. The whole world was falling into a sickening slump. In disdain, Margot hooked herself into the svelte new corselette that she supposed she would have to wear if she was going in for these form-fitting gowns. "Now, my beloved Aunt Ella, talk about behinders if you can!" She cast off a bleak thought of Frankie's hard little unfledged figure. Well, she had hated herself, had felt inferior when *she* was unfledged, and at fifteen had worn ruffles on her chest. Here was another wish come true! She saw before her a mournful future of tap-dancing, dessert-cutting, standing after meals, exercises to the radio, like that upon which K had belatedly entered. She wouldn't be left behind by these other women if she was going to take her place among them. Now Margot felt in herself, almost to her surprise, that almost untouched stratum of meticulous Ferguson competence, that had caused her to keep exquisite notebooks in school and bring home good marks on her report cards. How queer to have that old despised family quality to fall back upon! Yet—midwestern, firm and sound—it lay beneath hedonism, and she knew it. She made up her face carefully with her new cosmetics, and foresaw another mournful future. The old egoistic joy had gone out of having shampoos and facials, when they had seemed a mystic preparation, like a long-drawn-out bridal toilette. Now they would be only necessities—"the smart thing to do," as Sarah Rosen said. Margot had seen at once, with the sharpened acuteness that had sprung into life with Aunt Ella's comment, exactly what Ethel Spencer was doing to her face—and what was undone! The married ones had to do it too! She felt an angry desire to hunt out Bruce, beat out that other woman, show her she wasn't so secure!—get the security for herself . . . but then she would have to work and strain forever to keep it. And what would it mean, with all the best gone? She felt the hard challenge of her own solitude; no longer with defiant exhilaration, but with stark brutal actuality. But if she was going to push through, she must have money, and if she made money she must put her mind to it, crush out the old sensitive readiness, follow a steely course. She heard the hard click of women's heels on the floor of the lobby in the tall building where Sarah Rosen had her office. When you got older, it was money, money everywhere! She felt a sudden, impatient, contrite sympathy for her own father, with his caution and his steady, astute looking toward future safety. At least, when the folks lost their teeth, they could afford to get good false ones! She *would* be successful. She wouldn't fall back on the folks some day. They could never, never get her in the end. She wouldn't get faded and valiant and intelligent and philosophical. Another tag-end of poetry came treacherously into her mind.

> "But me
> They cannot touch,
> Old age and death, the strange
> And ignominious end—"

Death might touch her—but age she would fight with teeth and nails—why, she had always really supposed that she and youth were synonymous! She did yet. And she remembered how she used to admire Aunt Louie, for being pretty and unused, and think that she herself would be like *her* and not like mother. She could have what she was after now, because inside she hated and disdained it. That was the strongest, meanest armor.

Margot had had dinner with Sarah tonight, after having stayed late to finish some work. Sarah had evidently regarded that as a great favor, which would keep her flattered and wildly industrious for about a month. Margot pulled down her mouth sardonically; but all the same, she liked the thought that she had made good with the boss so quickly, and remembered, with considerable pleasure, the look of envy and curiosity in that blonde girl's eyes.

Now, Margot had a cool, easy feeling as she sat in K's low armchair, reading a little, but too tired to take the reading seriously. The time was about to come, no doubt, when she would be the perfect tired business woman, disdaining literature that disturbed the brain, and reaching for a detective story every night. She had carefully refrained from touching K's beautiful little pile of expensive wood. This was her next-to-the-last night in the apartment. Tomorrow she would have to begin the good old search for a place of her own. But this was the first night, Margot realized, when she hadn't minded being alone. She thought, again with that sardonic twist of her lips, of how people in books, after some great sorrow, "plunged into work" and came out bright and new, finer than ever, with something gained—a deeper note in the work. "I wonder if I'm putting a deeper note into cosmetics!" Well, she didn't find that quite such a simple recipe as it was cracked up to be; and yet, now that she had got started, and hadn't taken to drink, or followed the plan of *The Green Hat* woman, *pour le sport* (which once she had regarded as quite romantically effective), it seemed as if she *could* work, and a little better than before —out of a kind of disdain, as if to prove to everything in general how little she cared about it. The feeling gave her a bleak but slightly cocky superiority.

The telephone rang.

"Oh, damn!"—when she had just got decently settled in K's chair. If it was Daggie, she would harden herself, and tell him she was too dead to talk to anyone tonight. She was ashamed—but she didn't want to go back to Daggie. She didn't want to be intimate. But doubtless it was just somebody else calling for K.

All the time that Margot was telling herself this—as if she were repeating it to convince someone invisible—she was aware of the same discredited expectancy underneath. She "told herself" these things, but they were only stagy. She lifted the

French telephone, deriding herself for the way her heart had started beating. Oh, if she *still* had to be such a fool! It was just something left over, meaningless now, like a horrid effect of an old disease.

"May I speak to Miss Ferguson?"

"This is Miss Ferguson."

"Margot—"

The world seemed to turn in a slow, dizzy amazement. The miracle had happened. Bruce was calling her. Margot didn't know whether to be glad—or what to feel. She didn't feel in any way, except that she was trying to right herself in this dizzily turning universe, and to choke her heart down to where it belonged instead of letting it beat in her throat.

"Margot, this is Bruce. I want—"

"How on *earth* did you know I was here?" Margot demanded. Her voice broke in absurd indignation. All at once she could have cried for rage.

"Oh . . . I tracked you down."

"But—for heaven's sake! I don't see *how*."

"You don't seem exactly pleased." She could hear Bruce's laugh—"mirthless," a book would call it.

Margot didn't seem able to think of anything to say.

"Listen, Margot. I want to see you."

Margot felt moments go by as she kept on sitting at the table. She sat there in transfixed silence, as in one of those dreams when she found herself unable to make a move at the crucial instant.

"Did you hear?"

"Yes, I heard."

"Well?—you haven't answered."

The moments went by again—almost as if they were marked and separate, and she could feel each one in itself, an entity. But she couldn't seem to get her lips open. Under her frozen muteness, she had the wild realization that if she was to save any of her pride, and the possibility of the new existence, now was the time when she would have to say something bitterly, decisively final. This was her chance. But she was pierced by the humiliating knowledge that she couldn't do it—she was going to be unable to hold out against Bruce. The most she could do was to give in as slowly, grudgingly and temporizingly as possible—and she was almost too weak even for that!

She said foolishly, in a girlish-sounding voice, "I don't know just why you want to come."—Furious because it sounded hurt and lofty.

"I want to see you," Bruce repeated.

"You don't know where I am."

"How do you suppose I called you?"

Silence. Margot's face burned with the childishness of her retort.

"Margot—" Bruce insisted.

"Well, I . . . suppose you can see me."

"I'll be up in a few minutes, then."

Margot put back the telephone. She had a ghastly desire to laugh at this picture of herself sitting like the heroine of a movie who had just received the great message that brings on the happy ending. She got up, pushed back the little chair angrily, groaning in self-contempt and humiliation as she felt with what ease and swiftness she had succumbed. Her pride was hurting as if it had been an actual living tissue which had received a physical wound. It wasn't that she had let Bruce come—but that she couldn't help herself!

Yet all the time her blood was singing in a terrible jubilance. Bruce had called her—he hadn't let her go. She would see him and be with him. She felt—oh God, she didn't know how she felt! All seemed to converge toward a center of sickening fear. Why was Bruce coming?—why hadn't she asked him? demanded to know before she had given him leave? Because already she had built up an immense edifice of expectations. What if he wanted only some little thing? If he still had something of hers that he wanted to return?—or to get back something of his that *she* had? Margot wrung her hands and groaned again, jeering furiously at herself. But still . . . he must have gone to an immense amount of trouble to find out where she was, with no clues at all that her imagination could discover. She wondered again who could have told him. But when her mind started to go over the possibilities, it seemed to stop in a bitter impatience. The fact that Bruce had called, was coming, and that she didn't know what he was going to say, was an immense obstacle against which every other thought stopped dead.

And now there was the dreadful problem of getting through the time until he came. Margot walked back and forth through the rooms, into the bedroom and out again, into the kitchen, wringing her hands, moving a chair—anything to get through this gap of time. She tried to find some way to harden herself against anything she might hear. Against hope, first of all; and the sickening fall of disappointment. She didn't even know exactly *what* she hoped! She wanted to be cold to Bruce, and to tell him that everything was over in exactly the way that would hurt him most . . . and all the while she was trying to keep herself from the wild belief that miraculously this *was* the happy ending! She was listening with painful acuteness for the sound of the bell, wishing she could get where she couldn't possibly hear it, but afraid to end the torture that way. For a while she stood staring into K's mirror. Then she threw down the powder puff. She wouldn't let Bruce think she had got herself up for him. And what did it matter, anyway? She could never look prettier than she *had* looked. Not even so pretty. Now it seemed to Margot that the little marks under her eyes were stamped with such a hideous sharpness that they were all anyone could see of her. She went back into the living room and sat down again in K's chair.

Her mind went over and over what Bruce had said in a fruitless effort to be prepared. She felt with a sort of awed joy that there had been a suffering reluctance in Bruce's voice underneath a dogged decision. She tried to ward off any treacherous sympathy at the perception. But she couldn't keep her mind from ranging to the limit of the possibilities of what his coming might mean. She knew now, no matter what contempt of herself the knowledge gave her, that she couldn't bear to let him go again. She wanted Bruce to marry her.

But even that couldn't be a happy ending. Not now. Too much had passed. Too much water had flowed under the bridge. Nothing could be quite the same after that night of solitary agony when she had lain out on the ground. Time had worn at the love between them and laid scars upon that shining tissue which nothing could erase. What had happened was irrevocable. Yet Margot felt, with she did not know what mixture of rebellion and deep emotion, that the frayed fabric of love still held. And it was better, in some way, marred and tarnished as it was now. She looked back on her day of perfect happiness, and the happiness seemed shallow. She could not put away this deep undernote of pain. She had thought that she had learned then what it was to love; but she hadn't known until now, when she actually could not help herself, and was letting Bruce have his way against her will.

"Now love has bound me, trembling, hands and feet."

Horrible fool! She hadn't got rid of poetry even yet. It had sprung up again, like "the purple flower which the heel has trampled" . . . and everything around her was quiveringly alive.

The bell rang. It was pressed lightly and quickly, but the sound was piercing. Margot felt the restlessness of her terror suddenly leave her. She could walk forward quietly and easily. But her hands were cold. She opened the door. When she saw Bruce standing there, she suddenly felt that she was in the paralyzing center of fear—and that was why it was so still.

"Oh, hello," she said foolishly.

Bruce didn't answer. But he stepped quickly inside. When Margot saw how solemn he was, her heart began to thud with heaviness. She was too concerned with controlling herself really to see him now. Each was paralyzed with fear of the other. Margot stood aside, while Bruce turned and took off his coat, folded it carefully, and laid it on a chair with his hat on top. It was just as she had seen him fold his coat a hundred times; and she had a dizzy feeling that they *must* be in the old apartment in the little house in Twelfth Street. It was crazy that they should be here together—and yet in terror of each other, and apart. They could somehow annul all that had happened, if they would.

Bruce turned back. He looked at Margot now. He smiled

slightly, and she saw his lower lip tremble. Her resentment and constraint melted.

They stood facing each other, and their eyes met in naked helplessness. Margot felt instantly, in a rush of sympathy and truth, that pride was shameful and petty, it was left behind. She saw that it had been as hard for Bruce as for her. He, no more than she, could keep apart. Perhaps less—he had come to her. This time had a strange solemnity. Margot did not know which one made the movement that brought them together now. Both seemed to do it with a single, spontaneous impulse; to be drawn together by something inevitable and outside themselves. Their kiss was strange and solemn too; and Margot, trembling, felt that Bruce's lips were cold, although now her whole face was flaming. There was fear, reluctance, confession, gladness in the kiss. But again Margot felt that the depth of this emotion made up for the loss of the old pure happiness.

Bruce shifted his position a little, as they stood there together, and then led Margot over to the couch. All this time neither of them had said a word. They had reached each other again. That was enough. The feeling was so solemn that only now a little realization of bright joy was beginning to make its way through the first emotion of reunion. Bruce slowly drew her up to him more closely.

"Margot, we can't separate like this."

She murmured tremulously, "I know it."

"Yes. But what are we going to do?"

They had turned toward each other again. Margot heard with a shock of incredulity that tone of suffering reluctance in Bruce's voice; and now she saw the same thing in the hurt, strained look of his eyes. She had a moment of panic. Her lips opened and at first she could not answer.

"It isn't fair to you," Bruce said heavily. Now he was staring straight ahead. "I knew damned well I oughtn't to come up here. But I couldn't help it. That was all. I've been crazy."

He turned toward her again, with a dazed, bewildered motion, as if he had lost all comprehension of himself. Margot struggled with a sudden wild pity. Perhaps there was a love even beyond hers, that would be still more merciful, and set him free. But she closed her eyes to it in the force of her own jealous passion. Bruce drew her up against him almost roughly. She sat weak and dizzy in his arms. She knew now that for the first incredibly blissful moment of reunion she had believed that they were to be together for ever and ever. But now, bit by bit, the comprehension that Bruce didn't mean that had been forcing its way through her. Margot could only wait, while her heart beat in suffocating disappointment and suspension.

"You ought to put me out," Bruce muttered bitterly.

He turned away from her and put his face down upon the smart, square, new cushions at the end of the couch,—as crisp and cool in their linen freshness as K's own common sense. It made Margot feel that she was defending Bruce against Katherine—against everyone. She felt a fiery impatience with the way K looked at things, mixed with an angry suffering at being herself drawn away from that clear coolness.

She waited. What Bruce had said to her just now Margot felt as a slow hard blow that was gradually opening up a whole undesired vista of comprehension. Irony was returning to her, after her brief belief in the miracle. Her "great passionate love affair" was flawed and fragmentary—after all, it was her own! And the person who really pursued her, and could be wax in her hands, was Hec! No doubt even Dr. Redmond wouldn't have propounded divorce nor offered marriage!

Then she felt her heart thudding, and understood why it was. Bruce was crying. The sound seemed to enter and open up the very center of her heart, with a piercing pain that made her helpless; just as long ago (so she felt it now), on a beautiful lost day, this same man had reached the very center of her physical life and brought her to ripeness in a single hour. She had thought that then, finally, she "knew love." But this was something deep under that ecstasy of gratitude—this feeling that the sound of Bruce's crying was within herself, was more hers than her own. It made the earlier happiness incredibly shallow and immature.

She whispered, "Don't, Bruce. Don't. Please don't. I can't bear it."

And that was true—literally true. She felt wildly, like a mother with a hurt child, that she would do anything to stop it —with a quick disdain of herself, as if against that sound she no longer counted. She took Bruce in her arms, and tried to console him, by any words she could find to say—anything was better than having him away from her.

Bruce finally drew away from her, wiping his face, and trying shakily to get back into his character of a responsible man. He said:

"I know it's damned wrong. But I can't get along without you just the same."

Margot was silent. She felt the painful sweetness of that confession wrung out of him. She waited. But she realized that he was not going to say anything about his family. She felt with wild bitterness that it *was* unfair. She resented the assumption he was tacitly making that they stood together in comprehension, both taking it for granted that he must be what he called "loyal" to his family, that all that was settled, and she agreed and would be resigned to taking the small end. After all, in spite of the realms of golden air they had reached and dwelt in together, Bruce was himself and she was herself. He *had* taken that time as something really set apart; had never understood or shared with her (except humbly, tentatively) her own religion of love—that, if it *was* the best thing mortals could know on this earth, they were cowards not to make it take precedence over all lower things; and now he had slipped down, with some disappointment, pain and loss, and yet with bewildered relief, to the old regions that he knew better. But there was nothing to do with her bitterness and resentment except to let it turn in upon herself. Because, all the same, this was the man she cared for; the only one who, even by his imperfections, could make her feel to the utmost of her capacity, and a little beyond. By the very thing for which she had asked, she was entangled now—on the off side, to be sure— in the ordinary world of mortal love from which she had fled. She couldn't bear to be without Bruce.

"Well . . . it looks as if we can't help ourselves, that's all."

He heard the tone of bitter derision in her voice.

"Did I—bust up something for you, Margot?"

"Oh—" she laughed. Bruce looked at her almost timidly. "Just the fond notion that I could get along by myself."

Bruce took her hand, and kissed it. He said humbly:

"Well, I had that idea myself. I wouldn't have believed I'd come after you again, after I'd once had the guts to leave you. I guess I simply couldn't stand it any more."

Tears sprang into his eyes again. He made a grimace, and looked away from her.

Margot had to swallow the implications of that statement. But after a tiny space of cold, hurt aversion, she put her arms around Bruce again. Tears were thick in her own eyes. Even as she fondled him, there was a wounded resentment deep within her, that some day must bear some kind of fruit. Bruce hadn't wanted children from her. He didn't think of her "in that way." Again it was what she had asked for—it was what she had asked to be to him. The trouble was that *now* she wanted to be all things . . . as he was to her. She understood that the fight was not ended, even after she had won a victory. Again Margot had that larger sense of a turn of events, making the light shift and fall upon another space than that in which she moved, leaving her in a different kind of shadow than the cold earlier one. Her figures of Lilith and Eve were eternal combatants. The contest was never really ended. But Lilith, Margot felt bitterly, was always getting a little the worst of it, was always getting submerged at the close. The old weary battle was on again. But Lilith could put a finger in Eve's fine pie!—and she had her victories. Well—she would snatch what she could. She wouldn't retire tamely from the contest. What she had must always be snatched and fragmentary, it seemed, even after she had reached fulfillment. And here again, as if by the turn of the ball, the old fatal flaw was revealed.

"Well, I guess I'm a fool," Bruce said. He tried to grin at her.

But he had accepted her fierce consolation. If she was willing . . . why, then it was all right.

"I've got you again, anyway," he said, putting his arm around her.

There was an obtuse masculine fatuousness in those words. Black sparks were in Margot's eyes. Did he suppose it could be just the same again? That they could go back to their old relationship, when she had lived in the little house on Twelfth Street, and he had come to see her there? The meaning would be gone from it now—from the little meals she got ready for him, with the card table and the candles—if now he was to be hers only on the difficult precarious terms that he was making. She sprang up, ready to deliver herself of not a few bitter words. Yes, he thought he could have her just as he wanted her! But it couldn't be the same again. He needn't think that. He had broken off their love when it was just at its best, and let her get through it, and now he came back for just as much as he pleased.

Bruce listened doggedly. But his face was set in that way Margot knew, and which made her shake inwardly. Even her anger was crippled at the center by the knowledge of how necessary he was to her.

"Don't think it's easy for me, either," Bruce reminded her. "You always think how things will affect you, and how they're going to suit some idea you have beforehand. I tell you, this business is harder for me in plenty of ways than it is for you, Margot. I thought I was putting myself straight that time I left you. You think I'm gypping you! Maybe you think I haven't given you anything. I've busted up my integrity, if that means anything. It does mean something to me. Not that I blame you—I did it myself. But I can't give up all my responsibility," he repeated stubbornly. "It's just one thing I can't do." Tears started to his eyes again. "I tell you, we're in this thing together."

Margot sat and stared at him. She trembled, knowing that she could not lose him. His words sank into her, bowing down her head. Her defenses against him seemed gone, now that that hard little enclosing sheath was broken.

"I still love you better than anyone else, whatever you think," Bruce said.

Margot looked away, biting her lip and clenching her hands, and then looked back again. She saw Bruce, all at once, as Daggie and the others used to see him. A bald light shone upon their whole relationship, stripping it of any special and peculiar claim to romance. Bruce was just like other men. He wanted his wife and his mistress both, and he would keep them both as long as they would let him. But all that he said, his dogged insistence upon his "responsibility," no matter what incongruities and injustices it entailed, was making him all the time so fearfully much more valuable. Margot loved him unwillingly for his conscientiousness, aware of her own ruthless lack of scruples, in which at times she gloried; and at the same time she felt bitterly that he hurt her more than by an act that could be despised. She loved him because she couldn't overthrow him. And yet she *did* despise him, because he couldn't let love have its way—love that was like genius, greater than either of them. Only lovers who so felt it could act out a great and fatal drama. She and Bruce were different, and theirs was half-and-half.

"You can tell me to get out if you want to," Bruce said. "You've got the right to. I know I had no business barging in again, at this late date. I was the one that started things this time."

Margot's lips trembled at the queer, conscientious gallantry of that admission. But it didn't make it any the easier! She could see that before, when she had thought she was in love with Bruce, "crazy about him," she had been taking him really as the partner who could best bring about the fulfillment of her fairy tale. Now he was himself to her. That was less, in a way, but it bound her to him even more tightly. She struggled even now for a complete and perfect ending; but she couldn't bear to give up to the other woman; or to face the emptiness if Bruce went away. Life was going on again—only it was on his terms, not hers. In that there was a kind of deep-lying, wry justice, as if slowly the balance must be righted, if at last they were to stand for a moment in perfect equality. It seemed to be a law which she felt a racked, sacrificial consecration in fulfilling. She had asked for a "fatal" love—and here it was.

She had wanted it to be her whole life, and now it was. Here was where her fine hard independence went to pot! She felt herself again transfixed in that painful, humiliating readiness, which was yet too sweet to be given up. Nevertheless, the stratum of Ferguson practical ability in her was real, under all her romanticism; and now that she had fallen back upon it, it would keep demanding its right to assertion. Margot could already feel herself struggling to weld the two needs together, knowing that they were eternally opposed. She acknowledged the bitter justice of her plight. She felt herself looking down that long vista of which she had had a glimpse before, seeing the tortuous ways of her great love affair. But what she couldn't see was any ending.

"Are you going to let me stay, Margot?"

Margot was still sitting half turned aside. Now she turned back to Bruce. Her lips were helplessly parted, her eyes darkly strained with the sense of all she couldn't communicate.

Oh, yes, she was going to let him stay!

This slow, mute embrace was not like the first joy of reunion, with its false rainbow miracle of promise. Beneath it lay reservations, resolves, reluctances, streaks of hardness, half-estrangement. After they had once made the Great Renunciation, it seemed a little silly, even, to be getting together again. Margot felt silly, as if she were going on acting after the curtain had come down. All the same, this embrace had a mutual quality they had never quite felt before. Perhaps in guilt, perhaps in defeat—anyway, it was there, and it joined them together. The painful sweetness of desire was awake again; the broken habit of intercourse demanding its conclusion. They were ashamed, joyous, defeated, proud—all within the compass of that mortal bond, which for the time being at least, was stronger than anything. They had recovered life—on what terms it seemed they could—although it was jumbled and precarious, touched with derision, and they no longer knew where to find their footing.

Part Five
The Youngest

AN agent selling silk stockings rang the bell at the Ferguson house. No one answered, and after ringing again and waiting, he retreated. Only when he had got past the place, he saw "the lady of the house" out in the garden talking to a workman. He thought of seeking her there. But the poor fellow (who had started out as a preacher in a humble denomination) was secretly glad of an excuse that allowed him to cut any house on his beat. He had never overcome his stiff reluctant shyness, his nervous dread of intrusion, in spite of needing the money. So Mrs. Ferguson escaped, as Mrs. Morgan, frankly looking out of her window to see where the fellow was going next, observed with satisfaction; and the agent himself doubtless missed an easy sale to a soft-hearted customer.

The "workman" was Uncle Ben. Mrs. Ferguson had just mentioned, after the service last Sunday, that they must get hold of someone to put in their garden; and Ben had said he would come over. She wouldn't have thought of offering her brother-in-law this little bit of wages. But she could see that Ben really wanted the job. In his few bleak years of retirement, he had grown increasingly lonely for the work on the farm. Sometimes he went out there, but Ella didn't like it, and twitted him. "What do we give part to a renter for if you're going to go out there and do all the work for him yourself?" When Ben had first appeared this morning, Annie had noticed how aged and disconsolate he looked. The eternal bickering between him and Ella, once a joke among the relationship, had grown to bitter proportions now that they were housed up together with so little to keep them busy. Ella got after Ben for sitting idle, and then she scolded him for all his meager activities— going over to one of the neighbors to do a little tinkering, fussing over the storm windows, wandering off downtown to stand on the corner and talk with the other retired farmers. Ella had grown fat and complacent since they had moved into town; Ben, older and grayer.

But now he was more like himself. He loved to work in the earth. Even Grandpa Ferguson had admitted that Ben was a natural born farmer, although he was almost too slow and careful ever to get things done. And this was the very kind of work he liked best, small and puttering, where he could take infinite workmanlike pains. He and Ella had their own garden of course—a model one—but Ella always had to come out and pester him for being so slow. He and Annie could talk things over together. Since Annie had more on her hands than Ella, she wa'ant so pressed for time, Uncle Ben thought with sardonic pessimism.

"Well, now, Annie, I'll tell ye. I dunno as I'd put any small flowers right there, for they'd be a little too much in the shade of those cosmos later on. Ain't that where ye have yer cosmos?"

Ben had brought over the fork that he had been using on his own garden. 'Twasn't hardly worth bringing in a horse and plow from the country for these little patches o' ground, he said. Easier to do it by hand. But he was in no particular hurry to get to work. He was enjoying his sister-in-law's company. The spring air was somewhat chilly, but the sunshine was bright, and the ground had a good loamy smell. Mrs. Ferguson had put on her old coat with the worn beaver collar.

"Annie, do you remember that sociable out to the old schoolhouse where Joe Brownback got you for a partner in Wink 'Em, and wouldn't let go of ye, and Fred was so mad? I dunno's I ever saw Fred so mad."

"Oh, he can get mad!"

"Yes, sure, I know he can—wouldn't be a Ferguson otherwise," Uncle Ben said with feeling. "But 'tain't so very often Fred right outs and shows it like he done that night. I thought they was going to be a real fight between them two boys before the evening was ended. Well, they wa'ant the only fellows liked you pretty well, Annie, in those days."

She laughed and colored. Tall, his big shoulders bowed, in his ancient brown vest and work pants, Ben with his kind slow voice took her back to her girlhood days when she had come out to Buck Creek as the pretty new teacher whom all the fellows tried to get a chance to meet. She remembered the small county fairs where "the young folks" drove together, with the big farm horses snorting as they climbed the hill. She thought of the oak grove behind the little district schoolhouse;

526

of the polished brown leaves littering the hollows in the fall. A vision of these things overhung the April garden.

"Well, Annie, I'll tell ye, I'll get the ground ready today, that'll be a fair morning's job, and tomorrow we can decide for sure where to put the flowers. I s'pose *she'll* want me this afternoon."

Shivering a little, Mrs. Ferguson went back to the house. That bitter touch at the end made her sad, remembering the days when they had all been young people together.

The house seemed modern and warm and bright after standing out there in the garden with Ben.

The Fergusons had been a little slower than other people of their financial status in doing over their house. Fred had held off, with characteristic caution, until the children were pretty well accounted for, and he could exactly see his way. Then at last the place had undergone the prescribed metamorphosis of all the well-to-do homes in Belmond: with the parlor and living room thrown into one, the old downstairs furniture relegated to the attic or bestowed upon Essie Bartlett and her mother, new fixtures in the bathroom, new flowers and a trellis on the lawn. The warm easy atmosphere of the living room seemed an age removed from all that Ben had been talking about—seemed almost to be in a different world. There was an early American quality about Ben that Annie could recognize and yet had never really known: something sylvan, like the homemade hunks of maple sugar his cousins back in Pennsylvania used to send him every year, and that he would slyly take out of a special drawer in the back porch (supposed to be hidden from Aunt Ella), pounding off with a hammer a sharp-edged, crumbly, dark golden piece for some child who had come to woe, warning "Don't ye let the others see it!" The rustic air that had lingered about him even in his prime was enhanced by his retirement. He was an anachronism, authentic but of the past, here in Belmond. Ben was an old man. But she and Fred were not old people!

Now that she felt the spring in the air, the bright exciting change of the season, Mrs. Ferguson realized how pleasant this winter had been that was nearly over. There had been just enough to do, with club work, church work, the little journeys to and from Geneva, the happy break at the holidays when Bun had come home from the university and they had had "Carl's folks" here. The snowy winter, "an old-fashioned winter," people called it, when they had put up the car during the coldest months, had taken on just a flavor of old days . . . If hard times were around, they had not struck Belmond; and Mrs. Ferguson believed that it was somehow protected from them—just as it had never had a cyclone. Life seemed to be running along its appointed way, only with natural prosperity and well-earned comforts added. Now their peaceful, secluded, winter routine would be broken. But pleasantly broken! Soon the little excursions would begin, with the Lowries or the Vieles, the Fergusons taking along someone else who would enjoy the ride, like Mrs. Dunn or Ada Rist, and all of them bringing lunch. People were beginning to look up all the little waterfalls and odd-shaped rocks and interesting buildings that this good farming country could offer in the way of "scenery." Summer would be busy. Some of the children would come for visits. Bunny might drop in for any week-end now. He had a third-hand roadster which dad had let him get—dad remarking with dry humor that Bun had raised them to the status of a two-car family, they could count themselves among the big bugs now.

All at once, Mrs. Ferguson felt the old hunger for her children. She put down her magazine and went up the back stairs to look into Bun's room and see if it was ready. She thought with a shudder of Ben and Ella and their barren life in that narrow frame house they had bought on a side street. This had been Carl's room before it was Bunny's. It was still really "Carl's room" to his mother. Her gladness at having Carl so close—the only thing she admitted to other people—was overshadowed by a deeply hidden, sympathetic knowledge of his dissatisfaction, and the outcome that seemed to be confused between defeat and victory. Now, in the empty chill of the room, with the back window overlooking the garden patch in which Ben was slowly moving, she could stand alone with the pain of comprehension. She thought of Carl as he used to be, with his bright, confident, too sensitive eyes. How was it that she couldn't go to him?

But Bunny was always happy. When his mother thought of her youngest, a smile of fond contentment curved her lips. She could truly say that he was the one of their children who had "never caused them a moment's trouble." Coming late, he had seemed just to fit in quietly, with a mixture of affectionate youthfulness and queer, understanding maturity. Perhaps it was because he was the last—a gift suddenly vouchsafed them when they had given up thought of other children—that she and dad had both felt from the first they could relax their responsibility and simply enjoy him as their baby. Now it seemed to her, if she could *have* a choice (and of course she couldn't, it would be treachery to her mother's heart), she would say that the last was the best of all. He was *theirs* in a peculiar way that the other children weren't. Carl was hers, and Dorothy was her father's. Margaret—whose *was* she? Too much her own to be anyone's! The thought of Margaret brought guilt, hunger, frustration and pain. Her visit last summer had been really no assuagement. The mother's soft face took on secretive lines as she stood looking into the springtime vacancy of the room.

Well! Margaret took her own way. Mrs. Ferguson gave a quick shrug of her shoulders. She made up the narrow cot that Bunny preferred to a bed, as more rigorous and manly, smiling to think that she still had her youngest.

The telephone rang. That was a regular thing at this time of the morning. Fred always called up from downtown to ask what he should bring home for dinner. Some of the men stayed down at noon now, eating the forty-cent Business Men's Luncheon in the redecorated dining room of the Belmond House. But Fred liked to come home, except on the day of the Rotary meeting. Hotel fare tasted stale compared to mama's cooking. Now that they were alone, they could go back to the old country custom of having the main meal at noon—much to the girls' disgust if they had known it.

"Hello, Annie. That you? What do you want me to bring

home this noon? I wondered how about a little steak. They've got some that looks pretty nice here at Helmholz's."

"All right. Yes. Bring that if you want to."

But she pursed up her lips and then laughed as she hung up the receiver. She didn't doubt that dad had the steak already bought and tied up in a package. "That you?" Who else did he ever think it could be? And his asking what he should bring home was about as cut and dried as one of those Republican meetings in the courthouse to elect county officers. The men had once chosen Mrs. Hoagland as one of the delegates, out of courtesy to the ladies, after woman's suffrage had come in; and Mrs. Hoagland had gone there all ready to nominate Fannie Allison for a county office, because the ladies had agreed she needed it more than some of the men. But the meeting had slid off like greased clockwork, and before Mrs. Hoagland knew it had even started the same old ticket had been confirmed. "All in favor say aye, opposed no, motion carried, Mr. Brownback is our nomination." Those men had the whole thing fixed up before anybody went there.

Mrs. Ferguson turned away from the telephone. In the dimness of the closet, among the umbrellas and rubbers, some of the children's old things were still hanging. The big jardinière for flowers was empty. Margaret used to keep that filled.

"Well, if I'm going to have dad's dinner ready—"

She hurried out to the kitchen to fix the potatoes. Dad always wanted mashed potatoes with his steak.

Still, there was no need to hurry. There was fresh lettuce in the ice box, but Fred actually preferred canned vegetables. He was incorrigible in some ways! Soon they would have their own garden stuff—he liked that. Mrs. Ferguson looked out of the window. The garden soil lay freshly turned. Ben had gone home. Ella would raise a big to-do if he wasn't there strictly at twelve, just as if they still had all the work to get through on the farm! A bird settled on a rich black clod. Mrs. Ferguson looked more closely, thinking for a moment it was a new variety. She and Lillian now had a mutual interest in birds, vying with each other in the number of varieties that visited their lawns, the earliest that came back in the spring, the number that stayed over winter. Now, though, if Margaret would have consented to stay at home, they would have let her have a cat!

The clock struck dimly in the empty living room. Soon she wouldn't be able to leave her meals until the very last minute. As long as the steak was good, dad was satisfied. But it would be nice to have to set the big table in the dining room again. It was still a little too cold for the porch; but Mrs. Ferguson had arranged a breakfast nook, just for herself and dad, near the sunny kitchen window. She set the painted table with the green and white linen cloth she had bought at a sale in Geneva —she and Lillian had got some just alike. Then, feeling a little sentimental because they might not have many more meals out here together, she looked around for some flowers. The bouquet of straw flowers seemed dusty and stale. She might as well cut the last red tulip from the Easter plant that her Sunday School girls had given her. She put it in the little old twisted green glass vase she had got down from the top shelf of the cupboard, where it had been stuck away among other supposedly superannuated ornaments that had come from the division of Grandma Ferguson's possessions. Some of those despised things were turning out to be treasures! The girls would probably want this vase if they saw it. But she didn't know whether she was going to let the girls have any of Grandma's things or not!

While she was mashing the potatoes, Fred came into the house.

"Annie!" He came on into the kitchen. "Oh, I didn't know where you'd gone to!" He always wanted her right where he could find her. "Got your frying pan hot? This steak won't need any extra grease."

The steak hissed in the iron skillet, and the good smell went through the warm kitchen mingled with that of the coffee. Fred must always have his coffee. Fred washed his hands at the sink instead of going up to the bathroom. And he always used the toilet in the cellar by preference. He waited with his meal until she sat down. He was never willing to eat or sleep without her.

"I see the garden's plowed. Ben come over?"

"Yes. I hated to have him do it."

"Oh, I guess he wanted to. This is good butter. Rolfe bring it in? I don't like that butter you get downtown."

"Why, dad, it's nice."

"Well, it ain't like the homemade."

"Goodness! Nobody churns any more."

"Vina does."

"Well, she thinks she has to, you make such a fuss if you can't get butter from them."

"Ella did her own churning. All country women used to, and plenty in town."

"Yes, but you know they don't any more, Fred. How can you act as if they did? And you're a great one to talk, dad! When you won't even mow your own lawn."

She knew he still felt guilty about that self-indulgence. But he had got used to counting on the boys, and when they were gone he couldn't make himself go back to those old chores, as he still called them.

"Well, we don't have to eat the grass."

He felt satisfied at having got it back so neatly at mama. And he didn't worry about Vina. He gave her plenty for all the little extras she did. The steak was good, and so were the potatoes; and he had selected both. He still ordered the staples for the household. He was better at a bargain than mama. She looked after the rest of the stuff.

"Pretty nice dinner," he said.

It never failed to please her when he mentioned that her cooking was good. A dim pink flush returned to her cheeks.

"Fred, do you think you could get home just a little bit early? I'd like to drive out to the greenhouse and get some pansy plants this afternoon."

"Well . . . yes, I guess maybe we'd better go. May not come many more such good days for setting things out. Four o'clock suit you?"

2

After dinner, Mrs. Ferguson went upstairs to take a nap. This still gave her an almost guilty feeling of self-indulgence and luxury—for to lie down in the daytime, when a body wasn't sick, Fred's mother had always regarded as little short of a crime. Ella wouldn't do it yet. She would putter around all afternoon at nothing rather than—as she called it—give up and lie down. Mrs. Ferguson took a book along with her, as a further luxury, one that she had heard reviewed in the Woman's Club in Geneva when she had gone there with Lillian. Perhaps she herself would review it in the club here at home. This last year or two, she had begun to pluck up courage and take quite an active part. She had made a hit in the club with a portrayal of Ruth in a pageant featuring "Women of the Bible." Mrs. Hoagland—large, assured, pleasantly dominating —was the Naomi; and beside her Mrs. Ferguson, with her innocent conception of the extremely efficient character of Ruth, had seemed tender and almost maidenly. The words "Entreat me not to leave thee" she had always thought the most beautiful in the Bible. Beneath her shy, gentle, somewhat tremulous voice as she spoke these lines had run a secret strain of personal feeling that gave them a frail, touching sincerity. They made her think of the early days when she had entered the Presbyterian church with Fred, forsaking the ways of her parents. Her parents, long dead—the little Ohio town in the spring—the peaceful graves in the small burying ground, wooded and far away. None of the family lived in Woodbine now.

She dropped the book, feeling not quite up to it, and reached for the household magazine that she had sneaked along with her "instructive" book. First she dutifully looked over the recipes, then turned to a lushly sentimental story which she began to read in comfort. In the midst of a love scene, she drifted off to sleep.

She heard sounds outside. A car stopping. Then footsteps coming up the front walk. The screened door banged; and Bunny's voice called:

"Hello, mother!"

Mrs. Ferguson sat up. She hadn't really expected Bun today. The flurry of feeling her plans changed—and being still only half awake—upset her a little. Bunny came running up the stairs. Mrs. Ferguson got up and put on her kimono, and opened her door. When she saw his smiling, young, sunburned face, she was truly pleased.

"Well! We didn't expect you before tomorrow!"

She kissed him. Then she saw that there was someone else standing downstairs in the hall.

Bun, seeing her glance, said slightly abashed, "I brought Charlotte Bukowska along with me."

A girl?—and what a funny name! Bun ran downstairs. But then, Bunny liked all the girls, he was friendly with all of them. His mother smiled.

After a few minutes, she herself went down, nicely dressed. The low, intermittent sound of voices in the living room stopped. Bun stood up as his mother entered; and she noticed that slight awkwardness about him again. A girl sitting in the big chair got up too, after a moment of hesitation. Mrs. Ferguson felt a slight shock as she went forward to greet this guest.

"Mother, this is Charlotte Bukowska. I thought I'd bring her along with me—give her a chance to taste some good cooking." Bun grinned.

Mrs. Ferguson smiled. She shook hands graciously. But all the time, it seemed to her that she was barely covering that shocked feeling. The girl was large—that was partly what made her seem so strange—with frowning, heavy eyebrows. Black hair was combed from a solid broad forehead and fell in a heavy shock almost to her shoulders. The touch of her firm, large hand was strangely evasive and cold. After the introduction, the girl stood there awkwardly. She wore a careless sweater and old wool skirt, with crumpled white socks and low heelless shoes. She might have dressed a *lit*-tle more carefully if she was coming to visit people she had never seen! But what struck Mrs. Ferguson most was the strange ice-blue of the eyes under those frowning, unfeminine black eyebrows. There was something almost frightening.

What a funny girl for Bun to choose! Mrs. Ferguson couldn't help thinking that, although she instantly tried to be hospitable. She had always encouraged Bun to bring his friends home, feeling that they had made a mistake in that way with Margaret. But her smiling manner covered deep uncertainty. There was a queer air of tension and smothered hostility. Or did she just imagine it?

She said nervously, "We thought Bun might be home tomorrow. But the earlier the better! It must have been lovely driving today."

"Pretty swell," Bunny answered.

"Well, it's nice you could get through in time to come."

The girl did not speak again. She sat down at Mrs. Ferguson's smiling request. She was looking around from under straight frowning brows, letting Bunny and his mother talk together. Mrs. Ferguson began to feel an uneasy, wounded hostility, based on she couldn't have said just what. This girl seemed so big and strange . . . rough, almost. There had been a frightening indifference in the touch of her hand. But Mrs. Ferguson kept going back to that sensational contrast between the blue eyes and the heavy black brows and hair.

She tried to keep up the right air of cheerful welcome.

"Let me get you something to eat. You must be hungry after that drive."

"Children," she had almost said. She would have said it happily and naturally with any of Bunny's other friends. But with this girl—she didn't want to, and she didn't dare.

Bun said with embarrassment that they had stopped on the way for lunch.

"Wouldn't you like a little something more? Some fruit— or a piece of cake? We have some sponge cake. I was counting on Bunny to help us eat it up! Dad and I eat so little."

Bun glanced obliquely at his guest. "Like something, Charlotte?" She signified mutely that she didn't. "I guess we've had plenty, mother. We'll wait and keep an appetite for supper."

"It's too bad you didn't get here a little earlier. Dad brought home such a nice steak."

Mrs. Ferguson tried to give a quick smile at the guest, but it met a surly blankness. The girl was looking down now, and her mouth was sullen. Mrs. Ferguson began to feel upset and resentful.

The uneasiness grew until they were all silent. Finally Bun broke this silence with an obvious effort.

"I guess maybe we'll take a little drive," he said to his mother. He tried to smile. "I'll take Charlotte out to see the farm."

"Dad will be home in a little while."

"Well . . . I guess maybe we'd better go now, though, while it's warm."

"I expect that would be nicer," his mother valiantly agreed. "Well—" she tried to smile too—"you'll be back for supper, both of you."

When they left her at first she felt in a kind of daze. At least she would tell Bunny that he might teach his friends better manners! Not that the girl had really done anything, but she was so—just so. . . . And now Mrs. Ferguson thought she would have to call up dad and tell him that after all they couldn't go for the pansy plants. That little excursion was spoiled! She made a quick calculation about supper. She wanted to make something nice to impress that girl. Why did Bun bring *her* with him? Mrs. Ferguson was half provoked with Bun. It must have been charity. Those scuffed shoes, and that old skirt and sweater. The girl couldn't really be a *friend* of Bun's! But Mrs. Ferguson felt herself trembling and strange, judged somehow by alien eyes. She felt those cold blue eyes, remote as mountain water, still upon her; and there was a sensation she had never experienced before, as if she were being taken to task for all her innocent words and actions. She was almost glad to have them out of the house!

Bun and Charlotte walked out to the car. Bun felt with despair that they were far apart. He wanted to break down the fierce reserve into which Charlotte had retreated. But he seemed impotent and weak.

They started out in silence. Charlotte could take the custard pie for silence, anyway, Bun thought, half resentfully, half wistfully. He stole another of his oblique glances at her. He had just experienced the sensation of seeing his home through totally alien eyes—and it didn't make him comfortable, either! It seemed as if he ought to apologize for its easy bourgeois comfort. He had never realized before how complete that was. It had everything that belonged in the picture: radio, victrola, piano that nobody used any more, overstuffed davenport. It might almost have been a cartoon! And yet a stubborn adherence to his own people, an understanding of them that he could never communicate to Charlotte, a hurt perception at his mother's loyal and confused attempt at kindness—kept him still.

But he thought, damn it! He understood Charlotte too. He saw that her face was pale. Beneath a faint tinge of sunburn that had lingered through the winter, it had a sick greenish cast. Bun knew that Charlotte was weighing the possibility of their union all over again, and coming to the conclusion that it was no go. She was lumping him in with all of his household. He felt sick himself. That sense of impotence held him. And yet he wouldn't submit to it. At bottom it wasn't true. Bunny veered away from the straight blankness of despair. With fond guile, he began to plan a course of winning Charlotte from her surly muteness and from the decision before it was actually made.

They had been driving for about three hours today. Nevertheless, Bun felt fresh again. Perhaps it was fear spurring him on and giving him his second wind! He couldn't help taking his old, affectionate, tolerant, slightly cynical interest in these familiar things. He wanted wistfully to win Charlotte to some interest. At least, to make her *see* these things. But he knew that to her all towns were alike—places where the jobs were a little better or a little worse; except for a queer, inalienably American hope that each new place might somehow prove to be the Promised Land! Evidently she didn't think that of Belmond.

"Why the stern silence?"

He got a fiercely cold glance from those blue eyes. Charlotte looked straight ahead. No use to point out any of Belmond's spots of interest to her—"On your right, madam, the public library, presided over by Miss Vanchie Darlington, Belmond's most distinguished spinster—

> No such record of strict virginity
> Has ever been known in this vicinity."

That old gag the kids used to whisper when Vanchie sent them out of the library for disturbing the peace! Bun realized with a grin, half rueful, half like a naughty schoolboy's, that he didn't dare risk breaking into Charlotte's fierce concentration with any such trivialities. How different their tradition was! If you could call Charlotte's a tradition. If it was a tradition not to allow any tradition! None of these homely, intimate, small town things on which he had grown up meant anything to her.

"Your mother doesn't like me."

She announced that out of the blue. Bun felt indignation rise in him. It put him on his mother's side. He wanted to say, "I shouldn't think she would after the way *you* acted." No wonder Charlotte had seemed formidable to his poor mother! She did even to him. She was built altogether on a different scale from anybody in the Ferguson family. Margaret could certainly raise the roof at times, when the folks and she disagreed; but beside Charlotte she was a fragile flower. Bun felt an angry dismay. It was no use talking to Charlotte! She had one track and she went ahead on that like a locomotive. Went ahead with such force that she left the opposition paralyzed! Looking at her, he was aware again of her intense monumental seriousness, of a kind he had simply never met before, and about which Bun's tricksy spirit was forever playing, partly because he did respect it so tremendously '. . . and as always, ever since he had known Charlotte, queerly and almost wryly mingled with his admiration and passion for her was a sense of her pathos. What he kept seeing in her—but only in flashes—was a frightened, sullen child at bay. The impulse to combat her head-on faded. Instead, Bun put his hand on her knee and shook it slightly—with the old thrill, bitter-sweet, at the touch of that firm flesh.

"That's not half as bad as you think."

He could feel that his touch had slightly weakened her opposition, although she still sat locked away from him in that blue-eyed silence. But he believed that he knew the methods of gradual beguilement against which, in her stormy simplicity, Charlotte was never quite proof. It made Bun smile wickedly to himself, pitying her because he could outwit her, loving her because he pitied her—and yet aware that he had to go very carefully, all the same! Perhaps what he liked best of all was the danger.

"You had mother scared," he told Charlotte. "Yes, you did, you had her regularly buffaloed. It scares anybody when you turn on that scowl."

She still sat sullenly dumb. Bun was unhappy. She muttered: "I don't see why you brought me here."

They drove nearly a block before Bun answered. "Well, because," he said slowly, "I told you. I'm going to let the folks in on this. This isn't going to be any sneak business."

"I don't know what difference it makes."

"I know you don't. But I do. That's just the difference." Charlotte's face was hard. Bun said, "You can't expect to sit there like an Indian from a hostile tribe and have mother fall for you. You've got to give the folks a *lit*-tle chance. Mother was nicer to you a damn sight than you were to her."

Charlotte was still staring straight ahead. Yes, his mother had *acted* nice, if Bun expected her to be fooled by that! But Charlotte felt the essential firmness, under the boyish tenderness and easy gaiety, that always brought her up with a thrill of hard respect. She slowly, almost shyly, put her hand on *his* knee and returned his pressure. He watched her large mouth curve into a lovely smile.

"Well, gee—I felt like a roughneck," Charlotte admitted, like a surly truthful little boy. She turned away her head.

Bun was suddenly joyous. He grabbed her hand and held it hard. Charlotte could stand up to it. You could always count upon that. It was one of the things that made him love her, that good hard realistic intellect of hers, with its infusion of the loftiest idealistic passion (whether she admitted it or not)—all her strange, half-crude, half-seasoned mixture, at the same time

539

so childish and so experienced. His thin boyish body quivered to her strong attraction. But whether she realized it or not, he was a match for her. She had given him the shock of his life, but she hadn't overthrown him. Even if he wasn't one of those tough eggs she used to know! His kind of wily steel was out of her ken, so that it almost made Bun ashamed at times to triumph over her. It *did* make him humble, in a way he couldn't explain to her. Still, he'd better not talk—he hadn't triumphed yet!

Charlotte suddenly and passionately caught at his hand. They frankly pushed against each other in the car like two young animals. And it was perilous fun for Bunny to keep driving fast ahead just the same.

Now there was an almost delirious happiness in the brightness of the early afternoon—the scudding of white clouds across the blue April sky. The country earth smelled good. Town was pretty small, but it was big out here. They seemed to have the road to themselves. A few cars passed, but somehow didn't count. If only they could be alone together like this always! They could understand each other then. But they couldn't. This sense of there being no one but themselves alive in the whole spring world had only a transient truth. Bun knew that, young as he was. Just the same, this little time was theirs. And he intended to make use of it. He slowed down the car.

"Well, here are the Ferguson ancestral acres!" he announced.

He felt Charlotte's instant frown, which he had meant to provoke. He stopped the car after grandly circling the windmill.

"Come on," he said. "It's pretty nice, if the folks do own it."

He stared impudently straight at her and grinned disarmingly. Charlotte had to smile again, reluctantly bewitched by his casual charm, which she was aware she didn't quite fathom. She could feel that she was being maneuvered, but she got out of the car and went with Bun across the driveway. There was a look of distant reservation in her ice-blue eyes.

Bun took hold of her arm and pressed it up against him. "Have I made you sore?" She wouldn't answer. "You know, Charlotte—" He stopped. "I'm not making fun of your ideas. Jesus Christ, I more than—! I love you for what you believe."

He could feel Charlotte quiver. Then she turned to him and passionately raised her full red mouth. Their embrace almost overwhelmed Bun's slight, tall, boyish frame. But he held his ground. "I just want to make you live too, my sweetheart. I want to *have* you." His voice broke with earnestness. She gave him her lips but never her eyes. It seemed for a moment, in despair, as if there were too many things around them, and between them—as if they were caught in a network of circumstance that would defeat them in the end.

But he wouldn't admit that—didn't. He gave a sly glance around to see if Rolfe or Vina might have been watching. It would have been a nice eyeful for them if they had! Bun slightly shrugged his shoulders. Charlotte was like the rain and the sun. You had to take her favors when they came. He had an admiration, deep and humble, for her untutored simplicity that could ignore surroundings. But it brought his impish spirit up again.

"Well, come on," he said slyly, pulling her along with him. "Let's see what a mess things are under private ownership. Then we can have some direct action, kid."

He grinned, not expecting a response. But he was uneasy too. Beside his beloved, he felt himself mild, unseasoned . . . beside her adventurous, embittered young life, without rules, uncharted, nomadic, now here, now there, the code all different from the bottom up . . . And yet he felt himself so much older! His mind could see around her elemental simplicity. He knew what Charlotte was feeling. But she could never seem to fathom him, and this, although it sometimes pleased him, left him solitary. She didn't try to do it. He had never really impressed himself upon her, after all. Perhaps he couldn't. He was just too slight. He felt that way even beside his brother Carl (whom Bun considered pretty much of a mess psychologically) just because Carl took things so damned hard. Bun felt a touch of that despair again.

Right now he could see that Charlotte was disturbed. She could never meet his oblique playfulness. It was out of her range. She was scowling. To her it seemed trivial and indirect. She was used to going straight at things. It was the only way she knew. Bun had a fleeting, tender, remorseful perception that his manner sometimes made her feel clumsy—and naturally she didn't like that, poor kid. Perhaps he had unwittingly brought up old memories of her childhood, some of the things she had told him about, speaking in a flat, hard, matter-of-fact voice, when they had sat huddled up together in that old deserted tool shed they had discovered: of the time when she had started to school, a little Russian peasant girl among the American kids in a western town. He didn't want to be joining in with those little devils, some of his girl's first enemies! But if she only knew what she made *him* feel like about half the time!

Charlotte walked a little distance ahead of him. Bun let her have her way. He knew he hadn't actually made peace with her yet. The trouble was that what she thought about the folks was true enough—and yet it wasn't true. Charlotte ruthlessly simplified everything. Bun saw the complexities of every situation. He had artfully put a leash on her. And yet it didn't make him any more sure that he possessed her. He felt the thrilling challenge of that. Their feeling for each other must be true at every instant, not just in the long run, or all things considered, or in a general way. If ever the truth died out of their union, she would not have him. The ceremony in itself meant even less to Charlotte than it did to him, and that seemed little enough. He felt the perilous, striving, moment-by-moment integrity of such a union as he was attempting—a different kind of integrity from that of the folks in their taken-for-granted partnership, and one they would never grant or understand. Yet he intended to snare his beloved—forever, if he could. Bun followed, smiling to himself. There was a queer, old subtlety in that boyish face. Charlotte, his new Atalanta. If her beau—Atalanta's—wasn't such a whiz of a runner, still he had his technique of overcoming his girl wonder. Bun felt he had Charlotte bothered, all the same.

He had to smile again at the thought of the classical instance compared to this almost stern modernity. He saw Charlotte's scowling face above her old white sweater, and her strong bare legs with the crumpled ten-cent-store socks. The shock of black hair was held back with the sort of Alice-in-Wonderland comb that just now the girls were using. Russian ancestry showed in the height of the cheek bones and the width of the face. But she was a good deal more American than Russian. Bun felt in her something so new that it was crude. And yet something that he thought of as pre-classic. Archaic. She was a young archaic goddess of some genus never met with in the world before.

Well, it was a good break that Rolfe and Vina weren't around! Bun had slyly ascertained that their car was gone. They must have driven into town this afternoon. Charlotte didn't seem aware that anybody *might* be here. She looked at the old place, so familiar to Bun from his childhood, with a direct, refreshing impersonality. The whole countryside seemed deserted in the spring sunshine. No, not so much deserted as never yet inhabited. The farm lay off the main road and not many cars went past. It purified everything—this sunshine, alternately so chilly and so warm, the trampled bare ground of the pigpen, the broken pale cornstalks, the dark water in the tank. It seemed to Bun at this moment that he was following his sweetheart into a morning world.

The big barn door was closed. Bun pushed it open with a running shove, the kind he had always loved to give it when he was a kid, feeling very proud of himself. The semi-dusky interior, both impressive and homely, was nearly empty. That gave a strange feeling, too, of walking in a pre-dawn stillness. Some calves looked up with soft, dark, watery eyes from a bedded stall. The girls—Dorothy and Margaret—would have gone straight for them. Almost any girls he knew. But Charlotte glanced at the little buggers with a sort of troubled reserve, and said nothing. Two were lying down, one stood on knock-kneed long legs. Bun himself, as he passed, gave a hasty caress of the knobby baby head between the two soft ears. It was all right. They didn't have the calves here for pets.

He led Charlotte artfully on to the machinery. Rolfe kept the things he wasn't using conscientiously under cover. Dad always told Aunt Ella that Rolfe was about as good a renter as she could hope to find. If Aunt Ella had chosen to descend upon the place this afternoon, and give Charlotte *that* example of private ownership, it would have been all up with Bun Ferguson! Aunt Ella was too much even for dad.

"Here's the stuff. Hm?"

The big binder gleamed in the dusk. Charlotte went straight to it with frowning, direct interest. So this was what took his goddess's heart! Bun grinned trying to imagine his mother and sisters making for a binder! They could look at it a hundred times and still not know what it was for—or even ask. It made him feel tender toward them, and even more tender toward Charlotte. Well, what was funny? Charlotte came by her interest honestly. Those long blazing days of her childhood, out in the beet fields, working by hand, had ground into her a kind of respect that the university intelligentsia who were talking now about "the machine age," either praising or damning it as their temperaments demanded, simply didn't comprehend. Charlotte stored up fine photographs of machines (most of them torn out of library books and magazines, he must admit) just as Margaret, at one stage, used to collect Perry prints of the Old Masters, and colored reproductions from the *Ladies' Home Journal*. Bun saw that it was an idea Charlotte had got from reading about the new Russia. She had a bunch of proletarian magazines published in obscure places. . . . Let her look at her machines. Here in the dusk of the barn her lover felt her womanhood. He had not yet got into the very center of that rich, potential warmth. He was still on sufferance, he knew.

Bun let her look for a while, and then pulled her away, feeling jealously that he wanted this day for himself. He foresaw that the night would be difficult. He felt with a quick desperation that he must make her his or lose her, after all. He had only this little hour vouchsafed him. He had brought his bride into the midst of alien conditions, half knowing the danger, and now he must make her feel that in spite of them he was closer to her than anybody else in the world. It put him on his mettle. . . . Of course she *was* his—just now. He had won passionate response from her. But he knew that their love must rest on something more. She had given response to others, according to her code; and although she had yielded to him, fascinated, perhaps partly bewildered, she had not yet acknowledged him as standing alone from all the rest. Charlotte made no secret of the others. Bun had to hear about them and bear it as he could. He would use any method if he had to, he realized with sudden grimness. But no, he didn't want to! It would be half defeat. He felt in her somewhere an untouched purity that matched the blue mountain coldness of her eyes.

"Come on. You've seen enough."

He pulled at her, with a grim insistence beneath youthful boisterousness.

He was surprised at the meekness with which she followed him along. But Charlotte had these funny moments of docility. She had told him once about an English teacher who had had a great influence over her for a little while in a college in Missouri that Charlotte had attended for about six months. "She was going to make me lead a new life. She wouldn't let me cuss any more. I was going to be a true woman." Bun grinned, recognizing the authenticity of the quotation. But the funny thing was that Charlotte didn't cuss. Her language was soberly stripped of even schoolgirl profanity. Sometimes it had a queer awkwardness; almost—if anybody but Charlotte had spoken that way—prissy. Charlotte reminded him at times of a bad little girl trying to talk grown-up people's language. Humorously, but lovingly, Bun secretly cherished these contradictions in her.

"Now we're going over and look at the ancestral pile."

The old rock house stood pale gold and cool in the April sunshine. It seemed to Bun to have a sad dignity. The window glass glared disconsolately over the drawn green shades. Bun tried all the doors.

"Can't get in. All locked up."

Charlotte was standing back, still docile, and waiting. She asked in a queer awe:

"Is it empty?"

"Stark empty."

Bun was going on to explain the situation, but it didn't seem worth while. The familiar middlewestern routine of starting out farming and then moving into town meant nothing to Charlotte. It was such a matter of course to Bun that it simply signified "American." It was funny, when he came to think of it! His Grandfather and Grandmother Luers had been born in Germany, and his Grandma Ferguson in Scotland. Yet Charlotte was "immigrant" in a way that he wasn't, that he couldn't conceive of his family as ever having been. He had always thought of his ancestry as just ordinary American, when he thought of it at all. Charlotte would cover the complications of his family history with the one scathing word "bourgeois." It was so much more mixed up than that, that Bun didn't seem to have any recourse except to fall back on facetiousness.

"*We* can live here next summer. Or next winter. You can run the binder for Rolfe and I'll take photographs." He stole a sly glance at her. "The folks own this joint."

He grinned. But he didn't know that he wasn't half in earnest. Well, this had been a pioneer home, and Charlotte was a pioneer—more than any of his grandfather's descendants!

Charlotte was still staring at the house. She said soberly, "I would have called that a mansion." Here it was—just standing empty. She thought of the little tar-paper shack on the plains where all of them used to be crowded,—blazing so in the heat of the western sun that it was one shimmer when you looked at it from a distance. The whole family had worked in the beet fields together, except the baby, and he almost did—the mother had to take him along because she was nursing him. Bun always talked as if he, and his folks, were American. Well, that was American too! She had told Bun about her father, and the way he used to lick the kids to make them all work; but when Bun had started to get indignant on her account, Charlotte had turned around and defended her father. "He had to make us earn our bread." Now, remembering, her mouth had a cynical hardness. She looked with hostile eyes at the empty house. A mansion!—a palace was what it would have been. She hated Bun and the whole Ferguson family.

Bun knew it. He felt that there was nothing he could say. Her experience was out of the class of his. But he wasn't going to let her feel separated from him, all the same. He at least knew enough to appreciate the way things were. With a kind of timidity, he put his arm around her. Charlotte's body yielded to his touch, unconsciously, it seemed. Her eyes looked into his with a stricken appeal.

But she had to pull herself away and say again, "I'm going to be free just the same!"

"Sure. So am I."

Bun grinned to see the passionate flash of her eyes and the clenching of her hands. He felt inside the quivering sweetness of that fierce possessiveness she could show. All that he had felt up to now seemed shallow and colorless. Last summer he had thought he was developing a case on little Frankie Weyant— slightly detached and humorous, because she was such a kid. In fact, he had liked her being such a kid. It gave him a lot of time! He had dallied with a romantic fancy that he would wait for her to grow up and then come back for her. The appropriateness had appealed to him as idyllic. He could see that the folks were pleased at the idea of his falling for Frankie. Bun had always liked every girl for what she was. His sensitiveness had a peculiar faculty of finding out the hidden symbol in each of them, which his detachment had permitted him to appreciate at its full value. He had gathered girls, transiently loving each for what she signified to him. But Charlotte was the strange new element on which he hadn't counted. There seemed to him a sense of distance and of potential magnificence about her that bowled him over. He found his vague but changing social values —first aroused in that summer when he and Joseph had gone bumming West—suddenly concentrated and personified in this girl, with her hard, alien experience. But he couldn't say that Charlotte was just this or that. She seemed to him unique.

That was what had first interested him when he used to see Charlotte in his English class last fall, sitting miserable and silent, but sullen and hard. She wouldn't recite, because she had been shoved into the class by the registrar and didn't care anything about the subject. To the other students, she had been just a nut—their easy classification of anything incomprehensible. But her surly ability to stand alone had wakened Bun's admiration, mixed with the compassionate understanding he always had for neglected elements—why, his friend Joseph always said was contrary to all psychology, since if anybody

547

had an easy time it was Bun Ferguson! Bun had wanted to explore her strangeness. All girls whom he classed as interesting, according to his own special exactions, excited Bun's curiosity; but Charlotte—well, it did seem, uniquely. If the fellows thought it was a queer choice, and that he was getting out of line, let them go ahead and think so. They had learned some time ago that Bun Ferguson wasn't as amenable as he looked. The reason that Charlotte had given for coming to the university tickled Bun. She had been hitch-hiking, and she had hit the university town just at the opening of school. She had entered the best hotel to go to the ladies' rooms (Charlotte's entire experience of good hotels was confined to these democratic refuges) and in the lobby she had picked up a blurb put out by the Commercial Club stating that this was "the chief agricultural state in the Union." Charlotte had the idea of going some day to work on a communal farm in Russia—when she got put out of the country, she said. So she thought she might as well stay here in the chief agricultural state and see what she could learn. She told the fellow with whom she was traveling —he was a salesman for hardware gadgets—that he could go on without her. She guessed she'd stay and go to the university a while. The Dean had been interested in her and had found her a place where she could work for her board and room. That salesman had actually lent her enough money to pay for her fees. Of course she wasn't taking a single agricultural subject! They were trying to give her "culture." But partly out of the fatalism that was blended in her with a fierce and lofty enterprise, she had thought she might as well stay until her money ran out. Bun was tickled, too, because at the little denominational college, she had told him, the one where she was going to be made into a true woman, she had raised a great rumpus by registering herself as "Charlotte Corday." Hadn't she known they'd spot that for an alias? Bun had asked her. The faculty had made her give her "real name," of course; but she had stuck to the Charlotte, discarding her own stereotyped Russian name, Sonya or Marya (she wouldn't tell him what it was), and now she passed as Charlotte Bukowska.

"Why didn't you go to the agricultural college?"

"Have they got one?"

"You're a prize!"

She was like no one else he had ever known on earth, and he wasn't going to let her get away from him. But he felt the difficult necessity of explaining her to the folks, and reconciling if he could the two elements. He knew what he meant to the folks as their youngest. Bun suddenly felt as if he had too much on his boyish shoulders. As if he had started to carry the whole weight of a changing world.

But now he wanted to stop thinking. He wanted just pagan revelry in the spring sunshine . . . his girl's magnificent body. . . . Charlotte was still brooding over something; and Bun divined shrewdly that it was the meeting with his mother. Charlotte stuck to her guns. But there was still—when she encountered someone like his mother, with her fine unconscious gentility, the soft evidence of an easy life—a hurt uncertainty, almost humility, that bitterly shamed her. It was what had kept her docile under the teacher in that little school.

"Come on. Let's wander."

Bun caught hold of her hand and made her come along with him. Her face had grown pink in the chilly wind that was tossing her black hair. She looked again like an archaic goddess. Charlotte had told Bun once why she had chosen that name— because once in a library where she had gone to get warm, and where the librarian kept watching her, distrusting her looks— she had seen a picture of Charlotte Corday: one woman, she said, who had guts to up and kill a tyrant—even if she did wear silly-looking ruffles on her cap. It made Bun laugh—and yet he didn't laugh. At the center of his feeling for Charlotte, deeply and shyly hidden, was an acknowledged adoration for some element of the heroic that he felt in her.

But she was as much little girl as goddess. More, at this moment, when she suddenly broke away from him and went racing along. She stopped, panting, turned toward him. Her eyes had an open clarity, although her lips kept their sullen line. Bun had noticed that before—her mouth had been shaped by experience; at times it had a spread, sensual look; but her eyes were those of a cold pure child. Her woman's spirit had been only half brought to life. The brutality of her childhood was ground into her, making her forever distrustful, setting her always on the other side. It made Bun tremble with inchoate wrath. The thought of it was mixed strangely, religiously, with his love for her. Now he felt that love drenched deep in pity. He no longer wanted to enjoy her body. That seemed like an old treachery committed too often before.

"What are these trees?"

"Oh, this is a little stretch of timber that got left."

"Does it belong to the farm?"

"It does."

"I suppose we can go in, then," Charlotte said with such obvious sarcasm that Bun had to grin.

"Yes, we have the entrée."

All along, Bun had felt Charlotte's wariness in committing herself to any expression that might denote approval or even pleasure. It griped him, the way Charlotte lumped things all in together. The folks were "owners" in her vernacular, and that was enough. He didn't suppose she knew the difference between a nobleman's estate of the *ancien régime* and this middle-sized middlewestern farm! The things she knew were the craziest mixture of the bitterly realistic and the utterly romantic that he had ever come across!

"Oh—it's got a fence around it!"

"Sure. Do you want the cattle to get in?"

"I wouldn't care." She gave her shoulders a shrug.

"You're a swell agriculturist! You're going to teach the Russians a hell of a lot when you get over there." She scowled. It made her look big and clumsy. Bun took hold of her shoulder. "Come on, kid, don't be sore." He was a little sore himself. He had looked forward to bringing her out here. He respected the pattern of her life. She might be just tolerant to his! He could see all at once how his own history went back to this farm and was held—so far—in simple unity of design. But Charlotte's experience had been broken, outrageous, un-unified, made up of brief sojourns in unrelated places. It seemed to Bun as if he had taken Charlotte's experience into himself; and now already a profound break had come in that old feeling of unity.

He was looking at this beloved patch of timber as if from a distance.

"Come on. You want to see the woods. There may be some flowers up by now."

"I don't care anything about flowers."

Bun gave another of his sly grins. But he felt that this hour was somehow momentous. His hands were cold as he unfastened the loop of wire and pushed the wooden gate scraping back so that they could squeeze through. He let Charlotte go ahead while he fastened the gate. She was waiting for him now at a little distance. Bun felt the stillness all around them; and within the quiet spread of land, suddenly the fresh, bright, new magic of a wordless but admitted intimacy. He put his arms around Charlotte, and they made it up silently. She was the foreign bride, he thought, whom he had brought to this place from a strange land. Nevertheless, it was he, the almost despised stranger, who had divined the untouched spring in her that had kept her whole through deteriorating experience. She seemed again childish and pure at this moment. She had never really given herself, for no one had yet found her. Bun felt his hunter's instinct sharp and alert, crafty and deep, wanting to waken what no man had yet roused from slumber.

"Come on. This time you'll have to let me go ahead. You're liable to lose yourself in here."

The old sunken tracks of a wagon road led into the small stretch of timber, that seemed so dense, and was so brief. Bun remembered how, when he was a little boy, he always used to feel something mysterious in this patch of woods after the openness of the fields and pastures. He felt it now. The trees grew too thick and bushy. Nobody had taken the trouble to thin them out. The season was still so early, and the sunshine so scarce in here, that some of the trees were barely budded. The old fallen leaves made a mat, soggy underneath, that covered the cold, black, watery, springtime newness and ancientness of the ground.

The wagon road had petered out, and he and Charlotte had to go single file along a little path Bun well remembered, where their feet sank into the leaves and broke the flaking sticks with an Indian-sounding stealthy crackle. It was like one of the old games the kids used to play. Bun went ahead and held back the branches for Charlotte, snapping off the dead ones. It pleased and touched him that she followed him with docility. He had the feeling that this place was his, and that in bringing Charlotte here he was revealing a precious childhood secret to her alone.

Charlotte's eyes had that look of clarity. It made him feel again how the ancient—the dawn-ancient—and the half-formed new were mingled in her. In this strange, this unique creature, whom he alone had discovered. It was her ignorance that touched him so, along with her hard-bitten wisdom. His friend Joseph could say what he pleased, and Bun knew himself that she spelled plenty of difficulty—but he felt that all other women would be forever tasteless and trite beside her.

He let her wander around just as she liked now. It was fun, but it was pathetic too, to watch her. She made him think of a child catching sight of something beautiful and not knowing what it was. She put both hands against a tree trunk and leaned her forehead against it. She was used to roads—perhaps the stillness and the trees of this little place he happened to be able to offer her seemed like a refuge. At home, in the house, she had looked clumsy and out of place. But here she seemed beautiful. Bun loved her at this moment more than he had ever dreamed of loving anyone.

He called, "Charlotte!"

She went over to him in plunges through the mold and the leaves.

"I've got something for you."

She looked up at him, wondering, reaching up to settle the comb in her black hair. Bun drew back and made a little downward motion with his head toward a clump of leaves at his feet. Charlotte bent down and touched the white blossoms that the leaves sheltered, looking up at him again.

"What are they?"

"Bloodroots."

She touched the white petals, almost in awe. Bun was going to laugh at her, and tease her a little—he thought she didn't care about flowers! But he didn't feel like doing it now, as he watched her. Her touch showed a girl's peculiar love for flowers, different from any man's—something intimate, personal, akin —it was something he recognized, although he couldn't have explained it. But it was strangely touching to see this feminine revelation in Charlotte. Bun reached down and picked one of the bloodroots. The orange-red juice stained his fingers, making him smile to himself.

"Here—this is your flower."

He took hold of Charlotte's hand and put the bloodroot blossom into it, closing her docile fingers around the bleeding stem. The flower seemed strangely alive in the cold white purity of its petals.

Charlotte looked away from him. He saw her bite her lip, and tears come into her eyes. But he felt that he knew what she was thinking. His love for her seemed to make him almost clairvoyant at this moment. He knew without words what she wanted to tell him—that this was what she would rather have had said to her than anything in the world. He had found her hidden symbol, and by finding it, had given her to herself. She looked at him now, and gratitude overflowed in the tears that brimmed her eyes, washing out distrust. That color, that depth of pure blue, was imprinted on his sight. Bun shyly touched her. Her whole splendid body was yielding and soft. Humbly, with gratitude of his own, and proudly, Bun felt the mutuality in this embrace, different from their others. How simple it had been!—the gift she had wanted.

"Shall we go back?" he asked finally.

Charlotte nodded. She followed him blindly out of the woods. When they were in the car, she still had her flower, and he saw her fold it carefully and softly in her handkerchief.

The nice supper promised was almost ready for them when they got home. The table was laid festively in the dining room, with a spring centerpiece of jonquils and narcissus. It was too early yet for fries; but dad had been able to get hold of a nice fat chicken to cook with hot biscuits—Mrs. Ferguson remembered that Bun liked chicken pie almost better than fried chicken.

There was still a glow upon the two young people when they took their places at the table. Their faces were fresh from the spring air. A new unity held them together. It showed in their voices—although Charlotte's was muffled—and in the quick, radiant glances of their eyes. The surly line of Charlotte's lips was indefinably softened. Bun's mother had caught the meaning of this at once; although as she talked nervously, asked them about the farm and urged them to eat, she was struggling to deny it. The pleasant warmth aroused by the consciousness of having got ready a lovely meal for Bun and his guest was struck with horror. She had divined that this girl was older than her boy, exaggerating the actual three years that lay between them. She was aware, too, of experiences of which she had no real knowledge, and they both repelled and intimidated her. But she tried to tell herself that Bunny had always liked all the girls. It had never been serious. And this would be the same . . . although she knew already that it wouldn't.

But gradually Bunny saw Charlotte's light dimmed. She was silent again, awkward, and obviously out of her element. She ate the good things almost timidly, trying with childish care to curb the frankness of her appetite. He had never seen her so uncertain and downcast as this. And he divined why it was—he had won her to him, and so dissolved her strength. Now she could no longer stand on her surly independence. She was softened, bewildered, and on the defensive. He could almost have cried as he felt her shy, awkward efforts to make herself acceptable to these "bourgeois," whom until now she had always been able to regard out-and-out as her natural enemies. It was as if she had just become conscious of her old sweater and scuffed shoes as things of which to be ashamed instead of proud. And he didn't want that change! He felt to blame. She was awed by the pretty dishes and the filet lace which his mother— ironically!—was using in her honor. The large hands that had learned hard work too early were pitiful now handling clumsily the best silver and the delicate cup—were clumsy instead of splendid. Bun felt again what lay ahead of him. It was hard, perhaps not to be done . . . In a sense, he was giving away the freedom of his youth.

Seeing Charlotte here at his own table made him realize all over again how different she was from any other girl he had known. He despaired of the folks ever understanding her—or why he had made this choice. He remembered how pleased they had been when he had brought Frankie back with him once last summer, after he and Frankie had taken a hike together. They had treated her almost like a daughter then!—his mother had given her the pretty red-and-gold cup that the girls had always loved, and his father had trotted out his array of dry little jokes. Now they were even more bewildered by Charlotte than she by them. But Bun kept to his stubborn determination to give the folks their chance.

After supper, there wasn't much to do. Charlotte never thought of offering to help with the dishes. Maybe she didn't know that it was required of her. They sat down in the living room. Mr. Ferguson tried to make conversation by asking a few questions about the university.

"What course are you taking?" he said to Charlotte.

"Not any, I guess." She reddened.

Bun turned on the radio, turned it off—played a Paul Robeson spiritual on the victrola.

"Why don't you find something more lively?" Mr. Ferguson asked jestingly.

Mrs. Ferguson called to him then. For a while, the folks scrupulously left the young people to themselves. Bun went over and sat on the arm of Charlotte's chair. He put his hand on her shoulder, but he couldn't think of anything to say. He was restless with the sense of what lay ahead of him. He got up and went over to the piano and played a few meaningless chords, trying to work himself up to his announcement. His strained uneasiness showed in every move. Charlotte looked curiously subdued and disheartened.

Then his mother came into the living room, dutifully smiling, and saying that she would show Charlotte to her room.

Bun got up from the piano stool. His freckled face was pale.

"I guess I might as well break the news," he said.

Dad had come back into the living room too. In the silence that had followed his announcement, Bun heard the steady ticking of the clock on the bookcase. He saw the suspended anxiety on his parents' faces.

He went over and put his arm around Charlotte, and faced them. His face had a strained, appealing look, both boyish and old, as he tried to smile. The words seemed to him now almost more than he could speak.

"I gave myself a kind of birthday present, mother, a few weeks ago, that I haven't told you about. Charlotte and I got married."

He could see the shock in their faces. It was worse than he had thought. His mother looked actually as if she had been stabbed!—and as if she was just beginning to realize that it was her son who had done this. Bun felt himself trembling all over. He still forced himself to keep his strained smile. But he could feel that it made his face ghastly—and foolish. He stood his ground with gallant courage. He needed it more, it seemed to him, than in a stand-up fight, for he could perceive the blow that he was dealing them, and knew they wouldn't retaliate. And he knew how it must seem to them, this sudden flat announcement, with nothing to precede it—as if they had been betrayed. That was just what his mother was feeling, and he realized why. He felt for a moment as if he would break to pieces, beset on all sides. There was so much that he just couldn't tell the folks . . . how he must take Charlotte when he could get her . . . and how it was partly for their own sake—he was trying to be above-board. He couldn't give Charlotte up, no matter what happened; and yet he had been determined, when he saw that his love was not a momentary affair, to have it in the open, so that the folks would know—would hear it from himself and not from others. Mother was thinking, doubtless—he could see it—that Charlotte had lured him into this! And he would never be able to make her believe how little Charlotte had cared about the marriage. She had only gone through it to please him, half shrugging her shoulders, and believing that he was incomprehensible. Bun could have laughed. Now he was scrupulously bringing Charlotte home, to introduce her to the folks, as he would have done with any bride.

After a while his father said slowly and carefully, "Well—this is quite a surprise!"

His mother couldn't speak. Her hands were trembling.

Bun gave a shaky laugh. To have them say anything was a relief!

"I suppose it is!"

He had seen his father's eyes turn toward his mother, in uncertainty, to see how she was taking it. Dad expected mother to give the cue, and she wasn't giving it. Bun felt that he had to blunder along, in that awful hush, now that he had begun the thing, and go on scrupulously with the account he had so long been preparing in his mind. But his face had got red with the guilty realization that he wasn't so scrupulous as he was trying to make himself out to be. Because he had counted on their affection, and indulgence—he had known that if the marriage was all over when he came to speak to them, there was nothing they could do but accept it.

"Couldn't you have waited till the end of the year?" his father commented finally.

Bun colored again. "Well, it didn't seem as if we could. It seemed as if we were wasting our time when we weren't together." He tried to grin, but got no response. "You can't always wait." He put his hand on Charlotte's shoulder, and felt that firm flesh.

Charlotte was pale under her sunburn, and dumb.

Still those awful silences followed everything he said. It seemed to Bun again that he was going to pieces. Anger flared up in him. What was so terrible about this after all? They had tacitly trusted him to do as he liked all his life—and now he had made a choice, and it didn't suit them. Why should the folks be pitied? Their lives had gone smoothly, they had never run into any but minor troubles . . . except, perhaps, with Margaret—and Bun had long ago shrewdly decided that that was as much their fault as hers. But it was just *because* they were so innocent of tragedy that it seemed he had to pity them —and because it was he who was giving them their first actual blow! All his tenderness for them suffered. At this moment, it was *they* who were the children.

His father asked at last, "Where did this take place?"

Bun told them bravely, "We went to the justice of the peace."

He could see his mother's horror at that. Her eyes turned for a moment toward Charlotte. To the folks, there was something wrong in the very sound—something hasty, secular . . . well, that was true.

Bun felt with shaken relief that he could talk to his father, however. It was all turned around—mother had been the one to whom they had gone to interpret things and set them right with dad. Bun looked at his father in appeal. His mother had not spoken all this time. Bun saw her wounded eyes and trembling hands. At last she had been caught off her guard, struck too deeply to keep the situation smooth, as she had always done before. Bun knew well how all this seemed to her! The blow came from his hand—but he couldn't help it. This was his first actual experience of what it meant to make a choice. It might sound heroic—but, actually, it was a tearing in two.

With dad, queerly enough, there was almost a feeling of sympathy!

"What'll the college think of this?" Mr. Ferguson asked now.

"I'm not going to tell them," Bun said.

"Well—is that right?"

"Maybe it isn't, dad. But I can't help it." For the first time, Bun felt his lips quiver. He kept his grin with difficulty. "They can find out for themselves. But I wanted you and mama to know about it."

The clock ticked again in the suspended silence. Bun could feel that he was bathed all over in a cold sweat. He felt for Charlotte's hand. It was numb and unresponsive. She was almost cowed. . . . This was his appeal. It was the only one he had to make.

"Well," his father said finally, "I guess you're twenty-one, all right." He permitted himself a smile. His look tried to take in Charlotte too.

But Bun could see that even dad was mystified and hurt. He felt now that he could never make them understand. The most he could hope was that they would believe he had been taken off his feet, and "wasn't responsible"—and they must make the best of it. All at once, the future of their youngest child had got out of their hands, and out of their comprehension. Bun had always been aware of a certain inner detachment from his family—as if already, young as he was, he had a maturity that the others didn't have, and he must get things worked out in his own mind. That was why he had chosen the university in the first place—because none of the others had gone there, and he had felt the necessity of taking some step outside the family paths. He had met mild bewilderment, mild argument. But he had never encountered genuine misunderstanding before. It made him feel strangely helpless. The lines of existence were drawn far more sharply than he had ever known—and just tenderness and tolerance for all concerned wasn't enough. He could never make the folks see what Charlotte meant to him. He shrank with horror from the thought of bringing that deeply hidden personal secret to light. He would rather have them misunderstand him! They couldn't feel his hot haste to live all of his life that he could with this strange girl whom he had found. His world wasn't the same as their world had been when they were young, and had felt that they had all the years before them. Now—who could tell? But in that summer when he had struck out and left them, he had felt the ominous first thunder. They didn't even understand his desire to bring them and Charlotte together! His mother thought that Charlotte was "designing"—it was the old, primitive explanation, and mother had fallen back upon it, although it was unworthy of her. Yet in a way he had to accept it, since it was her special love for him, her youngest, that had thrown her off her balance.

Anyway, he stood clean before them. Now they must just make what they could of it! He trusted, half with relief, half ashamed, to their kindness, which had never failed him.

He saw his mother pull herself together. She had always so hated any suggestion that the whole family didn't stand together in perfect harmony!—and she couldn't bear that before Charlotte, this stranger. She managed to call up a wavering smile.

"It *is* a surprise," she said.

They all felt the inadequacy of this faint remark. But they accepted it with relief. Bun saw his mother give him and Charlotte a strange glance; and now for the first time he couldn't tell all that was in her face. But she came up to Charlotte, trying to smile.

"Bun is our baby, you know. It's hard to believe he's really married."

She said this in appeal—but perhaps, too, there was a deft touch of spite. Bun was all at once aware of depths of feminine craftiness struggling with feminine tenderness. But the tenderness was too much—the gentleness, the life built on affections. It broke her down. She kissed Charlotte gallantly, but in defeat, with her eyes full of tears.

"Your folks don't like it."

"Yes, they do."

"They don't!" Charlotte looked at him, outraged by the falsehood.

"Well," Bun pleaded, "we had to expect they'd be taken by surprise."

For a moment, he was afraid of the storm that Charlotte might raise. His mother had put them in the guest room— Dorothy's old room. The pastel-colored furnishings, the dainty curtains, still seemed to breathe the soft fragrance of his sister's tender placidity. He wanted to rest here now. He couldn't go through much more.

But he saw that Charlotte had been hurt through her hard youthful armor of sullen defiance. There were all the old hurts in it too, which he wanted to assuage. He thought of telling her that she had made no response, had forced his parents to do it all. But he couldn't. He could only soothe her.

When he put his arms around her, she turned to him passionately, and he felt the savage innocence beneath the hard coating of experience. *She* claimed him now. Her kisses annulled the other claims.

"Your folks wouldn't want me if they knew what I was like,"

she told him bitterly, turning against herself. Her eyes were wild.

"Well, it isn't my folks. I'm the one that wants you. Don't you believe I'll stick by you?"

"You can't," Charlotte muttered, looking down. Her sullen mouth quivered. "All bourgeois stick together."

"Charlotte, you don't mean that. Not about me," Bun pleaded, holding her tightly.

He couldn't get her to look at him, and he was hurt.

"Wouldn't you have wanted me to be decent to *your* parents?"

"No."

"Well—" Bun said with difficulty, "I *do* want you to be decent to mine."

But how could he go on even seeming to upbraid her? His own heart was sore from the dubiousness of the folks' welcome, although he might comprehend the cause. And he felt remorseful in a queer way. A few weeks ago, Charlotte would have laughed off such a meeting with bitter carelessness. But now, in her bent head, and her eyes that wouldn't look at him, he could feel her humiliation. She had wanted the folks to like her after all. She even cried a little, biting her lips, but yielding helplessly to the tears. Bun felt a painful tenderness at this evidence of the very human side he had awakened in his goddess, bringing down her old defenses. Now the natural girlish desires which he had discerned with excitement beneath the strength of her harsh independence were alive in a sensitive confusion. Charlotte *wouldn't* have asked him to accept her parents. Neither he nor she would have cared whether they accepted *him*. But he had tried to draw her into his home circle, where once again she was made to feel solitary and at bay. There was nothing he could do about it except to make her feel his own love again. Exhaustion gave him a feverish strength.

She was more yielding than she had ever been before—more yielding, more concerned, straining toward him now as he toward her, seeking a confirmation of the gift he had made to her when they were alone together. But even in the moment of fulfillment Bun knew that their first passion had changed. They

561

had let the world in on it. It was no longer all their own. The moment could not stand for what it was in its own rapture of the present. The future lay in it too. Bun knew well how little the fact of marriage meant to Charlotte. She couldn't understand what it had been to his parents, the kind of mutual thing —with her own father a brute, her mother a drudge, the sweetness of passion gone long before she was conceived. But he had grown up in the accomplished placidity of that mutuality. Bun felt with humiliated uncertainty that perhaps he was "bourgeois" after all. His marriage would mean to him all that he could make it—although he would take it as he must. No one would ever know or love Charlotte as he did, anyway! Surely that would always be a bond? He couldn't help struggling toward permanency. It seemed again for a moment, in a still more impotent despair, that the forces against him were too much for his slight powers.

"We're going to make a go of this," he whispered brokenly to Charlotte as he held her. "I can't let you get away. That's why I took you when I could. You mean the most. Charlotte. Don't you believe that? You mean the most."

He had convinced her, for now at any rate. He let himself rest for a little while in the splendor of her body. Yet even while he felt her strength, knowing it superior to his, there was in him the self-respect of his own comprehension that enveloped her.

Charlotte, satisfied, went to sleep. But Bun, after a spent shallow interval, was awake again.

Now the difficulties so unlooked-for in his easy, happy youth were heavy upon him in this dim hour. The future was clouded by them. Bun lay frowning. The fresh night air came in through the sheer curtains and centered in the little bowl of crocuses that his mother had placed scrupulously on the guest room table. There was a fragrance too delicate to be defined. Life was turning out in a queer way—a jolt had come in the early simplicity, and things no longer hung together.

He could feel in Charlotte an alien force that drew, repulsed, and held him. With a sigh now he relinquished the old idyllic thought of Frankie, youthful and cool as this fragrance in the night. Yes, he saw now, in another moment of clairvoyance coming this time largely from exhaustion, that he had really cherished the idea of some day—when she was older, when it suited him!—loving her. All would have been so clear and straight and easy then. This strange force had come suddenly between them, new, unpredicted and unpredictable. . . . That summer in the West had been the first of it, when he and Joseph had worked in the factory—that had been his first actual glimpse of what lay outside, after his gay easy boyhood and his warmly cherished childhood. He hadn't been really contented ever since. Something kept drawing him out from the old pleasant ways. That queer maturity of which he had always been conscious, that oldness in his youth, which came from being the youngest—an after-thought! Bun smiled wryly—had endowed him with a comprehension that wouldn't let him turn back. And now Charlotte's bitterly matter-of-fact stories of her childhood hardships had somehow made them his own. They repulsed him, in a way—the hard brutality—but he could never turn his back upon them. Her wandering, inchoate youth, after Frankie's that was clear and fresh and all of a piece—struck deeper. The folks had made his inheritance *too* pleasant, and that was why he couldn't accept it. That summer experience of his seemed kiddish and shallow after the harsh realities upon which Charlotte had been nourished—the immigrant childhood, the long broken journey West, the dawn-to-dark primitive labor in the sugar beet fields, the good old American attempt to rise ending this time in bitter resentment . . . and now the dream of a new Promised Land rising far away and slowly superseding the old dream of America. . . . He was meeting something, perhaps his match and more. But he felt stubbornly that he had something to give, something still fresh and inimitable, that couldn't be relinquished.

He felt the strangeness of Charlotte in this pastel-colored room that had belonged to Dorothy with her bright girlhood and her traditional marriage. He remembered that marriage now, on the radiant June day, out under the maple tree on the lawn; he himself so proud of his station as best man; all the church people and the relationship gathered around in a close and still unbroken circle. Already that seemed to exist in a past golden day which had been the culmination of the life here at home.

Bun raised himself on his elbow and looked at Charlotte asleep. His lips curled irresistibly at the thought of her loftily ridiculous name. Charlotte Corday Bukowska. This was his bride. His—Bun Ferguson's! The romance of this strangeness gave him a secret youthful joy. His lips quivered sensitively and settled into a troubled line. Charlotte's black hair was tossed back from her face on the white pillow. The heavy scowling eyebrows were serene in sleep. The startling ice-blue of the eyes was veiled by the smooth lids, and what he noticed most was her mouth, marred and blurred by experience . . . now she had the drooping lips of a hurt child.

He looked at her for a long time, with the feeling of tears burning behind his eyelids.

He turned restlessly away, thinking again of his easy youth, in this favored place—the warm home, the little local town in the pleasant shade of maples and elms, with the great rich country surrounding it. He felt an almost religious consecration in the vision of making up to his beloved for all that she had been made to suffer, and he hadn't—and the thousands of whom he was aware through her, of whom she had given him his revealing glimpse. His shyly hidden religious feeling could flower in the night. It was something which even the folks had never suspected. The old religion had never meant much of anything to him, although he had cheerfully admitted it and made allowance for it as a fixed fact in his parents' lives. All his own turned to this girl, the symbol of what he felt in the world outside. He himself was slight, young beside her—with her three extra years, her hard-bitten experience—but old, much older too. He wanted to take all this that was alien on himself and somehow absorb it. He felt the failures of his own family—Carl with his childish clinging to the old ways marked by sharp defensive irony; Margaret with her passionate exile leading nowhere. He, Bun, coming later, had escaped the need of these. It seemed as if all the elements of his home and family were lodged in his mind and affections to be held and comprehended by him alone;

and that somehow he must make a synthesis of them. But his home would never be the same to him after tonight. His easy life as the youngest was over. His beloved would lead him along very strange ways; but he had to go, holding all the while to things of which she was unaware and which he had inherited, fusing the two in some difficult reconciliation . . . perhaps impossible. He seemed already to be far from the folks, although he would never relinquish his youthful love for them, his tender, comprehending appreciation. He and his bride were the inheritors of a stormy future, even here in the pleasant fastness of this middle-aged frame house on the familiar local street with the tall trees all up and down the asphalt.

3

"Hi, Fred."

"How-do-do, Harry."

"Aren't walking, are you?"

"Yes, I had to leave my car at the garage."

He had got so out of the habit of walking that the familiar street at this hour looked almost strange to Mr. Ferguson. It was even stranger to have his acquaintances greet him just as always. He turned and looked at Harry Burbank as if it were someone he didn't know. Town was noisy with all the cars going home. But it seemed to him to lie within a hush of unreality. The pause that had intervened between those last two brief, momentous statements—his, "Well, Richard, I guess the time has come for me to pull up stakes," and finally Richard's, "Well, Fred, that's for you to say—" persisted still. After those words had been spoken, reality, the old reality, had ceased.

He passed the brick hotel building on the corner. The Rotary met there in the dining room on Thursday noons. Mr. Ferguson did not glance at the familiar windows. He had stepped out of his place. He was no longer one of the business men. The sound of his own footsteps had no meaning. He felt himself walking in vacancy.

He turned off from Main Street, so he wouldn't have to meet so many people.

Of course, there was no reason to feel any shame. It had been his own action entirely. It ought to be, really, a matter for pride. His affairs were in good shape. This was a day supposedly, to which he had been looking forward all his life. But a certain shame persisted. At the conclusion of his talk with Richard, Mr. Ferguson had got out of the bank as quickly as he could, not wanting Ray and the other employees to know.

Now he began to be really aware of the pain of that break; and yet running surreptitiously through it a strain of relief. He knew now that it wasn't just because of Annie. For a long, long while, he had been silently, secretly preparing for just this day. When he looked back, he could see that it had been inevitable from the start. He and Richard had never really pulled together. It was a wonder they had got along for as many years as this! He, Fred Ferguson, was an inheritance from the Old Man Spencer's day, too valuable for Richard to discard, but a drag on him all the same. There was a new order of business to which he didn't belong. Richard said that he was afraid of expansion; that he wasn't willing to meet the new prosperity on its own terms. He was the old style of banker, he could now admit that freely to himself. An account to him was a trust rather than an opportunity. His money he had expected to make through his own investments, by a slow shrewd adding of dollar to dollar. He had gone too far now from Main Street to be able to see the bank even if he had looked back. All at once the image of the new building had become dim to him; he knew that he had never been at home there; the dark interior of the old building, narrow and homely, was again the reality to him.

He looked around him at the stream of cars speeding past on the asphalt. The town lay in a bright summer light. He hadn't realized all the building that had taken place within the last few years. They hadn't seen much of it on their own street, which was long settled, and belonged to an older day. At another time he might have regarded all these evidences of growth with a natural pride. They were what he himself, along with the other business men, had hoped for and had helped to bring about. But now all at once, as he looked at the bright new glaring oil station opposite, and the roar of the cars hurt his ears, he had the feeling that things were getting out of hand. He started to cross the street and stepped back nervously out of the way of a car. What did the fellow think he was doing, anyway? They all thought they had to go just as fast as they could, these days! Mr. Ferguson suddenly found himself on the side of the pedestrians. For the moment he felt confused, outmoded. He had to realize that now when it came to walking, he wasn't so spry as he once had been. He felt a helpless outrage at the noisy indifference of that fellow who had made him jump.

"Don't he know there's anybody but himself on the road?"

Well . . . it looked as if Richard had the town on his side. The rush of cars, the glitter of sun on the red gasoline tanks, the smell of mortar from the tearing down of the old brick house next to the corner—all spoke for Richard. A woman going past said brightly, "How do you do, Mr. Ferguson?" A flutter of chiffon and a scent of powdered fragrance seemed to linger after her. Mr. Ferguson stared. She had spoken to him, but he didn't know who she was, all dressed up that way. He passed the Hoagland home, a large brick house with heavy porches. Young Bert Hoagland and a tall girl in white were playing in the tennis court. Their voices had an easy ring, their movements a summertime casualness. If the Hoagland bank, "the other bank," actually was in trouble, as some people thought, it didn't seem to bother this young Bert any! Mr. Ferguson thought he didn't know, maybe he was sorry he hadn't made more use of his opportunities to get as fine an establishment for his family as Henry Hoagland's over there. It was less than an hour since he had given up his place—but now already time had flowed past, and he couldn't have gone back to it. A great syringa bush near the walk was heavy with fragrance. The summer brightness pulsed with activity. A truck went roaring and lumbering past piled with brand-new furniture for somebody. All seemed fair, and more than fair. And yet all the same, he didn't trust it. There was some presage of a storm that he could smell far off in the air. There was nothing but his native canniness to back him up—Richard had all the arguments, so far as anyone could see.

But everything was so much the same on the surface that it was hard to realize he had done something irrevocable.

He thought perhaps he had better stop at the manse before going home and inquire about Mrs. Lowrie. She had been ailing a good part of the winter, and last Sunday she hadn't been able to attend church. It wasn't anything serious, Mr. Lowrie had cheerfully insisted; but then, they might feel hurt if folks took them too much at their word, and nobody stopped in to inquire. The way Annie had been feeling, he didn't like to ask it of her.

The street on which the church stood was older than his own. It had a look of shabbiness, with its rather small frame houses. The manse itself was in need of painting. Mr. Ferguson was ashamed to see it like this. It seemed to proclaim the dwindling meagerness and poverty of the congregation, and to be a slur upon himself. But he couldn't do everything! Once the ladies would have attended to such matters. But now the real workers were dying off, or getting old, and the younger ones, it seemed, weren't willing to bother with bazaars and big suppers. Besides, the church had got into the habit of counting upon him for everything. Well—he wasn't in business any more. He would have to think before he put his hand into his pocket. It was a queer sensation to know that now he had as much as he was ever going to make.

"Maybe I shouldn't have stopped."

He knocked, but nobody answered. The paper lay out on the walk. Mr. Ferguson picked it up and put it carefully inside the screened door. Reverend Lowrie had mentioned once last winter that if Mrs. Lowrie didn't improve, he believed they would drive over to the clinic in Geneva; and so perhaps that was where they had gone today. That would mean she was pretty sick, then. Mr. Ferguson felt a sense of heaviness, touched with shame, because he didn't want anything to happen before he and Annie got away—if they were going.

While he was here, he thought he would go around and take a look at the cistern that Mr. Lowrie said was leaking. It was at the back of the house, near the back steps. Mr. Ferguson lifted off the wooden top and squatted to peer down inside. He saw that the whole thing needed recementing. Yes, things were in poor shape all round. The barn had some shingles loose, and the doors were rotting. The church had never had the barn made over into a garage. It had stood empty for years. Reverend Lowrie was the first minister who had owned a car. He used the building just as it was. Mr. Ferguson had a sneaking feeling, snooping around this way when the Lowries weren't at home; although of course it was justified, since the repairs were up to him. Mr. Lowrie always put in a neat garden. But it wasn't so nice this year as in other years. "I guess his wife took up a lot of his time." Mr. Ferguson shook his head. He didn't see how he was going to get away. It had been one of the chief accusations against the old Montgomerys that Mr. Montgomery hadn't known how to make garden, and to manage. Mr. Lowrie had been active and thrifty, a small town man, keeping things up fine at first; but now it began to look as if his time was running out, like that of all the others.

Mr. Ferguson turned away with a feeling of sadness. He ought to go over to the church, too, and have a look at that stain in the plaster the snow had made last winter. He looked at the faded brick church, the narrow Gothic significance of the pointed windows; and felt he didn't want to go in there and see some more things that needed doing. The heavy leaves seemed to darken the street. The little spurt of renewed activity after the war, when they had first got Reverend Lowrie, was petering out. During the winter, the congregations hadn't been so bad, but now that summer had come they were smaller than ever. Mr. Ferguson was uneasily aware that the old talk about disbanding was going around again. Everything devolved upon a few—Mrs. Dunn, the Weyants, Essie Bartlett, Mrs. Rist and Ada—all of them willing enough, but the paying was up to him. For years this little band had fought all talk of joining the Congregationalists. But how would it be when they were gone, when the question was left to the young people? Mr. Ferguson felt he couldn't say much, since his own children had stopped coming to church. Now that he had dropped one load, it suddenly seemed as if this other was too heavy. There had been a pride and consolation in being the mainstay. But now he felt that he was carrying the whole church on his shoulders. The pain that had begun this afternoon spread and deepened. If folks didn't want the church, or the bank as he would run it, then it was time for him to leave. Let them get along without him! He could feel how much it had hurt when Richard had let him drop out with so little argument—and with a sly off-glance of the eyes that said he, too, had long been thinking. What was the use of keeping the church up for a few, at his expense, if the young folks didn't care about it? Mr. Ferguson felt that he'd like to make these repairs that were needed, and then get away from the whole thing.

He was tired, he wasn't used to walking. All his mild elderly aches and pains had come to the surface, and he went along slowly.

Mrs. Ferguson had stepped out into the back yard, and Mrs. Morgan saw her and called to her:

"How's the bridal couple? Aren't they coming back here this summer and let us have a look at them?"

She tried to speak brightly. "I don't know!"

But she knew very well! She went back into the house, and automatically finished the little task that she had begun, laying the flowers that she had cut on a newspaper on the kitchen drainboard, and with trembling hands picking off some of the leaves. She kept hearing that question over and over in her mind, and the strain of pretending was simply more than she could bear. The eyes of her neighbors, she felt, were upon her all the time, penetrating beneath the falseness of her smile. Oh, for Louie—somebody!—Fred was no use. All he did was try to soothe and console her—just as false with her as she with him! For the first time the smooth surface of a beautiful family life that she had always been able to keep, even when they were having so much trouble with Margaret, was cracking and straining. Before people in town, she could never let down for a moment from being Mrs. Ferguson, a fortunate woman, satisfied with everything just as it was. Once she had gone over to Mrs. Bird's, with some vague idea of talking to her—Mrs. Bird didn't belong to their church, and she was different. But Mrs. Ferguson simply hadn't been able to spoil the dear old lady's image of her as the happiest of wives and mothers, completely fulfilled in her beautiful brood of children. She was just barely able to restrain herself from sweeping flowers and paper together and throwing the whole thing into the wastebasket: acknowledging to herself by this out-and-out act that there was no use in making pretty bouquets, her home and her whole life had gone back on her. She crowded the flowers hastily into any kind of a bunch, stuck them into a vase which she reached for blindly on the cupboard shelf, and then left her bouquet standing there, and went on into the living room.

She sat down in the big chair. Her hands went lax on the arms. She lay back in a luxury of suffering, now that for a little while she didn't have to keep up before anyone—feeling almost as if she were drowned.

But the silence was too much. She was afraid of it. She had to do something. She walked around the room for a while, and then out into the empty hall. Without knowing just what she meant to do, she went upstairs, and then blindly into Dorothy's room for comfort. The dainty motionless curtains kept the room in a summertime hush. But this was the room where those two had slept. She had forgotten that when she came in. And Dorothy was too far away! Mrs. Ferguson wrung her hands.

She went out into the hall again. The door of Margaret's room was closed—just as Margaret's life was closed against them. Mrs. Ferguson couldn't bear to go into her own room. No help for her there. She dreaded to have Fred go off in the morning and leave her to face the blankness of another day; but in the night she was in a fever of impatience for morning to come. She lay outwardly relaxed, so that Fred wouldn't suspect, but inwardly she was hard and closed against him. She had to keep practicing her old code even now. Oh, if she could tell Fred how she did feel, let him into the awful blackness of the emptiness before her!—but her voice seemed to be drowned under years and years of womanly silences and bright pretenses. At the same time, she kept struggling to preserve her old attitude toward him, to withhold her secret from him, in which he had no share. The once that she had burst out at him, although it hadn't begun to rid her of pent-up grievances, had made him uneasy and strange with her ever since.

She went downstairs again, took up a magazine, and for a

little while felt quite calm again. The Vieles had spoken of getting up a group to drive over and see the Hanging Rocks, and momentarily Mrs. Ferguson was able to look forward to this. But then she thought of how Bunny used to do the driving for them, when he was at home, taking along little Frankie or some other girl. The pain of Bunny's marriage was what still filled her mind. She felt the marriage as a cross-blow that had struck at the roots. When Fred tried to get her to say just why she was taking it so hard, she couldn't admit her real feeling about it, she could only give the surrounding reasons: the girl was older, she was so rough, she wasn't their kind. Fred just didn't see how alien the girl was. Her terrifying strength!— against Bunny's youth, his slightness, his tender rearing. Mrs. Ferguson herself didn't understand the girl, couldn't make her out; but she had an intuition all the same that she was drawing their boy away to some threatening distance. There was a sharp blade of fear cutting into her confused hostility toward this alien. She couldn't give Bun's wife a name, she could only say "that girl." Bunny had chosen that girl . . . and now some hope—something—was dead.

Her youngest. She could stand to lose any of them but him! She had somehow known that she must give up the others— but never this youngest! Her last, and she would have no more. She felt that with blinding, piercing bleakness, as she wandered in anguish through the empty rooms. She had never taken in its significance before. Because they had Bunny, their gift to comfort and complete them, to throw a light of youth over their age. They had loved him in a bright security—and if *that* was gone—! Now there was no one but herself and Fred.

Terror came upon her. The whole house seemed unreal. The familiar furnishings were all around her but they had lost their meaning. She dreaded to have Fred come home, because it seemed as if he, too, meant nothing to her now. He had things outside, she charged that up against him—the church, the bank. She had nothing. All her pleasant activities, the club, the efforts at civic improvement, existed only on the circumference of her life. Her children were at the center. The home was nothing without them, she knew it, and she knew they were gone.

Now a deep resentment seemed to be struggling through her fear and emptiness. She was fighting to get back the memory of her girlhood. Then she had seemed to exist in herself, not to be dependent upon other people. Locking up the schoolhouse at the end of the day, going down the road with some of her "scholars" clinging about her, hot moist little hands loosely clasped in hers —out drying her hair in the sun, spreading out the shining light brown strands tipped and feathered with gold—she had been happy, and needed nothing else. She used to go after flowers in the woods and make careful little copies of them in water colors. This had seemed to afford her a lovely satisfaction, precise yet dreamy . . . but now she couldn't even recall what the satisfaction was. She couldn't go back to making water colors! She thought of the time when she and Fred were in love . . . the picnics in the woods, when the buggy wheels crushed narrow paths over the moist fresh grass, and the others sent them off to get the water for the coffee out of the spring beneath the big rock . . . and the cool breath from the stones, the hot sunshine in the open picnic place, had been illumined with a marvelous significance . . . which had never quite failed—until now. It was not just a sentimental saying that this love had crowned her life. It had blossomed in marriage and borne the fruit that she had craved. She could never say that her marriage had not been happy, in spite of all its secret failings. Nevertheless, her own separate life had gone down beneath it; and now that she needed that life again, she could no longer find it.

The whole town was empty. She had come into it a stranger, and now it seemed that she—she *herself*—was a stranger still. She had pretended to accept all kinds of things she had never actually accepted. Now when she tried to look ahead, there wasn't anything that she could see. The children hadn't known her as herself. Fred, either—or if he did once, he had forgotten. Maybe there *was* no self any more. It was all dissolved and lost. She had gladly given it away—but now she felt defeated.

Mr. Ferguson came within sight of his own house, substantial and roomy on its nice piece of lawn. The hedge of bridal wreath was still in bloom, which they had put in between their yard and that of the rented house next door, hoping it would keep out the dog and the children without need on their own part to keep shooing them away. There was no sense of heaviness here. All lay serene in the late afternoon light.

But as he approached the house, Mr. Ferguson was aware of a sense of emptiness that couldn't have been guessed from the pleasant exterior. The old home life had changed, and something vital had gone out of it. Ever since Bun's marriage, things hadn't been the same. Their pleasant, settled ways of living were upset. Sometimes he came home and found that Annie hadn't got any supper ready—an unprecedented thing! She didn't feel like cooking just for the two of them, she said. It wasn't worth the trouble. Well, then, they would go down to the restaurant, he told her. But neither of them enjoyed that very much. Gradually he had come to feel that there must be a change, something must be done for mama; and now that the change was upon him he felt relieved. He had a hurt feeling when he looked at the house. His old, constant satisfaction seemed to be gone. He traced it to the thought that his own children had pulled out—there were none to succeed him, in the house, in business, in the church. All at once he understood fully how mama felt. What was the use of keeping up everything just for themselves? Mama said he didn't feel as she did about the marriage. Maybe he didn't, just as regarded the girl herself. Her healthy robustness appealed to him, and she couldn't be so bad, he thought, or Bunny wouldn't have chosen her. But he realized now how he had counted upon his youngest son. He had always had the idea of setting Bun up in some business here at home, that would appeal to him—maybe something that he himself, when he got ready to leave the bank, could go into with Bunny. He had never supposed, any more than Annie, that they would lose Bun.

He opened the screened door and went into the house.

"Mama?"

No answer.

At first, he felt furtively relieved. He could put off the fuss of his announcement a little longer—make up his mind what he really did want to do about going away.

He went out as usual to get himself a drink. He always liked to do that when he got home. He turned off the faucet but for a few seconds the water slowly dripped. Now he began to feel heavily the silence of the house, that had only seemed to him a peaceful quietness before.

"Annie. Mama!"

All at once he went quickly and stealthily upstairs; and it wasn't until after he had opened the bedroom door, and seen the room unoccupied and in order, that he felt the heavy beating of his heart. This was where he had found her that Sunday morning, after Bun and Charlotte had left, lying huddled up on the bed and crying in such an abandonment that he had been terrified. He was only now realizing just how deep that shock had gone. At first he hadn't known what to make of it. He knew the marriage wasn't what they would have chosen, but he thought they had agreed to make the best of it. Hadn't mama reproached him often enough for not seeing the children's side? And now it seemed as if he had learned that lesson and mama had forgotten it! When he had tried to talk to her, how she had flown out at him! He couldn't get over it even yet. All at once she had opened up—mama!—and let out grievances against him that he saw she must have been cherishing for years. It had seemed to turn everything upside down! No, he *didn't* take on as she did—that was what she had told him; and it was because he had never cared for the children in the same way. "If you did, you wouldn't have to have things pointed out. . . . You know Margaret was with some man last summer." He hadn't known it. Mama had never said so before. Had Margaret told her? "Of course she didn't tell me! Do you suppose she'll ever tell us anything?" And then she had gone back years, while he had stood there dazed and bewildered—until finally he had realized that now she was blaming him for the way he had treated Margaret when she was sent home from the normal school. That had hurt him terribly. It hurt him still. Because he knew, and had long ago come to acknowledge, that maybe some of the things he had said then had been a mistake. But he had supposed at the time he and Annie had felt just the same! Of course he had been the one to do the punishing, since Annie was no good at it; and it was partly because Annie had felt so bad . . . he was going to see that this time Margaret knew what she had done. Last summer, when Margaret was at home, he had tacitly tried to make up for their mistakes, giving Margaret her money just the same as he had done with the others (he had given Bun his money too) and not even suggesting what she ought to do with it. The pained, guilty feeling that somehow they had failed with Margaret had made him more lenient to the others. He had tacitly come over to mama's side. And this was all that mama saw of it! Talk about *his* not understanding—! An old hot stubborn anger that he hadn't felt in years had flamed up in him, and he had turned and left mama to think what she pleased, and gone downstairs. There he had sat for a while, grasping at the arms of the chair, and trying to get hold of his anger. It was hard, painfully hard, for him to admit it—but he had never felt right about Margaret. Maybe, when you started wrong, you couldn't get the wrong undone. All right—if Margaret *was* carrying on (so he thought of it), then he guessed he was ready to bear his share of the blame. Still, that was a reason—so he wanted to tell Annie—why they oughtn't to make things hard for Bunny and this girl. The things Bunny had said—his arguments against the social order he knew his father had helped to build, his resolve to go off and start somewhere with Charlotte all on his own—these had hurt, and hurt still. They had driven the first wedge of doubt into Fred Ferguson's conception of things. But he and Annie ought to stand together, not apart. He hadn't been able to stay away from her long, or to keep his anger. It made him guilty that he *didn't* feel this quite as she did. She had always been more to him than the children, and he felt humbly that he wasn't more to her.

"Annie, we oughtn't to take sides on this. We ought to stand together."

She had agreed—or seemed to agree. Nevertheless, ever since then there had been a feeling of separation.

He felt suddenly lost. He hadn't the business, he hadn't the children any more to build and make plans for. Only Annie—and he would do anything to get her back.

Again he felt that unreasonable fear. It turned him cold. He went hastily downstairs again, and through the house. Then he saw her working among her plants in the back yard. In that one moment of terror, he knew how much she counted with him—yes, when you came right down to it, more than anything else ever had or ever could. He had proved it at last, by leaving the bank, something she hadn't believed he would ever be willing to do. He felt the desire to go off, to let everything else slip—just to be together, and to enjoy themselves, before it was too late.

As he crossed the back yard, he knew already that he was leaving. He saw all the familiar things with incredulous pain—the garden, the old workshop long empty, their apple tree. The beauty of the summer light of late afternoon lay over it all, more beautiful than he had ever seen it. He saw her small figure, in the thin summer dress, the gentle, fine movements of her little hands. He felt a surge of lonely anger against the children for hurting her. What she had said, the way she had chided him, although she had seemed to repent it with tears, had sunk into him deeper than she knew. Once she had told him that he never did anything just for her. "Anything extra—anything just for me." The accusation held justice and injustice both. Maybe he was jealous of the children, now that he saw how she missed them. But they were themselves as well as "the folks."

Yet when he came to make his sober announcement—the first time he had spoken it to anyone but Richard—it sounded incredible in his own ears.

"Well, Annie, I have something to tell you." He saw her startled face. No, it wasn't about the children, either—not this! "I'm going to close up my account. I've decided to leave the bank. . . . So I guess you and I'll go off and have a good time together this winter."

Part Six
The Folks

ALL this week it had been warm. And yet, most of the leaves were gone, showing that it was almost November. The trees stood branching dark against the blue, and around the heavy trunks the leaves lay thick, yellow and yellow-green, still soft, almost tender, and freshly fallen.

But it had been pleasant like this for such a while that Mrs. Morgan didn't feel she ought to trust the weather much longer. Now was the time to look after her plants.

Anyway, she wanted to be out here so that she could be sure to go over and say good-bye to the Fergusons.

At first she hadn't been able to get down to work, expecting them to come out any minute. But the car stood empty in the driveway between the two houses, ready for the journey. Of course, it always took folks longer to get off than they had planned.

Mrs. Morgan was bending down over her flower beds with her back to the street. "Funny she cares so much for flowers. It don't seem to go with the rest of her," Mrs. Viele had once remarked to Mrs. Ferguson. Mrs. Morgan didn't really care for flowers in the way that so many women did; or if so, she stood apart from that naïve delight, regarding it with dry harshness touched by humor and holding a strangled sense of defraudment: perhaps most of all with a stringent shyness. She knew it wasn't in keeping with her looks. She could tell herself that better than anyone else could tell her—she wasn't going to give anybody else the chance. People wondered why she had so much nicer flowers than others! Well, because she made a business of it. When anybody suggested that she must have "the knack," Mrs. Morgan scoffed. She said she guessed the knack was just hard work and doing things when they had to be done. She didn't wait around to get Loren to do the hard part for her. She wasn't afraid of getting her hands dirty. A slightly contemptuous, slightly shamed knowledge of these things was always in Mrs. Morgan's mind when other women exclaimed over her flowers. When she worked with them, decorating the lodge hall, or one of the churches for baccalaureate services, she felt awkward and never seemed to fit in; but at any rate, she could supply the decorations!

She also took a dry, sardonic pride in keeping the Old Lady Morgan's grave beautifully decorated—who had lived with her and Loren, and who *had* shown herself plenty feminine.

Mrs. Morgan had become so absorbed in her work with the dry, brown, matted plants spread fernlike on the sunwarmed ground that she almost lost the sense of where she was in time. Then she would look up and see the Fergusons' car out there in the driveway, and realize that her neighbors were leaving her. Mr. and Mrs. Ferguson! It didn't seem as if *they* could have reached the well-known stage of being left alone, with all their children married, or at any rate gone from them, and now getting ready to close up their home and go out to California! Mrs. Morgan had seen plenty of changes come over her street during the thirty-five years she had lived in this house. But it wasn't until now, when the Fergusons were leaving, that she felt the first real shock of time and change, and thought, It won't be the same any more.

A sense oppressive, and yet half ghostly, of slow, subtle, inevitable alterations was all around her, as she stood up, straightening her back, and protesting. It gave her the feeling all at once that so much and so little had come to pass. There had been so few marked happenings in the Morgans' own lives that Mrs. Morgan, with a kind of bleak curiosity, avid, caustic, and yet at bottom not censorious, because of her inner shyness, had noted outside events all the more clearly. She was very likely the most just observer on this street. But this morning all that she saw, in reality or in imagination, was made heightened and strangely moving in the light of her neighbors' departure.

She thought of the street as it used to be, years ago, and as she had scarcely realized until now that it had ceased to be. In the warm, deceptive beneficence of the October sunshine, that time was more real than now. She felt around her the air of that day, preserved only in glossy old photographs, and in memory.

Here stood the same houses—and yet how they seemed to have changed! Her own house the most of all. Photographs again, in a woven Indian basket given Mrs. Morgan as a Christmas present years ago, were the only things to recall the low frame house, plain and spare, with the hard-coal burner in the front room, into which she and Loren had come to spend the difficult, constrained first years of their married life with Loren's mother—years of which Mrs. Morgan now secretly thought with a harsh but half-resigned embitterment that had never received any answer. They had done nothing to the house until after the old lady had died. But now it was already a good while, as local history went in Belmond, since the Morgan house had worn this modern aspect, standing low on the ground, dampish under heavy trees, the porch blackly screened, and the rough coating of cement darkening through the changes of middlewestern weather.

No, not all the same houses. But it was a good while, too, since the old Grandma Davis house had been slowly carted off on wheels, to the great diversion of all the children, and the squarish frame house built next the Fergusons' on the other side, where renters with varying supplies of children had lived, but always it seemed with a yelping dog of one breed or another to endanger Mrs. Morgan's yard and flowers.

The white house across the street seemed not to have changed so much, although the old Gilberts who had built it were dead and it, too, had been given over to renters. Large, rambling, remotely and coldly Maine-style in the touch of classic severity given it by the doorway, not even the tourist sign in the front window had entirely bereft it of its native dignity. But the beautiful Yankee neatness of the woodpile in the back yard was gone—the ring of the ax on frosty mornings— the sight, sad in its sense of age, of belonging to another time and place, and yet in those very things somehow stabilizing and dignifying, of old Mr. and Mrs. Gilbert sitting silently together on their porch in the summer evenings. For as long as he could get about, Mr. Gilbert had gone muffled, limping, but true to his duty, with a shining little tin pail down the icy walk to the creamery on Saturday mornings. The sense of that long evening of life of the old couple, homely but formal, almost a work of art in its precision, could never quite leave the long sad windows and the chill whiteness of the closed front door.

The history of the Brattle house in the next block had a tragic tone out of keeping with that of the others. Someone regarding it—not Mrs. Morgan!—might have put the whole story together in the form of a drama called starkly "Pride," and almost too clear-cut in its pitiless unfolding. This story, however, had values beyond Mrs. Morgan's power of plain judgment. She was able to regard it only as a moral lesson—to be learned chiefly by the protagonists themselves, one of whom was now beyond learning. Its outline was too hard and recent for the drama to have sunk back into the softening light of memory that shone over the Gilbert place and the shortcomings of reticence and thrift on the part of old Mr. and Mrs. Gilbert. It was long enough past, even so, with the house standing empty on its big corner lot, for the gray-white paint to have faded, the fancy balconies grown precarious and dingy, the shingles begun to roughen and curl on all the silly little to-boggan slides of roof, and the wooden ball from the front porch railing to have fallen and lain cracked and half embedded in the grass. The house stood now like an ugly monument to the played-out pretensions of an early aristocracy in Belmond. It would soon be a disgrace to the whole street.

Pride was the beginning and the end of it. And what good had their pride done them?—Mrs. Morgan thought with an outraged, rankling resentment. It had caused those two to marry in the first place, and then had been the means of keeping them apart. There had been no merging in that marriage, even less than in hers and Loren's, in which each stealthily recognized the solitude of the other. None of the home girls were good enough for Lawrence Brattle, and he had had to show the town his superiority by choosing this girl "from away." Pride on Ida's part had never permitted her to yield to the life of the little town which she had entered unwilling and contemptuous. On Lawrence's part, it had forced him to despise and defend the town which he had never been willing to leave, since that would have been yielding too much to Ida. It had made him both overcareless and overfastidious about his legal cases, always spending more money than he earned, until his practice had become the worst pretense of all.

Well, anyway, it wasn't true, Mrs. Morgan could think with feelings too mixed and far-reaching for analysis, that to have children was the one thing needed to make a marriage real! It hadn't worked that way with the Brattles. But it seemed as if their one child was more the outcome of pride than of love. Each claimed her above the other. All the feelings that should have gone out to each other were concentrated on Virginia, forcing *her* pride too; until, by the terrible overemphasis of their love for her, they had lost her love for them. That was how the shrewdest observers were now making out the story: a story of tragic check and balance ending in blasting negation. Lawrence had seemed the winner for a while. Showering all that he had upon his one daughter, making her the justification for all, refusing to be separated from her, sitting with his arm conspicuously around her as if to warn every rival away—some people had thought that relationship "beautiful," but Mrs. Morgan had always doubted it, the excessive quality of it had offended her. And the result had finally been to make Virginia break away from the confines of his love, go as far from him as she could, and end by loving no one! The father whom she had overidealized at the start, she hadn't been able to forgive, as she might have forgiven one who had meant less to her. The whole idyll of his love for her had seemed tarnished and falsified. So that perhaps Virginia couldn't be blamed so much after all (as the strict notions of filial duty still prevalent in Belmond did blame her) for refusing to leave Paris where she lived all by herself, Ethel Spencer had reported, in a dubious little hotel, and come back to her stricken father, or to her mother left penniless and alone. But Ida had gained no more for herself by her immaculate virtue. Perhaps even less. Ida had been too proud to turn to anyone! Virginia had loved her father too well to forgive her mother either. This was what Ida Brattle had got for keeping *her* child so scrupulously apart from the rest of the children, nothing but white good enough for her to wear, nothing but expensive and distant schools good enough for her to attend—Mrs. Morgan could remember when not even the Ferguson children were good enough to play with Virginia Brattle! After Virginia had left them, Lawrence couldn't stand the bleakness of his home. He couldn't endure Ida's contempt without the exquisite support and retaliation of Virginia's preference. It was as if all his emotions were left stranded in helpless and chaotic agony. So it was no wonder that he had turned to a more easy-going woman to give him ease and sustenance—or a pretense of them; one who still thought that a Brattle *was* somebody. And then, after his whole quivering, shameful history of domestic and financial failure had been uncovered to "everybody," that same pride had forced him to cut his throat; and when that had failed, like everything else he had attempted—hadn't even brought back Virginia, had kept her away in fierce fastidiousness—to die slowly, and bitterly, away from home, where nobody knew him, in some cheap sanatorium. Of course Ida couldn't stay here either. Ethel Spencer had reported (with some pleasure, since Ida hadn't even quite accepted *her*) that she was acting as a kind of companion, or nurse, nobody knew just what, in a wealthy family in Chicago. That was how she had finally got away from Belmond! She had left Lawrence to cut his throat, and to win at least the pity of his neighbors for himself, and their chief condemnation for *her*-self—and to lose her child just as irrevocably as Lawrence had done.

No, sir, Mrs. Morgan decided firmly, it didn't do for any man to think himself better than his neighbors. If he did, it just showed that he hadn't the good sense to know where his own weakness lay. The neurotic values of the decadence of an aristocracy, however small, however local, were only a fading overtone in the life of such a town as Belmond.

The Ferguson house was the one that was always the same. Mrs. Morgan looked now, and saw it standing there on its familiar lawn, that was narrow on her side near the driveway, but wide on the side toward the rented house, with the big maple tree under which Dorothy had stood to be married, and that urn that had come to be one of the landmarks of this street. The house was nothing special. Both the Brattle and the Gilbert house had overshadowed it in their day. But now they had lost their glory; and the Ferguson house, freshly painted in its light clear yellow, the lawn always so well kept, the porches screened, the barn made over into a neat garage, all finished and settled and looking as if it belonged where it stood, shone out among the other houses. Other families had moved away, or died out, or lost their money. But the Fergusons, although they had their faults like others, were the kind of people who could always be counted upon. When Mrs. Morgan occasionally said, "Yes, we have some pretty nice folks living on this street," she really meant the Fergusons.

And now if *they* were going—! When Mrs. Morgan had said in her first dismay to Mrs. Ferguson, "This town will just be lost without you folks," she had meant something real. The hard times that were beginning to be felt around them had not yet touched Belmond. When the Morgans had heard of disasters, of banks failing—they had always had the feeling—well, *their* bank was safe as long as Fred Ferguson was there. Mrs. Ferguson wasn't the managing kind, like Mrs. Stark, or Mrs. Hoagland, but she had her part in almost everything that went on in Belmond. She was the one neighbor whom Mrs. Morgan trusted to understand that she herself meant more kindly than her manner might sometimes lead folks to think. Mrs. Morgan felt that now she knew why, when the town had lost its character, when too many folks had died, and control had passed to the younger ones who could never seem to measure up to the older, people who could afford it just went away, to spend the days they had left out there in the sunshine. But somehow she had never expected the Fergusons to go! Their full, busy, well-fixed household had always been a kind of center. She felt as if the house next door had stood in the full bright glow of a long noon sunlight, and that when it was empty, that glow would have passed away from the street, and twilight come.

Mrs. Morgan saw Mr. Ferguson come out to the car laden with suitcases. She carefully wiped her neat green trowel and laid it on the porch step. Then she went over to the driveway.

"Well, looks like the baggage man is here!"

"Yes," Mr. Ferguson said, "I guess we'll get loaded up now." He opened the door of the sedan and began stacking the suitcases neatly on the back seat. There were already some boxes in there. Mrs. Morgan stood watching him, wanting to help, but feeling awkward about it.

"All that stuff looks as if you were going away for a long while."

"Well . . ." Mr. Ferguson would never quite commit himself. "It's hard to tell just what we're going to need."

"Yes, I guess so," Mrs. Morgan agreed.

Much as she hated to see them leave, she began to feel buoyed up now by the excitement. There was a shout, and they turned to see the Vieles crossing the lawn, Mr. Viele raising his hand in jovial salute, and Mrs. Viele with arms hugged tight around a package. That gave Mrs. Morgan a qualm—she hadn't thought of giving any present to the Fergusons! Mrs. Viele was the kind who always remembered such things.

"Well, we thought we'd have to see the travelers off!" Mr. Viele was announcing, panting. "I see there's somebody here ahead of us." Both the Vieles cheerfully greeted Mrs. Morgan. "Where's the missus?"

"Oh, I guess she's still inside there primping."

Mrs. Ferguson came out now, wearing her fur coat, and a new hat that she must have got when she and Mr. Ferguson were in Geneva last Saturday. It was a small folded toque with a little veil, and gave her a curiously festive aspect.

"*Does*-n't the lady look sweet!" Mrs. Viele exclaimed.

She went over to Mrs. Ferguson and put the package in her arms, hugging her and whispering to her. It made Mrs. Morgan feel more remiss and awkward than ever. "Oh, you shouldn't have done that!" she heard Mrs. Ferguson exclaim; while Mrs. Viele made the proper protests, saying it was just a little to nibble on if they got hungry—and to remind them of home.

"We don't need to be reminded of that!"

Mrs. Morgan said, "You folks ought to have let me give you some breakfast."

"Oh my, no!" Mrs. Ferguson cried. "It was just lovely of you to think of it, but Ella and Ben want us to stop in there— I guess they begin to think by now we aren't coming!"

588

"Well, these things always take longer," Mrs. Viele consoled her.

"I could have heated you up a cup of coffee, anyway," Mrs. Morgan said.

"Oh, no, we both had a cup when we got up, and we feel just fine."

The three women stood aside while the men were busy loading up the car. Mrs. Morgan felt chagrined because Loren hadn't stayed to help his neighbors get started. But he thought he must be in that store by seven-thirty even if the sky fell. As Mrs. Morgan said with dry bluntness, nobody with good sense came into a hardware store any more in these days of ten-cent stores. But Loren still took a stubborn pride in the excellence and wearing quality of all his tools and cutlery and gadgets. Mr. Viele always seemed to be able to get away from his office!

"My, don't we hate to see them go!" Mrs. Viele mourned.

"I do, all right. I guess everybody does."

"Oh, well, we want them to have this lovely time too," Mrs. Viele cried, putting her arm around Mrs. Ferguson.

And it was true, even if the others couldn't go along, and enjoy the sunshine, nobody begrudged the Fergusons their winter in California. They had earned it, if anyone had. It was coming to them, Mrs. Morgan thought—even if she and Loren did have to stay here and shovel coal as usual. The Vieles had had lots of trips—nobody need pity *them* if they had to stay at home this winter.

"Can you get this in somewhere, dad?" Mrs. Ferguson asked, holding out her package to Mr. Ferguson. "Put it where we can get at it."

"What's this? Still more?" Mr. Ferguson demanded.

"Why, it's a whole lot of lovely things to eat that this naughty woman went to work and got ready for us."

"Well! Looks as if we weren't going to have to buy many meals on this trip!" Mr. Ferguson exclaimed.

The people in the rented house were out in the back yard keeping an eye on proceedings. The children were getting a little farther all the time over the boundary line into the Ferguson yard. They didn't feel quite the same as the people who were settled and owned property on the street.

Mrs. Morgan said, "Just wait a minute!"

She went into her own house, and into the dining room, where she kept some of her best plants in the sunny south window. She took a bright little scissors out of the buffet drawer—all her tools were first-class, they got *that* much, anyhow, out of keeping a hardware store!—and cut off the two beautiful purple blossoms from her famed gloxinia. She had never done such a thing before for anybody. She searched through the soft flannel leaves of her housewife until she found a long black-headed pin the right size—"Wonder I'd have it!"

The folks were just getting into the car when she went back to them. She took Mrs. Ferguson's arm and drew her aside.

"Here—let's decorate you up!" she said gruffly.

Bending, so that Mrs. Ferguson couldn't see the tears in her eyes, she carefully pinned the flowers onto the collar of the thick fur coat. Mrs. Ferguson craned her neck to look down at them.

"Why, Mrs. Morgan! Just see what this woman's done—"

She stood back, so that they could all see her decoration. They were as lovely as orchids!—Mrs. Viele cried. Mr. Viele was hearty in his appreciation. "You ought to keep those, somehow, till you can get out there, show those folks what kind of flowers we can raise back here in Iowa." Mrs. Ferguson's cheeks were flushed. She couldn't say how pleased and moved she was. She knew how Mrs. Morgan hated to spoil any of her sacred plants.

"She looks like a movie actress!" exclaimed Mrs. Viele.

"Fred, you must feel like you folks are going off on a honeymoon."

"That's right," Mr. Ferguson proudly agreed.

They all laughed. Mrs. Morgan, turning aside, managed to brush off the tears that had now overflowed, and gave a sniff and a cough to cover the proceeding. She didn't have a handkerchief in the pocket of this old jacket—she never had one when she wanted it—and now her nose was beginning to run.

She contrived to wipe it with her sleeve, pretending that she was scratching it.

"Well, sir," Mr. Viele now said, "looks like we've put in all we can."

"Yes, I guess she's pretty well loaded."

"Now comes the season of sad farewells. Well, Fred—"

"Well, Melvin—"

The two men shook hands.

Mrs. Viele, smiling and tearful, embraced Mrs. Ferguson. Mrs. Morgan was standing awkwardly aside. She dreaded this. But now her turn came. The soft fur of Mrs. Ferguson's collar brushed her face. "Well, I just hate to see you folks go," Mrs. Morgan muttered. She couldn't keep from crying again, or help folks' noticing it this time. Mrs. Ferguson gently patted her shoulder. Much more than could be spoken was expressed in that embrace. The years of neighborliness—all the little visits, the gifts of cookies and melons and slips and flowers, the helping out at this time and that. Mrs. Ferguson's fine little face, with its delicate wrinkles and gentle eyes, and her little veined aging hands with the wedding ring and the old-fashioned engagement ring with its thick gold hoop and tiny stone on the small ring finger, seemed so tenderly feminine to Mrs. Morgan that she felt a compassionate, adoring patronage toward Mrs. Ferguson, as toward a young girl. Now Mrs. Ferguson's face was flushed, and that, with the fashionable hat and the wisp of veil, gave her a kind of after-glow of girlishness setting out on her journey.

The Fergusons got into their car. Mrs. Morgan had to turn aside, grimacing, from the embarrassed sympathy of the others, and accept the handkerchief that Mrs. Viele pressed into her hand. Mrs. Viele's own tears flowed so easily that they embarrassed no one—certainly not herself.

The Fergusons were now nicely settled, with the lunch box, the handbag, the rug in case of need, all disposed of, with Mr. Viele's help. The people from the rented house had come over too, now, and were standing back from the others, the mother trying to restrain the children.

Mrs. Morgan, her face still drawn into a grimace, said, "I'll take care of the plants."

"Oh, I'm sure *they'll* be taken care of! I expect I won't know them when I get back!"

"Oh, you'll see such flowers when you get out in California," Mr. Viele told her, "that you won't look at your own when you get back." They all laughed in relief. Mrs. Morgan blew her nose. "Now," Mr. Viele warned them, "we don't want any of those pictures of picking roses in February, when we're buried in snow back here!"

"That's just what you're going to get," said Mr. Ferguson. "You didn't spare us any when you were down in Florida. And that was about the coldest winter we had!"

"My, it was lovely there," Mrs. Viele murmured aside to Mrs. Morgan.

"Have you got everything, Annie?" Mr. Ferguson was asking. Yes, she had. "Well, you want to be sure. Though I don't see how we'd get much more in this car."

During this last week at home, Mr. Ferguson had been depressed and taciturn, making Mrs. Ferguson turn often to say to him, "Well, Fred, if you don't *want* to go—" But now he seemed to have drunk of the excitement of departure. Usually on pins to get started when they were going anywhere, now he was ready to sit here and exchange the usual banter with Mr. Viele—even if Ella was waiting for them, and they hadn't had their breakfast either.

"Remember, they're not to keep you out there!" Mr. Viele cried above the sound of the engine starting. "They're great ones for trying to keep folks when they get hold of 'em, those California-ites."

"Oh, I guess we can get away from them when the time comes."

"My, I hope it's this nice all the way!" Mrs. Viele said. "But you'll soon be away from the cold weather." She nodded brightly.

Now Mr. Ferguson was getting anxious to start. Mrs. Ferguson sat smiling, reaching up once to wipe her eyes. Love to Dorothy, they were all telling her. "Kiss those dear children for me," Mrs. Viele cried.

"Remember, you're coming back! You tell Dorothy and that man of hers they can't keep you. Say hello to those grandchildren. I expect *they'll* want grandma and grandpa to stay."

The loaded car moved slowly out of the driveway. The neighbors were all waving. The woman who lived in the old Gilbert house was standing in her doorway now. She waved.

"Drive careful, Fred!" Mr. Viele shouted.

Everybody laughed. The whole town knew Mr. Ferguson's caution.

"See to it that the folks get you well fed up—you'll have to live on oranges out there in California! . . . Guess he didn't hear that."

They all waved hopefully again as they watched the car drive off down the street where the yellow leaves were sprinkled. They still stood for a little while.

"Well, they're off," Mr. Viele announced.

A momentary friendship seemed to have been formed among the neighbors. They were all being left behind. "My, don't we hate to see them go," cried Mrs. Viele tearfully. They all said how lonesome it was going to be without the Fergusons—but how nice they *could* go.

"Not everybody can these days!"

Certainly it seemed to make the street very empty. Already the Ferguson house had a closed-up look. Another empty house on this street! What was happening to it? And the Ferguson house had always been so busy, so full.

The others left, but Mrs. Morgan and the Vieles still stood talking together, as more intimate friends of the Fergusons. There wasn't much to be said now except repetitions. Mrs. Viele hinted at how badly Mrs. Ferguson had felt about Bun's marriage. It was a dreadful blow to her. And after Margaret . . . But Mrs. Morgan, somehow, didn't want to say much— she felt as if she knew more about the family affairs, living next door, and she didn't want to betray them, even to Mrs. Viele. She felt too lonesome and sore, with the Fergusons gone.

"Well, sir," Mr. Viele said finally, "I wish *I* was going to California."

Mrs. Viele said with smiling loyalty, "Well, we've got just as good a place as any right here."

They all agreed—Mrs. Morgan a little doubtfully. It didn't seem very good with the Fergusons gone. Yes, she guessed they hadn't so much to complain of—except the snow.

"Oh well," Mr. Viele said, "a little snow don't hurt us. Keeps us limber, shoveling."

But whatever they said was an anticlimax now. Mr. and Mrs. Viele agreed that they'd better be getting home. "Business goes on for the rest of us as usual." Mrs. Morgan went slowly across the driveway when they left. She had taken off the old gloves she had been wearing while she worked among her plants. The finger tips had been cut off, and now she noticed that her own fingers were dirty. She expected Mrs. Viele had been noticing that too, for all she was so soft-spoken and nice!

She went into her kitchen. It was not much like the Old Lady Morgan's kitchen of other days—this fresh room with the bright linoleum, all the modern appliances. The breakfast dishes were still on the table. Mrs. Morgan gathered up the silverware and took it to the sink.

She stood a moment, and then went into the other room.

Mrs. Ferguson's plants were in the front room. Mrs. Morgan fingered the lacy fern. It made her think of Mrs. Ferguson, it was so dainty—and of all the warm, busy life of the house next door. Well, she'd have plenty of time to look after the plants this winter. Loren was getting so he liked less and less to drive anywhere. Her house seemed bleak. Its neatness was no comfort. It was years, now, since she had got things fixed the way she wanted them. The memory of those first years under the supervision of the Old Lady Morgan had left bitter dregs. But even so, without that . . . maybe she just wasn't the kind. She didn't know as she could blame either herself or Loren. But now she couldn't help begrudging Mrs. Ferguson a little, much as she loved her. If Dorothy was the fairy-tale princess of the street—yes, she and not Virginia Brattle! with her rich handsome husband, her beautiful marriage, her lovely home—Mrs. Ferguson seemed to Mrs. Morgan the queen. She had all a woman could ask for. Family troubles, which Mrs. Morgan had noted more shrewdly than her manner gave any indication, only made her life more rich and deep and full. There was a dry shame in Mrs. Morgan's own heart.

Mrs. Morgan went back into the kitchen. She detached the shining toaster from the wall and carried it to the sink. All these shining appliances made her think of Loren. Thin, grayish, noncommittal, his natural taciturnity grown upon him during all these years in their trim, silent house—neither of them talkers or readers or people to go—and wearing an old gray striped coat that didn't match his pants, Mr. Morgan was as much a part of the hardware store as the bright scissors of graduated sizes in the showcase and the washing machines at the back end of the room. When someone would remark, "I don't see how hardware stores make much money these days," Mr. Ferguson would reply with a worried, dogged belief in the business excellence of his town, "Oh, they do it on their stoves and wash-machines." Mr. Ferguson was one of the kind who still wanted the tools he bought to be of the best and to last when he got them. But folks like that got fewer in Belmond year by year. And the hardware store, such a good business when Loren went into it, now was getting dusty and left behind. It seemed that they were going to have less instead of more as they got older. The best years, meager as they had been, were left behind.

"I'm not going to wash those dishes until I feel like it."

Anyway, they had their own place. They could do as they pleased. Now there wasn't even a neighbor to notice.

Mrs. Morgan went outside again. She wouldn't look at the Ferguson house. She felt ashamed and disgusted at having broken down and shown her feelings to all those people. There was a flatness, now that the folks were gone.

"Whoo! Scat!" Mrs. Morgan said suddenly.

That nasty dog—well, anyway, it had traipsed a little too far this time and lost out on the proceedings. Mrs. Morgan always hated to be as fierce toward the animal as she felt, for fear of what Mrs. Ferguson would think of her. But she couldn't bear to have the ugly beast around.

"You get out of here and quit leaving your calling cards in my yard!"

2

Even before they finished breakfast, the skies had begun to cloud over; and by the time they left Belmond, it was plain that the weather was in for a change. Later in the day, it had begun to rain. Going down through the southern part of the state, the autumn fields had turned dark and sodden, there was a patient, local, reproachful look about the wet frame houses and the farms with their leafless groves. The dark brooding sky seemed to tell the Fergusons that winter was coming on, and that never before had they been away. It gave them a feeling of shame and of flight which they never quite lost all through the alien stretches of the desert country. Their last view of home should have been that happy one of their house and their neighbors in the sunshine; but instead it had been of the little group of relatives and church people—Ben looking old and stooped, Mrs. Lowrie frail and faded—standing out in front of Ella's narrow frame house, shivering and left behind, under a darkened sky.

Through all the earlier part of their trip, the Fergusons had felt like strangers in a strange land. The scenery was splendid, of course. But Mrs. Ferguson had been nervous on the mountain roads. She didn't really trust dad on roads like that, although she sat tense and still, and wouldn't have told him. She longed for Bunny. The pain of that—to her—incomprehensible marriage dug its way even deeper into her, as if it were a wound that was slowly spreading from nerve to nerve. She had been afraid crossing the desert, where it was so far from town to town. The few people whom they met were dark and alien. At the Indian pueblo where they stopped, in the late afternoon, almost twilight, a chilly wind blew across the open space of the plaza in swirls of dust. The earthen houses looked stark and bare, the whole place ominous and strangely deserted, as if it belonged to another age. They didn't see how Margaret could have said she wanted to live there! "Oh well, Margaret likes anything that isn't what she's accustomed to." At the Grand Canyon, of course, it was wonderful. It was glorious, they soberly admitted that. But Mrs. Ferguson had drawn back from the railing, trembling a little. Dad could take refuge in statistics. But his arm was her only protection against this feeling of mightiness and of her own terrifying insignificance. There was something about that uncharted sublimity that dwarfed and threatened all the sanctities that she held dear. In her secret heart, it was not only terrifying, it was distasteful. Had she told the truth—which she would never do!—she would have admitted that she hated it.

But the moment they crossed the California line, the Fergusons had a feeling of safety. This was novel and strange, but it was an extension of what they knew. It was where Dorothy, and Louie, and many of their old friends lived. The word "Arizona" had a foreign sound—a western story, or a movie, Indians, or a health resort—but the word "California" was rich with familiarity. The desert all at once became friendly and interesting; and in the blaze of the far-famed sunshine, that last dark vision of home faded away.

It seemed as if things *did* change at once. They found such a nice tourist camp, even if it was out on the desert. With its neat stucco houses, with the fine windows and the real curtains, and the cactus garden, it was almost like a little town.

"Well, mama, maybe we better stay here tonight."

"Oh, yes, this looks nice," Mrs. Ferguson replied happily. "It doesn't look like that other one."

They pulled up at the office building. It was almost evening. But fear had fallen away from Mrs. Ferguson now. She was only a day's ride from either Louie or Dorothy. A very nice man owned the camp.

"Yes, sir, I've got a cabin for you—showers, toilet, kitchenette, everything you could ask for. I try to have the best there is going. Now if you folks'll just sign the register—"

Mr. Ferguson signed.

"Ioway, hm?" the man said, looking at their car. "We get

597

a good many folks from out there. M'wife and I used to live in Missoury."

"That so? Well, that's a pretty good state too," Mr. Ferguson conceded.

"Yeah, it sure is, it's a pretty good place. But *we'll* never go back there."

"Like this better, do you?"

"Well . . . you don't have the cold weather."

The man took them proudly to their cabin. Mrs. Ferguson exclaimed over how nice it was. It had bedding and all—good bedding. "You can count on it," he told her, "that bedding's clean. M'wife sees to that."

"Oh, I can see that," Mrs. Ferguson said happily.

It was nicer than a hotel, she thought. It was really like a little house of their own. Before this, she and dad had disliked the tourist camps, with all the noise of people coming and going. But now the time had come when she was ready to be pleased with anything. Their holiday was actually beginning. The man was telling them, why, some folks stayed a week or more—they'd had one family stayed a month! Said they liked the camp and might as well just squat here. Oh, this air was fine! There was nothing like it. "You know, folks pays a lot of money for desert air, in Palm Springs and those places. These scientific fellows are saying now it's got more of these vitamines or whatever you call 'em in it. Here, you can have all of it you can breathe for a dollar and a half. And if you've once breathed it, you'll never be satisfied with any other."

Mr. Ferguson listened silently. The fellow was kind of a boaster, he had decided, but he had a nice place here, so maybe he had a right to talk. There was even a relief in this familiar loquacity after the dark taciturnity of those Indians and Spaniards. At least it was language they could understand, like what they heard at home, only more so. If Annie was satisfied . . . Now Mr. Ferguson stepped in to ask if there was a place to eat.

"We can fix you up right here! Steaks, ham and eggs—whatever you want. M'wife's a good cook."

Mrs. Ferguson was happily sure of that. Well, then they'd try it here, Mr. Ferguson said. They washed their hands in the nice little bathroom. The water *was* hot, just as the man had said. The supper was nice too. Mr. Ferguson enjoyed his steak for the first time in days. Mrs. Ferguson, not wanting such a heavy meal, had chosen bacon and eggs. She was pleased with everything here. She felt at home among these people. The little waitress was nice about getting her more hot water for her tea. A pretty girl too, although perhaps with hair a trifle too golden. "You folks had all you want?" the girl asked sociably as she made out their bill; and the proprietor's wife, a perspiring fat woman with scanty bobbed hair, came waddling out to ask anxiously, "Was everything all right?"

"Oh, yes," they assured her, "it was fine."

After they had eaten, they decided to walk around for a bit. There wasn't much of a town, they could see, but the oil stations were all brightly lighted up, giving it the semblance of a metropolitan air. At this hour, the place really seemed more imposing than Belmond! Now Mrs. Ferguson felt that she could enjoy the novelty of the desert. The air was colder now, but it *was* wonderful. She looked with pleasure at the delicate colors of the sky. They didn't care to walk along the road, because of the cars; so they turned back toward the camp. Mrs. Ferguson stopped to look at the cactus garden; and Fred was interested too, since this wasn't just pretty, but something of a curiosity. Must take a lot of watering, though, he observed. He was wondering if this camp business was profitable. He could see that it took work and meant quite an outlay. Well, if they just didn't get too many of them, and run each other out of business—

"Look at this, Fred! Isn't it pretty?" Mrs. Ferguson touched the soft white plumes of a tall pampas.

"Better not touch it, mama. These cactus things have spikes."

"Oh, well, this hasn't," she said, stepping back nevertheless. "Oh, and see, this is pretty too! I didn't know cactus could *be* so pretty. Those huge big things looked so awful when we were driving along. Still, I wouldn't want things in a garden, it doesn't seem, that I had to be afraid of."

Everything was beginning to seem to her interesting and amazing. She had a childlike trust in the wonders of California.

The air was a little too chilly now, so they went inside. Mrs. Ferguson took out her knitting. She was making a little sweater for Rosemary. She had thought she would get it finished on the trip, but until now she had been too tired to work much on it in the evenings. Fred said he thought he'd step over to the office and see if they had a paper. He was gone quite a while—perhaps he was talking to the man. But she didn't feel lonesome or afraid. She worked happily away at her knitting, taking delight in its tea rose-pink, picturing the harmony of this delicate shade with Rosemary's brown eyes and fair hair. Pleasure had suddenly opened up again to her in her old diversions and there were new ones ahead of her. The little kitchenette painted in apple-green was so pretty that Mrs. Ferguson almost wished they had been staying here long enough for her to do some cooking in it. She was anxious, of course, to see Dorothy, and Louie, and all the folks. But in this place, she had a strangely blessed sense of being far away from all anxiety and trouble, and contented in a way she hadn't been for months.

Fred opened the door.

"Annie, you ought to come outside," he said. His voice was proudly excited. "Just come and see what a big moon there is."

She put down her knitting without protest, and went out with him, feeling excited too. He led her out behind the cabins of their snug retreat, away from the brilliant showy lights of the road. It seemed strangely wide and still—the noise of the cars was far away; and the moon was so marvelous it made a kind of fairyland. "You can see to read!" Fred exulted. Yes, it was certainly the biggest, brightest moon they had ever seen. All the desert was bathed in silver. And she could enjoy this beauty—because this was California, their goal, and she felt that the dangers of their journey were over. Fred put his arm around her; and just before they went into their cabin, standing in the dark little space between the doorstep and the car, he reached down and pressed his cheek against hers.

"Are you having a good time, mama?"

She nodded.

"Well, I don't know as I'd like to stay here, though," he said, after they were in bed—referring to the proprietor's assertion that he wouldn't go back to Missouri. "I guess you'd want something besides air after a while."

The next morning, after a good breakfast and fine coffee, they started out on the last lap of their journey.

"Well, stop again on your way back, folks," the proprietor of the camp told them.

"We'll certainly do that if we come this way."

"Everything was lovely," Mrs. Ferguson called back brightly.

The air was as pure and clear in the morning as at night. They were in California at last. It gave them an elated holiday feeling.

The towns were bigger now—different, of course, from those at home, but the difference was the kind they had wanted to see, not something to disturb them. They were looking at everything with eager eyes. They drove through a whole forest of branching cactus—"Joshua trees," a man at a filling station said they were called. "Well, sir, I didn't know there were so many kinds," Mr. Ferguson kept repeating. "My, there's a lot of waste country, though," he soberly added. "I don't suppose it's good for a thing but these cactus and stones." Mrs. Ferguson said nothing. She was already so pleased with California that she wouldn't agree.

Every moment now the landscape was changing. The long hard stretches of the journey were past. They felt as if they had been set free in the light golden sunshine. Now they were driving along a sort of avenue between tall palm trees and orange groves. They were beholding that, to them, almost miraculous sight—oranges growing! The globes of the thick-skinned fruit were still green-gold among the dark glossy leaves. Mr. Ferguson felt better now that he was where he could see things growing. Although the ground was hard and dry still—it must all take a lot of watering. He liked places that were settled, he said. But the mountains were not so

601

terrifying and strange beyond these pleasant homes. Everywhere there was evidence that people—their own kind of people —were living just like anywhere else; and yet it seemed to the Fergusons, on this bright morning, that the whole land existed in the midst of eternal holiday. Old anxieties, stringencies, responsibilities seemed to be gone. The estrangement of the last few months had been magically healed in the moonlight. They felt that particular happiness in being together, which, close as these two were, only visited them at rare unpredictable intervals.

They passed enticing roadside stands with oranges and figs and nuts for sale. Everything seemed to have a kind of theatrical, festive air. The beautiful fresh dates!

"Do you want to get some?" Mr. Ferguson asked.

They stopped and got out of the car. Mrs. Ferguson was pleased at Fred's easy readiness. He was always "good" to her of course, but now he seemed to stand back, anxious to make her happy . . . almost like the old days of courtship, when he had driven her into town with the best team of horses, and wanted to buy her ice cream, popcorn, everything they saw, in order to beat out the other fellows who were shining around the pretty teacher. It was *their* vacation, for which they had been working all their lives, living thriftily and soberly for all their increasing ease and prosperity. Now they had their chance to enjoy themselves, and they were taking it, both of them together. For the first time, she was really glad that none of the children were along.

Some of the dates were ready boxed "to send back home to the folks in the East." Mrs. Ferguson was elated because Fred seemed just as much taken by the idea as she was.

"Think we might get some of these, Annie? Might send a box to Ella and Ben, in return for that nice breakfast."

She assented happily. Too often, when she and the girls were taken by this or that on their earlier brief excursions, dad had wanted to drive along, saying cautiously they didn't want to be in too much of a hurry, they might see something better by and by—and it had ended in their going home empty-handed! Their lives *could* change—they still could change. Something might yet be in store for them. The stuff looked pretty nice, dad was saying—maybe they might get a box to send to Carl's folks too. The boys would enjoy it. Better for them than candy. She let him determine the size of the boxes, since he was doing the buying. But when dad *did* do things, he did them right. She would have liked to send back something to the Vieles and the Morgans. But she couldn't ask dad to get so much. He picked out a nice box for Ben and Ella, and a larger one for Carl and Lillian. Then he himself suggested, looking a trifle shamefaced at the way he was blowing himself for the stuff, that it might be nice to send a little something to Reverend and Mrs. Lowrie—and maybe to Essie Bartlett and her mother. Mrs. Ferguson felt a sense of smothered impatience that it must always be the same ones, dad's own folks, and the church people, *his* friends; but she was ashamed to make any protest—dad was so good, he always thought of the people he looked after, and of course they *were* the ones who needed it. She could pick up some little presents for Mrs. Viele and Mrs. Morgan later on. And if dad hadn't been intent all these years on looking after and providing for his own, he and she could never have taken this trip together!

"I suppose it's too far to send a box to Margaret," she did suggest, somewhat wistfully.

Dad said it was. "And anyway, she can get plenty of things in New York," he added dryly.

Mrs. Ferguson silently agreed.

But this was only a faint, transient shadow on the fresh beauty of the morning. The gifts had canceled the memory of that small aging group standing shivering under the darkening sky. Now they were really free for their own enjoyment! Everywhere along the way there was something to take her eye. She would have liked to sample all the fruits she saw, and to lay in great supplies of possible presents. The golden globes of oranges piled in pyramids on the open stands were simply too much for both of them. Fred had to admit that these people out here knew how to make a show of what they had!

"Well, I don't know, we had a good breakfast, but these oranges kind of make my mouth water," he said.

He stopped again and bought a big sack of them. Might as well have some, the things were so cheap—they could give Jesse and Dorothy what were left. He did wonder how they could sell them so cheap. Must be kind of hard on the folks who had to do the producing. Mrs. Ferguson shrugged impatiently—she didn't want to think about that. Anyway, this seemed like too good a chance to lose.

"Don't spoil your dinner," she warned Fred.

"Oh, oranges won't spoil my dinner. They're mostly all juice."

He put the skins carefully in a piece of newspaper, not wanting to litter up the roads—some people were so careless, and as a respectable town father he didn't believe in that kind of business, even if they were a long ways from home.

They drove into a medium-sized town for lunch. Dinner they would have when they got to Dorothy's. But that was a long while from now. They both admitted that they were hungry. It pleased and amazed them to find that the sun was almost *too* hot at noon. It made them wonder what kind of weather they were having back home—Mrs. Ferguson exultant because this was so lovely—it bore out her desire to come to California.

"Well, they might be having pretty nice weather back there too," Fred said loyally.

"Yes, but it was getting cold even when we left."

They drove through the bright new business section. Mr. Ferguson liked the ordinary restaurants and Mrs. Ferguson had a weakness for tearooms. But this noon they found a place that suited them both. "Home Cooking" was what attracted dad. It was a frame house, of gray shingles, what they recognized now as a California type. There was a beautiful great palm tree in the yard, which was enough to give the place a pleasingly exotic air. The rooms inside seemed to them a little chilly; but the woman—a plump, flushed woman, in a bright pink bungalow apron, with somewhat dubious mahogany-colored hair—obligingly lighted a small gas fire.

"Folks from away seem to notice the cold more," she said.

604

She was smiling and friendly, seemed nice in spite of her hair; and she sociably let them in on the details of the meal.

"Excuse me for being kind of slow, but I hurt my foot yesterday," she confided. "I don't know how I come to do it, but as I was coming downstairs, it just sort of turned over. Guess I'm kind of heavy on my feet."

It made them feel a trifle uncomfortable to have her waiting on them. But she seemed to get around all right, Mr. Ferguson noticed. They were both of them too hungry to want to be very sympathetic. She brought them fancy pink napkins and green-tinted glasses of water.

"Now what can I give you folks? I have Swiss steak, pork chops—"

"I believe I'll have the Swiss steak."

"The Swiss steak is lovely," she said approvingly.

"Well, I believe I'll have that too."

While they were eating, the woman sat down in the other room, just beyond the open doorway, ready for conversation.

"You folks from out of the state?" she asked.

They said they were.

"Well," she assured them, "you'll enjoy it this winter."

There weren't quite so many people through this year, she confided, when she came to get their plates. Times weren't so good. "I guess we don't feel it here like they do some places," she said brightly. "We don't have the cold weather to contend with, anyway." She hobbled out to the kitchen and back, making no attempt to conceal her infirmity—far from it; she was martyred but cheerful, and evidently quite proud. She came from back East, too, she told them. But she had been out here fourteen years, so she called herself a Californian.

"It's a wonderful place," Mrs. Ferguson said.

"Oh, it sure is."

She thanked them effusively when they paid the bill, and begged them to stop in again. You couldn't say folks out here weren't cordial, Mr. Ferguson noted—anyway, when they had something to sell! Had they enjoyed their meal? They assured her that it was very nice.

"Well, most everybody likes my meals. I have lots of folks comes regular, all the time."

Yes, and you couldn't accuse them of hiding many of their lights under bushels! But Mrs. Ferguson didn't want to hear even this much censure by this time. She did have a fleeting wonder as to what that woman did to her hair. But it was no use speaking about that to dad. *He* would never notice. And since it seemed to reflect a little bit on California, the woman being now a citizen, she didn't want to speak of it anyway.

She had one moment of sorrowful reflection as they got into the car and she saw the oranges. Once it would have been Howard and Jennie they would have thought of first of all, when they were buying those presents. It would have been nice to send Howard some of the dates anyway—but she wouldn't have dared suggest that to Fred. To him, it would have meant "countenancing" that woman.

"I believe I'll swing in somewhere, Annie. I don't quite like the feel of that back tire."

Mrs. Ferguson assented. If she *had* been afraid on those mountain roads, she could at least trust dad always to see that the car was in good shape.

They turned into the yard of a service station across the way.

"Guess you'll have to get out. This is going to take a little fixing."

She assented again. She didn't mind waiting out here in this sunshine. There was a place for the lady to sit down, the oil station man said politely, nodding toward a bench. She thanked him smilingly, and came back to it, after a trip to a clean, bright restroom. Everything was nice out here, she thought. Some of the restrooms she'd seen on this trip—! She felt flattered in her status of tourist. As she sat resting, she saw that some old fellow had come up and was talking to dad.

"From Ioway, are you?" the old fellow said. "What part?"

Mr. Ferguson told him.

"Don't know as I'm familiar with that section. I come from Ioway myself. Abbotsford, down in Scott County. But I been out here four years now, guess I rate as a native Californian."

Mrs. Ferguson sat and listened while the two men talked. Dad was always stiff with strangers at first.

"Belmond! Say, I did use to know a fellow there, come to think of it! Relative of my wife. Ran a grocery store. Allen, was his name. Jim Allen. Don't believe he's living now. Ever know him?"

Allen! Why, of course they knew him. Mrs. Ferguson was amused. She knew Fred hadn't thought so much of Jim Allen, but it was exciting to run across a man who knew anyone at home. He began to loosen up and get friendly at once.

"How's the son doing with the business?"

"Well, not quite so well as the old man did," Mr. Ferguson admitted. He didn't like to say that Gardner had run it pretty well into the ground, or cast any kind of reflection on his own town.

"Well, yep, that's often the way," the old fellow was saying wisely. "These young folks ain't brought up to work the way their folks did. Well, it's our fault. That's what I always tell m'wife when she don't like the way the children act. It's our fault, I tell her, we was the ones that raised them." Mr. Ferguson soberly assented—to Mrs. Ferguson's indignation. Yet she secretly agreed too—it hurt her when she thought of Margaret —of Bun . . . "The way my son's going," she heard this old codger proclaim, *"he* won't be able to retire and take it easy when the time comes—he's taking it too easy all along!"

And Fred assented again—as if Carl didn't work as hard as you could ask *any*-one to do! and Bunny too, learning photography in that place in Chicago, and getting almost nothing for it—certainly he was *work*-ing hard enough.

"Well, I'll tell you, though," the old fellow confided, getting down to business now, "with these chain stores and all, storekeeping's not the business it used to be. *I* wouldn't stay in it. No, sir, not these days. I'd go into the *gar*-age business if I was to start again. That's what the folks are after now! All on the go—the whole country's on the go. They'll buy gasoline if they can't buy bread and butter."

And what did he think *he* was doing, out here in California? And how had he got here? Mrs. Ferguson uneasily agreed with part of what he was saying, but she was indignant, defending her children.

"How's times back there?" the old fellow was asking now.

Fred answered cautiously, they were pretty fair.

"You'll stay here," the old fellow told him.

Of course Fred wouldn't agree to that.

"Sure! Why, your wife won't let you go back!" Fred shook his head, and Mrs. Ferguson laughed. Now she was beginning to think the old fellow a character. She felt herself siding with *him*. "After you've been here one winter, you'll never go back to shoveling snow."

And now he began to spread himself and expatiate on the awful climate back there in the East. "Hot? Why, the summer's hotter than anything I've experienced in the four years I been here." That irritated the Fergusons, while it made them uneasily respectful. His voice had taken on a proud, boastful note they were beginning to recognize. "Why, let me tell you, just two miles from where we were living, just two miles as the crow *flies*, I see a cyclone that ripped a fellow's barn right off its foundations and then set it down hind side to! That's a fact. And say, did you ever get caught in a blizzard?" It seemed he'd been closer than they ever had to a great blizzard too. Cyclones in the summer, blizzards in the winter—life at home was one running to cover, to hear him talk! The Fergusons laughed, both shaking their heads now, Fred somewhat nettled, as the old codger went on with his stories. "Earthquakes! Oh, yes, we have an occasional earthquake—not so many as the folks there try to make out we do. But an earthquake just lasts a minute and then it's all over—the Lord just gives us a little shake, to let us know He owns the earth."

Fred put in dryly that he didn't think some of this land out here was so much to own!

But the old fellow didn't hear that. It was evident that *he* was the one who was doing the talking—the quips and the tall tales were *his* special property. Mrs. Ferguson, although she sympathized, began to feel sorry for his wife. "Course, it can do some damage," he admitted, with a confidential, off-the-record air, "but we don't have 'em here like they do up there in northern Californy. I wouldn't live *there* for anything you was to offer me!"

But when he had said his worst, he let down, and conceded that Belmond was a pretty nice town. (Mrs. Ferguson began to think that his wife might not have such a hard time after all.) Abbotsford was too. Sure, he never went back on Abbotsford. Couldn't go back on the place where he'd made his money! All at once there was something pathetic about the old man, for all his big talk. They remembered how fast he had come hobbling over the moment he saw their car.

"Well, you know, you like to hear about the old place," he told them. "I tell you, the climate may be the worst on God's earth" (which Fred by no means was admitting!) "but you can't find any nicer folks than you can find right back there. No, sir, not anywhere. Well, when we get 'em all out here"— he perked up again—"then we'll have *every*-thing!"

The Fergusons had to laugh; and they returned his good-byes heartily. They watched him go hobbling off, solitary and chipper, down the street.

The car was ready now. They climbed into it and drove away. For almost three weeks, it had been their chief home. Soon they could put it away for a while. Now Mrs. Ferguson began to feel tired. She wondered if she hadn't taken a little cold, after all, sitting out on that bench. She couldn't look any more at the groves, the palm trees, the flowers. They didn't want to stop to eat anywhere before they reached Dorothy's, and it took them longer than they had supposed it would. She seemed to have had enough of oranges!

But as they finally drew near the city, both of them brightened up again. On the whole, it could scarcely have been a lovelier day. There was almost a reluctance in taking up ties again, in leaving this golden freedom, which they had shared. Evening brought a different kind of beauty. There was a strange limitless breath from the sea. At last they saw before them the misty fairy lights of San Diego—it was as if they were driving down into an enchanted land, where their lovely and fortunate daughter dwelt, and was waiting to welcome them.

They cruised around for some time among the unfamiliar streets, Mrs. Ferguson sitting tense and staring out at the houses, able to think of nothing now but her closeness to Dorothy. Suddenly she told Fred to stop.

"Look! Isn't that Jesse?"

A tall young man was standing near a parked car. Now he came toward them, waving. It *was* Jesse. They saw with excited pleasure how handsome he looked in his light overcoat and his light felt hat. Mr. Ferguson drew up to the curbing. Now they saw Jesse's dark eyes and the flash of his white teeth.

"Hello, there!"

He shook hands with Mr. Ferguson, hugged and kissed his mother-in-law; and he kept his arm around her, with a light flattering tenderness, as they all three stood together beside the car.

"Well, did you come out here to make sure we knew where to stop?"

"I came out to hail you. How are you?"

They told him, fine.

"It was sort of hard to find the place at this time of day," Mr. Ferguson admitted. "That's the house, is it?"

"Well, that's it," Jesse said laughing but slightly embarrassed. "But as a matter of fact—oh, say, there's Petey in the car. Poor little mutt, he's been waiting all day to come and meet you. Here, Pete—"

Jesse opened the door of the big car parked farther down the curbing, and helped out the little fellow, now almost in tears.

"Here they are—here's grandma and grandpa."

They crowded around the child, who lifted his little arms in a bewildered, half-frightened way. "Well, *Pe*-ter!" Of course he didn't know them. All day he had been looking for them; but now when he saw them, he realized all at once that they were strangers. He turned back, clutching a fold of his father's overcoat around him. He would know them soon, Mrs. Ferguson said compassionately. She wouldn't let Jesse make him come to them. But she kept looking down at him, and smiling, as they stood there, trying to make out this little face that she had only seen when it was a real baby face. Both Dorothy's children had been born at home. The child's bright eyes were clouded at first. Then they began to grow interested; even a little flirtatious. He began to swing in and out of the fold of the overcoat daringly.

"It won't be long before he knows us."

Mr. Ferguson said, turning toward the car to get out their suitcases, "Well, maybe we better go inside."

That slight embarrassment came over Jesse's laughing face again. They realized all at once that there was something strange —the car here, Jesse in his hat and overcoat, and Dorothy not running out to meet them.

"Nope. Not that way." He grinned.

"Why! Didn't you say this was the place?"

"It's the place all right. But we don't live here."

"Don't *live* here!"

They stared at him in astonishment. At first, they could scarcely take in what he was telling them. It was the house, sure enough, but for the time being it was rented. Well, they had struck a good chance—and things weren't so hot right now . . . "Guess you know that, dad, if you've got any stocks." Jesse was a little vague in his explanations. But the upshot of it seemed to be that he and Dorothy had seen the chance to make a little money out of the place—these people from the East had seen it, and it was just what they wanted—and so Jesse and Dorothy were living for the present in, "Well, a little joint that was for rent.

"You know, everybody does that around here. Everything's for rent. So we're just being cagey for a while."

Jesse laughed easily, turning off their bewilderment. It wasn't until they were in their own car, following Jesse's as he had instructed them, that the Fergusons seemed to get back their wits and wonder just what it was all about. But Mr. Ferguson was fully occupied in keeping up with Jesse, who drove too fast like all these young fellows; and Mrs. Ferguson was still in too excited and confused a state really to consider what it meant—although she *did* wonder why Jesse and Dorothy hadn't written them.

They drove up and down hills, and swung around corners, at a much faster clip than Mr. Ferguson liked, especially in a place with which he wasn't familiar. It began to seem as if Jesse was taking them out to nowhere. But at last he stopped in front of some sort of little place—they scarcely noticed what it did look like in their excitement. Now Dorothy *was* running out to meet them. Her mother, fumbling with the door of the car in her haste, had her own beloved child again. And Rosemary—

"Well, I should say we *do* see her! *She* knows grandma, doesn't she?"

Laughing and talking at once, after the greetings, they all went into the house.

It was some time before they calmed down enough to look around them and take much account of the place. After all, it was almost four years since they had seen Dorothy—almost that long since she had last come home to stay with them, the summer that Peter was born. Rosemary wasn't much more than a baby when they had seen her last. And Peter was *just* a baby. Mrs. Ferguson had enough to do in noting with pleasure that Rosemary's hair was still light, although her eyes were brown —that Peter was fair like Dorothy, that he looked like Carl at the same age—that Dorothy . . . but wasn't she thin? Oh, that was what the girls strove for these days, Jesse said laughing. It was fine, it suited him! When they were first married, he used to have to bring Dorothy a box of candy every week. Now she wouldn't look at the stuff!

"Here, old lady," he chided, putting his arm around her, "what are you weeping for?"

"Well, I'm just glad to *see* the folks," Dorothy said.

She let Jesse wipe her eyes with his handkerchief, to the children's wonder, and got back her smiling composure. But underneath it, she was still fluttered and excited, her mother could see. Now they must take off their wraps, and be shown where they could wash. A whole array of Dorothy's pretty towels was ready for them in the bathroom. The queer little coop was crowded with brushes, lotions, contraptions. But there was no time now for really looking at the place.

"I know you're just starved, mother," Dorothy said, with a touch of breathlessness. "Dad, are you starved? We have everything ready."

The little breakfast nook, too, where it seemed they were to eat, was crowded with dishes. The candles softly glowing above the beautiful bowl of roses gave the place such a festive air that at first Mrs. Ferguson was dazzled and scarcely noticed how small it was. But the children—

"Oh, they're going to have their own little table."

When the four adults had squeezed into the two painted settles, they felt—Mr. and Mrs. Ferguson, at least—as if they were trying to eat in a doll's house. The somber elderly colored woman who served them made things still more complicated. Was this all the dining room they had? Visitors were going to make things pretty crowded! Dorothy's face was flushed, her mother thought. She was carrying it off well, following Jesse's lead of acting as if the whole thing were a good joke. But it wasn't a joke to her. Mrs. Ferguson could see that well enough, and felt anxious. Dad, she could tell, was worrying too, and trying to make things out. There was an undercurrent of anxiety all through the meal, which had been better planned than cooked, and which the colored woman served dubiously. Why, the Fergusons had supposed that Dorothy and Jesse had everything they wanted! Dorothy's marvelous good fortune was still one of Belmond's favorite topics. But dinner, of course, wasn't the time to ask about it. And Jesse didn't seem to be worried at all.

Dorothy laughed. "I hope you like my dishes, mother!"

"Are these yours?" Mrs. Ferguson looked at them for the first time.

"Yes? Aren't they lovely? No, they're what we get with our handsome house."

"Somewhat augmented by Woolworth additions," Jesse observed.

Their own dishes, Dorothy explained, had to be left in the house. Oh, yes, that was customary. The people wanted to rent the place just as it stood; and if she and Jesse were going to get the price they asked for it—well, they had to agree. They were lucky enough to find people who wanted to pay such a price at this time! "I did snitch a few—a few little things," Jesse finished hastily, with a sidelong glance at Dorothy which she sedately refused to meet. He remembered now, with an inward chuckle, that "the folks" were strict Prohibitionists. It amused him, and somehow he rather liked them the better for it; he liked to tell at parties that Dorothy's parents were Bone Drys; although it seemed incredible, almost legendary, actually to find people like that.

"But aren't you afraid to have other people use your lovely dishes?" Mrs. Ferguson was asking.

"Oh . . ." Dorothy shrugged her shoulders.

"Oh, they won't break as many as we did," Jesse said easily. "You ought to see them, mother. They're an old couple from the East, as sedate as two old ducks, come from Boston. I believe they think they're really braving the wilds, coming out here. Always have gone to Europe before on their vacations. Never been west of the Hudson before. That's the kind. No, the point is, the furniture's really getting a rest, without the kids there!"

"I don't break furniture, daddy," Rosemary said, from the little table.

"Don't you? Well, I meant Peter!"

"No! No!" Peter cried.

The grown people laughed, and the grandmother sided with the children.

Well, Jesse made light of it, but there was *some*-thing behind it. The dinner was really very nicely planned. A little wine would have helped it out, Jesse thought somewhat ruefully. Mother, he surmised, would have taken it all right—yes, and enjoyed it; but dad—hardly. Well, "the folks" were all right, just the same, and he was glad to see them. His father-in-law's slow, provincial caution always amused Jesse. He rather liked its old-fashioned quality. Dad was a big man in his own town— Jesse appreciated that. Dorothy was using her own filet doilies, and her own pretty napkins.

"You see we kept out the coffee set," Jesse hastily told the folks; but Dorothy wouldn't let him catch her eye.

It was that lovely little after-dinner coffee service that one of Jesse's aunts (almost a stranger to her nephew, but dutifully honoring the occasion) had sent the children for a wedding present—Mrs. Ferguson recognized it. Aunt Ella, she remembered, had thought it was funny, saying, "Don't these things look old? Funny his aunt would send an old set,"—not realizing that the faded purple and gold was the very thing that made the cups so charming. Dad, of course, would have liked a bigger cup. He hadn't thought much, either, she could tell, of the avocado salad—he had never grown to like salads, or "those sauces" as he persisted in calling the dressing. However, he was doing manfully and making no complaint, although the poor man didn't have room to move his arms.

They all talked about the trip, about the children, about people and conditions at home. So dad was now a man of leisure! Well, this was the place for him to come. Dad didn't quite like that. He was careful to call the trip "a vacation." Dorothy seemed more like herself now. Her mother was getting used to the new way of combing her hair, swept severely off the forehead, as all the girls were wearing it now. It looked very *chic*, Mrs. Ferguson admitted. Still, she missed the soft waves about the face. Perhaps this hairdress was partly what made Dorothy look thin. She seemed to be radiant-eyed and glowing. But she had all she could do, looking after the children, and managing the colored woman who had been brought in for the occasion—their own maid, Jesse had said, laughing at the solemnity of this helper, went with the house. "This one looks as if she's about to shed tears all over the dishes." "Well, Jesse, maybe she has trouble or something at home." "Well, let her keep it there, then—we haven't got room for it," Jesse said. The frozen dessert, ordered from a catering place, was very fine. Still, it was a relief to have the dinner over.

"We'll drive around by daylight and see our late palatial residence," Jesse promised the folks.

Jesse would have liked a little evening's entertainment. But the folks were tired, Dorothy said, and they admitted it. The children were upset, too, with the excitement. Peter hadn't got used to his grandparents yet. Tomorrow they could have a good time. Tonight it would be better for them to go to bed.

The Fergusons were even more tired than they had acknowledged. But going to bed wasn't such a simple matter, either. It seemed that there were only two bedrooms, and one of those was really a sun porch. The children had that. So what *they* had must be Jesse's and Dorothy's room!

"But where are *you* going to sleep?"

"Now, mama, don't say anything," Dorothy pleaded, fearful that mother was going to think there wasn't room for her and dad.

"Look here, mother," Jesse proclaimed.

He took hold of an odd-looking handle on the wall and partly drew out a wall bed, with a flourish, pushing it in again.

"There?" Mrs. Ferguson marveled.

"There. It's a California bed," Jesse said laughing. "People sleep around anywhere out here."

"But I don't like to take your room."

"Forget it, mother. We're just picnicking, anyway."

Mr. and Mrs. Ferguson had to take the bedroom. Dorothy would have felt dreadful otherwise. She had fixed this nicely for them, with flowers, and her beautiful down coverlet. Those people must have let her keep out a few things anyway.

But the bedroom itself wasn't any too comfortable for Mr. and Mrs. Ferguson used to the quiet of their roomy house. This little house seemed to be made of paper. They could hear the children out on the porch. Peter was restless. Overexcited, poor little fellow. Mrs. Ferguson said "Sh!" to Fred, not wanting Jesse and Dorothy to overhear them. The bathroom was scarcely large enough for so many towels.

All in all, it was pretty much of a come-down after that lovely Spanish house of which they had so proudly showed everyone at home the pictures. The Fergusons couldn't help feeling that, although they didn't like to say much. Surely, if the children had to move, they could have found something better than this! The place wasn't much more than a tourist cabin.

"Oh well, when they're here by themselves they have room enough."

The bed was pretty fair, however—and the bedding was lovely. If only those two children were comfortable in there in that funny bed! Jesse had insisted that it was as good as any other. But their things were all in here, of course. It couldn't be very comfortable for them, this way.

"S'pose those kids are going to keep it up like that all night?"

"Oh, they'll calm down after a while. They're just excited. Sh!" Mrs. Ferguson warned as an after-thought.

She was more uneasy and wakeful, though, than dad. She supposed there wasn't really any cause for worry. Jesse, in fact, acted as if the whole thing was a lark. They hadn't found out much except that he had had some losses in the stock market. Mrs. Ferguson was ashamed to acknowledge part of the sources of her disquietude. But she had always counted upon Dorothy as the fortunate one, who had "everything she wanted." And now she didn't want to take up the old maternal anxiety again, which she had thought to put away, as futile, after Bun had disappointed her so. She didn't *want* to worry about Dorothy. That was one reason why she had come out here! This "vacation" at least—if that was what it was—must be all sunshine. But she could see that Dorothy was chagrined too. Treacherous sympathy for her child struggled with her own desire for this season of undisturbed pleasure. Hadn't they served their time? She turned restlessly.

"Aren't you going to sleep, mama?"

She hadn't meant to say it so soon, but she did. "Fred, I just wonder if we ought to stay here."

He was silent for a while. She thought he might have dropped to sleep, and perhaps not heard her after all. But he had just been mulling the situation over.

"Well, why didn't they tell us they'd moved?"

"Oh . . ."

Dorothy had been afraid they wouldn't come out, then. She knew that was the reason.

He was thinking it over some more. She waited in distress.

Now she looked back to the lost freedom of this day as a golden memory.

"Well—do you mean, we should go on to Louie's?"

She didn't want to say what she did mean. Of course they couldn't leave Dorothy after just this tiny visit. Fred had counted on staying here. Dorothy and Jesse had asked them so often. And they had thought there was plenty of room. She didn't like to suggest any extra expense. But she counted stealthily on dad's desire for comfort, which had been growing with the years. He told her finally:

"Well, better go to sleep now. We'll see about it in the morning."

That amounted to a promise from dad!—so she did go to sleep.

This morning, it was dad who didn't wake up. That was almost unheard of; but the driving had tired him out. Mrs. Ferguson, although she had slept fitfully, was uneasily wakeful from the time it began to be light, listening for sounds in the other room. She couldn't let Dorothy do everything, with those children to attend to, as well. Mrs. Ferguson thought with considerable chagrin of how proudly she had always told the other ladies about the servants Dorothy had—her cook, and the nursemaid for the children, and the man who looked after the grounds. That would make it harder for the poor child now, being used to help. Jesse might talk about picnicking; but she doubted if this was a picnic for Dorothy!

It was none too early, at that, when she heard them stirring. Dad would never be able to stand it, on other mornings, if they were as late as this. She suspected they would be. As soon as she heard Jesse go to the bathroom, Mrs. Ferguson went softly into the living room. She was tired, frayed, and secretly much irritated to find work awaiting her when she had expected such a beautiful rest. "I expect at Dorothy's you'll be treated like a queen!" Mrs. Viele had said. But she was concerned, really concerned for her child; and long training would not permit her to refrain from offering to help, in fact from insisting, no matter how she felt.

618

"Let me do that." Dorothy was hastily making up the wall bed. The living room was strewn wildly with clothes.

"Oh, mother! You didn't have to get up so soon."

"Well, I was awake," Mrs. Ferguson said evasively.

"Did the kids make an awful fuss?"

"Oh, they didn't bother us for long," Mrs. Ferguson lied brightly.

"They were so excited."

"Yes, I know they were excited. They always are when someone comes. You don't know how you children used to be whenever Aunt Louie came to see us."

"Were we awful?" Dorothy asked, laughing.

"Oh, no, not *aw*-ful. You never were awful."

"I was afraid dad would be up before now. We're sort of late risers."

"Well, he slept this morning—for some reason."

She couldn't help a touch of dryness in her voice.

The wall bed went up quite nicely, although it was rather heavy to handle. Jesse might have done this for Dorothy, Mrs. Ferguson couldn't help thinking. Jesse had a beautiful disposition, but she could see that he had never been used to exerting himself, or going outside his own inclinations. She perceived already, shrewdly—and with a sigh—that it was Dorothy who did the adapting. Mrs. Ferguson sighed again impatiently at having to give up—it seemed—the cherished notion of her younger daughter as a petted household queen. After all, she had only seen Dorothy and Jesse together on occasions when Dorothy naturally held the center—at the time of the wedding, and when Rosemary and Peter were born. Mrs. Ferguson hurriedly put the room into some kind of order so that Dorothy could go out to start the breakfast. Already the two women had entered into an unspoken conspiracy to get things going smoothly before the tempers of their menfolk could be ruffled.

"Oh, what lovely juice!"

Dorothy told her how cheap fruit was in the markets. She said what a grand electric refrigerator they had in the other house. "It's just too *bad* you can't be there!" she burst out.

"Oh, well . . ." her mother said consolingly. "It's you we came to see, not the house."

"I know it, darling. But—"

Now Mrs. Ferguson *was* ashamed to admit that there could be any disappointment.

The children were awake. Jesse did look after them, it seemed. Mrs. Ferguson was mollified when she heard his voice. Dorothy, however, had half her attention on the other room. She had refused to let her mother do anything more about the breakfast than to set the table; but now, when she hastily turned down the gas flame under the bacon to rush into the other room, Mrs. Ferguson turned it up again and finished things herself. She couldn't help looking anxiously at the clock, knowing that Rosemary went to school—and thinking how dad used to worry about their all being on time in the mornings. Well, there were advantages, too, in having the kind of husband who took things on himself. She had a fleeting remembrance of how poor Mrs. Christianson used to look upon *her* as the wife who had everything she could ask for. "My, if all the husbands treated their wives like Mr. Ferguson does you—!" Rosemary came in now, shining and fresh; and her grandmother had to stop and give the child a hug and kiss, saying she hadn't really seen her last night. Little Peter followed, shy but subtly mischievous. In the morning, she saw with triumph what beautiful children they were, the kind of children Dorothy *would* have —more robustly handsome than Carl's boys, she might have thought, if it hadn't been disloyal. Jesse, handsome, big and smiling, stood now in the doorway.

"Well, mother, is this where I find you? Come here, you didn't come out to California to fry bacon. Come on, kids, let's take grandmother out and show her the poinsettias."

"Oh, Jesse—" Dorothy had come back into the room. "I'm afraid there isn't time."

"Sure there is."

"Well, look at the clock!"

"Oh, I'll have all morning to look at things," Mrs. Ferguson said hastily—flattered, in spite of herself, by the clasp of his large, well-tended, sun-browned hand.

But she was on Dorothy's side. She knew too well what it meant to get breakfast for company and get children off to school at the same time. Dad had got up pretty good-natured after his long sleep, she saw with relief—she didn't know how it would be after this big trip. *She* could be out of sorts, but she could hide it better than dad. He greeted the children with unaccustomed joviality and helped them to squeeze into the breakfast nook. There wasn't time to put up the little table this morning. It worried Mrs. Ferguson that Dorothy wouldn't sit down with them and made *her* do it. Already she was assuming her old protective maternal rôle. But she knew how it was—and Dorothy could really have a better breakfast when the rest had gone and left her in peace, and she didn't have to look after them all. Jesse didn't quite like that: to have his wife standing and serving them as if she were the maid. He could be a trifle lordly at times. Well, Mrs. Ferguson thought, *she* didn't like it, either. It was much too reminiscent of Grandma Ferguson severely refusing, according to her code, to be seated when she had invited the folks all to dinner, and waiting assiduously on the menfolks but on the women very grudgingly. Not that soft little Dorothy was in the least like Grandma Ferguson!

Mrs. Ferguson didn't quite like a number of things. That Rosemary had so little time for her breakfast, for instance. Surely they might have got up a little earlier! Well, perhaps they did sometimes. Anyway, she mustn't allow herself to say anything, even if she did see that Dorothy had her difficulties. But she couldn't keep herself from half-wearily planning ways to help.

Jesse gulped his coffee and put down his napkin.

"Well, friends, I'll have to leave you. I'm a business man."

"Yes! Tell them *what* business," Dorothy said, delicately jeering.

"He's got some land business, hasn't he?" Mr. Ferguson said. He had never rightly known exactly what it was that Jesse "did"; although, of course, it didn't so much matter, since Jesse had money.

"Yes, dad, but I regret to state that the real estate business is not at present exactly flourishing in the land of sunshine. I've had to turn to my native talents for the nonce and set up a little competition for Ely Culbertson."

The folks didn't just know who Ely Culbertson was. Their education in bridge was not extensive. Jesse had to tell them. Jesse was giving bridge lessons, it seemed, along with a friend of his, or an acquaintance, to the grandes dames of San Diego. The acquaintance having formerly built a block of swank little shoppes, on spec, and most of these shoppes being now on the rocks, these two had set up shoppe for themselves—trying to get a little use out of the building. The Fergusons were not exactly shocked; the old taboo against card-playing was long ago lifted; still, it didn't seem like a *business,* to dad. Folks seemed to get into all kinds out here. They had noticed, as they drove along, a lot of funny signs on the houses. They were not yet used to Jesse's lordly young plutocratic way of treating life as a game in which he was sure to get the best breaks eventually. It was out of their experience; and somehow it seemed to put their own caution in the wrong. Before they could think of what to say, Jesse had left the table and gone into the other room.

He came back now, with his light overcoat over his arm. They didn't seem to have cut down on their clothes, either Jesse or Dorothy—Mrs. Ferguson had noticed that. Jesse looked too big for this little house. He hadn't grown a day older since the time of his marriage, so far as they could see. His hair was shining black. No one could resist that attractive smile. With his smooth, handsome, sun-tanned skin, he looked like a splendid young play boy who had nothing harder to do than keep up his tennis and lie out on the beach—he might have posed for a magazine advertisement; not at all like the father of a household, Mrs. Ferguson couldn't help thinking. And when he spoke, he did seem to make the whole thing sound like a kind of easy, adventurous stunt, which it was provincial to take too seriously.

"Well, mother and dad, you just loll about this morning, while I'm instructing the dames how to snatch the prizes from each other. Then we can take a drive this afternoon, maybe go out and have dinner and see a show tonight."

"You mustn't do too much for us," Mr. Ferguson said uneasily.

"Oh, we want to go ourselves! You're our excuse."

He caught Dorothy and gave her a kiss. She called breathlessly after him—"Jesse—Rosemary!"

"Oh, come on, Rosie. Almost forgot you. Come on and hop in."

They heard the noise of the engine outside. The car was gone.

Well, no doubt there wasn't any need to worry. It *was* just a temporary thing. After all, Jesse would inherit when his grandfather died. So perhaps he didn't need to get into any regular business. It was not a way of living that the Fergusons understood; but away from home, they could accept it more easily. Somehow, Jesse's mere presence was flattering. Helter-skelter as things seemed to be, there was really more pleasure in being here than at Carl's. Mrs. Ferguson thought that surreptitiously. Lillian often made her secretly impatient. But she couldn't hold her complaints against Jesse.

The whole household seemed to be lower-keyed when he was gone. If she had come out with her real feelings, Mrs. Ferguson would have admitted that she missed him. The situation became a little more realistic without him, however.

Now there was the question of what to do with dad while she helped Dorothy. He never knew how to occupy himself away from home. He didn't care much about the radio. Too much of this dance music, he said. But he was being more amenable than she had expected.

He said, "Oh, I'll just look around. Maybe Peter and I'll take a little walk around the place."

Well, that disposed of Peter too. The little fellow seemed to have accepted his grandfather. How splendid he looked in his little sun suit, husky and blond, with his strong bare legs and the straps over his fine square shoulders. When the children were so healthy, why worry?

The whole house seemed full of leisure when they had got the menfolks out of it. Now at last there would be the chance for a good talk with Dorothy. Mrs. Ferguson felt anxious for it, but slightly nervous.

"Mother, you don't have to help with these dishes."

"Why, do you think I'm going to let you do them all alone?" Mrs. Ferguson asked indignantly. "I guess I know what it means to entertain company, with children."

"*You're* not company."

Dorothy all at once hugged her mother in her old little-girl way, hung upon her, finally pushed her over to a chair and sat down in her lap.

"Big baby," Mrs. Ferguson said laughing.

A pang shot through her. Her real baby was lost.

Dorothy was heavy to hold, thin as she was. But her mother wanted her. She hugged her closely, straining for consolation, thinking emotionally that this was the one child whom she understood. She pushed back Dorothy's waved, brown-gold hair, taking her old pleasure in its softness. Now that she was keeping house and doing her own work, like the rest of them, Dorothy seemed to have descended to her old familiar status. She was no longer the silken smiling lady of leisure whose visits had been proud events in Belmond. Her mother missed the old splendor. But she felt that she and Dorothy were comrades now. She studied Dorothy's face anxiously, holding back the loosened waves of hair. It *was* thin. Tiny lines were etched about the lips. Of course this western air was dry. The skin was fair, but the old roselike bloom was gone. It made the mother indignant for a moment, thinking of Jesse's handsome smoothness. She divined that there was a little strain for Dorothy in keeping up with Jesse's requirements. He wouldn't know that she couldn't work and play at the same time. And Dorothy was too much like herself: Dorothy would feel that she *must* be what her husband expected and desired; otherwise—even if that was contrary to her own way—she had failed. Dorothy closed her eyes luxuriously under her mother's stroking hand. But she did not let go of her restraint. She wouldn't permit even a suggestion that her married life wasn't perfection. And Mrs. Ferguson had to approve that, although she longed to be closer to her child. It was her own code—the code of all women, she somewhat complacently supposed; unless they *weren't* what she thought of as womanly.

624

Peter had come in and was staring at them.

"You didn't know mama sat in grandma's lap, did you? Well, she's one of my babies, just as you're hers."

The little scamp looked mischievous, and tried to get into Dorothy's lap. He made his grandmother think of Forrest, just such another rascal. And yet this one's brand of mischief was subtly different. They were all different from each other. She felt the endless fresh interest of children . . . a complacency, a pang because it seemed Margaret was going to miss that— foolish girl! she thought with a rather confused indignation. And Bunny—who could tell about that girl, and what *she* might want? But it was too much, when Peter climbed on— they all had to get up, spilling him.

"Now let's go and do those dishes."

There was an intimate pleasure in working with Dorothy. Mrs. Ferguson longed to tell her about Bun and Charlotte, and her fears for Margaret, to get the solace of her understanding and sympathy. If Carl was closest to his mother's heart (or Bunny—who could say?), Dorothy was like a part of her own self.

"Isn't it too much for you to have us here? If we had known you were living in this little house—"

"That's why I didn't tell you."

"I know it was." Mrs. Ferguson sighed.

"Now, Mama Ferguson, you aren't going away! Jesse thought—" Dorothy looked confused—"maybe if it was too tight quarters here for you and dad, you might take a little place nearby. There are all kinds of them." Her voice was anxiously pleading.

"Well, I don't know," Mrs. Ferguson said vaguely. But then, Dorothy understood that she would have to ask dad first. "Oh, it isn't for myself—*I* wouldn't mind it." Which wasn't strictly true—but at the moment she thought it was. "You're the ones it's really hard on."

"No, it isn't," Dorothy lied valiantly.

At any rate, there was no use talking about it now. Dad would be the one to decide—although she might do the suggesting. They chattered about a lot of small things while they were washing the dishes, and then they went into the living room.

The place didn't look so bad when they had put it to rights —if it hadn't been for the glory of the other house.

"Oh, mother, I want you to see our house! It makes me mad we're not living there—I mean, while *you're* here. Everything is so sweet."

"I want to see it. Do you like the renters?"

"Oh, yes." Dorothy laughed. "They've taken possession, though! Except when anything's the least bit wrong. Then they're quick enough to suggest that the place is ours! 'I thought perhaps you'd like to know, Mrs. Woodward, that the enamel in the breakfast room has sev-er-al scratches. They were made before we took the house. No doubt you'll want to see to them before they get worse,' " she mimicked. Her mother made a face. "Couldn't dad have rented your place this winter?"

"*Our* house? Oh, dad would never have done that."

Although she hadn't meant it to sound like a criticism of Jesse—

They heard the toilet running. Dorothy jumped up. "Oh, that awful thing!" Dad must have left it. She hurried into the bathroom to fix it; and then came back laughing. She plumped down in her mother's lap again.

"What are *you* laughing about?"

"Oh, I was just thinking about our other bathroom—it would be a new experience for Aunt Ella."

She giggled, and leaned childishly against her mother's shoulder, playing with a little tendril of silver-brown hair. Her mother had to laugh too. Aunt Ella was well-known throughout the family as a connoisseur of toilets. It was a very ancient joke with Margaret and Dorothy. What particular pleasure Aunt Ella found, no mortal could say. But well did they remember, even out on the farm in the old days, how they had gone prancing and whimpering in childish haste, while Aunt Ella sat placidly ensconced reading old yellowed newspapers she wouldn't look at anywhere else, and Grandma said bitterly, "You might as well give up, when *she's* in there, I can tell you that." On all their drives, Aunt Ella kept an eye out; and whenever they stopped at a service station, she was off, saying, "Well, I'll try this one"—and returning with heavily whispered detailed reports, in a state of disgust or of great complacency, as the case might be. In any department store, the restroom was her first goal. Dorothy giggled.

"You naughty girl." Her mother shook her a little. "You were both naughty girls."

Mrs. Ferguson sighed—Margaret had got so far away from them.

Dorothy slid off her mother's lap and sat on the floor, resting her head against those familiar comforting knees.

She asked dreamily, "How did Meg look when she was at home? She's simply spiffy in the picture she sent us."

"Oh, she looked—very nice."

"I think she's got terribly good-looking, mother. I don't know. Sort of stunning. She's found her style."

"She *looks* fine. She was a little . . . Dorothy, did you know anything about it?"

"What? That man?"

"Oh, you *did* know!"

But how much she knew, her mother couldn't ascertain. Dorothy was always able to keep her own counsel. It hurt dreadfully to think that Margaret might have let her sister into the secret, and not her own mother. But that was the way with the girls! There had always been a bond of alliance between them, different as they were. She would never find out from Dorothy! It made her feel, with a lonely pain, the gulf that separated the generations. She saw now that Dorothy might even defend Bun's choice, and she shrank from revealing her own feelings. She was thrown back on dad, after all.

"I don't think there's anything to worry about, mother," Dorothy said consolingly, almost as if she were talking to a child. "You know Margaret always did go her own way."

"But do you suppose she still . . ."

Dorothy shrugged her shoulders. "*Quién sabe.*" She didn't want to talk about it.

Fortunately Peter came in again. The children were always a

safe topic. Rosemary ate her lunch at school, Dorothy explained, and Jesse brought her back in the afternoon.

"Does he always have to take her both ways?"

"Oh, yes. It's all right. I'm really glad of it. It gets him up in the mornings. Jesse does hate to get up."

"Yes, and dad gets up *too* early."

They both laughed.

Dorothy said, "Oh, the men are awful duds." She burrowed her head into her mother's lap.

"Of course you know, mother, we're just living like this for the time being," she added, looking up, and forestalling the possibility of criticism. "We aren't hard up like this *all* the time."

"Oh, no, of course not," her mother said quickly.

"Jesse wanted me to have someone in to help while you were here. I suppose we *would* have more fun. But I think that's silly, if we're saving money," Dorothy said with severe good sense. "We ought to be able to do it. *You* used to. I can remember when you used to entertain the folks from Nebraska, that whole big bunch."

"People don't work as hard as they used to do."

"Oh, mama—you just mean the people you know!"

"Well—maybe. . . ." Her mother assented.

But she didn't quite like that. It made her feel old.

"I think we *ought* to work . . . well, something . . ." Dorothy's voice shook a little. She sat up. "I just mean—oh well, nothing, I guess." She slumped against her mother's knee. Her eyes darkened.

Her mother sighed uneasily. It was hard to give up her old dream of the fortunate child! She didn't really *want* to hear anything more. It was as dad said—they must work it out for themselves. She felt a slight resentment against Dorothy for not being contented with good fortune. Well, she and dad had had enough work! She thought again of yesterday, seeing it all in a golden light. Her own trouble had always been that dad was *too* industrious—and now, it seemed, Dorothy was going to suffer from the opposite—! Did there always have to be something? She looked with a sudden sharp curiosity at

Dorothy's face, perceiving the determination that lay under that softness . . . Dorothy, her own child, was a Ferguson, after all. A fleeting thought touched her with pain, that she might have missed some point of likeness with Margaret, who had seemed so different, so alien, because she had Grandma's black hair . . .

But she had seen her girl again. She was *with* her. She could understand the troubles of Dorothy, the married one. The actual, tangible sunshine came in through the windows. Life worked itself out—some way—and maybe there was no getting around it. If dad was just willing to take a place here, she could see enough of Dorothy's household and no more.

Mrs. Ferguson was awake again before dad was. Dad was getting to be quite a late sleeper. They all carefully encouraged him in that—Mrs. Ferguson trying to close her ears when he said, well, there was no use in getting up, nothing to do around here. But taking this apartment was his own choice! He was the one. Dad had declared for a place with a furnace. He had regarded the little gas heaters with a profound contempt, saying often— she telling him "Sh!" for fear Dorothy would hear—"might as well have stayed at home if we're going to be *this* cold." She felt secretly triumphant, that he had come to be so tied to familiar comforts—she could have given up those things far more easily, if only she had fresh interests, places to go and see, touches of real luxury. But she remembered, with resentment that had never quite died out, the stern frugality of Fred's folks, and the restrictions it had put upon their early married life. This place was a long way from Dorothy's, and she had thought she must protest about that. Actually, she was relieved. And why shouldn't they have the comforts they wanted, and spend their money upon themselves?—if they couldn't have their children anyway. She felt a horror at her own secret selfishness, along with a strained triumph. Something active and maternally anxious seemed to have died out of her when she had lost Bun to that girl—she had felt the blow at the time, recognized it, but only now was she realizing the actual results.

She didn't want to get up before dad, even if she was awake.

She wouldn't interfere in any way with this fine new laziness that he was developing. He would never admit himself to be "retired"; would only say cautiously, well, he had "pulled out of the bank," would let "a younger man have charge"; and that he and mama were enjoying a little vacation. What his real plans were, she didn't know, and dared not ask. News from home worried him at times—"Conditions," as he phrased it. Mrs. Lowrie had had another sick spell; this one and that one had dropped out; a bank at Hanging Rock had failed. He "didn't like the looks," dad sometimes said. But she would close her eyes, would not believe that existence was not working out in the ordained way to which they had always looked forward. And this winter sunshine was on her side, bore her out.

It was not really late, of course, when they did get up. They were earlier than most of the people in the house. Mrs. Ferguson went out to the kitchen, while Fred went out to the near-by drug store for the Los Angeles paper. Sometimes he got to talking there. The girl at the drug store had shocked Mrs. Ferguson once by saying, "Oh, I do enjoy talking to your husband, I think he's the nicest old man!" Silly little thing!—no doubt every man over thirty was "old" to her, with her mat of overly golden curls, and her real eyebrows shaved off and others painted on, à la Hollywood. And dad was silly too, enjoying talking to that girl! But Mrs. Ferguson wouldn't say a word if he was late—she was only too glad to have his set, industrious routine broken. Every deviation from it was to be adroitly and preciously guarded.

Their kitchen was rather dark. The front room got the sunshine. There was no real dining room in this apartment. Mrs. Ferguson had persuaded Fred to let her set the table in the living room instead of in the kitchen nook, it was so much pleasanter. That seemed to him rather a frivolous way of doing; but he was getting very indulgent. "You fix things the way you want to, Annie, you're the one." It was more like play, eating in here. She set the little gate-legged table with the bright Mexican cloth she had bought one day when she was shopping with Dorothy. The dishes were all good enough in this place, but they were perfectly ordinary. Mrs. Ferguson secretly made pretty little additions to them from time to time, trusting Fred not to take notice. Well, he had told her that this time belonged to her. She was justified in doing as she pleased.

He was back on time. He was getting to be a great devotee of the paper, read it from cover to cover. His wife was amused to see that he didn't even miss the movie items. The fashion notes were about all that he passed up. Sometimes he would say, "Here, Annie, here's a show you might like to see—Rosemary would enjoy it." He had always considered the movies a waste of time at home, and put them with the things that were undermining the churches. Jesse joked, and said that dad was developing leisure tastes, and losing his morale. Dorothy was too tender to make fun of him. She smiled, but she kissed the top of her father's head, softly rubbing her cheek against the thin hair. Perhaps she knew too much about leisure tastes by now! She seemed to be more anxious for her dad to have a good time than her mother. Mrs. Ferguson resented that a little. Jesse and Dorothy both seemed to trust her to enjoy herself— or maybe they didn't think she had worked, and was in such need of enjoyment; but they were always thinking up things for dad. The boys would have been tender of *her* . . . only both the boys were lost to her. Yes, Carl too. Since that unfortunate time—of which none of them directly spoke—Carl had taken the reins of his life in his own hands. His smile, gentle and affectionate, admitted a secret distance from his mother, which she must help him to maintain.

The place was pleasant at this hour. They liked having their breakfast to themselves. They had suffered more than they would have admitted from the cramped quarters at Dorothy's. Poor child!—so anxious to make everything nice for them, and knowing all the time that they were uncomfortable. Mrs. Ferguson had been taken with those little Spanish-style apartments in the court that Jesse had shown them. But of course she hadn't expected Fred to like those. He had accepted this apartment with relief—it was more like home, not so "crazy." It was one of the two upper apartments in a large shingled frame house with palm trees and a border of enormous geraniums on the lawn. It stood on a nice wide street, one of the older streets, that looked as if middlewesterners had settled there. It had their own atmosphere—too much of it for Mrs. Ferguson's taste! The rooms were large, with good ordinary furnishings, nothing attractive but "all in good shape"—that was what men noticed in a place, workable and adequate equipment, not charm. "Now, Annie," Fred had said with satisfaction, "we've got everything we need here." He didn't want her to spend her time on housework, she was to take it easy. But she couldn't help making little purchases, putting on new cushion covers, getting the place to seem more homelike. She couldn't stand something just adequate and no more.

They sat long at their meal. Dad was finishing the paper. Mrs. Ferguson tried to get a glimpse of the shopping items as he read. But she didn't really like to go downtown alone— and of course she wouldn't have dad hanging around waiting for her; there was nothing he hated worse than that. It disappointed her that she and Dorothy could so seldom go shopping together. She had looked forward to long happy days. It was a job taking Peter; and Dorothy couldn't often get away. Jesse wanted her to get help; but as she said (with a touch of indignation) what was the use being hard up, if they still had everything they pleased! In a way, Dorothy actually relished their situation!—again like Grandma Ferguson, who had liked to feel that she had grim, hard tasks on hand. But if she counted on its changing Jesse in any essential way (as her mother surmised that she did) she would be disappointed. And surely the grandfather would leave them money. Why couldn't Dorothy take things as they came? Mrs. Ferguson had tacitly put aside any real shopping until she was with Louie. She was getting more and more secretly anxious to be with Louie. They enjoyed their nice breakfast, with the orange juice, and the muffins. Fred had said they would get some of their meals at a place nearby; but when she saw with what relief he returned to her cooking, she couldn't hold him to that. Secretly she resented cooking a single meal. Wasn't this her vacation? Fred liked to make excursions to the markets, to pick out the meat as he did at home, to select the fruit and vegetables, smoothing the pears carefully with his hand, satisfying himself that each one he paid his money for was the best possible value. And she couldn't interfere, for he had to have something to do. Much of her time was occupied in subtle attempts to keep him contented and occupied. Her own activities—although this was *her* vacation—had to be slipped around the edges.

They heard the bell.

"Is that ours?"

Before they could get up, they heard feet running up the stairs. Jesse appeared, handsome, and fresh as the morning, in the doorway.

"Hello, there, folks! Well, you're getting to be great dawdlers. I thought I'd find you through breakfast and dad out sprinkling the lawn."

"Oh, we're not so much earlier than you are."

Jesse agreed cheerfully when they asked him to sit down with them. "Mother, you know I never refuse any of your cooking." He ate the muffins that were left with unabashed appetite. Mrs. Ferguson thought again how young he was. She couldn't resist his big, healthy, handsome presence. Even the clothes he wore—the thick rough suit of English tweed—gave her a feeling of elation. She felt still more impatient with Dorothy—why couldn't she be satisfied, and take things as they came, when she had a husband as attractive as this!

"Well, mother, I've come to lure your husband from you."

Dad looked dismayed.

Mrs. Ferguson was instantly on Jesse's side—and dad knew it. She tried not to show it in her face.

"Aren't you going to the office?" Mr. Ferguson asked. That was what he had elected to call Jesse's "shoppe."

"No office today. Only three dames coming and Mark can handle them. I only take the good-looking ones."

Jesse grinned. His mother-in-law smiled forgivingly. Dad made no comment.

No, Jesse said, he had to take a drive—go out and see some of his unproductive property; and he'd thought maybe dad would give him the pleasure and consolation of his company.

"Where's that?" Mr. Ferguson asked.

"Oh, a sort of dude ranch I own shares in, out in the desert," Jesse answered carelessly.

They hadn't known Jesse owned such property. He had all kinds of irons in the fire—all of them white elephants in the present beautiful state of affairs, as he said cheerfully. At the same time, he laughed at the business prospects of southern California—surely not the way to regard his own community, Mr. Ferguson thought. He told about the grafts, but wherever he himself thought there was a chance, he said with good-natured cynicism, why not? As well I as another. Sure, it's all a graft. It wasn't a way of doing business that they understood; but Jesse came of a moneyed family, so they were half respectful.

"Isn't that a pretty long drive?" Mr. Ferguson asked cautiously.

"Oh, no, only about a hundred miles."

Mrs. Ferguson kept discreetly silent, knowing that Jesse's "about" might mean a hundred and fifty. Jesse never set minimums.

"Why shouldn't you go, dad?"

There was no reason why; and so, to her pleasure, she saw him forced to consent. Jesse said he would enjoy seeing the ranch. There weren't many dudes, worse luck, but it was swell country. Dad said he didn't think much of the desert.

"Oh, Fred, you know you liked that place where we stopped!"

Mrs. Ferguson would have enjoyed going far more; but she perceived that Jesse was sidestepping the idea of asking her. Now he came out with the reason. Dot's bridge club met this afternoon, he said, and he thought maybe mother would keep the children—if she could stand the little rascals.

"Oh, of course," she said at once.

"Yes, mama'd be glad to do that," dad asserted, with relief.

Maybe she would and maybe she wouldn't! It didn't exactly please her, if they had known it, this readiness of the menfolks to think she enjoyed nothing better than doing things for them all!

But anyway, she wanted Fred to go. Jesse said, stopping and

giving her hand a squeeze, he was going to run off with mother one of these days! He'd thought she wouldn't enjoy this long drive (oh, wouldn't she!—a lot more than dad would) but some time he was going to make off with her, and they wouldn't tell any of them where they were going, either. She understood the cajolery. But still she was flattered by his touch, and his good looks.

"Well, Annie, what'll you do this morning, before the children come?"

Oh, she'd get along.

Maybe she could go over and see those people from Dike, he suggested.

She didn't reply—but she didn't intend to do anything of the kind.

From the front window, she watched the two drive off together, with very mixed feelings. It gave her a little thrill, the nonchalant ease with which her son-in-law handled the low-slung car. Even Carl didn't have that light hand on the wheel.

Mrs. Ferguson let the dishes stand. She settled down in the big chair to read the Woman's Page at her leisure.

But she didn't want recipes. She was sick of cooking! She had a feeling of forlornness. Not that she had wanted Fred to stay. No, there was a sweet, secretive, rare sensation in having this whole morning to herself. Fred never enjoyed things much if she wasn't with him. But she wanted to do things without *him*, sometimes—it gave her a sense of freedom and expansion, a hidden relief. She was always aware of his inclinations when she was with him—while he was so often innocent of hers. It made her angry to think of the easy way in which Jesse had turned the children over to her. No doubt his inviting dad to go off was partly a sop. Of course, she wanted Dorothy to have a good time. Her feeling horrified her. She remembered when she was a child, a tender-hearted little girl loving her dolls and all living things. How dreadful it had seemed to her to see the cat, their old three-colored cat, slap away the kittens when she had "got through with them." She used to scold the cat, spank her (very gently), try to make her return to her offspring. "Why, kitty, your *own* kittens!" And now, was *she* like that? Were people all just animals, subject in spite of themselves to nature? It was against all her beliefs about herself. No, it wasn't quite like that. Sitting here alone in the quiet room, she felt it, deep within herself, as a kind of strangled striking back against a deep, subtle hurt her children had given her—yes, all her children.

Those people from Dike! She didn't intend to be saddled with them. Well, she thought rebelliously, she had always tried to be nice to her neighbors. She had never let herself act superior to Mrs. Dunn, although—oh, dear! And now she ought to have a little time for herself. She hardened herself against the thought of the old couple's pathos. The pathos itself was an irritation—to her, the soft-hearted! But this was where she had come to have a good time. There was a callousness even in this empty golden sunshine; and with that she allied herself. She had so little time left . . . that was what she felt now, like a sudden step into cold shadow . . . except for this winter sunshine, in which the roses bloomed, which she could believe lengthened the time endlessly. Thought for others belonged at home, along with responsibility. Those people from Dike did, too, and that was one reason why she avoided them. They were like Mrs. Rist, Essie Bartlett, all the old couples in the church. She had faithfully filled her rôle there, as Mrs. Ferguson, but these had never been her own kind of people. The old couple lived a few streets away, in a dreary little frame bungalow with a drooping banana tree in front. They had come up to the Fergusons when the car was parked one day, because they had seen the Iowa license. And of course, that was enough for dad! They were out here all by themselves. The old man had chronic bronchitis. Their children had got together to enable them to spend the winter in California. And now here they were, and roses were blooming, and they didn't know what to do with themselves. Dike! that they talked about. She had never seen it, but she felt she knew just how the place looked—the scrubby little town, with only the main street paved; even the bleak house where those people lived, beside a row of evergreens. They had no car, and dad thought he must take them places. "Maybe those people from Dike would like to go along," he was always suggesting uneasily. They had come to be dreadfully typical figures, to Mrs. Ferguson—with their sad, vacant presence, the old lady in her cotton stockings, the old man with his mournful cough. Lately they had joined, they called it "united with," an evangelistic sect, and they were always trying to get her and dad to attend one of the meetings. They talked solemnly about the second coming of Christ, sadly and patiently, with an empty hope, looking for that to free them from all their troubles, to prove that after all they *were* better than happier people. Although they were what dad called "good people," Mrs. Ferguson always felt embarrassed, even shocked, at such references. Religion oughtn't to come into everyday conversation. The old couple counted on the Fergusons as their link with home.

"No, I won't get tied up in that again!"

She rose rebelliously. The light in the bedroom was somewhat dim. She saw herself in the mirror, in her trim housedress, wearing the pretty old-blue sweater that Lillian had knitted for her. Her looks were not entirely gone. Beside the old lady from Dike, she was a pretty, fashionable young lady! She thought of the elated excitement of their departure from Belmond—the neighbors, the good-byes, herself in her new hat and with Mrs. Morgan's flowers pinned to her fur collar. Perhaps this was the perfect time, at last, that she had seen shining ahead of her all the years—no matter how they had been driven to embark upon it. She had never really stopped believing in such a time. What she wanted was something for herself—before it was too late—just herself, in relation to no one else, in no other capacity. Oh, for this little while, she didn't want to know it, if other people had troubles! She knew that she had had a pleasant life, but had she ever really taken time to *enjoy* herself? She felt as if she were—not renewing her youth—but returning to an old phase of herself, where she had left off when she was married. If this holiday should turn out to be a disappointment, then in some subtle way it would infuse all her personal life with disappointment . . . the life that still hiddenly existed apart from her children.

She trembled at her own hardness. It made her feel as if she had been a fraud all her days. In some ways, she had! To offset it, she went to get the tea-rose sweater that she was knitting for Rosemary.

There was a knock at the door. Oh dear, if it was that old lady—! She wouldn't be able to help acting cordial and pleased. She could only be hard when she was alone. Then she recognized a cough outside the door, and called gladly, "Come in!"

"Well, so she's a widow lady this morning!"

"Yes, I'm a widow."

"I saw that man of yours go off!"

"I haven't even washed my dishes—" Mrs. Ferguson began.

"Oh, now, dearie, don't you go apologizing for that. Not to *me*. I'm not one of these snoopy neighbors. I guess you know that by this time. I never wash my dishes until I feel like it, anyway."

Only too well did Mrs. Ferguson believe that! She had once caught a sight of the kitchen next door.

This was their neighbor, Miss Marcella Potter. She had the other apartment upstairs. She was a large, somewhat masculine-looking woman, and unplaceable as far as they could see. The Fergusons couldn't just make out what her business was, except that she had a remote connection with some real estate office, and sometimes spoke with great enthusiasm of avocado lands. She often referred to Portland, Maine, but she seemed to be evasive when they asked, with natural curiosity, whether that was where she "came from." She said largely, "Oh, my dear, I couldn't begin to tell you where all *I've* lived." Once, it seemed, she had been a nurse; and at one time, a sort of preacher. Her apartment, into which Mrs. Ferguson had only once been invited, was as heterogeneous as her experience. Antiques were mingled with ordinary overstuffed chairs, draperies of the nineties, ancient sentimental pictures that had been relegated to other folks' attics for years, framed poems of Edgar Guest, a German soldier's helmet, some valuable English Wedgwood, and all of it cluttered and dusty and jammed together in such a way as made Mrs. Ferguson gasp. But she must have some money from somewhere, Mr. Ferguson had shrewdly surmised. The men laughed at Miss Potter, Jesse especially. She *was* a funny mixture. She had a heavy face, and quite a mustache, but her hair was waved and done in elaborate coils; and she wore heavy silk dresses, of expensive goods, although in the general style of 1912, and rings and bracelets that looked both valuable and old. Nevertheless, Mrs. Ferguson enjoyed her, and defended her against Jesse and dad. Dad said he hadn't seen mama take to a person so much in years. Miss Potter seemed to have taken mama under her wing, so that once dad said slyly, "Well, mama, that lady seems to be sweet on you—if she was a man, I'd have to be getting jealous." Mrs. Ferguson scoffed at him. But all the same, she found flattery and comfort in Miss Potter's attentions. And it was interesting to talk to Miss Potter, she declared. She knew a lot of nice recipes—yes, she did; but you could never tell when, in the midst of shrewd sensible talk, she was coming out with some highflown notion that took your breath away—if you could believe it. And it seemed that Miss Potter did.

"Well, what's my little lady going to do with herself, when she's all deserted?"

"Oh—nothing much. I'm going to keep the children when my daughter goes to her bridge club this afternoon."

"That's good," Miss Potter approved, sitting down and stretching her legs. Miss Potter was a firm believer in children and large families, she often said. ("Why don't she get some of her own, then?" Fred had once suggested.) "Well, she's a dear little mother, isn't she—you can tell that to look at her. She doesn't often go and leave them, doesn't gad around like all these women do now, as if they weren't mothers!"

"Oh, Dorothy's a very good mother. I like to have her get out."

"I wish she'd let me take her to my doctor," Miss Potter suggested firmly, with a gleam of the eye. "He'd put some flesh on her in no time. I've known him to build people up as much as twenty pounds in two weeks! He has his own method, dearie—it goes back to the ancient tribes. Oh, these little mothers, it's hard on them." She sighed voluptuously. "You ought to go to him too, little lady."

"I?" Mrs. Ferguson laughed, flustered. "Oh, there isn't anything the matter with me."

Miss Potter shook her head wisely, and sucked in her lips.

Mrs. Ferguson tried to laugh again. She knew that Miss Potter might be said to have her peculiarities; but all the same, she was flattered by these admiring attentions. It was a new thing to find someone who wouldn't let her do anything on her side, but wanted to do things for *her*. When she had gone with a plate of cookies to Miss Potter's door, in duteous exchange for gifts of dates, health candies, and vegetized breads, Miss Potter had pushed her straight out into the hall exclaiming, "Oh now, my dear little lady, you aren't going to cook anything for me—you're here to rest and recover your strength, and I'm just going to see that you *do* it!" Dad might grumble uneasily, "What kind of an invalid does she think you are?" But all the same, there was something flattering in such treatment. As a "dear little mother," Miss Potter thought that she was entitled to soothing and building up for the rest of her days. Miss Potter was horrified at the notion that they should ever go back to Belmond. "Why, it would be the death of you!" Miss Potter treated her as if she were a fragile thing, almost too tender to be about in the world—at corners, took her arm and swept her across the street, landing her safe but breathless. "There! I'm not going to have *you* run over."

Now Miss Potter pitied her richly for being alone; and Mrs. Ferguson, although she had the grace to be ashamed, knowing well that poor dad hadn't wanted to go, still couldn't help reveling in this attitude and responding.

"If hubby's out enjoying himself," Miss Potter now said—and there was severity in her tone, "why shouldn't we go on a little toot of our own? I can't have this little ladykins getting lonesome!"

The children—Mrs. Ferguson said weakly; but Miss Potter declared that they would be back in plenty of time. Oh, she wouldn't keep the *little ones* waiting! "No, my dear, I never forget the children." Miss Potter left her to get ready, to put on her best things in some kind of confused but happy expectation.

"Oh, here's her ladyship ally ally ready!" Miss Potter herself had appeared in a velvet picture hat weighted with feathers. *There* . . . she adjusted her charge's coat and buttoned it for her. "Why, she's just too pretty for words in that little *shappeau*. I don't see how hubby can let you out of his sight!"

Mrs. Ferguson tried to laugh. She felt guilty for letting Miss Potter talk as if dad were a careless gadabout. But all the same she liked it. She had the feeling that it was coming to her. She knew she didn't deserve pity on just these lines, but perhaps she was a little tired of being told that she had a good husband. Ella thought, too good! As for the being pretty and all, it was nonsense—but people *did* use to say such things about her. There was that young principal at the Teachers' Institute—and there had been others. Fred seemed to have forgotten such things, that once they had been her due; and the children had never imagined them! Unless Carl . . . and that she had to deny herself, tremblingly fearful for her son's good and happiness. She didn't want the praise of some other man. She had sense enough to know herself too old for such business. And besides—she was unable to imagine anyone besides dad. But she didn't see how it could hurt anybody if she let Miss Potter give her a little admiration!

Miss Potter's car was waiting—a good, but somewhat battered sedan. Miss Potter made the arrangements with elaborate care for her little lady's comfort, making Mrs. Ferguson feel fragile and small.

"There—let's fix that cushion—that's right. Now, all comfy, sweetness?"

Oh, yes, Mrs. Ferguson said, she was fine.

If any of the others had seen her, she would have felt foolish. But there weren't any of them around. She looked out happily as they drove along, feeling more at ease with someone else driving than with dad. The gold of the winter sunshine exhilarated her. She could never get over the romantic delight of the exotic trees and flowers. She loved to drive past all the nice houses and imagine what they were like inside.

"Now, we're going to have just as much fun on *our* drive as that hubby of yours is having," Miss Potter said piously.

Mrs. Ferguson blushed.

She caught her breath at the hills. After all, she wasn't so sure with a woman driving. She had a boundless distrust for as well as a boundless alliance with her own sex. But Miss Potter, breathing a little heavily, handled the car with reckless assurance. Miss Potter pointed out the beauties of the city, dilating upon them in true Californian style. When they exclaimed over the charms of a Spanish house set back in bowers of greenery, "That's the kind of place *you* ought to have," Miss Potter declared. "I can just see you in a place like that." She was going to show her little lady the glories of the land, and then she would never lose her. And it was true—Mrs. Ferguson felt the settled sanctities of the house at home fading in the sunshine.

"And now we're going to see the greatest sight on God's earth," Miss Potter said solemnly. "Do you know what it is?"

Mrs. Ferguson wasn't sure.

"The ocean, my dear."

"Oh—oh, yes."

They stopped the car at a point near the beach. It was not crowded at this time of year. A lonely man sat out on the sand. The gulls clustered at a place near the rocks. Mrs. Ferguson looked uneasily at them. They were like chickens and pigeons combined, she thought. It frightened her to think of their making their home on the waters. She felt that she ought to be thinking great thoughts instead of nervously taking refuge in details. Miss Potter would expect it of her. She watched the long breaking of the waves.

"Do you know what that power is?" Miss Potter demanded solemnly. "It's the power of God. Every one of those waves is the beating of His great heart."

Mrs. Ferguson said nothing. This kind of talk always made her feel embarrassed. It was different with the prayers in church —prayers belonged there, were an established part of "the service." Yet she *did* need something. Yes, she, however fortunate, was faintly embittered, lost, and alone. She looked out over the silvery expanse. Its immensity frightened her, making her quickly draw back her gaze. She could see no reassuring land. All the waste of water seemed to come out of emptiness. Beyond there was . . . nothing but China. She had a moment of believing that fearful things, *the worst*, might have reality—something with which her love for her children, and Fred's love for her, and their standing in their own community, were not able to cope. Of course, she nervously admitted this was beautiful. But it held some challenge that she couldn't meet. She wanted sheltered places. When her children were born, somehow she had lost that kind of courage—except for *them*. She didn't know how to explain.

Miss Potter took her hand protectingly.

She said in her deepest tones, "I want you to drink in God's power. Take it back with you to your little home. When those dear children come this afternoon, they will feel that grandma has a new strength to give them. That's why I brought you to this holy ground."

Well, perhaps it was true. Oh, yes, she *did* need something. There was a mysterious shining in the silver emptiness. All the same, she was glad when they drove back among houses again.

Miss Potter insisted on taking her to luncheon and picking out the foods most suited to her bone structure. "That's very important, my dear. We have to think of the material man as well as the spiritual. Be all-rounded beings. Don't we?" Mrs. Ferguson didn't like all of the foods; but still, it was fun eating new things. And maybe there was something in what Miss Potter said about the bone structure. Who could tell? Doctors didn't know everything.

She got home just in time to take off her things before Dorothy and the children came. She felt strangely elated with her excursion, as she hurriedly put away in the cooler the gifts of health-building fruits with which Miss Potter had showered her. She was half ashamed, half laughing; took off the pink camellia flower Miss Potter had pinned to her dress, telling her it was like her "own dainty self"; yet she felt a sense of renewed girlhood—a pleasant soothing of something long unsatisfied. She had already half decided that she wouldn't tell the others. As she took off her new hat in the bedroom, and loosened her hair, she gave her head a little toss. "Well, I don't care!" A subtle smile curved her lips. Something remained from her glimpse of the ocean—disturbing, or illuminating—she didn't know . . .

Dorothy was distressed because Jesse had asked her to keep the children.

"Why, my child, you know I *like* to do it. Of course you're going to go."

She *did* feel a mysterious strength—whether it was the ocean, or what. Now she really looked forward freshly to the afternoon with the children. But she intended to have a good time with them—she wouldn't pay too much attention to Dorothy's careful modern regulations.

Dorothy was looking curiously at her. "Mother, you look great," she said suddenly. "I believe vacation agrees with you."

Vacation—yes, they were very anxious for her to have a vacation! "Oh, I've been outdoors a little while," Mrs. Ferguson said vaguely.

Dorothy was wearing a smart little costume, with her hair waved and brushed glossily back, a dash of geranium-colored lipstick on her soft mouth. But her mother thought this mode didn't agree with her so well as the more girlish styles. Dorothy wasn't exactly meant for it. She noted again the slight strain in Dorothy's thin face. But she wouldn't listen when Dorothy tried to suggest that she would rather stay here than go to the bridge club. She knew that Jesse liked to have Dorothy go to things, and she wouldn't abet her daughter in her relaxation. And she herself felt impatient at the idea of her pretty child turning into too much of a homebody. That wasn't the way people did things out here! But she felt all too much wary compassion for Dorothy—she knew too well what being wife and mother meant, to have her own concerns sunk beneath those of others, submerged but still uneasily alive, as she herself might have testified—the delicately shaded fibs, the valiant lies that kept things smooth, and other people happy . . . she felt as if she had just risen out of that into possession of herself again. Oh, she approved Dorothy, disapproved Margaret, but all the same she could have told Dorothy some things!

She didn't lose that renewed feeling all day. She seemed to manage the children easily. They recognized some kind of seasoned maternal authority in her. After all, she wasn't wholly dependent on her family's consideration! When she and Jesse took that excursion, if they ever did, she might show him that his mother-in-law wasn't such a poor companion. Dad wouldn't be along, holding her back. That subtle smile lurked in her lips. They would laugh about today—the health-food restaurant and all. Well, she wouldn't tell them. She could say, if necessary, that she "took a little ride." Of course, there wasn't anything to keep from them. It was just that they didn't need to know.

4

The Fergusons were in Pasadena now, at Louie's and Henry's. They were up in their beautiful bedroom, getting ready for dinner. Their suitcases were where the maid had neatly and discreetly placed them, convenient, but not too much in sight. The maid had offered to unpack for them, but Mrs. Ferguson had refused, with a quick deprecating smile, knowing that Fred wouldn't like it. They would do it later themselves. Anyway, she felt, now she had seen the house, that her things, although nice enough, were not quite equal to what Mrs. Sands' sister should have. She couldn't seem to get down to the business of dressing. At first she had simply walked softly about the room, looking at the lacy bedspread, the pastel cushions, the charming ornaments here and there, drawing aside the curtains to look out at the little Spanish balcony—until Fred got uneasy and said, "Annie, you ought to get ready." How lovely everything was! She couldn't get over it. And they could stay here as long as they pleased, without feeling they were making trouble, since Louie had plenty of help. She sat down at the princess dressing table between the tall candlesticks of thick creamy ware. Every movement was a delight, with such beautiful things surrounding her. She had not truly known until this moment—or not admitted—the desire for luxury that had always been part of her. If she had been staying with strangers, she might have been oppressed and shy. But with Louie, her own dear sister, she could let out her delight and revel in her surroundings.

She warned Fred, "We'll have to put on our best things to-night, dad."

"Well, it won't take *me* long to choose," he answered dryly.

Mrs. Ferguson was in a state of soft excitement. Her face looked flushed and youthful in this becoming light. She was happy in calling attention to the lovely things, even if all she could get from Fred was a cautious, "Yes, pretty nice, all right." She felt an elated sense of possession since all this belonged to Louie. She was with *her* people. *She* had relatives too. A thrust of impatience went through her at the thought of Ella. How had she ever stood Ella and her flat comments all these years? . . . although a sort of sad remembrance sank down into her when she thought of Ben, and the little group standing out in front of the house telling them good-bye. But now she had the proud feeling of coming into her own.

She put on her black-and-white georgette. At home, it looked very nice. Here it was ordinary. Her only jewelry was the string of artificial pearls, and of course her wedding and engagement rings.

"Oh, I wish I had something nicer!"

"What's the matter with this? You look nice enough for anybody."

"Oh, Fred, but Louie—!"

Still, she felt like a different person—a different person, and yet never so much herself. She answered happily when the maid knocked at the door.

"Are you ready, Fred?"

"You're the one. I didn't have much getting ready to do."

Oh, if Fred was going to be dry and sarcastic about the place—! He had never wanted to acknowledge that she had a family just as much as he did. His family had always been "the folks." Still, there was Henry. Fred respected his business success.

She would never forget her first sight of the house looming before them in the misty twilight, when she had realized that this was where they were going to stay! She felt lapped in noiseless comfort. The little place in San Diego she now regarded with a shudder—those people from Dike—with a pang of stifled remorse at the thought of Dorothy courageously meeting the conditions of her new home. But the children could get along without her, no matter what Jesse said. Jesse would have liked "the folks" to stay as a convenient anchor for himself and Dorothy! Mrs. Ferguson had felt that clearly through all his flattering cajoleries. And she didn't *want* to be thought of like that. She had had enough of it.

She went down the stairs into the great living room. Louie's place in Kansas City had been lovely. It had always been an excitement to think of visiting Aunt Louie. But it was nothing like this! Here, in this new house, they all seemed to have entered a different plane of existence. Tonight the place had a Christmas air, from the bright fire of logs in the fireplace, in spite of the flowers blooming outside. The front window, huge and theatrical, looked out upon misty twilight, its heavy curtains only partly drawn.

Louie came to meet them now. Mrs. Ferguson was proud that this was her sister. How well she fitted the place, giving its newness an air of soft dignity—her fine ample figure in the long-sleeved lace gown of delicate color, with the elegant soft simplicity that was her note. This was little Louie Luers, who had been born in Woodside, Ohio! Annie thought of her in fat buttoned shoes, with blond bangs unevenly cut. Louie, the child of the gentle, simple father and mother from "the old country"—and she had become this beautiful woman! Louie put her arm lovingly around Annie and kissed her again. An aroma of delicate fragrance, expensive, and subtly personal, breathed from her lacy clothes. Annie noticed the dull gleam of the pearl earrings that set off the light-brown waves of her hair, now grained with wavy streaks of silver.

"Oh, Louie, I think this is the most beautiful house I've ever seen!"

"Oh, do you, Annie?" Louie was gentle and deprecating. "There are so many Spanish houses—still, we like it."

They moved to the window together and looked off at the distant airy glitter of lights.

"You look so young, Louie!"

"I?" Louie was deprecating again. She gave a little laugh and a shrug. "Oh dear, Annie, I'm afraid you won't think so by daylight!"

"Yes, I will," her sister asserted indignantly.

Mrs. Ferguson sighed, she scarcely knew why. How Margaret would enjoy this, she couldn't help thinking with triumph. If Margaret had been willing to stay with them, *she* might have been enjoying this too. Mrs. Ferguson thrust back her old pain and confusion at the remembrance of her exiled daughter.

Henry, small and dry, was still the host. His riches conferred authority upon him. Almost aggressively insignificant as he looked, the others listened to him with respect.

"Dinner is served, Mrs. Sands."

"Thank you, Joan."

They moved into the candlelighted dining room.

Annie's state of soft excitement was lifted almost to ecstasy by the roses, the delicate glitter of crystal and silver on heavy lace. She felt more than ever as if she had stepped into a story in which she had always dreamed of taking part. With a small motion of dignity, she let Henry seat her. If she had been visiting anyone else, she would have gathered all the details to write to Mrs. Viele; but she couldn't with Louie, her own sister, it would have sounded like boasting. Still, she might work them in. It was all like a play. Even the maid had a touch of theatricality. The golden shade of her hair seemed marvelous by candlelight, swept back and falling fluffily about her neck. Only a glimpse of her heavy ankles spoiled the vision at times. But everything was almost too beautiful to be true!

"She looks like Greta Garbo," Annie said to Louie, when the maid left the room.

"Oh, they all do, more or less!" Louie said. She laughed.

"I'm sure her real name isn't Joan. She calls it Jo-*ann*. I don't doubt she has dreams of the movies."

"She really looks pretty enough."

"Oh, Annie! You won't think so tomorrow. And the time that girl spends on herself—it's all she does when she's off duty. Well, thank heaven, the cook at least is no Garbo. She's really a treasure."

She certainly was. The food was delicious. Annie looked once or twice at Fred to be sure he wasn't leaving the wonderful mushroom soup because of the whipped cream. But he was eating valiantly, and without comment. At home, when she and the girls had tried using candles at dinner, he had always observed, "Well, are we back to candles again?" Mrs. Ferguson sighed luxuriously, as she broke her dainty bread stick. Now she would have Fred off her mind. He would have Henry. She could give herself up to sheer enjoyment of Louie and luxury.

The dark red roses and the green candles gave the table a festival air.

"We've put off our Christmas to celebrate with you," Louie explained. "Oh, Annie, we did so hope you could be here!"

Annie explained eagerly—Dorothy wouldn't hear of their going, the children would have been disappointed. Louie agreed, with her soft consoling acquiescence, her sympathy that seemed almost to breathe a fragrance. She asked after the children lovingly.

"Oh, they're all right. Rosemary is so pretty."

Annie felt that she couldn't stop to explain now. Louie thought the children were still living in their own house. She didn't want to spoil the festivity of this meal. But she looked forward voluptuously to a long talk with Louie in which she could unburden herself of all her accumulated anxieties, finding someone at last with whom she could be completely at home. Tears almost came to her eyes, as she felt the happiness of this reunion, that seemed not to have a jarring note.

She felt the past drop away from her. Here they were, all four of them, who had been young people together, having reached the leisure and ease and prosperity which was the certain reward of their time of life, and tonight enjoying it.

"Annie, you aren't eating anything!"

"Yes, I am. I'm almost too happy to eat. It's so good to see both of you again."

She had put in the "both" politely. But Henry now said with unexpected gallantry, "Better still for us!"

The wonderful meal was over. Annie couldn't have told just what there was,—the meal was a dream of delicately flavored delicious things, the tinkle of ice as the "glamorous" maid poured the water into the crystal goblets, the mint-steeped drink into the tall glasses, the placing and removal of the lovely dishes. Louie said they would have their coffee in the living room. Annie gave a quick glance at Fred. She was so afraid he was going to say that they didn't drink coffee at night. But he said nothing. She gave another luxurious sigh. She felt rebelliously that she didn't care whether she slept tonight or not. The meal was perfect, and she was going to enjoy every bit of it.

The sense of festivity remained as they seated themselves in the beautiful living room, she and Louie together on the wide low couch. Annie didn't care what the coffee might do to her, when she could drink it from these exquisite rose and gilt cups.

"Louie, you have all different dishes!" she exclaimed.

Yes, they had started new out here, Louie said. They had kept only a few of their old things. They might as well—the things were scarcely worth moving (think of being able to say that!); and although at another time she might have been shocked at the easy abandonment of all those nice furnishings, Annie now happily agreed. She felt rebelliously that *she* didn't care whether she ever saw anything at home again. *She* wanted to start new. If her lovely daughter (who had married the handsome prince) hadn't quite been able to hold her part as heroine of the fairy tale, Louie could almost take over the rôle.

Henry offered Fred cigars. Of course dad refused! "No, I guess not, Henry." Mrs. Ferguson felt a slight sense of impatience. In spite of the traditional feeling against the evils of tobacco, which she had always supposed she shared, now she realized the pleasant manly elegance of the blue twist of fragrant smoke rising from Henry's excellent cigar. But of course she couldn't hope to change dad! It was marvelous enough that he had eaten the whipped cream, and not carefully pushed aside the dressing on his salad to find the bare unadorned pieces of fruit underneath. Now the night beyond the great window had become a startling darkness that held a dramatic suggestion of mountains and sea—but they were secure, in this lovely room.

The whole evening was a sort of dream. It was New Year's Eve. There seemed a beautiful omen in that. What should they do? Louie asked. She had thought they would wait and see what Annie and Fred felt like doing.

"I hope you haven't refused any invitations because of us!"

"Why, Annie Luers, where would I want to go, when you were coming?"

They both laughed at the familiar name.

There were dozens of things going on tonight. But Louie had thought perhaps they wouldn't care for the noisier places. Fred said hastily that they wouldn't. Annie was well aware that he would rather have stayed right here, but this time she wasn't going to help him out. They couldn't get an admission out of him of what he would prefer. "Whatever you folks have planned." And they didn't know what a concession *that* was! Louie said finally, well, they might drive through the Mile of Christmas Trees. "That's a terribly folksy suggestion! Still, I *have* heard it's rather pretty." Annie thought it would be wonderful. Then they could just come back here, and talk, and perhaps hear some good music on the radio.

"But maybe you're too tired to go out."

Annie hurriedly disclaimed that. In spite of the long drive, with so many cars on the road because it was holiday time, she felt as if she could do anything. Louie might call the Mile of Christmas Trees folksy; but it was something that her friends at home would want to hear about.

She went happily to put on her fur coat. They might as well be dressed warmly, Henry had warned. It was colder than it looked at night. Oh, not really cold, Louie scoffed gently. "I don't believe Henry would be warm anywhere!"

Henry made no comment. But Annie put on her fur coat anyway. It was so much the nicest one she had. The flowers Miss Potter had given her on leaving—an odd assortment—were all wilted. She unpinned them and put them into the enameled wastebasket, making a queer little face. Now that strange companionship was so far away it seemed as if it had never been. She remembered, with a kind of wonder, half flattered and half embarrassed, Miss Potter's grief at seeing her go, tears dripping from her jowls as she went out with them to the car. She had made Fred angry with her warnings about taking care of the little lady. "Does she think I'm going to upset you?" he had wanted to know. "I guess I've taken care of you a good many more years than she has, and nothing's happened to you yet!" He had actually been jealous at the end! The subtle smile curved Annie's lips as she smoothed the fur where the flowers had been pinned. Still, she was glad to have that companionship over. It had become—well, just a little *too*—

At that, she was ready before the others. Jo-ann had come softly in, with a discreet but haughty air, and the stiff rich curtains were drawn. It was the start of the New Year. People were beginning to speak of change and trouble and suffering; but Annie, in the comfort of Louie's house, would not believe it. The curtains shut out everything unhappy from the warm spacious quiet of this lovely room. This night *was* like the beginning of a fairy tale. What she had first felt in the golden air was coming true.

The drive seemed to her the most fairylike of all. At times, she felt herself wanting to share all this with the children. But she checked herself. Why shouldn't she have something of her own? She and Fred were not *only* parents. Often Fred used to tell her that. Now *she* was the one. Fred was worrying still over the incomprehensibleness of Jesse's wide and handsome but seemingly "unsolid" business transactions. He wondered how Bun was "making out" in the city back there. Annie didn't want to be reminded of these things! Now she and Fred were with their own contemporaries. And certainly there was nothing relegated about Louie! The children were dear, but they were Dorothy's. She wouldn't feel responsible for them. She would only enjoy them. We can have some fun too, was what she thought.

They had scarcely heard the big, dark, gleaming car roll up the driveway. Annie felt still more luxuriously lapped and sheltered in the softly upholstered interior.

"You don't do the driving, Henry?" she heard Fred ask.

"No, I let Percy take care of that."

Percy, Louie explained in a murmur, was their man of all work—making a little face at Annie to express her amusement at the name. They could see that he was colored. "All our servants have such imposing names—except cook, bless her heart, she's just plain Bessie.

"Well, we really need a chauffeur," Louie explained further. "Henry can't take me everywhere I go."

Annie hastily and sympathetically agreed.

She was impressed by the way in which her sister spoke of "servants," as if they were a special class. Not at all the way in which she thought of Mrs. Entwhistle—or of dear Mrs. Christianson! But she thought that Louie had the right.

The car went purring out and down the curving driveway between the dark exotic shrubs and trees.

"I want you to see this in the morning, Annie. This whole slope is a bank of color."

Annie said warmly, she *wanted* to see it.

"Who takes care of this?" Fred wanted to know.

"A gardener," Henry explained. "Have to have one, you know. Hard to keep things growing out here."

"Why, Henry Sands! Where is it *ea*-sier?"

Fred was noncommittal. If Henry didn't drive the car, or look after the place, what *did* he do? Well, no doubt he could afford to do nothing.

They were still moving in a fairy tale. Annie had no idea of where or in what direction they were going, up and down hills, and along curving roads. When they reached the long avenue of heavily branching deodars (Louie laughed at the title "Mile of Christmas Trees," but *she* thought it was lovely), then she did truly believe that she had entered her fairy land. The cars were lined up blocks away, but they need have no fear with Percy's careful, smooth, assiduous handling of the almost noiseless gears. They slid between two other cars, one a little old Model T Ford rattling along like a mechanical insect out of some well-forgotten age, and the other a battered family sedan. Annie felt that *they* were a favored, almost royal party. She didn't quite believe in it, but she loved it. Even Fred was impressed by this evidence of civic activity. He gave it his highest praise. He said, "It's certainly pretty nice." Annie heard the two men. Let them talk about "conditions" and "the market," and figure out just how the lights were put up. The women sat happily together. Louie had to make no such effort to be interested in all Henry's concerns as Dorothy in Jesse's. She was with Louie, her own beloved sister—Louie in her soft moleskin coat, even that giving out some faint fragrance. Annie held Louie's warm gloved hand. All sad things faded out under the holiday glitter of the lights—and why need any of them ever worry or work hard again?

The holiday was extended, indefinitely it seemed. One pleasant event followed another.

On New Year's Day, there was the famous Tournament of Roses. Fred had been dreading that, for he hated getting into a crowd. But with Louie and Henry, all was made easy—as they might have known! Henry had engaged fine seats long ahead of time, so that there need be no hurry in getting there, no long waits; and then they had Percy to find a place to park—*that* was off their hands. The morning had started with a flat, chill, strange-smelling fog from the sea. Fred, of course, was uneasy. He was afraid that it might rain. He wanted to know if they had covering downtown there, in case. Louie said with smiling confidence, "Oh, it never rains on New Year's!" "The Chamber of Commerce won't let it," Henry put in dryly. Both the women contended that the fog was nothing, the sun would shine. "You'll see!" Everything out here, even the weather—Mr. Ferguson thought—sided with the women. By the time they took their seats in the grandstand, the sun *was* shining.

"You'll find us, Percy?"

"Yes, Mistuh Sands."

They felt the comfort of leaving the car to Percy, the delight of having the best seats reserved for them. The Fergusons were used to having things good, but not the very best, not the top-notch—not what Fred was still apt to speak of as "tony." Well, they *were* tony today. There were rich-looking elderly people in the grandstand—people needn't be young to have a good time, Mrs. Ferguson thought defiantly. That had been, still was to a great extent, the code of Belmond. She was excited by the crowd. *She* liked it, liked to be where things were going on. And with such seats, even Fred couldn't mind it. Even he must enjoy the beautiful floats.

"Margaret would like this," she exclaimed sentimentally.

"Oh, she'd find something to turn up her nose at," Fred said.

Mrs. Ferguson watched everything eagerly, gathering details to report to Mrs. Viele and the other ladies at home. If Mrs. Morgan could see *these* flowers! The precious gloxinia plant was far surpassed by these moving masses of exotic bloom. In fact, it was beginning to seem as if she could never bear to return again. Why should she?—when the children were all gone. She felt happy in the midst of this crowd. There was a joy in seeing people without ties. Doubtless there were many from home. But here in this grandstand, there was little fear of seeing any of those sad, reminding figures like the old couple from Dike. Fred got somewhat restive toward the end. Henry was polite but uninterested. But then, you never could tell about Henry. After all these years, Annie felt that she didn't know him any better than at first. She wondered if even Louie did. Annie drank in every bit of the spectacle—eager for color, for show, trying to satisfy all the tastes that she hadn't admitted in herself for years; that were the opposite of Fred's. Fred made fun of the blond beauties who sat swaying in thrones above the flowers. He said he should think those girls would be pretty cold in their bathing suits, must think they were in a picture show. But Annie stood up for them, too, for their beauty golden and empty like the sunshine, in its synthetic perfection.

"They don't look real."

"They look better than real!" she said triumphantly.

It was amazing whom they did run into! Of course they had known she was living out here, had meant to pay their respects to her, to call some day in state. They had walked down the street when the parade was over, to the place where Percy was to meet them—and there, in front of one of the hotels, was an old lady beckoning to them. It was old Mrs. Spencer! Wonderful that she should recognize them after all these years. Fred was inclined to be embarrassed, since he had had what almost amounted to a disagreement with Richard. But if the old lady knew of that, she gave no sign. It was years since she had left Belmond; years now since old Mr. Spencer had died. But here she was, tiny, withered, but quite regally dressed in purple, and still evidently very much alive!

Annie was proud to have such a sister as Louie to introduce to Mrs. Spencer. She saw an instant approval of the moleskin coat and the violets in those small, sharp, aged eyes. She was not at all sorry to be able to make a showing in front of one of the Spencers! The old lady had always been nice enough to them. She had sent Dorothy quite a lovely wedding present. But it had been rather in a gracious, grand lady way. In the old Spencers' time, Fred hadn't been much more than their clerk. They had looked upon him as the Fergusons themselves now looked upon Ray Seeley. However, the old lady seemed shrewdly and willingly to have accepted the changed status. She certainly couldn't expect to patronize Louie!

And now they were going to have the afternoon with her.

"You'll enjoy it, won't you?" Annie said anxiously to Louie.

She had feared that Louie might not be interested in such an old lady. But if Louie did feel that way, she didn't show it. The two sisters had a gala feeling starting out together. It was almost as they used to feel when they were young girls setting off for a party. They pretended to be remorseful about leaving the men; but they weren't. Fred had consented to go out with Henry to the golf links. He was proud that old Mrs. Spencer should have invited Annie. However he might regard Richard, he still kept much of the awed respect of other days for the old Spencers. Fred never seemed to think of anywhere he wanted to go by himself; and Henry couldn't live without his golf. In fact, that was why Henry submitted to living in California, Louie said with a little shrug—because he could play golf all the year round. *That* was what Henry did, Fred had discovered—he played golf. At home, Fred would never join the golfing crowd, Richard Spencer, Dr. Redmond and the others—they were too tony for him, he thought, and he didn't like golfing anyway, it was another thing that kept people from the churches. But it was different when Henry played—must be, since Henry was an able man, and his own brother-in-law, and since the game seemed to fill up the empty places of Henry's existence. For the two women, there was more than they could get in, all the time!

It was too warm today for their fur wraps. Louie wore a soft woolen ensemble; and Annie was having the chance to wear the new outfit she had bought in Los Angeles. It was black and white—she had worn that combination often enough—but it was the style that seemed to change her altogether. The price had terrified her. She couldn't tell Fred of spending anything like that simply for something to wear. But Louie was on her side. Louie had been determined that she must have that suit and no other. Louie had offered to make up the price herself. "Yes, Annie—now you must let me. I get tired of buying things only for myself." That vacant, dimmed look came over her lovely face, which Annie had noticed before. "If I can't do something for my own sister, for whom can I?" Annie had to agree. She wouldn't tell Fred, of course—it worried him, he thought they were accepting too much already. Dad wasn't used to doing less than his share. *He* was used to being the provider. But why shouldn't I take a present from my own sister? Annie had thought. And then she had to get a smart hat and shoes to match. She had left the shop elated. She felt the enjoyment of going into stores with Louie—the instant respect shown by the clerks. She herself always entered the stores in Geneva a little deprecating and uncertain—although not at home, where they knew her, and knew that Fred was well-fixed. But then, there wasn't anything much to buy at home! Of course, when she brought back her new purchases, Fred had to take her down a little. Not that he had any idea of the price! He wasn't going to commit himself, but he wouldn't say either that he liked the suit. Finally he came out with what was the trouble. It was a nice enough suit, he said, but she didn't look so much like herself in it. "Now, maybe you haven't known," Louie told him, "how Annie can look!" Annie stanched her disappointment with Louie's approval. She was going to wear the suit even if Fred didn't like it! But she had given up the idea of getting ear-rings. She didn't know why she shouldn't have some—but she just never had worn them. Maybe the thought of Grandma's sharp tongue was still in her mind; even now, she couldn't quite get away from it. Nevertheless, she felt smart and gay starting out, carrying the lovely bouquet of roses for old Mrs. Spencer that the gardener had cut for them. She felt much gayer than if Fred had been along.

She never could get over her gratification at their smooth arrival—at stepping out of the handsome limousine, noting the respectful glances turned toward them from passers-by. She stood aside happily while Louie made her arrangements with Percy. Already she had got out of the way of wanting Fred to drive her anywhere. It was all so much easier with Percy.

Old Mrs. Spencer was awaiting them in the lobby of the hotel. They saw her, sunk into a big soft chair, valiantly arrayed in her purple gown and hat, and with great pearl ear-rings fastened upon her withered ears.

She looked them over and greeted them with satisfaction. She still had the Spencer eye for appearances! But Annie felt that she was ready to stand the scrutiny.

"I thought I'd be here," she told them, "and not make you come to my bungalow. Later, I must give you a little tea there."

In fact, she was *very* welcoming. She held Louie's hand, and she actually kissed Annie! Yes, it was plain that they had passed her tests. The kiss signified final acceptance and approbation. She professed herself delighted with the roses. She made the bell-boy take them to her bungalow, giving him many instructions, all very definite, to which he replied with a seemingly respectful, "Yes, Mrs. Spencer, we'll see to that." Louie couldn't help smiling; not, however, disapprovingly. The old lady gave a slight grunt of satisfaction. She rose, grasping both their arms. They were to have a little theater party. There was a new bill at the movie theater across the street; and she told them that she never missed a change of program.

"I'm a great lover of the movies," she announced with firmness.

Both the guests declared that they were delighted to go. It was only a step. Perhaps they would walk over. "Oh, no, my dear—not worth while calling your car. Besides, this is my exercise. I'm so pleased to be able to go without Sarah—my maid. That's what it means to be old! I have to take her with me. *And* of course pay for her seat! Has to have just as good a one as I do." Louie raised her eyebrows slightly at Annie. This was going too far even for Louie. But they were affected, in spite of themselves, by the old lady's air of authority. They piloted her over the crossing. They could see how dreadfully old she was when they walked with her. Louie, with that gracious, sympathetic way which her sister so admired, took Mrs. Spencer's arm and carefully held her back waiting for the change of traffic—the old lady herself, it seemed, would have charged straight into the midst. Truly, she could scarcely lift her feet. At any moment it seemed as if those great earrings might come rattling down upon the pavement—as if there weren't enough of her any more to hold her adornments together. But she was chipper and determined, and she wouldn't lose a moment of her pleasure.

"Marlene Dietrich!" she said. "Beautiful creature! I never miss *her*."

Old Mrs. Spencer to be so fond of the movies! Annie had always associated her with the cool high-ceilinged rooms of the Spencer house, and with things like the old Shakespeare Club. She had been somewhat in awe of Mrs. Spencer's "culture." And this foreign actress, who was reported to be a "siren," and whom Mrs. Stark had once declared the kind who ruined the ideals of our young people! But then, Mrs. Stark—she was altogether *too* . . . Annie felt a strange flicker of unholy interest. Mrs. Spencer insisted on getting tickets at the window, opening her lustrous beaded bag with her tremulous fingers, and minutely counting out the change. Louie took her arm again as they went into the theater.

The show had not yet started. They stepped into the hushed darkness before the matinée. The theater was full of old ladies, coming in groups or by twos, the less decrepit helping along the feeble ones. Annie and Louie piloted their old lady. They exchanged glances of affectionate amusement, feeling delightfully young, since they had the use of all their limbs and faculties. Louie helped Mrs. Spencer into an upholstered seat, helped her off with her purple wrap, and then laid it around her shoulders. "Thank you, my dear," the old lady panted— but with firmness still in her tone. "Now I believe I'll let you take my hat off too. I'll enjoy the picture much better when I'm comfortable." Louie gently lifted the rich little purple hat from the thin yellow-silvery waves, that parted, showing the dry old scalp, and freed the veil softly from the great earrings.

"That's nice. That's very deft." The old lady commended. She patted Louie's hand. "*Much* better than Sarah could do."

Louie and Annie exchanged another smiling glance.

Well, they didn't mind, they felt so young, they *could* do things for the old lady.

Both of them were amazed at Mrs. Spencer's command of movie lore. They had feared she would get tired; but not at all, it was evident that she wasn't going to miss an item on the bill. "Oh, I'm a great lover of the movies!" she warned them again.

Even so, when she thought of the stately old frame house in Belmond, with the long windows and the cupola, it was difficult for Annie to associate Mrs. Spencer with the picture they were seeing now. Mrs. Stark would have been horrified! Mrs. Stark was particularly indignant against the unwholesome influence of "foreign actresses." The Woman's Club, she

660

believed, should take it upon itself to censor the pictures that came to town. Annie had never considered whether she really believed that or not. Maybe at home, she wouldn't have patronized such a picture, that certainly didn't hold up the right ideals. But it seemed that the old lady took an epicurean pleasure in the overripe luscious beauty of this subtly decadent European flower. She surveyed the clinging "love scenes" with satisfaction, fixing her sharp little eyes upon the opulent slow movements of the lovely figure on the screen.

"I like the way this man makes love to her," Mrs. Spencer whispered complacently. "I couldn't bear that last one. A perfect stick!"

The two guests were amused but somewhat embarrassed by their hostess's frequent comments in most authoritative tones.

The picture, certainly, laid too much emphasis on sex. That was what Mrs. Ferguson told herself. Was Margaret, was her own daughter, an initiate of scenes like this? But she, too, watched it all with a hidden wistful interest, half charmed, half alienated. The exotic flower-face of the star shone strangely luminous through the tawdry working-out of the mechanized story. Mrs. Ferguson noted all the details, the butterfly sweep of the brows, the deep-set evasive eyes, the hollow cheeks with their Old World beauty—the suggestion the actress carried of something old, passive, too tired to hold its burden of finished aristocracy, letting it slip, with a lovely contempt, into tawdriness . . . The lovely face held a spell of fatalism, against which the bland American brightness of the ladies rebelled. Yet they found themselves fascinated, and a little frightened.

"Well, my dear, whatever you may think of her morals in the play," Mrs. Spencer said with satisfaction, "she's a beautiful creature!"

Now there was the business of getting the old lady out of the theater. The sisters supported her on each side as they went slowly across the street in front of the panting cars. No, she wouldn't hear of their leaving. Not until she had entertained them in her bungalow. In fact, it seemed to Annie that she was clutching at them.

Sarah, a middle-aged, patient-looking woman, had everything ready for them. Mrs. Spencer had finally to acknowledge that with a grunt. She dismissed Sarah then; but Annie and Louie noticed that Sarah didn't take it very seriously—she didn't go far. She had a stolid seasoned look of humoring her mistress. It was fearful to see Mrs. Spencer lift the silver teapot with her trembling little hands. But she wouldn't let Louie take her place. They could see how she still enjoyed the authoritative rôle of hostess.

"Well, now," she said, turning to Annie, when the business of pouring was over. (Sarah, by the way, had appeared again to pass the cakes.) "I suppose you're expecting me to ask you all about Belmond. I'm not going to do it. All my friends are gone. I'm not interested in the others. So why ask?"

Annie couldn't help feeling a little shock, although Louie gave a soft spurt of laughter. Mrs. Spencer said that Fred had done exactly right in leaving the bank. There was no use in people working forever. "My husband worked too long. He couldn't enjoy his leisure when he took it. But I do, my dear," she said firmly. "Every bit of it. I suppose you wonder, too, why I stay alone out here. Well, why shouldn't I? What would be the gain in coming back to look after Richard? Ethel manages him anyway. And very proper. I admire her for doing it. If he isn't good by this time, he never will be. I've done all I can about it."

With that, the old lady seemed to have dismissed Belmond, where she had dwelt as a highly important citizen for so many years. Annie felt a guilty half-sympathy, a shock. Mrs. Spencer wanted to know where Louie lived. In fact, she inquired minutely. She nodded her head with satisfaction at the address.

"I had a house too," she said. "But after my husband died, I sold it. I didn't want the responsibility. The only desire I have is to enjoy the few years left to me. I suppose they're few! They're longer now than anyone gave me credit for. No, I don't want a house. Here, I live as easily as I could anywhere. They know me. They give me good service. I suppose, on the whole, I might as well make up my mind to put up with Sarah. Too much trouble to look for anyone else. When

I want to buy clothes—I still like clothes—I can step just a few doors down the street. And I can go to see my movies. I can't miss them!"

Louie agreed, with her fragrant sympathy. But Annie couldn't help that shocked, guilty feeling. It was as if things only dimly formed in her mind were now sharply visible. The living room of the small expensive bungalow had a clear-cut modern brightness. The tea things were exquisite upon the little table. Piles of bright-colored movie magazines stacked the shelves. Why not? Mrs. Spencer complacently demanded, sharply noting the glance. She had read the classics, she said, and she couldn't abide this modern stuff. All full of horrors and diseases, poor people, people she wouldn't have cared to know. She wanted to have youth about her! It was as if she were warming her little old body determinedly with pictures of golden hair and luscious, painted lips. Oh, yes, she kept up with them all, she said, nodding—Ann Harding, Greta Garbo, Joan Crawford—she knew all of them, all of these heroines of the day, deplored divorces, was pleased with rumors of romances. And this was old Mrs. Spencer!—the Mrs. Spencer they used to know: who had put on a sheer white apron with knitted lace to pour coffee from a silver coffeepot at the Congregational church supper—who had brought with her a breath of New England decorum whenever she stepped into the bank, so that the men shook their cuffs into place surreptitiously, and cleared their throats. It was always as if the sharpness and purity of New Hampshire snows had hung about her . . . and there was still a last, frosty glitter out here in the bland sunshine. But the sharp steeple of the white church had dwindled until it couldn't be seen. Annie Ferguson felt as if she didn't know the world any more.

"Now, my dear, I see I've shocked you." Mrs. Spencer was as firmly complacent as before. "But let me tell you. My old life has gone from me. Why reside in memories of it? That's what I tried to tell my husband. But he wasn't able to take it in. When I came out here, I put the past behind me. I believe in doing things thoroughly. I'm too old to make new friends. But the movies take the place. People are disappointing when you come to know them. I can take these as I see them. These young people may do wild things, but they're beautiful, and young. They do what I didn't do in my day."

Annie listened in mingled disagreement and sympathy. The old lady sat in her comfortable chair like a frail little derelict of another age—of an afternoon, when the dust was golden, when the old Spencer surrey went slowly and decorously down the residence street, the fringe shaking, the shining horses placidly trotting. Now the old woman was like a frail white shell left on a distant sunny beach, all affections, experience, feelings washed out of her by time and change, nothing left of her but her dauntless resolution. Annie felt a slight shudder in this heated air.

They drank their tea, and ate their delicious little sandwiches and cakes. Annie did try to slip in some mild praise for Sarah. Even when they had finished, it seemed that Mrs. Spencer didn't want to let them go. Even if she didn't care for people! At last she allowed them to slip on their coats and gather up their gloves and bags. But she held Annie's hand for a final word.

"Stay here, my dear," she said earnestly. "Don't let yourself get old until you must. You'll do for other people, and even so you'll have no one but yourself left in the end." The old lady nodded her head, an earring ominously rattling. "You'll find that out. Then get all the pleasure that you can. I deny myself nothing."

Annie withdrew her hand, half shocked, half pleased. The air had a hothouse warmth in the bungalow. It seemed as if the great rich roses were already too fully open.

Annie and Louie drove back in the late afternoon, through the flat, salt-smelling sea fog again. It blotted the avenues, turned the palms and graceful pepper trees to ghosts, pushed in waves against the lights of the car, thick but meaningless—like a spirit out of the emptiness beyond. Annie felt far from home. She was frightened at this moment by the distance, the dreamy unreality that had come over old attachments that seemed to be slipping away from her. Old simple truths were dissolved. Was *she* going back on them? she, one of the mothers? She felt again the passivity of the actress, the subtle emanation from something too old and fatal for her to understand. It seemed as if all behind her was settling, tottering—and before her was emptiness. The face of the star seemed to float luminous somewhere, with the butterfly sweep of the brows above the enigmatic eyes. All this chain of bright new cities had become unreal in the fog from the sea. And the land beneath them was old, was cruel, and strange—old, older than the Old World their ancestors had left behind, before the time of man. There was no beginning and no ending.

This was a cloudy day. Mist softened and darkened the brightness. The gas furnace kept the large house evenly heated; but Louie, shuddering a little at the cloudy chill beyond the space of the big bright window, had declared they must have a log fire to make the place more cheerful. Fred was sitting by the fireplace reading, glad, no doubt, that the weather was at last so bad that the two women couldn't urge him to go out to the links with Henry. But Annie felt restless and queer. She couldn't settle down to read. After a while, she went upstairs to find her sister. She knocked on Louie's door.

"Oh, come in, Annie!"

Annie had only a few times stepped into this bedroom. Its spaciousness made their own seem small. It was all in light, delicate colors, pale but warm. Now, in this setting of misty, darkened air, it seemed to hold a kind of feminine enchantment. Louie was doing her nails. Her paraphernalia was spread out around her. The glitter of bottles and jars made the large modern dressing table seem like the secret, shining, magic center of the house—an altar, almost. Annie went toward it with a wistful reverence.

"Oh, you do have such lovely things!"

She had to think of the meager equipment of her own dresser at home—the flowered china manicure set given her (by Louie herself) years ago, and still set out in state, although she used little articles from the ten-cent store. Except for that, and a bottle of toilet water, she had no extras. Unless she counted the lotions bought from Lily Weyant, because she had felt she must give Lily some help, and which were of such poor quality she had stuck them away and never used them.

She sat down in a little low, chintz-covered chair. Louie was half turned toward her, sheathed in her pastel satin negligee, holding up her soft, finely cared for, middle-aged hand toward the light. Annie had the somewhat excited feeling of having penetrated the secrecy of a hidden rite. She was not sure whether she ought to be here. She felt again, with a voluptuous realization—almost as if she were listening to music—how lovely Louie was. Yes, still, in her middle-age. The fading of her face made it all the more interesting, with the loosened fragrance of a rose just before the petals fall, holding about it the poetry and fragrance of a long afternoon of summer sunlight now slowly drawing to a close.

Annie drew back from the glimpse of herself in the glass, moving her chair self-consciously. It made her seem aged and commonplace. She felt like a fraud in this lovely room—she had worked too much, there were too many anxieties behind her. And there was something still unsatisfied in her heart, beneath all the pleasure. On this cloudy morning, while she was watching the leaping of the fire, she had felt unresolved troubles and fears suddenly alive.

"I haven't had any letter from Margaret," she said.

"Oh well, she probably has so much to do."

Annie watched Louie reach out for a small jar of paste and dab her finger deftly into it. Loneliness came over her. She moved restlessly. She felt that she had never been able to talk about Margaret to anyone who would understand, that she had been saving it all up for Louie. She couldn't betray her child to the neighbors; and of course, with any of Fred's folks she must be on the defensive. Now she was with Louie, now she was with her own. She heard herself confiding all her pain and fears. The words crowded to her mind—"Some man—I know she was with some man—" But when it came to speaking them, she could do it only haltingly, and not in the luxurious detail that she had imagined. Louie's face was turned slightly aside. Her brows were puckered; and Annie felt in her something polished and blandly unresponsive, something that she had met before when she had tried to talk about their uncertainty over Jesse's financial state. Louie would say only, "Oh well, it's just temporary—probably this little experience will be all the better for them." And now she felt with disappointment that Louie refused to take in the meaning of Margaret's escapade. The pearl-mounted nail buffer that Louie was manipulating was like some delicate weapon holding her away.

Louie had to say *some*-thing.

"Oh well, Annie, it may not be what you think. I'm sure it isn't. Young people act differently nowadays. We mustn't think too much about that."

"But, Louie, she made this trip with him—I know she did."

"But still it may have been just a pleasure jaunt, a little unconventional, but without anything more to it."

"Do you think so?"

"Why, yes, I don't see why not."

Annie was silent. She tried dubiously to look at the trip in that way. She didn't know how to meet Louie's bland, determined consolation, and tried feebly to gather her forces for assertion. Louie seemed to feel that she was not quite living up to the sympathy expected of her. She put down her nail buffer.

"Didn't you tell me about this man who sent flowers?"

"Yes, but *he* wasn't the one!"

"Now, Annie, he might have been. I think very likely he was."

Annie was forced to be silent again. She remembered Margaret's dark face—the sound of muffled crying, when she had stood outside her child's door, feeling too obscurely guilty, fearful and uncertain to go in to her.

All her fears for her children rose in her like the mounting of a dammed-up flood, that had been gathering through the years. She wanted to tell Louie—she wanted to speak to someone to whom she could at last admit the bitter truths and the painful intuitions which all this time had lain underneath her bright, covering repetitions . . . "Carl and Lillian—getting along nicely—oh, yes, much better"—when all the time, she had the dark knowledge, never given words, even with Fred, of what Lillian had done. She wanted to speak out her bewildered perception of Carl as defeated under his apparent success. To speak, and to have what she said comprehended, *acknowledged* —that was what she asked. Their trouble with Margaret—the feeling that they themselves might have helped to drive her away, the old guilty crying sense that this was the child they had never known . . . to say all that, at last—and to hear arguments persuasive enough to dispel it. It seemed as if she must have someone with whom she needn't keep it up, to whom she could admit failures, and then to have that person assert, "Yes, but, Annie, you did the best you could."

But now it seemed as if all the space of the large, uncrowded room was between her and Louie, and it couldn't be crossed. The worst of it was, that she recognized Louie's attitude! It was just the way she herself had acted, more times than one, when Essie Bartlett, for example, had tried to talk to her. For she hadn't wanted to feel the desperateness of Essie's situation, had tried to ease it and shove away realization with false cheer, not letting it spoil her content in her own better fortune. Not, of course, that *her* life could be compared to Essie Bartlett's! But it humbled her, the way Louie met her confidences, making her feel inferior. She saw herself as a dreary small town woman worrying tediously over her children. She still was careful not to catch any sight of herself in the glass.

No, it wasn't that. It was more that Louie was afraid of giving a response. Louie wanted to smooth the surface so that she need not open her heart to trouble. And all at once, Annie felt her greatest sorrow—Bunny's marriage—banked up in her, with no relief. She could taste the bitterness on her lips. She could imagine herself telling all about it to Louie and Louie meeting every point with that sympathetic sweetness which Annie now saw as masking in silk her disinclination to understand. Wasn't it the same way that she had wanted to meet trouble herself? "Oh, but, Louie, that girl is three years older!" "Yes, but, Annie, that doesn't really mean anything." "I know, if she were his kind—!" "Now, Annie, they may be more congenial than you think. Those marriages are often the happiest sort." It would be useless to try to make Louie understand about Charlotte—how her very existence threatened all the sunny peace of a settled life. And it was *she*, their antithesis, whom Bunny, their youngest, had chosen to love! The pain, fear, threat of that knowledge was alive again . . . but in a dull aftermath, since nothing could be done about it. It was there, no matter how far she ran away from it. But even to hint at the fear that it gave her was ridiculous and out of place in this lovely room.

Louie gave a little shiver. "This is a horrid day," she said deprecatingly.

She reached over for another of the thick, shining jars, took a dab of fragrant cream and spread it over her hands, then studied them thoughtfully. Annie watched her, wanting in some way to feel close again.

"That smells nice," she offered.

"Try it," Louie said encouragingly, handing her the jar.

Annie spread the rich paste listlessly over the backs of her own hands. But it was too late in the day to achieve the perfection of beauty that had formed part of her girlhood dream. And her pleasure in Louie's things had turned into a faint resentment.

"It feels nice," she murmured. "But my hands have seen too much work."

The glitter of the jars and bottles tired and disturbed her. She looked surreptitiously at Louie's face. There was something empty, almost querulous, in its softness. In that moment, she made a subtle revision of her pride in her sister's beauty, her modesty in regard to herself. Annie had always been accustomed to sorrow over the fact that Louie had no children. But now she could see that Louie had changed. It was as if she had crossed over an invisible boundary line— she had turned her back on her old longing, she would no longer acknowledge it. Perhaps, indeed, she did not feel it. If she *had* wanted children, she had fortified herself against the lack by comfort and ease and beauty. For so long, there had been no one but herself on whom to expend her efforts, that now at last—by a substitution, half merciful, half blighting— herself had come to be all in all to her. Louie was too deeply and softly embedded in the ease and luxury which she used to regard so deprecatingly. It was no longer possible to reach her.

Louie moved uneasily, and gave a little laugh. "I think the weather has affected us both. It just doesn't seem right when we don't have sunshine. I was wondering—wouldn't you like to drive down to Los Angeles and go to a matinée this afternoon?"

"Yes, that would be nice," Annie said carefully, but somewhat distantly.

Louie reached over and gave her sister's hand a little squeeze. "You don't know what a comfort it is to have you here to run around with me! I suppose Henry will have to have his golf, rain or shine!"

Annie returned the squeeze faintly, but said nothing. There was something that made her unhappy. It sounded in Louie's voice. She felt that Louie had no real respect for Henry, although she would never say so in words—no, she, too, must still keep up the pretense of perfect happiness according to the ancient feminine code! Annie moved uneasily again. Reluctantly she felt that she understood, and was ashamed to understand, the disappointment and dry failure of this marriage. She seemed at this moment to be looking straight down into it . . . aware of the gifts and the freedom from responsibility that Henry tacitly piled upon Louie—of a cautious defeat in the shifting of his glance—of the price that had been paid for this enchanted life, in which Louie's beauty still softly bloomed. Once the determination to admit nothing wrong might have been loyalty—but now it had overshadowed everything else, until Louie's gentleness and silence had become mere fear of trouble and desire for smoothness. Oh, but, Louie, to *me*—to each other! I would love you so much better— But it was impossible actually to say those words. Annie felt a disappointment that rose like a sob. And already she had penetrated too far. She had come too close to this shining altar. She had seen what her position as the fortunate one, the Lady Bountiful, meant to Louie, and how Louie couldn't risk endangering it by any impulse of confidence or intimacy. Louie sat at her altar alone. Her shining peach-tinted robe was a symbol of the immaculate good fortune by which her beauty was surrounded and it must not suffer a touch.

Annie said, somewhat nervously, but smiling, "I believe I'll go outside for a little while."

"It's chilly," Louie murmured.

"Oh, I won't take cold."

"Put on my cape, then, Annie. It's in the closet downstairs. I always like to slip it on in weather like this."

"All right. Thank you, dear."

Annie put on her own coat instead. The soft, too soft, enfoldment of the woolly cape seemed to her unreal.

But the garden, all the place, was unreal too. The blooming things were strange in the sea fog. The colors of the flowers were dimmed. She felt an alien sadness in the tall eucalyptus trees with their dark blots of foliage against the gray sky. Again the land seemed old—and this moment was like an interlude. She could not find its meaning in the stealthy fog. For the first time, she had a faint, painful thrill of homesickness. Yet all her anxieties lay back there still unresolved. She shivered, thinking of old Mrs. Spencer. Again she saw that image of the white shell, lying empty and cold in the sea mist. The stealthy distance grew between her and her only sister. Solitude drew in upon her from out of this ghostly mist. She thought, with a shudder, of the long, slow, empty sound of the ocean. The coast, to have come to the coast—she felt a meaning in that now—something hidden in the very heart of the fairy story.

She turned back and went into the house, almost with a sense of flight from ghosts. Fred was still reading beside the fire of eucalyptus logs—or, if not reading, solacing his idleness with the pictures in the *Geographic*. His glasses were pushed down upon his nose—there was something oddly comforting in that homely touch. He looked up over the glasses.

"Hello, mama. Well. That you?"

The days went on until they were almost losing track of time. More and more, Fred was aware that the others were

671

conniving to wean him away from thoughts of home and to persuade him that the holiday need never end.

"You'll stay," Henry predicted, with a dry twinkle in his eye. And Louie added complacently, "Everyone does, you know." Louie simply couldn't understand why they should ever think of returning to Belmond.

Even Annie was on their side, Fred saw, and joined in the conniving. She wouldn't come right out with it. But when they were alone, and he talked about Belmond, Fred could see that she was indifferent. She gave a little movement of impatience when he spoke about the church. When he mentioned Essie Bartlett and her mother, wondering whether their fuel was holding out, she didn't answer and turned away. She wouldn't even show any interest in how their own house was getting along. What had happened to Annie since they came out here? Of course he wanted her to enjoy herself—this was mama's chance; but sometimes he felt with dismay as if he didn't know her any more. Once she broke out, almost with bitterness, that they had done everything *they* could in Belmond, and it wasn't as if the children needed them any more.

"Well, what do you want to do, Annie?"

But she wouldn't give a direct answer to that.

Fred couldn't answer clearly himself. He didn't know just what he had intended when he came away, he didn't know what he intended now. He seemed to be waiting for something to turn him one way or the other. He would stroll around the highly developed landscaping of Henry's grounds, asking the gardener the names of the strange plants, and watching him run the water from intricate systems of irrigation. It was clever. But when he thought of finding a place out here for themselves and putting all this care into keeping a lawn green and queer plants flourishing, it seemed to him a puttering sort of life. Nature here didn't seem to do anything; it was all like hothouse gardening; Annie might enjoy the great roses and geraniums and lilies, but he couldn't interest himself in things that seemed to be mostly for show. Of course, it *was* pretty fine to go right out into your own yard and pick an orange off the tree. It still seemed marvelous to him to pick oranges, while to pick an apple was natural and commonplace. Not that he liked oranges better. No, there was nothing that could come up to a good apple.

"What would you do back there?" they demanded. He didn't want to go back into the bank.

No, he knew he didn't. But just the same . . .

It hurt Fred to think that Annie could adjust herself so easily. In fact, she was blooming in the freedom from care. She never seemed to have enough of gadding and jaunting. Sometimes he thought she was trying to put the children out of her mind; and then again it hurt him because she *could*. But it worked upon him. Whether he would admit it in words or not, what mama wanted "went a long way." He didn't say so to any of the others, for that would be conceding too much, but he kept his eye out for a modest place "with garden maintenance" where he and Annie might try it out for a while. After all, he told himself, he had finished his work. He wanted mama to be happy. He saw some streets that appealed to him, not so showy, with an older look, like that place where they had stayed in San Diego. He talked to the neighbors, where one of these houses was for rent, and discovered that they were ex-Nebraskans and Presbyterians, and were just about like folks from home. He even broached the subject cautiously to Annie.

"Well, mama, would you like to look at a few houses? I saw one place that seems pretty nice."

But Annie didn't take to the place. She didn't seem to care much for the neighbors. What *did* she want, then? he asked her. He couldn't get her to say. When it came to *her* making a decision, she seemed fluttered—she wouldn't answer, and turned her face away from him.

When bad news came from home, Louie and Henry thought this clinched it. Now they wouldn't consider going back.

The first real shock was the news of the failure of the other bank. And not only had the bank failed, and closed its doors, but Mr. Hoagland had vanished. Yes, H. L. Hoagland! who, since the death of old Mr. Spencer, had been recognized as the town's first citizen.

Henry didn't see why that need affect *them*. They had nothing to do with it. Fred was lucky to be out of there, Henry said. He'd better withdraw completely. Fred hadn't any good arguments against that—or any arguments that would seem valid to Henry. He wouldn't admit that he was worried about his own funds, for that would seem like a reflection upon his own bank; and although he was "no longer connected," he must uphold the honor of the institution. He couldn't acknowledge that he didn't wholly trust Richard. He had never done that, even to Annie. But he was made to realize, as never before, the difference in the way that he and his brother-in-law looked at finance. Fred was humble, and felt he couldn't say much, for Henry, in the common phrase, had "done better" than he had. Fred had been proud all these years of claiming relationship with a man who had made as much money as Henry. But now it gave Fred a secret shock to see how coldly Henry viewed these things. Henry did his business in cold figures; that was the way all the big fellows managed it; and maybe he just couldn't understand how it felt to be bound up with a place and the people there. Although Henry didn't say as much in words, Fred had the feeling that he didn't condemn H. L. Hoagland for getting away while the getting was good. He raised his eyebrows and slightly shrugged his thin little shoulders. If people lost, that was their own lookout. They shouldn't have trusted the fellow so much. And anyway, Fred wasn't involved.

But the next piece of news struck even closer. The church was gone. Mrs. Lowrie, who had seemed better when the Fergusons left, had suddenly taken a turn for the worse and died; Mr. Lowrie, unable to face his loss and carry on a dwindling cause, had resigned; he had gone to Montana to live with his son; and the church, hastily summoning a meeting, had voted "not to continue." The other element had won. They were going in with the Congregationalists.

At first Fred was so upset that he couldn't take in anything more than the fact itself. The church was gone. Now, when he looked back toward home, he faced a painful blank.

The others all tried to persuade him that it would have

674

turned out the same if he had been there. He couldn't have carried the whole thing forever on his own shoulders. And maybe they were right. He wasn't sure himself that he hadn't been expecting this all along. He couldn't say just how much the canny pre-knowledge might have had to do with his coming away. He couldn't expect to live forever; and after he was gone, who would there have been to take his place? Still they had taken such advantage of his absence! He could never get over that. Resentment, loss, a stony relief that the worst had come to pass without him—Mr. Ferguson didn't know what he *did* feel. One thing grew more and more sure—Belmond would never be the same to him again. Sometimes he felt in dazed bewilderment that he *had* no home. His day there was over. He was out of the bank, the church was gone, and there were none of his children to carry on his work. Then what had he been working for all these years? Perhaps the best thing he could do now was to stay and live out his days in the sunshine. He went again and looked at that house, trying, as he examined the pipes and the heating arrangements, to crush down his pain at the idea of putting his money and efforts into some other place than the one he had so long called home. It might be a great relief to attend a church, like that big flourishing one the people from Nebraska so proudly referred to, where he needn't feel that the responsibility rested with him. It even seemed to him that Louie regarded the news from home as providential! And maybe, for all he knew, Annie in her heart did also.

"Oh, you'll stay," everyone said with complacent triumph.

For a time Fred seemed to be adrift. He mutely accompanied the others on their excursions, viewing the wonders of California; taking a feeble hand once or twice with Henry at golf. He sat in the park at Los Angeles, while Louie and Annie did their shopping, and got into conversation with other old fellows who were sunning themselves.

But everywhere he heard the same thing: "You'll stay." He heard it at the great Iowa winter picnic, the one gathering which he really wanted to attend; although he didn't know

675

whether it gave him more pride or more disgruntlement to find so many of his fellow countrymen away from home.

Fred and Annie went by themselves. The others had encouraged them, saying the picnic was "a great spectacle"; but such a gathering didn't appeal to Louie and Henry. Fred was glad to be driving his own car. To be taken everywhere—well, it was pretty fine for a little while, but it didn't suit him. He felt as if he were getting soft. He was glad to have Annie to himself again. These folks hadn't been driven here by chauffeurs!—and he would have felt queer arriving in such style.

Cars were lined up around the park as thick as they could stand, and for two blocks on either side. There was a special policeman. Yes, it was a big occasion. Again Fred felt a thrill of dubious pride in realizing that he was part of such a crowd as this. His thoughts were confused as he and Annie joined the others. The world that he had left behind was not the same—perhaps he would find the memory of it here, among these people who had come together to honor their old home.

Parties were still eating dinner, at tables or seated on the grass. It made Annie and Fred feel out of things. At home, they would have had their own group.

"Would have been nice if those folks from Dike could have been here," Fred remarked.

But somewhere in a crowd like this they would be sure to find familiar faces. The grounds were divided up into the different counties, just as the papers had described. The Fergusons found Bell County and went there at once. Some twenty or twenty-five people were grouped around the sign. The Fergusons waited for their chance to sign the register that lay on the wooden picnic table. Fred put down their names with some self-consciousness:

Mr. and Mrs. F. W. Ferguson, Belmond.

Surely there would be someone to recognize that signature! But although one or two of the names were certainly familiar, and people looked at them hopefully, suspiciously, or just blankly, the Fergusons could see no one whom they had ever known before.

It was too hot right out in the sun. Even Annie admitted that by taking off her silk jacket. She hadn't put on her new black-and-white suit for this occasion, to Fred's relief. If they did meet old friends, he wouldn't have wanted it to seem that he and Annie were trying now to be different than at home. They wandered off into the shade of a eucalyptus tree, where they tried to watch the crowd for someone they might know, without too apparent a hopefulness. Other people, it appeared, were doing the same. Louie and Henry had told them that they would find so many old acquaintances today that they would feel more at home here than in Belmond.

Well, they might have known almost any of these people! The middle-aged and elderly predominated. Except for that, it could well have been taken for some big gathering at home. It was pretty good, Fred thought, to see just ordinary folks again. Those fellows around the golf links were too high-toned for him. They talked about nothing but the market and their scores. He was hungry for some of the old local topics. He wanted to hear about crops and conditions. He and Annie caught bits of conversation around them. A man said in a bright, chatty tone to a woman: "You know Lulu died"; and she answered eagerly: "Oh, did *Lu*-lu die!" There were some queer characters, of course. Bound to be, among this many people. They saw one old man with a long beard, like a Bible character. "Must not have cut it since he left home," Fred observed. "Look at those!" Annie said, faintly scandalized. She nodded toward a rough-looking family clad all in dungaree pants. They were the kind whom she and Fred had noticed sometimes on their drives, living in one of those little shacks on a canyon edge, that looked ready to be swept away in the first flood. Annie thought *they* didn't look as if they had come from home. But they weren't so different from the others, Fred observed. They might have come out with less money, only a hundred dollars or so; but for the same reason, the reason all these people had come—because they wanted a softer life. They all seemed to have the same look, when you saw them in a crowd like this—a kind of rootless, drifting, meaningless look, against the alien background of palms and gaudy tropical flowers. Well, Fred reflected, his life hadn't been soft. Maybe he would have liked to take his ease, like the rest of them. But it seemed as if he couldn't be easy thinking of the news from home. He couldn't take Mrs. Lowrie's death, for instance, in the way that those two folks seemed to be taking Lulu's. The eucalyptus in the shade had a bitter foreign scent.

"Well, mama, we might walk around again—see if we meet anyone."

They got up, and somewhat forlornly wandered through the great park. In such a crowd as this, they seemed to have lost their old identity. They, Mr. and Mrs. Fred Ferguson, so well established in Belmond, were only newcomers here, only ex-Iowans like the others. It didn't seem to Fred as if picking oranges from the tree and cutting roses in February could make up for that.

Well, there was one thing more that they could do. They could go over to the western county where Fred's brother Will had lived, and where they had occasionally visited, and study the list of names fastened to a eucalyptus tree. And here they *did* meet someone they had known. Fred was just turning around when he felt a hand on his shoulder.

"Wait a minute, wait a minute," a voice said.

He stared into round light eyes behind owlish spectacles—a face that could have been the face of half a dozen men.

"Now I've got it—your name's Ferguson! Am I right?"

Fred admitted that it was, and shook the proffered hand, dubiously at first, then heartily and in relief as the explanations followed.

"I knew you were a Ferguson the minute I saw you, even if your back was turned to me. Couldn't mistake *that!* But for a minute you had me up a tree. You looked so much like Will you gave me a turn—and I knew you couldn't be Will, since Will was dead. Fred. Sure. I place you now. Will's brother. Why, *I* met *you* when you came to Clarion. Lafferty—insurance—don't tell me you've forgotten that fishing trip!"

Fred hadn't forgotten it. And of course he remembered Lafferty now. Why, he was the fellow who had made the coffee! The two men shook hands again, long and heartily. And Annie nodded. Yes, she remembered Mrs. Lafferty. All three were beaming.

"So you've left the old town—that's right, Belmond!—and come out here where all the good folks go." Mr. Lafferty clapped Fred on the shoulder again. "Oh, sooner or later—sooner or later. We get them all."

No doubt that *he* had become a Californian! But now he was insisting that they must find the missus. "She'll be tickled to death to see you folks." They must have a little reunion of their own. With a hand at the elbow of each, Mr. Lafferty was pushing them through the crowd.

"Ah, *here* she is!" he cried proudly.

Now the Fergusons *did* receive a shock. For this could never be Mrs. Lafferty!—this vision confronting them in an effulgence of pink and gold, this face smiling coyly out at them from the girlish shade of a wide pink hat, this golden hair. Mrs. Lafferty!—whom Annie remembered, a plump middle-aged matron like the others, at the meeting of the Aid Society. It had astounded them to see the magnificence to which familiar geraniums and calla lilies attained in the sunshine. But this was the most astounding blossoming of all! It *was* Mrs. Lafferty, though. She was extending a fat, bejeweled hand.

"Well," Fred said feebly, as he took it, "I guess this climate agrees with *you*."

But they had little time for astonishment or anything else. Mr. Lafferty was taking charge of them. He seemed to be constituting himself their host, and to be presenting to them all of Southern California. Already, like everyone else, he had made up his mind that they must stay. Go back to Belmond? He laughed at the idea. They would laugh themselves, when they had been out here a little longer. Why, there was no place in the world that had the destiny of Southern California! Grapes, oranges, melons—he named the products. What was a little corn compared to all those? He made them feel humbly that corn was a back number. Mrs. Lafferty smiled, with coral-tinted lips, above the shining expanse of her bosom. The Fergusons were dazzled.

Now Mr. Lafferty was suggesting that they go over to hear the program. Listen to some fine entertainment. Join in the singing of the grand old song. He knew some of the speakers personally, they were men who counted out here. If Fred would like to meet them afterwards, Lafferty could arrange.

"Oh, no, I guess not," Fred said diffidently. He still had a great respect for "speakers." But he thought they would like to hear the program. "Wouldn't we, Annie? Since these folks are kind enough to show us around." Even if corn was just a rustic product, it would be pretty good to hear the old song again.

Already the music was playing, and they started in the direction of the sound. It made the Fergusons feel that they had some part in the gathering. Mrs. Lafferty tucked her hand brightly into the curve of Annie's arm. But Annie noticed that she was panting a little. Her plump ankles bent inward as she tilted along on her shining high heels. Annie gave a surreptitious glance down at her own matronly oxfords. At first she had been dazed by Mrs. Lafferty's transformation. But now she was recovering her equanimity. The flat, middle-western intonation of the voice that issued from those coral lips had not changed; and the golden hue of eternal youth hadn't quite reached around to the back of Mrs. Lafferty's head. Annie's eye was sharp enough to take note of the tell-tale ends under the pink shade of the hat. She tried to hide her embarrassment, since the Laffertys were being so kind.

The speaker's stand was at the edge of the grounds. The crowd was a little disappointing. There couldn't be more than a hundred or so. But Fred supposed they were late in gathering, just as they were at all picnics.

"You want to listen to this fellow," Mr. Lafferty warned. "He's slated for governor some day. Oh, I tell you, it's the good old stock that's making California what it is." He slapped Fred's arm jovially.

Fred prepared to listen with respect. The speaker, a round-bodied man with a rosy public face and half-bald head, was launched on the story of "the little red schoolhouse on the country crossroads" where he had got his start. There was emotion in his voice. Fred felt a nostalgia for his own boyhood. He thought of the old Buck Creek schoolhouse where Annie had taught. He could almost smell the milky corn and the warm summer dust. But he was disturbed when the speaker made a quick transition. "Those happy days, when we milked the cows and shoveled snow, are fine to remember, aren't they, folks?—At a distance—from beneath the sunny skies of California!" Everyone laughed.

In fact, the longer he listened, the more disturbed Fred grew. These fellows scarcely mentioned Iowa at all, except to tell how lucky they were to get away from bad weather. Every speaker was just the same. "Privileged to enjoy the blessings of this wonderful climate!" That wasn't what Fred had come to hear today. His local patriotism was outraged. He felt homesick and sore. This old fellow who was introduced as "ninety years young," up there cavorting on the platform, telling how he had found his youth beneath the sunny skies— when all his antics only served to show off to everyone how decrepit he was! All of them started from the little red school-house, but from there they seemed to reach the same point in the end: the "problems of the day" in California. Every-thing was perfect, of course, that they all must say, no one could doubt the great destiny. But there were unpatriotic, un-American elements coming in. There was more need than ever for having the right men in office.

Fred turned to Mr. Lafferty and said, "Why, these sound like political speeches."

Mr. Lafferty laughed easily. "Oh, sure. The Iowa vote is important," he explained; taking it for granted that Fred understood these little matters. "And we got too good a place, we can't let these radicals get hold out here."

Fred didn't answer. Well, maybe that was true, he thought. He himself was afraid of "radicals," although he was vague as to the meaning of the term. But he didn't like the notion of having to hear one thing when he had come to hear an-other. He didn't care to be made a fool of in that way. He gave a sideways glance at Mr. Lafferty. These fellows wouldn't get *his* vote, he thought privately, even if he were to stay.

But now the song leader was being introduced. Sleek, breezy, plump, with wavy hair, he stepped easily in front of the microphone.

"Ladies and gentlemen, good afternoon. I suppose you're all from Iowa or you wouldn't be here today. All *from* there." The crowd laughed. "Well, it's fine, isn't it, to get together like this once in a while, just to celebrate? Now, everybody knows Iowa as 'the state where the tall corn grows'—they don't grow our oranges and lemons and figs and dates, and all the fine things we're privileged to enjoy—but they *do* grow corn. So we ought all to be ready to join in a little burst of song. You know how the song begins.

We're from I-o-way, I-o-way—

Iowa, of course, *we* all know the correct pronunciation is, but the song calls for Ioway, poetic license I suppose, so we've all got to sing it as written. Now, folks, as we come to the line 'where the tall corn grows,' I want you all to raise the right hand—see?—just to indicate how high that old corn can get. Pretty high, you bet you. Higher than some of our heads. Will you do that? Fine!"

This was something like. Fred cleared his throat. He wasn't much of a singer, but what he lacked in voice he was prepared to make up in patriotism. He had read of the singing of this song by thousands, joining their voices, so the papers said, in praise of their native state. It was something he had always wanted to hear.

But this was another thing that didn't turn out according to the papers! If these folks had ever known the song, they seemed to have forgotten it. It was like a difficult hymn in church, one with too many turns and high notes. The leader sang cheerily, waving time, but only a few embarrassed voices joined. A few hands were timidly raised—but as for those thousands!

Fred could hardly keep from showing his disappointment to Mr. Lafferty. But he was getting a little wary even of the Laffertys. Their cordiality was almost too shining. Fred felt tired. He wanted to get away. At last he said that he thought they ought to be going home.

The Laffertys insisted on going with them to the gate. Mrs. Lafferty's smile was fixed now. She went forward with short stubby steps. Her panting was interspersed with tiny moans. Mr. Lafferty took Fred's hand when they came to say good-bye.

"Well, folks, we'd certainly like to see more of you. Old friends are the best. Isn't that so? Say, I'll never forget that fishing trip!

"I think I could help you," he added confidentially, drawing Fred a little aside, "when you decide on that house you want to build. Why not come over and have dinner with us some time? And first, I tell you—" he squeezed Fred's arm—"I'd like to drive you around to look at some sites. Oh, sure you're going to stay! They all do. Folks like you are just what we need."

The Fergusons got away at last. They did not look at each other. They had driven several blocks before Fred spoke.

"Well, mama, I guess I better get you home before summer begins, or else maybe *you'll* be blossoming out with golden hair, like this lady."

It was almost the only comment on the occasion that he made—except to say dryly, when Louie and Henry questioned him, yes, there had been lots of people there, maybe half as many as the papers said!

But Annie knew that she had lost her case. If, indeed, it had been a case! Her feelings were as mixed as Fred's. When Fred had suggested that they take a house, she hadn't been able to answer. Tears had glistened for a moment in her eyes. She couldn't after all these years assert her will directly above Fred's. If it *was* her will. When she thought of staying here, she felt a painful, secret triumph against her children—if they didn't want to come home, maybe they would find that home was no longer there! But the old loyalties wouldn't let her admit that her home wasn't the same to her as ever, or that any other place could be better in the end.

No, sir, when summer came they were going. Fred was sure of that now. He had really been sure of it all along. If mama had insisted . . . well, no, he wouldn't have stayed even then. And he knew that mama wouldn't insist when she understood his feelings. The news from home had been slowly sinking into him, and all the sunshine couldn't blot it out. He couldn't help feeling that this was no time to be sitting around and looking at roses. He remembered the day he had left the bank, that feeling of storm in the summer air. He couldn't be easy any longer in the sunshine. He felt as if he ought to be there to join with the others—ought to be there to look after things. Maybe, as the others said, his work was accomplished. But he couldn't be satisfied until he had seen for himself. It had appeared to be the destiny of all good Americans to go on toward some final rosy sunset. Fred supposed that he, like the others, had been working with that goal in mind. But now that he had reached the goal, he found that he couldn't accept it. He couldn't be like Mr. Hoagland. He didn't want to escape his share. He couldn't forget that little group of aging people left behind and standing out under the darkening sky; or their own house locked and empty in the midst of the snow. If a storm *was* coming, that was where he wanted to be. Belmond was his own stamping ground; and it was there that his sunset lay, in the somber glow that followed the long working day of the prairie.

5

"Well, mama, we've crossed over the line!"

Fred said that with scarcely concealed satisfaction. Mrs. Ferguson sat up, straightened her hat and smoothed down her skirt. At first she had an impulse to protest at being back, and then a feeling she hadn't expected swept over her. She let down the window a little more, and the warm morning smells of earth and clover came in to her. They seemed new—fresh-minted and new—and yet carried a sense of familiarity too deep to be described. She felt as if she had awakened from a dream into the freshness of reality.

Both of them were looking around them now with the emotion and excitement of return. How green everything was! And how good everything smelled! The ground smelled good, and the green, green grass. Even the strong rank smell of the pigsties had an odor of fertility. They drove between fields of alsike clover and a scent of honey and strawberries came warm from the pink clover heads thickly crowded. It seemed as if this air—no longer dry, rarefied and golden—held and intensified all the teeming summertime odors.

"Well, there's no soil quite like this," Fred said. "I didn't see anything to beat it."

He had a feeling of exaltation as they drove along—up and down, gently up and down, on the great smooth billows of the rolling country. Talk about the ocean! The land was just as big. The rich earth that spread on every side was rounded by the sweep of the globe. And yet it was all close, familiar, it was home. Always, at the end of the road, he could see the tall trees on either side, with one side overhanging. Nothing was waste, all was put to use, made into a compact pattern of farms. He looked out at the scattered clusters of house, barn, grove and silo, some of them hazy they were so far away. There was a short detour that took them along a narrow country road and across a little rattling bridge over a sluggish prairie stream with a dark sparkle in its muddy water. But it was almost all on paving now. Fred noted that with pride. The whitish miles of asphalt glaring in the sun gave a modern, all-connected look to the towns and farms. Why leave a country like this, he thought, such a good country, and just when they were getting things fixed the way they wanted them?

The fields they were passing now were crumbly and moist with fertility. He was proud to see the fat, black-and-white hogs out in the wet barnyards. Coming into a town, they rode through green caverns of shade. There was a sense of teeming thickness in the close-built streets under the heavy trees. The leaves were so dense that a blackness lay at the heart of the foliage. Then they came out into open sunlight again. Wild roses were in bloom along the roadsides, fresh in their morning stain of pink, but some of them, a few of them, bleached white already with the heat. It gave the feeling of having come into the warm, unconscious, breathing interior of the mighty continent.

They stopped at a restaurant at noon. They had struck a dreadful bed last night, in some little burg; and for breakfast, at the only café, they had drunk pale coffee out of thick white cups. This time they had a good dinner. No fancy fixings, but what Fred called real food—real chicken and noodle soup and fresh strawberry shortcake. The fellow at the filling station had recommended this place. A widow woman ran it, and she knew how to make coffee. Cooking-school teachers might palaver about fruit juices, Fred announced, all they were a mind to; but he would give all the juice ever squeezed out for a good home-fried chicken. He wiped his lips with heartfelt satisfaction.

But as they drove on, and it grew later, their first exaltation of homecoming sank into weariness. The view was misty at the end of the road; trees stood mournful against the orange sunset; the scattered farms had a lonely look; and they felt the underlying sober sadness in these great stretches of brooding fecundity.

It was almost dark when they drove into Belmond. Both felt tired and secretly dispirited. The town looked small and local under the heaviness of the trees. The air was hot and thick. The frame houses seemed to have settled close to the ground. Now they had returned to their old responsibilities and there was no more getting away from them. They drove down the small Main Street. How drearily small it looked! There was the closed bank. Fred turned his eyes away uneasily from the sad, evening stare of the windows. He didn't want to pass his own old place of business on the corner. There weren't many people on the streets. The Fergusons felt unwelcomed, as if the place had closed against them in their absence, and they didn't know it any more. And yet they knew it too well!

"Shall we go home or shall we drop in to Ella's?"

Fred knew that Annie would have preferred to go home. She didn't feel like visiting tonight. But nothing would be ready in the house. They hadn't written exactly when they would arrive. They drove past the place, undecided. How

strange to see it there in the twilight, closed against them too!
—the shades down, even the lawn with an air of vacancy.

"Might get out and see how it looks," Fred suggested doubt-fully.

There was a homesickness in his tone. They both got out of the car, stiff and tired, and stood on their own cement walk.

But the place seemed strange to them. They had always thought of their house as pretty good-sized. Now, after Louie's and Henry's great white house in Pasadena, their own was small and commonplace. They tried the door to the screened porch. But it was hooked and dusty. The key was over at the Morgans', and they didn't feel like going after it. Besides, there were no lights next door, the Morgans must not be at home.

"Well, I guess we better go over to Ella's for tonight."

But there seemed to be no lights at Ella's, either. Annie sat waiting in the car while Fred got out to see if there was anybody at home. Why couldn't they have stayed somewhere along the road, reached home in the morning? Fred wouldn't hear to that, of course, as long as he was near any of his folks. But *her* folks . . . Annie thought of her own sister, feeling the helpless, misty sense of distance that had grown between them. She turned her eyes away from the outline of the narrow frame house where Ella and Ben were living out the bleak end of their fruitless marriage. Fred knocked on the closed front door.

"They're not home!" someone called out from the porch next door.

She came out on the lawn now—Ella's neighbor, Annie couldn't think of her name.

"The folks went to Geneva yesterday," the neighbor said, staring, yet pleased to give information. "They took Mister to the hospital there."

Annie waited, her heart beating thickly, until Fred came soberly back to the car.

"The folks have gone to Geneva—"

"Yes, I heard."

"She don't seem to know just what the matter is, except

687

that Ben had a bad spell of some kind. They think maybe they'll have to operate."

The Fergusons considered the situation nervously, wondering what it might mean for them. But they couldn't seem to take it in tonight. They had got back too recently, and were half strangers still. Fred climbed into the car again.

"Well—" he said heavily. "Guess there's nothing we can do about it tonight."

And now what were they to do? Fred couldn't help a hurt feeling because none of their friends or relatives were around to welcome them. The Lowries, too, were gone. This little while away, and already the small tight group that had stood out in front of this very house telling them good-bye, had been scattered and broken. Of course there were other places—any of their neighbors . . . But it didn't seem right to come down on the neighbors without warning. Annie couldn't bear the thought of their own empty house.

"Well, shall we go to the hotel?"

It seemed foolish in Belmond, right at home here, where any number of folks would have been glad to take them in. As if they hadn't had enough of hotels on their trip! But mama was out of spirits, Fred could see, and if that was what she preferred . . . He wished himself that they had stayed somewhere else and reached here by daylight. Everything looked different then. This was pretty bad news to meet them at the outset. It didn't seem like much of a homecoming. Fred had an uneasy feeling of guilt and responsibility. He knew that he was the one who had wanted to come back.

They drove around to the Belmond House. It was a familiar enough place to Fred. He had eaten here every Thursday with the Rotary. But for him and mama to be staying at the hotel made them seem like strangers in their own town. They entered the close, leather-smelling, local interior of the elderly brick building.

The thin young clerk looked up at them, his face shiny in the heat. At first it seemed as if he *did* take them for strangers. Then he saw who they were, and they had the satisfaction of at least a little welcome.

"Well! I didn't know you at first. You folks been away a good while, haven't you? Going to stay with us tonight?"

"Yes, we didn't feel like opening up the place," Mr. Ferguson explained.

"Well, glad to have you with us."

The old fellow who used to work here seemed to be gone. Fred thought he would ask about him in the morning. He was too tired for any inquiries tonight. A young fellow Fred couldn't remember having seen before took their bags. They followed him up the wide stairway with the worn rubber matting. The door of their room stuck in the heat. The young fellow put down their bags and pushed with his shoulder. He opened the window, took a nonchalant look at the rack of towels, accepted Fred's tip, and was gone. The old man would have been more concerned about their comfort.

They had asked for a cool room, and it seemed pretty hot in here. But Fred didn't like to make any complaint. "Give you the coolest we've got, Mr. Ferguson," the clerk had promised. Fred wouldn't acknowledge anything amiss with their accommodations in Belmond. He disregarded Annie's tremulous look. It hurt him that she didn't seem more pleased to be back. He realized that he couldn't always tell about Annie. He couldn't be sure that he knew her mind. When they were out there, she had shown a side that he had never seen before. Both of them were feeling somewhat disconsolate, here in this hotel room, with the smell of varnish, the air coming faintly in through the screen, the grinding noise of cars outside. But no matter how gloomy things might look tonight, Fred knew that he was stubbornly glad to have got back.

Thank goodness, the bed was pretty comfortable! Fred let Annie have the side toward the window. They would find it a whole lot cooler, he told her, when they were in their own house again.

As things turned out, Annie fell asleep sooner than he did. He himself felt oppressed by the still heat, the brooding heaviness. The future weighed upon him. He asked himself what he was going to do now. He was out of the bank . . . the church . . . all to which he had given his life. . . . And yet

689

he couldn't get rid of the old sense of responsibility. He could feel the whole great fertile country, burdened with its wealth of farms and towns, surrounding him in the night, and seeming to raise a silent question. He remembered the desolate look of the house, with the grass shaggy along the sidewalks. None of his children were there, and he had built the house for them. What would become of it when he and Annie were gone?

The concerns of the family lay heavy upon him. Just by going away he hadn't got rid of them. He might turn his back upon them, but still they existed. Louie and Henry could take their ease; they thought of nobody beyond themselves. But he and Annie couldn't be like that. There was no use to worry about Ben until they had some further news. Still, whatever was going to happen, Fred knew that he would be the one, Ella would look to him. The children were gone, but they were on his mind. Margaret—he didn't understand her, what she was after, what was going to become of her. He and mama had had to give in, and let her go her own way, whatever it was, but that didn't absolve them of responsibility. He could understand Bunny even less. It hurt and bewildered him that the boy seemed to have gone back on all the old ideas. Just the same, Bunny was their youngest. Whether they liked the girl whom he had married or not, they had to regard her as Bunny's wife, and do their duty by her as best they could. Lillian . . . he had never spoken of this to mama, knowing how much she cared for Carl; but he knew things hadn't been right between Carl and Lillian. If Carl had failed her, then it seemed as if *he* ought to do something to make it up to her. Her own father had gone back on her too. Fred had never forgiven Howard. Dorothy they had always regarded as the one who was provided for. But now that he had seen how things were going with her and Jesse, Fred couldn't even be sure of that.

He turned uneasily, but cautiously, not wanting to disturb Annie.

He was aware of a sense of change pervading everything, although it wasn't a thing he could touch or locate. He couldn't say how or when it had happened, but the old simple surety seemed to be gone—the old bright, simple faith in the way things had started and were likely to continue. The church of his fathers was empty. Even his town, in which he had placed his trust, never doubting that it must follow a steady growth to a fine destiny, seemed instead to have come to a standstill. There was something beyond him, something that he hadn't taken into account, some force that he was only blindly aware of working stealthily and bringing a right-about-face. His own children were allied with that force. He had given them all their start, but none of them had yet taken his place. It was he who was still back of it all. They still depended upon him. He felt a heavy solitude. He wasn't sure of anything. Only that he was here again—back home—and that no matter what changes there might be, the old demands were still upon him.

There had been rain some time before morning. What a relief that was! Now the air that came through their window was bright, clean-washed and fresh. Now mama had no excuse for bringing up California. The Fergusons began to feel a genuine excitement in getting home. They were just saying, what should they do, get breakfast here, or what?—when the clerk called them and told them they had a visitor downstairs.

Mr. Ferguson went down. It was Mr. Viele!

"Well, well, well! Here's the stranger returned!"

The two men shook hands heartily, while the young clerk smiled, and one or two traveling men turned to look at them in sympathy. Fred almost forgot, in the pleasure of the meeting, that it was Mr. Viele, and not one of his own church members, who had come to welcome him. The familiar clock, advertising the jewelry store, was ticking above the desk; the boy was sweeping; and the big shabby room with its doors standing open had the summery aspect that Fred knew well.

"Just got in last night, did you?"

"How did you find out about it?"

"Oh, Ada Rist telephoned Mamie this morning."

Someone had seen them stop at the folks' last night, and the news had got around that they were back.

"Say, if we'd known you didn't have a place to stay! Why, we've got all kinds of room, you know, would have been tickled to death to have you."

"Oh, that's all right, Melvin," Fred answered, ashamed that he had thought no one welcomed them. "We wouldn't have wanted to trouble you."

"Wouldn't have been any trouble at all. What do you think your neighbors are for?"

At any rate, he had orders to bring them right along, to accept no excuses. Mrs. Ferguson had come downstairs, wearing a fresh new summer costume, smiling and pleased at Mr. Viele's hearty approbation. "They must have treated *you* well in California!" he exclaimed. But had they had their breakfast yet? The Fergusons looked slightly embarrassed, were forced to admit that they had not. That was fine, then! Just what he was hoping.

"Verne, I'm going to steal your best customers."

The clerk allowed this, smiling. Mr. Ferguson paid the bill, lying nobly—since this was Belmond—and declaring that they had had a fine night. Oh, yes, a little hot, but the rain had fixed that. The dark thought of change seemed only a dream as Mr. Viele ushered them both out of the hotel into the busy summer-morning noises. He led the way, and they followed him in their own car, dusty from travel—driving along the street that still glistened from the rain, looking out at the fresh lawns and flowers. There seemed to be an effulgent June-time warmth about the whole town. The air smelled of green grass and bridal wreath. Where had their dark thoughts flown? This was the same old place they knew. They were back in Belmond.

The Viele house stood trim and well-painted on its bright green lawn. Mrs. Viele, in a thin voile dress, was at the door to welcome them. The ready tears overflowed her eyes as she clasped Mrs. Ferguson. They stepped into the clean, fresh, homelike living room; breathing in, through the fragrance of a big bouquet of wet snowball blossoms, the crisp welcome smells of bacon and coffee.

692

Mrs. Viele was effusive with sympathy and self-reproach. "Oh, you poor folks! Getting here without a soul to meet you. And having to sleep in that hotel!"

Oh, it was all right, had a good bed, Mr. Ferguson assured her uneasily, not liking the hotel to be maligned.

But it was certainly nice to be here! With a long sigh of ease, Mr. Ferguson sat down in the living room to talk with Mr. Viele while Mrs. Viele was getting on the breakfast. Mrs. Ferguson took off her hat in the immaculate guest room, spending some little time with her hair at the mirror, and noting with some excitement how trim and modish this little cotton suit looked. It was nicer than any she could have got in Belmond. Her black-and-white costume she would save to wear to the club, when it met at Mrs. Hoagland's . . . forgetting that the Hoaglands were no longer here. She stopped to smell the snowballs on the living room table, burying her face a moment in the soft bloom, wondering how her own flowers were getting on, thinking with a sigh of Louie's.

"Well, folks, you can come now."

The breakfast, of course, was delicious. Mrs. Viele was a wonderful housekeeper. It was pleasant to eat again from the familiar flowered Haviland. Mrs. Ferguson laughed apologetically when Fred declared he had tasted nothing like this for months. "Why, Fred, you know we had lovely things at Louie's!" "Oh, yes, but we had to have that girl with those fixed-up eyebrows hanging around us all the time." The women both laughed, but with indulgence. Annie tried to explain about Louie's maid. "All the girls out there want to get into the movies. Well, you can't blame them. Think of the wonderful salaries they get." But the memory of Louie's sunroom was even now fading—with the great windows open, the great curtains drawn here and there against the light. . . . And she didn't know whether she was sorry or not.

The conversation seemed to consist mostly of broken sentences—the Fergusons starting to tell something about their travels, the Vieles breaking in with news of affairs at home. The failure of the other bank, of course, was the great topic. Some folks said one thing, some said another, but no one was

693

really sure. No one knew what had become of Mr. Hoagland. "She" was with her family in Illinois. Bert was left here with the whole thing on his hands. There was talk of a trial. "Think of a man skipping out and leaving his own son to bear the brunt!" "Oh, well, they're in cahoots," Mr. Viele said wisely. Mr. Ferguson shook his head, reserving his judgment.

Still, it was both exciting and comforting to hear the news of home, even when it wasn't good news. None of the people at this table were directly involved. There was no doubt about it—the last slight constraint between the two families had faded now that the barrier of the church was gone. They would no longer belong to different denominations. They talked about it a little, Fred noncommittal, Mr. Viele heartily consoling. "Well, Fred, I know how you feel, but if you look at it in this way—it's pretty nice after all to think that we're all united. For my part," Mr. Viele said boldly, "I'd like to see even the Methodists join in!" He looked triumphantly around the table. And it did seem to be true, Fred couldn't think of good arguments against it—in this way, all who believed in the churches and the work they were doing could make a real stand against the forces that were trying to overwhelm them. It made them feel that the older people and their ideals weren't, after all, a thing of the past. Of course, Mr. Viele added hastily, that didn't include the Catholics. The Methodists were as far as he could go. In the midst of breakfast, Fred was called to the phone to answer the call he had put in to Carl. And even this was good news. Or, at any rate, it held bad news suspended. Ben was in the hospital for observation, and it hadn't been determined whether he was going to need an operation. Well, he would have Carl and Lillian to look after him. He wouldn't be left entirely to Ella, who was notoriously poor help in sickness!—although Annie, of course, wouldn't have dared say this in front of Fred. Now they could finish their breakfast secure in the knowledge that there was no present need for them to go to Geneva. The Vieles, prosperous and optimistic, saw everything in its most cheerful light.

After breakfast, the Fergusons suggested that they had better go over to the house. But Mrs. Viele wouldn't hear of it. Oh, no, they needed a rest. She hadn't begun to ask all the questions she wanted to about their vacation. It seemed as if she and Melvin had done all the talking so far! But they were *so* glad to have the Fergusons back. And besides—she squeezed Annie's hand and whispered mysteriously—they didn't want her to go over there yet. Well, she might as well tell them why. Ada Rist had planned to get everything in order for them; she was working there now; and she would be terribly disappointed if they came into the place when it was looking *this* way. Mrs. Ferguson consented in pleased surprise, ashamed of her disappointment last night. They had barely got into the living room when the telephone rang again. This time it was Mrs. Dunn, who had heard that they were back, and was coming over to see them.

Now they were really getting their welcome. Their status of returned travelers shed a glory over them, which, after all, there need be no hurry in giving up. Indeed, what hurry was there about anything? Mrs. Ferguson tried to think of some, on principle; they must get settled, get their things unpacked, in a few days at least they must be going over to Geneva. But she was glad to have this overruled by Mrs. Viele's fond sympathy, and to sit, with a pleasing touch of fashionable strangeness in her new dress, ready to be seen and welcomed, and enjoying the scents of grass and flowers.

Mrs. Dunn, heavy and perspiring, came panting into the room. So they were back, she told them—everybody'd about given them up; thought maybe they liked it so well out there they weren't ever going to leave. She greeted them with solemn significance, bringing with her the odors of sickrooms and funerals, at variance with the freshness of the Vieles' nice living room. It brought back the dark thought of change again, and made Mrs. Ferguson feel guilty and uneasy.

"Well," Mrs. Dunn said, as soon as she was seated, "I suppose you didn't think you was returning to this!"

But of course (thank heaven! Annie would have liked to say) she couldn't be quite as mournful as she would have liked here in front of the Vieles, who were Congregationalists.

Soon she was rocking in heavy comfort, and finding plenty of consolation in recounting all the sad facts to Mr. Ferguson, shaking her head, sighing at intervals, letting out a little surreptitious gleam of funereal interest in the excitement and trouble from her small, suspicious eyes—wanting to see most of all how they were going to take it! Annie kept her face warily composed. Mrs. Dunn made mournful digressions, describing Mrs. Lowrie's death, groaning and predicting the worst for Ben. "My, it seems as if we're just losing everybody!" she said with gloomy relish. But the church—careful as she thought she had to be—was the main theme of her lament. One thing she could do, Vieles or no Vieles, and that was unburden herself to the full about "that other element." Fred shifted uneasily in his chair, hating to hear the private affairs of his church given out, even to such good friends as these; feeling guilty too, his wife could see, at Mrs. Dunn's accusing reiterations of "if you folks ud been here," and "we couldn't do nothing without you folks." It made Annie indignant. As if Fred hadn't carried the load of that church long enough! and now must be saddled with the blame of its going to pieces!—and all the more so, because Annie knew that in her heart she was glad to be on the other side at last from Mrs. Dunn, comparing her with those people from Dike, finding comfort in the knowledge that at last she belonged with her own friends, "the ladies," the nice people.

One thing, though, did cause her an unwilling pang. That was when they asked about Essie Bartlett and her mother. Even the Vieles then, resolute in their attitude of looking on the bright side, had to give murmurs of sympathy. Mrs. Dunn was only too willing to expatiate.

"Well, you know, she's kind of dropped out—it's real too bad." And Mrs. Dunn, it was apparent, had no idea of doing that. She was finding consolation aplenty in forming part of "an element" in the new congregation! There would be a struggle, Mrs. Ferguson could see with a sigh, between the old element of the Congregationalists and the new element of the Presbyterians. Mrs. Dunn was continuing, gloomy satisfaction creeping through her voice, "I guess the young folks didn't want Essie. Well, they've been getting tired of her for a long time, even in our *own* church." Mr. Ferguson made an uneasy movement again. "She was the one most set on the churches not uniting. I don't believe she'll ever be reconciled. The new minister called on her—"

"He's *so* nice," Mrs. Viele murmured placatingly.

"—but he couldn't get her to go. Essie's been getting awful kind of funny," Mrs. Dunn said, shaking her head. "She won't hardly go out at all. She don't even seem to want to see people. But I guess she'll be pretty glad to see *you* folks."

Mrs. Ferguson made a movement too. The Vieles, at once, were warm with consolation. That was too bad! It *must* be hard on her. People got notional living so much alone. Still, Mr. Viele said, that wasn't the way to feel. They were sure that the attitude of the young people had been exaggerated. Everyone was glad to welcome the other members. And she wouldn't feel that way long, Mrs. Viele was certain. The ladies must all call on her. And now that she has *you* folks back—! Mrs. Ferguson murmured her sympathy. But she didn't dare steal a glance at Fred.

Anyway, it was evident that most of the members had accepted the change. Fred saw that with an inward feeling of blank incredulity. The Vieles had taken it for granted at once that he and Annie were with them, and he didn't know how to demur, since they were such good friends.

Of course, it was hard on the older members. Well, it was hard on Fred! But Mrs. Ferguson at last was able to confide that she was glad Fred had the whole thing off his shoulders. She was glad that this had happened—since it *had* to happen, and she believed even Fred had seen that—while they were away. Of course he wasn't going to take it any too easily. She didn't know . . . But all seemed friendly and possible, as the two women washed dishes together in the sunny kitchen. Mrs. Dunn, thank goodness, hadn't stayed very long. But it was long enough for Annie to be relieved to be out of her sight, away from those suspicious glances that seemed to penetrate her long, loyal pretense of really belonging with the Presbyterians. Mr. Viele had left for his office some time ago, after

Fred had said, "Well, Melvin, we don't want to keep you"; and Fred himself had now gone to town to have the car looked after. He thought there was something wrong with the brakes. The two women had the house all to themselves for the moment. They could drop the feminine veil of sweetness and smoothness and acquiescence and gossip to their hearts' content. Even Mrs. Viele, once you got her alone, could gossip. Nothing unkind, of course, but she could go into things. Mrs. Ferguson herself could tell about Louie's beautiful home, denying even to herself the sense of distance that had grown between her and her sister, believing in the wonderful time she had had there; and Mrs. Viele could break in with long, satisfying, intimate stories of old Mrs. Bird and her fragile health—"She'll be *so* glad to see you"; of Mrs. Brattle and Virginia; of the people who had lost money in the other bank; and of the historic downfall of the Hoaglands. Annie kept the secret of Dorothy's and Jesse's fall in fortune, making use of Jesse's easy version of the whole thing as a kind of lark. She wouldn't mention Bun. She had assumed her old rôle of the wholly fortunate wife and mother. But many things could be confided, never spoken of before, now that the two women felt themselves really united: how, although everyone was sorry for Mrs. Hoagland, still some thought it was a comedown that she had deserved; how Mrs. Stark, now that they had lost all their money, had quite stepped off her high horse; how everyone wished that Fred had stayed in the bank and just couldn't feel the same about Richard; how *no* woman, they should think, could be content to cut herself off from her family as Annie said old Mrs. Spencer had done; and how Annie's sympathy lay with Ben and not with Ella. When the sink was scrubbed shining white, and the soft white towels hung up to dry, the two women returned to the living room, glowing and intimate, appeased, and slightly ashamed of themselves.

A long pleasant day stretched ahead of them. Fred had telephoned that he wouldn't be through, and thought he had better get a bite downtown. Mr. Viele never came home at noon. They themselves could eat just what they pleased. But at last they began to feel that they had given Ada time enough, and that they couldn't wait any longer to go over to the house.

It did have a different look this morning. Mrs. Ferguson began to have a feeling of excitement, of emotional return, mingled with disappointment, alienation . . . she scarcely knew what, as she and Mrs. Viele approached the place. The doors were open, she could see that the curtains had been freshly put up. The two women went inside. There were sounds from somewhere in the house, but the living room was empty. All was in shining order. Great rose-and-white peonies bloomed in a flower basket near the piano, and on the table stood a vase of Mrs. Morgan's choicest roses. The big fern, glossy with freshness, was set in its old place near the window.

"We can tell who's been here!" Mrs. Viele archly exclaimed.

The sound of their voices had disturbed the workers. Mrs. Morgan, wearing a newspaper like a medieval peasant cap, accentuating her gauntness, looked over the banisters and then came hurrying downstairs.

"Well, for the love of Mike! Ada! She caught us!"

The call brought Ada in from the kitchen, flushed, eager, awkward and shyly happy. Now there was a great embracing. Mrs. Ferguson emerged from it smiling, flushed, with moist eyes. The women were all talking together.

"We thought we were going to get all through before you came over. Mamie, you let her steal a march on us."

"I just couldn't wait any longer!"

"Well, anyway, it looks better than it would have if you'd seen it last night."

"Better! I don't see how anything could look as nice."

Mrs. Morgan cried: "The trip must have done you good! Look at her little suit. Did you ever see anything so stylish? Just look at her, girls."

Mrs. Ferguson stood blushing and laughing, turning gayly around to show off her splendor, once again the center of her own small admiring group. She answered their questions happily. She could never admit to these ladies the small disappointments of her trip. And indeed it was already glowing in a rosy retrospect. Mrs. Viele took one arm, Mrs. Morgan the other, and she was led triumphantly on an inspection of the house. Ada, clumsy and happy, breathing heavily, trailed along behind the matrons.

"Do you see what these women have done!" Mrs. Ferguson marveled.

Fresh flowers in all the rooms, the curtains newly washed—and in the kitchen a whole set of supplies for the next day. Loren Morgan had seen early this morning about getting the electricity, water and gas turned on.

"Well, we thought we'd help you young folks get started keeping house," Mrs. Morgan explained, embarrassed by the thanks, laughing them off. "Have to do something to keep you here now we've got you again."

When they were through with the house they went outside. It didn't look as nice as it might, Mrs. Morgan said, worried. Loren had been cutting the grass since Mr. Graham took sick; but of course he had to do it nights and mornings, he couldn't take a minute from that old store.

"I was going to get after the grass around the trees myself—if I'd just known you were coming."

As if she hadn't done enough as it was! Explanations had to be gone into—how they had written to Ella, thinking she would pass the news along; and of course Ella hadn't been here to receive the letter. Ben's illness had to be talked about a little, with expressions of sympathy.

"I noticed," Mrs. Morgan said, "he seemed to be working awful slow, the last morning he was over here. I wondered then if there wasn't something the matter. My," she added, "you ought to have seen the place when *he* was taking care of it! I believe there wasn't a single day he didn't come over."

A low, dull pain with an edge of threatening sharpness was aroused at the words. But Annie put it hastily away from her. She was going to enjoy her homecoming, anyway, since she had had to come home. The flowers were blooming. They weren't like Louie's, of course, but still the whole place looked nicer than she had secretly expected. The porches were swept, no longer did the screened doors have that dusty, dispiriting look. Ada had stayed away from work, and Mrs. Morgan had been over since seven o'clock this morning.

"Now!" Mrs. Viele said triumphantly. "You didn't have any neighbors like these in California!"

There were still a few things that they wanted to do. The Fergusons weren't to be allowed to move in before evening. Mrs. Ferguson accepted in happy gratitude.

She waited on the porch for Mrs. Viele, who was talking to the others inside. As soon as Mrs. Viele had finished, they would go over and see old Mrs. Bird. It was a comfort, Annie felt, that there was no longer anything to separate her from the other ladies. Fred had insisted that they should return; but still, he didn't have things *all* his own way. The rich grass glistened in the sun. She was aware, even here, of changes. The rented house next door was empty again. Mrs. Morgan didn't know where the people had gone. Across the street, in the old Gilbert house, she saw the faded tourist sign. But it seemed as if her own house still stood secure in the sunshine of the long afternoon. The busy sounds from within the house let her stay for a little while in the privilege of return. But she knew that the time was coming, was ahead of her, when she wouldn't be able to put off feeling included any longer. Everything that she saw, here at home, was significant with associations. Grandma's yellow rose bush was in bloom. The tree where the children had had their swing, beneath which Dorothy had stood to be married, cast its pleasant shade. The geraniums were blooming in the urn. Garden vegetables, which Ben had put in, were up and ready. Her great holiday was almost over.

Mr. Ferguson had taken the car to drive downtown. However, he thought that first he would stop a moment at Ben's and Ella's place and see if he could learn a little more from their neighbor. She was in the thick of her Friday cleaning, and he didn't talk to her very long; only long enough to say to himself, "Well, we'll have to go over there pretty soon." No matter what the folks had said this morning, he couldn't leave the whole thing to Carl. Ella was his own sister.

He felt a hurt, secretive desire to drive past the church. But he was afraid of being seen. Instead, he drove down the cross street, slowing a little when he came in view of the place. The building stood there just as always, with the manse next door. Only now, both of them were empty. The load of which he had often complained was off his shoulders at last. But the ache of it was still there. He wouldn't be seen looking, so he drove on past. The memory of the locked doors and the bleak windows stayed with him. Now he actually understood that the long years of work, loyalty, responsibility were over. And what had it all been for? Just leisure wasn't enough. The street blurred, and for a moment he was almost afraid to drive. The faith of his fathers was gone, which they had come to found in a new land, carry with them, make greater and stronger than ever before. And this had happened while he was away enjoying himself on the fruits of his own labor! Still, there was mama—she had claims too—for once in his life, as she had told him, he had to put her before the rest. He felt a numb sense of loss, rather than blame. Mrs. Dunn talked darkly about "the other element"; but something larger than any "element" had been at work. Even if he had carried the load a little longer, this same thing would have come to pass; and there was a faint relief that he had not been forced to face the very hour, which his canniness and foresight had long told him was approaching. He could remember years back when this church was built. Then his father had felt, triumphant, that he had done his work for succeeding generations. The church still stood, but the generations had stepped out beyond it. And Fred's own children had been among the first! He might have stopped them, he might have laid down the law . . . but he had done that once, and they had lost Margaret. He couldn't say how or why it had happened; the faith had just faded out; no good trying to revive what wasn't there. And now that the church was gone, he had a queer feeling that the faith had faded from his own heart. He didn't stop to analyze it exactly. But the feeling was there. The loss would deepen and spread, like the slow creeping of old age through his bones. Just sitting in the sunshine wouldn't have stopped it. His faith had been the church, which his father had left to him. It was the church that he had helped to build, the institution that he had tried to carry on. First the faith, then the institution to make it secure, then the faith diminishing and leaving the structure that was to hold it empty. It was the institution that had been left to him. That had been *his* place in this long sequence. Now that it was gone, what did he believe? Anything more than his own children?

He felt the false cheer of the talk this morning, brightly covering realities. In spite of all the arguments, the new congregation could never mean anything to him. He would always be a stranger there. He and his folks belonged to the other fold. But Annie didn't. He acknowledged now, in pained bewilderment, that she never had. He felt estranged—felt himself in a void. The intricate pattern of marriage held him enmeshed in invisible ties. For years, he had brought Annie with him. Now, at last, her day had come. She had drawn him away from the folks. He felt as if he had failed them, just as his children had failed him. Yet he was conscious of a strange new sympathy for the children, embedded deep in humility. He had made mistakes, even when he was doing his best. Now, at the end of his life founded on trust, he was coming into uncertainty.

But the old responsibilities, although broken and shattered at points, still weighed heavily on his heart. It didn't seem as if he could go to town right now. Instead, he turned, and drove into the fading side street where Essie Bartlett and her mother lived. He stopped in front of the low frame house.

Even before he had a chance to knock, Essie came to the door.

She cried, "Mr. *Fer*-guson!"

"Yes. We're back, you see."

He tried to summon a reassuring smile, as he stepped inside, embarrassed and more moved than he cared to be, by the hysterical joy of her greeting.

She tried to be arch and welcoming at first, fussing about to get him a chair. But he saw her haggard look, and the awful brilliance of her eyes. While she talked and exclaimed, he sat down heavily. The bleak poverty of the room struck him with a breath of cold that slowly enveloped him, tearing wider the hidden wound that the sight of the church had made. He noticed that the stove was still up. He would have to see about having it taken down. He could have done it himself easily enough. His time wasn't valuable now. But there would be someone who needed the job, small as it was—he would have to think who. Essie was asking about the trip, with a brave assumption of her old vicarious delight. How was Dear Daughter Dorothy? And the darling children! It was so beautiful to think they could have this time with Dorothy and her handsome husband in their lovely home. Fred could answer only in monosyllables. His holiday had turned bitter to him. He could scarcely bear to meet Essie's withered girlish animation. He wanted nervously to put off the subject of the church. He had expected Essie to refer to it at once, and yet she didn't. She seemed to be sitting amidst the emptiness of the ruins after the disaster had struck and passed. But all the while he could see her thin hands grasping and grasping at the arms of her chair. There was a smothered wildness that unnerved him in the ceaseless scrape of the rockers. She began to chatter bitterly, gayly, hysterically, in seemingly irrelevant snatches, after every hint of a pause; while Fred sat uncomfortably mute, in helpless, guilty sympathy.

At last they reached a glassy silence.

Fred roused himself then to the old question: "How is your mother?"

Essie summoned the old bright smile, as she answered valiantly: "The same." For how many years had she been saying that, while the old wrecked body sank by imperceptible stages further and further toward decay?

But wouldn't he come in and see mother? Now Essie put on her brightest company air, with which she always ushered visitors into the invalid's presence. Fred got up silently to go through with the inevitable rite. He stood in suffering masculine discomfort in the close air of the little bedroom. Its meager neatness was unchanged. The smell of medicines had sunk into the very carpet, thin and worn as it was, showing in dim patches the boards of the floor. It sickened Fred to hear the slow scrape of a branch against the window. Essie was trying with dreadful gayety to rouse her mother to recognize him, excited and buoyed up by his return. "Don't you see who's here, mother? Mr. Ferguson's come to see you. You haven't seen *him* for a long, *long* time!" Fred gave a step forward and put out his hand. But the old body was finally past response. Even a glance of the filmed eyes, a movement of the feeble fingers, was now too much. Essie shook her head. She whispered, with a bright whisper of apology, "She just lies there"; as she straightened the bedclothes, smoothed the pillow with scrupulous care. But the doctor had said she was no worse—might live a long while—no one could tell . . . Fred nodded mutely. The young folks had laughed at Essie and all her little ways. But she had done her best to keep her tragedy within seemly bounds, growing unseemly herself with the effort.

As they left the room, Essie suddenly burst into tears. Fred heard the sound, aghast. It was terrible in this muffled place. Then his sympathy and comprehension rose above his silent embarrassment. He took Essie in his arms. How seldom his canny reserve had allowed him to do that with his own children! Only with Annie—and that was different . . . The terrified clutch of Essie's hands told him that he was her one rock of dependence; and he could feel his own slowly abating strength gather itself to meet the need.

"Oh, I'm so afraid I'll go before she does!"

The frightened words came out, in cries and whispers, and he braced himself to meet their import.

"I'm so sick sometimes—getting worse—sometimes I can't stand it!"

Fred led her into the other room before he tried to answer. In spite of the shock he felt, it seemed to him that he had known this ever since he had stepped into the house. But he made no falsely soothing answer to silence her. His mind was already seeking ways and means. And mute anger was slowly mounting inside him at the blunt misunderstanding of Mrs. Dunn, the bland reassurances of the others, signifying to him at this moment "the world," as he shared with Essie her gnawing secret in the bleak silence of the little house. He felt that he was face to face with something more irrevocable than he had ever known. The old optimism and trust had come to the edge of an abyss. What lay there, in those awful mists? He didn't know. He never had known. He felt Essie trembling in his arms, waiting for what he would say, as her final authority. He sought refuge in his practicality—it was what had always been, still was, expected of him.

Had she been to the doctor? he asked her.

Essie whispered, no. Fred did not reply at once. He understood that she had been afraid of what the doctor might tell her.

"I don't care for myself, I have nothing to live for now that the church is gone, but I can't leave her to the care of others. Not after all these years. All I've done is take care of mama. Now if I should go first . . ."

Well, something must be said, beyond the hard mute grasp of the hand that seemed to be all people had for each other in extremity. Easy promises, such as other folks could give, even good people like the Vieles, were out of his power. He had never liked to make promises that he hadn't been reasonably sure he could keep. That was one reason he had broken with Richard. But he couldn't hold too sternly to facts and probabilities—he must give a little comfort. Essie whispered something now about "the bank." The bank was all right, he assured her stoutly, above his own freshly reawakened uncertainty. As long as they both lived, he would promise that she had enough to take care of her. He would see her through. That, at least, he could feel was the truth.

He urged her to see the doctor. It was the right thing, even if it was useless. "Maybe something can be done. You mustn't make up your mind to the worst before you know, Essie."

Essie shook her head in feeble terror. But Fred felt relief in the weakened clinging of her hands. She was looking to him, as all the rest of them had, even when they were going their own ways. The old sense of protectiveness was deeply stirred; but mingled with it, a cold breath of solitude—for he felt that there was nothing in the world *he* could count upon, as this one poor woman counted upon him.

For a while the room had been blurred. But now its sparse furnishings began to grow sharp and clear. Mr. Ferguson's mind was still soberly searching for ways and means. There were other calls—there was his family, Ben—and who knew these days what was safe? But somehow it must be done. He felt that for once he had risen above practicality. In a way, in the void of their shattered loyalty, he and Essie were closer together than any two people in the world. Annie was the one he loved. And he loved his home. But it was here, in this little house, that he was king. It came to him, with proud humility, with a deep wry solace—that he had this fruit at least of what he mutely believed a lifelong effort to do the best he knew how. For the first time, he was able to see an awful grandeur in irrevocability.

"Now, Essie, don't you worry. You're going to leave things to me." He said that in his old way, as he had said it so many times before, must say it still. He led Essie to a chair. "I want to talk things over with my wife." Essie nodded mutely, humbly accepting that. "She'll know better than I do—she'll be over to see you soon. Can you get along until then?" He felt guilty about worrying Annie with this so soon after he had brought her home, but it couldn't be helped. He began to be aware that he needed a woman's aid. He felt proudly that, fine and delicate as she was, Annie had never failed to rise to a call. Essie's hands lay exhausted and trembling, but quiet now in her lap.

Fred cleared his throat, calling upon practicality again. "First of all, I'm going to send someone over to take down that stove. You don't want that standing in here now. It's just in the way." He frowned at the stove. It helped him to be able to work up a little indignation about the thing.

At last he got away, and climbed heavily into his car. Now there was Essie to be looked after—and Ella and Ben . . . For a moment, it seemed too much. His strength seemed to creak and strain, too old and worn for the load he had tried to drop. But he would have to take care of things the best he could. He felt that this responsibility—now that the church was gone—was closest to his heart. Yes, in a way, the claim of poor Essie and her mother was deeper than that of his own children. He had given them the best start he could. What they did with it was their own affair.

The solemn light of grandeur slowly faded, leaving him with the ways and means of his task. And now it seemed as if the brightness of the morning welcome had faded, too, from the streets. He noticed for the first time that the frame houses had lost their newness. Even the town was getting elderly. After those bright new glaring towns in the West it looked settled, established, fixed in its ways. He had always thought of it as a young town, with all its future before it. But now it seemed that that "future" had become the present, was even here and there beginning to be the past. So long as Fred Ferguson could remember, trust in the future of the town had been as much a part of his life as his daily bread. The feeling wasn't gone, exactly. But now that he had done some traveling, Belmond was no longer a place apart. Well, anyway, it was where he belonged; it was still, to him, the best place on earth. Even if it never became any bigger, he could still say that it was a pretty good little town in which to live.

He hadn't exactly meant to stop at the bank, but it seemed as if he had to see for himself how things were getting along. In a way he couldn't have explained, it was a surprise to see it still standing there, just as he had left it. It was strange to be going into that familiar place and to feel that he was no longer a part of it. His footsteps seemed to have a hollow sound as he crossed the hard white floor. He was a little doubtful as to how they would meet him; was conscious of having broken his ties. In spite of himself, that gave him a guilty feeling.

"Well, F. W.—didn't know you were back!"

Richard had come out to shake hands, as spruce and jaunty as ever. His hair was slicked glossily back, and he wore a pink rosebud in his buttonhole.

"Yes, we got back."

"Well—how was the trip?"

As they stood and talked, some of the first embarrassment wore off. Nevertheless, the meeting between the two men was full of discomfort. Richard was carrying it off, but he wouldn't quite let his eyes meet Fred's. Ray came up now with a shy but quite evidently heartfelt greeting. Fred had to speak to all the staff. The girls smiled at him, told him they had missed him. Richard asked if there was anything they could do for him; and when he said yes, if they'd take his check, the others all laughed and made a joke of his being a stranger.

Customers came in then, and he had to stand aside. He cleared his throat as he put his bills neatly in his folder. He hated to leave without asking how they were getting along; and yet he didn't know that he had the right any longer. So far as anyone could tell, business was going on much as before. Still, he didn't know—there was something different. If H. L. Hoagland couldn't be trusted, who could? The bright new modern splendor of the building had an air of being prematurely faded. There was a false note somewhere in the jaunty cheer. Ray looked thin and worn. His back was bent as if he carried a secret burden. Fred had always thought of Ray as a young fellow; but he saw now that Ray was middle-aged. Even Richard was getting older. His shining hair was streaked with gray, and his teeth were bad. It gave Fred a curious feeling to be looking on while the others worked, and to be standing here idle himself. What had he intended to do?—he had supposed, get into something, some new enterprise. But now he doubted if he had the heart for that. He had given too much of his life to the bank. And besides, what new enterprises *were* there? No, he couldn't say that he was sorry now to be out of it. He had felt it due to his own family to get out when he hadn't liked the way things were going. What he saw, what he could feel in the air, only confirmed his decision. But he thought of Essie's poor little funds—Fannie Allison's . . . he felt as if he had betrayed them. And he couldn't tell them to withdraw, either— that would have been treachery to the bank and to business. Some of his own funds were left here, against his secret judgment, and he would have to let them stay. Life wasn't so simple as he had thought. All was in flux, all in doubt, and allegiances were divided. A right here made a wrong there. He wondered against all reason if maybe he shouldn't have stuck to his post.

"Well, Richard, I guess I'll have to be getting on."

"Well, good-bye, F. W. Glad you stopped in."

The others were busy. They didn't see him go. That was all right. He had stepped out of his own accord. He didn't want any fuss made about him. But it was a pretty queer feeling to be out of it after all these years. Retirement wasn't what he had pictured. Should he have stayed out there after all? Now, as on the day when he had broken his connection, he felt as if he were walking in emptiness.

Still he hadn't taken his car to the garage—the thing that supposedly he had come to town to do. The clock outside the jeweler's told him that it was almost noon. He thought he would assuage his guilt by stopping in and asking Hy if he couldn't look after the car a little later.

But there was a change here too. His sense of welcome met another check. Hy wasn't in the garage any more. He had sold out the business and gone down to Florida. To this young fellow, the name Fred Ferguson meant no more than any other. The car would have to wait its turn. He might get it around five this afternoon—they might not be able to touch it before tomorrow. It was a small thing. Fred couldn't expect the fellow to make time for him. But Hy had always done his work, knew what a good customer he was, and would have got the job in somehow.

Fred thought he would telephone Annie. He didn't feel like going back this noon. He shrank just now from explaining what he had been about all morning. The two women would have enough to talk about together, he thought dryly, even somewhat bitterly. Annie had always preferred Mrs. Viele and the other ladies in the club to those in their own church (unless maybe it was poor Jennie). It was for his sake that she had confined herself to them. Well, now she and those others could be as close as they chose. He wouldn't interfere. After all, Annie had always stuck by him. She, too, was lonely, with the children gone, and he wanted her to be

his folks. Ella stormed and stewed because the renters didn't keep it up as she had done. But Fred, although he hadn't come out and disagreed with her, felt a little differently about that. After all, good tenants as they were—as tenants went—they were only here at the owners' will. They couldn't be expected to put the same into the place.

For the first time, in this silence of country sunshine, Fred actually realized that Ben might go. In spite of his impatience with and criticism of his brother-in-law, that gave him a pang. He thought of their young days together, the days when he and Ben had both been young fellows taking out their girls. The boys used to tease Ella about her beau and his slow ways, ask her when they were going to get around to getting married, suggest methods of hurrying Ben to the point. Well!—it might have been better if they had just let things rest, when he thought of how the marriage had turned out. When the two had finally got together, they had never hitched. Fred had always taken the part of his sister, on principle, since she was one of his own folks; and it had been a slight cause of dissension between him and Annie because he had known that her sympathies were with Ben. Now it seemed as if he could look back and see the injustice in the criticism. Annie had been after intangible and he after tangible things. But now Annie's viewpoint seemed at last to be fused with his own. Ben's faults and lacks seemed no longer important. Fred thought of how kindly he had always been. He had meant well. Folks didn't know what they were doing when they made fun of that old phrase! Maybe it could be applied to them all in the end. Not that Ben's life had been exactly a failure. But it seemed as if he had deserved more than he had got. Fred could feel only a painful wonder that Ben's life, after the young days, was going out in empty loneliness.

Fred heard a cry, and saw Vina crossing the yard. She came up hurrying and breathless.

"Oh, Mr. Ferguson! Why, I didn't know you was back."

She had been out in the garden, she told him. Her hands were too dirty for her to shake with him. Some kind of bugs were getting into the vegetables. They had gnawed all the radishes. She had wanted Rolfe to get after them, but he didn't have time. One of the horses had hurt his leg and Rolfe had been doctoring it. Fred listened impatiently to the long recital. Renters were always behind. But he was a little ashamed, knowing that since the garden and the horses belonged to Vina and Rolfe, they had to wait until the rest of the work was done.

"I'll go in and get this dirt off," Vina said breathlessly at last.

"Oh, don't bother, Vina. Not on my account. Here—we can shake like this."

He took hold of her wrist and shook it heartily, while her soiled hand dangled. She gave a pleased, breathless little laugh. Fred knew that she liked him. She and Rolfe had always preferred to deal with him. He wasn't soft—no one had ever accused him of that—but he did have the reputation of being fair. And Ella wasn't always so easy to get along with—Fred admitted that to himself, although he wouldn't have done so to anybody else. Not even Annie.

Now Vina was talking on breathlessly. "My, but I was surprised when I looked over here and saw it was you! We were beginning to wonder if you was ever coming home."

"Oh, yes, we had to come back. Couldn't let you have things all to yourself."

"Well, I don't know as we want to." But she gave a little self-conscious laugh.

She asked him then if he had been over to see Mr. Graham.

No, they hadn't yet. But they had talked this morning to Carl. Yes, he seemed to be getting on fairly well. Fred was cautious of making any admissions concerning his own family even with a person he knew so well, and who was so interested as Vina. There was the self-consciousness between them of owners and renters. Fred felt as if he mustn't let down too much. But it touched him when Vina said with naïve sincerity:

"My, I hope it ain't going to be as bad as they thought!" Tears misted her faded eyes. She looked around for something with which to wipe them, and finding nothing—embarrassed at using her sleeve before Mr. Ferguson—stared straight ahead and sniffed. After a moment, she put up her hand and brushed her eyes, leaving a streak of dirt across her cheek.

Any display of feeling made Fred awkward. Besides, he was tired out after the session with Essie this morning. He made no reply. But a dull pain sank deeper into him. Somehow, the sight of Vina's tears made him see Ben in a different light. He understood how, to her, Ben had seemed better than Ella. Maybe even than himself. That hurt Fred. He thought he had always been pretty good to Rolfe and Vina. But he had stood on the other side.

"We sure do think a lot of Mr. Graham," Vina said softly, after a while.

Fred made no answer again. But looking off across the land, it was almost as if he could see Ben's slow, patient figure— hear his friendly, companionable talk to the horses in the evening, after he brought them in sweating from the field. And he could hear Ben's mild, half-humorous replies to Ella, for which they had always been inclined to despise him. It seemed sad now that in the long grinding strain of the years the mildness had slowly declined into a feeble bitterness. Yes, there were other values than he himself had been taught to acknowledge. Fred had always taken the Ferguson stand of activity, work, getting ahead. They might all have been kinder to Ben. Except Annie—she had always been good. But then, Annie wasn't a Ferguson. Fred used to dislike it because Ben took the part of the children. It had made Ben seem kind of childish himself. But maybe, Fred thought, if I had been closer to them, they wouldn't have got so far away. Now he could see that Ben himself had been only a tenant—the place had belonged to Ella and her folks. Was that what had lain at the bottom of the whole trouble, after all? And Ben, in some ways, had been more of a natural farmer than any of them. At least, he had the faculty of getting things to grow. Now, looking around, Fred saw that the place was as much Ben's as Ella's. Only it was pretty late to admit that now.

"Well," he said uncomfortably, "we'll have to be going over there to Geneva, I guess, pretty soon."

He asked Vina where Rolfe was.

She blinked her eyes to clear the tears. She said that he was out cultivating. Should she call him?

"Oh no, don't do that," Fred answered mildly. "I just came out a minute to see how things were getting on."

At that, a worried, half-secretive look came into her face. She launched at once into her troubles, her talk interspersed with little allusions to Ella, to which Fred listened uncomfortably.

"Oh, they aren't so good. Rolfe told Mrs. Graham, what can we do when hogs ain't bringing in more than they do? Rolfe can't get any more for things than they'll give him. My—I guess it ain't any too easy for us!"

It was a long, wandering recital. Fred had always been inclined to discount impatiently the grumblings of folks on the farm. That had been a prime tenet in town. "Oh, the farmers are always grumbling." And there was no real reason for it, town folks said, when they had the best land on earth. But Fred wasn't a business man any more. He couldn't help a feeling of fellowship as he listened to Vina's recital, as she stood with troubled eyes, speaking out of her simplicity. Fred had liked to think of the farm as a haven of quiet certainty; he had never paid much attention to the grumbling. Renters always thought they were getting the poor end of the deal, that things were against them. That was why they were renters. So Fred had always declared. But now it seemed to him as if he and Vina stood together in the grip of a long slow movement of change which neither of them could comprehend. Fred felt a sense of helplessness. Vina seemed to be appealing to him as if *he* could do something about it. He was the owner. He was the one in charge. Now that Ben was sick, the farm would, to all intents and purposes, or the care of it, return to Fred. He listened half incredulously to Vina's account of changes. A lot of farms were lost to their owners. The insurance company had got Ed Davison's. That was bad news—that hit Fred: for Ed's father had taken up that place when his own father had taken this. Fred felt his town faith at war with his country faith. It was the latter which was slowly rising and taking possession of him. He saw the land again as when

716

he had come into it yesterday morning. That feeling had not died away. He could see that Vina looked to him, even though there was a slight hostility somewhere in her manner. She said excitedly that some of the farmers were getting mad. Fred heard that with resentment and dismay. Yet when it came down to Ed Davison, his old boyhood friend and neighbor, it was pretty close. He couldn't think of Ed as a stranger. His sober, distressed sympathy was at war with his business man's policy of never admitting that things weren't going right ahead. He tried to tell Vina that things weren't so bad. That seemed to be required of him since he was the one in authority.

He said at last, "Well, I guess I'll wander around a little bit."

"Would you like to go into the other house?"

"No, I guess I'll let that go for today."

Vina's talk was a strange mixture. A feeling of disgruntlement, which Fred saw now had always been there at the bottom, ran through her respect for him. Yes, the disgruntlement was there, although she admitted, "Well, I guess we're better fixed than some." It made Fred feel lonely again, as if the old foundations were gone. But that didn't absolve him from the care of the farm. Vina and Rolfe might not be here at all if it hadn't been for his folks who had built up the place. They owed their living to that. Fred thought of all the little favors, all the little jokes: Vina making butter for him, anxiously picking out the best chickens when Annie was going to entertain; leaving bouquets of her best flowers when she came in with the eggs. Yet disgruntlement had lain at the bottom of it all, and now the times were bringing it out. And he himself —he was in it too; for while he always had done, always would do, the best he was able for Rolfe and Vina, still he knew guiltily that the interests of the farm came first.

He wanted to get off by himself. He had heard enough about people's misfortunes. It seemed as if folks were due to have peace, not more trouble than ever, after a lifetime of work.

Vina anxiously watched him go. She was afraid he would discover something to find fault with. But Mr. Ferguson had no desire to find fault. He felt too heavy-hearted for that.

He went out toward the field, thinking he might call to Rolfe. But then he thought better of it. He had talked to enough people today. He had his own troubles, too, although others might not think so, seeing only his prosperity. He began to feel the healing of the country stillness. It seemed as if he never had quite known what the place meant to him. It was the heart of his feeling of return.

As he walked about, in spite of his anxiety, that feeling grew. Rolfe had the twenty in sweet clover. The soil needed replenishing. The clover wasn't in bloom yet, but it was getting rich and green. There were small green apples in the orchard where the grass was long. Rolfe didn't have much time for the orchard. It looked rather neglected, but Fred wouldn't say anything about that. He knew from the waning of his own strength that a man could not do more than his powers allowed. He hated to see anything amiss. It hurt his thrift and his sense of ownership. But he felt humbly that after all this place didn't belong to Rolfe. He wouldn't feel toward it quite as if it had been his own. Fred looked soberly across the road at the Davison place. It wasn't right to think of others there. "Others" were here, on their own place—but he didn't consider that. He came to the edge of the cornfield. Rolfe was far away. He wouldn't disturb him at his work. "He's busier now than I am." He caught the smell of the hot rich earth overturned by the cultivator. He looked down the rows of young green corn. Old feelings long buried stirred. There was no smell on earth so good to him as this, now that he had been away and come back. He felt that he almost envied Rolfe. Now, after all these years, was he going to turn around and wish that he had stayed a farmer?

As he walked back toward the house, he wondered what was to be done with this place when Ella was gone? There were no children of hers to inherit it. His brothers, too, had gone away. Their sons had gone into this business and that. None of them into farming. And he didn't see any of his own children managing the place. As things stood now, it was more likely to become an encumbrance than anything else. Perhaps he ought to urge Ella to sell it while she could. But then there were Rolfe and Vina to be thought of. There were so many things to be thought of, all opposing each other, but all working in together. And he was the one who had to think of them all. Young fellows like Bun looked all toward the future, and could say just how things ought to be. But things were just as real in the here and now, and had to be dealt with according to the present facts. Suffering and injustice were suffering and injustice, no matter to whom and when they happened.

Some of Bun's notions had stuck in his mind, crazy as he had proclaimed them to be. They came back to him now. He thought furtively, as he considered ways and means—well, maybe the boy wasn't so far wrong. He would never have confessed such heresy; but he felt that he would almost rather see this piece of land go back to the government than coldly sell it. And maybe land so good oughtn't to belong to any one man, particularly if the man wasn't going to live there. He felt ashamed, as if Rolfe were doing *his* work—only that wasn't true. The folks were gone, anyway. Maybe they had done their own share in bringing the place to bear. Then his mind shifted half angrily. Bun ought to come out here and see what *he* could do, instead of talking about Russia. Let that girl of his live the life of a farmer's wife. They might find out a few things, both of them. Yet Fred couldn't feel real resentment against Bunny. He had a queer, respectful humility toward his youngest, who had had the best that they could give him. He himself had striven and worked to raise his children above the country life, as he had thought, and Annie had thought; but now he wondered. And what was going to become of the farm?

He walked along, noticing many things that weren't quite what they should be. He felt an old tree trunk with his hand. He touched the stones of the old house. That belonged to him. It was a shame to see it just standing here empty. For the first time, Fred felt there might be a sentimental value in fixing up the old place. It had belonged to the folks. He couldn't see it go to pieces before his eyes. Maybe some of them would be glad of it sometime.

The rich smell of the country surrounded him. It wasn't like those desert places, not wild. He remembered with scorn the big talk of those fellows at the picnic. He never could have gone back on the old place the way those fellows had done. The smell of the cultivated earth held peace. There ought to be peace and plenty for everyone. Wasn't that what had been meant at the start? He was in the grove now. His foot struck against something, he bent down to see what it was. An old pewter spoon buried in the ground! That dated back to their childhood when they had played out here. Ella had buried this spoon, when the boys wouldn't let her playhouse alone. She'd always been one to hold tight to her own! Well . . . Ella hadn't made much of her home, though, when she'd got it. Maybe she'd held too tight. And then again, maybe she wasn't to blame. She and Ben didn't hitch, weren't meant for each other. That made his own heart warm toward Annie, through all their differences. She had softened his sternness, had made life sweet and rich for him. When he thought of the meager lives so many people led, it seemed as if he and Annie had almost too much. But Ella—he defended her mutely, although he knew what Vina thought of her, and with reason. He saw the heavy black-eyed girl fiercely putting her playhouse in order, although she could never get the look to it that Grandma gave to whatever she touched. Ella just missed out somehow—she didn't quite have it in her. She felt it, too, although the others thought she didn't. Fred put down the spoon, shoved the dirt over it with his toe. He guessed Vina was luckier than Ella, after all. She and Rolfe had their children, and they stood together. The ground smelled good where he had disturbed it. He felt the rich growth all around him. There was almost a song of growth in the summer air.

Well, anyway, it was good land. His father hadn't made any mistake about that. It was good land, and they had owned it for a while, worked it, and received its benefits. This belief in the goodness of his native soil lay underneath the tottering structure of business faith, religious faith, everything. Whatever folks might do with it, the land was here. That was good. If folks treated it right, it would never let them starve.

The Fergusons had dinner with the Morgans. Then at last they went over to their own house.

Mrs. Ferguson waited while Mr. Ferguson opened the front door. This was a soft, balmy June evening, very different from the one before. Mrs. Morgan had put on her porch light for them. It lighted up the evergreens along the driveway and shone part way across the lawn. The place still had an air of loneliness, they had been away so long; but here in the soft evening, so pure and yet dense with fragrance, everything held a peculiar intimacy. Annie felt a wonder that she should actually be here. But Louie's place—all its exotic features, the great slope of the grounds beyond the spectacular frame of the window, with the flowers, the drooping sprays of the pepper trees, the ragged tall grace of the eucalyptus—had retreated into a dream. Only this was real.

"Well, Annie, you can go on in. I'll put away the car."

Mrs. Ferguson went into the house. It seemed different to her, entering it alone. It had a ceremonious air. This afternoon, she had still been a fêted guest. Now came the moment she had secretly dreaded: when she must come back, and take things up where she had left them, only with the prospect of less instead of more ahead of her.

But once here, the familiar objects made their mute appeal. She went into the living room, switching on the central light. She thought with gratitude again of all that those women had done! The welcome that she had received everywhere had opened her heart again. Now she couldn't believe in her own secret turning away. This was where she lived. The great bouquet of peonies warmly perfumed the silent air. The deadness that had lain over the place was gone. Now, on return, all was living again, in a shimmering texture of contentment and pain. Her small rebellion—smothered, only partly acknowledged even to herself—was over. Again she would have to make the best of everything.

She saw the pictures of the children, waiting for her. On the piano stood the family group taken a year or so ago of Carl, Lillian and the boys—showing, although Carl was smiling, that they had been through things, that her oldest was already middle-aged. On the wall hung the framed photograph of Dorothy in her wedding dress. There was no good photograph of Margaret. The silly child had always fought against having one taken, from some queer, perverse notion that she didn't like her own looks. When she was last at home, Margaret had been disgusted to find this old picture of herself, when she was a junior in high school, that her mother had dug out and set up among the others. It didn't do her justice. The mother looked with a mixture of compassion and bafflement at the dark little face with the big, alien eyes. Still, after Margaret was gone, she had put the picture back, for she couldn't bear to feel that she was leaving out any of her children. The dark eyes seemed to be looking straight beyond her with a fierce, unfathomable reproach, which she was never going to be able wholly to comprehend or to answer. The face, intense and reserved, was foreign among the others. But the graduation photograph of Bunny, youthfully solemn, brushed and thin, wasn't like him, either. It held none of his oblique, smiling charm. Familiar and beloved as that face was, it was unfamiliar too. The mother gave it a quick, beseeching glance, which she felt was only half returned. Now all her children were gone, matured and set in their own ways, and there was nothing any longer that she or dad could do about it. They had come to the place where they must accept what was. The ideal household which she had always dreamed that her own would become some day had vanished, even from the dream . . . unless for an hour it had existed, unrecognized, fragrant with roses, bright with tears, on Dorothy's wedding day . . . All the same, there was a richness in having these faces all around her, unsatisfactory as the pictures were. She thought with a faint, incredulous shudder of old Mrs. Spencer in her bungalow; of that one special view of the petulant emptiness of Louie's face. It seemed to her that she had escaped—although from just what, she didn't know. How could she have tried to deceive herself? She had made herself into a wife and mother, bent and shaped herself to that rôle; and she could never go back to what she had been before. Tenderness was in the marrow of her bones; and now, at this return, it was achingly alive again. She felt her love trying painfully to encompass even Charlotte, although it stopped, in bewilderment and fear. She would be here, at any rate, when the children wanted to come home. "The folks" would be here.

However, she didn't want to have dad catch her looking at these pictures. She turned out the light.

Mr. Viele had brought over their suitcases. They were neatly piled in the hall. When she went upstairs, she found more evidence of her neighbors' care. Those women had hung fresh towels in the bathroom and set out a beautiful fresh cake of soap! They all said Belmond was more like itself now that the Fergusons were back.

Her bedroom was in spotless order. On the dresser stood a bouquet. Ada had set it there. She recognized the old-fashioned mixture of flowers all squeezed into the blue glass vase with its scalloped edge. After all, the newness of homecoming had not yet faded. It would linger for a long while, spreading its brightness over familiar things. Now she thought of many things to which she could look forward: a visit with old Mrs. Bird, in the white house she had always loved; her first club meeting, when she would appear as a returned traveler . . . even if there had been changes, if other things not so pleasant lay ahead of her. But strangely enough, her greatest comfort lay in the thought of Ada Rist. To Ada, she could talk of the children as much as she pleased. Ada would never tire of hearing. And in long, intimate conversations with Ada, in the sleepy leisure of Sunday afternoons—showing pictures, reading bits from letters, before the hungry, happy shine of Ada's eyes—the illusion of the ideal household could shimmer for a while. She had come back to find the complete response she had longed for in this lonely, aging girl, who had never had much life of her own, and who looked upon "the Ferguson children" as figures of romance in a bright fairy tale.

Her holiday, her one great time "just for herself," had been and was over. She couldn't say it hadn't been satisfactory. Most people, her neighbors, envied her. But how brief it seemed now when she looked back upon it and thought, This is all I'm going to have. The one moonlit night, the one golden day, when she and Fred and been together again, in renewal of their early days . . . and then the queer little personal consolation of Miss Potter's worship. . . . She thought of the vision of the old sinking world far beyond the pale flower-image of the actress's face, and of the silver emptiness of the Pacific Ocean; and she was glad to be at home again with dad, now when night was coming.

Mr. Ferguson drove the car into the cemented coolness of the garage. He looked it over, carefully tested all the tires, and then locked it with a feeling of relief and satisfaction. It had taken them safely on their long journey and it wasn't much the worse. Now it was back where it belonged. He brought the garage doors together and pressed down the foot-bolt. He snapped shut the Yale lock.

He went through the warm semi-darkness of the back yard, where the apple tree was standing, and let himself in at the back door. There hadn't been time for him to see to the house before, but he would have to take a look at it before he could go to sleep.

He turned on the cellar light and went down the steep, somewhat rough wooden stairway, where he was met by the same old smell of cement. He tapped the body of the furnace, hearing the hollow sound. All seemed to be as he had left it, except for a vague mousy odor. That could be looked after tomorrow. He wondered if he could afford to put in an oil furnace, with all the other things he had to do. Mama and he, if they were going to stay here, might as well have things as comfortable as they could.

He climbed the stairs again and went back into the kitchen. The painted doors of the cupboard stuck. He pulled one open, and took out a glass, carefully choosing one of the old jelly glasses that were always saved for kitchen use. He got himself a drink of water before he went upstairs. The water was warm at first, and he didn't want to stop to let it run. But it had the familiar taste, no other suited him so well. He drank slowly, and then put the jelly glass in the sink.

There was no need for looking around much in the other

rooms. Mama would see to them. He didn't notice details, but he felt the familiar atmosphere around him.

He hadn't said anything to mama about Essie yet. That could wait until tomorrow. It gave him a guilty feeling that he had brought Annie back to so much trouble. They would both have to pitch right in again. Fred had always thought of himself as a worker, and scorned slacker men. If a man was willing to work, so he had always said, he and his need never want. But now it had begun to seem to him that, as things went, he and Annie had been let off pretty easy. What had happened to Essie might have happened to anyone. *He* might have died, as John Bartlett had died, before he had been given time to make provision. And if he had happened to have gone into the other bank, the provision wouldn't have counted for much, anyway. It no longer seemed to him just and inevitable that some should have and others not. He and mama ought to be willing to help out where they could.

At dinner, Fred had been quiet, admitting in answer to questions that he guessed he was tired. The memory of Essie troubled him now in the midst of his own peace and comfort. It seemed to him that he hadn't given her the consolation he might. Essie, like him, had held to the church. Yet what comfort had he been able to muster, when they had stared together at the abyss? He thought of her life of starved devotion—he wasn't willing to admit that this could be the end. Yet the only assurance he seemed able to give her was that she could count on his support until she died. He felt heavily upon him the support of others which had helped to shape and make up his life. Maybe Bunny was right, and the world was changing—Bunny had had all the advantages, there must be something in what he said—but he himself still had to think about ways and means if he wasn't to let down those who had been taught to look to him. He felt proud of his part, and disdained the others—yet he felt hurt, humbled, defrauded somewhere. Was that all he was for? And he wondered sometimes if the great day he had been building for his children—that they had been building, the folks—had turned out to be their own day, after all.

He looked to see that mama had locked the front door, and carefully hooked the screen. Then he took the suitcases they would need, and went upstairs.

"Well, everything seems to be in pretty good shape," he said.

It was a little warmer in their room than downstairs, but still it was comfortable. Now that the trip was over, he began to look back upon it with pleasure and satisfaction. He would never have taken it, except for mama. If it hadn't been for her, he would have stuck just like the rest of his family.

He was ready for bed, at that, before Annie was.

"Aren't you coming, mama?"

"Yes, just as soon as I've . . ." He didn't hear the rest.

He waited uneasily, not able to sleep until she came.

"Well, this is the best bed I've had for a long while," he declared, with a sigh of satisfaction, when she got in with him at last.

Now that they were at home again, he felt that he had got Annie back. At least he had been able to give her this trip. Even if some things had happened while he was away, that he might have prevented, he was glad they had gone when they did. Mama's claims came first. He believed he had made Annie happier than Henry had made Louie, even if he hadn't been able to give her quite so much. They had their home to come back to—some folks, when it came to the end, didn't even have that much. Folks as good as *they* were. That made him humble tonight. As things went in this world, he and Annie had no cause to complain.

And yet things had changed. The era of his effort had passed. It was left for him to wind up his affairs the best he knew how. New undertakings had to be left now to the young folks, and there was no telling what *they* would do. He realized that he was seeing their own lives in a certain completion. It had been a pretty good day for them. He had always trusted implicitly that his children were destined to do better; but now he was hoping they would do as well. Simplicities were shifting into complexities, and in the darkening

726

twilight that he and Annie faced, along with the others that were left, he couldn't see what was beyond. He reached over and felt for Annie's hand, and drew her up to him. "Well, mama . . ."